THE SHADOW WALKER

and

THE ADVERSARY

Michael Walters has worked in the oil industry, broadcasting and banking. Over the last decade, he has worked as a management consultant across the world, in environments ranging from parliaments to prisons. He lives in Manchester with his wife and three children. *The Shadow Walker* was his first novel and began the Nergui series, followed later by *The Adversary* and *The Outcast*.

THE SHADOW WALKER

and

THE ADVERSARY

Michael Walters

This omnibus edition published in 2009 by Quercus
The Shadow Walker first published in Great Britain
in 2006 by Quercus
The Adversary first published in Great Britain
in 2007 by Quercus

21 Bloomsbury Square
London
WC1A 2NS

A CIP catalogue record for this book is available
from the British Library

ISBN 978 1 84916 100 8

Printed and bound in Great Britain by CPI Bookmarque, Croydon

10 9 8 7 6 5 4 3 2 1

THE SHADOW WALKER

'In the country of the blind, close your eyes.'

—Mongolian proverb

So that was it. Cleaned out again. Right down to the last *tugruk*.

He fell against the wall, nearly lost his footing, then staggered upright again and continued his uncertain way down the empty street.

What time was it? After midnight, for sure. The street-lights were on in the square, but the narrow side-streets were lost in darkness. And it was cold. Bone-chillingly cold, and winter was hardly here. He had tried to bet his coat on the last game – it was the only asset he had left – but thank blue heaven they'd just laughed at him. They usually laughed at him.

He tripped again, stumbling on an uneven paving stone, and felt suddenly nauseous. He should stop this. Stop the drinking. Stop the gambling. Yet again, he had left himself with nothing to live on till the next public handout, days away. But what else was there? Endless empty promises. That was the story of this country; everyone made promises. But nobody kept them. At least the cheap vodka always delivered.

He stopped suddenly, feeling sick, realising that his bladder was painfully full. The city lights swirled around him, a dizzying scatter of neon logos proclaiming a future he had no part in. He took a step back, trying to regain his equilibrium, the freezing cold aching in his limbs.

Where was he? Still a long way from home, a long way to go. He looked around, trying to find somewhere to relieve himself. There was a cramped side-street to his left, unlit, thick blackness only yards from the main street. He glanced back. The city centre and the main square in the distance were deserted, bleak and wintry in the thin glow of the streetlights.

He turned and began to make his way cautiously down the unlit street. Some lingering sense of propriety made him try to move further into the darkness – he had no desire to get himself arrested, on top of everything else.

He could barely see now, his eyes not yet accustomed to the dark. Tall blank buildings rose up on both sides of him, the lights of the main street lost behind him. He took another step, trying to regain his balance and his bearings, and then he stumbled again, his foot catching on something. Something heavy lying in the middle of the street. Something soft.

He fell headlong, his arm and his shoulder scraping on the rough ground, the impact agonising even in his drunken state. He rolled over, gasping, and lay on his back, trying to catch his breath. Above him, in the narrow gap between the high buildings, he could see a brilliant patterning of stars.

His eyes were adjusting to the darkness now, and he twisted around, trying to see what it was that had tripped him. At first, he couldn't make it out. Just a blank shapeless mound, spread across the frozen ground. And then he thought it looked something like a human figure, but not quite like one. He rolled over, trying to clear his head, trying to work out what was wrong.

And then, suddenly, he realised what it was, and he screamed, the nausea that had been building in his stomach overwhelming him, acid in his throat.

He was still lying there, moaning and retching, when the police patrol arrived fifteen minutes later.

8

PART ONE

ONE

It was like one of the gates of hell.

They drove at speed away from the airport, northeast towards the city, as the setting sun cast crimson shadows along the road ahead. As night fell and the sky filled with stars, the empty steppe was left behind, replaced by a vast industrial complex dominating both sides of the road. Endless blank buildings stretched into the thickening winter darkness, interspersed by networks of heavy pipe-lines, scatterings of pale orange lights. Somewhere in the centre, there was a single guttering flare.

Nergui followed Drew's gaze. 'Mining. Mainly coal here, though there are gold reserves in the area also. A primitive operation. This would not now be allowed in your country, I think. The ugliness, pollution. But the Soviets were not too bothered about things like that. And neither are we, I suppose, so long as we maintain some kind of industry. We have been through difficult times.' He shrugged, and then smiled. 'But much of the country is unspoiled. I hope you will get the chance to see some of it while you are here.'

'I don't know—'

Nergui nodded. 'Of course, forgive me. Murder is not a trivial matter. Especially in a case like this. We will provide you with every support. This matter is a grave concern to us as well. I merely wish to be hospitable.'

Drew shook his head. 'No, that's fine. I'm keen to see something of the country while I'm here.'

'I will be pleased to be your guide, Chief Inspector.'

'Call me Drew, please.'

The Mongolian nodded slowly, as though absorbing this request. He had given no indication of his own rank or position. At the airport, Nergui had introduced himself to Drew – one of a handful of Westerners on the in-bound flight – only by the single name. It had appeared, from the phone-calls and e-mails exchanged prior to Drew's arrival, that Nergui was the officer in charge of the investigation, but he had not made this explicit. Instead, he had introduced the younger second officer, Doripalam, as the Head of the Serious Crimes Team.

But there was no doubt that Nergui was at ease in the back of this official car, with Doripalam in the front passenger seat and a silent underling driving them down this featureless road towards the city centre.

And there was no doubt, too, that Drew was a long way from home.

Home was five thousand miles away. Home was the soft chill of late autumn rain, not the harsh grip of approaching winter. It was the grey downpour that had greeted Drew as he crawled from his bed at some godless hour that morning, hearing the steady breathing of his sleeping wife, the softer synchronised breath of the children in the next room. The ceaseless torrent down the windscreen of the taxi thirty minutes later, the rhythmic sweep of the wipers. The overcheerful banter of the driver, on his last run of the night, looking forward to his own bed.

As always, Drew had arrived at the airport too early, with an age to wait after check-in, trying not to think about the hours of travel that lay ahead, about what might wait at the end of the journey. He was still barely awake as he boarded the flight to Heathrow, a compliant automaton, gripping his passport, fumbling for the hastily arranged visa, juggling his deck of tickets. The flight was, inevitably, late, stacked for long minutes over London, Monday morning congestion already building. He ended up with no time to spare, racing across the terminal for the connecting Lufthansa flight to Berlin, convinced he would be stopped at the gate. As he stumbled up the aisle of the plane, the other passengers had stared at him, no doubt recognising him as the one who had briefly delayed their flight.

This was, supposedly, the easier route to Mongolia. The alternative was a flight to Moscow and an Aeroflot connection to Ulan Baatar. The specialist travel firm that had organised the trip had warned against this, citing the inevitability of delays in Moscow and the notorious unreliability of the Russian carrier. Better to trust German efficiency and the enthusiasm of Mongolia's own state airline, MIAT, to bring tourists and their currency quickly into their country.

The advice proved sound. The Berlin flight was on time, and the transfer at Tegel smooth enough. Two hours later, he was sitting on MIAT's only 737, finally beginning to relax. This flight was also on schedule and the service was efficient, even if the style and catering were, to Western eyes, eccentric. The in-flight meal consisted entirely of a selection of meats – cured, roast, perhaps boiled – accompanied by an apparently unending supply of miniature Mongolian vodkas. Drew drank two of these, enjoying the warmth and pepper taste, with a growing sense of ease that the hardest part of the journey was past. Three vodkas seemed too many for the early afternoon, and he slipped the last small bottle into his pocket as a souvenir. His neighbour, a middle-aged Mongolian man in a smart-looking black business suit, smiled at him and raised his own glass of vodka in silent greeting.

Unexpectedly – to Drew at least – the flight was interrupted for refuelling at Irkutsk, on the far eastern Russian border. The flight circled in over the vast white expanse of Lake Baikal, the dark Siberian forests stretched out ahead. There was more queuing to display passports and visas, the wooden-faced official peering suspiciously at Drew's documents.

'Police?' he had said finally, in heavily accented English.

Drew nodded, drawing a deep breath to launch into some kind of explanation. He had in his pocket the formal letter of invitation from the Mongolian government, though he had no idea how much weight this would carry this side of the border. But, after a lengthy pause, the man had just nodded and smiled faintly. 'Good luck,' he said. Drew suspected that he had used the only English words he knew.

Drew and the other passengers had sat in the empty airport, surrounded by cheap pine veneer and grimy plate-glass windows, drinking strong coffee from the primitive bar. At one point, seeking air, Drew had wandered out to join the cluster of smokers on a small wooden balcony, with views out over the woodlands and lake. Although it was mid-afternoon, it was icy cold, the Russian winter already biting. He stood for as long as he could, the frozen air harsh in his lungs, looking out at the dense Siberian forests, the trees black against the pure blue of the sky, the landscape deathly silent. He had felt then as if he was standing at the edge of the world, with no inkling of what might lie beyond.

Minutes later, they were shepherded back on to the plane. As they walked back out across the tarmac, Drew looked around at his fellow travellers. Most were Mongolian, with the distinctive broad features and dark skin, though there was a scattering of Westerners and some who looked, to Drew's undiscerning eye, to be Chinese. Most were dressed in conventional Western clothes – suits, jeans, sweatshirts – but two older men were dressed in heavy, dark coloured robes, wrapped around with brilliantly-patterned golden sashes.

Later, as they approached Ulan Baatar, the plane banked low over the steppes, turning in sharply towards the airport. The sun was low in the clear sky, casting deep shadows across the endless green plains. Even the shape of the hills was different here – softer, rounder, distinctively Asian. As the plane descended, Drew glimpsed, startlingly close to the runway, scatterings of nomadic camps, round grey tents, figures wrapped in traditional robes, tethered horses, flocks of sheep and herds of horned cattle.

The sight was unexpected, but this was how the people lived here. The population was sparse – little more than one person per square kilometre of land – and half still lived in the traditional *ger* tents. Half of those remained nomadic, tending their herds, moving with the seasons, coping with the extremes of an intense continental climate. It was a basic lifestyle unchanged for a thousand years. And over the past decade, unemployment and poverty had driven increasing numbers back out to the steppes, struggling to eke out an existence from the inhospitable grassland, rediscovering traditional ways of living, the lure and challenges of the endless plains.

Minutes later, the plane landed and, as incongruous as if from another age, there were the strings of landing lights, the formalities of passport and customs, the baggage carousel that, to Drew's mild surprise, rapidly disgorged the luggage he had checked in hours before. All around, there was the anonymous glare and bustle of a shabby airport terminal that might have been any-where in the world.

'Drew,' Nergui said. 'Drew McLeish. That is a Scottish name, yes?'

Drew looked across at the heavily built figure beside him. 'My father was from Glasgow. But my family moved to Manchester when I was a boy, so I lost the accent long ago. You know the UK?'

Nergui nodded. 'I spent a year there. Studying.'

'Your English is excellent.'

'Thank you. I also spent some years in the US, so I talk about sidewalks and elevators.' Nergui laughed. 'But I liked England. A beautiful country.'

'We have our own ugliness and pollution,' Drew said. 'But some of it is beautiful.'

'We will show you some of the attractions of our country while you are here.' Nergui paused. 'It is good of you to come. We will need all the help and advice you can give us. You will find us very amateurish, I am afraid.'

This seemed unlikely. The police might be short of resources and experience, but it was clear, even from their brief initial contact with Drew, that Nergui and Doripalam were anything but amateurs. 'I don't know that there's much I'll be able to teach you,' he said. 'But I'll give whatever help and support I can.'

'This kind of crime is new to us, Chief Inspector. Drew.' He said the name as though trying it out, but seemed satisfied with the effect.

Drew shrugged. 'Thankfully,' he said, 'none of us comes across this kind of crime very often.'

That was true enough. Crime wasn't supposed to be like this, not here. Crime here could be violent and sometimes complex – which was when Nergui tended to get involved these days – but mostly it was trivial stuff. Nergui had read in the newspaper only a few days before that the single most common crime in Mongolia was the theft of cattle. A few months earlier, an English journalist had had his bicycle stolen by a man on a horse, though Nergui had no idea how this could have been done. And there was always the drunkenness, worse when the nights lengthened and the weather became cold, and worst of all among the growing numbers without jobs or prospects. The levels of alcoholism and drug abuse in the capital mounted with every passing month.

But, even in these dark times, crime was not like this.

When they found the first body, nobody was surprised. These things happened from time to time. They had always happened, even in the old days, though then the authorities had made sure they were never reported. In these more liberal times, the privately owned scandal sheets picked up on stories like this and tried to stir up some trouble. But such incidents were usually soon forgotten, either because the police knew immediately who was responsible or because they were never likely to find out.

The body had been found in one of the narrow unlit side-streets near the city centre, in the shadow of a long-abandoned clothing factory. Cocooned in his new role, Nergui had had no reason to be involved. But he felt some frustration that this potentially interesting case had arisen so soon after his detachment to the Ministry. Bored and curious, he had used his new-found authority to request a copy of the scene-of-crime report. To his surprise, it arrived promptly and without question. One of the minor privileges available to those who no longer had to deal with policing on the front line.

Not for the first time, reading through the turgid account, Nergui wished that the police were able to demand a higher standard of literacy from their front-line officers. But the basic narrative was clear enough. A local drunk had found the body, while making his way home in the small hours after a night spent gambling in some illegal bar.

Nergui had seen more than enough dead bodies in his career. He could only hope that, when the drunk realised what lay beside him, alcohol had lessened the shock. But he suspected not, given the copious amounts of vomit apparently spread across the body when the police arrived. The pathologist, faced with an already unpleasant task, had expressed outrage at this further disruption of the evidence. On the other hand, as Nergui glanced through the crime-scene photographs he had to admit that, even for a sober person, vomiting would have been an understandable response.

The body was severely mutilated; it had been decapitated and was missing its hands, the neck and wrists savagely chopped as though with a heavy blunt blade. There were multiple lacerations to the chest as if the killer had been unable to stop, slashing savagely at the body, tearing repeatedly through its thin clothing, long after life must have departed. There was no sign of the missing body parts.

The pathologist had concluded that, in fact, all this mutilation had occurred after death. The most likely cause of death itself was strangling or asphyxiation. There was little other visible evidence. The body was dressed in Western-style clothes – cheap trousers, a thin cotton shirt, a rough jacket. Apart from the tearings and blood stains, the clothes were clean and looked new. They were mass-produced items that could have been purchased anywhere although this late in the year, it was difficult to imagine that anyone had willingly gone outside dressed like that. The pockets were empty.

The local police had, characteristically, stumbled into the incident more or less by accident. A passing patrolman, shining his flashlight down the side-street, had been startled by the scene – the twisted body, the prone drunk. His first reaction was to call for back-up, and then to apprehend the still retching drunk who had offered little resistance.

It was a natural assumption. Most deaths and criminal injuries in the city were the result of drunken brawls. But a moment's glance at the corpse had been enough to tell the patrolman that, though the drunk might be a witness, he was unlikely to be the perpetrator. There was little blood surrounding the body, and it was clear that the murder and dismemberment had taken place elsewhere and some time before.

Apart from the additional lacerations, the murder had all the signs of a professional killing. The removal of the head and hands had presumably been intended to conceal the victim's identity, the clothes had been stripped of identifying marks. The body had been dumped here, in the dark but just off the main drag, so there had been no concern about its being found. It might even be that the discovery of the body, and its inevitable reporting in the media, was intended as a warning to someone.

The murder might have been committed for any number of reasons. The drugs trade had made its inroads here as it had in most impoverished Soviet satellites, especially among the younger unemployed. There were the usual networks of organised crime – much of it with its roots over the borders in China and Russia but gaining an ever-stronger foothold in the capital. This was a country with no money but plenty of potential. The perfect buyer's market for anyone looking to get a piece of the future action.

And, of course, there was no shortage of home-grown corruption. It was only a few years since the Mon-Macau Casino scandal had resulted in the trial and imprisonment of a prominent group of politicians on bribery charges. And that case had been just one high-profile example of what was becoming an endemic problem – a seeping corruption evident in all parts of public life. Even, as he knew only too well, among the police themselves.

The police would make a show of investigating, but they would probably make little progress. For all its horror, this was the kind of crime that wouldn't justify much investigative time; the chances of resolving it were too small and it was in nobody's interest to dig too deeply. And even the most honest policemen might think that the victim, whoever he might be, probably deserved his fate. Which, Nergui conceded, could well be the case.

So, after a small flurry in the press, the case aroused little interest. Nergui had the details logged in the Ministry files on the off-chance there was some connection to any of the fraud or other cases they were already investigating, but he didn't seriously expect any link; he had already dismissed the murder as just another manifestation of the criminal underclass that infested this city.

And then, a week later, they found the second body.

'You are something of an expert in this field, I understand?' Nergui said. Outside, the night and guttering lights rolled past them as the car entered the city outskirts. The heavy industrial sites gave way to row after row of featureless low-rise apartment buildings, a familiar testament to ugly Soviet pragmatism. Most looked neglected, paint peeling, the occasional window smashed. But virtually all seemed to be inhabited – there were lights at the windows, occasional lines of washing hanging limply in the cold evening.

Then, unexpectedly, in an open space between the tightly packed apartment blocks, there was another clustering of *gers*, a nomadic camp somehow lost in the urban anonymity. Drew stared out at the neat lines of identical round grey tents, the smoke rising steadily from their central chimneys. There were ranks of old-fashioned, brightly polished Russian motorbikes and a lone tethered horse, its breath clouding the night in the pale orange of the streetlights. As if to compound the incongruity, a group of denim-clad teenagers stood chatting around a single streetlight in the heart of the camp, cigarettes glowing in their hands, as though transported there from some Western inner city.

He looked back at Nergui. The Mongolian was watching him closely, as though his response might be significant. Nergui's face remained expressionless, his flat features and dark skin looking almost as if they might be carved from wood.

'That would be an exaggeration,' Drew said. 'But I've had to deal with a lot of violent crime. Including murder.'

'Serial killings?'

'It depends what you mean. I handled one case where we had a genuine psychopath. He killed twice before we got him, but if we hadn't I don't doubt that he'd have killed more. And I've handled several multiple killings, but those were mostly professional hits.'

Nergui nodded. 'Which may be what we have here.'

'I wouldn't like to speculate,' Drew said. 'From what I've read, the whole thing is just – well, bizarre. It doesn't sound like the random killings of a psychopath, but it's a strange way to organise any kind of professional hit.'

'Yes, indeed,' Nergui said. 'Well, we welcome your help. And we will do all we can to reciprocate. We understand that this matter is a concern to both our countries.'

In truth, it wasn't clear why Drew had been sent here. It

was not unusual, when a serious crime had been committed against a British subject, for an investigating officer to be sent to work with the local police. Often, it was little more than a token gesture, a demonstration to the public that the matter was being taken seriously. This was probably the case here. The brutal murder of a British businessman in a remote and largely unknown country was always going to create a stir in the tabloids, even though the full details of the murder had not been released.

The victim had been a Manchester resident, and Drew, as one of the more experienced investigating officers, had been offered the opportunity to make the trip. It was a difficult offer to refuse, although Drew could see little that he could bring to this particular party. Investigating any crime, even murder – especially murder – was generally a matter of routine, of systematically exploring every avenue, sifting each bit of information, until you began to make the connections. There was little doubt that Nergui and Doripalam would be organising that side of things very efficiently. Drew might facilitate some contacts in the UK, if there turned out to be any significance in the last victim's identity, but that was probably about it.

They had now entered the city centre. The road widened into a brightly lit avenue, lined with a mix of official-looking buildings, many studded with communist emblems, and newer commercial offices, some with Korean, Japanese or even American business names that Drew recognised. This could be any Eastern European city struggling to come to grips with life after the Soviet Union – the first shoots of Western capitalism alongside drab weathered concrete, poorly maintained roads and streetlights, shabby squares and inner-city parks. Familiar logos, neon-lit on the summits of office buildings, competed with stylised images of soldiers and stars

– the fading murals of communism. And then, off to the right, there was a sudden glimpse of a very different building, the monastery of Choijin Lama, palely illuminated against the dark sky – a jumble of curving gilded rooflines, copper and crimson colourings, towers and short golden spires.

It was not late, but the streets were largely deserted, except for an occasional passing truck or car – mostly old-fashioned former Soviet or Eastern European models. Nergui pointed to an imposing building on the right. 'The British Embassy,' he said.

Drew nodded. 'The ambassador wants to see me. I've an appointment for tomorrow.'

'For lunch?'

Drew laughed. 'I don't think so. I'm due there at ten. I'm probably not important enough to merit lunch.'

'A pity,' Nergui said, as if he really meant it. 'He gives a good lunch.'

Drew was vaguely wondering how often this senior policeman had cause to lunch with the British ambassador when the car pulled to a halt outside the hotel Chinggis Khaan.

Nergui gestured towards the extraordinary towering pink and black glass monolith, set incongruously among the featureless Soviet-style architecture that otherwise dominated much of the city centre. 'I hope you don't mind staying here,' he said. 'I was unsure whether it was tactful to place you so near the scene of the crime.'

Drew shrugged. 'At least I'll be on hand for the next one,' he said. Even as he spoke, he felt that his words were glib and inappropriate.

But Nergui gazed at him impassively, as if taking his statement seriously. 'Let us hope,' he said, 'that your help will not be needed.'

TWO

At first, the second killing changed little. The circumstances were different, and nobody connected the two deaths. The body was found in the early morning, sprawled in a narrow alley at the rear of the Hotel Bayangol, by a hotel cleaner heading in to work. She had nearly walked past, mistaking the corpse for one of the huddled homeless drunks commonly found sleeping in the meagre warmth of the hotel's rear entrance or scavenging in its kitchen bins. But as she got closer, she realised that the distorted angle of the limbs and the surrounding splashes of blood indicated a fall from a much greater height than street level. Her screams were loud enough to bring out a group of the hotel's kitchen staff who had been smoking by the rear exit.

By the time Doripalam arrived an hour later, the body had already been removed. One of the local officers was standing within the police cordon, apparently directing activities. Doripalam hoped, without much confidence, that everything had been done by the book. More likely, the priority had just been to clear up the mess.

'What's the story?' he asked.

The local man shrugged, looking mildly irritated at Doripalam's arrival. Doripalam was growing accustomed to this. He had once naively assumed that local forces – with their limited resources always stretched to the limit – would welcome the involvement of the Serious Crimes Team. Now he realised that as far as the locals were con-

24

cerned, his arrival simply heralded more complications and more work.

'Who knows?' the man said. 'Suicide, probably, or a drunk trying to close his bedroom window. We're checking the hotel guest list. Shouldn't take long.' He turned away, the sense of dismissal almost palpable.

But, by the end of the morning, when the case remained unresolved, the local team had itself been dismissed and Doripalam's men had taken over. Doripalam established a temporary base in the hotel manager's office, and sat with Batzorig, one of his junior officers, working through the data that had been collected. They were no closer to identifying the victim or to determining the circumstances of the death. Batzorig, with his usual blend of enthusiasm and rigour, was working painstakingly through his notes. 'It looks as if we've accounted for all the guests and hotel staff. We thought at first that one of the night porters was missing but he was just sleeping off a hangover.'

Doripalam looked up and raised an eyebrow. 'A hangover? Was he on duty?'

'Supposedly. I don't think our investigation has done his employment prospects a lot of good.'

Doripalam nodded. It was this kind of thing that made his team so unpopular. Solving serious crimes usually meant uncovering a raft of more trivial misdemeanours along the way. 'So what do we know, then?'

'Well, we know that the victim didn't fall through a bedroom window – all the rooms on that side of the hotel were either occupied or locked, and there's no sign of any disturbance. It looks as if the body must have fallen from the hotel roof.'

'Is the roof accessible?'

'Not easily, but you can get up there through a maintenance area on the top floor. You'd have to know about the access, though – it's not the sort of thing you'd just stumble across.'

'So this isn't just some drunk who went up to look at the stars and took one step too many?'

'It doesn't look like it. And, since he wasn't staying at the hotel, we don't know how or when he got in. But security wasn't particularly tight. They usually lock the doors at midnight, but if he'd come in before that he wouldn't necessarily have been spotted. We're checking the security cameras, but I'm not hopeful. We're still waiting for confirmation of the time of death – it's not easy to be precise because it was so cold out overnight – but it could have been midnight or even earlier.'

'And nobody saw anything?'

'We're interviewing all the guests and the staff. But so far nothing.'

'But this still could just be a suicide?' Doripalam was playing devil's advocate, but everything had to be checked. After all, suicide was not exactly unknown in the city, or indeed anywhere else in the country. Unemployment had been running at forty per cent or more in the post-Soviet era. Poverty levels were similar, although less severe in the urban areas. Many people were living at barely more than subsistence levels.

Batzorig shrugged. 'Well, yes, it could be. But the puzzle is the anonymity. We've got a body dressed in cheap, mass-produced clothing – empty pockets, no documentation, no identifying labels. Why would a suicide bother to clear his pockets? For that matter, why would he bother to break into a hotel to kill himself? I can think of plenty of easier ways to do it. It doesn't feel right to me.'

Batzorig's instinct proved correct; the body remained anonymous. The fingerprints matched nothing in the police records. The dental records provided no clues. The victim was confirmed as a male, in his late thirties, medium height, heavily built, and appeared to be a Mongolian national. Beyond that, there was no information. The story was reported in the media, and the police hoped that someone would come forward to identify him, but there was little else they could do.

The post-mortem revealed that the victim had died from the massive trauma caused by the impact of hitting the hard concrete. But, although the state of the body prevented a definitive judgement, the victim appeared to have been involved in some sort of violent struggle prior to death, and there were traces of a strong sedative in the victim's blood. There seemed little doubt that the man had been murdered.

To his surprise, Nergui had found that a copy of the scene-of-crime report arrived on his desk in the Ministry, this time unrequested. Clearly his authority was now such that his arbitrary demands were immediately interpreted as essential departmental routines. After all these years, he was finally beginning to understand the attractions of power.

Nevertheless, the coincidence of the two unexplained deaths sparked his interest. Murders happened in the city more frequently than most people liked to admit; but this was still a relatively stable society. Most killings were sordid and straightforward – crimes of passion, drunken brawling, domestic violence. Even the unexplained murders could usually be categorised fairly easily. If a small-time local hoodlum was found murdered, it might be difficult to identify the individual perpetrator, but the police would generally have a good idea why the killing had happened and what sorts of people were involved.

But this was different. His curiosity aroused, Nergui took the opportunity to set up an informal meeting with his former deputy, Doripalam. Doripalam was young and relatively inexperienced, at least compared with his predecessor, but Nergui respected his intelligence and judgement. He had tried to keep some distance since Doripalam's promotion, anxious not to be seen as interfering, but offering support and advice when requested.

For his part, Doripalam seemed happy still to treat Nergui as a mentor, and was keen to draw on the older man's experience. They had developed a routine of meeting once a month, in one of the new American-style coffee houses that were beginning to spring up around the city centre. Nergui was intrigued that, despite the chaotic state of the economy, money was still available to spend in places like this.

They had arranged to meet early, but the place was already busy with a mix of young people – students, for the most part, chatting and smoking between lectures – and serious-looking businessmen in dark suits, earnestly discussing business deals or making apparently urgent calls on mobile phones. There was a rich smell of coffee and the cloying scent of baking pasties.

Outside the sun was shining and the sky was an unsullied blue. Across the street, at the edge of the square, crowds of men clustered round tables, playing chess or chequers, taking advantage of what might turn out to be one of the last temperate days of the year. Some of the older ones were dressed in traditional robes, but most were in heavy overcoats, with berets or American-style baseball caps pulled down over their eyes against the glare of the mid-morning sun. The fug of countless cigarettes hung around them like a localised cloud.

Nergui looked with some displeasure at the large foaming cup that Doripalam placed in front of him. 'This isn't coffee,' he said. 'It's a nursery drink.'

Doripalam shrugged. 'It's what the Americans drink. Apparently.'

'So we must get used to it.' Nergui took a mouthful and grimaced. 'Though that may take some time, I think. But thank you anyway.'

Doripalam sat down opposite and sipped at his own drink. 'So how are you finding life in the corridors of power?'

'I think the power must be in another corridor. All I do is attend meetings and sign forms. While you get all the good fortune.'

'Do I? Remind me.'

'Two homicide cases in a week. And both of them more interesting than anything I had to deal with in the last five years.'

'Oh, yes, that good fortune. How could I forget?'

'What's your view? Do you think they're linked?'

Doripalam looked at Nergui for a second, then he smiled. 'This is a fishing expedition?' he said. 'Surely the Minister isn't interested in anything as trivial as murder?' He was still smiling, and his wide-eyed features seemed innocent of anything more than mild curiosity, but Nergui knew better than to underestimate him.

'This is purely on my own account,' Nergui said. 'I'd like to be able to claim some official justification, but it's just idle curiosity. Wishing I was back in the old routine.' He stared gloomily down at the absurd coffee, and, for a moment, Doripalam felt some sympathy for his former boss. Sitting here, his austere dark grey suit off-set by a characteristically garish orange tie, his large body hunched awkwardly over the table, Nergui looked uncomfortably like a man who no longer had a purpose in life.

Nergui's detachment to the Ministry of Justice and Internal Affairs had been a substantial promotion, requested by the Minister himself. Nergui had always been an aloof figure in the police department, well respected but not widely liked among the team. There had been too many rumours about his past, too much suspicion about his real motives. And, of course, Nergui had always made very clear his intolerance for the incompetence and petty corruption that was endemic in the civil police.

For many in the team, Nergui's transfer to the Ministry had been a confirmation of their long-held assumptions – that all along he had been an authority lackey, delegated to strip away the few meagre perks associated with their thankless job. Or, worse, that he was simply another opportunist, adept at riding the waves of political change, with no loyalty except to his current paymaster.

But Doripalam hadn't shared these views. He had no doubt about Nergui's professional commitment or dedication, and he shared the older man's distaste at the endless petty corruption that seemed to be taken for granted by most of his colleagues. On a personal level, he had always found Nergui straightforward and trustworthy, if enigmatic, and he had been grateful when Nergui had actively endorsed his own promotion to head of department.

He was not surprised that the Minister, looking for a trustworthy ally in an increasingly turbulent political world, should have seen Nergui as one of the few individuals with the necessary abilities and personal integrity. And, in the circumstances, he could hardly be surprised that Nergui had found the offer impossible to refuse. But he suspected that, for all the prestige and material rewards associated with his new role, the old man would never be comfortable shuffling papers.

'For what it's worth,' Doripalam said, in response to Nergui's question, 'I don't think the murders are linked. I think it's probably just coincidence. It's unusual to have two such murders in close proximity, but that doesn't mean it can't happen. Or maybe it's some small-time feud. If so, I don't think anyone other than maybe their mothers will be grieving too hard.'

So, in the face of this summary dismissal, Nergui's interest had remained casual. There were no evident tie-ups with the other cases that his team in the Ministry was currently investigating – the largest of which was a complex corruption case in the taxation office. In truth, there was no reason to justify even the limited amount of time he had spent on the murder cases. He told himself that it was useful to keep in touch with developments in other areas of the Ministry. But he knew he was fooling himself, trying to find some justification for dabbling again in his old area of expertise.

But that all changed when they found the third body.

It was discovered three days after the second, and Nergui took the call within thirty minutes of the body being found. It was not merely the usual routine passing on of information, but the Minister himself, clearly agitated. Nergui spoke with him frequently, often two or three times a day, and he knew that the Minister was not easily rattled. On the whole, Nergui had little sympathy with either the Minister's politics or his ethics, but he had already learned to be grateful for the politician's calmness in the face of crisis.

'You've heard they've found another body, Nergui?'

'Another body? When?' Nergui assumed that the Minister had only just learned about the second killing. His staff tended to brief him only on the day's essentials, and it was reasonable to assume that a sordid street murder would not rate highly in the Minister of Justice's priorities.

'This morning.'

'No, I hadn't heard yet.' He wondered how long it

would be before the neatly typed scene-of-crime report dropped unbidden on to his desk.

'This is becoming a dangerous place to live, Nergui.'

Nergui sighed inwardly. He knew that the Minister's primary interest would be how this would play in the media. Under the old regime, this would not have been a problem. These days, although the state still owned the radio and television, the clusters of privately owned newspapers made old-style censorship virtually impossible. There were times when Nergui wondered whether this was entirely a positive outcome. At least in the old days you knew where you stood, even if it was in a state of blind ignorance. Today, the media agenda was more subtle but equally pernicious, as a multitude of owners – from individual entrepreneurs to political parties – made sure that their own perspectives were appropriately represented.

'Does there seem to be a link to the other murders?' Nergui asked.

'To the first, anyway,' the Minister said.

'The decapitation?'

'Exactly.'

'Any clues on identity?'

'None, apparently. Just like the others.'

'Right. I assume you've spoken to Serious Crimes—'

'Nergui,' the Minister said. 'You know as well as I do that the state police department, Serious Crimes or otherwise, is divided pretty equally between the corrupt and the inept. They could barely cope with the theft of a tourist's bicycle. Why do you think I was so keen to co-opt the one decent brain I found in the place? From where I'm sitting, this is a priority. No, this is *the* priority. Forget all the banking and state corruption stuff. We can afford to let them steal a bit more. I want you back there to sort this one out.'

Despite himself, Nergui momentarily felt his spirit lighten, but his better judgement prevailed. 'I really don't think that's a good idea. And, with respect, your comments aren't entirely fair. Doripalam's an excellent man—'

'Which is why, if I recall, he got the job as your successor with barely five years' experience under his belt. As I understand it, he was the only one there with a degree of integrity and two brain cells to rub together. But he'll be out of his depth with this, and I want it sorted quickly. I've already told them you're going back. I've told them to give you whatever you need. But get it dealt with.'

Thanks, Nergui thought. The police always love being told what to do by politicians. Especially when it's the prodigal son returning from his cushy billet as the Justice Minister's favoured lackey. And for all their friendship and mutual respect, Doripalam was unlikely to be first in the welcoming committee. He was already fighting an uphill struggle to gain credibility with the longer-serving but much less able officers who were now reporting to him. The enforced return of Nergui at the first sign of difficulty was hardly likely to strengthen Doripalam's position in the team.

Nergui couldn't help feeling some irrational guilt. In his heart, he knew – and he suspected that Doripalam would also know – that this was exactly the development that he'd been quietly fantasising about throughout the whole of the last six mind-numbing months.

'Okay,' he said at last. 'If you say so, Minister. I'll do my best.'

The Minister hung up. Nergui stared for a moment at the receiver, wondering why it was that the politician judged it appropriate to dispense with all the standard courtesies in his dealings with others. Then, hesitating only momentarily, he dialled Doripalam's number.

'It's okay,' Doripalam said, before Nergui could launch into an explanation. 'I've already been told. At least now I know why you were so keen to meet for coffee.'

'Doripalam, that's not—'

'No, I know. I was joking. I'm not exactly overjoyed, but I don't imagine this is your fault. At least I hope not. We have to make the best of it.'

'I'll try to make it as painless as possible,' Nergui said. 'Really.'

'Yes,' Doripalam said. 'I'm sure you will.'

An hour later, Nergui stood silently with the young man, examining the desolate spot where the third body had been found. The body itself had been taken away for the post-mortem. Nergui had seen it briefly, but it had told him nothing except how disgusting a mutilated human body can look. Which was something he already knew too well.

They were on the edge of the city, the dark green mountains rising behind them. This was one of the areas where the population still lived largely in the traditional round nomadic tents, rather than in the endless rows of faceless apartments that had grown during the Communist era. The presence of the tents was commonplace, even in this urban environment, but Nergui, after his time in the West, found it jarring.

It was tradition, of course, a way of life uniquely appropriate to the climate and lifestyle of the country. But it was a strange way to live, he thought, as though the inhabitants were trying to deny the city's existence, desperate to be up and on the move instead. Or perhaps that was not so odd. In this land, it was the city, the presumption of permanence, that was the aberration. And there was no question that the tents were solid and comfortable enough with their wooden frames and brightly painted doors, the thick felt and canvas of the walls. With the central stove burning, a few glasses of vodka, and the shared body heat of a family, it was possible to repel even the harshest of Mongolian winters. And Nergui had to acknowledge that the clusterings of family groups, the *ails*, offered a sense of community that was different from anything he had ever known.

But the body had been found outside all of this, dumped in a scrubby knot of fir trees in a small ravine. It was a bleak spot, especially so late in the year when, even at midday, the low sun barely penetrated its shadows. There had been a stream running through here, but the dry autumn had left the ground parched and cracked. The trees and bushes were scattered with garbage, rusting tins and rotting cardboard discarded from the camp above.

Earlier that morning, an ageing guard dog, left prowling by the edge of the camp while its owner sat outside his tent boiling water for tea, had suddenly raced off into the ravine, barking endlessly. By the time the owner had caught up, the dog had been snarling at a bundle dumped in some bushes. Even without touching the object, the owner had had some premonition about its contents and had backed up the slope to track down the local police.

It was fortunate that he had not looked more closely. The state of the body was even worse than that of the first. The head and hands had been removed, the severed neck and wrists yawning bloodily, and there were similar large knife wounds to the chest, this time cut savagely down to the bone. There was little blood and the body had not yet begun to decay. The murder had clearly happened in some other location, and relatively recently. The pathologist had quickly concluded that death had been caused by the stab wounds, but that again the removal of the limbs had taken place after death. Given the cold weather, it was difficult as yet to pinpoint the time of death precisely, but the killing had probably taken place overnight or even earlier that morning, perhaps only some six or seven hours before. It was not clear how the body had been transported to this spot, although it would not have been difficult to get a van or truck close to the edge of the ravine.

The victim was dressed in a heavyweight burgundy *del*, the traditional garb of the herdsmen out on the steppes, a heavy robe wrapped around the body, tied with an ornate but faded belt, designed to combat the rigours of the Mongolian winter. Such clothing was still commonplace even in the city, particularly among the older residents.

'Can we identify the clothing?' Nergui asked. 'This isn't one of those mass-produced Chinese suits.'

Doripalam shrugged. 'We might. But I'm not optimistic. The *del* and the boots are both years old, though they've worn well. The labels have been removed. That stuff could have been made or purchased anywhere in the country. Probably goes back to Soviet times.'

'So what else do we have?'

'Not much. Another male, probably in his late forties, fairly short and stout, and definitely Mongolian. There are no other identifying features. No other possessions. In a word – nothing.' Doripalam shook his head and then kicked at the hard ground in frustration. 'Just another nameless corpse.'

It was a cold clear morning, and the temperature had dropped from the brief Indian summer of the previous week. Winter was on the way, and the young man had a heavy black overcoat pulled tightly around him. He was a slight figure, constantly full of nervous energy. He took several steps out into the scrubby wasteland and then turned back, as though pacing a room. His dark hair, Nergui noted, was perhaps slightly too long.

'They weren't making any attempt to hide the body,' Nergui said. It was a comment rather than a question.

'If they'd wanted to conceal it, they wouldn't have chosen this spot.' He gestured up at the rows of *gers* visible above the ravine. 'There are people down here all the time. People with their dogs. Children playing.'

'Lucky it was a dog found it, then,' Nergui said grimly.

Doripalam nodded. 'But you have to say,' he added, 'that it's as if they wanted it to be found.'

'That seems a potential link between the three killings,' Nergui said. 'The bodies were left in places where they were bound to be found quickly, even though in two cases the murders took place elsewhere. But the killer has gone to great lengths to make sure we can't easily identify the bodies. So why not hide the bodies as well?'

Doripalam shrugged. 'I couldn't begin to imagine the thought processes of someone who does this.'

Nergui had been peripherally involved in a couple of serial killer cases while liaising with his Russian counterparts, and he was well aware of the confused psychology that underpinned such acts. That, of course, was to assume that these murders were indeed the work of a psychopath. Taken in isolation, the apparent professionalism of the murders would have suggested something more cold-blooded, more calculated; a commercial transaction. But three professional hits in two weeks seemed unlikely.

'Do you seriously think they're linked?' asked Doripalam, reading Nergui's thoughts. He knew well enough why the Minister had requested Nergui's return. And, as Nergui had half-suspected, while Doripalam had been far from pleased at the implied judgement of his own abilities, he had to admit some private relief that if they really were facing a serial killer, it would be Nergui's handling of the case under scrutiny. 'I mean, the second body as well?'

Nergui shrugged. 'I don't know any more than you,' he said. It was always worth saying that, even though Doripalam wouldn't believe him. The police always assumed that the Ministry was privy to information denied to ordinary officers. If only they realised how rarely that was the case, Nergui thought. 'It's difficult to imagine that this one isn't linked to the first, but the second – who knows? But, given the timing, I guess there are enough similarities for us to at least bear it in mind until we've got some better ideas.'

They trudged back up the steep slope to where the *gers* were clustered. After the gloomy shadows of the ravine, the bright morning sunshine created at least an illusion of warmth. A group of middle-aged women, mostly dressed in dark-coloured felt robes and heavy boots, were standing talking, watching the two policemen with apparent suspicion. Other women were sitting at the south-facing doors of their *gers*, washing clothes in plastic bowls or carefully chopping vegetables, peering at the two men from under their tightly bound headscarves.

There was a man, a heavyweight brown *del* pulled tightly around his body, a grey beret clamped firmly on his head, crouching by the engine of an old Russian IJ Planeta motorbike, carrying out some kind of work on the engine. He had a lit cigarette dangling from the corner of his mouth, apparently unconcerned about his proximity to the bike's fuel tank. A small group of children, dressed mostly in Western-style jeans and thick sweaters, were gathered round him, watching intently as if he were some form of street entertainment. There was a radio playing in the distance, a keening traditional tune probably playing on the state channel. In counterpoint to the plangent music, a dog barked shrilly and incessantly. From somewhere, there was the rich smell of roasting meat and the softer scent of wood smoke. It was difficult to imagine a psychopath stalking this community.

'You've made enquiries among this lot?' Nergui asked.

'We've started,' Doripalam said. 'Nobody saw or heard anything last night, so they say.'

'Nothing?'

'So they say.'

Nergui nodded. It was always the same. It had, apparently, been the same at the hotel. No one had seen or heard anything. 'Still, we have to keep asking. We may get something eventually.'

'You never know,' Doripalam said.

Nergui shook his head. This was going nowhere. It was all just routine stuff, which Doripalam would handle as well as, if not better than he could. Forensic examination of the victims' bodies. Attempts to gather any relevant data they could from the records. Links to any previous killings – though Nergui could think of no obvious ones. Routine questioning of possible witnesses. The usual grind of investigative work. But, unless they could begin to unravel the mystery of who the victims were, Nergui couldn't see them making any headway. It wasn't the kind of thing he would say to the Minister, but the best hope of their making further progress would be for the killer to strike again. Ideally, he added to himself as an afterthought, without actually succeeding.

As it turned out, Nergui's unexpressed wish was soon granted, though only in part. The killer struck again, and unexpectedly quickly. Unfortunately, he was all too successful.

The call came at around eleven the following morning. Nergui was in his new office in police HQ, reading and re-reading through the police reports on the previous killings. He had not thought it appropriate to turf Doripalam out of the office that had previously been his own, and had been quite happy to lodge himself in a small, unused room at the end of the corridor, with only a cheap desk and an empty filing cabinet for company. He hoped that this was at least sending the right message to Doripalam and the rest of the team.

Even before he picked up the phone, his instincts were telling him that this was not good news.

'Nergui? It's Doripalam.'

'What is it?'

'There's been another one.'

'Already? The Minister was right for once – this is getting a dangerous place to live. Where?'

'The Chinggis. In one of the bedrooms.'

'You're joking.'

'I don't hear you laughing.'

Nergui was silent for a moment. The Chinggis Khaan was one of the city's newest hotels, built in response to the growing business and tourist trade in the city. Any incident there would have major repercussions, maybe even international repercussions. The Minister, it was safe to predict, would not be happy.

'Do we think it's linked to the others?' Nergui asked.

'It's difficult to say,' Doripalam said, after a pause. 'This one's different.'

'Different how?' Nergui asked, already dreading the answer.

'I think you'd better come and see for yourself.'

It took only minutes for Nergui to reach the hotel in an official car, sirens screaming. The Chinggis was a striking building, a successful attempt to bring Western-style service and luxury to the city. Some of the other hotels, including the Bayangol, had subsequently emulated its style, upgrading their previously basic facilities to something that might begin to meet Western expectations.

Nergui waved his ID pass at the reception and was directed across the expansive lobby to the lifts. He glanced around him at the dark mirrored walls, the thick-piled carpet, the clusters of Japanese and Western tourists waiting to start their morning's excursions. He'd been in the place a few times before for conferences and formal meetings, but hardly knew his way around. Nevertheless, it wasn't hard to find the room number that Doripalam had given him. There were officers dotted throughout the lobby and by the lifts, discreetly deflecting guests to ensure they didn't approach the crime scene accidentally. They nodded to him as he passed.

The bedroom also had an officer stationed outside. Nergui was glad they were doing this by the book, but hoped that the police presence didn't itself stir up concerns. Still, the hotel had more than its share of high-profile visitors from overseas. Probably the other guests would simply assume that some international celebrity was among them.

Doripalam waved him in. The room was impressive, Nergui thought, and compared favourably with those he had seen on his travels in Europe and the US. In other circumstances, he would have thought it luxurious, with its wooden panelling and plush king-size twin beds. As it was, his attention was entirely dominated by what lay on the nearest of those beds.

For all his experience, Nergui almost found himself gagging. The rich smell of blood was overwhelming, even though the scene-of-crime officers had thrown open the windows in an attempt to render the atmosphere of the room bearable. The two officers had stationed themselves, understandably enough, by the open window.

The white cotton sheets of the bed were thoroughly soaked with blood, and there were further splashes on the carpet and pale walls. The blood was beginning to turn from red to brown, but clearly the killing was relatively recent. The chambermaid had discovered the body when entering to clean the room in the mid-morning. Nergui thought that she could never have imagined how much her cleaning skills might be required, though he guessed she wouldn't willingly be back in this room for a long time.

The body was spread-eagled on the bed, dressed in blood-caked cotton striped pyjamas. Nergui would have described the body as lying face up, except that the face was definitely not looking upwards. The head had been severed from the body, but this time had not been removed from the scene. Instead it had been placed neatly on top of the television set, gazing impassively at its former owner on the bed.

Nergui opened his mouth but could think of nothing to say. Doripalam and the other officers stood silently, looking almost smug that for once there was a sight that had rendered the legendary Nergui speechless.

In fact, Nergui had been struck by two overwhelming thoughts almost simultaneously. The first had been sheer mindless horror at the enormity of the sight that lay before him. The second was the realisation that the mutilated figure before him was a Westerner.

What, he thought before he could stop himself, would the Minister have to say about this?

THREE

'I'm impressed,' Drew said. 'This is excellent. A lot better than most of the hotels I get to stay in.'

Nergui gestured him to sit down. 'I hope beer's okay. We still have good contacts with Eastern Europe, so can get some decent stuff.' He lifted the glass and gazed thoughtfully at the contents. 'Czech. They know how to make beer.'

'Beer's perfect,' Drew said, with complete sincerity. His early-morning departure from Manchester seemed a lifetime away, and the long and fragmented journey had only compounded his sense of disorientation. And now, in a country where half the population lived in tents, he was drinking beer in the kind of anonymous hotel bar that might be found in any capital city in the world. Soft piped music was playing in the background, a piano version of some pop tune that Drew half-recognised.

'Your room is okay?'

'Fine,' Drew said. 'Excellent.'

Nergui nodded. 'I should not say this, perhaps. But your room is very similar to the one where – well, where we found the body.'

Drew nodded slowly, unsure how to respond. It was difficult to imagine the plush bedroom despoiled by the scene he had read about. He looked at Nergui, sitting magisterially in the corner of the hotel bar, and wondered how seriously he should take him. He was an impressive figure, heavy-set and tall by Mongolian standards, with a stillness and physical presence that somehow enabled him to dominate the room. His even features were distinctively Mongolian, wide-eyed and broad-cheeked, his clean-shaven skin dark and almost leathery, as though it had been burnished by the sun and wind of the desert. His dress was mildly eccentric – a plain, dark, good-quality suit contrasting with a shirt and tie both in what Drew supposed was salmon pink. But it would not be difficult, Drew thought, to imagine him, centuries before, riding out as a member of Genghis Khan's armies, leading the conquest of the known world.

Nergui's bright blue eyes watched Drew intently, his blank face giving no clue to his thoughts or feelings. Doripalam sat beside him, a slighter and paler figure, toying aimlessly with a menu from the table, apparently disengaged from the conversation.

'I'm sorry,' Drew said. 'Is it okay if we speak in English?'

Doripalam glanced up, smiling faintly, brushing his thick hair back from his forehead. He had the same wide-eyed features, but on this young face the effect was of openness and eagerness, perhaps even naivety. 'We will teach you some Mongolian while you are here,' he said. 'My English is not so good as Nergui's but if you speak slowly I can follow.'

'I can translate for Doripalam if we need to,' Nergui said. 'But he is too modest. His English is really very good. More and more of us are trying to learn, since it seems now to be the international language.' He turned to Doripalam. 'We should tell Drew what we know so far about our fourth victim.'

'Well,' Doripalam said, 'as you know, his name was Ian Ransom. He was a geologist in the mining industry, with a contract with one of our mining consortia. He had been in the country before, on two occasions I think, working on contracts. We spoke to the company involved. They say he was an excellent employee – a specialist in his field, a hard worker, all of that. But we see no motive for the killing. He was not robbed – there was a wallet with currency and credit cards in his jacket in the wardrobe.'

'What about the work he was engaged in?' Drew said. 'Any possible motive there?'

Nergui shrugged. 'Mining is a difficult industry here. Rapid growth. Lots of money to be made. New players coming into it all the time. Massive foreign investment, not all of it particularly legitimate. We're a mineral-rich country and everyone would like a slice of it. So, yes, it's possible. But we can see no real evidence in this case. Ransom was a specialist, a scientist. He wasn't senior enough to get involved in anything risky, I would have thought.' He took a mouthful of his beer. 'But we're keeping an open mind.'

'There's not a lot I can add,' Drew said. 'We looked at Ransom's domestic circumstances, in case that shed any light. He was divorced, two children – two girls who live with his wife, who's remarried. He lived in Greater Manchester – decent house, decent area so presumably did all right financially. He seemed to have lived alone and, as far as we know, wasn't in any kind of relationship, maybe because he travelled so much. He had a doctorate in geology, and started his career after university with British Coal – that was our state mining industry, now largely closed down—'

'Ah. Your Mrs Thatcher,' Nergui said.

'Our Mrs Thatcher,' Drew agreed. 'Ransom took early retirement from British Coal about fifteen years ago, and has worked as a consultant since then, largely overseas. Worked in India, Australia, South Africa, China and, of course, here. Seems to have been a bit of a loner.'

'But nothing there that would provide a motive?' Nergui said.

'Not that we can see. I suppose when someone travels like that there's always the possibility that they might have got involved in something dodgy—'

'Dodgy?' Nergui asked. It was the first time he had shown any uncertainty in following Drew's English.

Drew laughed. 'Dodgy. Um – dubious, criminal. That kind of thing.'

'Ah,' Nergui said. 'I understand. Dodgy,' he repeated slowly, as though committing the word to memory.

'So, yes, it's possible. But there's no evidence of it. He didn't seem to be living above his means, for example, so there's no sign of him having an income from another source.'

Nergui nodded slowly. 'So we both seem to have arrived at the same conclusion,' he said. 'It's quite possible that there's no significance at all in Mr Ransom's unfortunate involvement in this.'

'You mean he was just selected at random?'

'Well, of course that is possible. If we really are dealing with a psychopath here, then it may be that the killings are simply opportunist. Perhaps the killer just spotted Ransom in the street. He would have – how do you say it? – stood out in the crowd here.'

'He certainly would,' Drew said. It was an unnerving thought, given that his own Caucasian features would presumably draw the same attention. He looked around the bar. Four men, all Mongolians, dressed in Western-style business suits, had come in and were drinking beers at the far end of the room. One of them glanced over and smiled vaguely in Drew's direction. Drew looked down at his beer, feeling inexplicably vulnerable.

The restaurant maintained the standard of the rest of the hotel. The food was nothing special, but certainly comparable with that provided by most business hotels in Europe. The atmosphere was pleasant enough – dark wood, dim lights, attentive service, even a cocktail pianist meandering though a selection of familiar melodies. Nergui remained an entirely charming host, advising on the food, suggesting they stick with beer rather than moving on to the mediocre and highly priced wine list. 'It's your choice,' he said. 'But the beer is better.'

In other circumstances, Drew would have found the experience thoroughly enjoyable. Here, though, it was impossible to ignore the looming presence of the killer. Drew looked uneasily around the busy restaurant, with its chattering mix of locals and Westerners, and hoped that the presence was only metaphorical. He couldn't understand why he felt so rattled – after all, in his time he had strolled willingly, if not always comfortably, around some of the rougher parts of inner-city Manchester. It was odd to feel this level of discomfort in an upmarket hotel dining room.

Nergui carefully dissected his prawn starter. 'I suppose that is the place we have to start – whether there is any significance in Ransom being the victim.' He shook his head. 'If he was simply chosen at random, then our difficulty is even greater.'

Drew could see the problem. The worst possibility, from the police perspective, was that they were dealing with a psychopath with no rational motive but a high level of lethal professionalism. There would be no way of knowing where the killer might strike next, and the likelihood was that the killer would be adept at minimising any potential leads or evidence. The only hope would be to wait until the killer made an error. And with the earlier victims still unidentified, at present the only possible lead lay with Ransom.

'You're not likely to identify the earlier victims?' Drew asked.

Nergui glanced at Doripalam, who shook his head.

'Who knows? We have gathered the forensic information. Perhaps there are more sophisticated tools in the West, but I do not know that they would tell us much more. We know as much as we can about the bodies, but we have no identities to link them to.'

'But you've had coverage in the media? Surely someone must know who these people are?'

Nergui smiled. 'This is not like your country. A quarter of our population is nomadic. Of course, there are close family ties in many cases, and these days most people are formally registered with the state for voting and social security purposes. It's easier than it used to be. But with all the troubles we've had over the last decade, there has been a lot of movement. In both directions. Nomadic people coming to the cities seeking work. And unemployed city dwellers moving out to try their hands at herding or farming – usually without much success. Some of those have lost touch with their families or friends. Some have drifted into crime or more marginal ways of surviving.' He finished the prawns and placed his knife and fork, with some precision, across the plate. 'It is most likely that the victims here were not from our stable middle classes. They will probably be from our growing underclass – criminals or those on the edge of criminality. We are trying to match them up with our missing person records and we may hit lucky, but I'm not too optimistic. If someone was missing these people, we'd have heard from them by now.'

It was a desolate but logical conclusion. 'And you're sure the four deaths are related?'

'Again, who knows? It's reasonable to assume that the first and third are related – the characteristics of the killings were identical. And the characteristics of the Ransom killing are sufficiently similar for us to assume a link. But the second killing was different – really, the only common factor was the timing and the anonymity of the victim. If you're asking whether we have only a single killer – well, I hope so. I don't like the idea of one murderer stalking the city, let alone two. But, yes, it's quite possible that the second killing was simply a coincidence, and we have to keep that in mind.'

'There's no possibility that the later murders were copycat killings?'

'Copycat killings?' Nergui frowned, puzzled at the terminology. 'That is one of your tabloid phrases, no?' He translated the phrase briefly for Doripalam's benefit.

Drew laughed. 'I suppose so. I just meant, well, that a second killer might have copied the characteristics of the first killing. It's not unknown.'

'No, I imagine not,' Nergui said. 'But it sounds unlikely in this case, unless we have two psychopaths on the loose.'

'Or someone who wants you to think that the subsequent killings were random,' Drew said. But even as he spoke he was aware that this was becoming fanciful, the terrain of crime fiction rather than real life. 'No, forget it. It's nonsense.'

Nergui shook his head. 'No, we need to remain open to every possibility, no matter how unlikely. As your Sherlock Holmes so rightly says.' He laughed. 'Although I think this is verging on the impossible, in fact. We have not published the full details of the earlier killings – the decapitation and so on. No doubt rumours have leaked out, but no one could have the full details except from the police. Though, of course,' he added, as an afterthought, 'the police themselves do not always demonstrate the highest levels of integrity. Another legacy of our recent history, I'm afraid.'

'What about some sort of gangland feud? Is that a possibility?'

'Of course. That may be the most likely explanation. Crime here has not tended to be that organised, but we cannot discount the influence of our friends across our two borders. Real organised crime is, sadly, becoming more prevalent. And it brings us back to Mr Ransom. If this is the fallout from some sort of feud, how did an apparently unimportant geologist get caught up in it?'

'There've been no further murders or similar assaults since Ransom's death?' Drew asked.

'Nothing. We have four brutal killings in less than two weeks, and then nothing. I'm glad to say,' Nergui added, in a tone that suggested this was perhaps only half true. Another killing or assault would be dreadful, of course, but might at least help to provide some further leads. 'No, I'm glad there have been no more, but it makes me uneasy. I'm waiting for—' He paused.

'For the second shoe to drop?'

'A graphic expression. Yes, precisely that. A sense of something incomplete.' He shook himself, and began to attack the mutton dish which had just been placed before him. 'We should stop talking shop and find something more pleasant to discuss. You enjoy football? Manchester United?'

'Manchester City, I'm afraid,' Drew said. 'The bitter rivals.'

'Ah, but not so successful, I believe?'

'You could say that. But we've had our moments. Do you play football here?'

Nergui nodded. 'Yes, we play. It's becoming more and more popular. And rugby. People still like the traditional sports – horses, archery, wrestling. The three manly sports, as we call them. But every day we become more part of the global community.'

'Do you want that?'

Nergui shrugged. 'What I want is neither here nor

there. Compared with the vast majority of people in this country, I am a global citizen. I've lived in Europe and the US. I've travelled regularly across Asia, the Middle East, Australia. I can see all the benefits of the changes that are taking place here. But I also see many losses.'

'What kinds of things?'

'Well, the losses are obvious. We're losing our traditional ways of living, of thinking. We're losing traditional family ties. This country has been through many changes over the last century. Things are improving now, but these are still difficult times. We have the potential to be a wealthy, successful economy, but we live in poverty and we are surrounded by predators. Not just Russia and China, but the West, too.'

'Predators?'

'Maybe I exaggerate. But I think not. I'm a patriot at heart, probably all the more so since I have travelled so widely. Most of my fellow countrymen take this country for granted. They have seen nothing else. They complain about the government. They complain about the police. They complain about the economy. All very understandable. They have been through difficult times. But I think they do not realise how much they could still lose.' He laughed suddenly. 'I am sorry. We start to talk about football, and immediately I plunge you into despair.'

'You get used to that,' Drew said, 'supporting Manchester City.'

Nergui laughed appreciatively. 'I'm sorry,' he said again. 'I am being selfish. You must be tired and I just sit here rambling on about the state of our nation.'

'It's very interesting,' Drew said, honestly. He found himself wondering again about this man's role and rank, and also, for the first time, wondering about his background. Mongolia had been, in effect, a satellite of the USSR until the beginning of the 1990s. It was unlikely that Nergui had risen to a senior role in the police without being part of the previous regime, particularly since the Communist Party, with its new-found enthusiasm for democracy, had remained in power here for much of the past decade. Drew's understanding was that the police, in its current civilian form, was a product only of the mid-1990s, so it was likely that Nergui's career had been formed in the government militia.

'Well, we will have more time to discuss such things this week, no doubt. I am at your service as your host. But, equally, please tell me if you desire time to yourself. I know how oppressive such trips can be.'

'Thank you,' Drew said. 'So what's on the agenda for tomorrow?'

'Well—' Nergui waited while coffees were placed before them. 'You have your meeting with the ambassador at ten?' Drew nodded. 'You saw the embassy as we passed – just a few minutes' walk away. There's probably not much point in your coming to police headquarters till after your meeting, so we can arrange a car to collect you from there once you're finished.'

'I don't know how long the meeting's likely to take, I'm afraid. Probably just half an hour's courtesy chat, but you never know.'

Nergui smiled. 'The ambassador will assume you know things he doesn't. Which is no doubt true, but not about this case – he's been kept fully informed. He'll also want to make sure you know which side you're on.'

'I'm not aware I'm on anybody's side,' Drew said.

'We don't even know what the sides are,' Nergui agreed. 'But he will remind you, very discreetly, that the British Government is your paymaster, just in case there should be any – conflict of interest.'

'Is there likely to be?'

Nergui shrugged. 'Not from me. But we are involved

in politics here. Politicians think differently from the rest of us. They perceive conflicts where we do not.'

Drew nodded, not sure if he was really following this. He recalled Nergui's earlier words: 'I'm a patriot at heart.'

'You seem to know the ambassador well?' he said.

'I come across him from time to time. In the course of duty. He's a likeable enough person.' Nergui left the comment hanging in the air, as if there were more he could say. 'Well,' he said, at last, 'tomorrow, then – I'll give you my office and mobile numbers, and then you can call me when you've finished and I'll send a car over.'

Drew found himself absurdly surprised that the country had mobile phone coverage. But, of course, in a remote country like this a mobile infrastructure made more sense than fixed lines.

'I think the best use we can make of tomorrow is for us to give you a short tour of the city, and show you where the four bodies were found. Doripalam can also talk you through the various crime reports and witness statements. They're not in English, of course, but we can give you the gist easily enough.' Nergui paused. 'There is nothing we can do, really, but press on and hope something turns up. And maybe we can throw a few stones into the pond and see what ripples we cause.'

Drew wasn't entirely sure what he meant but nodded anyway. He noticed that Doripalam was watching the older man closely.

Nergui rose slowly to his feet. 'But, as I say, you've had a long day. We will let you get some sleep. Give me a call as soon as you're free in the morning.'

Drew watched Nergui and Doripalam walk slowly across the restaurant, Nergui pausing to speak briefly with the head waiter. Suddenly, sitting alone, Drew thought about Ian Ransom, who had presumably eaten alone in this very room the evening before he was killed.

Drew would shortly have to make his way through the silent hotel corridors to a room identical to that where Ransom met his brutal death. The thought was far from comforting.

FOUR

It was stupid, he knew, and he'd spent the first three or four months trying to resist it. He knew what they thought, and told himself that he didn't care. After all, why should he have any respect for them? He recognised what they were, most of them, and given half a chance he'd have had them out of the place. But it was impossible; there were no alternatives. That, of course, was precisely why he had been given the job in the first place. Because, everywhere you looked, this place was desperately short of alternatives.

So he should have just ignored them. That was the advice that Nergui had given him, and it was the advice he would have given anyone else in the same position. But it was much easier to say than to do. He knew how much they despised him – almost, he supposed, as much as he despised them. He knew that they were watching, waiting for him to make his first slip. And he was determined not to give them the satisfaction.

So, against his better judgement, he found himself arriving earlier and earlier each morning, getting in before any of the others arrived, making sure he was fully on top of everything. And of course Solongo, who had initially seen his promotion as finally proving him to be a husband potentially worthy of her social aspirations, now began to complain bitterly about the amount of time he was spending in the office. There was, he thought, no way of pleasing everyone, but at the moment he felt he was pleasing no one, least of all himself.

And now, on top of all that, Nergui's return had made everything ten times worse. He didn't entirely blame Nergui himself, though he knew full well that Nergui would have been unable to resist the prospect of returning to the scenes of his former glory. But that didn't help his own position. To the rest of the team, Nergui's arrival had simply confirmed their view that Doripalam had never been up to the job in the first place. Solongo had tried hard to conceal her disappointment when he had informed her, but he was clear that she too now assumed that his promotion was only a stopgap and that Nergui would be kept in the role until a more suitable candidate was found. She had never really believed that her husband was senior management material.

In the face of all that, he should have told them what to do with their job. Or at least he should have ceased putting in all the extra effort that had become the norm over the past few months. And yet here he was again, stumbling into the building at six-thirty in the morning, the day not even light, preparing for another day of minimal achievement.

As he made his way along the corridor, he was surprised to see that the lights were already on in one of the other offices. The night shift would have been on duty, of course, but they were unlikely to have ventured up to the management offices. Then he realised. Even now, it seemed, Nergui couldn't resist demonstrating that he was always one step ahead of everyone else. Knowing Nergui's domestic circumstances, though, Doripalam wasn't sure whether to feel irritated or pitying.

He tapped lightly on Nergui's door and poked his head around. 'Good morning, Nergui. See you haven't changed your habits.'

Nergui looked up from the mass of paperwork. 'Usual story about old dogs and new tricks, I'm afraid.'

Actually, Nergui was sorry that Doripalam had found him here so early in the morning. He had always had a reputation for working absurdly long hours, which others found intimidating and which he knew wasn't particularly justified. There was nothing wrong with intimidating people now and again, but Nergui didn't want Doripalam to think he was engaged in some egotistical game. There was enough tension between the two men already.

The truth was that Nergui needed little sleep. He had a suspicion that he could probably survive with virtually no sleep at all. But over the years he'd gradually settled for around four hours a night, generally between around one and five a.m.

This morning, he had thought it worth getting in early. Although he had been through the case papers countless times, he wanted to re-read them before they met Drew again later in the morning. Nergui had no illusions as to why Drew had been sent here. He knew it was a token gesture aimed largely towards the victim's family and the UK media. He also recognised that there was probably little that Drew could add to the investigation in the limited time he was here.

However, his years of working in this environment had taught Nergui that it was worth making best use of whatever resources were thrown in his direction. At the very least, Drew would bring another perspective to the case – and a fairly astute one, as far as Nergui could judge – which might complement his own experience and Doripalam's perspicacity. More importantly, Drew was an experienced investigating officer, of a kind all too rare in this country. Nergui wanted to extract whatever value he could from his brief presence.

Since arriving in the office at five-thirty, he had read painstakingly through the case documents, highlighting apparently important points, making detailed notes, producing short English translations of anything he felt might be of interest to Drew, and reviewing again the innumerable, largely unpleasant photographs.

Doripalam gestured to the mounds of papers and files in front of Nergui. 'Surprised you managed to keep awake,' he said. 'Find anything new?'

'What do you think?' At least Nergui now felt that he was thoroughly up to speed with everything in the notes. Nevertheless, the overwhelming impression that he was left with was an absence of any serious leads, nothing they could pursue with any feeling of confidence. 'Apart from the usual routine stuff, which you've clearly got well in hand, I can't see anywhere else to go.'

Doripalam nodded. 'Well, I'm disappointed to hear you say that, but I wouldn't have been pleased if you'd found something I'd missed.'

'I'd have been astonished. I didn't see it in the notes, but I take it we've done DNA testing on the victims' clothes?'

Doripalam raised an eyebrow in mock reproach, though he accepted that Nergui was only checking that all avenues had been covered. 'Official reports aren't back yet,' he said, 'but unofficially they've told me there's nothing. There is some extraneous matter on the clothes but nothing that's consistent between the victims or that matches any of our records.'

Nergui nodded and sat back in his chair, looking vaguely around the office as though seeking inspiration. His temporary office here was smaller and more functional than his room in the Ministry, but only marginally so. He was not a man who sought comfort or domesticity in the workplace, or, for that matter, even in his home life, but just for a moment he was struck by the bleakness of the room – the cheap functional desk, the pale green Ministry-issue paint on the walls, an old metal filing cabinet, a two-year-old calendar on the wall. Suddenly he felt as if the state of this room simply demonstrated how thin their resources were, how pitifully ill-equipped they were to face whatever it was that lay out there.

Nergui did not underestimate his own capability, he knew he was ideally suited to the role to which he had, for the moment, returned. He hadn't always been successful. But where he had failed he was confident that few could have done more.

So normally, even in these circumstances, he would be approaching this job with relish and optimism, particularly after the deadening experience of recent months. He knew the pressures he was under; he knew that the Minister's job – and therefore his own – might depend on the outcome of this case. That didn't worry him. It was the price of entry to this level of the game.

But what did worry him, as he sat here looking at Doripalam's tired but still enthusiastic face, were the implications of this case for the city, maybe for the country. This was a fledgling nation in its current form, struggling to find an identity. It was still a primitive state in many ways – its people fearful after decades, even centuries of repression and hardship, where for generations life had been scraped daily from the bare earth, where nothing lay between man and heaven except a thin protection of wood and felt.

There was something about these killings that stirred a primordial unease in Nergui. It was not simply that the streets of the city might be stalked by a psychopath, killing randomly and brutally, Nergui could deal with that. Such a killer would eventually make an error, and might even choose to reveal himself. But what really disturbed Nergui about the killings was the sense of purpose. The sense of deliberate, planned savagery. The sense of some narrative, moving slowly towards its dark resolution.

He slammed shut the file in front of him. 'Come on,' he said. 'Let's get some coffee. I think we both need it.'

'I'm a United man myself, I'm afraid.'

'Oh, well, we all have our crosses to bear.' Drew wasn't surprised. Like all City fans, he believed that Manchester United had been invented for people who didn't really like football.

The ambassador laughed. 'I thought it was you lot who bore the stigmata.' Which, Drew noted, was exactly the kind of thing you would expect a United fan to say. Upper-class public school toffs who had never even visited Manchester, except maybe for a champagne dinner in the executive box at Old Trafford.

'Takes me back,' the ambassador mused. 'I was brought up in Wythenshawe, you know. Seems a long way away now.'

I bet, thought Drew, who had grown up in the neighbouring but substantially more upmarket suburb of Hale. Wasn't that just typical? You couldn't even be confident in your prejudices these days.

'Coffee?'

And it was true that the ambassador did seem to have left Wythenshawe a long way behind, as they sat in apparently antique armchairs in this oak-panelled room, a silver tray of fine china set out on the low coffee table between them. Drew wondered vaguely where Mongolia sat on the hierarchy of ambassadorial assignments. He couldn't imagine it was one that they were all clamouring for at the Foreign and Commonwealth Office. On the other hand, it was an interesting enough place, and pretty stable compared with some of the options on offer.

It was probably the kind of posting they gave to the bright young things on the rise, or to the loyal servants on the way to retirement. Judging from his white hair and tweed-jacketed manner, it was safe to assume that the ambassador fell into the latter category.

'Thank you.' Not only was the china very fine, the coffee was also predictably excellent.

'Well, Chief Inspector, thank you very much for sparing the time to see me this morning.'

As if I had a choice, Drew thought. 'Not at all. I was very keen to seek your opinion in any case, so thank you for the invitation.'

'I'll be happy to share whatever insights I can with you. I've been here for a few years now, and this region has always been one of my areas of interest. Wrote a dissertation on it at Oxford, as a matter of fact. It's an extraordinary place in many ways. One of the few substantial countries that's still relatively untouched by the forces of globalisation.'

'That must be changing, I imagine?'

'It is, but still relatively slowly. It's very remote here. There are still comparatively few tourists. Not that many nationals have travelled outside the country. Your man Nergui is something of an exception there.'

'He seems to have travelled remarkably widely,' Drew said. He had the sense that the ambassador was keen to impart information, presumably in the hope of receiving some back.

'So I understand,' the ambassador said, in a tone that implied a fairly comprehensive knowledge. 'Lived in the States for a couple of years, and in the UK, and he seems to have spent time in Europe, Asia – well, you name it.'

'Seems a little odd for a policeman,' Drew commented. 'Even a senior one. No one's offered to send me on my travels. Except here, of course.'

The ambassador laughed. 'Well, yes, I think it is a little odd for a policeman, especially here where they generally seem keen to ensure that the police are as insular as they can make them. But there's more to Nergui than meets the eye.'

It was clearly a prompt, but Drew decided just to take a slow sip of coffee and let the ambassador approach this on his own. He knew from endless hours of interviewing suspects that there was nothing more effective than prolonged silence for encouraging others to speak.

'He's an interesting man is Nergui,' the ambassador said finally, 'and I'm not sure I've got anywhere close to fathoming him. But there are certain things you should be aware of.'

Drew raised an eyebrow and reached out to take a biscuit. There was no point in making this easy for the ambassador, or in giving him any sense that Drew owed him any information in return.

'The first thing you should know is that he doesn't work for the police. Not formally.'

'He doesn't? But I thought he was in charge of the investigation here—'

The ambassador nodded. 'Oh, he's certainly in charge of the investigation. He has his remit from the Minister of Justice himself.'

'Then—'

'But Nergui himself now works for the State Security Administration. Another arm, as it were, of the Ministry of Justice and Internal Affairs.'

'And the State Security Administration is what?' Drew asked, already having a good idea of the answer.

'Essentially counter-intelligence, as I understand it,' the ambassador said. 'As a department, it deals with anything that potentially comprises a threat to the state. Terrorism. Espionage. Sabotage. All that.'

'Like MI5?'

'As you say.'

'So Nergui's a spy?'

The ambassador shrugged. 'Well, I'm not sure that that's necessarily the terminology they'd use. But, yes, Nergui is a senior officer in the intelligence service.'

'What's his background?' Drew asked, wondering what he'd got himself into here.

The ambassador frowned. 'Well, that's one of the odd things about our friend Nergui,' he said. 'No one seems to know too much about him. Or at least no one's telling us.' Drew was momentarily amused by the conceit that, since no one had told the ambassador, it must follow that nobody else knew either. 'He's a mysterious fellow. Something of a state hero, for reasons that aren't entirely clear. He rose through the ranks of the government in the days when it was essentially an oppressive arm of the Communist Party, but seems to have avoided getting too tainted by all that. Mind you, the rise of democracy and the fall of the Soviet Union haven't prevented the Party from retaining a large majority here over most of the past decade. We now have a reformed Communist Party promising to govern like New Labour.'

Drew resisted the temptation to ask whether the ambassador thought this was a good thing. 'So what's he doing dealing with this case?'

'Well, when the civilian police was formed in the 1990s, he moved from the old militia to become head of the new serious crimes team. Then some months ago he moved back into the Ministry in what appears to be an intelligence role. He seems to have an awful lot of authority across all parts of the Ministry, and across the government in general. He appears to be trusted to get on with things in the interests of the government and the state – assuming that those are congruent, which isn't always the case. The Minister in particular uses him as a kind of right-hand man to deal with problems as they arise.'

'You make it sound slightly sinister,' Drew said. 'As if he were a Mafia hitman.'

The ambassador smiled, faintly. 'Do I? I'm sorry, that's not intentional. I don't think there's anything particularly sinister about Nergui's role, though of course we always have to bear in mind that he's an agent of the state.'

'And therefore not to be trusted?'

'Well, no, I wouldn't say that. But, as the Gospels say, no man can be the servant of two masters. If there were a conflict of interest, it's clear where Nergui's duty would lie.'

'Is there likely to be conflict of interest?' Drew asked, finding himself repeating his question from the previous evening. 'In this case, I mean?'

'I shouldn't think so for a minute, Chief Inspector,' the ambassador said. 'I'm talking generalities here.'

'Of course. So what kinds of cases does Nergui get involved in? From what you've said, it seems a little odd to find him caught up in a murder case, even one on this scale.'

'Well, I think this is where you have to recognise that priorities here are probably different from those you're used to. As I understand it, Nergui's remit covers anything that's a potential threat to the state. In the UK that would mean things like terrorism, subversion and so on. Lesser crimes – if I can call them that – although serious would not be construed as a threat to the state, and so would be handled by the police.'

'The police handle terrorists,' Drew pointed out.

'In terms of arresting suspects and so on, yes, of course,' the ambassador said. 'But you would be working on the basis of information and guidance from Special Branch, MI5 and so on.'

If only, Drew thought, but didn't bother to interrupt.

'But here, you see, in what is still an emerging country, any kind of large-scale or serious crime can be a threat to the state – fraud, corruption, industrial sabotage—'

'And murder?'

'Well, not usually, because most of the murders are pretty mundane affairs. But this is different. Just the sheer scale of it. They don't know what they're dealing with, and my guess is that the Minister has intervened personally, which is why Nergui's involved.'

Drew sipped on his coffee, mulling this over. 'Do you think they know something they're not sharing with us?'

'I was hoping you might be able to give me some insights into that one. Not immediately, of course – I realise you've just got here. But it would be helpful to know how your thinking develops.'

I bet it would, Drew thought. At least now he knew why the ambassador was being so open with him.

'My guess, though,' the ambassador went on, in the tone of one accustomed to having his guesswork taken seriously, 'is that that's not the case. Of course, they're quite capable of not sharing information with us.' He shook his head, as if overwhelmed by the enormity of such behaviour. 'But I've got one or two sources of my own, and my impression is that they're as baffled as we are by this.' He paused. 'What's your take on the whole thing, anyway?'

'So far? Well, I've not yet been through the case notes in any detail – they sent me over some stuff but most of it would need translating, of course. I'm meeting with Nergui after this to go through it all with him. But, on the face of it, it seems an odd one. The most straight-forward explanation is that we're simply dealing with a psychopath, someone who's just picking victims at random. A Brady or a Sutcliffe.'

'But do – those kinds of people genuinely pick their victims at random?'

'I'm not a psychologist, but I think there's generally more of a common pattern than would seem to be the case here. Though of course we don't really know if there is any pattern given that the first three victims are still unidentified.'

'And if it's not just a psychopath killing at random?'

'The odd thing, I think, is how professional the earlier killings seemed to be. The removal of the identifying marks, emptying of pockets. The removal of the limbs apparently done with some precision – not that we're looking for a skilled surgeon, but I understand it doesn't look like the work of someone in a hurry, panicking at the scene of the crime. It's strange behaviour for a psycho-path, but then I guess that psychopathic behaviour is strange by definition. Equally, the scale of the killings would be odd if this were some sort of professional hit – unless we're looking at some sort of tit-for-tat feud.'

'What, organised gangs battling for turf? That kind of thing?'

Drew smiled. 'Well, it happens in Moss Side all the time. It must be a possibility. But it does raise the question of why so much trouble was taken to hide the victims' identities. If you're sending a message, you'd surely want to make it as unambiguous as possible. Although, of course, the identities may be crystal clear to those involved. But, as Nergui rightly pointed out to me last night, this does take us straight back to the question of Ransom's involvement. From what we know of him, he doesn't seem the type to get caught up in a Mafia turf war.'

'Stranger things have happened, I suppose.'

'Of course. But if we are talking about some kind of

local internecine struggle, I can't imagine that the parties would be keen to draw the attention of the Western media. Why go to all that trouble concealing the earlier victims' identities, then brutally murder a Westerner in his bed in the best hotel in town?'

'Perhaps that was the unambiguous message you were talking about?'

For the first time, Drew looked closely at the ambassador. Behind the externally amiable old duffer, there was a very sharp and no doubt highly political brain. Maybe it was the ambassador who knew something about this that he wasn't sharing. 'Why do you say that?'

The ambassador shrugged. 'Just my Foreign Office training, Chief Inspector.' He laughed, though without obvious mirth. 'If someone kills one of your citizens, particularly in this kind of brutal way, your first assumption is that they're trying to tell you something.'

'Like what?'

'I haven't a clue in this case. Our relationships with the government are generally good. There's no great resentment to the presence of Westerners among the general population. On the contrary, they tend to see us as a source of prosperity and stability – better the West than the Russians or Chinese. I'm sure there are those who think differently, but not many. No, ignore me, Chief Inspector, like you I'm just floundering around in the dark trying to find a narrative that fits this dreadful set of incidents. In my role, I naturally gravitate towards a political interpretation first, but I suspect that in this case the truth will turn out to be much more mundane.'

Drew was left with the sense that he'd just been given some sort of coded message but lacked the insight to decipher it.

'Well, Chief Inspector, I suppose I've taken up enough of your time. But I'm sure you'll agree that we need to keep in contact. Will you join me for dinner later in the week? Nothing fancy, but a change from the hotel. Thursday?'

'Yes, of course.' It didn't sound like the kind of invitation one could easily refuse.

'I'll get someone to pick you up from the hotel – around seven? You're off to the police HQ now? Do you need a car?'

'Nergui suggested I call and he'd send one of theirs.'

'Ah, very good. And do let Nergui know that he will be welcome to join us.' The ambassador rose and led Drew towards the door. 'I think it's very important that we keep all the lines of communication open here, don't you?'

Drew nodded, but with a strong sense that most of the current communications were probably going over his head. There were times when he was grateful to be nothing more than a policeman.

The ambassador stopped in the doorway, his hand on Drew's arm. He paused for a moment, as though considering the most appropriate form of words, then said: 'Stick close to Nergui, won't you? And watch your own back.'

Well, Drew thought as he made his way slowly down the embassy stairs, that sounded like another unambiguous message.

FIVE

'One of our local heroes,' Nergui said, striding quickly ahead. Drew was finding it hard to keep up with him. Doripalam strolled some way behind them, clearly accustomed to Nergui's ways and apparently unconcerned by any need to match his pace. 'Hero of the revolution.'

'Ah. Right.' Drew looked round the expanse of Sukh Bataar Square, dominated by the equestrian statue of the eponymous revolutionary hero. It was perhaps not one of the world's great squares, he thought, but impressive enough. Here, Soviet-style functionality was replaced by something approaching grandeur – the squat white Parliament House, the palatial government buildings, the imposing bulk of the city Post Office. The square was expansive but busy with people, some standing talking in the morning sun, most striding purposefully to or from the nearby shops and the open-air Black Market. The majority were dressed in Western clothes although the older ones were often clothed in traditional robes and sashes. A group of young people, dressed in baggy sweat-shirts and jeans with familiar designer labels, were gathered at one end of the square, eating ice creams from cardboard cones, outfacing the chill of the late autumn morning.

At this time of day, the streets were busy but free-flowing, the traffic moving slowly without the freneticism of a European capital. There were noisy buses, UAZ trucks and some old stuttering Lada or IZH vehicles, but also some newer-looking Korean Daewoos, Hyundais and Kias. Now and again, Drew caught sight of shiny Western cars – a BMW or Mercedes – indicative of the rising wealth of at least one category of Mongolian citizen.

'And our real hero,' Nergui said, still walking. He gestured towards a large hoarding depicting the squat image of Genghis Khan. 'He'll be watching you everywhere you go.'

Drew had already noticed this. The standard image was everywhere – in pictures in the hotel lobby, painted in large murals on the sides of buildings, inked in tiny faded posters pasted across concrete walls. Here in the city centre his ubiquitous image competed incongruously with the lingering emblems of communism and the familiar global logos, neon signs and advertising hoardings that, as capitalism had taken hold, had come to dominate the city skyline.

'I think he still has something of a negative public image in the West, no?' Nergui said over his shoulder. 'But not here. And in part perhaps rightly so. He was a ruthless conqueror, but a remarkable man.'

Drew was feeling too breathless to respond. He had already discovered that it was difficult to keep up with Nergui, both figuratively and literally. He had called Nergui on leaving the embassy that morning, and a car had been sent over with remarkable efficiency to take him to the police HQ.

He had found Nergui and Doripalam sitting in a small, anonymous office, with a deskful of files and papers in front of them.

'Welcome,' Nergui said. 'Please, sit down. How was the ambassador?'

'Fine,' Drew said, warily. He was still mulling over the implications of the ambassador's final words. 'He sends you his regards. Oh, and we're invited to dinner on Thursday. He made a point of inviting you.' Drew looked across at Doripalam with mild embarrassment. 'Just Nergui, I'm afraid.'

Doripalam made a mock grimace of disappointment, then laughed. 'I will contain my disappointment,' he said. 'Although if you could arrange an invitation for my wife she might appreciate it.'

Nergui smiled at him. 'It is the British way, of course. There is no situation so bad that it cannot be remedied with a good dinner. But I am invited only because he hopes for some gossip from the Ministry.'

'So long as it *is* a good dinner,' Drew said. 'I have my standards.'

'The ambassador will not let you down,' Nergui smiled. 'Not with regard to dinner, anyway.'

Nergui had carefully prepared all the files, and Drew was impressed by the Mongolian's detailed familiarity with all aspects of the case. The three men worked painstakingly through all the material, Nergui translating as necessary, highlighting any points which seemed significant or interesting. Despite their scrutiny, the process appeared to add little to their understanding of the case. Drew had expected this, he was far too experienced in such matters to imagine that some major lead would have been overlooked. Equally, though, he knew that this kind of repeated, exhaustive examination of the facts was the only practical way to proceed. Even if there were no new leads at this stage, there was always the possibility that some new development might provide some illumination to the mass of material in front of them.

'The other question,' Drew mused as they finished working through the papers, 'is where did the first and third murders actually take place?'

Nergui nodded. 'It could be anywhere in the city. There are plenty of deserted or partially demolished buildings where you could commit an act like that. We've had a couple of officers investigating some places, but it's an impossible task. Unless someone stumbles on it accidentally, we're not likely to find it. And it could have been in the back of a van or truck, somewhere like that. Or some old slaughterhouse or yard that could easily be hosed down. Anywhere.'

'So not likely to be much help there, then. I suppose the next thing for me would be to have a look at the sites where the bodies were found. I don't know what it's likely to tell me, but it would be helpful to get a sense of the places.'

'Of course,' Nergui said. 'I could arrange a car, but it might be better for us to walk. We can try to give you a feel of the city.'

If Drew had realised quite how quickly Nergui walked, he might not have taken him up on this suggestion. As it was, he found himself almost jogging behind him as they strode through the city streets, Doripalam ambling casually behind both of them. The city itself was initially unremarkable – a mix of blank-faced low-rise commercial buildings, concrete tower blocks, and the occasional striking new building. They passed stalls selling snacks and, around the square, tourist souvenirs such as the traditional brightly coloured *loovuuz* hats, apparently identical to that sported by Sukh Bataar's statue. Beyond, there was a large mural, formed in muted shades of brown, depicting stylised martial and equestrian images with, bizarrely, the words 'Welcome to Mongolia' emblazoned in English across the top.

But the overall effect was typical of a former Soviet satellite making its painful way into the free-enterprise world of the twenty-first century. They passed through

Sukh Bataar Square, and then walked down one of the side streets. Nergui moved quickly ahead, and then stopped suddenly, turning to face Drew. 'There,' he said, pointing.

Drew caught up with him and followed the direction of Nergui's finger. Another, smaller street led off from where they stood, dark between what appeared to be a residential tower block and an abandoned factory, its large windows long boarded up.

'That was where the first body was found,' Nergui said, walking slowly into the dim side-street. He walked twenty or thirty yards, then stopped.

'Just here,' he said. 'You can still see some of the bloodstains.'

Drew looked down. The street was paved at the junction with the main road, but within yards degenerated into hard-packed earth. But Drew could make out the darker stains on the ground in front of them. He looked up and around at the looming building on each side of the street and shivered inwardly. It was not pleasant, even for an experienced policeman, to think of the headless, handless corpse being found in this bleak spot.

'And nobody from there witnessed anything?' he said, gesturing at the tower block. Rows of blank windows stared down at them.

'It seems not,' Doripalam said, arriving behind them. 'We have had officers going door to door, of course, but so far nobody saw or heard anything. It may just be true. This street is not lit at night. The streetlighting only goes as far as there.' Doripalam pointed to the larger road they had just left. 'So if the body was dumped in the hours of darkness, there is no reason why anyone should necessarily have witnessed anything.'

'What's this place?' Drew asked, nodding towards the commercial building on the other side.

'Nothing now,' Doripalam said. 'It used to be a clothing factory. A state-run place. Made suits – like this one.' Doripalam gestured ironically at his own cheap-looking blue outfit, visible beneath his heavy overcoat. 'Not exactly your Savile Row, but the best we can get. But when the government pulled out of this one, it closed. So now the place is empty.'

'And no sign of any activity inside?'

Doripalam shook his head. 'We searched the place, of course. But no sign that it has been disturbed for months.'

There was nothing else to be seen here. Drew and Doripalam followed Nergui as he strode swiftly back through Sukh Bataar Square, past the edifice of the Post Office building and down Lenin Avenue. Nergui pointed to the square tower of the Bayangol Hotel. 'The second body was found by the hotel there,' he said. 'We concluded that the victim had fallen from the roof.'

Drew looked up as they approached the looming shadow of the hotel. The building itself was another example of undistinguished Soviet-style architecture, through the hotel had obviously been extensively renovated in recent years to cater to an international market. Nergui led him into the alley at the rear where the body had been found.

'You said he was killed at night?' Drew said. 'So how did he get into the hotel?'

Nergui shrugged. 'We're still trying to find out. There are various possibilities. It's possible that the killers actually took a room there, and somehow brought him in during the day. We've been following up with all the guests who were booked in that day, which is taking a long time – a lot of them are international visitors. But I'm not optimistic. More likely they just bribed someone to let them in. We've interviewed the staff, but nobody's saying anything. Hotel staff are used to being discreet.'

'Even in a murder case?'

'Especially in a murder case, I think. They don't want to get involved. They may even have been threatened.'

'It just seems incredible that someone could be drugged and then taken up to the roof and, well, thrown off, and nobody saw anything.'

'Not that incredible, really,' Doripalam said. 'It was a Saturday night. There are few places to drink in the city, especially if you are an expatriate. There would have been a lot of drunken people in the hotel. Who notices one more person being half carried along the corridor?'

Drew nodded. 'And the third body? You said that was found in one of the *ger* camps?'

'I'll get a car to take us out there,' Nergui said. 'It is a little way from here, at the edge of the city.'

The car arrived in minutes in response to Nergui's call, and they were driven a mile or so from the city centre to the *ger* encampment in the suburbs. For the first time, Drew found himself in an environment that seemed genuinely alien. The centre of the city had been distinctive, but the pervading atmosphere and architecture were reminiscent of those in much of the former Soviet Union. For Drew, who had travelled only a little in Eastern Europe, the city had recalled nothing more than the anonymous settings of 1960s spy films.

This, though, was very different. The car pulled up at the point where the metalled road gave way to a rougher track, and the three men climbed out. Ahead of them were rows of the traditional *gers*, forming what appeared to be an exceptionally neat and well-cared-for shanty town. A few men, women and children were visible between the constructions, chatting together like neighbours in any suburb, all dressed in the herdsmen's costumes, the thick felt pulled tight against the chill of the morning. There were tethered horses, dogs, even a goat.

Further along, there was a chicken run, the scraggy birds scratching at the dusty ground. As they emerged from the car, Drew was struck by the richness of the atmosphere, the mix of smells – the scent of wood smoke, the musky aroma of goats and horses, somewhere the acrid stench of burning oil or petrol, all interlaced with the enticing smells of cooking.

The camp was an extraordinary sight. To Drew, it appeared different in kind from the type of encampment which one might find in a Third World country or amongst displaced or refugee peoples. These people were living in this way apparently through choice, maintaining a lifestyle balanced between their nomadic roots and the increasingly urban demands of the twenty-first century. There was a sense that, for all the concrete and glass monoliths of the city centre, this community could, if it wished, simply pack up and move on.

'It is very different from Manchester, no?' Nergui smiled.

'It's different from – well, anywhere I've ever been,' Drew said.

'For most people here, this is simply the natural way to live. They may be compelled to work in the city for economic reasons, but they retain their links to the steppes, to the traditional ways of living. They prefer to live here rather than in a bleak tower block in the city.'

'Probably a sane decision,' Drew said.

'Definitely. But, having lived in the West, I'm not sure I quite understand this lifestyle any more.' Nergui laughed. 'I like having my creature comforts too much.'

'Where was the body found?'

'There.' Nergui pointed to the ravine that lay beyond the rows of *gers*. 'Come.' He led them along the track until they were standing on the edge of the ravine. A line of *gers* stood immediately behind them.

'There was no attempt to hide the body?' Drew asked, recalling with a shudder the graphic photographs he had viewed of the exposed and mutilated corpse.

'It seems not,' Doripalam said. 'We think they drove a truck or van over to that point,' Doripalam gestured to the metalled road that ran along the far side of the ravine. 'And then they just tipped the body over. It would probably have simply rolled till it hit those bushes.'

'But why leave it here?'

'I think it is the same as the first body. They probably wanted to take it somewhere where it could be disposed of quickly and easily, but where it would be found. The road over there does not run close to the *gers*, so no one would take any notice of a truck passing in the night. They probably barely stopped. As it happened, the body was not visible from this side, as the bushes shielded it. Otherwise, it would have been spotted an hour or two earlier.'

Nergui began to lead them back past the *gers* to the waiting car. Although the summer was over now, the sky was clear and the day was growing warmer. Nergui had told him that the autumn weather could be changeable. There had been a few flurries of snow earlier in the week, the first signs of the approaching winter. They passed an old woman, wrapped in the now-familiar dark robes and sash, carrying a bucket of water. She smiled and nodded a greeting.

Drew had opened his mouth to make some comment about the *gers*, but at the same moment Nergui uttered an incomprehensible cry and flung himself backwards toward Drew. Drew stumbled, taken aback, and lost his footing, finding himself rolling on to the hard earth. Nergui flung himself across Drew, and then Drew felt the other man pulling hard on his jacket.

'What are you—?'

'This way!' Nergui said sharply, tugging harder. Drew rolled over, and ended up lying beside Nergui, who was rapidly shuffling back behind one of the *gers*. 'Come!' he snapped, gesturing urgently at Drew. Drew crawled after him until they were both shaded by the tent. Doripalam had dropped to his knees at Nergui's shouted warning, and was now scrambling around beside them. Behind them, chickens clucked loudly, alarmed by the disturbance.

'What is it?' he said.

Nergui was breathing heavily. 'There,' he said, gesturing up at the front of the *ger*. 'But keep your head down.'

Drew peered tentatively around at the front of the *ger*. There, embedded neatly in the thick felt, was a crossbow bolt still vibrating from the force of impact.

It seemed ridiculous. More a scene from an old Hollywood Western than any kind of real threat. At the same time, Drew recognised rationally that the arrow was a lethal weapon. If there was someone out there shooting at them, their lives were in danger, as surely as if they were facing a sniper with a rifle.

'Where did it come from?' he whispered.

Nergui pointed to an apparently disused factory building that lay across a patch of empty ground. 'Up there, I think. Somewhere on the first floor.'

'Do you think they're still there?'

'I don't know. My guess is not. Too risky, even if they'd hit one of us. I think they'd have taken one shot then made a run for it.'

'What if you're wrong?'

'I'm not planning to bet my life on it.' Nergui carefully pulled his mobile out of his pocket, and dialled the number of the police officer driving the car. 'He can get the car along this dirt track,' Nergui said. He spoke briefly to the officer in Mongolian, and a moment later the car came

78

bumping along the track towards them. As it stopped, Nergui pulled open the rear door, and he and Drew bundled inside. Doripalam clambered into the front passenger seat. The driver rapidly reversed towards the main road, and then pulled out in the direction of the factory.

Drew realised he was shaking. 'Thanks,' he said. 'I thought you'd gone mad. How did you manage to see the bolt?'

'I don't know. Instinct, I think. I saw a movement in the air out of the corner of my eye, and somehow registered that it was something more dangerous than a bird. I wasn't sure where it was headed, but I threw myself back without really thinking.' He laughed, humourlessly. 'Mind you, if my instinct had been wrong, I might have thrown you into its path, so you shouldn't be too profuse with your thanks.'

'Or worse still, you'd have messed up my suit for nothing,' Drew smiled. Both of them were playing this down, but he suspected that Nergui's instincts were more finely honed than he was letting on.

'There is nothing worse that one could do to an Englishman,' Nergui agreed.

The car pulled to a halt in front of the factory building. The ground-floor windows were boarded up, and there was no sign of life. Above, the windows had been left uncovered and most of the glass had been smashed. Presumably it was from one of those that the arrow had been fired. They pulled the car up close to the doors to minimise the risk of being shot at from above.

'What are you planning to do?' Drew asked, peering through the car window at the concrete building. 'We can't risk going in there on our own.'

Nergui shook his head. 'Certainly not. It's bad enough that your life has been placed in danger once. The ambassador would never forgive me if I allowed it to happen a second time.' Nergui remained blank-faced, and it took Drew a moment to realise that the Mongolian was joking. 'I've sent for back-up,' he said. 'They will be here in a few minutes. We're risking allowing whoever it is to escape – I don't know if there's a rear entrance to this place, but I've asked for a car to go to the back. But we don't know what we might be facing here. If this is just some joker taking a pot shot at the police, then he'll be long gone anyway. But if it's our killer, and he's still in there, then we don't know what he might want.'

The moments ticked by. This wasn't the first time that Drew had faced the prospect of entering a building with a potentially dangerous suspect inside, but here he felt absurdly vulnerable, because he had no idea what to expect, what the norms were. He had never, even in his most paranoiac policing moments, expected to have an arrow shot at him. And he had never faced a killer capable of mutilating his victims' bodies.

'What's your guess?' he asked to break the silence. 'Do you think it's our killer?'

Nergui looked back from the window. 'My guess is not. My guess is some joker.'

'But why shoot at us?'

'You will be surprised to learn,' Doripalam interjected, 'that the police are not always popular here. I know that this is difficult for a British policeman to understand.'

Drew regarded the young man's blank expression. 'And you share our sense of irony, too,' he said. 'But how would he know you were from the police?'

'Probably recognised the car,' Doripalam said. 'Cars like this usually mean either police or politicians. A good target in either case. If it is just some idiot, he probably didn't mean to kill us anyway. Perhaps just to give us a fright.'

'He achieved that objective, anyway. Speaking for myself, you understand.'

'It was a good shot. He knew what he was doing. But we have many skilled archers in this country.'

'You need to get yourselves some cowboys.'

'Some would say,' Doripalam said, 'that the police are precisely that.'

Behind them, two more official cars drew up. Nergui signalled for their occupants to remain in their cars for the moment, then he and Doripalam carefully opened their own doors. Nergui pressed himself against the concrete wall, edging back towards the other cars, protected by the building from any attempted assault from above, Doripalam following closely behind. Drew started to follow, but Nergui gestured him back. 'As I say, the ambassador would not forgive me.'

Nergui motioned to the other police officers to join them. The other cars had also been parked by the walls, and four officers climbed from each, pressing themselves against the walls by Nergui and Doripalam. Drew heard the sound of other cars, presumably lining up against the rear of the building.

There was an external entrance to the building a few yards further along the wall, fastened with a chain and a large rusty padlock. Gradually, the group of officers edged towards it. Nergui peered for a moment at the door fastening, and then spoke quietly to Doripalam behind him, who inched slowly back to one of the cars and returned, moments later, with a crowbar.

It looked as if the wood was rotten. Doripalam inserted the crowbar between the door and the frame, and pressed his weight against it. The door burst open with a splintering of wood, and the chain and padlock fell uselessly to the ground. He peered cautiously round the frame, pulling a flashlight from his pocket. He shouted something loudly in Mongolian, and then shone the torch inside, flashing it around the empty factory space beyond, clearly ready to pull back immediately if there was any response.

Drew realised he had been holding his breath, and let it out steadily. Everything seemed to be quiet. Nergui signalled to the men behind him, and he slowly followed Doripalam into the darkness.

Drew shook his head. It wasn't possible for him to sit here quietly in this car while Nergui and his team were potentially risking their lives. He opened the door of the car, and slipped out to join the police officers still waiting to enter the building. The officer at the rear turned and looked at him in surprise, but then gave a grin of welcome. Drew pulled out the pocket flashlight he always carried and held it as if it were a weapon.

Nergui called out something from inside. Drew had no idea what had been shouted, but it didn't sound troubled. It was presumably an instruction to the rest of the team, because they all began to move slowly into the dark building.

Drew followed last. Stepping to one side so that he wouldn't stand out as a target in the doorway, he paused for his eyes to grow accustomed to the gloom.

Inside, the building was largely a hollow shell, an enormous space which had at one stage housed manufacturing machinery, but which now echoed emptily. He could see the shadows of the other officers positioning themselves around the walls. Above them, there was some form of walkway running around the walls at the upper floor level – perhaps once intended for machine maintenance. Some pale light came in through the broken upper windows, but there was little to be seen.

Nergui and Doripalam stood poised at the far end, standing in front of a large double door, which presumably led into a storage room. There was a thin line of light coming from around the doors, indicating that there was illumination in the room beyond. It was difficult to be sure from where Drew was standing, but it looked brighter than daylight alone.

Doripalam signalled to two of the men to explore the walkways, reached by stairs in the corner of the factory space, although it seemed that the upper area was unoccupied. As far as Drew could see, there was nowhere else for anyone to hide, other than in whatever space lay behind the double doors.

The remaining men gathered at each side of the doors. Drew followed the officers across the oil-stained concrete floor, and stood beside them. Nergui reached out and tried the handle of the left-hand door. It opened easily and a pale strip of light shone out across the concrete. Nergui raised his hand to Doripalam and another officer, who brought forward two handguns, handing one to Doripalam. Drew had not realised that the police were armed, but it was scarcely a surprise. He was slightly more surprised to see that Nergui himself was also holding a firearm.

Nergui motioned to the two armed officers to stand facing the door, so that between them they would be covering the whole area behind the door. Then shouting some kind of warning – probably the Mongolian equivalent of 'Armed police', Drew thought – he kicked back the door. A bright light flooded out into the factory space, momentarily blinding Drew.

There was silence. Then Nergui said something and walked cautiously into the room. Doripalam slowly lowered his weapon, staring into the brightly lit space, a blank expression on his face. At first neither he nor the other armed officer made any move forward. Then they slowly turned to look at each other, and followed Nergui.

Another officer started to follow them, but a shouted instruction from Nergui caused him to stop. The rest of the team looked at each other in bafflement, but no one moved.

Ignoring the command – after all, he told himself, he was not part of Nergui's team – Drew stepped out from behind the police officers, and moved round until he was directly facing the doorway. Then he walked forward cautiously.

Nergui was standing in the middle of the room, staring fixedly at the object spread out before him. Doripalam and the other armed officer stood to one side, both gazing at the ground. There was a bright spotlight shining across the whole area, illuminating the ghastly scene. Drew wondered irrelevantly what the power source of the light was.

The object of Nergui's gaze was a decapitated body, propped against the wall in the full glare of the spotlight, like a grotesque museum exhibit. Fixed between its two hands, as if mimicking some parody of a ghost, was the victim's own head.

Drew stood for a moment, transfixed. To his side, some of the other officers had begun to cluster round the door, their curiosity finally getting the better of them. One of them, one of the younger ones, moved forward to look at the scene, and then backed away, a look of shock on his face, his hand over his mouth. He turned and moved rapidly towards the entrance, retching as he ran. Others began to move back similarly, as if the bright room were somehow contaminated.

Nergui looked up, and saw Drew. He nodded and beckoned Drew forward. Drew approached the room, uneasily but with less disgust than was evident amongst the police team. Although he had never seen anything quite like this, he had seen enough in his time to be able to cope.

'You do not need to come in,' Nergui said.

'It's okay,' Drew said. 'I've seen – well, I can't say I've seen worse, but I've seen plenty.'

Nergui nodded. 'We both have. But, like you, I have never faced anything remotely approaching this.'

Drew looked back at the officers outside, most of whom had now withdrawn from the room. 'It must be a shock to your men.'

Nergui allowed himself a pale smile. 'You have no idea how much of a shock.'

Drew looked around at the two armed men, then back at Nergui. There was clearly something else here, something he wasn't getting.

It was Doripalam who turned to Drew, a look of horror etched in his young face, his handgun hanging limply at his side. 'You see,' he said, 'this is not just a brutal murder. Not just one of the most brutal murders I have ever seen. It is much more than that. We all know this man. He is a police officer. A senior officer.' He paused, as though struggling for breath. 'This is the brutal murder of one of our colleagues. And all set up here like some insane circus sideshow.'

And the most terrifying thing, Drew thought, is that we appear to have come here as the invited audience.

SIX

'This is really very good.' A long pause, broken only by the sound of their eating. 'I'm sorry – I didn't mean to sound so surprised.'

Nergui laughed. 'No, it is understandable. My country is not known for the quality of its cuisine. We are a nation of warriors, not chefs.'

'And, for that matter, senior police officers are not usually known for their culinary skills. I speak entirely personally you understand. But no, really, this is excellent.'

'Well, thank you,' Nergui said. 'I will assume that your comments are more than mere British politeness. I enjoy cooking. It's something of a hobby of mine, but I rarely get the chance to try it out on others.'

Drew looked round Nergui's apartment, wondering what clues could be gained to the character of the man opposite him. A few, no doubt, although he had the impression that Nergui was not a man who would expend much energy expressing his character through home décor.

Still, the apartment was comfortable enough, and surprisingly spacious. The narrow hallway led to a small but well-appointed kitchen, two closed rooms which were presumably bedrooms, and the large living and dining area where they were sitting. To Drew's inexpert eye, the furniture looked moderately expensive, and he wondered vaguely whether these heavy dark wood tables and plush crimson seats were manufactured locally or had to be imported from Russia, China or even further afield.

He had initially been surprised when Nergui had invited him over for dinner, as they were finally driving away from the factory after their gruesome discovery. The scene-of-crime and forensic teams were still working away, but the body had now been taken away for examination, and Nergui felt that there was little to be added by their presence.

'I thought,' Nergui said, as they drove away, 'you and Doripalam might perhaps join me for dinner at my home tonight? I would be honoured.'

'Well, that's very kind of you.' Drew glanced back at the dark silhouette of the factory. 'But – well, are you sure? I mean, you mustn't feel obliged to be my host. I realise this has been a shock.'

'A shock, professionally, yes,' Nergui said. 'We have never experienced anything like this before. Of course, we have had policemen killed in the line of duty. But nothing like this.' Before Drew could respond he went on: 'It is not that the victim was a personal friend, you understand. I knew him, had met him in passing a few times.' Nergui laughed, with an edge of bitterness. 'The last time, I think, I was reprimanding him a little because he had failed to sort out some papers I needed for a case I was working on. But I understand he was a good officer. And he was, I imagine, a friend to some of those who were with us today.' He paused. 'That is what is so horrific – that whoever did this tried to ensure that we would enter that place in force. He wanted to ensure that this body was found, not just by any passer-by, but those who knew him best.'

Drew shuddered. Nergui was right. It was a horrific thought, suggesting an extraordinary cold-bloodedness to the murder. It also raised the questions of what had motivated the murderer to behave in this way, and – even more chillingly – where this motivation might lead him next. 'But why?' he asked. 'Why would anyone behave like that?'

'Who knows? We appear to be dealing with some kind of madman, though I can't begin to conceive what kind. But we still don't know whether the victims, including this one, were selected randomly or deliberately targeted. Even in this last case, I suppose it is possible that the victim was selected randomly, but then the killer chose to expose the body in the cruellest and most spectacular way he could.'

'But equally it may not be a coincidence that the victim was a police officer?'

'As you say. In which case, perhaps the previous victims were also not selected randomly.'

It was like gazing into a pool of clouded water, Drew thought. Occasionally some object swam into view, and you began to feel that you could recognise the shape of it. But then the water clouded again, and there was nothing but greyness and uncertainty.

There was no doubt that even Nergui, calm professional though he appeared, had been shaken by the day's events. Nevertheless, he remained insistent that Drew should join him for dinner. 'It is my duty as your host,' he said. 'But, more importantly, I would welcome the opportunity to spend the evening with someone. It is not a day to be alone, I think.'

Drew was often grateful his domestic circumstances meant there was always someone to come home to. Sometimes he would share his experiences, but more often he would simply try to put them behind him. It made his working existence more bearable.

Ten years on from his marriage, he couldn't really

envisage life any other way, and he wondered what it must be like for Nergui, coming home every day to this comfortable but sterile apartment. He also wondered why it was that having faced a trauma like today's, he could call on nobody other than his deputy and a total stranger.

As it turned out, Doripalam chose to excuse himself from the dinner invitation. Drew could not work out whether this was a tactful judgement on Doripalam's part or, more likely, it was simply that Doripalam had access to those domestic comforts which were so notably absent in Nergui's existence.

Still, Nergui was an excellent host. He had arranged an official car to bring Drew over to his apartment, and greeted him warmly at the door. He was dressed in what, to Drew's eyes, appeared to be a leisure version of the herdsman's robes, a brightly coloured flowing gown wrapped with a gold sash, his feet enclosed in finely embroidered leather slippers. Drew wondered if this was the typical dress of the average Mongolian at home, or perhaps simply a more overt expression of the dandyism which, in his professional life, Nergui appeared to confine largely to his choice of ties.

As he entered the apartment, Drew had been surprised to find that Nergui was cooking the meal himself. He had hardly struck Drew as the domesticated type, so it was incongruous to see him standing before a cooker, stirring and tasting the contents of the array of pans.

'There. It is fine. It is all under control,' Nergui said, leading him into the lounge area. 'Fifteen, twenty minutes, it should all be ready.'

Nergui offered him a beer, and also produced two bottles of red wine for the meal. 'It's not bad,' he said, apologetically. 'Bulgarian. It's difficult to get any better out here.'

Nergui was a relaxed host, and Drew felt no discomfort

even though they initially sat in an amiable silence. It was clear that Nergui had much on his mind, and he said little until he had served the first course – a spicy soup containing chicken and prawns. Drew expressed his compliments on the quality of the food.

'I'm afraid it is far from authentic local cuisine,' Nergui said. 'But then you should probably be thankful that it is not authentic local cuisine.'

'I wish I could produce food like this.'

'You don't cook at home?'

Drew shook his head. 'Not really. I mean, basic stuff but nothing like this. My wife's the chef.'

Nergui nodded. 'You have children?'

'Two,' Drew said. 'Boys. Eight and ten.'

'That must be exhausting.'

'It can be. Especially for my wife, when I'm working long hours, which seems to be most of the time. So she tells me, at least.'

Nergui smiled. 'Does she work also?'

'She's a teacher. Primary school. Young children.'

'Hard work, then. I imagine you don't have an easy time, if you are both working in these kinds of jobs?'

Drew thought about it. The question might have felt intrusive coming from someone else, but Nergui just seemed genuinely interested.

'It can be,' Drew said. 'We both end up working long hours at times. Sue has preparation to do. And I think the work is very tiring for her. But we seem to get through all right, most of the time.'

'That is good,' Nergui said, sincerely. 'I enjoy living alone, but there are times when I envy people like you.'

'Well, likewise,' Drew laughed. 'Sometimes a bit of solitude would be welcome.'

'I'm sure,' Nergui nodded. 'I've never really known anything else.'

'You've never—?' Drew stopped, embarrassed, unsure how he had been intending to finish the sentence. Been married? Been in a relationship? Anything sounded crass.

But Nergui seemed untroubled. 'I was married once,' he said. 'Briefly. A long time ago.'

'Oh. I'm sorry.'

'Don't be. As I say, a long time ago. It was the reason I first went to the West.'

'Really?'

'A long story. I met a young woman – a journalist from the US. This was what, fifteen years ago? I was working for the government here. My task was to show her around, look after her.'

Something about the way Nergui spoke the last words made Drew look up. Again, it occurred to him to wonder about Nergui's background. What had been his role in the government, in the days when this country was still a satellite of the Soviet Union? And how precisely had Nergui been charged to 'look after' the journalist? For that matter, had he similarly been charged to 'look after' Drew? It seemed unlikely – Nergui was clearly the officer in charge of the murder case – but it also appeared that Nergui's current relationship with the police force was not necessarily straightforward.

'Anyway, you can no doubt guess how things turned out. We had a relationship. When she finished her assignment here, she left for the US and I decided to try to follow her. I didn't think it would be possible. Foreign travel was highly restricted in those days, and travelling to the US was almost unheard of. If I had been refused permission, I don't know how things would have turned out, whether I would have tried to leave somehow illegally. Probably not. I'm a very law-abiding individual, as befits my current role.'

'But you were allowed to go?' Drew said, with some incredulity.

'I was very fortunate,' Nergui said. 'Things were just beginning to change here and in the USSR. This was the days of Gorbachev. There was a lot of optimism in the air, but also a lot of anxiety. We were already encountering pressures from commercial forces looking to exploit the resources we have in this country.'

Drew wasn't entirely sure where this was leading. 'You mean minerals?'

'We are a potentially wealthy country. There were already people visiting our country who we suspected were engaged in – well, industrial espionage, I suppose. The interest was in discovering what resources we had, and how capable we were of exploiting them ourselves.'

'You're talking about commercial companies – multinationals?'

'Some of them. There was also support from various governments, of course – the US, China – preparing to get their fingers in the pie. The USSR as well, I think, saw the writing on the wall for its own future, and so was looking at commercial alliances as a means of protecting its own position here.'

'So how did this affect your being able to leave the country?'

Nergui laughed. 'Very simply, as it turned out. I had been involved in some work here in the field of – well, I imagine you would call it industrial development. It was primitive stuff, looking back, but we were concerned that, when we finally opened our borders properly, we should not be exploited by our more powerful and experienced competitors. When I decided I wanted to leave, I proposed the idea that I should go to study business studies at Harvard. I would be able to learn what our Western rivals did and bring the knowledge back.'

'And the government allowed you to do that?'

Nergui looked momentarily embarrassed. 'Ah, well, I do not like to – what do you say? – blow my own trumpet, but I had been a rather successful student during my time at university here. In academic terms, an outstanding student, I suppose. I was supposedly destined for great things in our government service, so it did not seem that outrageous an idea when I proposed it. A few years earlier it would have been impossible, of course, so I was very fortunate.'

'So you went to Harvard?'

'I did the MBA, yes. My friend – my girlfriend, I suppose she was by then – was based in Washington. But, from here, I thought that would be close enough. It wasn't, of course.'

'I'm sorry,' Drew said.

'These things happen. Our marriage was an attempt to keep it alive, but I think we both knew it was going nowhere.' He shrugged. 'It's not the first time it's happened. It won't be the last. And it was probably all for the best. All of it, I mean. If it hadn't happened, well, I would have spent my whole life here. Which wouldn't have been a bad thing in itself, but I'm glad I've got a sense of what the world is like out there. It's a privilege shared by few of my fellow countrymen.'

'I suppose not,' Drew said. Various intertwined thoughts were drifting through his mind. He was trying to make sense of Nergui's story, which sounded just a little too neat, a little too pat in its narrative arc from love, through pursuit and parting, to self-consolation. Maybe it was just that Nergui had smoothed out the details and airbrushed out the pain and uncertainty that must surely have accompanied this story. Or perhaps the story itself was simply fiction, a cover to explain Nergui's visits to the States and the UK. Would it really have been possible to make such trips from here, even in the heady days of perestroika?

Which led inevitably to the second question. Just why was Nergui telling him all this? They had just met, scarcely knew one another, had nothing in common other than their interest in five brutal murders. It wasn't even clear that their interests in the murders coincided. So why would Nergui unburden himself of all this personal material? Was it simply that he really did have no other friends he could share this stuff with? Was it just that he was taking his first opportunity in years to talk about himself with someone who could do nothing with the information?

It didn't seem likely. Nergui didn't strike Drew as someone fraught with unspoken sorrows. He had told his story in straightforwardly factual terms, no sense of welling emotion. It was as if he had merely thought that Drew might be interested. Just making conversation.

And then, of course, lurking behind all that was the ambassador's parting comment. Stick close to Nergui, but watch your back. What the hell had that meant? For a moment, Drew felt very tired and very far from home. He was a simple man – intelligent enough, certainly for his current job, but with no real interest in or aptitude for politics, large or small. He disliked game-playing, and it seemed like some games were being played here, even though it was far from clear who was involved. Drew very much wanted to trust Nergui, particularly in facing down the horrors they had encountered that afternoon, and his instincts told him that Nergui was trustworthy. But he knew that, so far from everything familiar, it would be madness simply to trust his instincts.

'So how did you end up in the UK?' Drew said, conscious that the silence had been prolonged.

'I finished the MBA, and then – well, I thought I'd carry

on. I spoke with the authorities here, and it was generally agreed that I should get the most out of it while I was in the West. I ended up taking a doctorate in business administration at your London Business School. It was hard work because I knew that I would not be able to stay more than a year.'

'You completed a doctorate in a year?' Drew said. Maybe the story was fiction after all.

Nergui nodded. 'As I say, it was hard. I'd already begun some of the research at Harvard, so I was able to build on that.'

'Even so,' Drew said, 'that's impressive.'

'Well, I don't know. I've always had an aptitude for academic work, research. It comes fairly naturally to me. These are skills I can still use in my work. You also, I imagine?'

Drew laughed. 'Not to the same standard, I'm afraid. I have a university degree but nothing special.'

'As I say, it's just a gift – a small one, but sometimes useful.'

If Nergui was making this up, he was doing so very convincingly. There was no sense of arrogance or boasting about his achievements. If anything, he seemed mildly embarrassed, with something of the air of a golfer who has just hit a hole in one but doesn't know quite how he did it. And, if it was true, there was no doubting Nergui's intelligence at least.

'What did you do when you came back here?' Drew asked. 'How did you end up in – your current role?' He realised, almost too late, that he didn't actually officially know what Nergui's role was.

'Another long story. But basically I came back as – well, what you would call an intelligence officer, I suppose. I was well-regarded, as you can imagine, especially with my newly gained experience and qualifications. By this time, we were beginning to approach something closer to what you Westerners would consider normality. People were actually being allowed to visit countries outside the Eastern Bloc. We had tourists coming here for the first time. Foreign investment began to enter the country. We even started to build some sort of relationship with China. So it was an ideal time for someone with my background.'

While he was talking, Nergui cleared the dishes into the kitchen. He returned, a few moments later, carrying steaming plates. 'Mutton,' he explained. 'I hope you like it.'

Drew did like it, though he would have been hard pressed to describe the tastes. It was a spicy stew, which Drew would have characterised as Middle Eastern without really having much idea what it comprised. 'Very good,' he said, truthfully. 'You were telling me about your career,' he prompted.

'Well, it's not that interesting,' Nergui said. 'I progressed fairly rapidly up the ranks here, mainly just because I was in the right place at the right time. I was attached to the militia, but mostly working on intelligence projects alongside our Foreign Ministry, in the industrial and commercial field.'

'When did you move over to your current role?' Drew realised that he was still dancing round the nature of this role.

'I joined the police when it was established as a civilian force ten years ago. Most of the new police force was drawn from the old government militia, as you'd expect, and at senior levels there was a need for those who'd had links with intelligence. We were not exactly overburdened with talent. As external interest in our country increased, we were encountering more and more instances of criminal activity – fraud, corruption, intimidation, industrial espionage, as well as more conventional crimes. Things were becoming more unstable in Russia. China was opening up to more commercial practices. You can imagine the growing pressure on this country.'

Drew could easily imagine it. He still couldn't quite understand Nergui's role in all this, though. The links between the militia and foreign investment seemed obscure, and Nergui's subsequent movement into the police service didn't sound an obvious progression. Unless, of course, these were all simply different outlets for the intelligence services.

'What kinds of cases does the Serious Crimes Team normally get involved with?'

'All kinds. Major robberies, homicide, corruption. Anything that doesn't fall into the norms of day-to-day policing.'

'But you've moved back to the Ministry now?' Drew prompted.

Nergui nodded. 'Six months ago, yes. Not particularly of my own choosing. There were those who thought my talents were – underutilised as a policeman. The police force does not have a particularly good reputation in this country – justifiably in many cases I think. We have invested insufficiently in its development and it does not attract the highest calibre of employees. These days, there are more opportunities for our graduates in the private sector. But there has also been growing concern about national security, so I was – how do you say it? – poached by the Ministry. It was one of those offers I could not refuse.'

'And what was your role in the Ministry?'

Nergui shrugged. 'In general, dealing with cases that are perceived to pose a threat, in some way, to national security or stability. Not terrorism – we have a separate unit to deal with that, though it has not to date been a major problem for us, even with the breakup of the

USSR. But things like major commercial fraud, corruption – anything that might pose a threat to, say, our economy, social stability or whatever.'

None of this made much sense to Drew. It sounded very different from any concept of policing that he was used to. 'And murder?' he asked.

'Not usually,' he said. 'But then we don't usually encounter murders quite like these.'

'You really see these murders as a threat to national security? Is that why you've returned?'

'I have returned only because the Minister asked me to. It is embarrassing. Doripalam is a very capable officer, despite his youth. There's nothing I can teach him, I think. But the Minister is anxious. He is protecting his back. As for security – well, who knows? If we are simply dealing with a psychopath, then of course the answer is no. If there is something more rational behind the killings – like a vendetta or whether at least some of the victims were targeted – then, well, yes, it's possible. And there is also our concern for the stability of our country. Compared with many other parts of the old Eastern Bloc, we have survived the changes remarkably well. We have been through very difficult times, but our society has stayed remarkably stable. This is quite a safe country. But the kind of fear that could be stirred up by these killings – well, so far we have managed to keep the full details from being published and we have not indicated any linkage between the killings. But we can't keep this up for long. The press have been used to doing what the government tells them, but that is changing. I do not know, for example, how long we can prevent them from reporting that a police officer has been killed.'

Drew nodded. 'And what do you think will happen when people find out?'

'I do not know. There are many things that people

fear. There are many interpretations they could put on these deaths.' He stopped, enigmatically, as though unwilling to put his anxieties into plain words.

'And what about today's killing?' Drew asked. 'Where does that fit into this?'

'It is intriguing, is it not? Horrific, but intriguing. As with your Mr Ransom, the question is whether there is any significance in the choice of this particular individual?'

'You mean, other than the simple fact that he was a police officer?'

'Quite so.' Nergui finished eating, and placed his fork and spoon neatly across the bowl. 'I do not like to say so, but today's murder may give us a little hope.'

'Hope?'

'Or at least somewhere to start in our investigations. To date, we have had nothing. No leads. We thought Mr Ransom might start to lead us somewhere, but it appeared not. Perhaps Delgerbayar might.'

'Delgerbayar?'

'Our unfortunate colleague.'

'So you think there might have been some significance to his death? Some reason why he specifically was chosen as the victim?'

Nergui leaned forward across the table, placing his fingertips together. 'I do not know,' he said. 'But I do know, having asked some brief questions of his fellow officers today, that Delgerbayar had been acting oddly in recent weeks.'

'Oddly in what way?'

'In a number of ways, apparently. Delgerbayar was not a particularly sociable person, I understand. People differ, of course. Our officers tend to be a gregarious bunch. You will generally find them after work throwing back the vodkas in one of our city bars. But there are exceptions to that, and Delgerbayar was one of them. He might join his colleagues briefly, but he would leave early in the evening. Nobody could ever recall seeing him at a party or a social gathering. I hope I'm not speaking ill of the dead, but he was generally seen as a rather – enigmatic character. He wasn't married, had no close family as far as anyone was aware. No one really knew what he did with his time. He had risen through the ranks largely because he was seen as a hard worker, I think, rather than through any great talent.'

It was an interesting enough character sketch, but Drew wasn't sure where this was leading. 'How had he been behaving oddly?'

'Well, out of character, let us say.' Nergui smiled. 'From what I hear, he had always behaved a little oddly. The first thing was that a couple of his fellow officers came across him one night in the bar in the Ulan Baatar hotel – another of our more upmarket places. It was only a coincidence that they were in there – the police don't tend to drink in the tourist hotels, as you might imagine. But they were there on duty, following up some petty thefts that had taken place in the hotel. And Delgerbayar was in the bar, sitting with a mixed group of Westerners and locals, apparently having a good enough time.'

'Do you know who was with him?'

Nergui shook his head. 'No, the officers didn't recognise any of them. They just thought it was an odd group to find with Delgerbayar – the Westerners looked well-off, business types. The locals also looked relatively prosperous – perhaps not the type you would normally expect to find associating with a police officer.'

'Criminals?'

Nergui shrugged. 'The term is a broad one,' he said. 'Maybe criminals. More likely those who have done well for themselves in our economy by – what is your phrase? – sailing close to the wind.'

'But wouldn't you recognise those types?' Drew asked. 'Surely they'd be well known.'

'I would probably recognise them,' Nergui said. 'But in many cases – except for one or two larger celebrities – these kinds of people would not be well known to an ordinary police officer. Though our officers would probably be well acquainted with some of their employees.'

'I understand. So, as you say, not the sort one would expect to find consorting with a senior police officer.'

'No, but the two officers didn't really think much of it – it's not uncommon for officers to maintain some dubious contacts, particularly if they think they might extract some information from them.' He smiled. 'I've been known to do it myself. So it's quite possible that Delgerbayar's contacts were – well, if not exactly innocent, still quite legitimate.'

'Do you believe that?'

'Who knows? With most officers, I would think it possible, though I might still be suspicious. From what I hear of Delgerbayar, it doesn't sound likely.'

'And was there other strange behaviour?'

'Yes, and a more significant issue. Delgerbayar had been involved in an investigation into some illegal gold prospecting—'

'*Gold* prospecting?'

Nergui nodded. 'Our country is rich in many minerals, including gold. The gold is, officially, being mined by a small number of companies which have acquired the appropriate rights. It is one of the ways you become wealthy quickly in this country.'

Drew could imagine. Like much of the former Eastern Bloc, this now appeared to be a country where substantial poverty could co-exist very closely with extreme wealth.

'Not surprisingly,' Nergui went on, 'there are those

who, lacking other resources, try to obtain their own small share of this wealth.' Nergui's face betrayed nothing of his feelings – positive or negative – towards such people. 'There are a lot of problems with people prospecting illegally for gold. In the right places, you can pan for gold in rivers. You will find small amounts, but those can still be enormously valuable – particularly to a poor family without other work.'

'But these people can be prosecuted?'

'In principle, yes, very much so. In practice, the police often turn a blind eye, unless there is a direct complaint from one of the mining companies or the illegal activities are on a larger scale.'

'So what was Delgerbayar investigating?'

'We'd had a complaint, apparently, from one of the mining companies about a small encampment that had been established near to one of their key sites. It wasn't clear how much gold was actually being found by this group, but they'd been there for some time and I think they'd become something of a visible challenge to the mining company. I think they wanted something done to make an example of them.'

'What was Delgerbayar supposed to do?'

'There were two officers working on this, Delgerbayar and one other. The usual routine is that they would just give some sort of warning to the camp members, get them to move on. At most, they might formally caution them. But I don't think they expected to arrest or charge anyone unless there was active resistance.'

'So what happened?'

Nergui leaned back in his chair. 'Something strange happened. The day before they were due to visit the encampment, Delgerbayar disappeared.'

Drew looked up in surprise. 'Really?'

'He appeared briefly at headquarters and left a message

for his senior officer to say that he had stumbled upon an important lead in the gold prospecting case and was therefore having to travel urgently south, to the Gobi.'

'To the desert? Why?'

'He didn't say. It's difficult to see how there could have been any link to the prospecting case, which seemed like a trivial bit of business. He gave the name of a tourist encampment in the Gobi, where he said he was going to meet a contact.'

'But surely he wasn't allowed just to disappear like that?'

'Of course not,' Nergui said. 'His senior officer was furious. It is likely that there would have been some disciplinary action taken, unless he'd come up with a very good explanation for his behaviour.'

'But—'

Nergui anticipated the question. 'But that didn't happen, no. He never came back – not alive, anyway. We don't even know for sure if he reached the tourist camp. So far, no one's admitted to having met him. He was booked on to a flight to the Gobi, and it looks as if he – or someone – may have travelled. But that's all we know. The next time we saw him—'

Drew nodded slowly. 'Today. But it does sound as if there's a potential lead there.'

'Exactly. Of course, it's possible that this is all coincidence and that the Gobi stuff wasn't linked to this – maybe it was just a young officer showing off, thinking he'd stumbled on something and going off without thinking through the consequences.'

'It wouldn't be the first time, in my experience,' Drew said, with a faint smile. 'I might have even done it myself, if I think back far enough.'

'But, from what I hear, that doesn't sound typical of Delgerbayar. If anything, he tended to be over-cautious.

People were genuinely taken aback when he disappeared – I think most people assumed there was more to it. Some sort of domestic crisis or something. There were some who thought he'd had some sort of breakdown.'

'So you have to assume a connection?'

'We do.' Nergui sat back slowly in his chair. 'I hope you enjoyed the meal.'

'The food really was superb, Nergui.' Drew realised that it was the first time he had used the Mongolian's name. He felt, just for a moment, as though he had fallen under a spell, as though the combination of the food and the alcohol and Nergui's openness had compelled him to lower his guard. He wondered whether this had been Nergui's intention, whether the unexpected openness about his background had been a deliberate ploy to gain his own trust.

Even as he felt this, he realised that the prospect didn't concern him unduly. He wasn't entirely sure whether Nergui could be trusted, but at the moment he felt some reassurance that at least they were in this thing – whatever it might turn out to be – together.

Nergui smiled faintly, as though reading Drew's thoughts. 'Now,' he said, 'I have three questions for you.'

'Go ahead.' Drew couldn't read the Mongolian's expression, didn't know whether or not he was being serious.

Nergui ticked off the questions on his fingers. 'Three simple questions. One – would you like some coffee? Two – would you like some of our excellent vodka with your coffee?' He paused, slowly tapping his third finger. 'And three – would you like to travel to the Gobi in the morning?'

SEVEN

'We should have travelled business class.'

'This is business class. You should see economy.'

Drew laughed. This was like nothing he had ever experienced. He wasn't sure he would ever want to experience it again, but for the moment it was sufficiently different to be worth enduring.

He had never seen an aeroplane so crowded. It was a small propeller-driven plane, but it appeared to be more crowded than any 747 Drew had ever seen. It wasn't quite true that there were people standing but it felt as if there were. Certainly, most of the passengers seemed to be carrying more than their allotted allowance of cabin luggage, which appeared to be stuffed into any available place.

'I hope this is safe,' Drew said, looking around them. As far as he could see, he was the only Westerner on board.

Nergui shrugged. 'A better safety record than Aeroflot, anyway.'

'That's very reassuring.'

It was only a ninety-minute flight to Dalanzadgad, but this was quite long enough for Drew. He still wasn't sure that it was a wise decision to accompany Nergui. He had a suspicion that Nergui's decision to make the trip was prompted primarily by a desire to get himself and Drew out of Doripalam's hair, to give the young man the opportunity to get on with some serious police work without interruption.

As far as Drew could see, there wasn't a lot that he would be able to contribute to the investigation. On the other hand, it was a perfect excuse for a trip to the Gobi Desert, and it would have been a pity to have left this country without seeing it. Drew, who took his work very seriously, was uncomfortably aware that his visit to this country was a glorified public relations exercise, and he now felt additionally guilty about engaging in what was little more than a sight-seeing excursion. On the other hand, he told himself, he had not asked to come here. He was undertaking a task which his superiors felt to be worthwhile. And there was the small matter of having already been shot at, even if, as it had turned out, his life had not really been in danger. So maybe he should just sit back and enjoy this.

Although sitting back was not easy, given the state of the aeroplane seats. He had the impression that the passenger behind him was trying to insert a large cabin trunk in the space between their respective rows. He was also sure that he could hear the sound of a chicken clucking somewhere towards the rear of the aircraft.

'What's the schedule today?' he asked. This had all been very sudden. The previous evening, after he had found himself agreeing to accompany Nergui on the trip, Nergui had made a couple of official-sounding phone calls to organise the tickets and accommodation. Drew had returned to his hotel – again in an official car – at around eleven, and had then been up at six to prepare for the journey. He had retained his room at the Chinggis Khaan at Nergui's suggestion and left most of his luggage there, taking only his small shoulder bag with a change of clothes. There was only one return flight each day to Dalanzadgad so they would have to stay overnight. The intention was to stay in the same camp that Delgerbayar had been intending to visit.

'We get to Dalanzadgad at around ten-thirty. I've arranged to talk to one or two people from the airline to see if there's any record or recollection of Delgerbayar coming through. It's a bit of a long shot, but somebody caught that flight so we may be able to get some idea of whether it was Delgerbayar or not.'

Drew wondered whether Delgerbayar would have been easy to recognise. Since the only time he had seen the man's face it had been detached from his neck, it wasn't an issue he particularly wanted to dwell upon.

'And then we go on to the camp. It's not too far – I've arranged for a jeep to take us out. I've set up an interview with the man who runs the place, and I've asked him if we can also talk to a few of the staff. You never know, someone might remember Delgerbayar.'

Drew settled back in his seat, still trying to make himself comfortable. 'This probably sounds a stupid question,' he said, 'but what exactly is a tourist camp?'

'Just what it sounds like,' Nergui said. 'There are a number of them, scattered about the Gobi. Permanent clusters of *gers* which people visit for vacations.'

'Holiday camps?' Drew said. 'In the desert?'

'Well, you could perhaps think of it as a large beach.' Nergui smiled. 'Though I admit it's a long walk to the sea.'

'So who uses them?'

'They're still very popular,' Nergui said. 'Some of them cater for tourists from the former Eastern Bloc – we used to get a lot of tourists from there, when it was impossible for them to go elsewhere. But now it tends to be either international tourists – for them, it's part of the experience of visiting our country – or Mongolians from the cities who wish to visit the desert on their vacations. The place we're visiting caters mainly for foreign tourists.'

'But – assuming that Delgerbayar's story was true or at least partly true – why would a contact have arranged to meet him in a place like that? Why not in Ulan Baatar?'

'That is part of the mystery,' Nergui said. 'I have no answer. It is a strange place to arrange an assignation. Assuming that Delgerbayar's story was true, then it's possible of course that the contact was a foreigner, maybe a tourist or someone posing as a tourist. But that still doesn't explain why they should have arranged to meet in such a strange location.'

'Maybe they thought it would be a discreet meeting place?'

'That's quite possible. Of course, there are discreet places where one could meet in Ulan Baatar, but not many. In practice, the city tends to be something of a small village. Too many people know one another, frequent the same bars, the same restaurants. Delgerbayar was unlucky enough to be spotted in the Ulan Baatar. No matter where else he went, there was always the risk that he might be seen by someone.'

'Which implies,' Drew said, 'that his contact – if there was one – was someone he didn't want to be seen with.'

'Indeed.' Nergui nodded, and not for the first time Drew had the impression that the Mongolian's thinking had already progressed several stages beyond his own. Nergui's face, though, was as inscrutable as ever. 'Now,' he said, finally, 'you should enjoy the journey. It is not every day you have an opportunity to see the vast expanse of the Gobi.'

This was true enough, but it was not easy to take Nergui's advice. Intriguing as the destination might be, the journey itself was anything but enjoyable. The take-off had been unnerving – there had been at least a brief moment when Drew was convinced they were going to plough off the end of the runway into the cluster of sheds beyond. The ascent was little more reassuring, since he had the impression that the small aircraft was having to use every unit of its limited engine power to lift its heavy cargo. And now they were at what would normally be described as cruising altitude, the aeroplane was small enough to feel every buffet of air turbulence. Drew found no difficulty in declining the meagre meal of dried meats and biscuits that was proffered, but accepted the familiar small bottle of vodka that accompanied it with relative enthusiasm. Across the aisle, a group of young men, dressed in grey overalls, had already produced a larger bottle of vodka which they were consuming at an impressive pace.

Nergui glanced across at them and smiled. 'Mongolians do not like to fly,' he said. 'We think it is unnatural. So we calm our fears with drink. Which of course does little for either our safety or our state of mind.'

Nergui had clearly noted Drew's discomfort, and devoted his time to distracting stories of the desert, the nomadic herdsmen who frequented it, and other anecdotes of Mongolian life. Drew also had the impression, perhaps unfounded, that Nergui was attempting to distract his thoughts from the case that they were investigating.

The time passed quickly enough, though, even if it felt much longer in the pit of Drew's stomach. Before long, first the buildings and then the vegetation fell away, and Drew could see the vast expanse of the desert spread out before them. Drew had never seen a desert before and his expectations were conditioned largely by filmic images of the Sahara – empty wastelands of sand baking in the eternally noonday sun, a few palm trees, tents and camels.

Some of that he would undoubtedly see over the next twenty-four hours. But the landscape they passed over was surprisingly varied – they passed over hills, forested areas and green plains. As they flew south, the undulating hills slowly gave way to something closer to Drew's ideas of a desert. But even here he was surprised at how green the land looked. It was sand, for sure, but there had apparently been some rain over the preceding weeks, and a fine sheen of green, burgeoning grass, had spread across the landscape. Although the grass was sparse, from this altitude it bore a startling resemblance to a well-tended British lawn.

As they flew above the expansive landscape, far below Drew could see few signs of life. There were occasional clusters of *gers*, with the movements of animals that, from this height, might have been horses or might have been camels. Now and again, there was a fast-moving cloud of sand which Drew assumed was a vehicle of some kind. But otherwise there was little to be seen until they began to approach Dalanzadgad.

The descent was as unnerving as the ascent had been. It felt almost as if they were plummeting from the sky, though he had to assume that the pilot knew what he was doing. Drew felt his ears popping from the pressure change as the aircraft banked and then levelled, preparing for landing. Drew was never particularly good with aeroplane landings and this was one of the worst he had experienced. He was convinced they were simply going to plough directly into the ground, and so he was hugely relieved when their tyres hit the runway and bounced. The impact was a shock, but they – and the aircraft – seemed unscathed, bouncing speedily across the ground towards the airport buildings. Even then Drew thought they were still going too fast, but somehow the pilot managed to keep control of the aircraft and they pulled up safely at the stand.

There was no polite waiting for the pilot to turn off the seatbelt signs. As soon as the aircraft stopped moving, the crowd of passengers jumped up, as though co-ordinated, and began to scramble for their luggage in the overhead compartments. Somewhere behind, Drew once again heard the sound of a clucking chicken.

Only Nergui remained motionless in his seat. 'There's no rush,' he said. 'We might as well relax.'

Drew didn't feel too relaxed, but he was glad of the opportunity to recover from his airborne ordeal. 'Is the flight always like that?' he asked.

'More or less. Not always that smooth.' Nergui smiled gently, and once again it was difficult to be sure whether he was joking.

With remarkable speed, the crowd of passengers poured towards the rear entrance, and Drew and Nergui rose to follow. Outside, the sky was clear blue and the sun was already high. This late in the year, though, the temperature was cool.

Drew followed Nergui down the stairs and across the runway to the small concrete airport building. There were no passport or customs controls at what was exclusively a domestic airport. The arrival hall was anonymous, another example of Communist functionality. A couple of uniformed policemen were standing conspicuously in the corner, watching the disembarking passengers without interest.

Nergui walked over and engaged them in conversation, pulling his formal ID from his pocket to show them. Instantly, both men jumped to attention. They didn't quite salute, but they showed Nergui a respect which had been noticeably absent in their earlier demeanour.

Nergui beckoned him over, and spoke what were

clearly a few words of introduction to the two officers. Both nodded towards him.

'They're going to take us to the airport manager,' Nergui said. 'I don't imagine there's much he'll be able to tell us himself, but I think it's only courteous that we speak to him before we start bothering his staff.'

They followed the police officers out of the main hall, and along a corridor to a small, sparsely furnished office. A small harassed-looking man was sitting behind a desk, scribbling figures down on a bundle of papers and occasionally stabbing numbers into a large, old-fashioned-looking calculator. He looked up impatiently as they came in.

Nergui spoke a few words and introduced Drew, who nodded politely. The manager brushed aside his papers and spoke brusquely to Nergui. Even without any understanding of the words, it was clear that he was not pleased to have them there. Nergui spoke a few quiet words in return, and the man rose, his chair scraping back across the polished wooden floor. He spoke angrily and stalked over to the window, which looked out on to grey concrete walls.

Nergui looked back at Drew and smiled faintly. 'We don't seem very welcome,' he said.

'I had that impression,' Drew said. 'What's the problem?'

'I'm not entirely clear,' Nergui said, still smiling. 'Our friend seems to be under the impression that we will disrupt the smooth running of his operation, and spread fear and anxiety among the passengers.'

'You've told him we'll be very discreet?'

'Of course. But he doesn't appear to be reassured.' The smile was still fixed on Nergui's face, but as he turned back towards the airport manager, his face returned to its familiar blank mask. He spoke a few more calm words to the manager, who once again responded angrily, stamping his foot petulantly on the floor.

Afterwards, Drew couldn't actually recall seeing Nergui move. But suddenly he was standing only inches away from the airport manager, his eyes blazing. Nergui spoke, still softly, not raising his voice. Drew had no idea what the words meant, but he could feel the sense of threat even from across the room. The manager blinked, and Drew reflected to himself that it was the first time he had ever seen the blood genuinely drain from someone's face. The manager's mouth opened once, twice, but no sounds came out. Nergui said something more, and the man nodded quickly, his eyes blinking.

Nergui turned back towards Drew and, like a light-bulb being switched on, the smile returned. 'That's fine,' Nergui said. 'Just a little misunderstanding, I think. We can see anyone we like, and our friend here will be only too pleased to make the introductions.'

Drew found that he could barely speak himself. 'That's very nice of him,' he said, finally.

'Isn't it?' Nergui said. 'But we're a friendly people.'

Nergui led the way out of the office, and back into the main hall, the manager now scuttling along behind him.

'What was all that about, anyway?' Drew said, as he hurried along behind Nergui. 'Just bureaucracy?'

Nergui spoke without looking back. He was heading towards a group of uniformed check-in staff, who were standing chatting by one of the desks. 'I don't know,' he said. 'I thought at first he was just being difficult – you know, the usual petty official protecting his turf. But then I got the impression there was something else, that he might actually be frightened.'

'I'm not surprised he was frightened,' Drew said, deciding that there was little mileage in not being fully open. 'You scared the life out of me, let alone him.'

Nergui laughed. 'No, before that,' he said. 'I was doing my usual, polite officer of the law piece, flattering him into helping. You know the kind of thing—?'

Drew knew it all too well. It usually worked okay with the petty official type.

'—and he was stonewalling. Not just being difficult, but looking genuinely anxious at the thought of helping us out. That was why I put the screws on a bit.'

'You think he's afraid of something? Or someone?'

Nergui shrugged. 'Possibly. Who knows?'

By this time, he had reached the group of check-in staff, who were looking at him with some curiosity, assuming that he was a passenger in search of information. Before Nergui could speak, the manager had caught up with him and interjected, gesturing backwards and forwards between Nergui and the others as he effected introductions.

Drew watched him closely. It was frustrating, tailing behind Nergui, unable to contribute meaningfully to any interviews, spending half the time wondering what the hell was going on. But the one advantage of his position was that he could at least watch carefully the expressions and body language of those that Nergui was addressing.

Nergui was right, he thought. This man did look more anxious than the situation justified. Even if one accepted the supposed reason – concerns about disturbing passengers and staff – this did not explain the gleam of sweat that had already appeared on the manager's forehead. It surely couldn't be the first time that the police had wished to investigate on site – this was an airport, after all. But as the manager hopped from one foot to the other, twisting his head and interrupting as though having to interpret to the staff what Nergui was saying, he did look scared. He was doing his best to conceal it, with over-eager smiling and laughing, but even some of the staff were regarding him oddly.

Nergui simply ignored him, talking steadily and calmly to the group of staff. After a few moments, he reached into his jacket and brought out the picture of Delgerbayar which he had copied from the police files. He showed it around the group, allowing them time to gaze fully at the face. Nergui had shown Drew the photograph during the flight. It looked to be a well-taken photograph, though Drew could not relate it to the white, bloodstained visage he had seen.

As Drew watched, one of the female staff in the group began to nod enthusiastically, talking hurriedly to Nergui. She was gesturing towards the photograph and then pointing towards a spot across the hall, close to the exit doors. As she pointed, she spotted a colleague walking slowly through the hall and called out to him. He looked up as she shouted, then hurried over to join the group. Drew wasn't clear what was going on, but it appeared to be important. Nergui was engaged in intense conversation with the woman, then, when the newcomer arrived, he turned and spoke rapidly to him also. The man was nodding and pointing over to the same spot.

Finally, Nergui turned to Drew and beckoned him to join them. Drew smiled vaguely at the group, who all simultaneously took a half step back as he approached. It was as if they didn't quite know what to make of a Westerner in their midst. There was no hostility in their response – just curiosity and a certain wariness.

'What is it?' Drew said. 'You've got something?'

'Looks like it. I didn't really expect it. You have to ask the questions, but you can't really imagine that anyone would remember one passenger amongst hundreds a week ago.'

'And do they?'

'Definitely. But only because Delgerbayar behaved rather differently from most other passengers that day.'

'How?'

'It looks as if he arrived on the same flight we did today. He disembarked from the aircraft, made his way into here, and then over towards the exits, where we assume he looked around for someone who was meeting him.'

'But how—?'

'It's not entirely clear what happened. Of course, nobody had particularly noticed Delgerbayar up to this point, even on the plane. We made enquiries among the cabin staff yesterday, but you saw how crowded the flights can get. Anyway, we assume that Delgerbayar got here and found the person he was due to meet. The first thing that anyone notices are some raised voices over by the exit doors. The whole room turns to look, and there are two men apparently having an almighty row. It's starting to turn into something physical – pushing and shoving, you know – when a couple of the airport police turn up to separate them.'

'What happened? Did Delgerbayar tell them he was an officer too?'

'Not clear, but we can check with the local police and find out who was on that day, see if anything was said. But my guess would be not. In fact, surprisingly, Delgerbayar and the other man both turn hurriedly and walk out through the exit together. They were being watched by our friends here—' Nergui said, gesturing to the two airport employees, '—along with everyone else. It appeared that they both jumped into the same truck and sped pretty rapidly away from the airport.'

'And they're sure it was Delgerbayar?'

Nergui nodded. 'As sure as anyone can be in this kind of situation, I think. I pushed them quite hard on that and they've both looked carefully at the picture, and they're sure it was him. The others here weren't close enough to be certain, but these two both happened to be walking by the exits when it happened, so they were only a few feet away.'

'So – we know he definitely came down here. And we know he met up with someone. Which suggests that at least part of his story was true.'

'Though of course we don't know if his visit here was really connected with the gold prospecting business, or whether it was something else entirely.'

As Nergui talked, Drew looked past his shoulder at the group of airport staff. The manager was hovering beside them, occasionally whispering something nervously. Drew raised an eyebrow to draw Nergui's attention to the scene behind him. Nergui picked up the signal instantly, but didn't turn round to look.

'He's asking whether any of them recognised the other man,' Nergui said, quietly.

'I think your hearing is better than he realises,' Drew murmured, smiling faintly.

'My hearing is very good,' Nergui said. 'I can hear them shaking their heads, and I almost think I can hear the relief in his voice. Or is that my imagination?'

'They're definitely shaking their heads,' Drew said. 'I don't know about the rest of it.'

'Neither do I. But I think we need to keep an eye on our friend here.'

Nergui turned to thank the manager and staff, smiling pleasantly at the group. Most of them looked excited to be part of some sort of official investigation, and a number wanted to ask more questions. Nergui made what were clearly polite noises, and then led Drew out through the exit into the sunshine.

'What did you tell them?' Drew said, when they were outside.

'Not much. Official investigation. Following up some routine lines of enquiry. The usual.'

A jeep was standing, engine running, in what appeared to be the No Parking area immediately outside the airport building. As they emerged into the daylight, the driver jumped up then hopped out of the vehicle. Without hesitation, Nergui walked over and tossed his bag into the back. Drew followed and did likewise, then they climbed into the truck. Nergui spoke a few words to the driver, and they pulled out into the road.

Drew was struck that, even down here, ninety minutes' flight from Ulan Baatar, Nergui seemed to be recognised instantly. Drew considered himself lucky to be recognised if he stepped outside his own office.

There was little to Dalanzadgad – a few concrete-built commercial buildings around the airport, some residential blocks, a sprawl of randomly constructed wooden huts, and the inevitable *gers*. The town was primarily a gateway to the southern Gobi, rather than an entity in its own right.

The jeep quickly left the town behind, racing initially along metalled roads, then dirt tracks, and finally hitting the desert itself. They pounded along at high speed, scattering dust and debris. Nergui sat beside the driver, looking relaxed, enjoying the cool sunshine and the open space. For the first time, it struck Drew that this seemed the natural habitat for these people – even Nergui, city dweller, international traveller, seemed more at ease out here.

Drew was overwhelmed by the emptiness, the sense of space, the enormous blue spread of the sky. All sense of scale was lost here. Apart from the occasional hut or *ger*, there was nothing to provide perspective. Looking back, Dalanzadgad already looked both immensely distant and still strangely close. Ahead, there seemed to be nothing, just endless blank miles to the horizon.

The landscape seemed deserted. Once, they saw a distant figure on a motorbike speed by, miles away from them. Otherwise, there were no signs of life. Incongruously, the driver had turned up the volume of the vehicle's tape deck, so that the jeep was blasting American rock music as they drove.

After half an hour, there were the first signs of an encampment rising above the horizon ahead of them. It was impossible for Drew to tell how far away it was, but he could see a wire fence, a clustering of *gers*, and some larger wood-built buildings around it.

Nergui pointed. 'That's the place.'

'Plenty of beach,' Drew shouted back, over the noise of the engine and the music. The camp seemed utterly isolated. 'How do the tourists get out here?'

'They run buses from the airport. You'll be surprised how civilised it is when we get there.'

It was a surprisingly long time before the camp drew near. As they approached, Drew saw that there were indeed tourists – a few of them, at least – sitting inside the fenced area. It was a surreal sight. In this deserted spot, apparently miles from any other life, tourists in tee shirts and shorts were lying on sun beds, reading novels, sipping beers, looking like holidaymakers on any beach anywhere.

'Doesn't look busy,' Drew commented.

'Very late in the year,' Nergui said. 'If you'd come in the summer it would have been full. The weather's too cool now.'

It was true. The sun was still blazing down from an unclouded sky, but the temperature was only mild. The sunbathers were being optimistic, trying to make the most of the sunshine, but it was barely warm enough to be sitting outside.

The jeep pulled up to the gate, and stopped in front of what was clearly a reception area. Nergui jumped out and grabbed his bag from the vehicle, Drew following behind, and then turned and entered the building.

The wooden building was warm and dark inside. It was sparsely furnished, just a reception desk and a couple of low chairs. The man behind the desk looked up as they entered and smiled at Nergui, uttering some words of welcome. Nergui nodded back, and gestured behind him, introducing Drew.

'Mr McLeish,' the man said, smiling enthusiastically at Drew, 'it is good to welcome you here.'

'You speak English?' Drew said.

The man nodded, modestly. 'A little,' he said. 'We have been receiving tourists from the United Kingdom and from the USA for a long time now – more than ten years. I have been trying to learn some of their – your – language.'

'You speak it well, Mr—?'

'Batkhuyag. I ask our visitors to correct me when I get it wrong.' He laughed. 'They are very happy to do so.'

Nergui said a few more words to him in Mongolian. Batkhuyag nodded, and pointed behind him. 'I have arranged a *ger* for you to use as a base,' he said, speaking English, clearly for Drew's benefit. 'I try to find the most – what do you say? – private one for you to use so that you can speak to anyone you wish to without being disturbed.' He shrugged. 'I really do not know if we can help you. The police down here came to ask some questions, but as far I am aware no one here was able to provide any real information. But we will help as much as we can. Please feel free to speak to anyone, to go where you wish.' He paused, as if unsure how to formulate his next sentence. 'I would of course ask that you try to disturb our guests as little as possible. I know you may wish to speak to them, but please come to me first so that I can prepare them.'

Nergui nodded. 'I do not know that we will need to speak to your guests. Would any of them have been here at the time that Delgerbayar – the officer we are investigating – was supposed to have visited?'

Batkhuyag nodded. 'That was a week ago, yes? In that case, some of them would have been, although most are here only this week.'

'Well, we will see how things go. We may wish to speak to some of those who were here last week, but I promise you we will be discreet.'

'Of course,' Batkhuyag said. 'I should not have raised the issue. You know your jobs, I'm sure.'

Nergui smiled. 'If you've had the local police round here asking questions, I can imagine that discretion was not always evident?'

'Well, they are local men. They are doing their best, I'm sure. But I need to do mine, and the tourists are important to us.'

'We want them to see our country at its best,' Nergui agreed. 'I will ensure that they do.'

Batkhuyag led them back out into the open air, then through the cluster of *gers* towards the back of the camp. He gestured to a tent which lay separated from the others, close to the wooden building which served as a restaurant and meeting place for the camp. 'I thought this would be best,' he said. 'We use it for staff during the busy part of the season, but it's empty now. You can use this to interview people and as your accommodation for this evening, if that's okay.'

It was clear to Drew that Batkhuyag was doing his

best to ensure that the hospitality of the camp was not unduly contaminated by the presence of the policemen. The *ger* was as far as it could be from the remaining tents, and was clearly not of the same standard as the tourist *gers*. But Drew didn't blame the man for seeking discretion. Subtlety wasn't a quality generally found amongst policemen, and he didn't imagine that the police here were any different.

Batkhuyag opened the door of the *ger* and showed them inside. The interior was dark but, to Drew's surprise, there was electric light. The place looked surprisingly comfortable. There was an ornately decorated table in the centre surrounded by rugs. Some hard wooden chairs had been placed, slightly incongruously, around it, but Drew imagined that those had been provided specifically for Nergui and himself. Around the far walls, there were two beds, again ornately painted. Sleeping here would certainly be an experience, but not necessarily an unpleasant one, he thought.

Nergui looked around and nodded, smiling faintly. 'It looks fine,' he said. 'Most comfortable.' It was difficult to be sure if there was a trace of irony in his tone. He gestured towards one of the seats. 'You will join us, Mr Batkhuyag?'

Batkhuyag looked surprised. 'Me? I didn't really envisage—'

Nergui made a slight bow. 'But, of course, Mr Batkhuyag, you are the first person we wish to see here. I do not believe that anything happens in this camp of which you are unaware, no?'

Batkhuyag looked confused. It was, Drew had to admit, a neat question, a cunning balance of flattery and threat. 'Well,' Batkhuyag said, 'I'm not sure I would say that—'

'Come now, Mr Batkhuyag, there is no need for false

modesty. I can see how well run this place is.' Nergui casually lowered himself on to one of the wooden chairs. Batkhuyag had no choice but to follow. Drew pulled back the remaining chair and turned it round so that he could sit leaning on the chair back. He carefully positioned himself slightly away from Nergui and Batkhuyag. As far as he was concerned, this had to be Nergui's interview. He would intervene only if he thought there was something he could add.

Nergui leaned forward in his chair, his hands together. 'Now, Mr Batkhuyag, how much do you know about why we're here?'

Batkhuyag shrugged. 'Not a great deal. Just what the local police chief told me when they visited.'

'Which was?'

'That you were investigating some internal case involving one of your officers, who you believed had visited the camp a week or so back. They really just wanted to know if he had been here. They showed me his photograph.'

'And had he been here?' Nergui said.

Batkhuyag shook his head. 'Not as far as I'm aware. I didn't recognise the photograph.'

'Is it possible he came without your knowing?'

Batkhuyag shrugged. 'Of course it's possible. The day in question was one of our turnover days – one group of tourists coming, another leaving, some staying put. Things get very busy. We tend to get deliveries on those days, too. There's laundry being picked up for cleaning, new laundry being dropped off. Food deliveries. All of that. I couldn't swear that your—'

'Delgerbayar,' Nergui said.

'I couldn't swear that he wasn't here for a while in the middle of all that. I'm pretty sure he wasn't staying here as a guest. Obviously, we had no one of that name, and that photograph didn't look familiar. Also our guests tend to stay for several days at least – as I understand it, your Mr . . . Delgerbayar would have come down only the previous day. That would have been unusual, so we would have remembered.'

'Did you ask any of the other staff if they recognised him?'

'A few,' Batkhuyag said. 'I mean, we didn't do it systematically or anything. The police weren't here long enough for that – I got the impression they were just going through the motions. Routine questions.'

'That would be pretty much it,' Nergui said. Watching the two men, Drew wondered about this. He didn't know how much the local police had been told. It was difficult to believe that they would be unaware of the brutal murder of a fellow officer. And why would they not have been told officially? Drew still had the sense of operating in an alien environment – superficially it resembled the world he was used to but it left him constantly wrong-footed. For Drew the murder of a fellow officer was still one of the most serious and dreadful of crimes. Partly this was because of the inevitable fear that it might be your own life on the line next time. But partly it was the recognition that if you tolerated that kind of assault on the forces of law and order, there was no possibility of holding any other line. It was difficult to believe that, if the police down here were aware of Delgerbayar's murder, they would have treated it casually.

'And nobody recognised him?'

'No, but that doesn't necessarily mean too much. We just asked a few of the staff in the restaurant and such like. They'd have been serving people meals, but they wouldn't necessarily get to know the tourists particularly well. On the other hand, around seventy per cent of our visitors are from overseas, so the staff tend to get to know the Mongolian guests better. They speak the same language, for one thing.'

Nergui nodded slowly. 'So it looks as if we can assume that Delgerbayar did not stay here as a guest, but it's quite possible that he did come here without your knowing.'

Batkhuyag shrugged. 'That's right. If he was here for a few hours, maybe meeting another guest, he could easily have come in and out without anybody particularly noticing, I think.'

Nergui rose, and began to pace slowly across the tent. 'I'm afraid we probably will have to conduct some more systematic questioning with your staff. And perhaps with some guests also.'

Batkhuyag raised his head. 'I am not in a position to prevent you,' he said. 'But can I ask you what this is all about?'

Nergui stopped pacing, and turned to look at him. Drew leaned back on his chair, his face studiedly blank.

Batkhuyag was watching Nergui closely now. 'I realise that you may well not wish to tell me. I ask because if you are going to cause some disruption in the camp, I feel I have a right to know why.'

Nergui remained silent. It was clear that he was not intending to assist Batkhuyag in taking this issue forward. At the same time, it was not at all clear to Drew how Nergui was going to handle this.

'I would ask only that you don't treat me as a fool,' Batkhuyag said slowly. 'I have lived in Ulan Baatar. I talk to people in the police. I am aware of your reputation. I am also aware that the police would not normally send someone of your . . . seniority to deal with an internal disciplinary matter. Or, indeed,' he added, turning to face Drew, 'an officer from the United Kingdom.'

Nergui laughed suddenly. 'Well, I'm very flattered that you think so much of me, Mr Batkhuyag. And you are quite right that I should not treat you as a fool. I am sorry if my approach has seemed discourteous.' Drew was reminded of the way Nergui had spoken to him as they had travelled back from the airport on the night of his arrival. This was Nergui the diplomat. It was not difficult to imagine him dealing with the British ambassador in the same manner – polite, but giving nothing away.

'We are not trying to deceive you, simply to exercise some discretion.' He paused. Drew wondered if Nergui was trying to work out how to finesse all this, but he continued smoothly enough: 'We are, as you rightly surmise, dealing with an extremely serious crime – it's a sensitive matter, and there are good reasons why I am unable to provide you with any more information at the moment. But, believe me, it is serious enough to warrant both my involvement and – because there are some Western interests at stake too – the involvement of my colleague, Chief Inspector McLeish.' He gestured towards Drew, who noted the use of the rank with some internal amusement. Bullshit with a capital B, he thought, but it seemed to be doing the trick. 'We believe there is a possibility that our colleague, Delgerbayar, has been involved in this, but we don't know precisely what his involvement is. That is why we are so keen to understand his movements down here.'

'My information,' Batkhuyag said, softly, 'is that your Mr Delgerbayar is dead.'

Drew looked up in surprise. He had assumed from Batkhuyag's earlier words he had no inkling of why they were here.

Nergui's face remained blank. 'And what information would that be, Mr Batkhuyag?'

Batkhuyag shrugged. 'People talk to me.'

Nergui leaned back in his chair, lifting the front legs slightly off the ground. 'Really? That's very interesting. You must be a sociable sort. Why didn't you mention this earlier?'

'I didn't think it was up to me. You were spinning me a line. That's your business. But I think it's better if we're straight with each other. I'm more likely to be able to help you if I know what it is you want.'

Batkhuyag was clearly sharper than he appeared, Drew thought. But then you probably didn't run a place like this without being a little streetwise.

Nergui nodded. 'You are no doubt correct, Mr Batkhuyag. You will appreciate the need for discretion. But, yes, I can confirm that Delgerbayar is dead.'

'Murdered,' Batkhuyag said. It was not a question.

Nergui put his hands behind his head, looking relaxed. 'Now, you do realise that your possession of this information raises some interesting questions for me?'

Batkhuyag said nothing. He was, Drew thought, giving nothing away unless he was likely to get back something in return. Funny, he thought, how these types are the same the world over.

Nergui frowned, as though he were working through some particularly abstruse conundrum. 'The situation is this,' he said, finally. 'The news of our colleague's demise is not exactly public knowledge. Even the police down here do not know – at least not officially. But somehow the information seems to have reached you. I'm curious as to how that might have happened.'

'As I say, people talk.'

'Not really good enough, I'm afraid, Mr Batkhuyag. You see, if I were the suspicious sort, I might come to the conclusion that the only way you could know about Delgerbayar's death would be if you were somehow involved in it.'

'So why would I tell you and put myself under suspicion?'

'You tell me,' Nergui smiled, coldly. 'I would hate to have to arrest you while we try to sort that mystery out.'

Batkhuyag did not look particularly troubled by the prospect. 'I don't know what the police down here are supposed to know officially,' he said, putting an ironic emphasis on the last word. 'But I listen to what they say. They know about your Mr Delgerbayar.'

Nergui raised an eyebrow. 'Do they?' he said. 'And what do they know?'

'They come out here to drink, quite often,' Batkhuyag said. 'There aren't many places to choose from down here, and we get decent beer for the tourists. We don't encourage locals, but I turn a blind eye to the police.'

'Of course.'

'There was a bunch of them here last night. We have some music on most evenings – the usual traditional stuff for the tourists. Place gets full. There were some police officers and others here most of the night, knocking back the beer and the vodka.'

'Mongolians?' Nergui said. 'The others, I mean.'

Batkhuyag frowned. 'I'm not sure. There was a group turned up early on – a few police people I recognised and one or two I didn't. Others joined them over the evening. A few of the tourists, mostly Westerners – we've got a fair number of Brits and some Americans here at the moment.'

'Is it usual for the tourists to drink with the locals?' Drew asked.

'It's not unusual,' Batkhuyag said. 'The language can be a barrier, but it's amazing how easily you can make yourself understood after a few vodkas. So, no, there was nothing particularly odd about that.'

'So what were they saying?' Nergui asked.

'Well, I can't pretend I was listening closely,' Batkhuyag said. 'But I kept picking up bits of the conversation as I passed by.'

'Of course,' Nergui said, stony-faced. 'You were working in the bar?'

'I do when we're busy. Anyway, I overheard them saying something about things up north, in the city. It was the usual stuff about how the Ministry doesn't know what it's doing, keeping people in the dark. You know.'

'I know,' Nergui said. 'And they mentioned Delgerbayar?'

'Not by name. But I put two and two together. What I heard – what I thought I heard – was something about a policeman coming down here stirring up trouble. They said – I'm sorry about this but it's what I heard – they said, well, in effect that he'd got what was coming to him.'

'And did they indicate why they thought that?'

'Not that I heard. Tell you the truth, I was a bit shocked. I mean, we complain about the police all the time, but you kind of expect that they'll stick together. Made me wonder what was going on. But also made me think that I'd be better off not enquiring too deeply.'

Nergui nodded, his face still giving nothing away. 'You're a wise man, Mr Batkhuyag. Have you anything else to tell us?'

Batkhuyag shook his head. He looked less composed now than he had at the start of the interview, as though Nergui's response – or lack of it – had for the first time confirmed to him that he might be on the edge of something serious here. 'Who else would you like to see?'

Nergui looked across at Drew, though Drew had the impression that this was more from courtesy than anything else. 'I think we need to see any of your staff who were working in the bar last night or who might have been around on the day that Delgerbayar was supposedly down here.' He handed Batkhuyag his open notebook and pen. 'Perhaps you could write down the names, and then we can see people in order.'

Batkhuyag thought for a moment, then dutifully began to write a list of names. 'I think that's everyone, but if there's anyone I've missed, I'll add them.' He rose to leave, but Nergui gestured him back into his seat.

'Two more brief questions,' he said. 'First, do you know the names of any of the guests who were with the police officers last night?'

Batkhuyag opened his mouth to speak, then stopped. 'No, I don't,' he said. 'At least, there were a number, but I don't know who—'

'Just some names,' Nergui said. 'We will be discreet.'

Batkhuyag looked from Nergui to Drew and then back again, clearly considering his options and realising how limited they were. 'Okay,' he said. 'There were a couple I can be sure of. I'll ask them if they can spare a few minutes to see you – they've been off on a tour of some of the prehistoric sites but they should be back soon.'

'Thank you,' Nergui said. 'And my second question—'

Batkhuyag had clearly already anticipated the second question. 'I recognised the police officers, but I don't know their names—'

Nergui raised his head and smiled coldly at Batkhuyag. 'Really?' he said. 'Well, I suppose I could always take you down to the police HQ and get you to point them out to me.'

'Look, a job like mine depends on discretion. If it gets around that I've been talking to you—'

'I can see that that would be a problem for you,' Nergui said. 'Just write the names down. I will tell no one.'

Batkhuyag looked between them both again, clearly anxious now. Then he shook his head, and bent down to write the names on the pad.

EIGHT

They spent the remainder of the afternoon working steadily through the list of interviewees. It was necessary work – the kind of balls-aching routine that, in Drew's experience, dominated any major enquiry. But it was clear that they were making little progress.

The rest of the camp's staff were either much smarter or much dumber than Batkhuyag – or, quite possibly, Drew reflected, they were both. Either way, they were admitting nothing. No, they had no recollection of seeing Delgerbayar at the camp. No, they hadn't particularly noticed any strangers on the site that day, though it was difficult to tell with all the comings and goings. No, they had not overheard any conversations last night. Maybe there were some policemen in the bar last night – there often were – but, no, they couldn't honestly remember for sure. And in any case it never paid to get too close to the police.

'It's a waste of time,' Drew said, as the final staff member had been ushered from the room. It was particularly so for him since few of the interviewees had spoken any English.

'It's always a waste of time,' Nergui agreed, 'but we have to do it. You never know when someone might let something slip. Look at Batkhuyag.'

'He was being smart,' Drew said.

Nergui nodded. 'I like it when people are smart. It's when they make mistakes.'

'He's just got a big ego. Likes to tell you what he knows.'

'That will get him into trouble in a place like this,' Nergui said.

'Maybe it already has.'

Nergui frowned. 'There are some patterns forming here,' he said, slowly, 'but I have no idea what to make of them. What are your thoughts?'

He sounded as if he was genuinely interested, though Drew suspected that he was being humoured. 'I've no idea,' he said. 'What have we got? Delgerbayar makes his unscheduled trip down here, meets someone presumably by arrangement, gets into an argument with them, slips away when the police arrive and comes here, though we've no definite sightings. The person he met may or may not have been a guest here.' It didn't sound all that much, now that Drew came to summarise it. 'Then somehow, somewhere, he gets himself killed, and ends up, headless, in the factory where we found him.' He plunged on, willing himself not to envisage that scene again. 'And then we find that, within hours, although the news has been kept under wraps, the local police are gossiping about his death and apparently saying that he brought it on himself. It's not a lot.'

'It isn't,' Nergui agreed. 'And we shouldn't necessarily make too much of the police down here. You're not likely to keep that kind of thing very quiet, especially when so many officers were involved in finding the body.' He paused. 'Which may, of course, be another reason why the killer set it up like that.'

'But why would they think he had it coming?'

Nergui shrugged. 'Maybe just the usual small-town resentment of HQ. Maybe they didn't like the fact that he'd invaded their turf.'

'Or maybe they know something.'

'Maybe. Which brings us to our group of tourists – those who were chatting to the police in the bar last night. We should talk to them next.'

'It's not going to be an easy conversation,' Drew said. 'Especially if you're trying to keep Delgerbayar's death quiet.'

'I think we should still keep it quiet. If the news is out there, I want to know who's spreading it, and I'd rather it wasn't me.' Nergui paused. 'Just a friendly conversation is all we need.'

Nergui had asked Batkhuyag to track down some of the tourists. They were back now from their trip and were in their *gers* or out in the setting sun, resting before dinner. Moments later, Batkhuyag returned followed by two quizzical-looking men. Both were middle-aged, one short and overweight, the other tall and deeply tanned. The latter was wearing sunglasses and made no move to remove them as he entered the dim interior of the *ger*.

Nergui watched until Batkhuyag had backed out of the tent, and then gestured to the two men to sit. 'Good afternoon, gentlemen. I am very grateful that you were able to join us.'

The overweight man scowled faintly. 'What's this all about? We're supposed to be on vacation.' He was an American.

'I understand. I apologise for interrupting your leisure. I will be as brief as possible.'

'That would be appreciated.'

'You have been here a few days, that is right?'

'Four days. We're flying back up to Ulan Baatar tomorrow. It's an organised tour.'

'I hope you're enjoying your visit to our country.'

'It's very interesting. But I'd be grateful if you would get to the point.' Drew was watching closely. It was clear that the overweight man had little time for small talk, but it wasn't clear if there was any agenda, beyond his desire to conclude their discussion. The other man, Drew noted with some interest, had still not spoken, but was watching the discussion with a faint smile playing across his face, as though he were nothing more than a disinterested observer of the interview.

'Of course,' Nergui smiled. 'As I think you have been told, I am a senior officer with the Ministry of Security here—'

'I was told you were a cop.'

'In effect, I am. I'm on secondment to the Serious Crimes Team. My colleague here—' Nergui gestured towards Drew, '— is most definitely a cop. He is a chief inspector with the British police.'

The overweight man looked across at Drew, baffled now. Whatever assumptions he had made about this meeting had clearly been overturned. 'What's this all about? What's a Brit doing here?'

'It's a long story, Mr—?'

'Collins.'

'Mr Collins. I won't bore you with the details, as I realise how precious your time is. We're investigating a potentially very serious crime in Ulan Baatar, which has also had an impact on some British interests there, hence Chief Inspector McLeish's presence. Sadly, it appears that the case may also involve one of our own officers who went missing a week ago.'

'What does this have to do with us?'

'Nothing directly,' Nergui said. 'Except that we believe that, after leaving Ulan Baatar, the officer in question came here.'

'Here? Why would he come here?'

'We do not know. As yet. He was seen at the airport, and we have some evidence that he came here. But we do not know what he did or who he saw. We are therefore interviewing a number of people – mainly staff, but also some guests – who may recollect him and shed some light on what he did here.'

'And why do you think we can help?'

Nergui shrugged. 'I have no idea whether you can or not. As I say, we are simply speaking to a cross-section of people. You have frequented the bar here in the evenings?'

'No law against that, is there? We tried that kind of law once. I wouldn't recommend it.'

'On the contrary,' Nergui said, 'it is encouraged. Though perhaps some of my countrymen partake with a little too much enthusiasm. No, I simply wondered whether you had seen the officer in question in the bar?' He handed the photograph over to Collins.

Collins scrutinised it closely, then twisted and handed it to the other man, who looked at it very briefly without removing his dark glasses, and shook his head. 'I'm afraid we can't help you,' Collins said.

'No? Well, we have to keep asking. Thank you for your time, Mr Collins and—!' He looked at the other man, who smiled and nodded back, but still said nothing. 'We are very grateful to you. I hope you will enjoy the remainder of your trip. Have you had a chance to meet any of the locals down here?' He added the last question as an apparent afterthought.

'Locals? One or two – I can see what you mean about them knocking back the booze. We've had one or two lively nights in the bar.' With the interview at an end, Collins sounded more relaxed.

'The local police use this place a lot,' Nergui said. 'We thought that might have been why our colleague came here. But they seem to know nothing about this.'

'They—' Collins began, then stopped. 'I don't know who we met. We couldn't really make ourselves understood. Except through the international language of the bottle.' He looked back at the other man, and Drew wondered whether some sort of signal passed between them. But Collins had his head turned away and the other man had not removed his glasses, so there was no way of knowing. 'Well, if you've finished with us, gentlemen, I think we'll go and prepare ourselves for another night of socialising and inebriation.'

'Please, be our guest,' Nergui said. 'Have an enjoyable stay. Everything in moderation, as they say.'

'Except moderation,' Collins said, as a parting shot. The door of the *ger* closed softly behind him.

Nergui waited a moment, swinging softly on his chair, then said, 'What do you think?'

'I think he's guilty as hell,' Drew said.

Nergui nodded slowly, as though contemplating this opinion and giving his reluctant assent. 'But of what?'

'Haven't a clue, I'm afraid. Probably nothing to do with this case.'

Nergui laughed and rose slowly from the chair. 'Come,' he said, 'we've spent enough time in the darkness going slowly round in circles. Let's at least step into the sunshine as we do it.'

Drew followed Nergui out of the tent. At first, the light was blinding after the dim interior of the *ger*. Although it was still only mid-afternoon, the sun was already low above the horizon, casting long shadows across the desert. The day was growing noticeably cooler.

'It will be cold tonight,' Nergui said. 'Zero or perhaps lower.'

They walked slowly out of the camp gates, and made their way across the sand, Nergui leading. There was no obvious destination. The undulating sands stretched emptily ahead of them. Off to the left, in the far distance – it was impossible to tell how far – there was a small clustering of *gers*, but little else to be seen on the expanse surrounding them.

They walked a few hundred yards away from the camp, and Nergui stopped, looking back. 'It looks very peaceful, no?'

'Miles from anywhere,' Drew agreed.

'Miles from anywhere,' Nergui repeated. 'Miles from civilisation, certainly.' He kicked the sand with his foot. 'Desert,' he said. 'Emptiness.' He began to walk again, heading away from the camp as if striding towards the desolate horizon. Drew followed, glad to be out in the air, but wondering where this was leading.

As though reading Drew's thoughts, Nergui stopped again, turning to face Drew. 'I do not like this,' he said, at last. 'I do not like the pattern.' He spoke as though commenting on an item of clothing or furniture, and for a moment Drew was unsure what he meant.

'The case?'

'The case,' Nergui said. 'I do not like the fact that we are down here in the Gobi. I do not like the involvement of the police. I do not like the systematic nature of these killings. I do not like the fact that – in the face of all that – we nevertheless appear to be dealing with a psychopath.'

'We still can't be sure of that.'

'No, we can't. Though I am not sure how else you would characterise such killings. But it is not just that. It is the totality of it that disturbs. It does not – how can I put this? – it does not fit together. And most of all, because there is a pattern here I still cannot read, I do not like the fact that we are down here, in this part of my country.'

Drew was lost now. He watched Nergui, who was striding up and down the sand, as though he were unable to stand still for a moment.

'I don't understand. What is it you find so disturbing

about this place? I mean, it's a desolate enough spot, but—'

'Desolate,' Nergui repeated. 'Yes, certainly. But it is the emptiness that disturbs me.'

This was all becoming a little too philosophical for Drew's tastes. He would not have imagined that Nergui was a man prone to these kinds of imaginative fancies, but then he did not understand this culture.

Nergui smiled. 'You think I am a superstitious fool?'

'No,' Drew protested. 'It's just—'

'I am expressing myself badly, trying to capture a feeling I have.' He shrugged. 'The famous detective's intuition. You have that?'

Drew smiled. 'I think it's usually just a polite word for blind guesswork when I haven't a clue what's going on.'

'That could well be the case,' Nergui agreed. 'But it is not entirely fanciful, I think, not in this case. We Mongolians are accustomed to the open air, to emptiness. It is our heritage. But today it feels to me as if we are surrounded by forces that are threatening that birthright. Do you know what lies that way?' He gestured towards the southern horizon.

For a moment, Drew was thrown by the apparent *non sequitur*. Then he turned to look where Nergui was pointing. The sun was beginning to disappear below the horizon, and the camp to their right was throwing huge shadows across the landscape around them. It would soon be dark.

Drew peered into the shadows. The line of the horizon was sharp against the deepening blue of the sky, but he could see nothing.

'You cannot see it from here, though it is not so very far,' Nergui said. 'Close to the Chinese border, down there, you will find one of our country's largest deposits of gold and copper, ready for exploitation.'

'Not yet being mined?'

Nergui shook his head. 'The deposits were discovered a few years ago. There are several different exploratory sites now, and there has been initial work carried out by various consortia – companies from Russia, Canada and the US, among others. Interest has been growing, as it's gradually become clear how substantial the deposits are. How much money there is potentially to be made. The Chinese are interested, as are the South Koreans. We are, as you might expect, nervous of the Chinese.'

'If there's so much money to be made, why has it taken so long to get off the ground?'

'Mining is a risky and expensive business – we are talking about investment in the billions. I think, until the scale of the deposits was known, there was a nervousness about becoming involved. Perhaps there still is, but there is beginning to be a jockeying for position. Everyone wants to get in on the act. I am no geologist, but I believe there is much more out there.' He paused. 'This could transform our country. That is also a cause for nervousness. We are talking about a level of investment that is more than our gross national product – maybe several times more. If China or Russia were to make that level of investment—'

Nergui was pacing across the sand, beginning to walk back towards the camp. The sun had set, and darkness had spread across the desert with startling speed. Already above them, the sky was filling with stars.

'What do you think they might do?' Drew asked, walking behind Nergui.

'Maybe nothing. But it is not an altruistic state. We have spent decades being a puppet of the Soviet Union, and before that centuries as a satellite of China. I would not like those days to return.'

Drew thought about Nergui's background in the

industrial sector, his experience in the US and Europe, his still unspecified role in the Security Ministry. It was not hard to see the connections in a society like this. 'And you think that has something to do with this case?'

Nergui stopped and turned. The scattered lights of the camp were bright behind him. 'I do not know,' he said. 'But we are here, in the Gobi, within striking distance of the exploration. We are here because we are following the trail of a murdered policeman who was supposedly investigating some trivial case of amateur gold prospecting. You are here because you are investigating the murder of a British geologist.' He shrugged. 'Of course, this may all be coincidence. But I feel something.'

This all sounded fanciful to Drew, who had never had much time for the notion of the detective's intuition. His earlier response had been flippant but it had also been pretty close to the truth. He didn't often trust his own instincts. When he did, he had generally found it to be a mistake. Certainly, some of the people they had seen today, like the manager at the airport, had seemed evasive. But people often had something to hide, usually nothing to do with the matter at hand. Probably Batkhuyag was taking back-handers from suppliers, or even maybe from the police, for some scam or other. He was the sort who wouldn't want the police digging too deeply into his business, but it was likely that his fears had little to do with the case they were investigating.

'But what kind of connection could there be?' Drew said. 'I mean, we're talking about brutal murders. The work of a potential psychopath. International mining companies may well have their ethical shortcomings, but I'm not aware they resort to that kind of stuff.'

Nergui stopped as they approached the gates of the camp. 'You are right, of course. I am probably just talking nonsense. It is hard not to be affected by the nature of the crimes we are investigating. It is hard not to see this as the beginning of the end of the world. The beginning of the end of our world, I mean. Things are changing here. I do not know what will emerge.'

He stopped and looked back out towards the open desert. Far in the distance, it was possible to make out one or two lights, but otherwise, beyond the camp, the darkness was complete. The sky was heavy with stars now, sharper and brighter than Drew had ever seen. The absence of ambient light, the clarity of the air, made Drew feel that they really were poised on the edge of the galaxy, at the edge of the universe. And he felt, too, that at any moment they might begin to fall.

NINE

'Finally,' Nergui said, 'you will have an opportunity to sample some authentic local cuisine.' He paused. 'I apologise in advance.'

Drew laughed. 'I'm sure the wine and vodka will compensate.'

'I am not sure about the wine, although I will see if I can influence our host. The vodka will be fine. But beware the airag.'

'Airag?'

'Fermented mare's milk. It is an acquired taste. But you may prefer never to acquire it.'

'Sounds – interesting.'

'It tastes interesting. But we are not likely to be offered that here. You might be offered it if you visited a family in a *ger*, and I'm sure they arrange for the tourists to try it. People even distil airag vodka, which at least means that the inebriation compensates for the taste.'

'You don't like it?'

'I love it, but I think you would not. But perhaps I am underestimating your Western tastes. In any case, as I say, we will not be offered that this evening.'

They were sitting at the end of a bench table in the large tent that served as the camp's restaurant and bar. The space was already filling with crowds of tourists – most of them apparently English speaking, a mix of Americans, Canadians and British to judge from their accents.

'I still find it extraordinary that people come here as

tourists,' Drew said. 'With all due respect, it's not an obvious holiday destination.'

Nergui smiled. 'No, only in the days when we had a captive market of those not allowed to journey beyond the iron curtain. We are working hard to promote our tourist industry, though – it is one of the ways we bring wealth into the country. These days, it is still mainly the serious travellers who come here, those who enjoy visiting the most faraway places. This is one of the last remaining wildernesses on earth. After all, it is little more than a decade since we had no Western visitors at all. Even now this place hasn't yet opened up in the way that Russia or Eastern Europe or even China have.'

'It is an extraordinary place,' Drew agreed.

'In a strange way, it is becoming even more extraordinary as the influences of the West begin to arrive,' Nergui said. 'We no longer know who we are. We were Communist, but never wholly subscribed to the creed. The Buddhists were suppressed but never really disappeared, and now they are stronger than ever. A large proportion of our people are still nomads and herdsmen. And many of those in the cities would like to be. But Western influences are growing. We are building our fancy business hotels. The large multinational corporations are investing in our development. We are sitting on vast resources which we and others would like to exploit. But we still drink airag. And we still eat this stuff.'

As he spoke, the first course of the meal was being served, and a waiter dressed in traditional crimson robes was hovering at their shoulder. Nergui gestured him to proceed.

As it turned out, the meal was edible enough, though scarcely luxurious. The opening course was a salad largely comprised of tomatoes and cucumber. Then there was some plain grilled meat – the ubiquitous mutton,

Drew thought, though it was difficult to be sure. Finally, some plain but not unpleasant cake. As the salad was being served, Nergui rose and walked over to the bar where Batkhuyag was standing chatting to another member of the camp staff. Nergui returned a few moments later, smiling and holding a bottle of red wine. 'It's the usual Eastern European stuff,' he said, peering at the label. 'Romanian. But it will help the food down.'

There was a water jug and glasses on the table. Nergui filled two glasses with the wine, and held his up towards Drew. 'To peace,' he said.

Drew returned the toast. 'And to our – your – success in solving this case.'

Nergui took a sip of his wine. 'I think the two may well go together,' he said.

'Thought you two gents would have found somewhere better to eat than this?'

Collins was hovering over them, a glass of beer clutched firmly in his hand. It was still early in the evening, though the meal was finished, but he already had the air of a not-quite-contented drunk.

'The options are limited,' Nergui pointed out, smiling.

'You guys are staying here?' He swayed slightly, then carefully lowered himself to the seat. There was no sign of the man in the dark glasses.

'Just tonight,' Drew said. 'We fly back to Ulan Baatar tomorrow morning.'

'Shame, shame,' Collins said, sounding almost sincere. 'We're having a good time down here, despite the lousy food.' He gestured with the beer glass, narrowly avoiding tossing its contents across Nergui. 'Beer's crap too, but at least there's plenty of it. And vodka.'

'There is always plenty of vodka,' Nergui said. 'That is one blessing.'

'No shit, sunshine.' Collins beamed at them both, as though they were his new best friends. 'Great stuff, the old vodka.'

'Have you tried the airag?' Nergui said, sipping at his own glass of wine.

'Iraq?' Collins said. 'We invaded that bastard.'

'No, airag. It is our traditional drink.'

'Thought vodka was your traditional drink.' Collins seemed to be losing interest in the conversation, his gaze wandering around the room as though in search of more stimulating company.

'This is our other traditional drink,' Nergui said. 'You will be offered it on one of your tours. You must drink plenty. You will like it and it is good for you.'

'Does it get you pissed?' Collins said.

'It is fermented,' Nergui said, simply. 'You can, if you wish, obtain airag vodka.'

'Sounds wonderful. I'll get some to take home.'

'Very wise. I'm sure it will be very popular in – where are you from, Mr Collins? I mean, where in the USA?'

'Texas,' Collins said. 'Dallas. Where else?'

'Where else indeed? I apologise, Mr Collins, it should have been obvious.'

Collins stumbled slowly to his feet. 'Good to see you again, guys.' He staggered slightly, then regained his balance. 'I'm back to the bar. Get you guys a drink?'

'That's very kind, Mr Collins,' Nergui said. 'Not just at the moment, thank you. But we will join you at the bar, if we may?'

'It's a free country,' Collins said. 'Hey, is it a free country?'

'Nothing is free, Mr Collins,' Nergui said. 'There is always a price.'

Collins looked at him, baffled, then clearly dismissed Nergui's words as some kind of obscure Mongolian

146

joke. 'See you at the bar, gents,' he said, lurching back-wards.

'Do we really want to spend the evening with him?' Drew said.

'I can think of more edifying ways of relaxing, cer-tainly,' Nergui said. 'But there are two good reasons why it might be a good use of our time.'

'Which are?'

'He is on his way to being very drunk. And he does not have his minder with him.'

'Minder?'

'Our anonymous friend in the dark glasses. Of course, I do not know if that is his role. But he joined our meeting today for some reason, and he seemed unduly reluctant to say anything at all.'

'Probably just shy. Found your presence intimidating.'

'Of course. That will be the reason. But, in any case, Mr Collins seems far more talkative in his absence. It is probably worth our while to listen.'

'We'd better not leave it too long, then. He looked as if he might well be comatose within the hour.'

'Come then,' Nergui said. 'Let me buy you a beer.'

Most of the tourists were still sitting at the tables, the babble of conversation rising as the evening progressed. Drew followed Nergui across the room to the bar, where Collins and a small group of other tourists were clus-tered. Batkhuyag saw them coming and moved over to serve them.

'Beers for us,' Nergui said, 'and perhaps we can buy Mr Collins and his friends a drink.'

Collins turned towards them, his face reddened by the alcohol. 'Gentlemen,' he said, loudly, 'let me introduce the cops. This guy's come all the way from the United Kingdom. They're looking for one of their friends who's gone missing. Anyone seen him?' Collins looked around the group, as if he were seriously expecting a response. The others looked slightly embarrassed, and Drew suspected that they were probably looking for an excuse to leave Collins to his drinking. Drew didn't get the impression that the presence of two police officers was likely to reduce the group's discomfort.

'We're off duty now, Mr Collins,' Nergui said. He held up his beer. 'As this demonstrates.' Nergui was still wearing one of his dark suits but he was, for once, wearing his bright blue shirt open-necked and without an equally lurid tie. Drew thought he look almost relaxed.

'You guys really are cops?' one of the others said. His accent was American, from the southern states. 'Collins isn't bullshitting?'

'Not this time.' Nergui smiled. 'But we are here to socialise now, nothing more.'

'Cops are always cops,' Collins said. 'You bastards are never off duty.'

'What makes you say that, Mr Collins?' Drew said, smiling as politely as he knew how. He noticed that one of the group had already discreetly peeled away and was heading back to the dining tables. 'Have you had many dealings with the police?'

Collins took a large swallow of his beer. 'Jeez, I'm a businessman. Can't get you bastards off my back. You and the fucking IRS.'

'So what line of business are you in, Mr Collins?' Drew said. He tried to make it sound like nothing more than a social enquiry, just making conversation, but he was aware that his real curiosity was too close to the surface.

'See what I mean?' Collins roared, gesturing to the remaining two tourists. 'Never let up, the bastards.'

Nergui intervened smoothly. 'Never mind,' he said. 'Tell us how you're enjoying our country.' He turned to face the other two men, directing his conversation away from Collins. 'This is your first visit?'

'Certainly is.' This was the man who had spoken earlier. 'It's a fascinating place.'

'It's a craphole,' Collins said, but the spleen had diminished in his voice.

Nergui turned. 'I'm sorry you think so, Mr Collins. It is, unfortunately, the only country we have.'

The other two men guffawed, and Drew noticed them discreetly exchanging a signal that they should leave Collins to it. He watched as the two men moved away and walked back to join a group of mainly elderly men and women at one of the dining tables. He didn't get the impression that Collins was particularly welcomed by the rest of the tourists.

Collins shook his head and laughed. 'You're right,' he said. 'I'm being a discourteous asshole. This country's okay. Not exactly Dallas, but okay.'

'What made you decide to visit our country, Mr Collins?'

He shrugged. 'I travel a lot. Europe. Middle East. Far East. You name it. I enjoy travelling. Business or pleasure. I like going to interesting places. This is an interesting place.'

'For a craphole, you mean?' Drew said.

'Hey, buddy, I was out of line. I apologised. Enough already.'

'Of course,' Nergui said. 'I take no offence. You leave here tomorrow?'

Collins nodded. 'Back up to Ulan Baatar, then into the north for a few days.'

'Well, I hope you enjoy it all. Forgive me, but you do not strike me as the type who would normally be undertaking an organised tour of this kind?'

Collins signalled to the barman for another beer. 'Spot

on, buddy,' he said. 'But I wanted to see the place, and this was the only way to do it.'

Nergui nodded. 'It is still not easy to be an independent traveller here.'

'Nope. I prefer to make my own way, usually, but I was advised against it.' Collins seemed slightly more sober now, though he was still drinking the beer at a fast rate. 'They told me it would make it harder to see the rest of the country.'

'That is probably true. It is not so difficult now as it was. But we do not tend to make it easy for people to travel on their own.'

'When do you cops ever make anything easy?'

'Well, that is not our job, Mr Collins.' Nergui smiled. 'Your companion from this afternoon. He is not here this evening?'

Collins seemed to hesitate, though only for a moment. 'Nah, he's gone off to bed early. Had a headache. Probably all that intensive questioning you put us through.'

'We did not manage to extract very much from your companion,' Nergui said. 'He is a friend of yours?'

'No, met him on the trip. We get along pretty well, though. Drinking buddies. Not sure why he came along with me, but he happened to be with me when your friend—' He gestured towards Batkhuyag behind the bar. '—asked me to join you.'

'You never did tell us your line of business, Mr Collins,' Nergui said.

'No, I never did, did I?' Collins said. 'And I wonder why you're interested.'

'Just making idle conversation, Mr Collins.'

'In my experience cops never just make idle conversation.'

'You seem to have a lot of experience,' Drew said.

Collins laughed. 'Yeah, too much experience not to be careful what I say to the likes of you.'

'You are very astute, Mr Collins,' Nergui agreed. 'I suppose that is necessary in the minerals business.'

Drew tried hard to conceal his surprise. Collins's surprise, though, was obvious. 'Jeez. Who the fuck told you that?' The belligerence was still there, but it was undercut now with a new hesitation. For the first time, Drew thought, Collins wasn't quite sure of his ground.

Nergui shrugged. 'It is my job to know such things, Mr Collins.'

'I thought you bastards had put the KGB days behind you. What have you been doing, bugging my *ger*?'

'Nothing so crude, Mr Collins. Your occupation was stated on your visa application. I thought it wise to make a few standard checks.'

'Did you?' Collins said. 'And what else did these – standard checks tell you?'

'Nothing to trouble you, I think, Mr Collins.'

Collins leant back against the bar and took another deep swallow of his beer. His eyes were darting around the room now, as if he were looking for someone to come to his aid. Behind them, the hubbub of conversation was growing louder.

Nergui was sipping his own beer very slowly. He smiled at Collins and then at Drew, who was watching all this with some fascination. He wasn't sure whether he should feel offended that Nergui had not chosen to share this information with him. 'I hope I was not being intrusive, Mr Collins. I made only the briefest of checks, looking at material in the public domain. But such things are always interesting.'

Collins said nothing. He had drained his beer glass, and was clutching it in his hand like a lifeline. Drew wondered whether Nergui really had anything incriminating on Collins. He suspected not, but the fact that Collins was reacting in this way was telling enough.

'For example,' Nergui went on, 'you obviously know that your friend – your acquaintance from this afternoon – Mr Maxon, I believe – also works in the minerals industry. And also lives in Texas, though in Houston. No wonder you get on so well. You must have a lot in common.'

Collins shrugged, still watching Nergui closely. 'We've barely talked about work,' he said. 'Don't think we're really in the same field. But I don't see it's any of your business.'

'No, you are right. It is not.' Nergui paused, as though thinking over the ethical implications of this. 'It is, in part, my business to be aware of who is entering our country, and to understand why they are here.'

'I'm a goddamn tourist, for Christ's sake,' Collins said. 'I'm here on vacation. What else?'

'I am not aware of anything else,' Nergui said. 'Unless you wish to tell me differently.'

'Jesus, you people.' Collins staggered backwards, as though the impact of the alcohol had suddenly overwhelmed him again. 'You'll never change.'

'How is that, Mr Collins?' Nergui continued to sip on his beer, smiling.

Collins slumped against the bar. He looked up at the barman who, without being asked, placed another beer by his side. Drew wondered at what point they ought to suggest that Collins had had enough. It was difficult to be sure – his drunkenness seemed to ebb and flow with his moods. But his speech was definitely becoming more slurred now. 'I don't know what the fuck it is with you people,' he went on. 'You have the chance to make something of this dump, but you want to keep control. You want to have it all your way. You'll go to any lengths to stop real money being made. You're all still bastard Communists under the skin.'

'I'm not sure I really follow, Mr Collins,' Nergui said, softly.

'Oh, you understand well enough,' Collins said. 'Bastard Communist.'

Nergui opened his mouth to respond, but a voice from behind them interjected. 'Jesus, Jack. You had too much already?'

Maxon had appeared behind them, unnoticed. He was still wearing the dark glasses, even inside at night. With his eyes hidden it was impossible to read his expression, but there was the same thin smile on his lips. 'I apologise, gentlemen. Jack can become a tad – aggressive when he's had a little too much.'

It was the first time they had heard him speak, Drew realised. His voice was soft, emollient, the intonation of a salesman used to dealing with difficult customers.

'Do not worry,' Nergui said. 'Simply an exchange of views.'

Maxon's smile was unwavering. 'I've told Jack before. It's never a good idea to exchange views too forcefully.' He paused. 'Especially with the police.'

'Wise advice,' Nergui said.

'I think I'd better help get Jack to bed,' Maxon said.

'Jeez, I'm okay,' Collins said, waving Maxon away, but stumbling noticeably as he did so. 'Fine for a few more yet.'

'I don't think so, Jack,' Maxon said. The words had the force of a command, rather than an expression of opinion.

Collins stared at Maxon, and for a moment Drew thought the aggression was going to return. Then Collins shrugged. 'Yeah, maybe you're right. Been a long day.'

He thumped his now empty glass down on the bar

and started to make his unsteady way towards the entrance, Maxon turning to follow him.

'Goodnight, Mr Maxon,' Nergui said. Maxon turned at the sound of his name, and for a moment Drew thought he caught a look of surprise before the blank expression returned. 'By the way, Mr Maxon,' Nergui went on, 'how are you feeling?'

'How am I feeling?' Maxon paused, and there was a slight, but definite edge of puzzlement in his voice now. He looked across at Collins, but he was turned away, fumbling with the door catches. 'I'm feeling fine. Never better.'

Nergui nodded slowly, as if he was giving this news serious consideration. 'I'm very glad to hear that, Mr Maxon. Very glad indeed.'

TEN

After Collins and Maxon had left, Nergui and Drew had decided to retire early. They had a brief, friendly chat with some of the other tourists – mostly Americans, but with a scattering of Europeans too – but had recognised that they were unlikely to extract any further useful information from the group. So they walked back through the cold night air to the *ger*. Drew started to say something about Collins, but Nergui raised a finger to his lips. 'We do not know where Collins and Maxon are sleeping,' he whispered, very quietly. Wait till we get to the *ger*.'

It was a long time since Drew had slept under a tent. He had bad memories of a few seaside holidays in North Wales as a child, spending days listening to the endless drumming of rain on the roof, always feeling just too cold to be comfortable. But Drew had to acknowledge that this particular tent with its wooden frame and thickly padded felt walls was a long way removed from the flapping canvas monstrosities he had endured as a child.

The felt, Nergui had told him, was made by hand, the rolled cloth being pulled behind horses across the desert. In the centre of the *ger* was an iron stove, its chimney exiting through a hole in the middle of the peaked roof. The stove had been lit for them earlier in the evening, and the warmth in the tent now seemed perfectly adequate to repel the chill of the desert night. Even so, Nergui had told him that in the depths of the Mongolian winter, *gers* could only be made habitable by the collective warmth of multiple occupancy.

Inside, the *ger* was comfortably, if not luxuriously, appointed. The chairs they had used for the interviews were scattered around the floor. There were two narrow but comfortable-looking beds arranged around the walls, laden with blankets.

Once they were safely in the tent, with the door fixed shut behind them, Nergui said. 'My apologies for not sharing the information about Collins and Maxon before. I had not intended to keep it from you. I called HQ earlier and asked them to look into the visa information. I picked up the message on my mobile just before we went into the restaurant.'

'Don't worry. It made it much easier for me to keep a straight face. Like Collins, I didn't know how much you really knew.'

Nergui laughed. 'Not much more than I said, unfortunately. I had checked on the occupations they gave on their visa applications. I got Maxon's name from Batkhuyag earlier.'

'Is there any indication of what exactly they do in the minerals business?'

Nergui shook his head. 'Not really. In both cases the form just describes them as "executives" and mentions the name of the employing company. I got HQ to check the company backgrounds, and discovered they're both part of a conglomerate involved in mineral prospecting and exploitation.' He paused. 'Mining, in other words.'

'They both work for the same company?'

'In effect, yes. Different operating companies. It took a bit of digging on the part of one of my people to trace them back to the same parent. It's a US-based group which seems to operate in a whole range of sectors – mainly minerals like gold, copper, even uranium, all of which we have here. They also have various energy interests – oil, nuclear power.'

'And they claim not to have known each other before meeting on this trip?'

'Collins claimed that Maxon was in bed with a headache,' Nergui pointed out. 'But he seemed to have made a good recovery.'

'But if they are out here for a reason, why travel as tourists?'

'My guess is that it's because it's the easiest way to get around out here without arousing too much interest. We don't actively discourage independent travellers these days, but we don't make their lives too easy either. The government are keen to encourage foreign investment and links with external business, but we like to know what's going on. So if people are travelling here outside of one of the organised tours that we've now got pretty well-regulated, we tend to keep fairly close tabs on them. If they're here on legitimate business, then we usually know all about it in any case. If they want to travel for, say, scientific or social reasons, then we're happy to help so long as we know precisely what they're up to. We get a lot of visitors who have a specialist interest in things like our archaeology or geology, or even things like our music or folklore, but we usually arrange to work closely with them.'

Drew again wondered just who Nergui was talking about here. Was this the police keeping tabs on people, or maybe some more shadowy government agency? But the implications were clear enough. 'So someone who wanted to come out here and wander about on their own would arouse some suspicion?'

'Well, let us say, some interest, at least. Even if their intentions were legitimate, we would want to know what they were.'

'And if their interests were not legitimate?'

'They would not get very far, I think.'

Drew nodded. 'So if you were looking to come out here for some illicit purpose, then coming as part of a tourist group might give you some cover.'

'Absolutely. Of course, it would constrain your freedom of movement, but if your main aim was, for example, to make contact with someone or have some discussions, then it might give you enough scope.'

'Which might explain why Delgerbayar came down to this place?'

'If they were meeting him. Or, more likely, if he was aware of a meeting taking place down here. Yes, perhaps.'

Drew lowered himself on to one of the hard chairs. 'Well, that closing little outburst of Collins's certainly suggested he was up to something.'

'I was relieved,' Nergui said. 'I had almost given up on the possibility of taking advantage of his inebriation.'

'But none of it makes any sense,' Drew said. 'I mean, even if Collins and Maxon are involved in something, it can only be some shady business deal. Why would that result in a series of brutal murders?'

'These things are not unknown. We are talking about some potentially very big deals here. There is a lot of money to be made. Those who were here early have gained some potentially major advantages. Others – some of them far from scrupulous – are now trying to muscle in on some of the opportunities.'

'But multiple murder—'

'I agree. It seems unlikely. We have been aware of some cases of – well, shall we call them "disputes" between different parties. And, I think, some of that has led to violence from time to time, though it is usually well concealed. But, no, nothing like this.'

Drew was unsure what kind of world he was getting involved with here. In his experience, serious business-men might well be unethical and even criminal, but they were rarely violent. If only because violence was too messy, left too many dangling loose ends. It was the real villains who got involved in violence, like the gangs fighting in the drugs feuds in inner-city Manchester or Merseyside. But most of these were small fry – little men with ideas far above their station.

At the same time, he could not ignore the fact that serious organised crime really did exist. It wasn't just the product of over-glamorised Hollywood movies. And over the borders from here, in both Russia and China, different forms of economic and social transition had created societies where such interests could thrive. It wasn't so far-fetched to assume that some of these forces might now be exerting some influence in this country.

If that were the case, Drew wasn't sure he wanted to be involved. This was unknown territory in every sense. In this world, he wasn't even sure where the boundaries lay between criminality, politics and business. It was already clear that for all his intelligence and charm, Nergui was like no policeman Drew had ever encoun-tered. Stick close and watch your back. But from whom?

'But do you think it's possible,' Drew asked, 'that this is all connected?'

'I do not know,' Nergui said. 'All we can do is try to trace out the patterns and see where they might connect. We keep returning to mining, to minerals. But then it is the future of this country. It already accounts for more than half of our exports and has the capability to change the fabric of our society. So it is perhaps not unexpected that it should dominate our thinking at every level, or that it should attract some dubious interests. But whether that is sufficient to justify all that has happened?

I do not know.' He paused. 'I am being fanciful again. But I have a sense of something working itself out. Something that is not straightforward. It makes me uneasy. I do not know where this is going.'

It sounded like the mother of all understatements to Drew, but there was also a sense of something unspoken, some understanding that Nergui was reaching that he was not yet able or prepared to share. Nergui stared, blank-faced, at the floor.

'We should get some sleep,' Drew said, finally.

'You are right,' Nergui said. He looked up and smiled palely. 'We do not know what tomorrow holds. We should sleep.'

Drew expected that sleep would not be easy to attain, but he was wrong. The lingering effects of the beer and wine helped, and he fell asleep very quickly after climbing into the narrow bed. He was wearing an old track suit which he had brought in place of pyjamas. Nergui was wearing some similar old garment, which looked as if it might be military issue. Despite the chill of the desert night outside, the tent felt warm and comfortable. Nergui had turned out the electric light, and the darkness was almost complete, except for a very faint glow from the stove.

When he woke, Drew had no idea how long he had been sleeping. The tent was still in utter darkness, but almost immediately he had a sense that something had changed. He stiffened in the bed, trying to pin down the sense of unease that was rippling through him. Was there someone else in the tent? He lay still and tried to listen, but could hear nothing. Not even, he realised, the sound of Nergui's breathing.

He slipped out of bed, and fumbled his way carefully across the floor until his fingers touched the soft wall of the tent. Although his eyes were adjusting to the dark, he could see virtually nothing and the glow from the stove appeared to have extinguished. He thought he could see a faint shadow which might have been the low table. He stopped momentarily, wondering if he could hear anything, but there was nothing except the unnervingly loud sound of his own breathing.

Drew began to move forward, keeping his hand on the tent wall until he found the door frame. He ran his hand across the wood and fumbled until he found the light switch. He pressed the switch and the *ger* was flooded with bright light. The tent was empty. There was no intruder, no evidence of any disturbance. And there was no sign of Nergui.

His bed was rumpled but unoccupied. The sheets had been pulled back, as though Nergui had climbed out in a hurry.

Drew paused. Why was he getting so worked up about this? In all likelihood, Nergui had just gone off to the camp lavatories to relieve himself of some of the evening's beer.

But, somehow, Drew felt that wasn't the case. Something felt wrong. He looked around the sparsely furnished *ger* trying to identify anything out of place, something that might justify his sense of unease. But other than Nergui's overcoat being missing there was nothing.

Drew turned and pushed open the door. The cold night air hit him in the face, startling after the warmth of the tent. He stepped back in, grabbed his own coat and thrust his feet into his shoes. Then he pulled back the door and walked out into the night.

The camp was silent. For the first time, Drew thought to look at his watch. Just after three a.m.

The perimeter of the camp was studded with small spotlights to light the walkways, but otherwise everything was in darkness. There was no moon, and the sky above was dazzling with stars, an even more brilliant display in the full night. The thick smear of the Milky Way stretched out above.

Drew walked forward cautiously, listening for any sound. There was nothing. All of the *gers*, and the larger administration and reception buildings, were dark and silent.

He walked a few more steps, then turned the corner into the main walkway that led up to the administration building. At the far end, in one of the *gers* nearest to the reception building, there was a light. The door of the *ger* was open, and the light from the interior stretched out across the walkway.

Drew walked up the path, his feet making no noise on the soft sand. He drew level with the entrance to the *ger* and moved forwards to peer inside.

Nergui was standing just inside the door, his back to Drew, motionless.

'Nergui?'

Nergui turned, with no obvious surprise. 'Drew,' he said.

Drew walked forward, and looked past Nergui into the interior of the tent. He was, he realised, not surprised at what he saw. The bed nearest to the door was coloured deep red by spilt blood. A body lay face down on top, its large frame half sprawled across the floor.

Across the room, another figure was lying next to one of the other beds, the body twisted, the head at an odd angle. There was no blood this time, but it was clear that this figure was also dead.

'I felt it coming,' Nergui said, quietly. 'But I was too slow. I didn't take it seriously enough.'

Drew stepped forward to look around the *ger*.

'Who—?' He looked more closely at the blood-stained figure. 'Collins,' he said.

Nergui nodded.

'And the other? Maxon?'

Nergui shook his head slowly. 'Batkhuyag.'

'Batkhuyag? But why?'

Nergui shook his head. 'I do not know. Perhaps they both said too much. But it is very strange.'

'You think it was Maxon?'

'That is the obvious explanation. But it is very strange.'

Drew wasn't sure what Nergui meant. 'How did you find them?'

Nergui looked at Drew as though he had just asked an unexpected question. 'You know,' he said, 'I am not sure. I woke up – I don't know why. I am a light sleeper, always, and I woke with a sense that something was wrong. That I should have acted before. That I was too late.'

Drew thought back to his own awakening, his own sense of unease. 'So what happened?'

'I put on my shoes and coat and came out. Just as you have done. I saw the light in here. The door was already wide open. And I came and found the bodies.'

Nergui was as blank-faced as ever, but Drew had the sense that he was genuinely stunned by this.

'You didn't see anyone else?'

'No. I think I heard the sound of an engine as I walked up here. Maybe a motorbike. But it was a long way away, and I thought little of it.'

'You think it was Maxon?'

'It may have been. But he could still be in the camp.'

The thought chilled Drew. If Maxon was the murderer here, then it was likely that he had also been responsible for the previous killings. The thought that he might still be somewhere in the camp behind them was not pleasant. Drew turned and peered into the darkness, looking for any movement.

'We should call for backup,' Drew said.

Nergui pulled out his mobile. 'I already have,' he said. 'But they'll be a while. All we can do is wait here, I think. We need to watch the scene, and we need to ensure that, if Maxon is here, he doesn't make a break for it.'

Privately Drew thought that he might not be too worried if Maxon did make a break for it. He certainly wasn't sure he felt like trying to stop him.

'You said it was strange,' he said. 'What did you mean?'

Nergui looked around. 'Why should he do this?'

'As you say, maybe he thought they'd said too much.'

'But why do this? Why here? Why now? At the worst, these two might have raised a few suspicions. We were leaving tomorrow, they would soon be gone. We had no evidence to detain them. Maxon wanted to remain low key, that was obvious. So why commit a brutal murder under our noses? Why turn himself into the only obvious murder suspect?'

Nergui was right. It made little sense. 'Maybe they had a fight of some sort. Maybe Maxon really is a psychopath. And perhaps it didn't take much to set him off.'

'It is possible. But there is something else happening here. I feel it.'

Drew felt it, too. He could feel the cold air of the desert penetrating this space, entering his bones. He could feel the cold glare of the empty galaxies above his head. He could feel the blankness of Nergui's gaze, who stared at these bodies as if he himself had been the perpetrator of their deaths.

This last thought was unexpected and struck Drew almost with the force of a blow. It was ridiculous, of course. The real killer was out there somewhere behind them, perhaps close at hand, perhaps far away. But watching Nergui's face, Drew was struck once again by how alien this world was, how little he understood. And he realised that out here, anything might be possible.

ELEVEN

'I'm very disappointed, Nergui.'

'Of course. So am I. I take full responsibility.'

Anxiety was etched into the Minister's face as he paced slowly up and down the room. He was a heavily built man, his dark hair thinning. He was wearing an expensive-looking Western suit, but he wore it uncomfortably, as though he would rather be wearing traditional clothes. 'Naturally,' he said. He smiled, though there was no obvious humour in his expression.

'I will of course tender my resignation, if you feel that to be appropriate. I should point out that Doripalam carries no responsibility for this.'

The Minister laughed. 'Don't be ridiculous, Nergui. I don't know that there's anything else you could have done. And even if there was something *you* could have done better, I'm sure that no one else could. Let's face it, at least you were in the right place at the right time.'

'Not quite at the right time, unfortunately,' Nergui pointed out. 'And it was only luck that I was there at all.'

'Nevertheless, the truth is, if you can't put an end to this, I'm sure nobody else can.'

Nergui nodded in acknowledgement. He knew the Minister too well not to engage in false modesty. 'You may be right,' he said. 'If so, the question is whether I can.'

'And what do you think?'

'I honestly do not know.'

'But you have some ideas?'

Nergui shrugged. 'I do not know whether I would even dignify them as such. There are some patterns. Some leads we can follow. That is all.'

'That isn't much.'

'It is all we have.'

'What about Maxon?'

'Another mystery. He is a Westerner, on the run in our country, potentially accused of a series of brutal murders. But he has vanished from the face of the earth.'

'That's not possible. Not here.'

'It is not. But it has happened.'

'The US Government has shown no signs of involving itself?' The Minister presumably knew the answer to this already but he waited for Nergui's response.

'No. I suspect they may be slightly embarrassed.' Nergui allowed himself a small smile. 'It appears that Mr Collins was a dubious character. The FBI had a large file on him, potentially linking him to a whole series of possibly fraudulent deals. Action had been taken against him by the US regulatory bodies in connection with various doubtful business dealings, but he had managed so far to avoid criminal prosecution. He also appears to have connections with organised crime interests. If we had known any of this, he would not have been allowed into the country. I don't think the US will be rushing to uncover any further dirty linen.'

'Well, that's one relief,' the Minister said. He slumped himself back down behind his large, virtually empty desk. 'And you're sure we've kept the whole thing tightly wrapped up in the media?'

'As best we can. There was no way we were going to keep this completely under wraps, given it happened in the middle of a camp full of tourists. And, frankly, we also wanted to get Maxon's picture in the media as quickly as possible so he could be picked up. So we've implied that this was some sort of bust-up between

American business associates, with poor old Batkhuyag getting caught up in the middle.'

'With no link to the murders here?'

'No. Those haven't even been mentioned. Some people may make the connection, but with so little information I wouldn't expect it.'

The Minister nodded. 'Well, that's something. And what about your Englishman?'

'I'm not sure. His presence here is something of a token gesture. He wasn't planning to stay more than a few days. But I'm keen for him to stay a little longer, if his bosses can be persuaded.'

'Why?' The Minister frowned. 'Do we really want some foreign policeman peering over our shoulders, prepared to embarrass us?'

'I don't think that's a risk. He's a dedicated policeman, not – with all due respect, sir – a politician.'

The Minister laughed. 'But he's in contact with the British ambassador?'

'The ambassador is in contact with him. Which is no surprise. But I don't think that's a cause for concern. The truth is, we can make good use of McLeish's experience and expertise in this case. We don't have too much of that among our own people.'

'That's true enough. Okay. I'll trust your judgement on this one, Nergui, for the moment at least.' The Minister paused, leaning forward over the table. 'But, Nergui,' he said, after a pause, 'remember – no more disappointments. We can't afford it. Not again.'

'So what do you *think* is going on?'

'As I say, I really don't have a clue,' Drew said. 'Nergui keeps talking about patterns, but there's no pattern to it at all.'

'So far as you can see.'

'So far as I can see,' Drew agreed, mildly irritated by the ambassador's implied superiority. Still, he imagined that the ambassador rarely implied anything else.

'But what about the mining connection? That seems to suggest some kind of link.'

'Well, yes, but I've no idea what. There's not really much to it, when you try to piece it all together. Okay, Ransom was a geologist. Delgerbayar, the murdered police officer, was involved in some supposedly trivial gold prospecting case. Collins and Maxon were both working in the minerals industry. That's about it.'

'Plus this strange convocation of visitors to the Gobi.'

'Yes, and that.' But at best, Drew thought, it was as if they had a few pieces from a much larger jigsaw puzzle. A couple of edges, a bit of sky, part of a face. But nothing that might make a picture.

'And this chap Maxon has really gone missing?'

'Apparently.'

'That seems difficult to believe.'

'That's how Nergui feels. He thinks it's virtually impossible.'

They were sitting in the ambassador's personal lounge, a comfortable room with low armchairs, thick-piled carpet and glossy mahogany tables. It was late morning and autumn sunshine was incongruously bright outside the window. The ambassador sipped his coffee. 'And do you believe him?'

Drew hesitated perhaps a fraction too long. 'I think so,' he said. 'I mean, I've no idea what to make of any of this, but I've seen no reason not to trust Nergui so far.' This was true. On the other hand, he also didn't know whether there was any positive reason why he *should* trust Nergui.

The ambassador did not look convinced. 'Well,' he said, finally, 'is it safe to assume that Maxon is behind all of this?'

Drew shook his head. 'No. Not necessarily. I mean, of course it's possible. He's been in the country longer than Collins – for nearly three weeks. And, interestingly, although he's now here as a tourist, it's not his first visit. He's been here, supposedly on business, a couple of times before – made visits to various of the mines in the north of the country. We're in contact with the FBI, but they're not telling us much. There's nothing to connect him to the murders here, so far as we can see.'

'But if he isn't, then it looks as if we have two psychopaths on the loose simultaneously. Quite a first for this place.'

'Assuming,' Drew said, 'that Maxon was responsible for Collins's and Batkhuyag's murders.'

'You think there's any chance he wasn't?'

'I really don't know,' Drew said. 'I mean, if these two murders had happened in isolation, of course he'd be the obvious candidate in the frame. But it's still hard to see quite why he'd have killed those two at that point. And it's hard to tie any of that in with the earlier killings.'

'Maybe they're not linked.'

Drew shrugged. 'Maybe not. In which case, as you say, we have two rampant psychopaths and one hell of a coincidence.'

The ambassador nodded, making a show of stirring his coffee again and selecting one of the luxurious biscuits from the plate in front of them. 'So what do you think they know?'

'Who?'

'Nergui's people. The Ministry. Intelligence. They must have more knowledge than they're letting on.'

'I don't get that impression. But then I wouldn't, I suppose.' He paused. 'To be quite frank, I'm feeling out of my depth in all this.'

'Out of your depth?' The ambassador raised his eyebrows. 'An experienced policeman? You're dealing with a bunch of amateurs here. Other than Nergui, that is.'

'It's not that,' Drew said. 'Though this case is like nothing I've ever had to deal with as a policeman. It's the politics. It's the sense that there's something else going on, coded signals I'm not picking up.'

'Ah, the *politics* . . .' The ambassador sat back in his chair, smiling. 'Well, I'm with you there. Even though it's my job.'

Drew didn't bother to add that he saw the ambassador as part of the problem. He thought it was probably better to move on. 'But to go back to your question, no, I don't get the impression they know more than they're letting on. Certainly not at the operational level, anyway. It's difficult to tell what Nergui might know, as I'm sure you've experienced. But I think he's as disturbed by this as anyone. More than most, in fact. And I think that's because he doesn't usually come up against things he doesn't understand.'

'Well, that would make sense. I think Nergui's used to being in control of things. And I imagine he must be under a lot of pressure, though we'd never know.'

'Pressure?'

'From his Minister. If all this has just been the work of some lone psychopath, that would have been bad enough in terms of its impact. If, as it appears, it's something more complicated than that, then the Minister will be getting very anxious.'

Drew finally got around to taking a sip of his coffee, which was already growing cold. 'Why?'

'Well, there's a lot of noble talk about, you know, protecting the fabric of society and all that – and I'm sure Nergui genuinely believes some of that – but for the Minister this is just our old friend politics once again.' The ambassador paused, as if he were wondering how openly to speak. Drew had already decided that the ambassador's apparent willingness to take Drew into his confidence was simply more game-playing. He would share only what he needed to, Drew had concluded, in the hope of getting something back. 'It's the problem with democracy, I suppose,' the ambassador went on. 'Since this country introduced democracy at the beginning of the 1990s, there have been many changes but the Communist Party has largely retained power.'

'So what's the problem? Aren't the Communists firmly entrenched now?'

'To some extent, but there's a lot of public unrest. There are plenty who think the country's going to hell in a handcart. Who knows what's around the corner? A psychopath on the loose for too long wouldn't be particularly helpful to the career of the Minister of Security. But if it's something more than that – particularly if there are commercial interests involved in some way – well, that could really be a knockout blow.'

'So the Minister will want this sorted?'

'One way or another, yes. And quickly.'

'What do you mean – one way or another?'

The ambassador shrugged. 'I'm sure you must encounter these kinds of problems from time to time. Politicians want solutions. They don't really care whether the solution really solves the problem, so long as they can be seen to have done something.'

'That kind of thing doesn't usually get down to my level, I'm glad to say.'

The ambassador smiled, coldly. 'Then, young man, you should count yourself very lucky. Enjoy it while you can.' He spoke as though Drew's privileged status might change at any moment.

It was only after Drew had concluded his meeting with the ambassador that he remembered that he and Nergui were due to have dinner at the embassy that same evening. The relative light-heartedness he had felt at finally getting away from the ambassador melted away. What he had said was true. He was increasingly feeling out of his depth in this world, unsure who to trust or what to think. The prospect of an evening between the ambassador and Nergui was not an enticing one.

And how long was he supposed to stay out here? The original plan had been for him to fly home at the end of the week, with only the possibility of a return. But then he had received a message on his mobile from the Chief Constable's office to say that Nergui had requested he stay here a few more days, with the Ministry picking up the expenses. It was made clear that in the interests of international relations – not to mention the PR – Drew should accept the request.

There was also a message from Nergui suggesting that they meet in the bar of the Chinggis Khaan for a drink before dinner. He had last seen Nergui during their flight back from the Gobi that morning. Drew had been feeling exhausted after their disturbed night and although Nergui had the same brightness and energy that Drew had noted from the start, he looked troubled by the events of the night.

Their conversation on the return flight had been desultory, partly because of Drew's tiredness and partly because there seemed to be little worth saying and the case was, in theory, being handled by the local police chief, but there was no doubt that in practice he reported to Nergui. The relationship had been obvious to Drew, watching their conversation at the murder scene, even though he could not understand what was being said.

Compared with the previous murders, these were straightforward. Collins had been stabbed repeatedly in the chest and back, and appeared to have died from the loss of blood. Batkhuyag had been strangled, probably with a belt. Although no precise time of death had yet been established, both had been dead for some time before Nergui had found them, which explained how Maxon had been able to make his escape. The working assumption was that Maxon was the killer, and only Nergui seemed to be treating this as anything other than simple fact.

Even before they had embarked on their morning flight back to Ulan Baatar, a full-scale manhunt was underway. The local police chief had confidently expressed the opinion that Maxon would be picked up by the end of the day. After all, he had pointed out, how easy could it be for a Westerner to hide in the Gobi?

Nergui had called as soon as their plane had touched down to see whether this prediction showed any sign of being fulfilled. The answer was no. No one had yet reported seeing or even hearing of Maxon or any other Westerner outside the tourist camp. Police officers on motorbikes were making the rounds of all the surrounding *gers*, but so far to no effect. Still, it was, as the chief kept repeating, early days.

Drew assumed that by the time they met that evening, Nergui would have something more concrete to report. As before, Drew came down from his hotel room to find Nergui holding solitary court in the corner of the bar. Drew was pleased to note that he had already ordered the beers.

Before Drew could ask the obvious question, Nergui was already shaking his head. 'Nothing,' he said. 'No news at all.'

Drew sat down opposite Nergui and took a long pull on his beer. 'When did you last check with them?'

'Twenty minutes ago. They've promised me they'll call as soon as they have anything to report.' He smiled. 'But

I'm not sure I trust them to be assiduous enough so I'll probably call them again later. Just in case.'

'Someone must have seen him.'

'You would have thought so, wouldn't you? I don't see how a Westerner on the run can stay unnoticed in the middle of the Gobi for long.'

'Is it possible he's being sheltered?'

'I suppose so. It's quite possible that there's some herdsman out there who's not heard the news – though many of them have shortwave radios, these days – and who's taken pity on him. But you'd have thought we'd have found something.'

'Maybe he's not trying to hide. Maybe he's committed suicide or just ridden off into the desert.'

Nergui nodded. 'I suppose it's not beyond the realms of possibility, if it is true that he's responsible for these killings.'

'You still think he might not be?'

'I genuinely don't know. It is the logical assumption. Although we then have to consider what the link is with the earlier murders, or we're left with two killers. But mainly it is that old instinct again, nothing more. I don't think it is as simple as that.'

'You think the same person is responsible for all these killings?' It sounded ridiculous, Drew thought. But the alternative seemed even more absurd.

Nergui shrugged. 'There is no point in speculating. But my instinct says no. Which is a truly terrifying prospect.'

'I understand you've asked my bosses if I can stay on here.' Drew realised too late that the statement sounded accusatory. He hadn't intended that, but maybe he was right to be annoyed.

Nergui nodded. 'I'm sorry,' he said. 'I have been thoughtless. I should have asked you first. But I had the impression you were keen to stay a little while longer. And I was certainly keen to draw on your experience.' He paused. 'But I was forgetting about your wife and family. That was inconsiderate. I am sorry.'

Drew wondered about trying to extract some moral leverage from Nergui's apparent embarrassment. But, in truth, he wasn't even sure how genuine this embarrassment was. Nergui struck him as a man who always knew exactly what he was doing. If he'd neglected to ask Drew first, this was probably because he didn't want to take the risk that Drew might decline. Much easier to go above Drew's head and get the deal done that way. Maybe in Nergui's position he'd have done the same. Maybe.

'Well, I think I've managed to square that side of it. Sue isn't best pleased, but I think she accepted that it isn't my choice. But what I can't really understand is why you want me to stay. I'm not sure there's really much I can add.'

'You are too modest,' Nergui said, in a tone that suggested sincerity about this at least. 'Other than Doripalam, most of our men are amateurs or worse. We have never had to deal with anything remotely like this.'

'Who has?'

'Well, you have much more relevant experience than any of us.'

Drew wasn't convinced by this. His own suspicion was that Nergui wanted to have him around because he was a neutral third party. He imagined that Nergui's professional life was almost as lonely as his domestic life seemed to be. He had no obvious peers in the police, other than Doripalam, and the relationship there was uneasy. His relationship with the rest of the team seemed to be distant and untrusting. And no doubt his relationships with the Minister and his other political masters were far from straightforward. It was probably a relief to find himself working with someone who had no particular axes to grind.

'Well, I'll accept the compliment,' Drew said. 'To be honest, I'd be sorry to have gone back now. Partly because there's nothing more frustrating than leaving a case before it's resolved. And partly because I want to see more of your country while I'm here.'

'I am surprised it holds many attractions for you any more,' Nergui said. 'The presence of corpses tends to take the edge off the tourist trail.'

'Is that what your Minister thinks?'

'It is one of his concerns, of course. Our tourist trade is growing, partly because this is seen as being one of the last unexplored parts of the world. But also because we have a relatively safe environment.'

'And the presence of a serial killer – or, worse still, two serial killers – doesn't particularly enhance that reputation.'

'Quite. But I think his bigger concern – *our* bigger concern – is that there may be something more behind this.'

Drew took a large drink of his beer. There seemed little point in holding back his thoughts. He was unsure what games everyone else might be playing, so there was probably some mileage in being completely straightforward. 'My friend the ambassador thinks you know things you're not sharing. Is that true?'

'Me personally, or the Ministry in general?' Nergui said, without hesitation.

'Either. Both. I mean, I think the ambassador's concerns are with the Ministry. But from what I've seen, I think it's more likely that you might know something you're not sharing with anyone else. On your side or mine.'

'Are we on different sides, then?' Nergui regarded Drew with something approaching amusement.

'You tell me. The ambassador clearly thinks we are. I hope not. But all this is new to me.'

'Much of it is new to me also, Drew. I do not think we are opposing sides in this. But then I am not sure what the sides are.'

It was only afterward, as they were walking through the clear night air towards the embassy, that Drew realised that Nergui had not answered his initial question.

The evening was already becoming chilly, and Drew pulled his overcoat more tightly around him. Nergui had told him that, as the winter approached, nights in the city became very cold – minus fifteen or more degrees. There was little cloud cover, and above the city lights and neon signs the skies were filled with stars. The main streets were well lit, and this early in the evening there were still plenty of pedestrians. The streets around the hotel were busy with cars and buses.

Away from the busier thoroughfares, though, the atmosphere of the city was very different. The side-streets were ill-lit, and in many cases disappeared into darkness only yards from the main road. As they walked briskly towards the embassy, Drew thought back to the first victim, the body dumped in one of these dark silent streets. Involuntarily, he glanced back over his shoulder. There were a few other pedestrians behind them, mostly swathed in heavy coats and hats, huddled against the deepening cold. For a moment, he had a sense of being watched, maybe even followed, though none of those behind were paying any obvious attention to himself or Nergui.

Nevertheless, he was glad when they reached the brightly lit gates to the embassy. As Nergui rang the bell, he looked back again. There was a figure standing, half in shadow, by the corner of the street opposite. It was only a silhouette so it was impossible to tell if he was looking in their direction. A moment later, he turned and disappeared into the gloom of a side street. Drew found himself shivering slightly, unsure if this was just the effect of the cold.

'Gentlemen, welcome. Do come in. It must be freezing out there.'

Drew turned and was surprised to see the ambassador himself greeting them at the door. He wasn't quite sure what he had expected. During his daytime visits, there had been a receptionist and other staff dealing with visitors. In the evening, Drew had half-expected a butler.

He followed Nergui into the brightly lit hallway, and was surprised at the sense of relief he felt when the large front door was finally closed behind them.

'This way,' the ambassador said. 'We're in my private quarters. Much more intimate than any of the official rooms.'

The ambassador led them along a corridor then up a flight of stairs. The door at the top of the stairs opened to reveal a small hallway, and then beyond that a comfortably furnished sitting room. A middle-aged couple were already sitting in armchairs, sipping sherries.

'Come in, come in, gentlemen. Let me take your coats.'

Again, Drew had been unsure what to expect from the dinner. He had vaguely imagined some kind of formal arrangement – perhaps waiter-served around a polished oak table. However, the ambassador had been insistent on informal dress, so some form of intimate gathering seemed more likely.

'Let me do the introductions,' the ambassador said, bundling their heavy coats into his arms. 'Professor Alan and Dr Helena Wilson.' He gestured at the couple, who had risen as Drew and Nergui came in. 'And Chief Inspector Drew McLeish and, from our host country, Mr Nergui of the Ministry of Security. I'll leave you to get to know one another for a few moments, if I may, while I put these down and get you both drinks. Sherry okay?'

He disappeared back into the hallway. The Wilsons stood looking at Drew and Nergui for a moment. In Drew's experience, the mention of his police rank wasn't generally conducive to small talk at parties. But Nergui, as ever, was fully up to the moment. 'Good evening,' he said, smoothly, gently gesturing them back to their seats. 'You both work in academia?'

Professor Wilson shook his head. 'Helena does. I used to, but I've been seconded to the Civil Service for a couple of years now. Working for the government,' he added, presumably for Nergui's benefit.

Nergui smiled. 'Ah, so we are both government servants,' he said. 'What is your field?'

'I'm a chemist by background,' Professor Wilson said.

'Ah. Very interesting.' Nergui nodded, as though giving serious contemplation to this information. 'I imagine there are few chemists in the Civil Service?'

'Well, not practising ones, no, except in the government laboratories. I'm a little unusual, I guess. I had a background in industry after completing my doctorate, with a parallel career in academia, so I bring a little commercial expertise to the policy field, as well as technical knowledge.'

'I understand,' Nergui said. 'My own position is not dissimilar.' He left the comment hanging in the air. 'And you, Dr Wilson, are you a chemist also?'

'Please call me Helena,' she said, smiling. 'No, I'm afraid I'm not a scientist at all. I'm an anthropologist by background, but for the last few years I've been working in the field of folklore and folk traditions. It's my fault we're here, I'm afraid. Alan's just tagging along.'

'It's hardly a burden,' he said. 'It's fascinating. You have an extraordinary country here.'

'You are very kind. You are here to study our folk-lore?' Nergui prompted.

Dr Wilson nodded. 'The music, mainly. But yes, all of it. I'm no expert in the field – I specialise in English folk-lore and folk song – but I was interested to find out more. So I used my sabbatical to arrange an exchange with the university here.'

'And you have found material to interest you?'

'Very much. I was excited to hear the *khoomi* singing – hear it live, I mean. I'd only ever heard it on record. And you have a tremendous wealth of folk material – songs, stories.'

'I am pleased to hear it,' Nergui said. 'I am afraid I can claim no expertise in the field, but of course I know songs and stories from my own childhood. Are these stories different from those in England?'

'There are parallels, and it's astonishing how often variants of the same stories recur throughout the world. But the stories here are distinctive. They reflect the geography, the history and the lifestyle here.'

'Everything here is different,' the ambassador said, entering the room with two more sherries. 'This is like no other country.'

'Have you been here long?' Drew asked.

'Three years now. They're looking to move me on, but I'm close enough to retirement that I think they might just quietly forget about me for the moment. This seems a decent enough place to wind down.'

'There must surely be more comfortable postings?' Nergui said. 'For all my loyalty to my country, I would-n't claim that it is the easiest place to live.'

'You're right but there are plenty of less comfortable ones too. This society is stable. The people are very hos-pitable. There is a wealth of history and tradition here which is different from anywhere else on earth. I can manage to get hold of most of the creature comforts I need.' The ambassador held up his sherry glass in demonstration. 'I'm very happy.'

'Then you're very lucky,' Professor Wilson said. 'I don't think many could claim that about their work.'

As though accepting a cue, his wife turned to Drew. 'And you, Chief Inspector—'

'Drew. Please.'

'Are you happy in your work?' She was smiling, but there was an undercurrent of seriousness that Drew couldn't quite pin down.

'I don't know if I've ever really thought about it. Mind you, I've never thought about doing anything else either.'

'The ambassador told us why you are here. It's a dreadful case.'

Drew exchanged a glance with Nergui. He wondered quite how much the ambassador had told the Wilsons. Had he just explained about Ransom's death – which had received some lurid coverage in the British press – or had he also discussed the wider series of killings?

'Well, I wouldn't take the press coverage too literally.' Drew wasn't going to give anything away. 'But, yes, it was a brutal killing. And it somehow seems worse when it happens to someone so far from home.'

Professor Wilson opened his mouth as if he were about to say something, but then stopped and looked across at his wife. 'We shouldn't pry,' he said. 'I realise that there must be things you have to keep under wraps.'

Nergui smiled, his face as inscrutable as ever. 'You are right,' he said. 'There are aspects of the case that we need to keep confidential, even in company as illustrious as this.' There was no way of knowing whether the final comment was intended ironically.

'But you really have no idea of a motive?'

Drew shook his head. 'As Nergui said, it wouldn't be

appropriate to say any more. We're progressing with our enquiries, as they say.'

'Of course, no. We understand. It's just a bit of shock when this sort of thing happens to a fellow Brit; it makes you look over your shoulder, particularly when you're in a place as – well, as alien as this.' Professor Wilson glanced at Nergui. 'I'm sorry, but you understand what I mean?'

Drew understood what he meant, all too well. Nergui simply nodded. 'Certainly. Our country is very different from the West. We are becoming more Westernised in some ways – though less so in others, as the Soviet influence has declined. I can understand why you would feel very far from home.' He sat back in his chair, as though musing on this idea. 'Mr Ransom's death was dreadful, and a real shock to everyone. All I can say is that, despite that, this is a very safe and stable country. Our crime rate is low, generally, and we have little violent crime.'

'But you have had other murders?' Professor Wilson said. 'Recently, I mean.'

Nergui gazed at him expressionlessly. 'This is a city. People get drunk, get into fights. We have the occasional mugging, the occasional assault. And, yes, the occasional murder.'

'And do you think they're connected?' Professor Wilson said. 'These occasional murders?' There was a definite edge to his voice now. Drew assumed that Wilson was a variant on the type of 'concerned citizen' who could always be relied upon to write personally to the Chief Constable.

'I really don't think it would be appropriate to discuss this any more,' Drew said. 'I'm sorry, but you're putting us in a very difficult position.' He was aware, even as he said this, that it was likely to be construed as a tacit admission that the murders were linked.

'I'm sorry, Chief Inspector, I had no intention of

putting you in a difficult position. I was just interested to know whether it is safe for us to walk down the streets at night.'

Nergui nodded, ignoring the undertone of sarcasm. 'I understand your concerns. But this city is safer than almost anywhere else you could be, believe me.'

The words were reassuring, and Nergui's calm demeanour was even more so. But Drew wondered whether Nergui's claim was true. And, more importantly, whether Nergui himself really believed it.

TWELVE

'What about you, Drew, do you believe in it?'

'No, I don't. Well, what I mean is, I'm quite happy to accept that there might be more things in heaven and earth and all that, so I'm prepared to keep an open mind in principle. But I have to say that I've never seen it work in practice.'

'Have you ever used it?' Professor Wilson said. 'In an investigation, I mean?'

It was nearly midnight, and they had become caught up in one of those conversations that only happen amongst strangers when too much alcohol has been consumed. Drew had noticed that the ambassador was adept at plying others with drink while minimising his own consumption. No doubt an invaluable tool of the trade.

'Not personally, no. But I've been involved in cases where it's been tried.'

'What kinds of cases?'

'Oh, well, you know, usually missing persons – particularly missing children. When there's a child missing, after a while the parents will cling to any hope – anything that might bring them some news, even it's bad. They'd rather know.'

'But you've never seen it work?'

'No, never. I've always had mixed feelings about it. We wouldn't usually initiate it – though I know there are some senior officers who take it seriously – but we wouldn't stand in the way if, say, the parents wanted to try it.

But I'm always afraid they're being taken for a ride. There are unscrupulous people out there, who'll take advantage even in a situation like that.'

'So you think these people – mediums, whatever you choose to call them – are all charlatans?' There was something forensic in Professor Wilson's approach, as though he were a prosecuting barrister trying to get the better of a hostile witness.

'I wouldn't say that,' Drew said, though privately he thought he would probably say exactly that. 'I mean, some of the people I've encountered seemed genuine enough. In the sense that they believed in what they were doing, at any rate.'

'But you never saw it work?'

'Never. There have been several occasions when we've all gone traipsing off, feeling slightly ridiculous, because one of these people had said we would find something in a particular location – a field or woodland or whatever. But we never did.'

'But there have been instances where the police have been guided accurately by mediums, haven't there?' Helena Wilson said.

'I believe so,' Drew said. 'I've read press stories about them, and I've met some senior experienced policemen who give some credence to it. But it's not been my experience.'

He wasn't entirely sure how they'd got into this conversation. It had started with some comments – apparently humorous – from Helena Wilson about her own 'second sight'. She had explained that she had grown up with a sense of being able to predict events or, on occasions, be aware of events happening elsewhere.

'It's one of Helena's hobby horses,' her husband said. 'As a man of science, I struggle with it a little.'

'Rubbish, I'm not suggesting anything unscientific. I'm

not even suggesting that it's necessarily true. It's not something I can turn on or turn off at will.' This was obviously an argument that they had rehearsed on many occasions, and there was no rancour in her voice. 'But I have had certain experiences, which I'd struggle to explain.'

'What kinds of experiences?' Nergui said, sitting forward.

'Oh, well, you know, having a sense that something's going to happen before it does.'

'Like predicting 9/11? There were, inevitably, people who claimed to have done that,' the ambassador said.

She shook her head hard. 'No, in my experience, it's something much more personal, much closer to home. It's the sense of – oh, I don't know, things like meeting someone and feeling that something bad is going to happen to them. And then it does – they have an accident or whatever.'

'And this has happened to you?' Nergui asked.

'Yes, exactly that. I've also, on a couple of occasions, been aware of accidents or illnesses affecting people close to me before I've been told about them.'

'That could just be coincidence,' her husband pointed out. 'It's the usual story. You factor out all the times you had that feeling but nothing happened.'

'I can't argue with that. But I honestly can't recall having that feeling without some resulting event. Which doesn't mean that there haven't been plenty of occasions when I've not had the feeling but the person's gone ahead and had an accident anyway.' She laughed. 'I'm not making any serious claims for this, you understand, just telling you what I've felt.'

'What about you, Nergui? Have you ever been involved in using mediums?' Dr Wilson turned to Nergui.

Nergui shook his head. Drew had noticed that although Nergui appeared to be accepting and consuming wine and port along with the rest of them, he was displaying no sign of inebriation. Drew wished he could say the same for himself. He was finding it increasingly difficult to string a coherent sentence together. 'I'm afraid not,' Nergui said. 'Though perhaps sometimes it would be better if we did. It might improve our success rate. I also think that attitudes are a little different here. We would not use a medium in the sense you describe, but many of my colleagues would see a spiritual dimension to their role.'

'What sort of spiritual dimension?' Professor Wilson asked.

'It varies. Religion and spiritualism have a confused history here, mainly resulting from the Stalinist suppression of religion. So now we have some people who are genuinely Buddhists, others who have adopted some of the Buddhist or Taoist principles, some who are following older shamanist traditions, and so on. Not to mention the increasing number of evangelical Christians – one of the growing effects of Western influences. But I think it would not be unusual to find officers who used – well, let us call them spiritual methods, such as meditation, as part of their work. And some of that, I think, would not be too far away from what we have been talking about.'

It was after midnight by now, and he looked at his watch. 'It is late,' he said. 'We should perhaps be thinking about going home.'

The idea of going home seemed powerfully attractive to Drew. The idea of returning to the Chinggis Khaan was rather less so, but he was conscious of increasing tiredness and inebriation. 'I think that would be a good idea, if you'll excuse us.'

The ambassador made a show of encouraging them to stay, but it was clearly little more than politeness. It had actually been a very enjoyable evening – not at all what he had been expecting, Drew thought. The Wilsons were not the kind of people he would normally spend an evening with, but their company had certainly been stimulating.

The ambassador led them back down the stairs to the main entrance hall. Outside, the air was icy, a thick frost already gathering on the street. Nergui had summoned an official car to take him back to his flat – Drew noted that such transport seemed to be available without difficulty to Nergui at any time of the day or night. They stood at the top of the steps, looking down at the car, its engine running in the empty street.

'Can I offer you a lift?' Nergui said. The Wilsons, like Drew, were staying at the Chinggis Khaan. 'It's a cold night.'

As the cold air hit him, Drew began to feel the effect of the alcohol. 'If it's all the same to you,' he said, 'I think I wouldn't mind the walk. It's only five minutes.'

The Wilsons looked at each other. 'I wouldn't mind a lift,' Helena Wilson said. 'These heels aren't ideal for an icy street, especially after a few drinks.'

'You're sure you don't want a lift, Drew?' Nergui looked at him closely. 'You're okay?'

'I'm fine,' Drew said. 'Should have taken a bit more water with it, that's all. Fresh air will do me good.'

He followed the others down the steps to the car. Nergui ushered the Wilsons into the back, and then climbed into the front by the driver. Helena Wilson started to close the rear door, then stopped, looking at Drew. 'Chief Inspector. Drew,' she said. 'Are you sure you won't come with us? There's plenty of room.'

'No, really, it's okay.' He had started to walk away, feeling unstable.

'Drew,' she said again. 'I—' She stopped as if unsure how to go on. 'Please. Take care, won't you?'

He turned, surprised by the sudden urgency in her tone. She closed the car door as the driver started to pull away, but was still watching him earnestly through the window. He thought, for a moment before the car moved, that there was a look in her eyes that was close to fear.

The car did a U-turn, and accelerated past him. He saw Nergui wave a farewell gesture through the front window. Helena Wilson was still watching him, looking back through the rear window. And then the car turned the corner, and was gone.

Drew straightened up, trying to maintain his equilibrium. He really had drunk much more than he had realised. That was the problem with whisky. The effects hit you suddenly, later. He stumbled slightly, and then began to walk slowly down the street, the large angular bulk of the hotel already visible against the clear night sky. The street was deserted and silent, white with the thickening frost.

He had walked only a few more feet when he heard a sudden tumble of footsteps behind him. He half turned, startled by the unexpected sound. For a moment, he caught sight of a shadow, the glint of something in the pale streetlight. And then he was pushed, hard, the force of the blow sending him sliding across the icy pavement. He tripped and stumbled, trying to regain his balance, as something hit him again. He rolled over, his eyes filled first with the glare of the streetlight, then with a jumble of stars and a looming shadow. And then with darkness.

PART TWO

THIRTEEN

'Nergui?'

Nergui looked up. Through the narrow window, he could see the sky lightening outside. He wasn't sure how long he'd been sitting here, reading through the case files.

'Brought you this.' It was Doripalam, holding two mugs of coffee.

'Thanks,' he said. 'I need it.'

'Well, I was making one,' the young man said. 'And I saw that you were already in.' He placed the mug carefully down on Nergui's desk. 'How was the ambassador's party?'

Nergui gestured him to sit down. 'Alcoholic,' he said. 'But otherwise better than feared. We met a couple of rather odd Brits. He was a chemist who was also a civil servant. She was an anthropologist doing some work on our folk traditions. Or something like that.'

'You're making my night at home sound more attractive by the second.'

'Just bear that in mind when they come to offer you a job in the Ministry,' Nergui said.

'That may be a little while yet.'

'Well, the way this case is going there could be a vacancy before long. Not that I'd necessarily recommend you take it.'

'That why you're in so early?'

Nergui looked up at Doripalam, wondering quite

what was going through the younger man's mind. He was probably feeling some relief now that it was Nergui's reputation on the line in this case, but Nergui guessed that his feelings were likely to be more complicated than that.

'Not really. Didn't get home till late. Then I couldn't sleep so I thought I might as well come in. But all I've been doing is re-reading the files. I keep hoping that something new is going to leap out at me, but of course it doesn't.'

'No news on our missing American?'

'Maxon? No, he's just vanished. Seems unbelievable. You'd imagine that a Westerner couldn't stay undetected for five minutes down there, but he seems to have managed it.'

'Maybe he's dead too?'

Nergui nodded. The same thought had, of course, already occurred to him. He had assumed that Maxon had been riding the motorbike he had heard accelerating away from the camp before he found the two bodies. But maybe it had been someone else. Maybe Maxon had been another victim, not the perpetrator. Certainly it would be much easier to hide a dead body down there than a living Westerner. But it still wasn't a straightforward explanation. If Maxon was dead, how had the killer managed to kill him and somehow dispose of the body, alongside the other two murders? They had searched the tourist camp very thoroughly, and Nergui was as sure as he could be that Maxon wasn't there, living or dead.

But Doripalam was right. It was a possibility they couldn't ignore. Though finding a dead body in the Gobi desert wasn't likely to be the easiest of tasks.

'I'm hoping he's alive,' Nergui said grimly, 'because he's one of the few decent leads we've got in this thing.

If he's dead – if he's another victim – we're no further forward.' He shrugged. 'But I have a horrible feeling you may well be right. Nothing makes any sense here.'

'I think everyone's getting rattled about this one. There are all kinds of stories flying about.'

'Inevitably,' Nergui said. They had done their best to keep the story under wraps as far as the general public was concerned. These days, it wasn't easy. The press was always keen to demonstrate its independence, and wouldn't take kindly to being excluded from a potentially major story. But the reporting of the initial murders had been low key, with no suggestion of any connection, and the Ministry had managed to ensure that none of the details were published. Delgerbayar's murder had been reported in a similar manner. It had been difficult to play down the Gobi murders, particularly given the need to try to track down Maxon, but they had not been linked to the murders in the capital city.

Nergui was unsure how long this relative quiet would prevail. While there were strict rules on police confidentiality, someone, somewhere, would eventually talk about this case to friends and family. Too many people – in the police, in the Ministry and other government departments – were aware of what was going on. And all of these people would themselves be anxious, perhaps feel the need to share their worries with someone else. Gradually the story would filter out, maybe in even more lurid form than the reality, if that were possible. And then the panic would begin.

Nergui knew that they had to make some progress, some real progress, before then. But for the moment progress continued to elude them.

'We're still working through all the routine stuff,' Doripalam said. 'All the door to doors, looking through all the missing person reports, combing the areas where the bodies were found – you name it. But it doesn't look promising.'

'No. Mind you, with that stuff, there's no way of knowing. We just have to keep hoping.'

'Anyone ever tell you you're too optimistic to be a policeman?' Doripalam said.

'Oddly enough, no. Though they've found many other grounds for disqualifying me for the role.' Nergui smiled, palely. 'There's no other way, though, is there? We can't give up.'

Once the young man had gone, Nergui continued reading through the papers. He was painstaking, but there really was nothing new, nothing he hadn't seen before. He had combed through every detail, every nuance of the report. Maybe another eye would see something different, though he doubted it. But there seemed to be nothing more that Nergui could contribute.

He looked at his watch. It was already eight o'clock. He felt as if he had been up all night, which was almost the case. It wasn't physical tiredness, more a sense of mental, even spiritual, exhaustion, as if he really was at the limits of his endurance.

There was no one here that he could talk to, not even Doripalam. They'd kept their relationship positive, despite everything, but it wasn't the time to start unloading his personal feelings on the younger man. He had enough to cope with. Was it too early to call Drew? He thought not. Drew had given the impression that he was an early riser, so even after the previous late night, he would almost certainly be up by now. He picked up the phone and called the Chinggis Khaan, asking to be connected to Drew's room. He heard the ringing tone, but the call was not answered. He looked at his watch again. Probably Drew was at breakfast.

Eventually, the operator came back on the line. 'I'm sorry, sir. There's no reply. Can I take a message?'

'Just let him know that Nergui called,' he said. 'He's got the number.'

He put the phone down, feeling unaccountably anxious. There was no reason to feel concerned. Drew would be having breakfast or had gone for a stroll. It was even possible he was still sleeping and had not heard the phone.

But Nergui could not shake off a feeling of concern. It was that silly Wilson woman. Nergui was not, by the standards of his countrymen, a superstitious individual. But her talk of premonitions and psychic powers, however rational the articulation, left him feeling uneasy. There was something about the way she had looked at Drew as the car had driven away.

Looking back, Nergui thought that he should have insisted on Drew coming in the car with them. Not, he told himself, that there was any danger in the city at that time of the night. It was only a few hundred metres to the hotel, after all.

But the thought kept nagging at him. Maybe his fears weren't wholly irrational. After all, there was a killer – maybe more than one killer – at large in the city. There had already been an apparent attempt on his or Drew's life. And, of course, one policeman was already dead. In the circumstances, maybe leaving Drew to walk home wasn't his finest decision.

And there were more rational concerns. Drew had been pretty drunk. It was a cold night, icy underfoot. Maybe Drew had slipped, hit his head. Temperatures last night had fallen many degrees below zero. It was beginning to reach the time of the year when those without homes were all too commonly found dead in the streets in the early mornings.

Nergui rose and paced across the office. This was idiotic. He was behaving like a mother whose son is late coming home from a drinking session.

Despite himself, he picked up the phone and dialled the number of Drew's mobile, which he had scribbled on a pad on the desk. There was a long, empty silence while he waited for the roaming signal to connect. Finally, there was a click and the sound of the overseas ringing tone. The ringing stopped suddenly, and for a moment, as the familiar voice reached his ears, Nergui thought Drew had answered it. But then he realised that, from apparently immeasurable distances, this was simply the sound of Drew's pre-recorded voicemail message. 'I'm sorry I'm not available at the moment, but if you'd like to leave a message—'

Nergui left a message, but somehow with no confidence that it would be picked up. His tiredness had fallen away, but it had been replaced by a yawning anxiety, an insuppressible sense that something was dreadfully wrong.

Blackness. Silence. Nothing.

Death must be like this. Perhaps, after all, he was dead. Or perhaps he had been buried alive. His body felt numb, and he couldn't tell if the numbness was internal or somehow imposed upon him.

But he must be alive. He was thinking. His mind was confused, uncertain, but he was slowly, step by step, piecing together a train of thought. Images. People. Voices. A cold white hard sheet. A burning orange light. Something unexpected. Something frightening.

Panic rose in him, though that surely must be another indication that he was alive. The dead didn't panic, did they? His breath caught in his chest. That meant he was breathing, at least, though for how long was another question.

He tried to hold his breath and listen. Could he hear anything? No. Nothing. Not even the beating of his own heart. Perhaps this was what death felt like, after all.

He was unsure how long he lay in this semi-comatose state. Maybe hours, perhaps only minutes. Gradually, though, he became aware that something was changing. The feeling was slowly returning to his body, the numbness slowly melting away. He could move his eyes, begin to move his fingers. He began, finally, to feel like a human being again. He was not dead. Or, if he was, death was much closer to life than he had ever imagined.

But the gradual return to sentience was neither pleasant nor reassuring. As the feeling gradually began to flow back into his limbs, he became increasingly aware of the pain. A dull throbbing ache that filled his arms and legs and head, the kind of painful lethargy that accompanies a serious bout of influenza. And more localised aches – bruises or contusions on his back, on his head. And on top of all this was a feeling of lassitude. Even in other circumstances, he would have struggled to rise from where he was lying.

As more and more feeling flooded back into his body, he became aware that his supine state was not voluntary. There was some kind of binding holding his arms, and something similar around his ankles. When he tried, painfully, to lift his head, he became aware of a cord around his neck, tight enough to throttle him if he tried to move more than a centimetre or two.

He realised – like a third party observing his own predicament – that he ought to be frightened. He had no idea where he was or what was happening here, his brain was not processing this at all. But one thing he could work out, what was happening here was clearly not good.

Slowly, slowly, consciousness came dribbling back. Why was he here? What was going on? Where was he? The questions came in no rational order, but at least he was beginning to formulate questions.

Suddenly, as if he had woken from a deep sleep,

clarity hit him. Whereas before there had just been a fog of sensation, now he could remember everything up to a point. He remembered the dinner at the embassy. He remembered the Wilsons, and the bizarre turn taken by their conversation. He remembered the strange behaviour of Helena Wilson. He remembered the car driving away into the frosty night. And then—

Then what? Himself drunkenly stumbling away. Something, someone crashing into him. And then nothing. And then this.

With full consciousness came a full sense of horror. He had no idea where he was or why he was here. But he was lying in the dark, with no sign of light or life, his limbs strapped down. And someone, for some reason, had brought him here.

FOURTEEN

'I'm sorry, sir. You can leave a message for him, but that's all we can do. I'm sure you appreciate—'

Nergui sighed and leaned forward over the reception desk. 'No,' he said. 'I do appreciate that you're doing your job, but so am I. If you don't have the authority to do it, then can I speak to whoever's in charge here?'

'I'm sorry, sir. I mean, I understand you're in an official capacity, but I've been told strictly—'

It would never have been like this in the old days, Nergui thought. There was a time when one flash of your official card would have been enough to terrify the wits out of any functionary who got in your way. In those days, they knew what the Ministry was capable of. It was still generally unwise to cross the Ministry, but there was greater willingness to take the risk these days, particularly if Western currency was involved.

Nergui straightened up, smiling. Then he turned sharply on his heel. For a moment, the receptionist looked relieved, assuming that she had dealt successfully with a troublesome visitor. The look of relief turned to a look of panic as Nergui calmly pushed open the door that led behind the reception desk 'Now, if you'll just give me a cardkey to open Room 204, I won't need to cause the kind of fuss that might disturb your guests.

'You can't—' she said. 'I'll call the police—'

Nergui shrugged, still smiling. 'I've told you. I am the police. Please do tell the manager if you wish to. He can join me in Room 204. Now please give me a key.'

She stared at him for a moment, then reluctantly took a card from the drawer beside her and ran it through the computer system. 'That will open it now,' she said.

'And if you or the manager should decide to call the police, you should mention that it's Nergui who has taken the key.' He briefly flashed his pass again. 'There, you see. If you tell them that, they will not be surprised and will not waste their time coming over here.'

He let himself out from behind the desk and made his way across to the lifts. Out of the corner of his eye, he could see the receptionist hesitate and then pick up the phone. He hoped that she was only calling the manager.

He knew he was being foolish. There was nothing for him to worry about, and he could have waited and done this properly. But the sense of anxiety had continued to nag away at him. It was eleven a.m. now. He had called Drew's room repeatedly, but there had been no response. Drew's mobile appeared still to be switched off or out of range. There had been no word from him at all. Nergui had even tried to call the British ambassador, in case Drew had for some reason returned to the embassy the previous evening after the car had left. The ambassador, fortunately or unfortunately, had been tied up in a meeting and had not yet returned Nergui's call.

Finally, when he could see nothing else to do, he had come across to the Chinggis Khaan. The receptionist had called up to Drew's room, but there was, as before, no response.

It was perfectly feasible that Drew was deeply asleep or had decided to get some air. Maybe he was out exploring the city, doing some of the tourist activities while he had the opportunity. Maybe Nergui had simply missed him and he was already on his way to the police offices.

Or maybe, Nergui thought, he had not been back here at all.

The lift opened on the second floor and Nergui made his way along the corridor to Drew's room. He slid the card through the electronic lock, and pushed open the door.

The room was empty. The bed was undisturbed, though if the chambermaids had already visited the room, it was still possible that Drew might have been here this morning. The room itself was very tidy, with only a few personal possessions – a hairbrush, a paperback thriller, a still unpacked suitcase on the stand – to indicate that it was occupied.

Nergui pulled open the wardrobe doors. There were a couple of suits and several shirts hanging up. Nothing else. A pair of polished black shoes on the floor. Policeman's shoes, Nergui thought.

'Excuse me, sir, I must ask you—'

Nergui turned. A short, overweight man was standing in the doorway. He was balding and his hair was badly combed across in an attempt to conceal the fact. He was wearing an expensive-looking Western-style suit. Presumably the manager.

Nergui nodded politely. 'Can I help you?' he said.

The manager looked nonplussed at Nergui's question and it took him a second to gather his thoughts. 'I'm sorry, sir, but this really is—'

'Has this room been made up yet?' Nergui said. 'Have the chambermaids been in here?'

The manager opened his mouth, clearly about to repeat his objections to Nergui's presence, then he stopped. 'I can check for you,' he said, finally. 'Can I see your ID first, though, sir?'

Nergui nodded. 'Of course.' He smiled and pulled out his ID again. 'Here,' he said.

'That's fine, sir. No problem. You understand we have to be careful.'

'Naturally.'

He followed the manager back out into the corridor. A group of chambermaids were standing by the lifts, chatting. The manager approached them and spoke briefly, then turned back to Nergui. 'They say that room's already been cleaned.'

Nergui smiled at the group of women who were watching him with some curiosity. 'Police,' he said. 'Room 204. Which of you cleaned that room?'

One of the women, young and pretty with dark hair, raised her arm shyly. Nergui looked at her. 'Had the bed been disturbed?' he said. 'Had anyone slept in it?'

She shook her head nervously. 'No,' she said. 'The bed hadn't been slept in. I thought it was a bit strange, as the room was occupied . . . but you don't know—' She giggled slightly and turned away.

'Thank you,' Nergui said.

The chambermaids giggled again, glancing back at him, then moved off together. Nergui turned to the manager. 'Do you know who was on duty last night? On the reception, I mean. After midnight.'

The manager nodded. 'We lock the main doors at midnight, so people have to use the entryphone to get in. I'll need to check who the night porter was last night.'

'Thanks. And can you make sure that no one goes into 204. I mean, no one. No chambermaids. No one.'

The manager nodded, looking anxious. 'I'm sorry,' he said, 'but what do you think has happened? I mean, after the last incident, we're all a bit on edge.'

'Trust me,' Nergui said, 'I'm as much on edge as any of you. As for what's happened, well, I haven't a clue at the moment. I'm hoping nothing's happened. But I'm fearing – well, I don't even know what I'm fearing, except that it's nothing good.'

Back down in the hotel lobby, Nergui commandeered the manager's office as a makeshift base. The manager himself seemed only too pleased to hand over leadership to someone else.

While the manager was checking on the identity of the night porter, Nergui made another call to the embassy. The ambassador was still busy, as Nergui had expected, so he left a message for him to call back urgently. If anything had happened to Drew, it would be highly damaging if the ambassador was not advised of the situation immediately. He had also left a message for his own Minister, briefly setting out the current situation. In the circumstances, he recognised that this was probably the least welcome news the Minister could have received. Losing one Westerner might be an accident. Losing two – and one of them a senior policeman at that – might well be construed as criminal negligence. Nergui's was not the only career that was likely to be on the line here.

Oddly, Nergui felt remarkably calm. As soon as he had realised that Drew had not returned to his room the previous evening, his personal anxiety had melted away, replaced by an almost glacial attention to the minutiae of his duties. This was one of his strengths – the capacity to detach himself from personal emotions and lock himself rigorously into the requirements of his job. It was, he suspected, not a particularly attractive personal quality, but it was one of the factors that contributed to his professional effectiveness. In this case, though, he was conscious that his own emotions were buried not far below the surface.

The manager returned a few moments later with the

night porter. He was a tall man, dressed in blue overalls. As the night porter sat down at the manager's desk, Nergui could smell alcohol on the man's breath. It was not clear whether he had slept since completing his shift early that morning.

Nergui nodded to him. 'I do not need to detain you long,' he said. 'Just a few simple questions.'

The night porter looked anxious. Nergui guessed that, in that line of work, there was always temptation to break the rules, or even the law in minor ways – drinking, petty theft. Probably the porter assumed that he had been caught out in some transgression and was about to be sacked, if not arrested. In other instances, Nergui might have been tempted to play that to his advantage, but that did not seem appropriate at the moment.

'You were on duty last night?' he asked.

The man nodded. 'Came on at eleven thirty, worked through to seven.'

Nergui paused, as though taking in this information. 'Were there any disturbances last night? Anything out of the ordinary?'

The man shook his head. 'Nothing. It was a quiet night.' He looked nervously across at the manager. Nergui suspected that the porter had probably spent much of the night asleep.

'I dropped off an English couple after midnight. Did any other guests return after that?'

'Not last night. We don't tend to get many. If tourists go out to eat, they tend to be back before then. There's not a lot of late-night entertainment. The bar here's open till one, so if people want to drink they usually stay here.'

'So there was no one else?'

'No one.'

Nergui leaned forward across the table, staring intently at the porter. 'You're absolutely sure of that?' he said. 'This is very important. I'm not trying to catch you out. I just need to be sure.'

The man nodded, more nervous now, but apparently telling the truth. 'I'm sure,' he said. 'Nobody can get in without using the entryphone. Even if I was—' For a moment, Nergui thought he was going to say 'asleep' but he went on: 'Even if I was away from the desk for some reason, they'd have to wait till I got back.'

'And it's not possible that someone else might have let anyone in in your absence?'

'Not last night. There was no one around. I was the only one on duty. The bar closed early – before midnight – because no one was in. So, no, I'm sure no one else came in after midnight.'

'Okay, that's fine. That's all. Thank you for your help.'

The porter looked surprised and relieved, as if he'd been reprieved from some major crime. He smiled and nodded, and looked across at the manager. 'No problem,' he said. 'I'm here on site if you need anything else.' He rose and hurried out of the room before anything more could be said.

'Assiduous chap,' Nergui commented.

'He'd have been asleep most of the night,' the manager said. 'Probably half drunk. Or more. But I'm sure he's right. Even if he was dead to the world, it would just mean that the doors stayed locked. We've got video cameras over the entrance so we can check the tapes to be sure, but I think you can safely assume that nobody else came in here after midnight last night.'

Nergui rose. 'We may need to talk to other staff at some point. But if he was the only one on duty, I don't imagine anyone else can tell us much.'

The manager shook his head. 'I wouldn't have thought so. I mean, we'll give any help we can. What's this all about?'

Nergui hesitated for a moment. The manager would have no difficulty looking up Drew's name or recognising that he was a Westerner. He might even have some knowledge of who Drew was. 'Look,' he said, 'this is all highly confidential. Nothing must leak out. I'm serious, if anything about this appears in the press, I'll be back here before you can open your mouth again. And you're likely to become closely acquainted with the inside of our magnificent prison facilities. So don't say a word to anyone. Not even gossip.'

The manager was wide eyed. 'I wouldn't—'

'Of course. But I can't take any risk on this one.'

'You think this guest – this Mr McLeish – has gone missing?'

Nergui was not surprised that the manager had already checked Drew's name. 'We don't know,' he said. 'All we know is he didn't come back here last night.'

'And is this connected to the previous – incident?'

Nergui was tiring of providing explanations, but he recognised the importance of treating the man with some courtesy. 'Probably not. As I say, it may all turn out to be nothing. But, especially given the previous incident, we can't be too careful.'

The manager nodded, with some enthusiasm. 'Of course, of course. I understand. As I say, if there is anything more I can do to help—'

'We will be in touch. I am very grateful for your kind assistance today. I am sorry that I was so peremptory in dealing with your receptionist, but you will appreciate I was in a hurry. Please pass on my apologies.'

Nergui thought that by now he had laid the politeness on quite thickly enough. 'But remember,' he said, turning as he opened the door, 'say nothing. To anybody.'

*

Outside, the day was bright but cold. Nergui hurried across Sukh Bataar Square, pulling his coat tightly around him. As he walked he checked his mobile which he had switched off while interviewing the porter. There were two messages – one from the ambassador's secretary to say that he was now free and could Nergui call back, and, inevitably, one from the Minister. The latter was not a conversation he was looking forward to. He procrastinated briefly by calling the ambassador as he walked.

Eventually, he was put through. 'What is it, Nergui? The message sounded urgent.'

'It may be. You haven't seen Chief Inspector McLeish since we left last night?'

'No. I waved you off, saw him start to walk down the street. That's all. Why? Has something happened?'

'It looks as if he never returned to the hotel.'

There was a long pause at the other end of the line. Nergui heard the vague swish of static, the sound of the ambassador's breathing. 'How do you know?' he said at last.

'I've been trying to contact him all morning. Left messages. For some reason, I got worried and went over to the hotel. His bed wasn't slept in. The night porter on duty has no recollection of letting him in after midnight.'

'It was – what, about twelve fifteen when you left here? But where can he have gone? It's only five minutes back to the hotel.'

'I know,' Nergui said, feeling an unavoidable sense of personal responsibility. 'That's why we let him walk. I mean, there's no doubt some straightforward explanation—'

'I don't know what it could be,' the ambassador said bluntly, echoing Nergui's own thoughts. 'I mean, he doesn't know anyone here, so if he didn't come back to the embassy, there's nowhere else he's going to go. He was a little drunk – I mean, is it possible that he ended up going to the wrong hotel or something stupid like that?'

Nergui glanced up at the imposing silhouette of the Chinggis Khaan, black against the clear blue of the sky, dominating the city centre skyline. 'It doesn't seem likely.'

'He could have collapsed or something.'

'Or slipped and hit his head. I hope that's not it, given the temperatures overnight.'

'Christ, if we don't find him, this is going to be a major incident,' the ambassador said. 'How is it possible to lose a senior police officer?'

Nergui had no answer. It was an excellent question, and one he suspected the Minister would also be asking in the next few minutes. In his own mind, he was conscious of the political ramifications of the situation, but was growing more aware of his own personal feelings. He had grown to like Drew in the short time they had spent together. Nergui was more than capable of detaching himself from the emotions involved, but he realised that underneath, for the first time in many years, he was feeling genuinely worried about another human being.

'I'll get back to you as soon as we know anything,' he said. 'That's all I can do.'

He delayed calling the Minister till he was back at the office, partly just to buy a few minutes and partly because he wanted to ensure that he was in as much control of the situation as possible. As it turned out, the conversation was easier than he had feared. The Minister's famous panic control mechanisms appeared to have kicked in, and he spoke calmly, even pleasantly.

'If you were anyone else, Nergui, I would have assumed that your message was exaggerated.'

'I'm afraid not, Minister. I set it out as clearly as I could.'

'You did indeed. So all you know is that he never returned to the hotel last night?'

'Well, we're as sure as we can be of that,' Nergui said, trying to remain as objective as he could. 'We know he didn't sleep in his room. The night porter on duty has no recollection of him returning after midnight. And it doesn't seem likely that he would have been able to enter the hotel any other way.'

'So when did you last see him?'

'Just after midnight. I gave the others a lift back in the car, and Drew – Chief Inspector McLeish, that is – insisted on walking back to the hotel.'

'Pity you didn't insist on giving him a lift.'

Nergui didn't need to be told this. But then Drew had been adamant about wanting to walk, the hotel had been literally a few minutes away, the streets were deserted. No one could have predicted that anything would happen. But Nergui knew there was no point in going through all this with the Minister.

'Indeed, Minister.'

'So what do you think could have happened to him? I take it that you're treating this as in some way linked with the other incidents?'

This seemed to be everyone's favourite euphemism at the moment, Nergui reflected. 'Well, we have to recognise that there could be a link with the killings,' he said. 'But there's no way of knowing at the moment.' He paused. 'If there is a link, who knows what the implications might be? It hardly bears thinking about. But there could be a host of more straightforward explanations. People do go missing, and sometimes for the oddest of reasons.'

'But they're not usually senior policemen on official visits to overseas countries.'

'True enough.'

'And, unless I'm missing something, it's not easy to come up with an explanation that doesn't have a potentially negative outcome?'

'Well—' Nergui hesitated. But the Minister was right. Even the simplest explanations – that Drew had fallen and hit his head, that he had collapsed, that he had been mugged – did not augur well for Drew's well-being. 'I suppose you're right,' he said.

'Which, in turn, doesn't indicate a particularly positive outcome for you or me, Nergui. Do you have any leads on this at all?'

'On the disappearance?'

'On any of it. This whole sorry mess.' Nergui noted that, despite all his own reservations, the Minister had immediately elided everything into a single case.

'Some, but nothing substantive. Everything that happens seems to take us further away.'

'We need to get somewhere on this, Nergui. And quickly. Especially after this. This is going to be a major incident. The British government will be all over us. The Western media will be all over us.'

'I know.'

The Minister, never one for niceties, ended the call without saying anything more. Nergui looked at the phone and nodded. 'Don't hesitate to pass on any ideas you might have,' he said to the now-dead receiver.

'Nergui?'

He looked up. Doripalam was standing in the doorway.

'I just heard. Is it true?'

Nergui shrugged. 'It's true he's disappeared. What that means – well, your guess is probably a lot better than mine.'

'I wouldn't have disturbed you, except – well, this is maybe not the moment, but I've got a bit of an idea. It's 'probably stupid, but I wanted to check it out with you.'

'What's your idea?' Nergui said. He knew that anything Doripalam came up with was unlikely to be a waste of time.

'Well, it goes back to Delgerbayar. You remember that he'd been involved in the gold prospecting case?'

Nergui nodded, wondering where this was leading. 'Some small-time thing, as I understood it. Dispersing one of the illegal camps. He was due to go up there with another officer the day after he went missing.'

'That's right. Well, I had a check back through the records. I don't think anybody picked it up, but I think Delgerbayar had already been up to the camp.'

Nergui raised his head and stared at Doripalam. 'What do you mean?'

'Just that. He'd been up to the camp before.'

Nergui was sitting up and paying attention now. He was also cursing himself for apparently missing something that might have been important. 'He wrote a report on the visit?'

Doripalam shook his head, looking slightly embarrassed. 'Well, no, that's just it. There was no report. No one knew that he'd been.'

'So why did you think he had?'

'I was having a look through the stuff that was cleared out of Delgerbayar's desk. I don't know why. Just clutching at straws, I think. We'd already been through it to see if there was anything important there. By the time I got to it, there wasn't much left apart from paperclips and old rubber bands.'

'And?'

'Well, his desk diary was still there. Someone had already been through it but Delgerbayar wasn't one for making detailed entries so there wasn't much in there that was useful. Mainly just single names or abbreviations.

Times of meetings, that kind of thing. Scribbled in there, usually. Obviously meant something to him, but wouldn't mean much to anyone else. But I went through it one more time, just in case anything new struck me. And what I noticed was that the phrase he'd written in the diary for the scheduled visit to the camp looked the same as something he'd scribbled in about a month earlier. I couldn't really read it, but in the end I became convinced the two words were the same.'

'Doesn't sound a lot to go on.'

'It isn't. But I've checked back in the records – it looks as if Delgerbayar had various things officially scheduled for that day, but none of them actually check out. Nobody noticed, because most of them were just routine activities, but there's no question he wasn't where he was supposed to be.'

Nergui looked at the younger man with some admiration. 'And you accused me of being over-optimistic. I don't know what this means, but it looks as if it's worth pursuing, especially as we've got nothing else to go on. Who was it spoke to the people in the camp? I mean, after we found Delgerbayar's body.'

Doripalam shifted uneasily on his feet. 'Well, that's the other thing.'

Nergui began to have a sinking feeling. 'What other thing?'

'Well, I've checked back in the reports and, well, it doesn't look as if anyone went out to visit the camp.'

'You're joking.'

'Well, it's not really all that surprising,' Doripalam said, looking uncomfortable. 'The original job was a pretty routine piece of work—'

'Police as the paid lackeys of the mining corporations?'

'If you say so,' Doripalam said. 'After Delgerbayar's

body was found in the city and there was all that stuff about his journey to the Gobi, it never occurred to us that the illegal prospecting stuff was relevant any more.'

Nergui shook his head. 'We never learn, do we? We tell ourselves that good policing is following up every avenue, no matter how trivial or potentially irrelevant. But then we all still manage to miss the obvious.' He caught Doripalam's expression. 'I mean all of us. It never occurred to me to think about the prospector angle, either.'

'Well, if it's any consolation, it looks as if the camp had broken up in any case before Delgerbayar's death. The visit that was due to happen the day after he went missing never took place. So there's no reason why anyone should have thought that it was worth following up.'

'Except you did,' Nergui said.

Doripalam nodded. 'So what do you think we should do about it?'

Nergui shrugged. 'I think I need to get out of this place. I think we should go exploring.'

FIFTEEN

'It shouldn't be allowed,' Nergui said. 'These are the people we should be treating as criminals.'

Not for the first time on their journey, Doripalam regarded Nergui with some amusement. It would be interesting to observe Nergui's interactions with the Minister, he thought. They must have some lively political discussions.

'Look at it,' Nergui went on. 'It's a shambles. And here of all places.'

Ahead of them, the grassy steppe swept up towards the smooth grandeur of the northern mountains. The rounded contours of these mountains were like nothing found in the west, Nergui thought. He remembered days spent walking up here in past summers, the grassy hillsides thick with wild flowers and darting butterflies, an extraordinary profusion of natural beauty.

But it was autumn now and late afternoon, the sun already hanging low over the mountains, reddening the slopes. It had been a long journey, and they were anticipating a further long trip back in the dark.

Their objective lay immediately ahead of them. The valley, as Nergui had accurately pointed out, was a mess. On the far side, there was a make-shift shanty town of *gers* and wooden huts, providing storage and accommodation. Closer to hand was the valley itself. Its sides were scarred and rutted with endless excavations, ripped randomly into the landscape. The summer's rains had turned the ground to mud, and now, with winter approaching, the earth was hard and frozen. On the far slope, a battalion of bulldozers and tractors worked away at the land, tearing rutted holes into the grass.

At the heart of the valley, the river was slick with spilled oil and other chemicals. Piecemeal dams and embankments had been built to shift the course of the river at various points, providing access to areas that had previously lain under water. From the sodden and disturbed state of the valley floor, it was clear that the river's path had been manipulated many times.

'It's not pretty,' Doripalam acknowledged.

This was one face of the country's expanding minerals industry. Not all the production sites were as ugly as this, but there were increasing numbers of opencast excavations in the land north-east of the capital. Some of the production companies were relatively responsible, taking care of the environment where possible, giving consideration to the local flora and fauna, restoring the landscape once the work was completed. But others – a substantial number of others – paid little attention to such concerns. They came, took what they wanted, and left an unholy mess behind them. This, Nergui presumed, was one of those.

The worst part was that it was all legal. These companies had obtained their licences quite legitimately. The government was only too keen to do deals, so long as investment entered the country and the government was able to take its share. Most of the mines were joint ventures involving companies from Canada, the US, China, South Korea, Russia and elsewhere. These opencast mines were the cheapest option, the minerals simply ripped from the ground. Over the last decade, much of the production had been here in the north of the country in areas like this. Inevitably the resources would be finite, but for the moment there was abundance, and the country had experienced an extraordinary gold rush as producers had converged here to seize their share.

In principle, the licences were subject to regulation in respect of environmental impact, health and safety, and other human considerations. In practice, there was no will or ability to enforce this regulation. Bureaucracy, the producers would tell you, was the enemy of enterprise. And enterprise, as the government well understood, lay at the heart of investment and growth. Who cared if a few landscapes – or even a few people – were damaged in the process?

And, with an all too familiar irony, the forces of law and order were directed not towards these despoilers of the environment, but towards those who tried to gather up a few crumbs from their table. The illegal camp that Delgerbayar was supposed to have visited was some way downstream from here. The inhabitants were former herdsmen whose livelihoods had been damaged or destroyed by years of economic chaos and a sequence of harsh winters. They were attempting, with some success, to scrape a living by panning for gold in the riverbed. They emerged at night, once the floodlights were extinguished, scanning the valley with their feeble flashlights. They called themselves 'ninjas', a reference to the cheap imported green plastic buckets they used for panning. As they worked their way across the valley floor, they strapped the buckets to their backs, in ironic homage to the ninja turtles of the cartoons.

No one with a grain of human feeling could blame them, but their actions were nonetheless illegal. The gold they found belonged to the ruthless predators operating in the valley before them. And the police were summoned like hired lackeys to do the producers' dirty work for them.

Nergui wondered vaguely why the encampment had broken up and moved on before the police had visited. It was quite possible that one of the mining companies had taken the law into its own hands, maybe irritated at the police's insistence on going through the proper channels. It would not have been the first time. But there was probably no way of ever finding out.

Their current interest lay not in the environmental chaos immediately in front of them, but in the cluster of *gers* that lay a mile or so beyond. It was here that, according to the records, some of those in the original camp had now retreated, hoping to find a livelihood among the fragments of gold. Nergui drove their Hyundai truck carefully past the pounding bulldozers and across the grasslands towards the encampment.

There was a group of men clustered around the *gers*, drinking beers and playing cards. They looked up, with some hostility, as the truck drew closer.

Nergui was unsure how to play this. The police were unlikely to be popular among this group, since they were seen as being little more than the hired hands of the mining companies. Except, Nergui reflected, that they weren't even hired. They did this dirty work for nothing.

But there was little point in hiding their identities as police officers. They had to give a reason for being here, and, if it came to it, it was always possible to indulge in a little official intimidation. Maybe, as so often, the simplest route was complete honesty.

Nergui pulled the truck to a halt and jumped out. Doripalam followed him, a step or two behind. Nergui thought the younger man was making a creditable job of not appearing nervous. Or maybe he was just more confident than Nergui.

The group of men looked at them, unspeaking and expressionless. Their ages were mixed – the youngest probably in his thirties, the oldest maybe late sixties.

They were all dressed in traditional clothes, wrapped warm against the chilly air.

'Good afternoon,' Nergui said, breaking the heavy silence.

No one spoke. Nergui sighed inwardly. This was not going to be an easy process.

'We're police officers,' Nergui said. 'We'd like a word.'

The youngest of the men smiled thinly. 'Well, well. I would never have guessed. I'm just surprised it took you so long.'

Nergui shrugged. 'I couldn't care less what you do down there. Someone may come to stop you, but it won't be me.'

'Oh, someone will definitely come to stop us. And soon. And I couldn't care less if it's you or someone else. But that wasn't what I meant.'

Nergui looked at the young man more closely. He sounded well-educated, much more articulate than most of the nomads he had encountered out here. He had, Nergui noted, already positioned himself as the spokesman for this group, despite apparently being the youngest of the men. The others seemed content to defer to his leadership.

'So what did you mean?'

'We've been expecting a visit from the police for some time now. It's taken you longer to get out here than I imagined. But I suppose it is off the metropolitan beat.'

Nergui nodded, slowly. 'You sound as if you're rather off the metropolitan beat yourself.'

The man laughed. 'It's still so obvious? After all this time. I thought I'd put all that behind me.'

This was all getting a little too opaque for Nergui's tastes. He had a sense that he was losing dominance of the conversation. It was not a common sensation for Nergui, and his usual response, in professional circumstances, was to engage in some intimidation. He had a feeling, though, that this approach would not be effective here.

'Can we sit?' he said mildly. 'I need to ask you a few questions.'

'I should perhaps be careful,' the man said. 'If you're here in an official role, I might incriminate myself.'

'Are there grounds for you to incriminate yourself?'

The man smiled. 'You'll need a more sophisticated approach than that, I'm afraid.' He gestured towards the *ger* behind them. 'Come in. We can talk in here.'

Nergui and Doripalam followed him into the dark confines of the tent. Inside, there were benches draped with blankets. He gestured the two officers to sit, and then squatted on the floor opposite them.

'My name is Cholon,' the man said. 'Tell me how I can help. Though I think I have an idea.'

Nergui hesitated for a moment. 'We are investigating a series of murders. Including one of a police officer called Delgerbayar.'

Cholon did not appear surprised at this information. He nodded, as if absorbing Nergui's words, but made no response.

'We have reason to believe that this officer visited an encampment of illegal gold prospectors shortly before his death.'

'This camp?'

'No, not here. Further downriver. But we also understand that some of the inhabitants of that camp are now living here. Is this correct?'

Cholon thought for a moment, as though about to respond in the negative, then he nodded. 'That is so,' he said. 'A number of us, including myself.'

'How long is it since you moved here?'

'In my case, about six weeks. But the camp finally broke up only about three weeks ago.'

Nergui shifted on the stool, looking momentarily distracted. 'Why did the camp break up?' he said, finally.

Cholon laughed. 'The usual reason. Intimidation. Violence. Threats.'

'From the mining companies?'

'Certainly not from any environmentalists.' Cholon laughed. 'Yes, of course from the mining companies.'

'Did the camp receive any visit from the police?'

Cholon lay back, stretching out his legs across the floor. 'Not while I was there. But I understand that someone – a senior officer – came after I had moved on. Doing the companies' dirty work as always.'

'Delgerbayar?'

Cholon shrugged. 'I don't imagine he was too keen to share his name with them. All I know is that it was the usual threats.'

'This was an official visit?'

'You tell me,' Cholon said. 'Surely you know what errands you send your officers on.'

'Suppose I were to tell you,' Nergui said, speaking slowly, 'that Delgerbayar was operating as – well, let us call him a freelance. Would that surprise you?'

Cholon smiled. 'Nothing about the police would surprise me,' he said. 'And nothing about the mining companies, come to that. You're both capable of anything.'

'I am sure that we – and they – are capable of many things. But I'm posing a serious question. Of course, there are corrupt police officers. The temptations are many. But you may be surprised to learn that the majority, the vast majority, are honest.'

Cholon raised an eyebrow, an amused smile on his lips. 'If you say so.'

'I say so. But some of course are systematically corrupt. I do not know if any are directly in the pay of the mining industry—'

'I thought you were all in the pay of the mining industry. In practice.'

Nergui shrugged. 'We are obliged to obey orders. We are obliged to enforce the law. It may on occasions be a bad law.'

Cholon snorted. 'I'm sorry,' he said. 'I don't see where all this is leading.'

'I thought you said you had some idea why we might want to talk to you.'

'I—' Cholon stopped, then laughed. 'So you do have more sophisticated approaches after all.'

'You would be surprised,' Nergui said, softly, 'how sophisticated I can be. But let us go back to Delgerbayar. I will be straight with you. In visiting your camp, he was not acting in any official capacity. We do not know in what capacity he was acting. Did you have any similar previous visits from the police?'

Cholon nodded. 'From time to time. Not just there, but wherever we were trying to prospect. The official visits – we had those too, but they were different. Then you'd just get a team of police turning up, with a warrant and a straightforward order for you to move on. You knew that if you didn't move within the defined time, you'd be arrested. So you moved. But the unofficial visits were different. That would be a lone police officer – usually armed. He would turn up with threats and innuendos, pretending he was just there to give you advance warning. Trying to help – but the message was always clear.'

'Was it always the same officer?' Doripalam interjected.

Cholon shook his head. 'No, I'm talking over a period of a couple of years. There were maybe two or three different officers – sometimes they turned up in pairs. The first time we thought it was a joke – that maybe they'd just failed or omitted to get the warrant for some reason and were trying to bluff their way through it.'

'And what happened when you ignored them?'

Cholon stopped, suddenly. 'That first time was two years or so ago,' he said. 'We were operating from a camp further downriver – a fair distance from here. Two officers turned up – no official paperwork, but warning us that if we didn't move things would become unpleasant. As I say, we thought it was a bluff. We've learned not to be intimidated easily. We're not going to back down just because someone in a uniform turns up—'

'I see that,' Nergui said.

'So we just sent them on their way, and waited for them to come back with a warrant.'

'And what happened?'

'They – the officers – didn't come back. But a couple of nights later, in the early hours of the morning, the camp was attacked.'

'By who?'

'They were hooded, dressed in dark clothing. It was impossible to see their faces. They came armed with shotguns, knives, you name it. Attacked individuals – beat up some, injured others and—' He stopped.

Nergui watched him closely, saying nothing.

'—and they killed two of the group. Including my father.'

'I'm sorry,' Nergui said.

Cholon shrugged. 'It is difficult to forgive them.'

'You reported this?'

Cholon smiled. 'In the circumstances, it did not seem prudent. We did not know for sure who attacked us – yes, the mining company was behind it, of course, but we did not know who had actually carried out the attack. We thought – and some of us still do think – that the police were in their pocket.'

'We are not hired thugs,' Doripalam said.

'Really? I've witnessed teams of police moving prospectors out of their camps, enforcing the law as you put it. Yes, this attack was more brutal than that, but the police can be brutal enough even on their official visits.' He spoke the last two words with bitter irony.

'And you had further – unofficial visits?' Nergui said.

Cholon nodded. 'As I say, from time to time. We took them seriously. The police came armed, but that was probably not necessary. We knew what could happen to us if there was any resistance.'

Nergui reached in his pocket and pulled out the now dog-eared photograph of Delgerbayar. 'Is this one of them?'

'This your Delgerbayar?' Cholon said. He peered closely at the image. 'Yes, I think he could well have been one of them.'

Nergui nodded slowly, putting the photograph back in his pocket. 'Yes, I feared so,' he said. He paused, adjusting his posture on the hard wooden stool. 'And what happened to your brother?'

Cholon stopped and stared at Nergui. 'My brother?'

'Your brother. Badzar. What happened to him?'

'How—?' Cholon leaned forward, wrapping his arms tightly around his legs. 'I can see I have underestimated you.'

Nergui smiled. 'You are not the first. But tell me about your brother.'

'I assume you don't need me to tell you, given your apparent omniscience.'

'Humour me, Mr Cholon.'

'The way you've been humouring me?'

'Not at all. You have told me much that I did not know. Some that I did not wish to hear. But your brother. What happened?'

Cholon hesitated for what seemed a long time, as if he had determined not to proceed. 'Okay,' he said at last, 'I'll humour you. I presume you know the background?'

'I know some of the background. Let me tell you the little I recall, and then you can fill in the gaps. I first came across you, Mr Cholon, or at least your name, in the late 1980s. You were something of a revolutionary, as I recall.'

'Hardly,' Cholon said. 'Although perhaps, yes, in your terms I was a revolutionary. I considered myself a democrat.'

Nergui nodded. 'Campaigning against the government, against the dominance of the USSR. Some might have called you a freedom fighter. Or a terrorist.'

Cholon snorted. 'On a pitiful scale.'

'There was sabotage. And a bomb.'

'None of which worked. We were amateurs. Students playing at it. Copying what we had seen happening in China, in Eastern Europe.'

'Nonetheless, you – and your brother – gained a certain notoriety at the time.'

'My brother more than me. He was the one with the grand ambitions.'

'So I recall. He was arrested?'

'Shortly before everything changed. The great tidal waves of democracy. The fall of the USSR. I'm still not sure what would have happened to him if that hadn't happened. He would still be in prison, I imagine.'

'And what did happen to him? For that matter, what happened to you?' Nergui smiled. 'You were a spokesman for your generation. Now you are an illegal gold prospector.'

'Maybe not so different,' Cholon said. 'Doing my bit for freedom and the real redistribution of wealth.'

'No doubt. But it's quite a shift.'

Cholon shrugged. 'So you say. Not much changed, to be honest. My father had been a herdsman, a nomad. He had worked hard and moved back to the city, getting a job in one of the state manufacturing businesses. We were fortunate in getting a good education, going to university.'

'The benefits of the old state against which you rebelled?'

'Possibly, but education is possible even in democracies, I understand? Anyway, things were going well until the economy collapsed.'

'Brought down by the end of the Soviet Union.'

'The irony didn't escape me. Though, as you well know, that is only part of the story.'

'So what happened?'

'My father lost his job, and tried to return to herding, but those were harsh winters and nothing worked. My brother and I had to leave university, and we both decided that the best thing would be to follow our father back out here. Since then we have done our best to scrape a living.'

'Until your father was killed?'

'As you say.'

'Your brother is still out here as well?'

Cholon looked at him closely. 'You are not so omniscient after all, then?'

'What do you mean?'

'I thought that was why you were here. I thought you were looking for Badzar.'

Nergui noticed that Doripalam had drawn closer to them and was listening intently.

'Why should we be looking for Badzar?' Nergui said.

Cholon shook his head. 'I said that I should not incriminate myself. Should I incriminate my brother?'

'That depends,' Nergui said slowly, 'on what your brother has done.'

227

Cholon looked from Nergui to Doripalam, and then back again. 'That is really not why you are here?' he said. 'You are not looking for Badzar?'

'We were not here to seek Badzar. We weren't even here looking for you.'

'But you knew I was here?'

'No. As you say, I am not so omniscient. I did not recognise you until you told me your name. But then I do have a good memory for the cases I've been involved with.' Nergui stopped, as though he had finished. Then he said: 'But you must tell us about your brother. What has he done?'

Cholon opened his mouth to speak, then stopped. There was a genuine anxiety in his eyes now. 'I do not know,' he said. 'I do not know for sure.'

A chill was beginning to creep down Nergui's spine. Once again he had a sense of something moving, circling, coming closer towards resolution. Behind Cholon he could see Doripalam shifting in his seat. There was an expression in Doripalam's eyes which Nergui could not read.

'What is it,' Nergui said, 'that you do not know for sure?'

Cholon stood up, slowly, as though his limbs were aching. He began to pace across the floor of the *ger*. 'I thought that was why you had come,' he said, again. 'I – I dreaded you coming, but I also hoped that you would. So that at least I could know.'

Nergui sat in silence, hoping that Doripalam would not break in with a question. Cholon needed space to speak, to articulate whatever thoughts were twisting inside his brain. Nergui knew this moment well from his interrogations. An inappropriate question would provide Cholon with an escape route, allow him to defer whatever it was he needed to say. Silence would allow him no exit.

'I need to know,' he said at last. 'I need to know what my brother is capable of. I need to know if – if he can really be the one.'

'Behind the murders?' Nergui said, his voice quiet.

Cholon looked up at him. 'You are playing with me? That is it. You do know.'

Nergui shook his head. 'We know nothing, Cholon. But you need to tell us what you think.'

'My father's death was a terrible thing,' Cholon said. 'It was not simply that he was killed. It was how he was killed. He was – butchered. The only blessing was that he must have died very quickly. But it was a horrible death—'

'Your brother witnessed it?'

'I think so. He would never say. But, yes, I am sure he saw it all.'

'And what happened?'

'The death – the whole incident, but especially our father's death – affected us all very badly. I was thrown into – well, depression is what you would call it, I suppose. I found it hard to rebuild things, to carry on. I did not want to work. Everything seemed pointless.'

'That is not so very surprising. In the circumstances.'

'No. But it took me a long time, months, before I was able to move on. And even then it was not like before. But it affected Badzar far worse.'

'Worse?'

'Very differently. I found myself unable to work, unable to move on. Badzar became angry. Furious. At the injustice. At the inhumanity of it. He wanted revenge.'

Nergui was feeling cold now. The day was drawing late, and the sun would be setting outside. It would be an icy night, but the cold that flowed through Nergui's body was internal, the chill of fear. 'What sort of revenge?'

'Initially, he went crazy. He went to the mining operations down here—' Cholon gestured through the walls of the tent in the direction of the valley floor. 'He was convinced – rightly, I'm sure – that it was the company behind what had happened. He stormed into their camp, found the office of the site manager, and attacked him. With his bare hands, but he did a lot of damage before they dragged him off. He had a knife in his pocket, though he had not used it.'

'Was he arrested?'

'No. The man was battered and bruised but not seriously injured. I imagine that they did not want the police probing around too much into Badzar's accusations. He was thrown off the site, that was all. But they probably imagined they could get their revenge in some other way.'

'And did they?'

'Badzar was too smart. He left here, kept moving. I didn't know where he was, though I heard stories of him joining other camps, other groups of nomads in the area. He had a motorbike and some money we had got for the gold.' He paused, as if hoping that Nergui would interrupt. 'And there were other attacks. Workers – managers, mainly – from the mining companies. There were several cases – attacks at night. Some were injured, in one case very seriously. One was killed.'

'You think this was your brother?'

Cholon nodded. 'I cannot be sure. The company blamed us, and we had to suffer more assaults from them. But, as far as I know, none of the attacks was reported to the police.'

'Not even the killing?' Doripalam said.

'Not even the killing.'

'So where is your brother now?' Nergui said. He was watching Cholon intently now, his eyes unblinking.

'Again, I do not know for sure. But I think he is in the city.'

'Why do you think that?'

'I saw him last about a month ago. He turned up here one day, on his motorbike. He looked . . . wild-eyed, disturbed. The way he talked was different. He talked slowly, as if he was drugged, and he talked about destiny and the need for action. He told me he was going away, and that I should not expect him to return.'

'He mentioned the city?'

'Not specifically. But he borrowed some more money. He was not staying in this area. I do not know where else he would go.'

'And you think he is responsible for the killings?' Every word was like a pebble being dropped into an icy pond.

'I do not know,' Cholon said. 'Genuinely, I do not. I don't want to believe that he could be capable of that.'

'But you can believe that he was responsible for the attacks out here?'

'He is a disturbed man. I saw the look in his eyes. I heard the way he was talking. I do not know what he is capable of.' Cholon stopped, as though he had finally run out of words. The silence stretched on. Finally he said: 'But yes, in my heart, I think it is possible. It is possible.'

SIXTEEN

By the time they emerged from the *ger*, the sun had already set. The sky was a deep mauve and darkening quickly. Glaring spotlights illuminated the waste of the valley floor, and the bulldozers were still slowly patrolling the landscape, tearing up earth and grass. Even at night, the noise was extraordinary, a ceaseless roaring echoing back from the surrounding hills.

'You will need to come back with us,' Nergui said. 'You will do that.' It was not a question.

Cholon nodded. 'If you think it will do any good.'

'I do not know. We do not know that your suspicion is correct. But we have nothing else to go on. No other ideas. And time is growing short.' He had not mentioned Drew to Cholon, and he felt again the rising fear that he had been trying to suppress throughout the day. 'At the least, if your brother is in the city, we need to find him. And you may be able to help us in that.'

'Perhaps. There are people I can speak to, who might have seen him, might have some idea where he is.'

Nergui wondered whether he should be calling back to headquarters, getting officers out trying to round up some of these contacts, ready for their return. But he was worried that any sudden flurry of activity might drive Badzar to ground long before they arrived. At the same time, he could not guess at the possible implications of any delay. In the circumstances, the prospect of a four-hour drive through the night was not an attractive one.

In the event the drive was even worse than he had anticipated. There was only a single route from here to the city – it could hardly be dignified with the title of road – composed from years of horse and motorised traffic pounding down the hard earth. It was badly rutted along its length, the ground broken and pitted, and Doripalam had to drive carefully, peering into the light of the headlamps, to avoid being caught in any of the larger holes. In the darkness, it was impossible to gain any more speed, and Nergui found the slowness of their pace increasingly frustrating.

He sat in the back of the vehicle with Cholon. Cholon was chewing his fingers, looking anxious, with no evidence now of the superficial confidence with which he had greeted them earlier. It was as if he had been hiding some truth from himself, and now could no longer pretend.

'What do you know about the killings?' Nergui said. He was still trying to piece together the story in his mind, wanting to understand why Cholon should have harboured these suspicions. This could all, he thought, just be nonsense – evidence perhaps of Cholon's disturbed state of mind rather than his brother's. Perhaps they were merely chasing phantoms, in this endless, dream-like passage through the empty night.

'Only what I have seen in the newspapers. They get brought to us out here, though usually a few days old. I saw the story about the Westerner killed in the hotel but didn't think much about it. It seemed a world away. I saw he was working for the mining companies which didn't surprise me. It is a corrupt world.'

Nergui listened, feeling every bump in the interminable road. 'And you read about Delgerbayar's killing?'

'That was when I first began to wonder – I saw the picture of the policeman in the newspaper. I wasn't certain – just as I still wasn't when you showed his photograph to me – but I thought he was one of those who had visited the camps. And by this time I knew the stories of the attacks out here. So I began to wonder – I had seen the way that Badzar looked when I had last seen him. I was not surprised when you turned up.'

'But you have no real grounds for suspecting that your brother is . . . involved in this?'

Cholon shrugged. 'No, of course not. But I know my brother. We were close. I would not be here – I would not be betraying my brother – if I did not feel that something was dreadfully wrong.'

Nergui sat back in his seat, watching the ceaseless passing of the rough terrain outside, just visible in the car lights. 'You know there have been other killings?'

Cholon turned to Nergui, his mouth open. 'Other killings? The same as the two I read about?'

'We do not know. Some of them have similar characteristics.'

'Characteristics? What do you mean?'

Nergui paused, unsure how to take this forward. If Cholon was being honest – and there was no reason to assume that he wasn't – it was difficult to know how much of the truth he could bear. 'The details do not matter,' he said. 'Let us just say that these were not straightforward killings.'

Cholon looked at him as though about to ask a question. 'I do not need to know,' he said. 'I do not know any more what Badzar might be capable of. I do not want to know.'

'There have been a number of killings,' Nergui said. 'Three more in the city, as well as Delgerbayar and the Westerner, Ransom. Possibly connected. We do not know for sure. And there were two more murders down in the south, in a camp near Dalandzadgad. The last two were different, and we have a suspect who is not your brother. But we think there might be a link.'

'I don't understand.'

Nergui laughed mirthlessly. 'Neither do we. Not at all. The common thread here is mining, mineral production, probably gold. That is the only factor that may link the killings, if they are linked at all. I do not know if your brother is involved. If he is, I do not know if he is the sole perpetrator of these killings.'

'And I thought you were omniscient.'

'At the moment, I would settle for knowing just one thing, anything, about this case with certainty.'

The truck rumbled on, Doripalam still silent, leaning forward over the steering wheel as he peered into the sparse light from the headlamps, occasionally twisting the wheel jerkily to avoid a pothole. It was as if they were suspended in time, as if the awful reality outside the vehicle did not exist.

'There is one thing more,' Nergui said at last.

'What?'

'There is a police officer, a detective, sent over from England. He came to investigate the death of Ransom, the Westerner.' Nergui stopped, suddenly realising the weight of fear that lay in his heart. 'He has gone missing.'

'Missing? How can a visiting policeman go missing?'

'How could one of our own senior officers be brutally murdered? None of this makes sense. All we know is that the officer was walking from the British Embassy to his hotel late last night. And that he never got there.'

'And you think—?'

'It is like everything else in this case. We do not know what to think. But we have to fear the worst.'

'I cannot – I do not know what to say.'

'You will appreciate,' Nergui said, 'that this is no longer simply a police matter, if it ever was. This will become a major diplomatic issue. I do not know what the outcome will be. But, whatever it is, we need to resolve it quickly. Do you think you can trace your brother?'

'I don't know. There are people he may have gone to. Places he might be. But it is all guesswork. I don't even know for sure that he is in the city.'

It was becoming hopeless, Nergui thought. He was losing whatever touch he might once have had. The plodding methodical police work was going on in the background, but seemingly going nowhere, and still managing to miss the few things that might be important. And here he was, rushing off on pointless wild goose chases, desperate for anything that might give him a lead, clutching at any straw. But he was surely experienced enough to know that such leads were almost always illusory. He could almost feel this lead melting away as he reached for it. And increasingly his judgement seemed flawed. Perhaps he should have stayed up at the mine, spoken to more people, tried to find out precisely what it was that Delgerbayar had been up to. Instead, he had gone racing back to the city, for what? Someone who might have nothing to do with all this, and who could be anywhere. It was madness.

And underneath all that, he realised, as the truck rumbled on through the night, was something else, something that was driving him on into this insanity. It was the feeling, deep down in his bones, that Drew was still alive but that, unless Nergui could find some means of playing against the most extreme odds, he would not be alive for much longer.

Blackness. Emptiness.

He had no idea how long he had been here. Even with the return of consciousness, time seemed to have stopped. The sensations that should have given him some sense of progression – hunger, thirst, the aching of his body – seemed to have been suspended. He was aware of the hard surface beneath him, and of the imprisoning bands around his ankles, wrists and neck, but it was as if he were somehow detached from this reality.

Even the horror that had overwhelmed him when he had first realised his position had, for the moment at least, abated. Something – psychological, physiological, he did not know – had calmed his mind, allowed him to think rationally.

It was insane. The whole thing was insane. Why should anyone attack him? Why had he been brought here, wherever this might be? Why should anyone want to imprison him?

Was this a kidnapping? His policeman's mind was working automatically now, suppressing the fear, thinking back to his negotiator training, trying to work through the possible scenarios, the potential options available to him.

If this was a professional kidnapping, perhaps politically motivated, then his chances of survival and release were much higher. There would be some demand which the authorities might or might not be able to concede. There would be some form of negotiation. His survival would be guaranteed for a time, as the kidnappers would not lightly sacrifice their only bargaining counter. Perversely it was encouraging that so far he had been kept, literally, in the dark. If his kidnappers did not allow him to see their faces or have any information, they would have nothing to fear from his eventual release. Professionals, he reminded himself, whatever their motives might be, did not like to kill unnecessarily.

If the kidnappers were just small-time crooks who were aiming too high, his future was highly uncertain. If things became too difficult, they would simply want to cut their losses and get out. And central to cutting their losses, he realised, would be his own elimination.

Suddenly, the real panic struck him, blasting chills through his body like an icy wind. He arched his back, pushing and pulling against the ties that held his limbs, struggling and struggling and struggling, unable to make any headway. And then all his detachment collapsed, and he was nothing more than a mindless frenzy of wrestling bones and blood, as he felt himself lost in the blackness, falling into the worst nightmare he had ever known.

The end came equally suddenly. There was a sharp searing light, burning into his brain. He screwed his eyes shut tight, and the light was red, as hot as the sun, agonising in its brilliance, like hot wires against his eyeballs. He had no breath to scream any more, and all he felt was a desperate longing for the previous cool darkness. If that had been his death, then surely now he was entering the outer realms of hell.

But then his beating heart calmed, and the pain in his eyes and his head lessened. He still could not see, but he registered that this brilliance was nothing more than light, ordinary light. Black dots and shapes danced in the crimson brilliance, gradually settling back into order.

At last, after what might have been hours, he found himself able to move his eyes. His eyelids remained shut, and he realised that fear had rendered them immobile. Partly it was fear of the brilliance of the light. Mostly, though, it was fear of what sights might greet him when he was able to see again.

He forced himself to try to relax, to breathe more steadily, suppress his sense of panic. And finally he was able, very slowly, to open his eyes.

The sight that met them was unexpectedly banal. Above him, the source of the searing light, were four bright fluorescent strip lights set on wooden beams.

Turning his head as far as he could, he could see concrete walls, metal shelving. Cardboard boxes with incomprehensible labels. Some items of anonymous industrial equipment, shaded with dust. A storeroom of some kind.

He was lying on a wooden bench, maybe a work bench. He twisted his head a little more, stretching his muscles to their limits to try to see his arms. His wrists were tied with plastic twine, coiled repeatedly around, fastened underneath the bench itself. His ankles and neck were presumably tied in the same way. He turned his head as far as he could. A water bottle – the kind used by cyclists and runners – had been taped to the bench beside his mouth enabling him to reach the nozzle. He twisted his head and, with considerable discomfort, managed to suck down some of the water.

The room was silent. He stopped moving and tried to listen. At first, he could detect no sound of any movement, other than the seemingly deafening beating of his own heart and the rasp of his own panicked breathing.

He forced himself to hold his breath for a moment, listening hard. And finally he thought he heard it, like an irregular echo of his own heartbeat. It was the soft but insistent sound of another's breath. He tried to lift his head but it was impossible. All he could see were the beams, the lights, the concrete walls.

But somewhere outside the constrained field of his vision, someone was watching him.

SEVENTEEN

By the time they reached the outskirts of the city, it had started to snow, thick flakes whirling in the glare of the streetlights. There had been some flurries earlier in the week, but this was the first serious snow of the winter. Perhaps it was as well they had travelled back when they did. Being stranded on the steppes in this weather would not be pleasant.

It was nearly one a.m., and the streets were deserted. For the first time, Nergui found the emptiness unnerving. Against the brilliance of the settling snow, the gloom of the unlit sidestreets seemed threatening. Nergui felt uncomfortable until they pulled into the enclosed car park at the rear of the police headquarters. Even then, he looked uneasily behind him as they bundled out of the truck and hurried through the snow to the entrance.

Inside, it was warm and reassuringly prosaic. There were one or two officers on duty, but most were lounging in the rest room, sipping coffee. Nergui led them through and up the stairs to his office. It was only once he was in there, settled behind his desk, with Doripalam and Cholon sitting opposite, that he finally felt fully secure.

What was happening to him? He had been doing this job, or something like it, for most of his adult life. He had a reputation for fearlessness. He was in the police building, surrounded by high-level security and staff who would jump at his every whim. And yet here he was, behaving like a skulking rookie, terrified of his own shadow.

For much of the journey there had been no network signal on his mobile. The networks were good in the cities and towns, but much more sporadic out in the countryside. As they had re-entered the city limits, his mobile had bleeped obligingly to let him know that there were messages for him. He gestured to the others to go and get coffees for the three of them, then sat down to listen to the messages.

The first, inevitably, was from the Minister. 'Nergui, I don't know where you are,' he said, an edge of threat in his voice. 'I'm trusting that you know what you're doing. But things are starting to get seriously out of hand here. I'm stalling the British government as best I can, but I can't put them off for long. We need some answers, and we need them quick. Call me when you get in. Whatever time that is.'

Nergui looked at his watch. One fifteen. He knew from experience that the lateness of the hour would be no excuse for failing to contact the Minister. He wasn't sure, though, that he had anything to report.

The second message, equally predictably, was from the British ambassador. 'Nergui,' he said in English, 'I've been trying to get hold of that bloody Minister of yours. Seems to be permanently in meetings.' Clearly, Nergui thought, the Minister was following the ambassador's own example. 'I know the Foreign Office is in direct contact with him now, but I'd like an update. Nobody's telling me anything—' Even in these circumstances, it was difficult not to be amused by the plaintive tone. 'Give me a call in the morning, Nergui. I really want to know what's going on.'

That was one, at least, that could be safely left. Nergui waited, and listened to the third message. It was a voice he recognised. Batzorig. 'Sir. You're probably out of mobile range at the moment – don't know exactly where you are. Can you give me a call as soon as you pick this up? I'm not sure, but it might be urgent. We've had a message left for us that I think you ought to—'

Nergui thumbed off the phone and jumped to his feet. In seconds, he was out of the door and jumping, three steps at a time, down the stairs to the rest room. He burst into the room, banging back the door. The three officers sitting drinking coffee looked up in surprise. Doripalam and Cholon were at the far end of the room.

'Where's Batzorig?' Nergui said.

'I think he's upstairs, in his office. He said to tell you—'

'So why didn't you?'

The officers looked confused. 'Well, he didn't say exactly—'

'Forget it.'

Nergui turned on his heel and stormed out of the room and then back up the stairs. Batzorig's office was at the rear of the building, down the corridor from Nergui's own. It was a large room he shared with three other officers, though he was the only one currently on duty.

He looked up from his desk as Nergui pushed open the door, and jumped to his feet. 'Sir,' he said. 'Did you get my message?'

'Just a few minutes ago.' Nergui sat himself heavily down opposite Batzorig. 'What is it?'

'Well, it may be nothing, sir. But we received a message this evening. Just came through on the out-of-hours line, and I happened to pick it up.'

'What sort of message?'

'Well, I was able to record most of it, sir.' There was a facility for recording all incoming calls, no doubt a legacy from the days when surveillance was more commonplace, but still useful nonetheless. 'As soon as I realised it might be important. I changed the tape so there was no danger of it being recorded over.'

'Very good,' Nergui nodded. Why was it that all these young officers felt the need to try to impress him? Had he been the same in his younger days? He feared that he probably had.

Batzorig held up the tape and slipped it into a cassette player he had set up on the desk. He had obviously been preparing carefully for Nergui's return.

For the first few seconds after he pressed the play button, there was nothing but the faint hiss of the turning tape. Then suddenly a voice, low and sibilant, cut in. '—Have something that might interest you. It may be possible to arrange its safe return. But this will require co-operation. I will call again at nine a.m. tomorrow.' There was the sound of Batzorig trying to extract some more information from the caller, but it was clear that the caller had already hung up.

'What time did this come in?' Nergui said.

Batzorig consulted his notes carefully. 'Just after ten,' he said. 'Seven minutes past, to be exact.'

Nergui nodded. He wondered whether the caller had known he was out, had seen him leave with Doripalam. Had, perhaps, also seen him return.

He looked up at Batzorig. 'Go and fetch the man I brought in. He'll be with Doripalam, either in my office or down in the rest room.'

Batzorig hurried to do Nergui's bidding. Nergui sat, staring in silence at the tape machine. Then he leaned forward and pressed the play button again. He heard the same words: '—Have something that might interest you. It may be possible to arrange its safe return. But this will require co-operation. I will call again at nine a.m. tomorrow.'

It could be a hoax, of course. It was likely to be a hoax, in fact. Drew's disappearance had now been reported in the media, so they could expect their fair share of lunatic calls over the coming days. But something told Nergui that it was, at least, worth taking seriously. It didn't sound like a crank call – too short, too deliberate, too little desire to make an impression. There was something about the tone that unnerved him, a sense of emptiness, of uncaring.

The door opened and Batzorig returned, followed by Doripalam and Cholon. Nergui gestured Cholon to sit. The others hesitated, unsure whether they were part of this, but then came in and closed the door behind them.

'Listen to this,' Nergui said. 'Do you recognise the voice?' He had no desire to lead Cholon, but his question could mean only one thing.

He played the tape again, listening intently himself to the repeated words.

'—Have something that might interest you. It may be possible to arrange its safe return. But this will require co-operation. I will call again at nine a.m. tomorrow.'

Cholon looked at the tape machine. 'You mean is it Badzar?'

Nergui nodded, watching Cholon closely. He was still unsure how far Cholon could be trusted to give an honest response about his brother.

'Can you play it again?'

Nergui pressed the play button once more. He could recite the words verbatim by now, but they were still telling him nothing.

Cholon shook his head. 'I don't know. It could be. It could well be. But I can't be sure.'

Nergui played the tape yet again. The voice was obviously being disguised in some way – the deep timbre, the

244

odd sibilance. But it did not sound as if it was being artificially distorted, other than by the phone itself.

'There's not much to go on,' Nergui conceded.

Cholon stared at the tape player, as if the answer would emerge from the machine itself. 'It's no good,' he said. 'I can't be sure. It doesn't sound like him, but there's something about it. Maybe I just don't want to believe it's him.'

'Well, all we can do is wait until the morning. See if they call again.' Nergui looked up at Doripalam and Batzorig. 'We shouldn't make too much of this. It could well be a hoax.'

He looked back at Cholon. 'If your brother is in the city, we need to find him. Do you have any idea where he might go if he came back here?'

'There are a few people he might go to, at least to try to get somewhere to stay. Old friends from university days.'

'Are they contactable by phone?'

'Most of them, yes, though I've only got the numbers of a few. They're generally working for the government, these days.' He smiled wryly. 'I'm not sure whether that's selling out or not.'

Nergui looked at his watch. 'It's late, but we can't waste time. Can you start phoning round? We'll probably get a better response if you do it, rather than making it an official police call.'

'I'm not sure you'll get a particularly good response to any call at this time of night.'

'We can't afford to wait till morning. We'll work with you. Maybe if you tell them that your brother's gone missing, that you're afraid he might be ill—'

'He has. I am,' Cholon said. 'Otherwise I wouldn't be here.'

Doripalam led Cholon into another office where they

could begin the process of telephoning. Nergui didn't have high hopes of any result, but it was the only place to start. Batzorig excused himself with an offer to fetch the coffee that was presumably still waiting for Nergui downstairs.

Nergui looked at his watch. Nearly two. He couldn't put off ringing the Minister any longer. He had a suspicion that the Minister genuinely didn't sleep. No matter what time Nergui called, there was never any sense that he had been woken or disturbed by the call.

Nergui dialled the number, wondering what further ways he could find of articulating that, no, there was still nothing of any substance to report. The Minister's phone rang at the other end of the line, but there was no answer. In Nergui's experience, this was almost unprecedented. The Minister usually turned his phone off in the presence of the President, but there were few other exceptions to his rule of constant availability. After a few seconds, the voicemail cut in and he heard the Minister requesting him to leave his message after the tone. Nergui simply gave his name, noted the time, and invited the Minister to call back when he was free. He ended the call, feeling an absurd mixture of relief that he hadn't had to endure yet another content-free discussion with the Minister, and concern about what the Minister might actually be doing.

Before Nergui could allow himself the luxury of worrying further, Doripalam stuck his head round the door. 'We've got something,' he said.

'Really?' Nergui had not been expecting any serious results from the calls, let alone so quickly.

Doripalam nodded. 'Cholon started with the most likely candidates. The real old friends. Struck lucky almost straightaway.'

'What's the story?'

'Couple who were at university with Cholon and Badzar. Same year as Badzar. He's a civil servant, she works for the tourist agency. They've got a small flat near the centre. Badzar just turned up, a few days ago, apparently, out of the blue, said he needed somewhere to stay until he was able to rent somewhere. They hadn't seen him for years, but put him up. Stayed a couple of nights, then disappeared.'

'I presume their night has been well and truly disturbed by now,' Nergui said. 'Let's get over there and see if there's anything more they can tell us.'

'Do you want Cholon?'

Nergui hesitated. 'Might be as well,' he said. 'They might speak more openly with him there.'

Nergui grabbed his coat and hurried back down the stairs. Doripalam went to fetch Cholon, and the three of them met at the entrance to the car park. The snow was coming down thicker than ever, the sky lost in the swirl of flakes. Already, since their return, an inch or two had settled on the truck.

'I carried on calling,' Cholon said. 'Managed to lose a few friends in the process, probably. But no one else had seen him. Most hadn't seen him for years.'

'But we know he's here now,' Doripalam said. 'We know he's in the city.'

Nergui shivered, telling himself it was due only to the blast of cold air that hit him as he stepped out into the night. The snow was coming down heavily, and the concrete underfoot was already becoming hazardous.

They climbed into the truck, Doripalam driving, and pulled back out into the city streets.

'Take it carefully,' Nergui said. 'We don't want to write off a police vehicle on top of all our other problems.'

The roads were icy but Doripalam drove skilfully.

Snow was a familiar problem and there were already snow ploughs and gritters out in the city, so the main roads were relatively accessible. By morning, much of the worst of the snow would have been cleared. The biggest problem was the lack of visibility. Doripalam peered forwards into the drifting snow, trying to spot any other vehicles that might be on the road. But, apart from the occasional snow-clearing lorry, the streets were deserted.

The flat was just a few minutes' drive away. It was part of a long, low-rise tenement, built of looming grey concrete overlooking a small park. Most of the building was in darkness, apart from two or three windows, one of which, Nergui assumed, was their destination.

They parked by the roadside, and Nergui led the way into the dimly lit entrance lobby, which to his surprise was unlocked with no sign of any security staff or concierge.

'Flat 23,' Cholon said, from behind.

They made their way up the stairs to the first floor and along the dark corridor till they found Flat 23. Nergui knocked loudly. After a few moments, the door opened and a short, harassed-looking man peered out. He looked at them carefully for a few minutes as though deciding whether to welcome them or not. They he recognised Cholon and nodded, with a half smile.

'Come in,' he said. 'But please be quiet. The baby is asleep. She is easily disturbed.'

They followed the man into a small, neatly furnished living room. A woman, presumably his wife, was sitting on the sofa, looking nervous. Nergui stepped forward, his presence filling the small room. 'Thank you, Mr—'

'Oyon,' the man said. 'And my wife, Odyal.'

'I am sorry that we have to disturb you. Please be

assured that we would not unless it was very important.'

'I don't understand,' Oyon said. 'I thought that
Cholon was looking for his brother—'

'That is correct,' Nergui said.

'But I don't understand why the police—'

Nergui held up his hand. 'It's a long story, and we
don't need to bother you with most of it. But Badzar has
gone missing and we have reason to believe that he may
be very ill. We are trying to trace him as a matter of
urgency.'

Oyon frowned, as though trying to make sense of this
information. It was clear that he realised that more lay
behind this simple statement, but he also recognised that
there was little point in pursuing it. 'I don't know if I can
help you very much,' he said at last.

'When did you last see Badzar?'

Oyon looked across at his wife. 'Just the other day. He
turned up unexpectedly. Out of the blue.'

'You had seen him before that? Recently, I mean?'

Oyon shook his head. 'Not for years. I mean, we spent
some time with Badzar and Cholon after university,
when we were all working here. But we lost touch
when—' He looked up at Cholon, suddenly embarrassed.

Cholon smiled. 'We lost touch with everyone then. We
were closer to you than to most. At least we exchanged
the occasional letter. I kept meaning to visit you, but I
never came back to the city.'

'So it was a surprise when he turned up?' Nergui said.

'A complete surprise. A bit of a shock really. I mean, it
was good to see him. Or at least it would have been—'

Odyal intervened: 'He seemed like a different person.
I would not have believed that it was the Badzar we used
to know.'

'Different in what way?'

'Well—' She looked awkwardly at Cholon. 'I don't know when you last saw your brother, Cholon—'

'Only a short while before he came here. A few weeks ago.'

'Perhaps he had changed over the years. Perhaps it would not have been evident to you?'

Cholon shook his head. 'No. It was obvious to me, too. These changes had come about only in recent months. When I saw him again, he was . . . very different.'

'At first, I was not even sure that it was really him,' Oyon said. 'He had aged – I mean, we have all aged but he looked much older than he should. He looked . . . disturbed in some way. I wondered about drugs. I was worried about his health so I am not surprised that you say he is ill—'

'His illness is not a physical one, I think,' Cholon said softly.

'You mean that he is—' Oyon glanced at his wife, and then at the door leading into the baby's bedroom. It was clear that he was wondering just what sort of person they had been harbouring, why the police should now be interested in Badzar's whereabouts.

'We believe that Badzar may have had some sort of breakdown,' Nergui said, smoothly. 'We are concerned for his welfare. It would help us if you could tell us as much as you can about his visit here. Anything he said. Any indication of where he might be going.'

Oyon sat back in his chair. 'Well, let me think. He turned up the other night, Tuesday it must have been. Quite late, about nine. As I say, completely out of the blue. The doorbell rang, and when I answered it, there he was. He was dressed in clothes that looked . . . well, unsuitable for the time of year. A thin shirt, a jacket, no coat. He was carrying a small bag, a holdall. That was all. I suppose I must have stared at him at first, wondering who he was, because he said: "It's me. Don't you remember? Badzar." And, of course, as soon as he said that, I knew who he was, though I could still hardly recognise him. He looked so different from the person I knew.'

'And what did he say?' Nergui prompted.

'He said he'd returned to the city on some business. I mean, we knew the story, how you—' He nodded towards Cholon. '—how you had returned to the steppes with your father. But we knew very little else. He didn't explain what his business was, and, well, I didn't like to enquire.'

'You thought it was something criminal?'

'Well, no, not really criminal. But I knew that he had had to make ends meet as best he could, so it would not have surprised me if he had been involved in some things that were . . . dubious. As a government employee, I thought it was best not to know.'

'What else did he say?'

'Not much. He said he'd arranged to stay in the city for a few weeks and had organised some lodgings. But there'd been some sort of administrative mix-up and they wouldn't be available for a day or two. So he was throwing himself on our mercy, as it were.'

'Did you believe him?'

Oyon frowned. 'I'm not sure. I mean, it was a plausible enough story as far as it went. It seemed a bit odd that he should have made these arrangements but then had nowhere else to go other than to people he'd not seen for ten years. But Badzar was never the most conventional of individuals.'

'So you let him stay?'

'Of course. What else could we have done? I mean, as

you can see, we've hardly any room here, so all we could do was offer him the sofa, but that was okay for a day or two. We brought him in – gave him a meal, shared a few glasses of vodka. He relaxed a bit after that, seemed more his old self. We talked a bit about the old days. He was happy enough talking about university, but I had the impression that he didn't want to talk about what had happened after that.'

'And he didn't give you any clues as to his business in town?'

'Not at all. I mean, he wasn't obviously secretive about it. But it never came up, and, as I say, I didn't want to enquire.'

'And how long did he stay?'

'Just two nights. We didn't see much of him, to be honest. We saw him on Wednesday morning, as we went off to work. The baby goes to Odyal's mother when she's working. We gave him a key, and I had the impression he was out most of the day. We got back around six. He reappeared a bit later than that. We had another meal. He'd brought a bottle of vodka, so we had a bit more of that, and that was really it. He didn't give us the impression he was going to be going the next day, but again he was around till we'd gone off to work. When we got back, he wasn't here and the key had been left on the table there. We weren't sure whether to expect him back, but he never reappeared. To be honest, we were slightly annoyed that he hadn't bothered to come back to say goodbye. But, as I say, Badzar was always unpredictable.'

Nergui nodded. 'And he gave you no clues about where he was going?'

Oyon frowned. 'Nothing very clear. I had the impression that it was somewhere nearby.'

Nergui leaned forward. 'Why do you say that?'

'I'm not sure.' Oyon looked across to his wife for assistance. 'It was something about the way he talked on that second night. We'd had a few drinks. It was all a bit more relaxed than it had been, though Badzar still seemed pretty tense. He was saying something about his journey here. He hitched a lift with some truck driver part of the way. Had everything set up here but then – what were his words? – there had been developments. I think that was how he described it. So he couldn't imme- diately move in where he'd planned. And he found himself on our doorstep—'

'That was it,' Odyal said. 'It was the way he said it. Almost, well, insulting. The impression he gave was that it wasn't so much that he'd been keen to see us after ten years, but that he didn't know where else to go and we were the nearest people he knew. We'd drunk a bit so I didn't really take it in, but I can remember feeling a bit irritated by the way he spoke.'

'I think he realised what he'd said,' Oyon said. 'He'd drunk more than we had – was on the way to being drunk, really. He apologised a bit, said he'd not meant it to sound like that – that he'd actually come out of his way specially to see us. But I don't think I really believed him.'

It was an interesting question, Nergui thought. Had Badzar started apologising because he was concerned he'd insulted old friends, or was it because he was worried he'd given something away about his proposed whereabouts?

'Is there anything else you can think of?' Nergui said. 'Anything else he might have said? Any other impres- sions you formed? Even the most fleeting thought or idea might be useful to us.'

'I don't think so,' Oyon said. 'As I say, he didn't talk at all about why he was here or what his business was. It was obviously something that was ... I don't know, urgent, important to him. He seemed keyed up the whole time he was here. As if he was keen to be getting on with whatever it was he was having to delay.'

'Did he seem threatened?' Doripalam said. 'I mean, was there any sense that he was being pursued or that someone was looking for him?'

Oyon looked blankly at Doripalam. 'I don't know. Is that why you're looking for him?'

Nergui shook his head. 'We've no reason to believe he's in trouble. But we don't know why he's come to the city in this way. We don't know what he might be involved with. We're just trying to piece the picture together.'

Oyon and Odyal were looking at each other, both clearly wondering what it was they had become entangled with. 'I don't know,' Oyon said. 'I mean, he looked tense, as I've said, and unwell. But I didn't really get the impression that he was afraid. It was more that he was – I don't know – involved in some task that was proving challenging or demanding, maybe more than he'd expected. I can't put it any better than that.'

'You've been very helpful,' Nergui said. 'I'm sorry if this has been an ordeal for you. And again I'm sorry for disturbing you at this time. We would not have done it if it hadn't been important. I'm sure you understand that.'

'Of course, of course. I hope we've been of assistance.' Oyon might have appreciated the importance of their visit, but he was also clearly very keen to get them out of the flat. It was evident that this was a visit that he wanted to put behind him.

'I'm sorry we've had to put you through this,' Cholon added. 'And I'm sorry if Badzar has caused you any difficulties. It would be good to come back again in different circumstances.'

Oyon was ushering them gently but firmly towards the door. 'It's always good to see you, Cholon. I'm sorry we've been out of touch for so long. Please, you're welcome here any time.'

But, Nergui thought, there was little sincerity in his voice.

EIGHTEEN

Outside, the snow was falling faster and thicker than ever. It was scarcely possible to see to the far side of the road, and there were already heavy drifts against the walls of the tenement block behind them. Nergui glanced at his watch. Three fifteen. He had left his phone switched on during the visit to the flat in case the Minister should call back, but so far there had been no calls.

The three men bundled into the truck, and Doripalam started the engine and turned the car around. The wheels were gripping but only just. If the snow continued, they would need snow chains until the roads were cleared.

'Back to HQ?' Doripalam said.

Nergui hesitated for a moment, and then nodded. An idea was beginning to form in his mind, coalescing around Oyon's final comments about Badzar's possible whereabouts. Perhaps it was possible that Badzar was really close at hand. Nergui looked back down the snow-filled street, his mind racing.

'Yes. For the moment.'

Doripalam pulled back out into the road, and made his way cautiously back to HQ. At each corner, Nergui could feel the wheels sliding, as Doripalam battled to keep control. It was a night to be indoors. But Nergui had an increasing feeling that their activities were only just beginning.

As they turned slowly back into the HQ car park, Nergui's mobile rang. He thumbed the call button.

'Nergui. It's me.' The Minister, of course.

'Minister. You called earlier, I think.'

'Where are you, Nergui?'

'Just arriving back at HQ. It's early days, but we might have a lead.'

'Excellent.' The Minister sounded unexpectedly distracted, as if somehow his thoughts had already moved on from the murders. 'Look, Nergui, I need to see you. Urgently.'

'Now, Minister? But—' But what? It was only at that moment that Nergui realised that, in some dark corner of his mind, he had already begun planning other activities for the rest of the night, that he was already beginning to pursue a half-formed idea.

'Now, Nergui. As soon as you can get here. I have some things I need to discuss.'

This did not sound good, but Nergui was past caring about the Minister's political positioning, even if this meant that he might end up as the sacrifice on this occasion. He looked at his watch. Three thirty.

'How soon can you get here, Nergui? I'm in my office.'

'I'll come immediately. The snow's awful. Maybe ten or fifteen minutes.'

'Make it ten.' As always, the call ended abruptly.

Nergui turned to Doripalam. 'I've got to see the Minister. I'll be an hour, no more. I've got an idea I want to follow up. I may be wasting everyone's time but we can't afford to delay. We should get snow chains put on the truck if we're going out again.'

Doripalam nodded. 'And I take it we are going out again?' There was a note of irritation in his voice.

'Trust me, Doripalam. I'm not keeping any secrets here. I've just got a hunch. I'll explain when I get back, though it's probably too half-baked to waste anyone else's time on other than my own. But I would be grateful for your support.'

Doripalam looked at the older man for a second, then nodded. He twisted in his seat and looked at Cholon. 'I should organise you some accommodation.'

'What you're planning,' Cholon said to Nergui. 'Is this about my brother?'

'It may be.'

'In that case, can I be part of it?'

Nergui looked at Doripalam, who shrugged. Nergui said: 'I don't know what's involved and I don't know what kind of risk we might be talking about. And we can never afford passengers. So we'd be insane to let you come.'

'I understand.'

'But I think we're past the point of sanity on this. I don't know what we're doing any more. Chasing phantoms. So, yes, if you want to chase some phantoms with us, you can come. But do exactly what I tell you. I may be going mad, but I'm not completely reckless.'

Nergui climbed out of the truck and slammed the door behind him. He watched as Doripalam and Cholon trudged slowly into the building. Then he pulled his coat around him and began to walk through the billowing snow towards the Ministry building.

After the impenetrable darkness, now incessant light.

Slowly, as he lay there, he had begun to regain a sense of his own body, the belief that movement was possible, that he was still alive.

He struggled at first, pulling against the bonds that held his wrists and ankles. But there was no give, no shifting of the cords that held him, only the burning pressure of the ropes against his skin. He was held firmly, tied with professional skill to the wooden bench.

The blind panic that had overwhelmed him in the

darkness had passed now, but the terror remained. Somebody had done this to him. Someone was waiting, perhaps somewhere in this very room. Something, eventually, would happen.

There was something surreal about his predicament. Trapped, held by an unseen and unknown assailant, in a brightly lit industrial building. Moments went by when he really didn't believe it, when he half-expected to wake from a dream or somehow find that it was all an elaborate hoax. Then the reality hit him again, and fear chilled his heart. And at that point the silence would become the biggest threat of all, building around him like a tangible object, taking his breath from him. And he listened, straining his ears, waiting for whatever would happen next.

It was a long walk across Sukh Bataar Square, pushing against the buffeting of the strong winds and the frozen blast of the snow. The Square was silent and snow-covered, the statues shapeless under the gathering drifts. The snowstorm had settled in thickly now, and even the snowploughs and gritting trucks appeared to have given up on their work.

In normal conditions, the Ministry buildings were a five-minute walk away, on the far side of the square. Tonight, he had already been walking for ten minutes and still had some way to go. He pulled his shapeless old trilby down over his eyes, and his thick winter coat more tightly around him, and trudged on through the deepening snow.

As he walked, he wrestled with the thought that had begun to form during his interview with Oyon, putting his problems aside at least until he reached the Ministry, trying to work out the next steps in their search for Badzar.

Oyon, for whatever reason, had formed the impression that Badzar's destination was not far from Oyon's own flat. Nergui was inclined to trust that judgement. He had noted that Oyon seemed to be genuinely affronted that Badzar had turned up on his doorstep only because he was already in the neighbourhood.

Even it was true, there were still many places where Badzar could be holed up. There were numerous tenements around there, more concrete legacies of the old communist functionalism. Badzar could be staying with another contact, or could have rented a flat of his own, assuming he had the money to do so. More simply, there were also likely to be a number of unoccupied flats – those awaiting a change of tenant, even one or two blocks that were due for renovation or demolition under the government's continuing drive for renewal. Badzar could have broken into one of these.

But there was another possibility. The tenement block they had visited was on the edge of one of the industrial districts, close to where the concrete landscape of the city centre gave way to the sprawl of the *ger* encampments. In that area, there were some thriving businesses, some still state-owned, some the first fruits of burgeoning entrepreneurs. But, as throughout the city, there were many disused industrial units, left over from the period of economic madness when the country had adopted all the worst elements of free-market economics to disastrous effect.

And one of those disused units, only a half mile or so from Oyon's flat, was the factory where they had found Delgerbayar's body.

Was it simply a coincidence? After all, there were dozens of disused factories and warehouses across the city. Even if Badzar was holed up in one of them, why should it be that one? Surely he would not risk lingering around an area where the police had been engaged in a large-scale investigation.

Except, of course, that that could be precisely the point. There had been a tendency throughout this case to disregard the obvious because it was seen as irrelevant. They had thought nothing of Delgerbayar's intended visit to the illegal prospectors because it had appeared to be a red herring, just another part of the routine pattern of his life. So maybe this was similar. They had assumed that the location where Delgerbayar's body was found was simply a convenient stage set. It was just one of many large empty buildings, isolated from any domestic dwellings, with a suitably intimidating entrance and an appropriate setting for the body to be found. Nergui had had no doubt that the killer had chosen it with some care to maximise the impact of their find. But they had all assumed by the time the police reached the building, the killer would have been long gone.

They had searched the building rigorously, and subjected it to forensic testing where there appeared to be the possibility of finding any material or data potentially linked to the killer, but they had found nothing. There was no sign that the building had been occupied, other than by the spectacularly positioned corpse of Delgerbayar.

But Nergui had been working through the timescales in his mind. The day that they had found Delgerbayar's body was the same day that Badzar had appeared unexpectedly on Oyon's doorstep. Was it possible that, having committed the murder, he had set up the body as they had found it, and then moved to lie low with his former acquaintances for a few days?

He shook his head, leaning forward into the wind and snow, treading cautiously to maintain his footing. It was a ridiculous idea. Why would Badzar simply turn up unannounced? Wouldn't he have made some arrangements beforehand, arranged some safe place to stay? But that might be the reason. If Badzar was involved in this, he was leaving no pre-arranged trail, no plans, even assuming that his actions were premeditated at all. Oyon and Odyal would recall his turning up with some surprise, perhaps, but they had commented on his unpredictability. Under pressure from the Ministry, the story of Delgerbayar's murder had been suppressed and only limited information had been reported in the media, as Badzar could have predicted. There was no reason why Oyon and Odyal should have made any connection between Badzar's appearance and the murder.

Still musing on the implications of this, Nergui finally reached the anonymous concrete block that housed the Ministry of Security. The building was almost in darkness at that time of the night, lights showing in only a few windows. The front doors were locked, but Nergui had a key. He unlocked the door, struggling slightly with his gloved hands, and then stepped inside, snapping the lock closed behind him.

After the icy chill of the night, the warmth of the building struck him immediately. A profligate use of the Ministry's resources, he thought. He made his way slowly up the stairs towards the Minister's office on the second floor.

Most of the offices here, including Nergui's own, were bleakly functional – bare tiled floors, grey-painted walls, metal desks and filing cabinets, chairs built for sturdiness rather than comfort. The Minister's office, inevitably, was different. Nergui was unsure where the Minister had obtained his furnishings, since they surpassed even those used by the senior apparatchiks in the old days.

There was a light shining under the Minister's door. Nergui knocked and waited, knowing from experience that the Minister liked to keep visitors waiting, if only for a few moments.

There was the expected pause, then he heard the Minister's voice. 'Come.'

He pushed open the door slowly, and stepped inside. To his surprise, the Minister was not alone. A grey-haired man sat facing him, his back to Nergui.

He turned in his chair as Nergui entered.

Nergui raised his eyebrows. 'Professor Wilson,' he said. 'This is a surprise.'

Wilson nodded. 'I was very sorry to hear about Chief Inspector McLeish,' he said. 'There is no more news?'

Nergui glanced briefly at the Minister. He had no idea why Wilson was here. He had understood that Wilson was not in the country in any kind of official capacity, but was merely accompanying his wife's research. Perhaps he was here to complain again about the lack of progress the police were making, particularly given Drew's disappearance. But it seemed unlikely he would be making an official complaint in the small hours of the morning. There was no helpful signal in the Minister's expression.

'Nothing we can make public, yet. There are some leads, but it's too early to say.'

'Are you assuming that Chief Inspector McLeish is—?' Wilson left the sentence hanging.

'We're assuming nothing,' Nergui said. 'I remain optimistic for the moment.'

Wilson nodded, clearly sceptical, but made no rejoinder. Nergui looked across at the Minister, wondering if he was going to offer any kind of explanation for Wilson's presence.

'You asked me to see you, sir?' Nergui was beginning

to find the situation irritating. There was no way of questioning the Minister's authority, but Nergui couldn't see why he was wasting time here when he needed to be getting on with the search for Badzar.

'You still don't seem to be making much progress, Nergui,' the Minister said in English.

'We have some leads, sir,' Nergui said. 'I appreciate the urgency. In fact, you took me away from a potential investigation to bring me here.' He presumed that the Minister had not just brought him over here to receive a public dressing-down.

'An investigation? What sort of investigation?'

Nergui glanced at Wilson. He had no intention of saying any more until he was at least clear why Wilson was here. 'We're tracking down someone who we believe may be able to help us with our enquiries.'

The Minister nodded. 'That is why I called you over, Nergui. Professor Wilson may also be able to, as you put it, help you with your enquiries.'

Without being asked – not always a wise action in the Minister's presence – Nergui sat down beside Wilson. 'Really? In what way?'

Wilson coughed. 'I'm afraid I was not entirely straight with you last night,' he said. 'My visit here is on a some-what more formal basis than I indicated.'

Nergui shot a glance at the Minister, who responded with a barely perceptible shrug.

'I understood that you were here to accompany your wife?'

'I allowed you to understand that. My wife's research is quite genuine, but it is not the primary reason I am here.'

Nergui was growing tired of the game-playing. 'I am sorry,' he said. 'It's been a long night already and I have much more to do. I don't particularly enjoy being lied to. I would be grateful if you could get to the point.'

The Minister looked for a moment as if he was about to intervene, then he sat back. Wilson went on: 'I told you that I worked for the British government. That much at least was true. I am here in that capacity.'

'In what capacity, exactly?' Nergui could feel anger rising. He was unsure where this conversation was going but he did not like the feel of it.

Wilson sighed slightly. 'As you may be aware, the UK government is one of the parties with an—' He paused as if seeking the appropriate word. 'An interest, I suppose, in the development of the gold fields in the south.'

Nergui looked from Wilson to the Minister, who was wearing his most accomplished blank expression. 'I wasn't aware that the UK government had any interest in the gold fields,' he said. 'My understanding was that a range of commercial businesses were involved.'

'That is correct. Our involvement is an indirect one.'

'I'm afraid,' Nergui said, 'I really don't understand what that means.'

Wilson nodded. 'I'm trying to express this as delicately as I can. My position is a difficult one.'

'I think so,' Nergui said, 'if you are in the country under false pretences.'

'Well—' Wilson hesitated, and for the first time looked slightly unsure of his ground. 'We will return to that, I'm sure. But let me try to explain my position. There is a substantial investment in the gold field development from a consortium of UK companies—'

'Along with substantial investment from a range of other international companies, I understand,' Nergui said.

'Quite so. This is an entirely commercial transaction.

The British government's role – my role, that is – has simply been to ensure that British interests are being protected.'

'Which explains why you're here. It doesn't explain why your presence is so covert.'

'We have had concerns about this project for some time,' Wilson said. 'In particular there has been some evidence of . . . well, tension between the partner organisations.'

Nergui had been aware from his own professional interest that the project in question had not been proceeding entirely smoothly. The identification and potential extraction of the gold reserves had been more problematic than had initially been envisaged. Increased investment had been required, and while the size of the potential returns was still unquestioned, the timescale for realising them had become increasingly uncertain. Further investment had been sought particularly from the Russians, and Nergui understood that relationships between the parties had become strained.

'I'm aware of some of that,' Nergui said.

'Were you aware that Mr Ransom was also involved in this project?'

Nergui sat forward in his chair. 'My understanding—' He glanced across at the Minister. 'Our understanding was that Ransom was working for one of the companies prospecting in the north.'

Wilson nodded. 'That is correct. But he was a freelancer. He'd recently been recruited – covertly, to use your word – to provide some advice to the consortium in the Gobi. Primarily, as I understand it, to validate some apparently suspect data being produced by one of the partner companies.'

'Were we aware of this?' Nergui asked the Minister.

The Minister gave a minute shake of his head. 'We

were not told,' he said. 'Ransom's visa was provided on the basis of his work in the north.'

Nergui turned to Wilson. 'So Mr Ransom was also acting illegally. Was the UK government aware of this?'

Wilson looked pained. 'We were not informed officially,' he said. 'But I can't pretend that we were entirely unaware. Mr Ransom had something of a reputation as a troubleshooter in such matters.'

'So are you telling us,' Nergui said, 'that Ransom's killing was in some way connected to the tensions you are talking about?'

Wilson shrugged. 'I honestly don't know. But it was Ransom's death that brought me out here. We didn't know what was behind it, but it set alarm bells ringing. I wanted to find out more about the state of play in the consortium. Make sure that our interests were protected.'

Nergui stared at him. He turned to the Minister. 'I take it we were not aware of this either? Or did you just decide not to share it with me?'

'Nergui,' the Minister said, 'we were aware of none of this. Of course I would not have kept this kind of information from you. Not in the circumstances.'

Nergui knew only too well that, in all circumstances, the Minister would share only what he chose to share. But it was difficult to believe that he would not have been open in this case.

'Which means,' Nergui said to Wilson, 'that you are also travelling illegally, in that you lied on your visa application about your reasons for entering the country.'

'Not entirely,' Wilson said. 'I indicated on my application that, although I was accompanying my wife on her research visit, I would also take the opportunity to consult with the ambassador and other UK representatives about trade matters. I just didn't specify the nature of the consultations.'

'Nergui,' the Minister said, 'I can see no point in raking over the question of whether Professor Wilson is here legally or not. I would have preferred a greater degree of openness, but that time is now past.'

'I had no intention to deceive,' Wilson said. 'I merely wanted my entry into the country to be as low-key as possible. I did not know – I still do not know for sure – what interests are involved here, and I wanted, as far as possible, to observe without being observed.'

'The fact remains,' Nergui said, 'that in effect you have withheld evidence that might have helped us progress more quickly in identifying Ransom's killer. Your information, at the very least, provides a possible motive for the murder, which to date has been missing.' He paused. 'If we'd been able to act more quickly, we might have prevented further murders. And,' he added, 'Chief Inspector McLeish might still be with us.'

Wilson nodded slowly. 'I know. I understand that. That's why I'm here. When I heard that the Chief Inspector was missing – well, I realised it was not appropriate for me to keep my silence any longer.'

Appropriate, Nergui thought. Brutal serial killings, a potential kidnap. And this man talks about what is appropriate.

'Let me be straight,' Wilson said. 'My concern is a simple one. Some of the interests involved in the project are, I believe, dangerous ones. I do not know precisely who is involved, but we know the kinds of organisations. And I suspect that some of those involved would be more than capable of murder.'

'So you think that Ransom was murdered because of his involvement in the project?'

'I think it's a possibility. Why he was killed, I've no

idea. Whether he had some knowledge, some information—'

'And why was he killed in such a brutal manner?' Nergui said. 'If these interests are as you say, then his killing would have been carried out professionally. There would have been no need for such a display. He would have been simply spirited away.'

'Like Chief Inspector McLeish?'

Nergui nodded. 'Exactly like Chief Inspector McLeish.' Nergui paused for a moment. 'Professor, I am sorry to be rude but I would very much like to speak to the Minister alone for a few minutes.'

The Minister looked as if he was about to interrupt, but Wilson said, 'Of course. I understand entirely. I will wait outside.'

'Thank you,' the Minister said, looking at Nergui. 'We will just be a few minutes, I think.'

As soon as Wilson had closed the door behind him, the Minister said, 'I don't want to hear your views, Nergui. We have to take this seriously.'

'I'm not suggesting for one moment that we don't take it seriously,' Nergui said. 'But I'm not at all clear what it means. Why should we trust Wilson?'

'He is here representing the British government.'

'He's here under false pretences, carrying out unauthorised enquiries into a UK citizen who was also working here under false pretences. He has withheld information relevant to a major murder enquiry. And not through any ignorance, either – when I spoke to him the other night it was quite clear that he knew full well how serious this was. He's only spoken up now because McLeish's disappearance could expose a major scandal. So why should we trust him? We don't know what his agenda is. We only know that he's lied to us, to the authorities, from the beginning.'

'Nergui, you're experienced enough to understand the

politics behind all this. You know we've had concerns about the funding of the project in the south. We've turned a blind eye because of the importance of the project, that's all – we needed the investment.'

'Of course, and we'll take money from anywhere if the price is right. I understand that well enough.'

The Minister shook his head, looking as if his patience was wearing thin. 'Nergui, it is not your place to be questioning government policy. Your role is to maintain law and order – a role you've signally failed to carry out in this case, as far as I can see.'

'It is not easy to carry out that role if information is being withheld from me.'

'Nergui, you are drifting into dangerous waters here. Respected as you are, like everyone else you hold your position in the Ministry through my patronage. There are people out there who would be only too pleased to see you fall—'

'I take that for granted.'

'I know your strengths, Nergui. I value your intellect, your honesty, your perception. These qualities are not common in an organisation comprised largely of incompetent yes-men. But I need you on my side.'

'In that case, you have to trust me. I can't operate if I don't know who or what to believe.'

'Nergui, believe me, I knew nothing of Wilson's story until this evening.'

'I believe that.' Nergui smiled. 'If only because it must be a painful admission for you. It is disturbing to find that for all our intelligence work, there are things we are unaware of.'

'It is very disturbing, Nergui. If there is any truth in Wilson's suppositions, it suggests we have a potentially very unstable situation in the south. If these people are prepared to act in this way—'

'But, I'm asking again, are we right to trust Wilson? He tells us that, for reasons unknown, he believes Ransom might have been murdered by – what? Organised crime? The Russian mafia? The triads? And they choose to kill Ransom in such a brutal way? I'm not sure if the story makes any sense.'

'It depends on what might lie behind the murder,' the Minister said. 'If what we're seeing here is a series of eye-for-an-eye killings – the kind of gang feud that we speculated about – then maybe a high-profile killing makes sense.'

'Well, maybe. But Ransom's was the fourth murder, at least as far as we know. So who are we suggesting started this round of killings – the Brits?'

The Minister shrugged. 'I don't know, Nergui. I can't make sense of it. But you don't seem to be making a great deal of progress either.'

Nergui nodded. 'I can't deny that,' he said. 'I feel as if I'm grasping at shadows here. We have another lead, but I don't know how it would fit with any of this.' He briefly outlined their visit to the illegal prospectors and their encounter with Cholon. 'It may well be another waste of time.'

'You have to take it seriously,' the Minister said. 'I'm not sure whether a lone psychopath makes any more sense than what Wilson's suggesting, but if there's half a chance it's true—'

'Then we have to stop him.'

Nergui started to rise, but the Minister gestured him to sit for a moment longer. 'But, Nergui, we also have to take notice of what Wilson says. As you say, we don't know what his agenda might be. We don't know if he's telling the whole truth or, indeed, the truth at all. But if there's any substance in what he's saying, then one of our major national investment programmes might be on the point of turning into a bloodbath.'

'It's not much of a choice,' Nergui said, rising. 'A serial killer or a mafia feud.'

'It may be worse than that,' the Minister said. 'It may be both.'

NINETEEN

The weather had eased slightly by the time Nergui made his way back over Sukh Bataar Square. Snow was still falling, but less thickly than before, and Nergui could now see his way through the haze of streetlighting to the far side of the square. The landscape was heavily covered in snow, buildings and statues rendered shapeless by the drifts. There was no sign of human life across the vast area of the square, though a snowplough was standing, apparently abandoned, in one of the main streets.

Nergui glanced at his watch. Four thirty. Time for the next leg on his goose chase. Nergui realised that he was operating almost entirely on instinct. It was a strange sensation. For all his occasional talk of intuition, Nergui's normal approach was one of painstaking rigour. He knew from experience that crimes were much more likely to be resolved through a systematic sifting of the evidence than through wild hunches or undisciplined guesswork. But in this case, though enormous efforts had been devoted to working steadily through every piece of evidence, the results had been virtually non-existent.

Not that this made Nergui's actions any more sensible or justifiable. He knew that if he had caught a junior officer racing across the country in the way he had been doing, he might well have been taking disciplinary action by now. He smiled, grimly. Everyone knew that the rules did not apply to Nergui, so he was unlikely to be challenged from within the police. But if he did not start to deliver some results soon, his position might indeed become untenable.

He was gratified to see, as he trudged back into the police HQ car park, that the four-wheel-drive vehicle had been prepared for snow travel, with chains and additional spot lamps. As he stepped into the warm building, he saw Doripalam sitting with Cholon in the rest room. He waved, and both men jumped to their feet and came out to meet him.

'Everything's ready,' Doripalam said. 'I got the vehicles prepared. We're ready to go when you are.'

Nergui nodded. 'You have firearms?'

Doripalam glanced at Cholon. 'For you and me, yes.'

'That's fine. I hope that they will not be needed, but we should take no risks.'

'Should we take other back-up?'

Nergui shook his head. 'It's your choice but I would prefer not. We may well be wasting our time. I would rather that we did not waste that of too many others. But we should have whatever resource is available standing by.'

'I've arranged that.'

Nergui smiled. He was beginning to suspect that Doripalam's approach to this case was much more rational, more cool-headed than his own. He turned to Cholon. 'Are you sure you wish to accompany us? I don't know what kind of risks might be involved.'

Cholon shrugged. 'If this is my brother, then my presence may be helpful.'

This was true enough. Nergui did not know what they were stepping into. But if they did find Badzar, it was conceivable that he would behave more rationally towards Cholon than to others.

'Okay,' Nergui said. 'But it's your decision. And you must do nothing unless we tell you to.'

Cholon nodded, and the three of them trooped back outside to the waiting vehicle. The snow had almost stopped now, and the sky was clearing, with a few stars already visible. The weather would become colder before dawn, Nergui thought, the roads more icy and treacherous.

Doripalam climbed into the driver's seat. Nergui sat beside him, and Cholon climbed into the back. 'Where are we going?' Doripalam asked.

'Back to the place where we found Delgerbayar's body. The disused factory.'

Doripalam turned to stare at Nergui. 'Back there? You really think we're likely to find something there?'

Nergui shook his head. 'I really have no idea,' he said. 'I'm flying blind. If it were you behaving like this, I'd have you on a charge by now. But there's something – I don't know. It's close to the flat where Badzar stayed for those two nights. The timing of that coincided exactly with Delgerbayar's killing. I have a feeling about it, that's all it is. But I want to check it out.'

'But the place was thoroughly searched after Delgerbayar's body was found.'

'I know. But I think he may have been back there.'

'He'd be taking a big risk.'

'Maybe not. It's no riskier than anywhere else. Maybe less than other places. We assumed that the factory had no particular significance. We searched it thoroughly, then left it. We saw no reason to have it guarded or under surveillance. He might have realised that, once we'd finished our business with Delgerbayar, it was the last place we would return to.'

Doripalam looked far from convinced, but shrugged. 'Well, as you say, it's worth a try.' He turned on the ignition and pulled the vehicle slowly out into the street. Even with the snow chains, driving was precarious and they could feel the heavy vehicle slipping slightly as they turned into the main street. Conditions would become worse as the snow gradually turned to ice under the clear skies.

The factory area was not far, but the journey took them close to thirty minutes as Doripalam fought to maintain control of the vehicle. Finally, they turned into the shadowy concrete yard outside the factory.

The sky had cleared fully now, and there was a nearly full moon shining brilliantly above the horizon. In the pale moonlight, the thick silent snow was eerie, deadening the sound of their movements. It lay thick across the yard, and had drifted deeply against the empty factory itself. Nergui jumped down into the snow, feeling it crunch under his feet. Even here, in the lee of the buildings, it was a good six inches deep.

He walked slowly across to the door through which they had gained entry on the previous occasion, Doripalam and Cholon following behind. Other than the sound of their own footsteps in the snow, the silence was absolute. The low moon lengthened the shadows, so that the side of the factory lay in darkness.

The door had been boarded up following their previous entrance. It appeared to be undisturbed but Nergui was aware that there were several other entrances around the building, which might allow access.

He turned towards Doripalam who was carrying the large crowbar they had brought in the rear of the truck. Doripalam was standing waiting, but Cholon had stopped some yards back, caught in the moonlight, staring at the massive building in front of them.

'Is something wrong?' Nergui half whispered, the sound of his voice muffled by the snow.

'I've just realised what this place is,' Cholon said. 'I came here only once or twice, and I did not recognise it in the dark.'

'What do you mean?' Nergui moved to take the crowbar from Doripalam, watching Cholon closely.

'It's the factory where our father worked. It was when he lost his job here that we were forced to move out of the city.'

Nergui nodded. With a slight sense of shame, he realised that his primary emotion was one of relief, an acknowledgement that the shadows he was chasing might, after all, prove to have some substance. He could see that Cholon's emotions, by contrast, were confused, his recognition of the truth battling with a realisation of its implications.

'We must press on,' Nergui said. He inserted the crowbar behind the first of the nailed boards and slowly eased it away from the door. The doorway had been expertly sealed and it took some time to remove all the boarding to the point where the entrance was accessible. Finally, though, they had it cleared, and Nergui kicked the door open.

After the deadened silence of the landscape outside, the echo of the opening door was startling, booming around the enormous vaulted space beyond. Nergui waited a moment for the sound to die away, and then stepped carefully into the darkness. He waited again before preparing to turn on his torch, allowing his eyes to grow accustomed to the blackness.

As his eyes adjusted he realised that the darkness was not complete. The large factory room itself was unlit, but at the far end of the room was the faintest of lights hardly visible from this distance. Nergui squinted, trying to orientate himself to the shape of the building. It was, he realised, a glimmer of light shining under a door. The door of the room where they had found Delgerbayar's body.

*

The waiting. That was the worst of it. The knowledge that something was going to happen, but not knowing what or when. The sense that something or someone was waiting, just outside his vision, and might appear at any moment.

And the silence, the unearthly, unending silence. Other than the faint sounds of his own breath, his own heartbeat, he had heard nothing for – how long? He had no idea. It felt like hours, but was perhaps only minutes. There was no way to measure time. His body felt as if it was in suspended animation – he had long since ceased to feel any pain, any bodily needs or feelings at all. It was as if somehow he was existing beyond time.

And then suddenly the silence was broken. It took him a moment to register. Was it the sound of movement, of footsteps? He concentrated hard, trying to listen, trying to work out precisely what it was he had heard.

At first, he could hear nothing, then he heard it again, more clearly this time. It was the sound of someone, something moving somewhere close at hand. He strained to move his head to try to see something more, but the binding around his neck held as tightly as ever, and all he could see was the glare of the ceiling lights.

The sound grew louder. It was the sound of footsteps, not quite steady, not quite even, as though the person was dragging some heavy object. And there was something else, a scraping, something metallic being pulled along.

And then, for a breathless moment, there was silence once more. He could hear his own heart beating, faster and louder than before, the blood pounding in his ears.

For the first time since his initial panic attack in the dark, he was terrified. Up to now, his mind had detached itself from this reality and he had almost allowed himself to believe that the silence, the waiting, might continue forever, as if time really were suspended.

But the approaching sound of footsteps had brought

him back to the reality of his predicament. There was no way out of this. He could not move. He could only lie here, his heart pounding, as he waited for what would happen next.

He strained his ears again listening for some clue, some indication. The footsteps resumed, uneven as before, backed by the strange metallic scraping, growing ever louder, ever closer. And then he heard something bumping against wood, a hollow echo. The footsteps paused again, and he heard, with a sickening emptiness in his stomach, the door at the far end of the room slowly being opened.

'It's the same room as before,' Nergui whispered. 'The room where we found Delgerbayar.'

Doripalam and Cholon had clustered close beside him. The factory was icy cold, and they could feel the further blast of chilled air from the open door behind them. The three of them were looking down the length of the room. Nergui was holding a large spotlight, shining the beam down the dusty empty space towards the closed door at the far end.

The main factory area was as empty and deserted as before. Nergui had shone the torch around the large vaulted room, peering into the corners and up on to the ramps to make sure nothing had changed. At this time of the year, there were not even any rats scurrying in the corners. There was simply an eerie, hollow silence that seemed to close around them as they stood together in the freezing night.

Nergui turned to Cholon. 'You don't need to come any further. Go back to the car. If we're not out in ten minutes, radio for back-up.'

Cholon hesitated. 'I'd still rather come with you. If it is Badzar—'

'We don't know what we're going to find here.' Nergui's mind was already conjuring up images of their last discovery in this place. 'It's better if you go back and wait.' Up to the point when he had spotted the glimmer of light from the far room, he had not really believed they were going to find anything here. It was a hunch, something that had to be checked out, but all his professional experience had told him that it was a waste of time. But his hunch had been right. There was something here.

Cholon paused a moment longer, but Nergui said: 'Go. Now.' Cholon nodded, and turned back to the open door. Nergui suspected he would wait outside, desperate to find out what lay behind this. That was okay – at least he would be in a position to radio for help if it should be needed.

Nergui nodded to Doripalam, and they began to make their way slowly along the length of the room. Nergui kept the spotlight trained ahead of them, trying to avoid it shining directly on the door so that there was less chance it might alert anyone in the room beyond.

By the time they reached the door itself, Nergui was convinced he knew what lay in the room. He wasn't sure what alerted him first – some instinct, perhaps, but then he picked up a smell he knew only too well. It was the smell of blood and decay. It was the smell that lingers when human remains have been left to rot. The smell of death.

He gestured silently to Doripalam to stop. Then he whispered: 'Step back. I do not think we are in any danger here, but I suspect that what lies beyond that door will not be pleasant.'

Nergui put down the spotlight and pulled out his pistol, his eyes locked on the doorway. Then he reached out and threw open the door, holding his breath, preparing for whatever lay beyond.

Even so, he was taken by surprise.

The room, as he had expected, contained no living creature. It was as silent and empty as when they had found Delgerbayar's body. And it was again lit by a spotlight attached to a car battery, providing the setting for another grotesque display.

But the centrepiece was different. There was no body on the table. Instead, there was a bloody mess, a horrifying parody of a butcher's tray. Nergui blinked, trying to take in what he was seeing. Finally, his breath coming in short bursts, he was able to decipher the extraordinary sight in front of him.

Lying on the table was a mass of severed human body parts. There were four hands, cut off at the wrist. And there were two human heads, their eyes empty and staring, placed precisely in the centre of the table.

Nergui turned to Doripalam, who had positioned himself behind Nergui and was staring, horrified, into the room. 'I think,' Nergui said slowly, 'that Badzar has decided to fill in the gaps in our collection.'

TWENTY

It was nearly eight by the time Nergui arrived back at police HQ. Doripalam had called out forensics to collect the body parts, and Nergui had waited, tramping backwards and forwards in the deep snow, until they and the scene-of-crime officers reached the factory.

Doripalam had asked for a full alert to be put out for Badzar's arrest, and officers were being called back on to duty to attempt a full-scale manhunt. At least now they had a clear suspect, but Nergui knew from experience how easy it was for a fugitive to hide out in this city. He was not hopeful that Badzar would be apprehended quickly.

He had sent Doripalam and Cholon back, telling them to get some rest. He had briefly informed Cholon what had been found in the room, but had not allowed him to see the grotesque display. As he spoke, he had seen the look of horrified emptiness in Cholon's eyes. It was no longer possible for Cholon to deny, to himself or anyone else, what his brother had been capable of. 'I'm sorry,' was all that Nergui could say, but he could sense the years of uncomprehending anguish that lay ahead for Cholon.

Cholon began to walk, dead-eyed, back to the truck. Doripalam turned to Nergui. 'You'll be all right here on your own? Do you think it's safe?'

Nergui shrugged. 'I imagine so. I can't believe that Badzar would have hung around after setting up that little show for us.'

'He's smart, though,' Doripalam said. 'How did he know we would come here? I mean—' He looked slightly embarrassed. 'I mean, it was only a hunch on your part. I – well, I wasn't sure anything would come of it.'

Nergui smiled grimly. 'Neither was I, if I'm honest. But once the thought had occurred, I couldn't ignore it. But the truth is that that display could have sat there for a long time. The light was on a timer, and I suppose Badzar could always come and replace the battery at intervals if necessary. At this time of the year, the flesh wouldn't decay quickly. He could just wait until we – or someone – happened to stumble upon it.' He paused. 'And of course, if our phantom caller really is Badzar, then he might have used his next call to lead us here.'

'But what's he up to? Why go to all that trouble to dismember the bodies, apparently to hide their identities, and then give us the missing body parts anyway?'

'I don't know, but I have a sense that this is moving towards some endgame.' It was what he had felt all along, the sense of something moving slowly but ever more certainly towards a purpose, towards some sense of resolution. He couldn't square this feeling with the brutal and apparently random nature of these killings, but he now felt this sense of purpose more than ever. He shook his head. 'There's something about this,' he said. 'I think endgame is the right word. There is some game being played here, and I have an awful feeling we're being treated as the pawns.'

Doripalam nodded, clearly baffled by Nergui's speculations. 'You don't want us to wait till the back-up arrives?'

Nergui glanced across at Cholon, who was leaning over the bonnet of the truck, looking like a man who had had all the life beaten out of him. 'No, you need to look after Cholon. I can't begin to imagine what he's going through. Get him a hotel room, see if he can get some sleep, but keep an eye on him.'

As soon as the truck had driven away, Nergui wondered if this had been a wise decision. There was no telling what Badzar might be planning. Perhaps he was observing him at this very moment, waiting until Doripalam and Cholon had driven away before moving against Nergui. Just as, Nergui thought, he might have been waiting for Drew on the night they left the embassy.

He looked uneasily around him. The yard beside the factory was silent and deserted. It was still dark, though the glow in the eastern sky heralded the approach of sunrise. In the distance, the city would be starting to come to life, the snowploughs out clearing the streets. But there was no sign of that here. Nergui flashed the spotlight around the yard, catching unnerving shapes and shadows as the beam circled. He moved himself slowly back against the wall of the factory, trying to ensure that there was at least no risk of his being caught from behind.

Nergui was far from being a nervous individual, but the next twenty minutes, until the back-up team arrived, were among the most uncomfortable he had ever endured. He stood, with his back to the factory wall, regularly arcing the spotlight beam around him, trying to minimise the risk that anyone might take him by surprise. He kept his hand in his pocket, resting on the cold handle of his pistol, ready to draw it at any sign of movement.

The snow was helpful to him because any figures crossing the open area of the yard would be thrown into relief by the stark whiteness, and it was virtually impossible to walk silently across the crisp drifts. The moon had risen too, and the yard was bathed in its pale light, although there were still too many shadows and dark corners where an assailant could hide.

Nergui told himself he was being ridiculous. There was no possibility that Badzar would have hung around here, no chance that he had witnessed their arrival. The risks would surely have been too great. But, clearly, they were not dealing with a rational man. It seemed there was no limit to what he might do, no way of predicting his actions.

However much he tried to rationalise his position, Nergui could not shake the uneasy feeling that he was being watched. His mind went back to the arrow that had been fired at himself and Drew, and he realised how vulnerable his position might be.

He remained as still as possible, listening for any movement, any sound that might reveal the presence of another person. Now that the snow had stopped falling and the sky had cleared, there was a faint chill breeze blowing through the yards and alleyways between the factory buildings. He heard, once, the sound of something scattering, perhaps a paper blown in the wind, or maybe the echo of footsteps in the snow. He turned in what he judged to be the right direction, straining his ears, but could hear nothing more.

And then he heard another sound, off to his left. Unmistakable this time, the sound of scraping, snow being dislodged, someone moving. He directed the spotlight towards the sound, able to see nothing. The white sweep of banked snow rose towards a concrete wall at the far end of the factory yard. And then his spotlight caught something, raised upon the top of the wall – a shape, a shadow, moving swiftly, dropping behind the concrete. He tensed, shining the light backwards and forwards at the spot, but could see nothing more. Just the snow-covered top of the wall, perhaps a smudge or two where the snow had been disturbed.

He peered into the light, trying to see more. Perhaps it had been an animal of some kind, though that seemed unlikely on such a cold night. And in his heart he knew that someone had been watching him. Perhaps was still watching him

Nergui shivered. The prospect that he was being observed by the person who had been capable of such unspeakable acts of murder and mutilation, who had perhaps been responsible for Drew's disappearance, sent a chill through his body. He crouched down, trying to present as small a target as possible, his eyes concentrating on the area where he had seen movement, but also constantly darting around the yard in case assault should come from another direction.

Finally his concentration was disturbed by a far more welcome sound. It was the noise of a car engine, closely followed by a second. Headlights flashed around the edges of the yard as two marked patrol cars pulled slowly to a halt in front of the factory.

Nergui rose, peering over the cars to see if there was any sign of movement beyond. Three police officers emerged from the front car. The rear car contained the pathologist and a specialist scene-of-crime officer.

Nergui spoke briefly to the three officers. 'Come with me. I think I saw someone over there. It may be our man. But be careful. He's extremely dangerous.'

He led the way cautiously across the yard to the snow covered wall where he had seen the movements. He flashed the spotlight across it. He had been right. The snow had been disturbed in the centre, as if someone had been trying to clamber over the wall. The wall itself was no more than six feet high, not difficult to scale in normal circumstances but made more treacherous by the drifted snow. There was no obvious gate or other entry point.

Nergui handed the spotlight to one of the other officers, and stamped his way through the snow drift to reach the wall. Aware that he might be making himself a sitting target, he reached up and pulled himself up till his head was above the top of the wall, ready to drop back if there was any evidence of a threat from the other side.

There was nothing, just a further area of snow-covered concrete, then the ground fell away into some form of wasteland – the ruins of some demolished building, though it was difficult to tell in the snow. On the other side were more factories and industrial buildings, tightly clustered.

Beyond the point where the snow on the wall had been disturbed, there was a line of jumbled footprints, leading down into the wasteland area. It was possible that they might provide some sort of trail, but Nergui suspected that the trail would be lost in the factory buildings opposite, where the narrow alleyways had avoided the worst of the snow.

'Was it him?' one of the officers asked.

Nergui shrugged. 'I can't imagine anyone else being out here on a night like this. Get over the wall and see if you can make anything of the trail of footprints over there – anything at all from the footprints themselves. And then see if you can find where they lead. They probably just disappear on the far side, but it's worth a look. Take care.'

The officers began to clamber up onto the wall. Nergui watched them a moment, and then began to walk back across the yard to where the pathologist and crime-scene officer were waiting. He nodded to them without speaking, and then led the way back into the factory.

Even for Nergui, returning to the scene, the display of body parts was still shocking. He could see the crime-scene officer visibly paling at the sight before them, and even the hardened pathologist appeared shaken.

'I'm assuming,' Nergui said slowly, 'that these items correspond to the two unidentified corpses already in our possession. That is, I am praying that we are not now faced with two further killings.'

The pathologist nodded. 'Let us hope not.'

'And the second thing is to try to get some idea of their identities. If these were removed from the original corpses, then it should be much easier to identify them, I presume?'

The pathologist nodded, staring at the display with a mix of horror and bafflement. 'There are no guarantees but at least we will have fingerprints, dental records. It looks as if the killer is trying to assist us.'

'So it would seem,' Nergui said. He turned to the crime-scene officer. 'I want you to review every square centimetre of this place. Anything you can find – *anything* – may be critical. We think we know who we're looking for now, so we're going to need evidence to prove he was here. I can't imagine he's going to have left fingerprints, but there may be other forensic evidence.'

He left the two men working in the room, still lit by the battery-powered spotlamp, and made his way back outside. The three officers had climbed back over the wall and were making their way back towards him.

'Nothing,' one said, shaking his head. 'The footsteps up at this end are too jumbled to make anything of. And over on the other side there's a whole network of sheltered alleyways that the snow hasn't touched. We followed the trail a few yards into the alleys, but then it disappeared.'

'This man knows what he's doing,' Nergui said. 'He's not going to make it easy for us.' He gestured back to the factory. 'Two of you had better stay here, just in case.' He looked around in the darkness. 'I cannot imagine he is still in the vicinity. But then I didn't seriously believe that he was here in the first place.'

He turned to the third officer. 'We've got a full scale search going on of the area?' he asked.

The officer nodded. 'As best we can. We only had the night duty on, but we're calling in as many officers as we can. The snow's not helping. They're gradually getting the streets cleared, but this is the first serious snowfall we've had this year so it's taking time to get it sorted. We've got patrol cars all round there now, but it's taken a while to get them in place.'

'Okay. There's not much more we can do. If you take me back to HQ, you can get your car out with the rest.'

As they drove back Nergui noted that most of the main roads were now largely clear. Lorries laden with huge cargoes of ploughed snow were ferrying along the major routes, trying to open as many as possible before the morning came.

Nergui looked at his watch. Seven twenty. The sky was lightening now in the east, and it would not be long before the sun rose. He would not be sorry to see the back of this particular night, but he was apprehensive about what the coming day might bring. The anonymous caller was due to ring back at nine. Was this a hoax or was it really Badzar? And if it was, what might he tell them?

Assuming that the limbs were those belonging to the original bodies, it looked as if Badzar was now trying to communicate something. Was this just coincidence, or did he somehow know that they had stumbled across his identity? If Badzar had been observing him over the previous days – which Nergui, with an inward shudder, increasingly felt to be the case – then it was possible

289

that he had seen Cholon accompanying them. Maybe he had realised that Cholon had betrayed him. If so, they should ensure that Cholon himself was protected. He pulled out his mobile and dialled HQ, asking for Doripalam. It took Doripalam a few minutes to reach the phone, and when he eventually spoke he sounded breathless.

'I wanted to check that Cholon was okay. What have you done with him?'

'He's still here. I tried to persuade him to get some sleep, but he was keen to stay here, at least till the next call comes in. And I thought this might be the safest place.'

'We need to keep an eye on him. It's possible Badzar has seen him with us.'

'You think Badzar's been watching us?'

'I think he was watching us in the factory tonight. I think he was watching me after you and Cholon left.'

There was an intake of breath at the other end of the line, as Doripalam took in the implications of this. 'I'll take care of him. But I wanted to tell you, I've been doing some more digging since I got back here. There are some things I need to update you on.'

Nergui glanced out of the car window. 'I'm just a few minutes away. I'll find you when I get there.'

The centre of Sukh Bataar Square was still thickly covered in snow, looking oddly pastoral under the smooth drifts. The roads around the square, though, were now clear. They turned off the square and pulled into the HQ car park.

It was only when he finally entered the HQ building that Nergui realised how cold he was. Through the glass he could see Doripalam sitting in the rest room with Cholon, a large pile of official files behind them. Cholon had finally fallen asleep, curled awkwardly in one of the large armchairs.

Doripalam jumped up as he entered, one of the files in his hand.

Nergui smiled faintly. 'I need some coffee before I can take anything in. I'm freezing.'

He filled the electric kettle that sat among the debris of used coffee mugs on the table at the end of the room and then turned back to Doripalam. 'What is it?'

'A few things,' Doripalam said. 'I was wondering about Delgerbayar and where he fitted into this.'

It was a good question. Cholon's description had suggested that, at the very least, Delgerbayar had been involved in some business on the side. It was, of course, one of the first questions they had asked in the light of his brutal murder, but there had been no indication of any wrong-doing on Delgerbayar's part.

'A thorough search was carried out of all Delgerbayar's files and materials after his death,' Nergui said.

'I know that. It was all scrupulously clean. Maybe suspiciously so, knowing what we know now. But I had a look through the file again this morning, and something struck me. We'd asked for a copy of Delgerbayar's recent bank statements to see if there was any evidence of unexplained payments.'

Nergui nodded. 'As I understand it, there was no indication that he was on the take. The incomings and outgoings were pretty much what you'd expect for a man in his position.'

'They were. But I had a closer look at the statements. Most of the payments were what you'd expect, but there were a number of small transfers of cash in from another account. Always just small amounts as if he needed to tide himself over to his next salary or whatever.'

'Maybe he had another account,' Nergui said. 'A savings account or something.'

'Well, yes, that's what I assumed. But I thought I'd better check.'

Take nothing for granted. One of the first rules of investigation, Nergui thought, and precisely the one they'd been guilty of neglecting all the way through this case. 'Not an ideal time of the day for checking bank details,' he said.

Doripalam smiled. 'No. So I called the manager at home.'

'Bet he was pleased. What time was this?'

'About six. He was up already, at least. But he knew it was a murder enquiry and, well, I mentioned your name so he was happy to help.'

Nergui nodded. 'There goes my chance of an overdraft. And he gave you the information without asking for authorisation in triplicate?'

'He did once I'd mentioned your name. It turned out there is another account. It was opened by Delgerbayar's father. The thing is, Delgerbayar's father died five years ago, though the bank weren't aware of that.'

'And what was in this account?'

'I didn't push the manager to give me the exact amount, because he was beginning to feel a bit awkward about talking to me. But clearly a lot. The manager was told some story about the father being in some sort of export business. So most of the payments were in dollars. In cash, apparently.'

'And the bank never thought to question this?' Nergui said. It didn't surprise him. The country had increasingly stringent regulations in place, having subscribed to international standards on money laundering. But they were frequently flouted. Nergui guessed that in this case a small proportion of the cash had also found its way into the manager's pocket. Maybe that was one small fry to deal with later, if they ever managed to deal with the big fish in this case.

'I think by the time he realised what we were talking about, he wished he hadn't been so helpful,' Doripalam said.

'So Delgerbayar was on the take, and in a fairly big way. And it obviously made him at least one serious enemy. We need to get someone over to the bank before the manager starts destroying any evidence.'

'I already thought of that,' Doripalam said. 'I didn't know who we could spare from the search for Badzar. I'd have gone myself but I wanted to stay to update you. In the end, Batzorig volunteered. He's gone over to the bank and told the manager to meet him there. Batzorig's going to go through all the papers with him and bring back anything he can find that looks remotely relevant.'

'Sounds sensible,' Nergui said, 'though it may well be a waste of time. If the manager's smart, he'll have kept any written evidence of this to a minimum. And it was a clever move of Delgerbayar to use his father's account – that way the setting up of the account would have pre-dated the introduction of the money laundering checks. It's quite possible that the manager can be faulted only in that he allowed substantial sums to be paid in without checking the source. And I bet that's true of every bank manager in the country.'

'There are a couple of other things,' Doripalam went on. 'I did a bit of digging in one or two other areas as well. I thought it was worth doing a bit of checking on the mining company that Delgerbayar seems to have been involved with. Turns out it's a largely Russian-owned company. Got some state investment from us. It's part of the consortium involved in the Gobi project. In fact, the two biggest investors are the Russians and a US company.'

'Strange bedfellows,' Nergui commented. He looked

at his watch. 'How did you manage to find out all this in the space of about an hour?'

'Not difficult, actually. Did a bit of searching on the internet – got some basic information. Also got some data from government systems – not sure whether I was supposed to be on there officially, but I got one of the IT guys to do me a favour.'

'You're making me feel old. This US company – wouldn't have any links to Collins and Maxon, would it?'

'You're not over the hill yet, clearly. Yes, part of the same group. Another operating company.'

'And what about the Russian company?'

'MN Mining. It's based in St Petersburg. They're part of a wider group, but MN is exclusively focused on mining, primarily gold, in Mongolia. They've a major office in the city here. The Chief Exec is a Russian, Sergei Kartashkin, based here.'

'And where does the US investment come in?'

'Well, that's where it gets interesting. To start with MN was established as a subsidiary here to carry out opencast mining in the north – the kind of stuff we saw yesterday. It looks as if they got some government funding from our end so it was essentially a joint venture. But then they began to chase some of the prospects in the south where more deep mining is needed. It's a much more expensive process – even establishing where the reserves are costs a lot, so they had to look for more investment. MN eventually became part of the consortium with the US company, a company from the UK, and some South Korean interests.'

'All supposedly legitimate?'

'Difficult for me to tell. It's more your area than mine,' Doripalam said.

Nergui nodded. All kinds of money was flooding into

the country, some honest, some much more dubious. There was a lot of incentive for organised crime to use this isolated republic as a route for money laundering, particularly if they could realise a return on their investment in the process. This didn't mean that the investment in this case was necessarily crooked, but a number of the Russian-based companies were known to have criminal links. Nergui was also aware that there were growing links – as well as significant tensions – between organised crime in Russia and its counterpart in the States. It would not be a surprise to find some unsavoury elements involved in this particular deal.

'Well, at least we now know that they've got interests in the south, which might begin to explain Delgerbayar's mysterious trip to the Gobi, given that he was on their payroll. And, given the background, even putting aside what we know about Collins and Maxon, I guess I'd be very surprised if they were entirely above board. I've no idea what all this is telling us, but we've started pulling at some interesting threads so maybe this thing might start to unravel. Though what it looks like underneath is anyone's guess.'

Nergui looked at his watch. Eight forty. The promised telephone call was due in twenty minutes, assuming that the first call hadn't simply been a hoax. 'Okay,' he said, 'we need to get everything set up for this call, if it comes. I want us to start trying to trace the call as soon as it comes in on the switchboard. Tape every word of it. I don't imagine he'll be careless if he's true to form, but we can't afford to miss a trick. You go and get things set up. I'll stick down here with Cholon for the moment.'

Doripalam turned, on his way upstairs, but Nergui called after him. 'Doripalam, you've done well. Very well. I think we're finally starting to get somewhere.

Once we've seen whether our phantom caller returns, what do you think about a visit to Mr Kartashkin? I feel in the mood for a business meeting.'

TWENTY-ONE

At first they thought that the call wasn't going to come. Nergui had positioned himself at a desk which was secluded but within sight of the switchboard operator, so that they could signal to each other if necessary. Doripalam had set up the tape machine and was in contact with the telephone engineer who was going to try to trace the call. The attempt would probably prove futile. The call would almost certainly come from a mobile. Although it was theoretically possible at least to identify the area from which the call was being made, this would only be achieved if the caller was considerably more garrulous than on the previous occasion.

Nine o'clock approached and the small team tensed, waiting for a call on one of the external lines. If any other calls came through at the same time, the operator would put them on hold without warning to avoid distraction from the job at hand.

Nine o'clock came and went. At four minutes past, a call came in but it was only someone trying to report a stolen wallet. The operator, true to the plan, put the caller on hold and waited. 'Hope he's still there when I get back to him,' he commented.

'We don't know how long that might be,' Doripalam said. 'How long do we keep waiting?'

His question was answered almost immediately. They recognised the voice instantly from the night before. The tape was already running, and Doripalam had triggered the call trace.

'Nergui,' the voice said. The operator signalled to Nergui, and then transferred the call.

'This is Nergui. Who is this?'

'I'm here to offer you help,' the voice said. 'I have something valuable which I think would interest you. I'm seeking only your attention in return.'

'What do you mean?'

'As I say, I have something of value. I am seeking no reward except that you listen to me.'

'This is nonsense,' Nergui said. 'I'm too old to be playing games. Tell me what you want or get off the line.'

There was a long pause and for a brief moment Nergui thought that the caller really had hung up. Then he heard the faint sound of breathing down the line. Nergui held the silence, willing the caller to speak first.

'I have McLeish,' the voice said at last. 'The police-man. I want to meet you. Only you. I'll call again.'

'How do I know you're—?' Nergui began, but the line had already been cut. Nergui slammed the handset down hard, frustrated at the lack of information. This could all still be a hoax, a stupid waste of time. He looked up at Doripalam who began to walk over, shaking his head.

'No chance of tracing it. Far too short. I think they'd got it pinned down to the south of the city, but that was about it.'

'That would put him close to where we were last night,' Nergui said.

Doripalam nodded. 'It would, but it's not much to go on.'

'He must have known we were trying to trace him. That's why he hung up so quickly,' Nergui said. 'He's a smart one.'

'You don't think it's a hoax, then?'

Nergui shrugged. 'Well, it could be. But he knew McLeish's name, and that's not been in the press so far. So if he's a fake, he's a fake with good connections.'

'So what now?'

'We're no further forward. In fact, it feels like a step back because we don't know when or if he'll contact us again.'

'He said he would.'

Nergui nodded. 'Well, if it's not a hoax, then I think we can assume he will. The question is how soon, and what happens in the meantime. We've got to keep the momentum here. Make sure that everyone available is on the search for Badzar. We want every building in that area scoured.' He turned to the switchboard operator. 'If our friend calls again, put him through to my mobile. We're going out – probably an hour or so.'

Nergui stalked towards the door, grabbing his coat from the chair in passing. 'Come on,' he said to Doripalam, 'we're going to pay a visit to Comrade Kartashkin.'

After the sound of the opening door, there was silence. He tensed, straining his ears for what might follow, listening for the sound of movement, of footsteps. But there was nothing. At first, he thought he could hear the faint distant sound of breathing, but it was impossible to be sure.

Panic and despair overwhelmed him. He had been terrified of what might be about to happen, but at least there had been the prospect of some sort of resolution. This was worse. It was as if he was still held in suspension, endlessly paused, waiting for some change that would never come.

That, presumably, was the idea. This was a form of torture. He tried his hardest to suppress his rising panic and to concentrate. Someone had opened the door. Someone was out there. Someone was waiting.

He listened again, trying to distinguish some external sound from the beating of his own heart and the rasp of his own breath.

And then he heard the footsteps again, not close, still outside this room, the same unevenness, the same accompanying scraping. And something else.

The sound of a voice. Little more than a whisper, soft and sibilant. It was impossible to distinguish any words. It was impossible to tell if this was someone talking to himself or to a third party, though only one voice could be heard. It was as if someone was pacing up and down, waiting, counting out time.

And then the footfalls became more purposeful, no longer aimless pacing, but moving as if towards some goal. Were they receding? At this thought Drew felt relief coursing through his body. But he knew that this was ridiculous. Whatever respite he might be gaining could only be temporary.

He was right; suddenly the footsteps returned, growing louder, before he could draw in his breath again. The unevenness was still there, but he could no longer hear the sound of the scraping, just a slow purposeful footfall coming in his direction.

Then a change in the quality of the sound told him that whoever had been pacing around outside had at last entered the room. Watching him as he lay bound on the bench. All rational thought left him. He was helpless, consumed by a primordial terror, every instinct screaming to escape.

He tried to speak, but the words were trapped in his dry throat. He moved his arms and legs agonisingly against the plastic binding and tried again to lift his head, but still could see nothing but the roof and the lights.

The footsteps came closer and now he could hear the faint sound of breathing, the rustle of clothing. Someone was standing immediately over him, though still invisible to his constrained vision.

He held his breath. Expecting almost anything. A gunshot, a knife, a physical blow.

But there was nothing. The footsteps stopped. The faint breathing continued. Drew waited, his hands gripped white, for what might come next.

'I'm afraid he's tied up all morning.' She ran her index finger slowly down the page of the desk diary in front of her, as though she needed to confirm her statement. 'I might be able to find you a slot towards the end of the afternoon.'

Nergui glanced at Doripalam, who looked back blankly. He smiled gently at the receptionist. 'I don't think you quite understand,' he said. 'We're the police. We're investigating a murder. Several murders, in fact. We need to see Mr Kartashkin now.'

Her mouth had dropped slightly open at the mention of the murders, but she still didn't seem inclined to give way. 'I've been told very strictly that he shouldn't be—'

But Nergui was already walking past her and up the stairs to the first floor. She jumped to her feet as though to try to stop him, but Doripalam motioned her to sit. 'It's easier for everyone if you don't get involved,' he said.

'But you can't just come—' She looked wildly around her.

'We can,' Doripalam said, smiling. 'We are. Incidentally, just to save time, where will we find Mr Kartashkin?'

She stared at him as though he were insane. Then she shook her head as though realising that there was little point in arguing. 'He's in the Boardroom. Top of the stairs, first on the left.'

'Thank you,' Doripalam said. 'See how helpful a little co-operation can be.'

He bounded up the stairs after Nergui. Nergui had clearly caught the beginning of the conversation below, and so was now waiting at the top of the stairs, smiling back down at Doripalam. 'Where did she say he was?'

'Boardroom. First on the left.'

Nergui strode off again, just a few yards down the corridor to a sturdy wooden door. A well-polished brass plate confirmed that this was the Boardroom.

Nergui, not one to minimise the impact of his entrance, pushed down the handle and flung open the door.

Four men sat round a large mahogany table, files and papers spread between them. They were all staring in astonishment at the intrusion.

'Good morning, gentlemen,' Nergui said. 'Which of you would be Mr Kartashkin?'

A large, bald man stood up at the far end of the table. 'I am Kartashkin,' he said calmly. 'I trust that there is some good explanation for this intrusion.'

'I believe so,' Nergui said, smiling faintly. He produced his ID card from his top pocket and waved it airily in front of the men. 'Ministry of Security,' he said.

Kartashkin looked as if he was about to protest, then clearly had second thoughts. 'I am not aware that our company is of any interest to the Ministry,' he said calmly. 'I have not gained this impression from the Minister.'

Nergui smiled. 'No, well, perhaps he does not share all his innermost thoughts with you. Perhaps you would like to give him a call to check?'

Kartashkin stared at Nergui's impassive gaze, then

suddenly looked down. 'No matter,' he said. 'I am of course always happy to co-operate with the Ministry in any way possible.' He looked around the table, smiling blandly. 'Perhaps, gentlemen, you will leave me alone for a short while with Mr—?' He glanced at Nergui.

'Nergui,' Nergui smiled. 'And my colleague, Doripalam. This should not take long.'

The other men shuffled out, and Kartashkin sat smiling at Nergui and Doripalam. As soon as the door closed behind his colleagues, Kartashkin's smile vanished. 'What the hell's this all about? I do not appreciate being invaded in my own offices.'

Nergui's smile was as bland as Kartashkin's had been. 'This is a very important matter, Mr Kartashkin. We are investigating murder.'

Kartashkin regarded him closely. 'And what does murder have to do with me? I'm a businessman.'

'As you say, Mr Kartashkin. And a very well-connected one. We understand that at least one of our officers was on your payroll.'

Kartashkin's head jerked up. 'What do you mean?'

'What I say.'

'That's ridiculous. We don't—'

'Delgerbayar, the officer in question, is now dead. Murdered. Brutally murdered.'

Kartashkin rose to his feet. 'I must ask you to leave. I'm not sure what you're implying, but it sounds like the most outrageous—'

Nergui slowly raised his hand. Kartashkin, imposing figure as he might be among his own colleagues, fell silent. 'I am not trying to imply anything, Mr Kartashkin. I am simply stating some facts and seeking your help with our enquiries.'

Kartashkin slumped back down into his seat. 'You can't prove—'

Nergui lifted his hand again. 'Mr Kartashkin, we are both adults. Let us not waste each other's time. You do not know what I can prove or not prove. I know that Delgerbayar was on your payroll. It may well be that other senior officers are also in your pocket. I do not know that, and at the moment I do not particularly care. But I do care about Delgerbayar because he is now dead, and I want to know why.'

Kartashkin hesitated, looking from Nergui to Doripalam and then back, as though hoping that some other approach might be forthcoming. Finally, he said: 'I don't know what you're talking about.'

Nergui shook his head slowly. 'That is disappointing, Mr Kartashkin. I had expected a more intelligent response.'

Kartashkin looked at the door as though expecting that someone would walk in and interrupt them. Perhaps, Doripalam thought, someone really would contact the Minister on his behalf.

'What are you proposing to do? Arrest me?' The words were defiant, but the tone much less so. Kartashkin had suddenly become a different figure from the blustering demagogue who had first greeted them. This was a man, Doripalam thought, on the verge of fear. But fear of what? This would not be a man troubled by the legal consequences of his actions. He did not seriously fear arrest. It might be that he was engaged in corruption far more serious than the bribing of a few police officers, but in this society foreign investment was always well beyond the law. Whatever he was afraid of was something far more troubling. As he watched Kartashkin, and saw sweat breaking out on his neck and forehead, Doripalam thought back to the board meeting they had apparently interrupted. They had caught only a glimpse of the grouping of men before they had responded to Nergui's interruption, but Doripalam had the impression, from the expressions and body language, that it had been some sort of crisis meeting.

Nergui nodded. 'If I have to take you in to police headquarters to get the answers I need, then so be it. It would be an unfortunate interruption to your day. I am sure you have much to get on with.' Nergui glanced briefly across at Doripalam, and it was almost as if the older man had been reading his thoughts.

Kartashkin shook his head. 'I am not prepared to say anything on the record. If you want a formal statement, you will have to arrest me.'

Nergui smiled softly. 'But off the record?'

'I don't know.' Kartashkin glanced at the door again. 'This is not a good time. I am in the middle of things.'

'We will keep you no longer than we need to.'

'I . . . Well, we are facing some difficulties.' He paused, clearly trying to think what to say. 'You are right. Off the record. Delgerbayar was known to us. He did the odd bit of business on our behalf. Nothing corrupt—'

'I understand,' Nergui said, his face blank.

'I do not know why he was killed. But I want to know why. We have been having some business troubles.'

'You are involved in one of the Gobi projects, that is right?'

Kartashkin looked sharply up at Nergui, then nodded. 'I think you know more than you are saying. Yes, we are involved in the Gobi.'

'It is not going well?'

'It is proving more difficult than we envisaged, yes. There is enormous potential, but the initial investigations are proving difficult. It has required more investment than we expected. Considerably more.' He paused, clearly wondering whether he had said too much.

'You are the major investor?' Nergui said. 'Along with our government, I mean.'

Kartashkin hesitated. 'It's complicated,' he said. 'We were the major investor, initially. It was virtually a joint venture between ourselves and your government, with a little investment and expertise from the US, the UK and Korea. But as the projected costs have risen, we've struggled to keep pace, so the other parties have increased their stake. Especially the US.'

'The US government?' Nergui said.

Kartashkin shook his head. 'There is government investment and support, as there is in all the partner companies, but this is a private company.' He smiled, bleakly.

'But you have raised the required investment?'

'We have raised the required investment. But it has not been easy. There have been tensions.'

'And murders?'

'We do not know if Delgerbayar's death is linked in any way—'

'Mr Ransom, the Englishman, was also on your payroll, was he not?'

For the second time, Kartashkin raised his head and stared at Nergui. 'You are playing with me,' he said.

'Believe me, Mr Kartashkin, I do not play where such matters are concerned. We know that Mr Ransom was working for the consortium.'

'He was working for our British partner. In the north. He was advising on the opencast mining—'

'Mr Kartashkin, please do not underestimate me. We know that Mr Ransom had been carrying out some work connected with the Gobi project. We understand that he had been called in to verify some disputed data.'

Kartashkin's eyes were wide now. 'In Russia, I think we have ceased carrying out secret surveillance on our citizens. I can only assume that this is not yet the case here.'

'Assume as you wish,' Nergui said. 'But we do like to be aware when visitors to our country are acting illegally.'

'Hardly illegally,' Kartashkin said. 'And you will need to take this up with our partner. It was they who requested—'

'He was working outside the terms specified on his visa,' Nergui said. 'But that is unimportant. We have two murder victims, killed in very similar circumstances, both apparently employed within your consortium. Such coincidences spark my curiosity.'

'I do not know what is happening,' Kartashkin said. 'I am speaking the truth. I am out of my depth in this project, I admit it. I'm a businessman – a pretty hard-nosed businessman, I thought. I don't always do things by the book. But this is beyond me.'

'What is beyond you, Mr Kartashkin?' Nergui said.

'This project. There are people involved in this who scare me. On all sides.' He glanced at the door again.

'Even on your own side?'

Kartashkin leaned forward, his hands clasped together. 'Yes, even on my side. We're a legitimate business. But we needed more investment here to keep in the game. We've always walked a fine line.'

'What do you mean?'

'We're based in St Petersburg. It's not easy. Organised crime there is . . . well, it dominates the business world. Not all businessmen are criminals, but we all have to make accommodations.'

'I understand. And you have been making accommodations in respect of this project?'

'More than ever before. We were desperate. We'd already sunk so much into this that if it had fallen through we'd have gone under. And there was increasing investment from the other partner countries, so we began to be afraid of being squeezed out. So we had to look for further investment at home.'

'And you found it?'

'We found it. But only by doing business with people that we would not normally wish to go near.'

Nergui nodded, and looked at the door. 'Your colleagues,' he said. 'These are the people you are talking about?'

'Two of them, yes. The other one is my deputy. But the other two directors—'

'Do you believe they are responsible for the murders, Mr Kartashkin?'

Kartashkin shook his head. 'No. I mean, that would make no sense. Why would they want to kill Delgerbayar and Ransom?'

'So who did?'

'Well, this is what scares me. If we assume that the two murders are connected, then that suggests that they were committed by someone else in the project. Someone trying to harm our interests.' He paused. 'That, at least, is how my new colleagues appear to think.'

Nergui nodded. 'And they think this because this is perhaps how they would behave themselves?'

Kartashkin shrugged. 'I do not know. But I know that they are taking the killings as – how do I put this? – as an affront to their honour. The way they talk disturbs me.'

Nergui nodded. 'I think you are a brave man, Mr Kartashkin, to state your views so openly.'

'I am anything but brave,' Kartashkin said. 'But I am trusting you with this. I do not want more bloodshed.'

'I could insist on you coming back with me to give a formal statement,' Nergui said. 'And I may yet have to do so. But for now I think it is better if we treat our business as concluded. You have told me nothing.'

Kartashkin nodded, the relief showing on his face. 'Thank you. There is little else I can do, but I would help if I could.'

'I would give you one piece of advice, Mr Kartashkin. Get out of this. As soon as you can.'

As they left the boardroom, they saw two of the men who had left the meeting now standing at the far end of the corridor, watching them. Nergui made a gesture of apology. 'I am sorry for disturbing your meeting. I hope that I did not keep you waiting for long.' He walked slowly along the corridor towards the two men, who were watching him warily. One was tall, thin, shaven-headed. He wore dark glasses even indoors, in the middle of winter. His stare was blankly intimidating. The other was shorter, his hair combed tightly back, his eyes bright and blinking.

'Routine questions, I'm afraid,' Nergui said. 'We're investigating some illegal prospectors near one of your sites in the north. I just wanted to check whether you had actually met the prospectors, whether you could provide any information about them. But Kartashkin says no. Is that your recollection also?' He gazed impassively at the two men, a faint smile on his lips.

There was silence for a moment, then the taller man spoke, scarcely above a whisper. 'We know nothing of this. We simply wish for the police to enforce the law.'

'It is what we try to do,' Nergui said. He nodded slowly, as though musing on his words. 'But thank you. And my apologies again for the disturbance.'

He turned and made his way down the stairs, Doripalam close behind, feeling the men watching him until he had walked across the reception and back out into the street.

As soon as they stepped back into the cold morning air, Nergui began to stride, with characteristic speed, back towards HQ. Doripalam hurried to keep up. 'Nasty bunch,' he said.

'Very. I was keen for them to know that Kartashkin had told us nothing.'

'What do you think about Kartashkin? About what he said, I mean?'

'I feel,' Nergui said, 'as though he has provided us with another piece of the jigsaw, but I have no idea about how it all fits together. If it's true that Ransom's and Delgerbayar's deaths are somehow connected with the Gobi project, then where does Badzar fit in?'

'Maybe Badzar's working for one of the partner groups. Perhaps he's a hired killer.'

Nergui stopped suddenly and turned to look at Doripalam. 'It's possible, I suppose, but I can't see that it makes much sense. Who would hire a madman? And what professional killer would leave the bodies the way these were left?'

They crossed the road, stepping over the thick piles of greying snow left by the snowploughs. The roads were largely cleared now, and the morning traffic was becoming busier.

As they turned the corner back towards police HQ, Nergui's mobile rang. He pressed the receive button, holding the phone to his ear as he walked.

It was one of the junior officers. 'We've had another call, sir. From our friend.'

'Is he still on the line?' Nergui said. 'I asked for him to be put through to the mobile.'

'We tried, but he wouldn't hang on. Obviously thought it was a ruse to give us time to trace him. But he left a message.'

'What message?'

'Said he wanted to meet you, sir. Just you. On your own. He's still claiming that he's got the British officer. Says he's prepared to release him but only if he can meet with you.'

'Did he give us any reason to believe that McLeish is still alive?'

'Not really. Didn't stay on long enough.'

'So what next?'

'He wants an answer from you, sir. As to whether you're prepared to meet with him. The implication was that if you don't, the British officer won't be alive much longer.'

'Assuming he's alive now. Okay, we're only a few minutes away. Did he give you any indication when he would call again?'

'He said in fifteen minutes. And that we should be ready with an answer.'

'In that case, I'd better try to come up with one.'

He ended the call and relayed the gist of the message to Doripalam.

'What are you going to do?'

'I don't know,' Nergui said. 'He's got us over a barrel, as he's no doubt fully aware. We can't just ignore this. The political ramifications are too great. But it would be crazy to go into a one-to-one meeting with a psychopath like this. Especially since we don't even know if he does really have McLeish or, if he does, whether McLeish is still alive.'

'You could go in with some back-up.'

'It would be a risk. If McLeish is there and alive, we don't know what Badzar would do if he thought we had him cornered.'

'And it could all be just a hoax?'

'As you say. It could all just be some lunatic trying to make idiots of us. Not that that's been particularly difficult in this case.'

They had arrived back at HQ. Despite the brilliance of the morning sun, the place still looked depressing, its dark concrete looming over them. The thick snow by the entrance was already grey from the tread of countless feet. Nergui did not feel at home here. He felt that the regular police resented his presence, were suspicious of his motives. But equally, he realised, he no longer felt comfortable back in the Ministry. He had always considered himself an astute political player, a survivor, but he was increasingly beginning to feel that this world was leaving him behind.

Inside, the offices were almost deserted, most of the officers engaged in the manhunt for Badzar. So far, he appeared to have slipped away without trace.

Nergui stopped by the telephone switchboard. 'When do we expect him to call back?' he asked the operator.

The operator glanced at his watch. 'Ten minutes,' he said. 'Maybe a little less.'

Nergui nodded. 'I'll be in my office,' he said. 'Put him straight through.'

He led Doripalam into the office and sat himself down behind the desk, gesturing Doripalam to sit opposite. The files on the case lay untouched in front of him.

'I don't think I have a choice,' Nergui said.

'What do you mean?'

'I think I have to do what he says,' Nergui said. 'Meet him. Alone.'

'Even though we don't know whether McLeish is even still alive?'

'Especially because of that. The Minister can't keep a lid on this story much longer. The Western media are going to be all over us in the next twenty-four hours.'

'The story won't be improved if we end up losing one of our senior officers as well,' Doripalam pointed out.

'You're right.' Nergui grimaced at the thought. 'But,

as I say, I don't think there's a choice. All I can try to do is minimise the risks. The risk to me. And the risk to McLeish, if he's still alive.'

'And how do you do that?'

Nergui shrugged. 'I've got my own talents in that direction. And I'll be armed. And I want you as back-up.'

'Me? But I not sure I'm the best—'

'There are highly trained officers I could take with me, but I'm not sure who to trust here any more. I don't know who Badzar is working for, if he's working for anyone. And I don't know who or what he knows. I have a feeling that if I set this up as a formal mission, he may well know. And that may mean the end of things for McLeish.'

'But I'm still not—'

'Doripalam, we've no idea what we might be letting ourselves in for here. We don't know what's driving Badzar. We don't know why he's suddenly decided to make himself known. It could be a trap. But why bother with a trap? We presume he's already got McLeish – if he's got demands, then he's already got more than enough leverage. If he wanted another victim, he could find one easily enough without putting himself at this risk. He could have killed me while I was waiting at the factory last night. I think it's more likely he wants something.' He paused. 'And maybe *he* doesn't know who he can trust, either.'

Doripalam nodded and opened his mouth to speak. But then Nergui's phone rang. He picked it up, listened and reached out to switch on the intercom. 'It's him,' he mouthed.

The same sibilant voice emerged from the low-quality speaker. 'Have you had time to think?' it asked, without preamble.

'What is it you want?' Nergui said.

'To see you. Alone.'

'How do I know McLeish is safe?'

'You don't. You won't until you meet me. Now, please stop wasting my time. Are you prepared to meet? Just you. If there's any other police presence, McLeish dies.'

'If he's still alive.'

'As you say. Yes or no?'

Nergui paused and glanced across at Doripalam. 'Yes,' he said. 'Just tell me where and when.'

TWENTY-TWO

Not quite silence.

Drew lay, straining every muscle to try to see or hear something, to try to gain some clue as to what was happening.

Someone was watching him closely as he struggled, in one more vain attempt, with the ties that gripped him. He didn't know how he could feel the presence of this other person.

But there was not quite silence.

It seemed like hours since he had heard someone enter the room, but was probably only minutes. And even though he knew that whatever happened next was unlikely to be pleasant, a part of him still refused to accept this, still somehow believed that his current state would continue indefinitely.

Why did his captor not simply get on and do whatever it was he intended? Why this endless torturing uncertainty? Was it simply an attempt to wear down his resistance? But why? Drew had nothing – no possessions, no information – that was likely to be of interest to whoever had kidnapped him in this country. If the intention was to extort some demands from the government, either here or at home, there was nothing obvious to be gained through this kind of psychological torture.

He continued to alternate between struggling with his bonds, and lying as still as possible, trying to gain some sense of what might be happening. But both activities were equally fruitless, nothing more than an empty gesture, a vain attempt to demonstrate to his captor that he had not yet ceased to resist.

And then, suddenly, unexpectedly, he felt the soft touch of a hand against his, the startling warmth of human contact. The touch was so gentle that at first he thought that he was imagining the sensation. But then he felt his hand being grasped firmly in another's grip, a strange feeling because the hand felt harsher, drier, than human flesh. He twisted his head, trying at least to see the hand, trying to see what was gripping his fingers.

And then he saw it. It was, indeed, simply a human hand clutching his own, but the fingers were enclosed in the kind of protective glove worn by those handling food in a shop or café. The kind of glove that might be worn by someone who did not wish to leave any trace of fingerprints.

Drew arched his back, trying to see more, but could still see only the hand and, beyond that, a wrist surrounded by a white shirt cuff. The hand was grasping his own tightly, pulling it hard to one side. He felt his heart beating loudly, his breath pounding through his chest as he wondered what would follow.

And then he heard something metallic, something heavy, being lifted from the ground. He could hear his captor's breathing, the slight strain of someone lifting something heavy, high above his head.

Drew tensed as he felt the momentum of the object through the air above him, his mind jumped back to the sights of the dismembered bodies, the thought of how those limbs had been removed. And as he felt the draught of air above him, he did not even have the breath to scream.

He felt, rather than heard, the heavy thump of metal on wood. He remembered, crazily, stories of those who had lost limbs initially feeling no pain, not even recognising that they had been injured.

But then his breath and his senses returned, and he realised that he was genuinely not hurt. He twisted his head to look at where his captor's hand was still gripping his own.

In the bench just by his hand, a large axe was buried a centimetre or so into the wood. His hand had been pulled back to avoid the axe, so the blade had instead cut neatly through the bindings around his wrist.

Drew opened his mouth to shout, though he had no idea what words he might utter to this still unseen figure who was unlikely to speak any English. Before he could speak, a handcuff was slip around Drew's untied wrist. He felt his arm being pulled again, and was then aware that the other half of the handcuffs had been firmly attached to an object, as yet invisible to him. He twisted again in his remaining bonds but could still see nothing.

The figure moved behind him, and his other hand was gripped and pulled aside. Again, there was the swish of the axe falling through the air and he felt another bond fall free.

He tried to move, but the remaining bonds on his ankles and neck still held him firmly in place. He caught a glimpse of his captor as he moved rapidly around the room, a black shadow passing swiftly across his constrained vision. The figure was down at his feet now. Again, Drew felt the hand on his leg, holding his feet to one side as the axe fell again, severing the bond on his left leg. And then the same on his right. His legs were free, and only the tight binding on his neck still held him in place.

His captor moved slowly alongside the bench. Drew twisted his head as much as possible, and for the first time saw the figure who was standing beside him.

The man was unremarkable. He was of average height, stockily built, dressed in a cheap-looking, black Western-style suit. He wore a white shirt, open at the neck. He stopped now and stared at Drew.

He was wearing a black skiing mask which entirely covered his face except for two small eye-holes. And, whereas the rest of this figure was unexceptional, the eyes were striking. They stared fixedly at Drew, reddened, burning, unblinking. It was impossible to read the emotion that lay behind them, there was just an emptiness, a blankness, that seemed almost less than human.

Up to now, Drew's terrors had been substantial but unfocussed, nothing more than a fear of what might be impending. Now, though, the threat was real and immediate.

Drew lay still on the bench, his legs and right arm free, but his neck still pinioned to the bench. He shifted his head further, feeling the bindings cutting painfully into his neck, and saw that his left arm was fastened with the handcuffs to a ring on the end of a metal pole. Drew pulled hard on the handcuffs, but it was clear that the pole was set into some heavy, immovable base. It was this, perhaps, which Drew had heard his captor dragging along the floor.

The figure stood motionless, watching Drew. The axe hung loose in his left hand. And, in his right hand, held equally loosely, was what appeared to be a pocket knife, gleaming brightly in the room's stark illumination.

Drew stared back in terror, as the figure began to move slowly forward, raising the knife before his face. His eyes still seemed expressionless, empty of thought or feeling.

As the knife approached his face, Drew suddenly felt as if life and feeling were flooding back into his inert body. Too late, he kicked out with his legs, trying to thrust himself free, feeling the grip of the bond around his neck, preventing him from throwing himself off the bench. The knife rose above him, and Drew screamed, the echoes bouncing ineffectually around the walls and empty spaces.

Nergui had been here before.

How long was it? Three years, maybe four. Something like that. But the sights and sounds and smells – especially the smells – of this place had stayed with him ever since.

It was a place he would dearly have liked to forget. He remembered what he had seen here, at a time when he thought that his country was finally succumbing to irrevocable chaos. This place had seemed almost like a symbol of those miserable days, an image of the depths to which the nation had sunk and from which it had seemed unlikely ever to arise.

But things had changed, and Nergui supposed that this augured well for the future, even if his cynicism did not allow him to entertain excessive optimism. This place was as eerie and unnerving as ever, but its connotations were changing. Already the past was being put behind it.

Visually, the place was extraordinary, a tortuous tapestry of black twisted pipes and billowing steam. It was the entrance to a sewer pipe, a massive construct built in the Soviet days. The pipe network had been built to transport not only sewage but also steam heat from the then thriving factory units around to domestic buildings in the neighbourhood. It had not been a particularly efficient arrangement, in that substantial amounts of steam billowed out into the frozen air. But it did ensure, with characteristic Soviet ingenuity, that heat that would otherwise have been wasted – and which, in the West, would perhaps have been discarded without a thought – was transferred to a practical use.

But, with the collapse of the economy, the steam tunnels had been transformed into something more than merely practical. For some, in the most unpleasant and tragic circumstances, they had become life-saving. This area, only a few years before, had been overwhelmed by those with no other homes to go to – the majority of them children or teenagers.

Whatever their various backgrounds, the hordes of homeless young people had congregated here, trying to find some way of enduring the bitter cold of the icy Mongolian winter. The steam pipes had provided one source of warmth, and the homeless had come in their hundreds to shelter inside, braving the stench of the sewers in exchange for survival.

Initially, the authorities had largely turned a blind eye. If these people were able to fend for themselves, however harsh the conditions, then so much the better. But crime levels had risen, and the groups of semi-feral children became seen as a scourge by those in more fortunate positions. Pressure was placed on the police to deal with the problem, and Nergui recalled numerous raids on the area. Children were picked up in their dozens, and shipped off to shelters that were often only marginal improvements on the makeshift hovels they had left behind. Inevitably, many of those picked up simply ran away again within days, and the whole miserable cycle continued.

Gradually, though, things had changed. Crucially, the economy had slowly improved, and some foreign aid had been obtained to deal with some of the specific problems of homelessness. There was a growing number of decent children's hostels, many of them run by international charities. Work was now more plentiful, and many of those who had been homeless were able to fend for themselves.

Nevertheless, this still tended to be a place where the homeless would cluster, particularly as the winter approached. Many of the formerly thriving factories now lay abandoned, and it was possible to find shelter close enough to the steam pipes to stave off the rigours of the winter nights.

Now, though, the area looked deserted. Alleys ran off between the factories, deep in shadow. In the open areas, the ground was thick with snow, melting only where the steam continued to billow, filling the frozen air with a dense white fog. Nergui stepped slowly forward, straining his eyes. He could see only a few feet in front of him.

He glanced at his watch. Nearly three, as Badzar had stipulated. Behind him, across the city, the sun was already setting, and the shadows were lengthening between the buildings.

This was insane, he thought. He had sought no permission for coming here, nor even told anyone, other than Doripalam, where he was going. This solitary action went against every rule of policing. On the other hand, he did not see much alternative. The Minister, if he had been consulted, would probably have seen things the same way, though might have felt unable to say so overtly.

The proper thing to have done would have been to initiate a full-scale police operation. They should have surrounded the area, given Nergui full back-up, ensured that, whatever else might happen, at least there would have been no chance of Badzar escaping from this alive.

Instead he just had Doripalam, his gun, and his cell phone with Doripalam's number already dialled. They had agreed that if Nergui should call the number without subsequently speaking Doripalam should summon back-up immediately. But Nergui had no illusions that back-up would arrive in time to prevent Badzar's escape.

However, if the worst did happen and Drew was

killed, the Minister could present this as a maverick escapade, not officially sanctioned. At worst, they would be back where they started, and Nergui would be left to take the responsibility, probably posthumously. At best, though, this might just conceivably produce the positive outcome that would never be achieved through more orthodox means.

The afternoon was already growing dark. Nergui pulled out his flashlight and shone it down the narrow alleyways, though the illumination was almost useless within the dense clouds of steam. He could make out only the cracked and stained concrete of the old factory buildings. Above, there were lines of smashed and boarded-up windows. Below, there was just scattered rubbish, the debris of abandoned industry, white shapes under the snow.

Badzar had not indicated precisely where he would be, or how he would make his presence known. He had simply told Nergui to come to this spot at three, and then to wait.

Nergui flashed the light up and around him, occasionally glimpsing, as the steam momentarily cleared, the dark towering factories. Once, far above, he caught sight of the densely star-strewn sky. There were no working streetlights down here, though behind him he could see a faint glow in the distance behind the mass of buildings. Through the mist, the sky was darkening from red to a dark purple as the sun disappeared. Soon, the darkness here would be thick and heavy, softened only by the continually billowing steam.

The atmosphere was getting to him, and the shifting clouds of steam created phantoms as he moved forward. He thought of the headless corpses and, despite the cold, the sweat trickled down his back. He told himself that if Badzar wanted him dead he would have killed him the night before. But the thought did nothing to calm his nerves.

Nergui carefully moved the flashlight around him, watching the thickening shadows, the constantly shifting clouds, trying to keep his back close to the wall. The only sound was the insistent hiss of the escaping steam, the rustle of his own footsteps in the frozen snow.

And then, without quite knowing how, he was aware of another presence. He peered forward into the gloom and the steam, trying to make out any movement. Just when he was almost convinced that he had been mistaken, he saw something, across the open space, at the entrance to one of the many alleyways. At first, it was nothing more than a movement, undefined, a sense of shifting space. And then it resolved itself into a shape, a silhouette, half obscured by the darkness and the drifting steam.

'Badzar?' Nergui called. He pointed his flashlight towards the shape, but the beam made little headway in the foggy night.

There was no immediate response. Nergui was sure now that the figure was that of a man, dressed in a long dark garment, but could still make out little more. His hand clutched at his pistol in his pocket and he began to move slowly forward.

He walked forward some metres, holding the flashlight steady, watching the black figure emerge slowly from the darkness. 'Badzar?' he said again.

The figure remained motionless, apparently watching him without concern. It was still little more than a silhouette, the face featureless.

He took another step forward, and at last the figure moved, raising its hand. 'Stop there.' It was the same deep sibilant voice he had heard on the phone.

'Badzar. It's not too late to put an end to this.' As he spoke the words, Nergui knew that he was lying:

something had been set in motion here that lay far beyond his powers to resolve.

'Stop,' the figure repeated.

Nergui obeyed, holding the flashlight out towards the figure. As far as he could make out it was dressed in a long black coat, some sort of hood pulled over its eyes.

'What is it you want?' Nergui said. 'Why have you brought me here?'

'The British policeman is safe,' the figure said, as though answering the question. 'He will remain so as long as you have done what I say.'

'Where is he?'

'He is here. Close at hand. Are you alone?'

Nergui gestured with the flashlight. 'Completely. As you can see.'

'How do I know that?'

'How do I know you have McLeish?'

'You don't.'

'Likewise, then. You have to trust me.'

The figure nodded, as though considering this. He continued to stare towards Nergui, his face invisible. 'I trust you,' he said. 'For the moment.' And then he turned abruptly, and disappeared back into the darkness of the alley.

Nergui stared after him for a moment, then walked rapidly across the open yard to where the figure had been standing. There was no one there.

Nergui shone the flashlight down the alley. A trail of footprints disappeared across the icy snow. Nergui traced their path to where they ended at an open doorway leading into one of the factory buildings. For a moment, Nergui felt bizarrely reassured by the sight of the footprints – as, he realised, he had the previous night. It was as if he had to keep reminding himself that Badzar was, after all, only human.

He made his way cautiously down the alley, occasionally glancing behind him, in case this was some kind of trap. The silence had returned, and he could hear nothing other than his own footsteps.

There was no light showing beyond the doorway. The door hung open, and Nergui saw a broken padlock on the ground nearby. He stopped by the opening, conscious that he did not wish to make himself too visible a target. 'Badzar. Stop playing games. Tell me what you want.' He could hear his voice echoing in the empty spaces beyond the doorway, an unexpected contrast to the muffled snowbound world outside.

There was no response. Nergui switched off the flashlight, aware that it would only betray his position. He pulled out his pistol, thumbed off the safety catch and stepped forward into the darkness.

Once through the doorway, he stepped rapidly away from the door, moving himself along the wall so that his position would not be obvious. He stopped, his back pressed against the wall, and held his breath, listening for any clue as to what might lie inside this vaulted room.

There was nothing. The silence and the darkness seemed complete, other than the very faint greyness coming from the open doorway. He had no idea what was in the room, whether it was simply an empty abandoned space or filled with equipment of some kind. He did not know if Badzar was really in here, and if so whether he was here alone.

He stayed motionless by the wall, wondering what his next move should be. If there was no other response, he would have little option but to switch on the flashlight again. He felt absurdly exposed in here, recognising that Badzar was playing with him, leading him into a position where he had no choice but to reveal his position, to present himself as a target to an unseen enemy.

He pressed himself back against the wall, his pistol clutched tightly in his hand, his finger resting on the trigger, preparing for what might happen when he switched on the torch.

And then the decision was taken out of his hands, so suddenly that he almost fired involuntarily. The great vaulted space was suddenly flooded with light, rows of fluorescent tubes flickering into life along the roof beams.

Nergui tried to keep his eyes open, but was dazzled by the unexpected brilliance and for endless seconds could see nothing. He held the gun tight, wanting to be ready for whatever might be waiting, but aware of the risks of shooting into the unseen.

But nothing happened. And finally his eyes cleared, and he was able to look across the vast factory floor to what lay at the far end of the room.

TWENTY-THREE

The knife rose, the silver blade glinting in the bright overhead lights, then came down sharply. Drew's screams were still echoing round the vast empty room as the blade struck, the blade snagging hard against the tight cords.

Drew gasped, all the breath expelled from his body, his mind dazed, his terror now beyond even screaming. He felt, momentarily, the icy steel against his neck, then nothing more. It took him a moment to realise that he felt no pain, and several seconds more to accept that he remained unharmed, except for a mild tingling on his neck where the blade had grazed him.

He twisted his head, trying to see what was happening, and found that, for the first time since he had awakened in this place, his head was free. The stroke of the knife had, with consummate skill, sliced neatly through the cords that held him while barely touching his skin.

His captor was standing calmly, a few feet away, watching as Drew twisted his body to see. Behind the woollen helmet, his eyes were unblinking.

Drew's body was aching and stiff from the lengthy period of captivity, and at first he was barely able to take advantage of his new freedom. He was held now only by the handcuffs which, as he looked around him, were attached to a ring embedded in a large piece of concrete. He pulled hard on the handcuffs and the block shifted slightly on the floor. It would have been possible to move it, but only with considerable effort. His captor must be considerably stronger than Drew himself, accustomed to moving heavy loads.

His muscles in agony, Drew pulled himself into a sitting position. His captor still stood watching, motionless, with the air of a scientist observing an experiment. Drew looked around him. As he had surmised, this was some kind of disused factory building. The room they were in was a storeroom of some kind, with empty metal shelves stretching around the walls. Here and there were abandoned items – a paint pot, some rusty-looking tools, a few pieces of wood and metal. Drew himself had been lying on a wooden workbench, set in the middle of the concrete floor.

The room was a relatively large one – maybe ten metres square – but through the door behind his captor Drew could see a further, much larger area. Probably the original factory floor, he thought.

It was as if, once his body had been freed, Drew had come to life again, returned from his state of suspended animation. During his captivity, he had been largely unaware of pain or other bodily needs. Now, suddenly, he was aware not only of the stiffness and aches arising from the discomfort of his imprisonment, but also of other pains – the bruises and grazes he had sustained while being attacked and kidnapped. But more immediately, he was acutely aware of a need to urinate.

He stared at his captor. 'Who are you?' he said. 'What do you want from me?' He was conscious that even if his captor was prepared to engage in dialogue with him, he was unlikely to speak English.

There was no direct response. His captor continued to stare at him. Drew pushed himself down from the bench and put his feet on the floor. His legs shook from the effort, but he forced himself to stand upright. 'Why have you brought me here?' he said, in a last effort to make himself understood. He tried to move forward towards his captor, stretching himself away from the handcuffs as far as he could.

The other man still did not move. He was standing several feet beyond Drew's reach. As Drew tried to stretch towards him, he continued to watch, apparently with mild curiosity.

Finally, the man took a step back, still watching Drew. He turned suddenly and began to walk towards the open doorway. At the door, he paused momentarily, and looked back over his shoulder. 'Come,' he said in English. 'This way.'

Drew stared at him for a moment in astonishment. The words had been in English. The accent had sounded American, or at least the accent of someone who had learned English in the US. Drew watched as the man disappeared into the far room. Then, slowly and painfully, he tried to follow, dragging the heavy concrete block behind him.

He moved a metre or so along. Then he stopped and, with feelings mixed between relief and a sense of futile rebellion, he unzipped his flies with his free hand and began to urinate copiously across the concrete floor. It was only when he was finished and the liquid was running in rivulets across the empty room that he recommenced his slow progress towards the open door.

Nergui's sight cleared slowly, and he stared across the room through a haze of colours.

This was the old factory floor. It was a vast room, with a high vaulted ceiling crossed by metal roof-beams. Large windows stretched along each wall, although the majority of these were broken or boarded up. It was clear that the room had once contained some form of production machinery, but now, apart from a few discarded pieces of rusty metal, the large space was empty.

At the far end of the room, a man stood. It was the figure Nergui had seen in the darkness, dressed in a long black overcoat, with a hood over his head. Even in the bright light of the numerous fluorescent tubes, Nergui could barely make out the man's face in the hood's shadow, though it was clear he was a Mongolian.

'Badzar?' Nergui said.

'You know who I am,' Badzar said. It was a statement, rather than a question. 'I saw my brother,' he added.

Nergui took a cautious step forward. It was not evident that Badzar was armed, but Nergui had already taken too many chances. 'It's not too late to stop all this,' he said.

Badzar shook his head. 'I think it is too late,' he said. 'Not for me, but for others.'

'Where's McLeish?' Nergui said. 'The British policeman. You said you had him. Where is he?'

'He is not here,' Badzar said. 'It is not true that I have him. Not quite true.' He held up his hand as Nergui started to speak. 'But I know where he is. He is close by. He is, as far as I know, safe for the moment.'

'As far as you know? What do you mean?' Nergui felt a small tremor of relief. He did not understand Badzar's responses, but they were bizarre enough to suggest that they could be true, that McLeish might after all still be alive. 'Where is he?'

'Close by,' Badzar said. He shrugged. 'I am happy to take you there, though I do not know what will happen after that. I want an end to all this. It is not what I expected.'

Nergui gently shook his head, trying to make sense of what he was hearing. Maybe it was simply that Badzar was insane, beyond all reason, disconnected from the enormity of what he had done, the crimes he had committed. But it did not feel like that. It felt, as it had to Nergui all along, as though something was emerging here, something he could not yet begin to grasp.

'It's easy for you to put an end to this, if that's what you want,' he said. 'Take me to McLeish. Hand him over. We can deal with things from there.'

'It is not that simple,' Badzar said. 'It cannot be that simple again. There have been so many crimes and this is just the start.'

Nergui took some more steps forward. Badzar did not appear to react to his approach, his hands hanging limply by his side. Nergui's hand was in his pocket, clutching his pistol.

'What do you mean,' Nergui said, 'just the start?'

Badzar shook his head. His face was visible to Nergui now, caught in the fluorescent lights. He was staring ahead, his eyes blank, his face expressionless. He did not look like a driven man, he did not look like a threat. He looked like a man who was lost, who had somehow travelled too far, too quickly, and now had no idea where he was. Nergui realised that Badzar was not staring at him as he had assumed, but was looking through him, beyond him, as if at something in the far distance. Nergui glanced behind him, wondering if this wasn't after all some kind of trap. But then it became clear to him that whatever Badzar might be staring at, it was not anything in this room. It was not anything that was visible to the human eye.

'What is it?' Nergui said. 'What are you talking about? Where's McLeish? Take me to him.'

Badzar blinked, and his eyes focused on Nergui, as if seeing him for the first time. 'I'll take you to him,' he said. 'I want to take you to him. I think he is safe. At the moment.'

'Quickly, then,' Nergui said. He did not begin to

understand what Badzar was saying, but it sounded as if, for whatever reason, McLeish's safety was far from guaranteed. 'Take me to him.'

Badzar stared at Nergui. His eyes were no longer staring into nothingness, but were now fixed on Nergui. The effect was no less disconcerting. 'It was him, you see,' Badzar said, as though responding to Nergui's instruction. 'He was the one. He told me to do it. He helped me.' He paused, his eyes pleading. 'I would not have done it without him. Not in the same way. Not so much. Not so many.'

'Who told you to do it?' Nergui said.

'He did. He led me into this. He told me it was the only way. And then we just went on. There was no way out. No way back.'

'Who do you mean? Who are you talking about?'

'Him. He told me.' Badzar was shaking his head now, repeatedly, obsessively. His eyes were still blank. 'He told me.'

'Where is he? Is he with McLeish?' Nergui looked around him at the empty, brightly lit room. He could not follow Badzar into his apparent descent into madness. Was there really some third party? Or was this just some bizarre symptom of Badzar's insanity? If so, there was no guarantee that McLeish was still alive, no guarantee that McLeish was here at all.

'He told me to call you. To bring you to him.'

The words stopped Nergui, chills running down his spine. 'He told you to call me? To bring me here?'

Badzar shook his head, looking impatient. 'No, not to bring you here. That's just it. He told me to bring you to him. He doesn't know we are here yet.'

'Where is he, then?'

'He's – nearby. I said I would bring you to him. But I wanted to talk. To tell you. That it was him.'

'What was him?'

'Everything was him. Everything. He told me to do it. All of it. And he – was responsible.'

'Who is he?' Nergui said again.

'He is nearby.' Badzar stopped and looked at his watch. 'We have no time. We have to go to him. Otherwise—'

'Otherwise what?'

'We have to go. Now. But I wanted to tell you.'

'Take me to McLeish.' Nergui pulled the pistol from his pocket. 'Take me now.'

Badzar looked down at the gun, but barely seemed to register its existence. 'I need to take you now,' he said again.

He turned and began to walk slowly towards the rear of the factory. There were wide double doors there, clearly designed to provide access for large machinery. To the right of the doors, there was a smaller entrance for everyday access. Badzar reached it, Nergui following close behind, and pulled open the door.

Nergui followed him out into a dark narrow alleyway. It was unlit, but Nergui could see both ways along its full length. Another factory building loomed over them.

'I will take you to him,' Badzar said. He began to walk slowly along the alley, staring at the ground. Nergui followed behind, his pistol clutched in one hand, the flashlight in the other.

The alley opened into another open yard area, with a cluster of factory and warehouse buildings around it. The yard was covered with frozen snow, apparently undisturbed since it had fallen. Above them, the sky remained clear and star-filled.

Badzar walked slowly across the yard, leaving a trail of footprints in the virgin snow. By now, Nergui had no idea what to expect. It was clear only that Badzar was beyond any reason.

There was another, wider alleyway at the far side of the yard. Badzar started to walk down it, but almost immediately stopped and turned to his left. 'Here,' he said. 'Here it is.' He gestured towards the wall of the adjacent building. Nergui followed close behind and saw that there was a narrow doorway, that had been left ajar. 'In here,' Badzar said.

Nergui waved the pistol at him. 'You first,' he said.

Badzar nodded, and slowly pushed open the door and stepped inside. He walked a few steps forward, and Nergui followed carefully, still suspecting a trap.

Beyond the doorway, there was a short unlit passage-way. At the far end were more double doors. They were closed, but around them shone a thin line of light.

'In there,' Badzar said. 'He is in there.'

'McLeish?'

'Yes, McLeish is there. And he is there. I hope we are not too late.'

'I hope so too,' Nergui said. 'You go in first.'

He still had no idea what to expect, how to gauge Badzar's sanity. His greatest fear was that McLeish's corpse lay beyond this door. It was not clear what else might be waiting.

Badzar stepped forward and pushed open the door. Light flooded through the opening. Nergui paused, allowing his eyes to grow accustomed to the new bright-ness. He did not want to be caught out again.

Badzar stood, holding the door for him in a parody of conventional politeness. Nergui stepped forward slowly, holding the pistol in front of him, and entered the room.

It was another large abandoned space, this one prob-ably an old warehouse, as the walls were covered in racks and shelving. As he walked forward in the brightly lit room, Nergui wondered irrelevantly how it was that these deserted buildings still had access to electricity.

Then he stopped. Badzar had paused a few feet in front of him, his arms limply at his sides as before.

The room was not empty. Drew was here, as Badzar had promised, and he was not yet the corpse that Nergui had feared. He looked, though, as if death might not be far away. He was sitting huddled on the floor at the far end of the room, his face pale and drawn, his eyes haunted. He was hunched forward, dressed in the clothes he had been wearing when he left the embassy. One of his arms was handcuffed to a post, the kind of device that one might use for tethering a dog or a horse.

And next to him was another figure, dressed in black, a black ski helmet pulled across his face, hiding everything but his eyes. He held a pistol loosely in his hand, the barrel pointing towards Drew.

The figure turned to them, and Nergui was sure that behind the mask, his face was smiling. 'Good afternoon,' he said. 'You are just in time. Only just in time. I'd begun to think that you weren't coming.' He raised the pistol in front of his face and looked at it, shaking his head. 'So I will not need this just for the moment.' He looked back up at Nergui, leaving the gun barrel pointing at Drew.

'But I'm glad you came,' he said. 'We've a lot to discuss.'

TWENTY-FOUR

Nergui slowly lowered his pistol, but kept it in his hand. 'I suppose I should have expected this.'

'You're a smart man, Nergui,' the masked man said, 'but you're out of your depth here. I think we all are.'

'Even you?'

'Yeah, maybe even me.'

'Drew. You're okay?' Nergui looked across at Drew now, ignoring the masked man still pointing his pistol at Drew's head.

Drew nodded slowly. 'I think so, for the moment.'

'He'll be okay,' the masked man said. 'So long as you're sensible.'

'Forget it, Maxon.'

The masked man nodded slowly, then reached up to peel off the helmet. 'As I say,' Maxon smiled, 'you're smart. Smart enough to help your friend McLeish here, if you're sensible.'

Nergui shook his head. 'It's too late, Maxon. Even if you get away from us, you won't get away from them.'

'Smart again, Nergui. But you're wrong this time. I've been in this game too long to be caught out now. All I need is a little help.'

'Not this time. It's gone too far.'

'You've no idea how far,' Maxon said. 'It's beyond you now. This isn't about law enforcement or morality, it's about politics. Nobody wants the truth, they just want a politically expedient outcome. You can be a hero.

You walk out of here with McLeish safe and the killer in custody.' He gestured towards Badzar. 'He's in no state to resist.'

'And in exchange I let you get away?'

'You *help* me get away. I need shelter for a couple of days and help getting out of the country, that's all. I might manage it on my own, but with your help – with official help – I'll be safe.' He shrugged. 'Nobody loses.'

'Except Badzar.'

'Jesus, he's a killer. He's a serial fucking murderer. Why do you care about him?'

'I don't care about him. I want to see him given the treatment he deserves, whatever that might turn out to be. But I care about you. If he's a killer, what are you?'

'I'm a professional,' Maxon said.

Nergui shook his head. 'Maxon, you are, as you would no doubt say, a piece of fucking work. Okay, so what if I don't help you?'

'Then we all lose. Let's think about it, shall we? You don't play ball, first thing I make off with your friend here. You're back where you started.'

'You won't get away for long. We're combing the city for you.'

'Yeah, without any success till I gave you a small clue. Like telling you exactly where I fucking was. And the point is that I know exactly how much of a political storm is brewing about our friend. You've been able to keep the lid on it so far, but not for much longer. Soon as the Western media realise you've no idea where he is – or, worse still, if my patience runs out or my trigger finger slips – you're in deep shit. Particularly if it's made known that you had me in your clutches but let me slip away.'

'This is insane, Maxon. Even if I do go along with this, what happens once you hand McLeish over? What's to stop us picking you up then?'

'Because I'll make sure you don't get McLeish till I'm well on my way. You didn't think I was going to just hand him over on your word as a gentleman, did you? No, it's quite simple. I take him away to another little hidey hole. You get me the clearance and the papers I need to get me out of here to some place of my choosing, and then I give you a call to let you know where to find him.'

'You're crazy. Why would we go along with a deal like that? Easiest thing would be for you to shoot McLeish as soon as we're off the scene. That way it's minimum hassle for you, and we wouldn't know till it's too late.'

'Jesus, you know, Nergui, you should be in my job. I'd never thought of that. Well, there you go. But as I see it, you've got no option but to trust me. But okay, you take Badzar with you, anyway. Gesture of good faith and all that. That way, if it all goes belly up, you'll at least have captured the dreaded serial killer. Sounds a smart deal to me.'

'You're a bastard, Maxon.'

Maxon shook his head, smiling faintly. 'No, like I told you, I'm a professional.'

'So how did a professional get mixed up in a mess like this?'

Maxon shook his head, impatiently. 'There's no time for this crap, Nergui. I'm sure you've got the story all worked out for yourself.'

'Some if it. You had a cosy deal going on the Gobi project. Yourselves, the Brits, the Russians, Canadians, the Koreans. All amicable. All legit business.' Nergui paused, watching Maxon. 'Legitimate businesses, but a nice front for laundering money through an obscure country with the potential for substantial profits at the end. And our government maybe only too keen to encourage it. Once again, everyone a winner.'

Maxon was watching him closely, though the aim of the pistol towards Drew never faltered. 'Cut the crap, Nergui.'

'But then things started to go off track. The explorations weren't going as well as expected. More investment was needed. The Russians and the locals kept telling you there were problems. Your people – and the others, the Brits, the Canadians – were suspicious. The figures didn't add up.'

Maxon moved the gun closer to Drew's head. 'Okay,' he said. 'Let me finish so we can all get moving and so that your friend here understands what this is all about. The Russians knew we weren't prepared to invest any more without a fucking good reason. So they announced they were investing more, demanding a bigger stake. We were being squeezed out.'

Nergui nodded slowly. 'But surely this kind of dispute could be resolved amicably? After all, our government is in charge of the project – they have the final say.'

Maxon laughed, mirthlessly. 'You know, Nergui, that might just have been the fucking problem. It's not for me to judge, but I got the feeling that there were some people there not batting on our side.'

'So you decided to act on your own initiative?'

'It's my job,' Maxon said. 'I'm an enforcer. It's what I do.'

'Except you didn't do it, did you? Where did you come across Badzar?'

'You're wasted in this business, Nergui. You're pretty professional yourself. You could make some real money. Yeah, I came across Badzar when he started launching one-man guerrilla attacks on our sites in the north. I was supposed to – discourage him. But then I heard his story.'

'And your heart bled?'

'—And I thought he was more useful to us alive than dead. I brought him back to the city, initially. But then I managed to persuade him that I was on his side.'

'You must have impressive powers of persuasion.'

'Yeah, and not all of them involve violence. I reinvented myself as an agent of the US government looking to undermine Russian dominance of the mining industry here.'

'Not so far from the truth, then?'

'The best lies never are. Badzar didn't exactly trust me, but he could see that we were working towards the same ends. And I also took the precaution of introducing him to one or two addictive substances. It's amazing how amenable people can be when you're the sole supplier of something they need.'

'And your involvement was always deniable?'

'Exactly. Badzar had no real knowledge of me. Always useful if things go wrong.'

'Which they did.'

'On the contrary, they went better than we might have dreamed. It's just that the Russians were such stubborn bastards.'

Nergui nodded. 'The first killing – the dismembered body – that was one of the Russian team?'

'One of their geologists. One of those who'd been producing the dubious data. We thought that would give them a clear message.'

'And they didn't report him as missing because that would have exposed the whole sordid arrangement. Instead, they just responded in kind.'

Maxon nodded. 'Pretty much so. We underestimated them, I guess. We thought that, compared to us, this was just a two-bit bunch who would back off at the first sign of trouble.'

'Pretty naïve, Maxon.'

'Yeah, well, I guess I'm used to operating in more civilised parts of the world.'

'So the second victim – the one who was helped off the hotel roof – he was one of yours?'

'Same thing. One of our geologists. I think the message was clear.'

'But you didn't take it?'

'Shit, no. I mean, this was a goddam battle of wills now. We directed Badzar very gently towards another of their team. Someone closer to the top guys.'

'The body we found dumped in the ravine, and they responded by killing Mr Ransom, who I take it was one of yours?'

'Exactly. Ransom had been doing some work for us, trying to verify the data that they'd been producing. He was our expert in that field. Poor bastard. He wasn't involved in any of this. Just doing his job.'

'Another professional,' Nergui said. 'But I suppose you could say the same about the geologists you killed.'

'Those bastards knew what they were doing,' Maxon said. 'They were in it to their necks.'

'So how did our Mr Delgerbayar get involved in this?'

'We didn't know how they'd got on to Ransom. He was basically a backroom guy that we'd had crunching data for us. Had barely been down to the Gobi and certainly wasn't anyone they'd see as a threat, unless they had some inside knowledge. Delgerbayar had been on the consortium's payroll for a while, but he wasn't just doing our dirty work, he was also helping out the Russians as well. They were paying him to do some digging about what was going on. He'd been up in the north asking questions, and then headed back south to talk to the Russians in the Gobi. He was getting rattled because he thought if there was a scandal his neck would be on the block. But it was clear he knew something about Badzar. That didn't worry me particularly – Badzar was always disposable – but too many people were beginning to know too much. Down south, everywhere was alive with rumour. We thought that Delgerbayar's death might make a suitable gesture. And it wasn't difficult to persuade Badzar.'

'Why not?'

Maxon laughed. 'Didn't you know? Delgerbayar was one of the leaders of the group who broke up the prospectors' camp. I don't know whether Delgerbayar actually killed Badzar's father himself, but it's possible. Badzar didn't take much persuading.'

Nergui nodded. He could still see, in his mind, the grotesque vision of Delgerbayar's dismembered body stretched out in the factory where Badzar's father had once worked. The horror of the scene remained unchanged, but his response to it – his assumption of a clear distinction between victim and perpetrator – had changed forever. It was, he thought, the loss of another kind of innocence, long after he had assumed that cynicism had made him invulnerable to such shifts.

'And it was after that that we came across you in the Gobi?'

'Yeah, and you bastards scared the shit out of me. I thought that the Russians might have been on to Badzar, but I assumed I'd kept myself out of the picture pretty thoroughly. I headed down to the Gobi to brief Collins, who was liaising with our people down there. We headed out to the tourist camp to avoid being seen at the mines, and then you bastards turned up.'

'Just coincidence. We were following Delgerbayar's trail.'

'Yeah, because everybody heads to the same place down there when they're trying to be incognito. Jesus, Nergui, ever thought that maybe this country of yours lacks some leisure facilities? Anyway, I thought they were on to us. Good job I tend to jump to conclusions, because it turns out I was right. I spotted a couple of guys lurking round the camp, and thought I'd better make myself scarce. Collins was pissed in the tent. I invited whatsisname, the guy who ran the camp, in to join us for a few drinks. Then I slipped away, supposedly to the john.'

Nergui raised his eyes. 'You invited Batkhuyag in there deliberately?'

'Sure, so there were two guys. But also Batkhuyag had some inkling what was going on. He kept his eyes and ears open a bit too much. Another rumour merchant. I thought that, in the dark, it was quite probable that the killers wouldn't realise I wasn't there – they probably wouldn't know what I was supposed to look like. At the very least, it would buy me some additional time to get away. So that's what I did.'

Nergui was still staring at Maxon. 'I see what you mean by professionalism. But how did you manage to get out of the area?'

'I'd got Collins to organise me a motorbike. I think it was stolen. Anyway, I had that, with a decent supply of petrol, so I just headed north into the desert.'

'Pretty risky at the time of year.'

'Maybe. But what you don't know don't kill you. I was well prepared. Always am. I headed north – I'd got various equipment including good GSM navigation equipment with me. I just drove and drove through the night. Eventually got back here. Probably not thinking too straight by that point.'

'Which is why you kidnapped McLeish?'

'No, I thought that through pretty well. I knew the Russians were after me. I suspected that your government wasn't likely to do me any favours. So I had to try to get out of here. Which wasn't likely to be easily achievable by any conventional means, as far as I could see. Then I thought of you and McLeish. You struck me as being, well, smarter and less corruptible than some of your compatriots and that McLeish would provide the leverage I needed.'

'But how did you track him down?'

'Not difficult. I aimed to phone round all the major hotels asking for him, so I could see where he was staying. As it turned out, I hit pay-dirt first time at the Chinggis Khaan. I just waited there till he came out and followed him. Ended up at the embassy. I had a cold night waiting out for him to emerge, and then I thought it was wasted because he was going to get in the fucking car with the rest of you. But he didn't, and so here we all are. And now you and your friend can see how serious this fucking situation is.'

'So where do we go from here?'

'Simple,' Maxon said. 'You take Badzar with you, claim the credit. Meanwhile, I look after McLeish while you make the arrangements to get me out of your goddam country.'

Nergui glanced at McLeish. 'I don't know if it's that simple,' he said. 'I'm still a policeman. I don't know whether I can go along with just letting you go. And that's putting aside the question of how much I can trust you in any case. If I let you out of here with McLeish, I can't expect to see either of you again.'

'Jesus, what are the options here? I need to get out of your fucking country as soon as possible. Those bastards are only a step behind me. I'm not going to do anything to jeopardise my escape. But you need to act fast. And as for your fucking scruples, well, don't you realise you're the only one left who seems to have them? Your fucking government are behind the Russians on this one all the way. They just want to get the best deal. They happily got into bed with my people when that looked the most lucrative option, and now they've just as happily switched sides.'

He paused, suddenly, and then unexpectedly smiled. He turned and gazed at McLeish, who was slumped against the concrete block, looking drained, beyond words. 'And anyway, Nergui, what are your fucking scruples worth? It's McLeish's life you're gambling with, not your own.'

The last comment hit home. Maxon was smart, right enough. While Nergui had been talking, trying to buy time, Maxon had still been one step ahead, taking the opportunity to make sure that he and Drew understood the full significance of what they were involved with. Turning Nergui's own scruples against him. Pushing the only button that might make him co-operate.

Nergui shook his head and turned towards Drew, not knowing what he was going to say, let alone what he should do next.

It was as if Drew had taken Maxon's words as a cue. He suddenly seemed to gain new and unexpected strength and flung himself across at Maxon, dragging the metal post and concrete block behind him. Maxon staggered backwards, startled by the energy of the sudden lunge. His gun went off, firing randomly into the vaulted spaces above them. Almost simultaneously – and Nergui could never be sure what he had or had not seen – the factory space was plunged into sudden darkness. Nergui reeled at the total blackness, dragging out his gun but afraid to fire. He fumbled in his other pocket for his flashlight, which became frustratingly tangled in his coat.

Another shot echoed around the empty building, and then another. From somewhere just ahead there was a sharp cry of pain, and then a third shot. Then there was a long, agonising silence.

Nergui rolled across the floor till he felt the cold stone of the wall against his back. His ears and eyes were straining, trying to discern some movement, to gain some clue about what had happened. Finally, moving as silently as possible, he pulled the torch from his pocket and, throwing himself into a crouching position with his pistol held in front of him, he shone the light around him.

The room was completely silent now, eerily so after the echoes of the gunshots. Nergui carefully moved the flashlight beam around, and then realised that another torch was shining from somewhere across the room.

Ahead of him, Maxon lay on the concrete floor, blood pouring from a bullet wound in his chest. Next to him, Badzar also lay on the ground, his head apparently blown open by another bullet. Behind them, Drew was slumped against the concrete block. For a moment, Nergui thought that Drew had been hit as well. He was staring blankly into the light, his face white, his body shaking. Nergui realised with a deep sigh of relief that he was apparently unharmed.

Nergui shone his own torch back towards the approaching light. 'Who is it?' he called, first in Mongolian, then in English.

The voice that replied was English, softly spoken, British. 'I'm sorry to startle you,' it said. 'The darkness was a risk, but necessary.' Nergui could make out a silhouette now, walking slowly towards them. He raised his pistol, prepared for anything that might happen. The approaching figure raised its own gun, but in an unthreatening manner. 'Infrared sight. Seemed the best way.'

Finally, the figure stepped into the beam of Nergui's flashlight.

'Wilson,' Nergui said. 'You realise I will have to arrest you for murder?'

Wilson nodded thoughtfully. 'Whatever you say, Nergui. Though I think a simple thank-you might have sufficed.'

TWENTY-FIVE

Outside, the snow had begun to fall again, thick and fast from the night sky. Nergui sat at an angle to the window, watching the falling flakes caught in the streetlights of Sukh Bataar Square, barely listening to the conversation.

'McLeish is all right, then?' the Minister asked, tapping together a sheaf of official-looking papers. As always, his desk was immaculately clear, except for an old-fashioned blotter and inkwell. Nergui suspected that the sheaf of papers was similarly decorative, something for the Minister to leaf through when he wanted to appear busy.

Nergui pulled himself away from the hypnotic swirl of the snowflakes and looked back at the Minister. 'Physically, he's fine. We had the police doctor check him over. He sustained a few minor cuts and bruises in the original kidnapping, and he'd been without food or water for some time, but there wasn't any serious harm done. He's been patched up and given a decent meal, so he should be okay.'

The British ambassador was sitting in the Minister's other armchair, flicking aimlessly through a thick file on his knee. Nergui had no idea whether the file had any significance, or whether this was just another piece of window-dressing. He was beginning to realise how little of this world he really understood.

'Still, I imagine it must all have been something of an ordeal?' the ambassador said.

'You might say that,' Nergui said. This was, he presumed, another instance of that famous British understatement. Or possibly just crass stupidity. 'He was very shaken. Who wouldn't be? As to the long-term impact, well . . . I'm no expert.'

The ambassador nodded. 'The police are well-versed in those matters. I've spoken with the UK Home Office. They've got well-established procedures for post-trauma counselling, all that stuff. We're having him flown back tonight on a specially chartered flight via Vienna, so we can get him out of here before the world's media cotton on to what's happened. He'll have access to the best treatment as soon as he gets back.'

'That's good to hear,' Nergui said, sincerely. 'He's been through hell. I don't think we can begin to imagine what it was like.'

'Though fortunately Maxon wasn't the killer,' the Minister said.

Nergui turned to look at him, his mouth half open, biting back his instinctive response. 'I suppose it depends on how you look at it,' he said, finally. He paused momentarily, then continued. 'Speaking of which, what happens to Wilson?'

The Minister hesitated, then looked to the ambassador. 'Professor Wilson's been handed over to our custody. We'll take care of him,' the ambassador said, smoothly.

'Which means what?' Nergui asked.

'Just that,' the ambassador said. 'We have it in hand.'

Nergui looked from the ambassador to the Minister. Both faces were untroubled, giving nothing away. He shrugged. 'Well, I'm sure I can depend on your country's integrity, ambassador.'

The Minister nodded. 'Quite right, Nergui. I think we can all be justly pleased at how this has all worked out, in the circumstances. Especially you.' Nergui detected just the merest undertone of threat in the last two words.

'I did my best, sir. It was Doripalam who made the critical links. I can't in all honesty claim much credit. Or pretend that I wasn't lucky in the end.'

'Well, these things are never straightforward, Nergui.'

'No, sir, not with so many interests involved. It's not easy for a simple policeman.'

The Minister stared at him. 'I don't think I would ever class you as simple, Nergui. That may be your problem.' He paused, then smiled broadly. 'But I'm deeply grateful for what you've achieved here. McLeish is safe. We've removed a dangerous psychopath from the streets.'

'Two dangerous psychopaths, I suspect,' Nergui said.

The Minister shrugged. 'Well, Maxon was a common criminal. The US had nothing on him officially but it looks as if they knew more than they were saying about his background. We're liaising with the FBI on that but they don't seem too surprised that he might have killed here. That kind of infighting isn't uncommon. I don't think he or his associate will be missed.'

Nergui shrugged. 'As you say, sir.'

'You know, Nergui,' the Minister said, 'you're a good man. We'll be pleased to get you back in here where you belong.'

'I'm sure you will, sir.' Nergui smiled thinly. 'And I'll be pleased to get out of Doripalam's hair, I suppose. He deserves some kind of recognition for this – he did a superb job.' He paused. 'But I'm thinking about my future. You might not think so, but I really am a simple man. I begin to think that I am much more comfortable with the kinds of crime I understand.'

'I think the ambassador was a little put out,' Nergui said. 'Saw this as his territory.'

McLeish smiled. He stretched out his aching legs as far as he could in the rear seat of the car. 'I really couldn't face it,' he said. 'Another hour at the airport with that sanctimonious bastard congratulating me on my part in bringing a serial killer to justice.' He laughed bitterly. 'Lying motionless on a bench for two days.'

'You did more than that at the end,' Nergui pointed out.

'Probably would have just got myself shot if Wilson hadn't intervened.'

'We don't know that Wilson did intervene,' Nergui said. 'Perhaps he was just holding the gun for a friend.'

'Of course,' McLeish said. 'Jesus, what a world.'

'Anyway,' Nergui went on, 'I don't know that Maxon would have shot you. I don't think he knew what to do. He was desperate, or he wouldn't have tried such a half-baked plan, but you were the only bargaining chip he'd got.'

'And he was right to be desperate. Someone was right there behind him.' McLeish paused. 'I can't follow it, though. Do we assume that Wilson was working with the Russians?'

Nergui shrugged. 'Who knows? I think we can assume it was the forces of stability and global capitalism. They don't care where the money comes from or goes to, so long as they get their share and nobody rocks the boat. Maxon had become a liability. Probably even to his own people. Or am I too cynical?'

'From what I've seen here, you're nothing like cynical enough. I just hope you can keep it up.'

They fell into silence as the official car pounded through the empty night. As they approached the airport, they passed through one of the mining districts. Nergui stared out of the car window as they passed, watching the chaotic floodlit acres of heavy machinery, makeshift buildings, pipelines and trucks. McLeish turned back and looked at Nergui. 'You know, when I first saw that,' he said, 'I thought it looked like a gateway to hell.'

Nergui followed McLeish's gaze into the darkness. 'I think perhaps you understand our country better than you realise,' he said. 'But I hope that you are wrong.'

THE ADVERSARY

To Christine, James, Adam and Jonny

They are out on the steppe, miles from home. Miles from anywhere.

It is late afternoon, early spring. The immense sky is clear, just a few wisps of cloud against the rich blue. Everything – even the snow tipped mountains that surround them – is dwarfed by comparison.

The sun is already low, and the mountains are casting vast shadows across the green plain. Behind them, the distant hazy sprawl of the city is still drenched in bright sunlight, windows and towers blinking as they speed towards their destination.

He has been told to keep his head down. But it is difficult not to look around. He has never been this far from the city, never seen such openness, such unfilled space. He has lived on the steppe and the mountains were the boundaries of his world, but he had no idea that, after driving for mile after mile, they would still remain so distant and unreachable.

He looks back at the endless strip of dirt road behind, gazing through the wake of dust at the old car that follows their gleaming truck.

He looks forward along the same road, wondering how far it will be before they reach their goal. And he looks out as they pass an occasional camp, grazing goats and cattle, old men on horseback who watch their passing without evident interest.

There are four of them in the Jeep. He sits in the rear with the boss. The boss's eyes are closed as though he is sleeping, but he suspects the boss is awake, listening to the aimless conversation of the two in the front. He has never seen the boss sleeping, though clearly he must. He finds himself nodding from the motion of the truck but tries to keep awake by guessing how far they have to go.

On their return, there will be five of them in the truck, so it will be more crowded. He imagines the boss will sit in the front then.

At some point he falls asleep. When he opens his eyes, the sun has almost set and the truck is slowing. It seems they have reached their destination, though when he looks out of the window this place looks no different from the endless miles of empty grassland they have already passed.

The truck pulls to a halt, and the boss instantly opens his eyes. The driver twists in his seat to look back at him. The boss says nothing but nods faintly. This is the place.

Behind them, the car draws to a stop. The boss opens his door, and they all climb out and stand around the truck, as the car driver manoeuvres his vehicle around them. He stops, finally, thirty or forty metres away. They watch as the driver climbs out, opens the rear door and pulls out two metal petrol cans.

The sun has nearly set now, just a brilliant red sliver visible over the mountains. The mountaintops and the western sky glow crimson, and the remaining sky is a deep mauve, the first stars beginning to emerge.

In the far distance, the city is a tiny bundle of smoky light. But otherwise, the steppe seems deserted.

In the dim light, they watch in silence as the car driver systematically pours petrol across the roof of the old car. The rear door is still open, and he leans inside to pour more of the liquid across the rear seat. When both cans are empty, he throws them back inside the car. Then, as if making a final adjustment, he unscrews the cap of the car's petrol tank.

He pauses and looks across at the boss who gives his usual almost imperceptible nod. It is not clear whether it will be visible to the car driver in the twilight, but it seems that he has received the signal. He begins slowly to walk backwards away from the car, watching where the spreading pool of petrol has begun to seep across the grass. He pauses and pulls something from his pocket. He makes a sharp movement with his hand, and then he tosses a glowing object on to the damp ground at his feet.

He pauses, momentarily, to ensure that the discarded match has ignited the petrol. Then he begins to walk, much more rapidly, to where the rest of them are standing.

He nods to the boss with a faint smile, and then they all turn to look back at the car. It is almost dark, the clear sky laden with stars, and the spreading wall of flame is dazzling in the gloom. They watch as it sweeps unstoppably across the body of the car.

Without a word, the boss turns and climbs into the passenger seat of the Jeep. The rest follow, three of them squeezing into the rear seat, and then they pull away, turning back on to the road towards the city.

The young man looks back through the rear window. The car is burning, a meaningless beacon on the vast empty plain. He watches as it diminishes behind them. The glare expands briefly as the petrol tank ignites and the car explodes. And then it is disappearing once more, soon little more than a tiny earth-bound echo of the star-filled night.

And, as the Jeep pounds back along the dirt track towards the city, he is still unsure whether it was only his imagination, or whether he really could hear, in those moments before the fire caught hold, the pounding of fists and the crying of a panic-filled voice from inside the spreading wall of flame.

CHAPTER 1

The court room faced east, its large windows looking out across the city and the blank expanse of Sukh Bataar Square. At mid morning, early in the year, the low sun streamed across the pale wooden benches, silhouetting the figures of the room's few inhabitants.

Judge Radnaa leaned forward, momentarily dazzled by the sunlight, blinking impatiently. 'So you are saying we cannot proceed?' she said. She could barely make out the features of the man facing her, could not read his expression.

'It is complicated,' he said. 'We need more time.'

Judge Radnaa looked across at the panel lined up on the bench beside her. Two other, less experienced judges, and three citizens' representatives. The maximum possible representation, reflecting the seriousness of this case. Behind them – as if to remind them of the gravity of their responsibilities – the court-room wall was adorned with the striking red and yellow geometries of the national flag.

'We have already been sitting for two weeks,' she said. 'And, before that, we spent a long time in preparation. You assured us that the prosecution case was comprehensive.'

'As I say, it is complicated,' the man said. 'There have been developments.'

'But you are not prepared to enlighten us as to the nature of these developments?'

'It is—'

'Complicated. Yes, Mr Tsengel, I think we have grasped that. I understand that you are relatively new to your role in the State Prosecutor's Office. It may surprise you to learn that the law is frequently complicated.'

'Yes, but—'

'I do not think this is acceptable, Mr Tsengel. We have already invested very substantially in this case. We have listened to the evidence that the State Prosecutor's Office has so far presented. This is clearly a very important case with many ramifications—'

'Well, that's exactly—'

'And yet, now, two weeks into the case, you are seeking a significant adjournment because of – developments. And yet you are unwilling to share with us the nature or significance of these developments. That is, I think, an accurate summary of the situation?'

'Yes, but, well, it is—'

'I think we understand very well what it is, Mr Tsengel. I think we should perhaps now seek Mr Nyamsuren's views on this topic.'

Tsengel opened his mouth as if to intervene, but remained silent. He was a short, rather awkward young man, who looked uncomfortable in his cheap, Western-style suit. He shifted from one foot to the other, as though keen to make his escape from the judge's presence.

Judge Radnaa looked across at the two other men,

who had been sitting at a desk in the middle of the room, whispering incessantly to one another during the previous discussion. She gestured to one of the two men, a tall slim figure in a black suit of considerably better quality than Tsengel's. He rose slightly, acknowledging her gesture.

'Mr Nyamsuren,' she said. 'Will you join us for a moment?'

Nyamsuren exchanged a glance with the other man, a heavily built middle aged man with a shaved head, and then rose to approach the bench, a quizzical expression on his face. 'There is a problem?'

'So it would seem,' Judge Radnaa said. 'The State Prosecutor's Office is seeking an adjournment.'

Nyamsuren raised his eyebrows. 'Really?' He looked across at Tsengel, smiling vaguely. Tsengel stared down at the floor. 'There is some difficulty, Mr Tsengel? Mr Muunokhoi has already been substantially inconvenienced. I presume we are not talking about a long delay?'

Tsengel looked up, his face pale. 'Well, it's difficult to say. I mean—'

Nyamsuren turned to stare at Tsengel, as though in astonishment. 'I am sure this is some simple misunderstanding, Mr Tsengel. The State Prosecutor's Office is always very thorough. And my client has co-operated fully with the authorities at every stage. I cannot see what further developments might have occurred at this point.'

Tsengel coughed, looking between Nyamsuren and the judge. Behind them, the other judges and the citizens' representatives had been watching the discussion with close attention. 'Well, yes, but the situation is very—' He caught the judge's eye and coughed again. 'The situation is very difficult. You will appreciate that I am in an awkward position—' He trailed off, as if unsure what to say next.

'You place us all in an awkward position, Mr Tsengel. I think Mr Nyamsuren would be entirely within his right to object very strongly to your proposal.'

'With respect,' Nyamsuren said, his glance moving from the judge back to Tsengel, 'I am still not entirely clear what Mr Tsengel's proposal actually is.'

'Mr Tsengel?' The judge gestured pleasantly towards the young man.

Tsengel shifted awkwardly. 'Well, we're seeking an adjournment of the trial. While we resolve the issues that have arisen.'

Nyamsuren smiled without any evident humour. 'I see. And how long an adjournment are you seeking?'

'Well, I can't exactly—'

Nyamsuren laughed. 'I must confess, I had not previously been aware that the State Prosecutor's Office possessed a sense of humour.'

'I'm sorry, I don't—'

'Mr Tsengel, Mr Muunokhoi has been continually harassed by the police and by the State Prosecutor's Office for many years. Statements have been made about my client's business activities which verge on the libellous. He has been accused of trafficking everything from heroin to, I believe, uranium. And yet, not only has my client never been prosecuted, until now no charges have ever been brought against him. Six months ago, for reasons best known to themselves, the police decided that they had amassed sufficient evidence to justify my client's arrest on various charges including—' He glanced down at his notes, as though the precise charges were a matter of indifference to him. 'Including charges of, ah, underpayment of import duties. Since then, he has been subject to the most stringent bail conditions, severely curtailing his ability to conduct his legitimate business. And now, when my client finally has the opportunity to demonstrate his innocence, you come forward to seek an indefinite adjournment on the grounds of some – difficulties which you are apparently unable to share with us. I can conclude only that this is an elaborate joke.'

Tsengel looked miserably at the judge, as though pleading with her to take pity on him. 'With respect, the core charges relate to illegal imports. Rather more serious than the underpayment of duties—'

'Yes, of course,' Judge Radnaa said. She raised her eyebrows inquiringly towards Nyamsuren. 'I take it that you are not prepared to accede to Mr Tsengel's request?'

Nyamsuren smiled. 'I think you can take it that that is our position,' he said.

She turned to Tsengel. 'And you are not in a position to present the State Prosecutor's evidence?'

Tsengel hesitated, as though trying to come up with an alternative answer. 'As we speak, no,' he said, finally.

She nodded slowly, and then looked back at her colleagues. 'We will need a brief adjournment to consult,' she said, 'but as I see it we have only two routes available to us.' She paused. 'First, we can continue the trial on the basis of whatever evidence you can present. I take it that this would not be your preferred option?'

Tsengel blinked and nodded faintly.

'Or,' she went on, 'since Mr Nyamsuren is, quite reasonably, not prepared to agree to an indefinite delay, we can perhaps agree to a short adjournment while the Prosecutor's Office considers its position. Perhaps until tomorrow morning?'

'It is not your fault. You need to realise that.' Nergui was sitting in Doripalam's office, leaning back in his chair, his ankles resting neatly on the corner of the desk. Doripalam thought that he had never seen him looking quite so relaxed. He only wished that he could share Nergui's composure.

'It's a mess,' Doripalam said. 'The whole thing's a mess.'

Nergui shrugged. 'We know that. But nobody's blaming you.'

Doripalam leaned forward across the desk. While they had been talking, Nergui noticed, Doripalam had been doodling aimlessly on the lined pad in front of him, large spirals, starting at the outside and working down to a tiny enclosed point in the centre. 'Maybe you're not blaming me,' Doripalam said. 'Because you know what this place is like. But others will be.'

'Of course. There will always be ignorant people looking for scapegoats. But this is not your fault.'

'It's my responsibility.'

Nergui carefully dropped his feet from the desk to

the floor and leaned forward. As always, his clothing was an apparently unstudied blend of the conventional and the eccentric – a dark, well-cut business suit, offset by a lemon shirt and a louder-than-usual tie in varying shades of yellow. His socks, Doripalam had noticed as Nergui had balanced his ankles on the desk, had apparently been selected to match the shirt.

'And what form should your responsibility take?' Nergui said. His dark features were as expressionless as ever and his tone was casual, but Doripalam felt obliged to take the question seriously.

'I don't know,' he said. 'But if it's thought that I'm not up to the job, then I shouldn't be in it.'

'So you would resign?'

'If it came to it, well, yes, I suppose I would.'

'Then I suppose I would have to ensure that your resignation was not accepted.' Nergui smiled. 'If it came to it. But I think we can assume that it will not. Not over this, anyway.'

Doripalam pushed back his chair. 'But it's a mess, though, isn't it? After all this time. After all the effort we've put in. We nearly had Muunokhoi. And now the whole bloody thing's down the pan.'

Nergui shrugged. 'We have to be philosophical. You are sure there's no chance of salvaging it?'

'Some of the evidence we've got holds up. So it's not quite dead, but it's as good as. It's all tainted by the fake stuff, so nobody's going to take the case seriously. We tried to buy ourselves some time, see if we could make more of the evidence we've still got, but they weren't having it.'

'No, well, that is not so surprising.'

Doripalam smiled for the first time. 'No, but at least we forced those smug bastards in the Prosecutor's office to do some work. Though I imagine that's the last satisfaction we'll get in that direction.'

Nergui nodded slowly. 'They are looking for an enquiry, you know?'

Doripalam rose and walked across to the window. It was a cold clear spring day, the sky a brilliant cloudless blue beyond the clutter of grey buildings. The view from his office was not impressive – the back of a disused office block, most of its windows smashed. Between the two buildings, there was an abandoned yard, filled with the detritus of the failed business – an old desk, some office chairs, even a broken filing cabinet. Somewhere beyond all this, he thought, there was the open steppe, the mountains, the miles of emptiness. 'I didn't know,' he said, 'but I presumed they would.' He laughed faintly. 'They behave as if they're the ones who've put in all the work. Perhaps we should institute an enquiry into all the times they've messed up our evidence.'

'We could have only so many enquiries,' Nergui said. 'But, no, I don't think we can avoid it this time. There will be too many questions.' He paused. 'I have put my own name forward.'

Doripalam turned from the window. 'You have?'

Nergui shrugged. 'Why not? I understand the operations of this place better than anyone. Of course, if you are uncomfortable—'

Doripalam shook his head. 'No, of course not. But wouldn't they see a conflict of interest?'

'If I were to chair the enquiry? I don't see why.'

Doripalam leaned back against the window, his thin figure silhouetted against the daylight. 'Well, for a start, you appointed me.'

'But I am clear,' Nergui said. 'This is not an enquiry into you or your performance. There is no suggestion that you were even aware of what was happening.'

'I know that,' Doripalam said, 'and I hope you know it too. But I'm sure that others will be only too keen to think the worst.'

'There are always such people,' Nergui said, apparently with genuine regret. 'But I think the situation here is straightforward. I know what you inherited here – not least, because I was the one who bequeathed it to you. And the Minister knows all this. He knows that the civil police force was a shambles from the start – the ones the military didn't want, the detritus who couldn't find a better government job. He knows how much we've done to develop some professionalism—'

'Or at least come competence,' Doripalam added softly.

'As you say. He also knows how much we have done to change things, you and I. And how unpopular we have made ourselves in the process.'

'Very gratifying,' Doripalam said, with only a mild edge of irony. 'The Minister's good opinion does of course mean a great deal to me. But I'm not sure I see the relevance.'

'The Minister is no fool. He knows the problems you are facing. An enquiry is necessary, but he does not wish to make your life any more difficult.'

'So he wants a whitewash?'

'On the contrary, he wants a thorough and rigorous enquiry into all the circumstances behind this case. He wants transparency and openness. He wants, I suppose, an appropriate apportionment of account-ability and blame.' As Nergui mouthed the ministerial vocabulary, it was impossible to tell whether there was any undertone of satire. 'He wants to ensure that you have the resources to resolve the situation.'

Doripalam nodded. 'And the Minister wants all this? He is taking such a personal interest in the case?'

'He is aware of it. I speak on his behalf, you under-stand,' Nergui said. 'Perhaps, from time to time, I paraphrase.'

Doripalam shook his head. 'You cunning old bastard,' he said.

'So I'm fired?'

Doripalam shook his head. 'It is not within my power to fire you, even if I wished to. You know that.'

He's playing games, Doripalam thought. Why does he continue to play games, even now? 'But of course you are suspended from duty,' he added. 'On full pay. Pending the outcome of the enquiry.'

'So I will be fired? In due course. Pending the outcome of the enquiry.'

Doripalam sighed gently. An apology would have been nice, he thought. Some kind of recognition of the inconvenience, the embarrassment, that Tunjin had put them all through. Not to mention the implications of Muunokhoi potentially being out on the streets again, more untouchable than ever. Doripalam had intended to approach this interview in a spirit of equanimity and fairness, but he found himself losing his temper. 'You do realise what you've done, of course? I mean, you do understand the implications of your actions?' He was talking to Tunjin as if he was some sort of imbecile, rather than an officer with thirty or so more years' experience than his own. But he found it hard to regret either his tone or his words.

Tunjin leaned back in the seat facing Doripalam's desk. He looked considerably more relaxed than Doripalam himself. 'I'm sure I do. But you may care to remind me. Sir.' Tunjin presumably assumed that his long career was already over, and was behaving accordingly. Or, more likely, he well understood the impact of this kind of behaviour on Doripalam, particularly when exhibited by junior but more experienced officers.

'Do you know how long we have been trying to get to this point?' Doripalam asked, almost instantly regretting the question.

'For many years,' Tunjin said. 'Since well before your time. Sir.'

Doripalam nodded slowly, trying hard to control his anger. 'I am sure you can tell me precisely how long, Tunjin. I am told it is at least fifteen years.'

'I think it's longer. Sir.'

'Well, I am sure you are right. So – how long? Eighteen, twenty years. Perhaps longer—' Doripalam held up his hand, sensing that Tunjin was about to provide the relevant information. 'And, now, when we get so close, this happens. No. I am sorry. I underestimate your contribution. *You* make this happen.' He paused. 'And so, after whatever it is – nineteen, twenty years – we are back where we started. Which in my view is precisely nowhere.'

Tunjin, gratifyingly, seemed rather taken aback by Doripalam's short speech. 'With respect, sir—' Doripalam was pleased to note that, for the moment, neither of the latter words sounded entirely ironic. This, he supposed, was progress. He decided to press on. 'No,' he added, as if after some thought. 'I am wrong. We are somewhere. We are deeply in the shit. The criminal world sees us as a laughing stock. The Prosecution Service believes that we are considerably worse than useless. The Ministry believes that we are either corrupt or inept, or more likely both.' He paused, but not long enough to allow Tunjin to interrupt. 'I find it difficult to see any positive aspects to this position. And there's only one person responsible for our predicament.'

Tunjin was, he noted, finally beginning to lose his temper. Doripalam was unsure whether this was desirable, but, given his own current state of mind, it was at least moderately satisfying. 'With respect, sir,' Tunjin repeated, with the ironic note now reinstated, 'given that we had, in effect, made no progress in the last two decades, I thought my actions were justified. The evidence we had wouldn't have stood up on its own. I thought it was worth the risk.'

For the first time, Doripalam's anger and irritation were overtaken by something close to astonishment. He sat back in his chair and stared at the figure sitting opposite him. Tunjin was a mess – physically and, it was beginning to seem, perhaps mentally as well. He was a short, fat, shapeless figure of a man, completely bald, who stared back at Doripalam over a stack of badly shaven chins. He was wearing a cheap black suit, worn shiny at the elbows and knees. The jacket and trousers were dotted, at disturbingly frequent intervals, with what were presumably stains of spilled food.

'Worth the risk?' Doripalam repeated finally. He was finding it difficult to come up with any coherent response. Tunjin sat watching him, playing with a badly-chewed ballpoint pen, apparently unconcerned.

Doripalam shook his head, trying to find an appropriate form of words. 'This is what I find so extraordinary,' he said. 'This will no doubt sound patronising, but you're one of the best – the most experienced – policemen we have in this team. We have problems – you know the problems we have. I have little respect for some of your colleagues, and doubtless they have little respect for me. But in your case—'

Tunjin had placed the end of the pen in his mouth, and was proceeding to mutilate it still further. After a moment he withdrew it, gazed thoughtfully at the dog-eared tip, and then inserted it carefully in his ear. Doripalam watched the process as though hypnotised.

After a pause, he tried again. 'We have not always seen eye to eye,' he said. 'I have often found your approach cavalier, lacking in discipline.' Tunjin had proceeded to prod his inner ear methodically with the pen, and Doripalam was finding it increasingly difficult to sustain his train of thought. 'But I saw that you achieved results. I recognised – I thought I recognised – your integrity, your honesty, compared with some of your colleagues.' He hesitated, increasingly convinced that he was wasting his time. Tunjin's manoeuvres

23

with the pen were an almost literal demonstration of his deafness to Doripalam's words.

'It had not occurred to me,' he said, finally, 'that you might be guilty of this kind of act. Of falsifying evidence.'

Tunjin withdrew the pen from his ear and peered at whatever he had managed to extract. Finally, he looked up at Doripalam and shrugged. 'I am a police officer,' he said. 'I just do what I can.'

Doripalam stared at him in bewilderment. 'But can't you see,' he said, 'that, even if you had succeeded, this kind of behaviour, this kind of manipulation of justice, is just not acceptable for a police officer? Especially for a police officer.'

Tunjin shrugged again and inserted the chewed end of the pen back in his mouth. 'So,' he said, 'it is clear. In due course, and no doubt after due procedure, I am fired.'

'So – we are now in session.' Judge Radnaa looked closely at Tsengel, who was sitting hunched behind the pale wooden desk. 'Are you now able to clarify the situation, Mr Tsengel?'

Tsengel shifted awkwardly and then climbed slowly to his feet. 'Yes, madam. At least, in so far—' He paused, as though words had deserted him.

'Mr Tsengel?' Judge Radnaa looked around the almost empty courtroom. Trials were normally open to the public, and even the most mundane case usually attracted at least a few idle visitors with time on their hands. A trial of this nature would normally have attracted queues of sightseers, not to mention the full representation of the press. But it had been clear right from the start that this was in no sense a normal trial, and the Ministry had insisted on a closed courtroom on the grounds of protecting its intelligence sources. The defence team, perhaps recognising that their case would, if anything, be strengthened by this anonymity, had raised no objections.

Tsengel seemed to gather his wits. 'In so far as I can,' he concluded. 'I have consulted with my superiors,' he said. 'Our position remains the same. We have run into some difficulties with our evidence. We would ideally like to seek an adjournment to see if these can be resolved.'

'And are you now able to specify the proposed length of this adjournment?'

Tsengel hesitated, and then glanced across at Nyamsuren, who was sitting, apparently relaxed, next to the accused. 'Well, we do not believe that we are able to resolve our difficulties unless we obtain a substantial adjournment. A matter of weeks, at least.'

Judge Radnaa nodded slowly and then glanced over at Nyamsuren. 'I take it that your client's position has not changed in respect of such an adjournment?' she said.

Nyamsuren nodded and rose languidly to his feet. 'I am sure you appreciate our position, madam.' He glanced back at his client, who was still staring fixedly at the table, his shaven head bowed forward.

'Indeed.' She looked back at Tsengel. 'And on this occasion I can only agree that the defence counsel's position is entirely reasonable. I can see that you have some difficulties, Mr Tsengel, though I confess I am at a loss to understand precisely what they might be. But I think that the defence also has the right to assume that, particularly in a trial of this nature, the State Prosecutor's Office will be fully prepared before the case reaches court.'

Tsengel looked as if a literal burden had been dropped on to his shoulders. He nodded, miserably. 'I understand,' he said. 'My instructions are that, if it should not prove possible to obtain the kind of adjournment we are seeking, the State Prosecutor's Office wishes to confirm that it has no further evidence to offer. In short, there is no case to answer.'

Judge Radnaa stared at him for a moment. 'In formal terms,' she said, 'the trial has commenced. I do not believe, therefore, that we are in a position simply to dismiss the case.'

Nyamsuren rose. 'If you will permit me, madam?' he said. 'My client has been charged with an extremely serious offence, as well as being the victim of a continuous stream of unsubstantiated innuendo. In the interests of my client's reputation, I think it is essential that the verdict is reached on the basis of the evidence that has been presented—'

'Or, to be precise, not presented,' Judge Radnaa said.

'As you say, madam. But I believe that, given the seriousness of the charge, a clear verdict is needed in order to remove any doubts about Mr Muunokhoi's position.'

'I can only agree with you, Mr Nyamsuren.' The judge looked across at her colleagues and the citizen's representatives. 'We will withdraw and consider our verdict, though I imagine it will not take us long.' She paused. 'In the circumstances, I presume that the defence has no further evidence to offer?'

Nyamsuren glanced over at Tsengel, who was now sitting staring blankly at the floor. 'We had of course prepared a thorough defence. However, in the absence of a prosecution case, I think this is now superfluous.'

'As you say, Mr Nyamsuren. Very well. We will consider our verdict and then reconvene in—' She glanced at the clock on the far wall of the courtroom. Its convex glass face, she noticed, perfectly enclosed the reflected image of the Mongolian flag that dominated the wall behind the bench. 'Well, I do not think we will require more than thirty minutes.'

She rose and strode purposefully out of the room, followed by the team of junior judges and citizens' representatives. The door closed behind them, and the courtroom was silent. Tsengel still stared at the floor, avoiding Nyamsuren's eyes.

Nyamsuren was smiling. He nodded at the two silent policeman who had been stationed each side of the courtroom door throughout the trial. 'I think your escort duties are almost finished, boys,' he said.

The two policemen made no response, but looked pointedly back past Nyamsuren. Nyamsuren looked over his shoulder. For the first time, his client had ceased staring down at the desk and had raised his head. Beneath his bald head, his eyes were dark and staring, now fixed on the two officers who stiffened, fingers resting on their rifles. There was no evident humour or warmth in his blank eyes but, like Nyamsuren, he was now smiling.

CHAPTER 2

She should have gone with the others, taken the chance when there was still time.

But she had been afraid to leave, worried that her departure would reveal too much. After all, a mother would never leave her child, would not willingly return to the steppe with her son's fate still unknown. She had made that clear to the policeman. She had said: 'I won't leave. I won't move on. Not till I know where he is. What's happened to him.'

The policeman had nodded, jotted down some words in his notebook. She suspected that he was not really interested, that he would never look again at the sentences he was scribbling down. He was going through the motions, trying to make her believe that they were taking this seriously.

'We don't know that anything has happened to him,' he had pointed out, in a tone that was presumably intended to be reassuring, but which sounded merely dismissive.

She didn't blame him. He thought she was just another anxious old woman. Probably his own mother was the same. No doubt she fussed about the life he was living, about the risks he was facing as a police officer, about what his future might hold.

'I know,' she said. 'I know that something's happened to him.'

The policeman looked up at her, apparently surprised by the quiet certainty of her tone. 'But you've told us everything you know?' he said. 'You have no other information?' There was a mocking edge to his voice. He didn't care about any of this. He didn't care what she felt.

She stared back at him for a moment, as if she were about to say something. Then she shook her head. 'No. I've told you everything I can.'

It was true, she thought. She had told him everything she could. Not everything she knew. But everything she was able to say.

She had no idea who to trust. She certainly had no reason to trust this smiling, insincere young man. Outside her immediate family, she had no reason to trust anyone. All she could do was try to bring it all out into the open, make it public, arouse as much noise as she could.

And hope that this would be enough to stop him.

After the policeman had gone, she had sat hunched on the small stool at the entrance to her *ger*, staring out across the empty grassland. Behind her she could hear the soft movements of the horses, the clattering of equipment, the desolate cry of a baby.

Her family were preparing to move on. She would not be travelling with them. Not yet. Some of them had offered to stay with her, but she had said no, fully aware that they were also afraid. Afraid for her, afraid for her son. But, mostly, afraid for themselves.

They knew he would come.

The rest of the family struck camp a week later, packing up their tents and equipment with the characteristic efficiency of the nomad. When the horses and trucks were loaded, her brother had come back to speak with her.

'How long?'

'As long as it takes,' she said.

'We will come back for you. When we're settled. As soon as we've found somewhere suitable. It will only be a few days.'

'As long as it takes,' she repeated.

She had watched them go, feeling as if her heart was being torn from her body. A mother does not willingly leave her child.

She had not even been able to say what she felt. Had not trusted her emotions. But, also, had not trusted that somehow, in this vast empty plain, they might not be observed.

It had been a long time before the last black specks of the convoy had vanished into the pale haze of the horizon. Afterwards, she had returned to her *ger*, boiled water for tea, and sat down on her stool, nothing now to do but wait.

He would come. She was sure of that. Soon, he would come.

That night, she lay awake, listening to the faint sounds of the spring breezes rustling through the tent-frame, the occasional distant sound of a bird or a barking dog. She imagined him out there, perhaps already approaching, perhaps close at hand.

She imagined meeting him again.

The next morning, when her mobile rang, she was

almost certain it would be him. She was sitting outside the *ger*, her husband's old heavyweight *del* slung over her shoulders against the early chill.

She answered hesitantly, wondering what she would say.

But it was not him. It was the police, again. A different policeman, more senior than the one who had visited before. No, they had nothing more to report. But, yes, he would like to meet her, hear her story for himself.

She agreed to a time later in the week, not taking in what the emollient voice was saying. She did not fool herself that the call had any significance. It was the publicity, she thought. In that sense, at least, her plan was working. She was getting her story out there. She was getting it noticed.

Perhaps that would help to keep him away. Or perhaps it would bring him sooner. She was no longer sure which she preferred.

He came the next day. When he appeared, it was hardly a surprise to her and she realised that she had forgotten to be afraid.

He was alone. She had somehow imagined him arriving with an entourage, the centre of everyone's attention, because that was how she remembered him.

But of course he was alone. He parked his truck carefully, yards away from the remaining cluster of *gers*, and walked slowly across the scrubby grassland to where she was sitting. The morning sun was behind him, and he was little more than a silhouette, but she fancied she could see the empty depths of his eyes.

She remained seated almost until he reached her. Then she rose and slowly made her way into the tent, feeling his presence close behind her.

The discussion went as she had expected. He did not stop to question what she might or might not know. He did not bother with explanations. He did not attempt to bargain or cajole. He simply told her what he wanted and waited calmly for her to agree.

When she refused, for a moment he looked almost surprised. Then he repeated his request, quietly, in the same polite tone. The sense of threat was palpable.

She refused again. And then she told him what she knew, or what she thought she knew. She told him what she had, and what she would do with it.

She did not know what reaction she expected. Perhaps she had hoped that he would simply turn on his heel and walk away. Perhaps.

But when the first blow came, she knew she had been waiting for it. She tensed just for a moment as his fist struck her cheek, and then she staggered against the wall of the tent. His second blow struck her in the chest, and she fell back, her head hitting the solid wood of the tent frame.

She was semi-conscious, aware of an absurd disappointment that she should have succumbed so easily. She felt his foot slamming hard into her back. She thrust herself against the side of the *ger*, knowing now that at least this – all of this – would soon be over.

But then he was leaning over her, and she saw his eyes, blank and expressionless as he pulled a cigarette lighter from his pocket.

And she realised that it was all only just beginning.

*

'It's a new one. Really moves when you put your foot down.'

Doripalam didn't doubt it. He eased himself further down into the backseat of the Daihatsu 4x4, and tried to relax. This was something of a challenge when being driven by an over-enthusiastic young officer with a habit both of driving too quickly and – perhaps a greater immediate concern – of slowing insufficiently on the tighter bends.

'See that,' Luvsan said, twisting the wheel. 'Holds the road beautifully.'

'So far,' Doripalam agreed, feeling the dirt road slide beneath them. 'Though I am not sure how long the fates will be on your side.' That would be all he needed at the moment, he thought. A brand new vehicle written off by an idiotic young officer. Particularly if he succeeded in writing off his commanding officer at the same time. Though some might see that as a bonus.

Once again, Doripalam wondered quite why it was he had decided to take on this trip. The case had received some coverage in the press, for reasons he knew all too well, but he could hardly pretend that it was a major priority. The truth was that there was almost certainly nothing to it. Nothing that the police could deal with, at any rate.

Partly, it was about the public profile of the department, he supposed – a necessary but tiresome part of his job. Given the coverage that this story had received in the media, he needed to be seen to be taking some action, however much he might think it to be a waste of time. If questions were asked in the Great Hural, as they conceivably might, he could at least demonstrate his personal commitment to the case.

But, if he was honest, there was only one reason he was out here today, speeding north into the shadow of the mountains when he should have been firmly seated behind his battered desk. He was avoiding Nergui. He was avoiding his former boss, his mentor, who was making yet another return visit to what inevitably still felt like his home turf. Not that he could avoid Nergui forever, or even for very long. But by the time Doripalam returned to headquarters, later that day, Nergui should at least have completed the round of ritualised greetings and glad-handing. Doripalam knew Nergui well enough to recognise that he would neither welcome nor be fooled by such ceremony. After all, most of those who were acclaiming Nergui's return had previously been only too glad to see the back of him – and for much the same reasons that they now resented Doripalam. But he knew they wouldn't hesitate to use Nergui's arrival as yet another stick to beat their current boss.

So, all in all, this was a pretty cowardly excursion, and would probably end up producing precisely the opposite effect from that Doripalam had intended. On the other hand, it would give Nergui the chance to get himself installed without further interference. And it would perhaps give Doripalam the chance to prepare himself for – well, for whatever it was that Nergui was up to. He was still unclear about precisely what that might be. And, knowing Nergui's ways, that continued to disturb him.

They had left the city well behind them now, and

were heading north towards the mountains. It was another beautiful spring day, the sky a deep clear blue, the grassland lush and fertile at the start of the new year. Luvsan religiously consulted the truck's state-of-the-art GPS navigation system as they sped away from the city, but it was hardly necessary. The single hard-packed road stretched endlessly in front of them, and the landscape around them appeared deserted, mile after mile of rolling steppe.

'That's the place,' Luvsan said, unexpectedly. He gestured ahead of them, momentarily taking both hands off the wheel. The truck jerked and swerved slightly, until Luvsan calmly tweaked back the wheel with his left hand. 'See that,' he said. 'Handles like a dream.'

Doripalam sat back in the seat, breathing hard, wondering quite what kind of dreams Luvsan was used to. But he could see the encampment now – a small scattering of the traditional round tents, the *gers*, still some distance away across the empty grassland. It did not appear to be a particularly large camp, just five or six tents. Quite probably most of the group had already moved on, seeking new pastures for their animals now that the spring was here. If so, he thought, it was not surprising that the mother had decided to stay on here. He wondered how long she might have to wait.

As they drew parallel with the camp, Luvsan twisted the wheel with obvious enthusiasm, and pulled off the dirt road towards the cluster of tents. Doripalam relaxed, resigning himself to the bumps and bruises that would result from driving at speed across this rough terrain. He knew from experience how much this empty landscape could distort one's sense of distance, but even so he was surprised by how long it took them to draw close to the camp. Finally, though, they drew up by the *gers*, Luvsan hitting the brakes more abruptly than necessary so that the truck skidded slightly on the hard earth.

'You're sure this is the right place?' Doripalam said. The camp looked deserted, though he knew that the nomads would never abandon their *gers* as they moved to new pastures.

Luvsan twisted in his seat and gave Doripalam a look that bordered on the pitying. 'Of course it's the right place,' he said. 'I was up here about ten days ago, when we first interviewed the mother.' He paused, looking back out through the windscreen. 'There were more tents then, though. Some of them must have moved on.'

'It's spring,' Doripalam said.

'They've not left much, though,' Luvsan said. 'I don't see any animals.'

He was right, Doripalam thought. One would normally expect to see grazing sheep or goats, as well as the tethered horses used for transport. And it was unusual to find a camp of this kind which wasn't jealously guarded by at least one over-sized dog, running out to greet any passing truck. But here there was nothing. No animals, no sign of life at all. Not even one of the ubiquitous motorbikes that were increasingly becoming the preferred mode of desert transport. Just the small cluster of *gers*, a tiny island of human construction in the middle of the vast natural landscape.

'Maybe the rest haven't moved far. Probably Mrs Tuya is waiting for us, and then she will join them.' Doripalam had arranged this visit a few days previously, speaking to Mrs Tuya on a surprisingly clear mobile phone line.

'And how's she planning to travel?' Luvsan said.

Doripalam shrugged. 'I presume the rest will return to collect her.'

Luvsan looked sceptically at him. Doripalam shook his head. 'Okay, you tell me.'

But Luvsan was right again. Doripalam's suggested narrative didn't make much sense. Mrs Tuya travelled with her family, a tightly knit community. It was conceivable that some might travel ahead to seek out the more fertile areas, but it was unlikely that they would leave her alone to deal with the police. Especially given her state of mind, and everything she had been through over the preceding two weeks. This was supposed to be a routine meeting, but for the first time Doripalam felt a stirring of unease.

He slowly opened his door and climbed out into the cool morning air. The summer was some way off, but it would be warm later, he thought. Apart from the whisper of the wind through the sparse grass, there was almost complete silence. Behind the *gers*, the steppe stretched out until it merged with the darker green of the snow-tipped mountains.

'It's eerie,' Luvsan said from behind him. 'The silence.'

'Not something you often encounter in your own company, I imagine,' Doripalam said, but the jibe was half-hearted. 'What state was Mrs Tuya in when you interviewed her?' he asked finally.

'She seemed okay,' Luvsan said. 'I mean, worried, as you'd expect, but relatively calm in the circumstances.'

Doripalam nodded. He wondered just what 'relatively calm' might mean, given these particular circumstances. A missing teenage son. Disappeared on his first significant journey away from the family. A puzzling final phone call which indicated that he had found a new job. And then nothing.

'I read the transcript of the interview,' Doripalam said. 'She seemed calm enough but she wasn't giving much away as far as I could see.'

'She answered the questions fully enough,' Luvsan said. 'But you're right. There was something closed about her.'

'You think she was hiding something?'

Luvsan shrugged. 'I'd guess not. But it's hard to be sure. People behave strangely when they're worried. And I think she holds us partly to blame for not making more progress.'

'She might be right,' Doripalam said. 'That's certainly what the press think. But it's hard to make much progress when we don't even know for sure that a crime's been committed.'

'You think he might have just taken off on his own?'

'He's a teenage boy,' Doripalam said. 'I don't think it's beyond the bounds of possibility, do you?'

There was still no sign of life or movement from the *gers*. Doripalam realised that both of them had been stringing out the conversation in the vague hope that someone might emerge from one of the tents, relieving them of the necessity of entering the *gers* themselves.

'It doesn't look as if there's going to be a welcoming committee,' he said, finally. 'I think we'll need to take a look for ourselves.'

Luvsan nodded and then, in an unexpectedly loud voice, called out: 'Hold the dog!'

It was the traditional greeting, called as one approached a *ger* as a visitor. Doripalam had always found it mildly absurd, and here – with no sign of life, canine or otherwise – it sound ridiculous. There was no response, so he walked slowly forward and pulled open the door to the leading *ger*.

He blinked, peering into the darkness. He ducked and stepped into the tent, moving slowly to allow his eyes to become accustomed to the gloom. Luvsan followed a few steps behind.

The *ger* appeared to be deserted. There were a few pieces of furniture in there – some brightly coloured chests, a cupboard, a low table with a white cloth thrown across it. Opposite the door, there was a single bed covered with a garish tapestry.

'No one here?' Luvsan said, stating the obvious.

'Doesn't seem so,' Doripalam said. 'The place is very tidy. Doesn't look as if anyone left here in a hurry.'

'But it looks as if they did leave,' Luvsan said, stepping past Doripalam into the gloomy interior of the tent. 'Not much sign of life.' He pulled open one of the brightly painted cabinets. Inside, the shelves, lined with old newspapers, were empty.

Doripalam turned and stepped back out into the bright sunshine, blinking from the glare. There was a stiff breeze now, whipping through the scrubby grasslands, and Doripalam realised that, despite the brilliance of the morning sun, he was feeling cold.

He walked across to the neighbouring *ger* and, without bothering to call a greeting, he pulled open the door. As his eyes grew accustomed to the darkness, he saw that this tent was as empty as the first. Again, it was tidy, still furnished with garish cupboards and tables. But there was no sign of habitation.

'Just the same?' Luvsan said from behind him.

'Exactly the same. Tidy but deserted.'

'How long do you think they've been gone?'

Doripalam shrugged. 'No way of knowing. I spoke to Mrs Tuya – when? Four days ago.'

'And there was no sign that she was planning to leave?'

'Of course not,' Doripalam said, with a touch of impatience. 'She didn't say much, but my impression was that she was planning to stick around as long as it took. Until she had some news.' He walked further into the empty *ger*, and pulled open more cupboard doors. All had been emptied, and no trace of any recent inhabitation had been left. 'And why would they clear everything but not pack up the *gers*? Nomads don't leave their *gers* behind.'

'Not through choice,' Luvsan agreed.

The two men stepped back out into the sunshine, Doripalam carefully pulling the door of the *ger* closed behind him.

'We'd better check the rest,' he said. 'Just in case.' There were three more *gers*, standing some metres back from the first two. 'You take that one, and I'll look at these two.'

Luvsan nodded and stepped across to the *ger* that Doripalam had indicated. Doripalam himself turned and pulled open the door of the next tent.

Even before he had fully opened the door he knew that this one was different. The smell was not strong and was quickly whipped away by the breeze, but, to a policeman of Doripalam's experience, it was unmistakable. He reached into his pocket and, for the first time, pulled out a flashlight. He suspected that he would want to spend as little time as possible inside the tent.

He switched on the flashlight and stepped forward cautiously into the darkness, holding the torch out before him. Once inside the tent, the smell instantly grew stronger, almost unbearable. In the sunshine, the interior of the tents was growing warm, and he could hear an incessant buzz of flies.

As his sight cleared, he moved the torch-beam carefully around the interior. At first, it looked much like the previous two – tidy, apparently deserted, no sign of life.

And then the light finally fell across the sight he had been anticipating. There was no sign of life here, either, at least not human life, but the life had, he thought, departed relatively recently.

The body was lying sprawled against the side of the tent, its limbs spread out across the earth. The head was set at an odd angle. Doripalam moved the torch to light up the body and saw, with a shock, that the throat had been brutally cut.

He forced himself to move closer, scarcely breathing, trying not to inhale the rich scent of human decay. It was the body of a middle-aged woman – probably late forties, through it was difficult to be sure as the face lolled unpleasantly away from him. She was dressed in a traditional dark brown *del,* the heavy robe bunched tightly around her twisted figure. A pair of highly polished black boots protruded from beneath the robe. It looked as if she had been attacked and then fallen back against the wall of the tent.

But there was something more, something odder. Reluctantly, Doripalam reached out and moved the body slightly. Its arms were trapped underneath the trunk, twisted awkwardly. As Doripalam succeeded in raising the body slightly, he saw that the figure's arms were tied, knotted with strong plastic twine at the wrists. The arms themselves were bare, the thick felt of the *del* apparently ripped away. Along the length of each arm, he could see an ugly tapestry of what looked to be bruises and inflamed burn marks.

Doripalam heard footsteps behind him, and allowed the body to fall back to the hard earth. He turned to see Luvsan standing in the doorway, silhouetted against the sunlight. He moved the torch light to shine full on the dead woman's face.

'Mrs Tuya?' he said.

Luvsan moved forward and stood behind him, all his previous energy and enthusiasm apparently sapped. 'I think so,' he said, finally.

'Anything in the other *gers*?' Doripalam said.

'Nothing like this. More or less like the first ones. Deserted. Cleared out. All the cabinets empty.'

Doripalam moved the flashlight around the interior. He realised that his initial impression had not been entirely accurate. Although this *ger* was tidy and sparsely furnished, it had not been cleared like the others. There was some crockery neatly stacked on a cabinet on the far side of the room, and one of the larger cupboards stood half open to reveal some clothes inside. In front of the cupboard there was a large metal chest, its lid thrown back, with a further pile of clothes and other household items – a kettle, some saucepans, a few cheap-looking ornaments – stacked inside.

'It looks as if Mrs Tuya was preparing to leave as well,' Doripalam said. Luvsan nodded, his mouth clamped firmly shut. His face was pale, and it looked as if he might be sick at any moment.

Doripalam nodded and then turned to lead the younger man back out into the daylight and fresh air. Once outside, he took a deep breath, relishing the cool of the morning breeze, the clean air smelling only of the broad empty grassland and the mountains. Luvsan followed close behind, and then slumped down on to the bare earth, breathing heavily.

'And it looks,' Doripalam said at last, completing his earlier observation, 'as if someone was very keen that she shouldn't go.'

CHAPTER 3

For a moment he thought there was someone in the outer office. He froze, his hands still deep in the drawer of the filing cabinet, mentally rehearsing the excuses he had prepared. All the good reasons why he should be here, searching through the records at this time of night.

He looked cautiously behind him and realised that the sound was nothing more than his mobile phone vibrating on the wooden desk. He had been half-expecting the call, of course. That was why he had left the phone out there. He hadn't dared switch on the ring-tone, in case there should be someone else left in the building. But he couldn't risk missing the call when it came. There was no room for sloppiness. He knew only too well the price that others had paid for missing their cues.

He picked up the phone and glanced at the screen. No calling number. He had no doubt that the call would be untraceable, if anyone should be inclined to try.

He thumbed the phone on. 'Yes?'

As always, there was no preamble. 'Everything is under control.' It was a statement, not a question.

He swallowed, his mouth suddenly dry. 'Yes. I've got it all in hand. Don't worry.' He immediately regretted the unnecessary reassurance. The phone was silent, and he thought for a second that the caller had hung up. 'I've got it all in hand,' he repeated, his voice cracking slightly.

Finally, the caller spoke again. 'There's one loose end.'

'Not here,' he said. He was aware that his voice was sounding over-eager, but he could do nothing to prevent it. 'I've checked and double-checked everything—'

The caller gave no acknowledgement of his words. 'You need to finish tidying up.'

'Everything—' He stopped, understanding what the caller was saying. 'He's no threat now,' he said. 'He's been suspended. His career's finished—'

'I want you to tidy everything up.'

'But wouldn't it be riskier—?' He was about to bite back the words, knowing how dangerous it would be even to ask the question. Then he realised that, in any case, there was no point in continuing. The phone was dead. The caller had already hung up.

He straightened up, suddenly realising how tense his body had been during the call, how tightly his hand had clutched the phone.

That was it, then. Tidy everything up.

He bent over and finished running through the files in the cabinet, though his mind was no longer focused on the task. He dropped the last of the folders back into the drawer, careful to ensure that his gloved fingers left no marks, that there was no trace that anything had been disturbed.

Tidy everything up.

It was not a surprise. But he had hoped that the task would be allocated elsewhere. This was all too close to home.

Which, of course, was precisely why he had been chosen. He knew well enough by now how this all worked. How quickly he had become implicated. How few options had been left for him.

He carefully slid the drawer of the cabinet shut, and then twisted the combination lock back to where it had been when he had entered the room forty minutes earlier.

He stood for a moment and looked around him, satisfying himself that he had left no sign that anyone had been in here. Then he quickly stepped across the room, gently pulled open the door, and left Doripalam's office.

'Have you been avoiding me?'

Doripalam looked up from the mass of files spread out across his desktop. Nergui was standing in the doorway, his shoulder resting casually against the framework. From somewhere behind him, the sun was shining and his heavily built body was visible only in silhouette.

'Why should you think that? I've been busy.' Doripalam gestured towards the papers in front of him.

'So I hear. Especially after yesterday.'

'Especially after yesterday,' Doripalam agreed. 'All we needed at the moment.'

'Killers rarely exercise any consideration,' Nergui said. 'What's the story?'

Doripalam hesitated. He had found himself increasingly reluctant to discuss current cases with Nergui. He was aware how quickly in these informal discussions they tended to revert to their former roles – Nergui the experienced chief, himself as the eager deputy lapping up the older man's wisdom and advice. It wasn't deliberate on Nergui's part, he thought, and Doripalam always tried hard to resist the tendency, but their old relationship was too deeply ingrained. And, whatever his motives, it was clear that Nergui still couldn't fully tear himself away from this place.

'I've no idea,' Doripalam said at last. 'There's not much to go on yet. We're waiting for the full pathologist's report. But she was clearly murdered – her throat was cut. Probably been dead for at least twenty-four hours. Maybe more. The body had been tied up – the wrists were still tied and there were rope marks around the ankles. And she had been subjected to – well, torture seems the most accurate word. The body was covered in bruises and burns – probably from a cigarette. At the moment, that's about all we have.'

'It sounds plenty. What about the rest of the family?'

'We're trying to track them down,' Doripalam said, finding himself drawn into the conversation despite his best intentions. 'It looks as if some of them must have moved on after we first interviewed Mrs Tuya, but we don't know where they are or why they abandoned some of the *gers*.'

'But some *gers* seemed to have moved on?'

'Apparently. The officer I was with, Luvsan, had been up there to conduct the original interview.

Reckons there were eight or nine tents then – probably more than twenty people in the camp. When we went back, there were just five tents.'

'And all deserted?'

'All deserted and cleared out, apart from the one where we found the body. Mrs Tuya was clearly in the process of leaving – there was a half-packed case. We found one or two other personal items in the other tents, but only the kind of thing that might have been left behind accidentally.'

'So why not pack up the *gers* as well?'

Doripalam shrugged. 'Who knows? Maybe they left in a hurry, if one of them was responsible for Mrs Tuya's death. Or, if they weren't responsible, maybe they were afraid of whoever was.'

'Doesn't take long to dismantle a *ger*, though, if you know what you're doing.'

'Maybe long enough, if you're really afraid.'

As they had talked, Nergui had sat himself down in front of Doripalam's desk. He was, Doripalam noted, carrying a box file labelled 'SCT Enquiry' which he placed unselfconsciously down on the corner of the desk. Doripalam wondered if he was supposed to ask about the file, but he decided to delay that for a while. All things considered, at the moment he felt more comfortable discussing the murder case.

Nergui leaned back in the chair, lifting the front legs off the ground. He looked the same as ever, Doripalam thought, and it was difficult to gauge whether he was going native in the Ministry. Doripalam had not honestly expected him to stay in that role for very long. Particularly after the incidents with the Englishman.

And yet here he was, more than a year on, apparently settled into his role as the Minister's bagman, supposedly dealing with issues of national concern but – as far as Doripalam could judge – spending most of his time processing files in his small but well-appointed office on the third floor of the Ministry. Except, of course, that he wasn't there at the moment. At the moment, he was sitting in Doripalam's office, once again sticking his nose into the business of the Serious Crime Team and engaged in – well, who knew what?

As always, Nergui's dark-skinned face gave nothing away. He gazed impassively at Doripalam as though he had been following every twist of the younger man's train of thought. 'Do you think it's connected with the son?' he said, after the silence had become uncomfortably prolonged.

'Again, who knows?' Doripalam said. 'Until now, I hadn't been taking the son's disappearance particularly seriously.'

'But you thought it was worth going up to talk to her yourself?'

Doripalam shrugged, still uneasily aware that he had, for whatever motive, timed the visit to Mrs Tuya to coincide with Nergui's return. He had no doubt that Nergui had noted the fact. 'That was a PR thing, mainly,' he said. 'You saw the kind of coverage she'd received in the press. Another example of precisely what we didn't need at the moment.'

'She had a relative on *Ardiin Erkh*, I understand?' This was one of the privately-owned national daily newspapers that had appeared with the arrival of democracy in the country.

Doripalam nodded. 'A cousin. Assistant editor or some such. That was how she got the original coverage. Then all the others jumped on the bandwagon.'

'Widow of military hero loses son. Police have no leads. That kind of thing.'

'Precisely that kind of thing. Except that the implication was "police can't be bothered".'

'Because you didn't take it seriously?'

'Well, we didn't particularly, to be honest. The boy, Gavaa, was nineteen. He'd moved to the city to take up a clerical job in one of the state departments. A large well-built boy who apparently took after his soldier father. Bright and self-sufficient. And, by all accounts, not on particularly good terms with his mother. Nothing there that made you think of him as a natural victim.'

'You thought he'd just taken the opportunity to leave home properly?'

'Pretty much so. All the signs were that he'd settled into the city pretty quickly and pretty successfully. He had a good circle of friends. For a young man without commitments, he was fairly well-paid. He was renting a flat near the centre, just a few hundred metres from Sukh Bataar Square. All in all, a fairly cosy lifestyle.'

'But you couldn't track him down?'

'Well, no, that was the mystery. That and the circumstances of his disappearance, such as they were.'

Doripalam was becoming aware that, once again, the two of them had indeed slipped back into their old familiar pattern of dialogue – Nergui asking questions, prompting Doripalam to think harder, underpinned by the same old desire to please and impress the older man. This was not, he thought, appropriate behaviour for the chief of the Serious Crimes Team. On the other hand, he was forced to acknowledge that, on the basis of previous experience, it might enable him to come up with some answers, or at least some new questions.

'I read that he got himself a new job?' Nergui said. Doripalam wondered precisely where Nergui had read this. Admittedly, the story had been well covered in the press, thanks to Mrs Tuya's cousin. But Doripalam was also aware that Nergui could gain access to pretty much any internal police information if he chose.

'We don't know for sure,' Doripalam said. 'He phoned his mother a couple of weeks before the time we think he vanished – though we don't have an exact date for that, or even know for sure that he really has disappeared. He told her he was leaving the Ministry, that he had a new opportunity in front of him which was too good to refuse.'

'But he didn't tell her what it was?'

'No, in fact, she said that he seemed very secretive. Kept hinting that there was more he could tell her but that he had to keep it confidential. That kind of thing.'

'Not a Government job,' Nergui said. It was not a question.

Doripalam smiled faintly. 'Well, I imagine you would know. But, yes, we did check that, because we couldn't think what kind of role might have any requirement for confidentiality.'

'If not a Government role, that suggests something more dubious,' Nergui said.

'Maybe. That is, if we take what the mother said at face value. By that time, she seemed keen to stir up as much trouble as possible. I wasn't directly involved, but I read all the transcripts of the interviews and I couldn't decide whether or not she was exaggerating what Gavaa had said. Making it sound more mysterious than maybe it was.'

'But he still vanished?' Nergui ran his fingers slowly through his thick black hair.

'Well, in the sense that we don't know where he is, yes. But his disappearance doesn't seem to have been particularly sudden. He'd given his landlord a month's notice on the flat, so was clearly expecting to move. He'd also given notice in his job, telling them that he'd found something that paid better, though he didn't say what. But he left both the job and the flat a couple of weeks earlier than expected. The landlord came to drop in some mail one day and found the place deserted.'

'Like the *gers*?' Nergui said.

'Well, yes, I suppose so. It was a furnished flat, and, from what the landlord said, I don't think Gavaa had many personal belongings in any case. Just some clothes, a few books and pictures. They'd all been stripped away, but I imagine they would have fitted into a small suitcase. The landlord was surprised he hadn't said goodbye, as they'd got on fairly well, but just assumed Gavaa had decided to move early for some reason. When we spoke to him, he seemed to think the whole thing was just a fuss about nothing.'

'What about the friends? If Gavaa had just moved to a new flat or a new job, surely they'd know where he was?' Nergui crossed his legs and rested one ankle delicately across his other knee. His socks, Doripalam noted, were pale blue today, matching the shirt and tie beneath his standard dark grey suit. Doripalam wondered vaguely how many colour combinations Nergui had in his wardrobe.

'You'd have thought so, wouldn't you?' Doripalam said. 'That's the only bit of the story that doesn't hang together, where the mother's concerns were understandable. He'd been out drinking with a group of the friends the night before he vanished – pleasant evening, no indication of anything unusual, no sign that he wasn't intending to go to work in his civil service role the next day. But he never turned up at work. Like the landlord, his employers just assumed that he'd decided or been required to take up his new job earlier than expected. They were a bit annoyed, but people often don't work out their notice, so they weren't surprised.'

'And the friends?' Nergui prompted.

Doripalam shook his head. 'We've spoken to all of those who were with him the night before he vanished, plus a few others who were known to be acquainted with him. They all claim they've not seen him since. I don't know whether they're telling the truth. Again, I wasn't directly involved, but I get the impression from the interview transcripts that maybe some of them were a little surprised to find themselves on the end of a police investigation.'

'You think they might have been lying?'

'Well, not all them. It's hard to imagine that they'd all have managed to stick to a consistent story. But I suppose it's possible that some of them are not telling us everything.'

Nergui frowned. 'But why would they bother keeping it quiet if they knew where he was? You don't think they're responsible for his disappearance?'

'I think it's more likely that, if he has just decided to make himself scarce for some reason, one or two of them might know where he's gone to.'

'Presumably we put some pressure on them in the interviews?'

Doripalam nodded, noting the 'we'. 'Of course. All the usual stuff. We told them that withholding information from the police is potentially a very serious offence – impeding the course of justice and all that. We also told them that this had the potential to become a murder investigation – which is certainly the direction that his mother was pushing us, even without a body. But looking at the transcripts, I don't think they were all that impressed.'

'That's the trouble with the youth of today,' Nergui said. 'No respect.'

Doripalam smiled. 'I think the trouble with the youth of today is that they're generally a bit too smart for their own good. And for ours. If any of them did have any information, they didn't see any reason to share it with us, and nothing we could say was going to influence that.'

'In my day,' Nergui said, 'you could have thrown them in jail until they decided to co-operate.'

'In your day, Nergui, I'm sure you could have done much worse than that if you'd chosen to,' Doripalam said. 'But things have changed.'

'Oh, I know,' Nergui said. 'But don't expect me to like it.'

'Anyway, that's where we are with it. Until now, I'd assumed that Mrs Tuya was over-reacting, that Gavaa had simply taken this as an opportunity to leave home properly, cut all the ties, that kind of thing. I thought he'd pop up again in his own time.'

'And maybe he will,' Nergui said, though with an ominous note in his voice. 'What about the relationship with the mother? What do we know about that?'

'Well, let's say it was strained,' Doripalam said. 'Not entirely clear why. The father was a soldier. Fought as part of our force alongside the Russians in Afghanistan.'

'And that's where he was killed?' Nergui said.

Doripalam leaned back in his chair and looked at the older man. Nergui gazed back at him impassively, his bright blue eyes revealing nothing of his thoughts. Doripalam had the uneasy sense, as he so often did with Nergui, that he was somehow being played with – possibly to his own benefit, but played with nonetheless. How much did Nergui really know about all this? 'Yes,' Doripalam said, finally, 'killed by a sniper, supposedly. Gavaa would have been little more than a baby at the time, so would hardly have remembered his father. But he grew up with – at least according to his mother – a rather idealised version of what his father had been like. He idolised him. The military allowed them to stay on in army accommodation after the father's death so Gavaa was brought up in army houses, in sight of the parade ground. Saw his father as part of the great Mongolian martial tradition. Wanted to follow in his footsteps.'

'But he didn't?'

'That was part of the problem. His mother didn't want him to follow in his father's footsteps – perhaps understandably, given what happened to the father. So she blocked and discouraged him. Then, when he was old enough, he went off without her consent and tried to join. And ironically enough he failed the medical. Suffered badly from asthma. So they wouldn't have him anyway. And that of course only made things worse. No doubt his mother couldn't conceal her relief.'

'Complicated things, children,' Nergui observed. 'I've generally managed to steer clear of them.'

'I imagine this wasn't helped by the fact that Gavaa was faced every day with the sight of a world he couldn't be part of. So, as soon as he could, he took the opportunity to get out there and find himself a job in the city.'

'How did the mother end up out on the steppes?'

'She came from a family of herdsmen. After it became clear that Gavaa wasn't going to return to the family home, she decided to return to her own family. Gavaa had already been in the city for six or seven months then, and it looks as if there wasn't much contact between them.'

'Is it possible that he was responsible for his mother's death?'

Doripalam nodded. 'I can see that your razor sharp mind hasn't been blunted by your time in the Ministry,' he said, smiling faintly. 'Yes. We're also looking at that possibility.'

'In any case, perhaps the news of his mother's death will bring him out into the open,' Nergui said.

'Perhaps. It will certainly receive enough coverage. I am sure that Mrs Tuya's cousin will see to that.'

'It's always good to have friends in high places,' Nergui said. He half rose, as though about to leave, then paused, holding out the box file. 'Speaking of which, you haven't asked me about the enquiry. I assume you're interested in its progress.'

Doripalam smiled. 'Of course. But I knew that if I didn't ask, you wouldn't be able to resist telling me about it anyway.'

Nergui sat down again, nodding slowly. It was impossible to tell from his smoothly carved features whether or not he was amused. 'You are right,' he said. 'Young people today are much too smart for their own good.'

CHAPTER 4

The apartment was a mess, there was no doubt about that. In fact, looking round it, he had to admit that that would be a polite description. The room was – there was no way of avoiding this conclusion – squalid. There were dirty plates and dishes piled in corners, gathering mould and perhaps worse. There was a large pile of unread newspapers, stacked unsteadily on the seat of the worn sofa. There was a bog-like pile of apparently unwashed clothes, outer-wear and underwear, squashed haphazardly against the filthy sink. There were arrays of glasses and cups, most half filled with vodka or other spirits, lined up across the table, chairs and floors. Several empty bottles lay under the table.

And, most of all, right in the middle of this panorama of filth, there was him. Spread-eagled, barely sentient, probably smelling worse than the rest of this mess put together.

How the hell had this happened?

He sat up slowly – he was incapable of moving with any greater acceleration – and looked slowly around him. He could scarcely believe what he was seeing. Admittedly, he had never been the tidiest of men. Some might say, he reluctantly acknowledged to himself, that he was one of the least tidy. But he had never found himself living in a state like this.

And, at least for the moment, he still couldn't quite remember how he had reached this point.

He had, he realised, a severe headache, pounding at the rear of his skull. His throat was parched, and tasted as if he might have tried to chew some of the discarded clothing before his collapse. As he stared at the stacked rows of empty and half empty glasses, the source of his condition became clearer. He was fortunate only that much of the contributory liquor remained unconsumed.

He pulled himself very cautiously to his feet, blinking as the sunlight from the uncurtained window caught his eyes. The cheap clock was still there above the sink, he noticed, its crimson plastic as gaudy as ever. Ten past eight. He assumed that was morning, though at this time of the year it could still be light at eight in the evening. In any case, he had no idea how long he had been unconscious.

He dragged himself across to the sink, found a relatively clean looking glass, rinsed it out and filled it with water from the tap. He drank the water down in one, then refilled the glass and emptied that one in the same fashion. He repeated the process a third and then a fourth time. By that point, he felt slightly more human, though now nausea was beginning to replace thirst as the dominant sensation in his body.

As he moved away from the sink, he caught sight of himself momentarily in the full-length mirror he kept propped behind the main door of the flat. The mirror had been his wife's, and he couldn't for the life of him think why she had decided to leave it with him.

Possibly only to maximise the unpleasantness of moments like this.

There was no way round it. He looked an even worse mess than the rest of the flat. He was dressed in a filthy cotton vest, stained with sweat under the arms and spilled food down the chest and stomach. Below that, he was wearing a pair of sagging old boxer shorts which were in a state some way beyond rational description. And he was even wearing a pair of socks with matching large holes through which each of his big toes protruded.

But all of that was relatively reassuring compared with his face. He looked like death. No, he looked like death in an advanced stage of decomposition. He had never seen any living person, let alone himself, looking quite as awful as this. In fact, over the years he had seen one or two corpses that might have been in a healthier state.

He was unshaven. That went without saying. Three or four days' growth at least. His pendulous stomach served only to emphasise the filthiness of his yellowing vest. And his hair looked as if it had been dipped liberally in some deeply unpleasant viscous substance – possibly oil, or possibly something sweeter to attract the lice which he suspected were breeding enthusiastically somewhere in there – and then held in a wind-tunnel for a considerable length of time. It was, he reflected, quite possible that this was exactly, or at least approximately, what had happened.

He couldn't remember last night. That wasn't unusual. What concerned him more was that he couldn't remember any of the preceding ones either.

He poured himself another glass of water, and then slumped down on the threadbare sofa, carefully moving a mould encrusted plate out of the way first.

So what did he remember?

Well, he remembered being suspended, that was for sure. Now, how the hell had that happened?

Partly, he'd just had enough. He put up with this crap, year in, year out, throughout his whole career, and he'd thought it was about time he did something about it. It wasn't as if he didn't take his job seriously. That was the main problem. He took it all a bit too seriously. That was why he was in the mess he was. He looked again round the devastation of the flat. One hell of a mess.

So he'd tried to get smart. But smartness wasn't his thing. Granted, he could call on some low cunning when he needed to, and he'd thought that would be enough to get him through. But he should never have tried to get smart. Not where Muunokhoi was concerned. That had been a big mistake.

The thought of Muunokhoi made him uneasy. He wasn't clear, even now, quite how much Muunokhoi knew. The word was that Muunokhoi knew everything, and on the whole Tunjin was inclined to believe that. He'd certainly managed to unravel Tunjin's idiotic plan quickly enough, though Tunjin had no idea quite how. It was obvious that Muunokhoi had sources on the inside, though Tunjin had thought he'd got all that covered. But they'd clearly worked out what was going on, and it surely wouldn't take them long to finger Tunjin as the perpetrator.

His suspension hadn't exactly been publicised – he was supposedly on sick leave – but he couldn't believe that it wasn't already common knowledge. And if Muunokhoi was getting the right information, it wouldn't take long for him to put two and two together.

And in the middle of all that Tunjin had taken the opportunity to render himself comatose for – well, who knew exactly how long? No, smart definitely wasn't his thing.

For a moment, panic almost overwhelmed him. If Muunokhoi was after him, he was finished. There was no question about that. He knew more than enough about what Muunokhoi could do to people who crossed him. He'd seen plenty of evidence of that, which is why he'd taken the steps he had. But all he'd done was make things worse, and put himself in the firing line.

He breathed deeply and forced himself to relax. That was the one thing you could say about blind panic. It could take the edge even off a hangover like this. Suddenly a pounding headache and churning guts seemed a relatively small price to pay for staying alive.

Okay, so he wasn't smart. But he was cunning and streetwise. He knew this city, and he knew more than enough about the lowlifes who frequented it. He ought to be capable of staying one step ahead of Muunokhoi, at least for a while.

But for how long? That was the question. He couldn't keep hiding forever. And he knew enough about Muunokhoi to recognise that he was a patient man. Ruthless. Unforgiving. Implacable. Vengeful. All of those. But nonetheless patient. Unlike Tunjin, he wasn't the kind of man who would rush into some half-formed scheme without a clue how it was going to end up. He would take as much time as it needed.

Tunjin might make himself safe today, tomorrow, maybe a year or more from now. But at some point, probably when he was finally beginning to relax again, Muunokhoi would be there.

And that, of course, was assuming that Tunjin managed to keep himself at least moderately sober. He shivered at the thought of just how vulnerable he'd been over the last few days, no doubt stumbling from bar to bar and then back here to knock back more dregs of vodka from all these scattered bottles. All things considered, it was surprising that he'd woken up at all.

Tunjin staggered up from the sofa, trying to force himself to think clearly. It was possible, of course, that he was simply below Muunokhoi's radar. Why would a big wheel like Muunokhoi concern himself with an insignificant mite like Tunjin? But then he knew the answer to that well enough. Muunokhoi would bother with Tunjin because he was the only person who had ever come close to putting him behind bars.

Tunjin looked around the flat. Maybe Muunokhoi's people had already been here. Frankly, they might have ransacked the whole place and it wouldn't look very different. Though maybe the smell would have been sufficient to discourage them. Taking care to avoid the scattered plates and bottles, Tunjin stumbled through into the bedroom. It was in a marginally better state than the larger living room, in that there were no plates of half-eaten food and only a single empty vodka bottle lying by the bed. The bed itself was disturbed, though he had no recollection of using it on the preceding nights. But then he had no clear recollection of sleeping anywhere else either.

He moved slowly into the bedroom, shaking his head to try to clear his thoughts, swallowing the panic that was once again beginning to well up in his stomach. And then he stopped, and for a moment the fear overwhelmed him.

There was something lying in the centre of the unmade bed. A grey cardboard file, bound with an elastic band. A file he recognised. A file he had last seen sitting, apparently unregarded, on the Chief's desk.

The case file relating to Muunokhoi.

He walked forward slowly and reached out to touch the file, as though suspecting that it was a hallucination. Stranger things had happened, he imagined, after the consumption of this much alcohol. But there was no question that it was real.

Had he somehow contrived to bring it home with him? Maybe sometime over the last few days, his drunken logic had somehow led him back to police headquarters with the aim of stealing the evidence. Though it was difficult to imagine that anyone would have let him in, and he couldn't believe that he had been in a state to enter without being spotted.

Maybe he'd somehow picked it up on the day of the interview with the Chief. Picked it up off the Chief's desk, without either of them registering the fact. It didn't seem very likely.

Or maybe someone else had stolen the file on his behalf and brought it here as – well, as what? As a warning? To incriminate him in some way?

He leaned over and carefully picked up the file, a wave of nausea sweeping over him as he did so. He pulled off the elastic band and opened the file, rifling through the stack of papers inside.

They were exactly as he recalled them. Including those notes and documents that he had either forged himself or had had painstakingly prepared by one of his contacts, a former fraudster, who had worked for nothing other than a few mild blackmail threats. Tunjin wondered, in passing, whether Muunokhoi might have expressed any interest in the person who had actually carried out this skilled work.

But Tunjin's more immediate concern was his own well-being. The papers in the file were almost as he had seen them last. But not quite. There was one small, but highly significant, difference. Slipped into the front of the file, on top of the pile of documents, was something new, something which Tunjin was sure had not been there when he had last seen the file.

It was a photograph. A high quality photograph, apparently taken in a photographer's studio, with the subject carefully posed. If the subject of the photograph had been, say, an actor or a singer, this might have been the shot selected for sending out, over the artiste's signature, to fans. There was no need for a signature here, though, since Tunjin recognised the subject only too well. It was Muunokhoi. His eyes were empty, but his mouth, as always, seemed to be smiling.

'I'm here to report a crime. Or a potential crime, I'm not sure. Is this the correct place?'

Sangajav, sitting uncomfortably at the reception desk, looked up confusedly. He had been working painstakingly through a series of statistics that

Doripalam had requested and now he had lost his place. 'I'm sorry?'

The woman before him presented an impressive figure. Probably around forty, he thought, with a severe haircut and features that were striking rather than conventionally attractive but still with a very decent figure. Very fashionable clothes, too, he noticed – an expensive-looking dark business suit, probably imported from the West somewhere. Sangajav had little aptitude for mathematics, but, at least in his own mind, he was highly experienced when it came to appraising women.

'Is this the right place to report a crime?'

Sangajav carefully gathered up his papers and looked up at her. 'Well, no, not really. I think you want the police station.'

'Isn't this the police station?'

Sangajav shook his head, as though dealing with a very elementary error. 'No, this is police *headquarters*.'

'And you're not a police station as well?'

'Well, no. This is mainly administration, and some specialist units—'

'But you are the police?'

'Yes, we are, but—'

'So why can't I report a crime here?'

'It's just that – well, you have to go to the police station.'

'But since I'm here, can't you deal with it anyway?'

'That's not really the way—'

'But why not? If you're the police and I want to report a crime, why can't I do so?'

Sangajav sighed. Why did this sort of thing always

happen when he was around? This wasn't even really supposed to be a reception. The building wasn't strictly open to the public, so the desk was really just here for greeting official visitors. But visitors were so few that there was little point in employing a permanent receptionist, so the informal procedure was that one of the officers rostered for administrative duties would sit here just in case anyone turned up. As far as Sangajav could judge, this only ever happened on his watch and it was always people like this.

'It just doesn't work like that,' he explained patiently. 'We're not an operational police station. That's on the other side of the square. As I say, we're mainly admin people here, and one or two specialist units like the Serious Crimes Team—'

'The Serious Crimes Team,' she interrupted. There was a faint hint of a smile around her mouth. 'Well, what if I wanted to report a *serious* crime? Could I do that here?'

Sangajav was beginning to suspect that, despite her impressive appearance, the woman was deeply insane. He wasn't sure quite how to respond. 'Do you want to report a serious crime?' he asked.

'I'm not sure,' she said. 'What constitutes a serious crime?'

Sangajav shook his head, despairingly. His only thought now was how he might get rid of this woman. It didn't seem appropriate simply to throw her out. 'It's difficult to say,' he said at last. 'Perhaps if you tell me what the crime is, I can tell you whether it's serious. But you'll still have to report it at the police station.'

She nodded as though carefully absorbing this information. 'What about a threat of physical violence?' she said. 'Would you consider that serious?'

'We might,' he said. 'It would depend on the circumstances.'

She nodded again. 'What if the purpose of the threat was to intimidate a member of the judiciary?'

'A member of the judiciary?'

'Yes,' she said. 'A judge. A judge who generally deals with major criminal trials. That is, what you might call "serious crimes".' She stared fixedly at Sangajav, and it was impossible to be sure whether she was being ironic.

'I think that might count,' Sangajav said. 'If that were the case.'

'It's the case,' she said, slowly. 'I'm a judge. And I've been threatened. It may just be nonsense. But it may not.'

Sangajav still wasn't entirely sure about her sanity. But if what she was saying was true, then it probably merited taking seriously. The Chief probably wouldn't thank him if he turned away a senior judge from the door. And, at the very least, it would give him a legitimate reason to fob her off on to someone more senior. 'I think I probably need to get someone to talk to you,' he said at last.

She paused, as if some thought had struck her. 'You said the Serious Crimes Team was here? It's just that I think I know the Chief.'

'Doripalam?'

There had been a look in her eye which Sangajav – experienced as he was in the appraisal of women –

68

couldn't quite read. But as he spoke, the look vanished with the suddenness of a light being extinguished. 'Doripalam?' she said. 'No, I don't know him. I was thinking of someone else.'

'Perhaps his predecessor,' Sangajav said, intrigued despite himself. 'Doripalam's not been in the job all that long. His predecessor was a man called Nergui.'

The same look, or something very close to it, reappeared in her expression. 'Nergui,' she said. 'Yes. It was Nergui I knew.' She hesitated. 'We had some dealings – oh, years ago. He has – moved on?' She asked the last question hesitantly, as though concerned about the possible nature of Sangajav's response.

'Promoted,' Sangajav said, bluntly. 'To the Ministry of Security.'

She nodded. 'That's good,' she said. 'Though hardly surprising, I guess. I'm sorry not to have been able to meet him, though.'

Sangajav had begun to see a way in which he might extricate himself from this increasingly insane conversation. She had expressed a desire to see Nergui, and that was good enough for Sangajav. 'Well, actually, you probably can,' he said. 'He's here at the moment, as it happens, carrying out some assignment.' Like most of the team, Sangajav was as yet unclear precisely why it was that Nergui had reappeared, though experience suggested that the impact of his return was unlikely to be straightforward or comfortable. 'I can try to track him down for you, if you like.'

She smiled fully for the first time, and Sangajav was forced to revise his original judgement. She was indeed a striking woman, but she was also, he realised, actually very beautiful.

'I would like that,' she said. 'I would like that very much.'

CHAPTER 5

'I still don't understand what exactly it is you're up to, Nergui. But I do know that I don't feel very comfortable about it.'

They were sitting in Nergui's temporary office. It was much smaller than Doripalam's, tucked away somewhere at the end of the corridor. When he had first received the request from the Ministry to provide some temporary accommodation for Nergui, Doripalam had been tempted to find him a broom cupboard, if only on the accurate grounds that they were already severely pressed for space. In the end, by reorganising some of the administrative staff, they had managed to vacate this room, which was an improvement on the proposed broom cupboard in that it at least had a window. In fact, it had a window which, unlike those in Doripalam's office, actually had a partial view, sandwiched between two adjoining office buildings, out over Sukh Bataar Square.

Doripalam was currently standing staring out at this view, trying to avoid catching Nergui's eye. He was getting better at standing up to him. At least now he felt comfortable saying what he thought. But he still felt faintly patronised, as though Nergui were patiently tolerating his comments rather than paying them any serious attention.

'I've explained,' Nergui said. 'I'm conducting the enquiry as instituted by the Minister. You know that we have to go through this.'

Doripalam was watching the traffic swirling slowly around the square in the chilly morning sunshine. There was the usual procession of battered old Soviet cars and buses, belching thick fumes. The square was thick with clouds of pigeons, scattering for bread-crumbs thrown by a small group of school children passing on the far side. It was still early, and there were relatively few pedestrians other than a few suited figures heading into the government and commercial offices in the streets around the square. 'I know *I* have to go through it,' he said. 'But I'm still not clear why you have to.'

Nergui shrugged. 'I thought we'd been through this,' he said. 'I know the team well. I understand all the pressures you have to face. I've no axes to grind—'

Doripalam turned, shaking his head fiercely. 'No axes to grind? Come off it, Nergui, this is your show from start to finish. It's nothing to do with the Minister, except that his signature has somehow appeared on the bottom of the terms of reference. What was it he thought he was signing?'

Nergui smiled. He was, as always, leaning back in his chair, his ankles resting on the corner of the desk. How did he always manage to look so relaxed these days? Perhaps after all the life of a pen pusher had turned out to suit him. 'I think you're getting much too cynical,' he said. 'It must be the job that's getting to you.'

Doripalam sat himself slowly down in the chair opposite Nergui, trying to control his exasperation. 'Okay,' he said. 'Tell me again, very slowly, what it is you're trying to do here.'

'It's really very simple,' Nergui said. 'We have had something of a political embarrassment. We know it wasn't your fault, and I know exactly the problems that you've been facing. They were problems I faced when I was in the role, and I never succeeded in resolving them. We've both made some progress, but we both know there's a long way to go.'

'You mean corruption?'

Nergui nodded. 'We all know that the civilian police was made up initially of every deadbeat that they wanted to kick out of the militia. We took people who could barely string a sentence together and then stuck them in positions of real power. And then we seemed surprised when that power became corrupted almost overnight.'

'There are some decent people in the team,' Doripalam said.

'I'm not denying it,' Nergui said. 'Especially among those we recruited later – as the present company amply demonstrates – though even there we were hampered by the poor wages we could offer. Who wants to come and risk their life in the police force when you can earn twice as much working in a shop?'

'I suppose I did.'

Nergui nodded. 'I suppose you did. And one day I'll have to make a serious attempt to find out why.' He smiled faintly. 'But you're the exception, along with one or two others. There's a hell of a lot of them out there who really just aren't up to it. The worst ones are corrupt – not seriously so, for the most part, but taking the odd quiet backhander just to turn a blind eye. The ones who aren't corrupt are just incompetent – they don't understand what the job is or why it matters. They don't follow the procedures. They lose us virtually every case we manage to get to court. And the few who aren't corrupt or inept are just lazy. They can't be bothered with the job.'

'That doesn't say a lot for my leadership.'

'Oh, come off it, you've only been in the job five minutes, and I know you've made some real progress. How long was I in the job? What does it say about my leadership?'

Doripalam knew better than to try to answer that one. 'Okay, so where does that get us?'

'It gets us to a point where maybe we have an opportunity to begin to put things right.'

'I'm not sure I follow.'

'Doripalam, when I was in the job, I pushed and pushed for more resources to get this place sorted out. I managed to get some, but never anything like enough. I imagine you've been doing the same, and I've certainly tried to use whatever influence I've got to support you.'

'Well, I'm sure I'm very grateful,' Doripalam said. He intended to sound ironic, but was conscious that he merely ended up sounding petulant.

'But no-one's interested. There's a flurry of excitement when something really serious happens – like our murders last year – but that kind of thing is generally too embarrassing so all they want to do is sweep it under the carpet.'

'As they did very effectively in that case, as I recall.'

'Indeed. They're politicians. Their job is to avoid embarrassment. And unfortunately they tend to see a team like this, not as a force for social good, but simply as a source of potential embarrassment.'

'And you think we're a source for social good?' he asked.

'Of course I do. You know me. I'm a patriot, for all my cynicism. I want what's best for this country. I think, in a thousand small ways, we're under siege. We're under siege from the West, from the East. And, potentially, we've already been infiltrated. Our defences are already being undermined.'

'Sounds a little over-dramatic to me.' From the corner of his eye, Doripalam could see the pedestrians strolling across Sukh Bataar Square on their way into work. There was a man, dressed in a grey business suit, sipping American-style coffee from a paper cup as he made his leisurely way past the large statue of the revolutionary hero towards the government offices. Close by, a couple of teenage girls, dressed in T-shirts with Western designer labels emblazoned across the front, had stopped to chat before going their separate ways. This did not look like a country under siege. On the other hand, young as he was, it did not look much like the country Doripalam had grown up in.

Nergui shrugged. 'Maybe I spend too much time with politicians. Too much rhetoric. But I think it's true. We expend all our time and energy on the big political questions – our relations with China, with Russia, with the West – while I grow increasingly afraid that it's the smaller crimes, the smaller corruptions that are undermining the stability of the state.'

'The state's always been corrupt,' Doripalam pointed out.

'Maybe. But, whatever we thought of the old system, things were under control. Now I'm not sure they are. Profit drives everything, and it's slipping away from us. I'm not sure anybody cares enough to fight back.'

'Except you?' Doripalam was unsure whether he intended his question to sound mocking or sincere.

Nergui smiled. 'I'm just a civil servant. Just doing my job. But I do want to have the resources to do it properly.'

'So what does this have to do with the enquiry?'

'We've suffered yet another political embarrassment. The Minister's ridden out the storm, as he always seems to, but the opposition have made serious capital out of it.'

Doripalam nodded. 'The Minister made that very clear to me. Kept assuring me that it wasn't my fault, but it wasn't clear who else's fault it might have been.'

'Certainly not his. But the point is that, for once, they couldn't brush this under the carpet. Which, by a very entertaining irony, was largely the Minister's own fault.'

'Because he extracted such political kudos from the fact that we were bringing Muunokhoi to trial in the first place?'

'Precisely so. If I recall correctly, I did warn him that

this might not be the wisest move, but he can be an impetuous fellow where political advantage is concerned.'

'Even if the case hadn't fallen apart quite so spectacularly, the Minister's comments might have been prejudicial to a fair trial,' Doripalam pointed out. 'I wasn't exactly pleased about that, though in the circumstances it didn't seem appropriate to bring it up afterwards.'

'I understand that Muunokhoi's lawyers were planning to argue precisely along those lines,' Nergui said. As always, it was not entirely clear how he had come by this particular piece of information. 'But the question was entirely academic, as things turned out.'

'And so now we – by which I mean you – have to investigate how Tunjin was allowed to get us into this mess? I'm not sure I quite see how that's likely to help us. I certainly don't see how it's going to help *me*.'

'I'm just being opportunistic,' Nergui said. 'The Minister has to be seen to be doing something if only to cover his own back. He wants a short sharp review that will result in a few suitable rolling heads.'

'With my name high on the list?'

'Of course not. The Minister can be impetuous, but he's no fool. He knows – not least because I've repeatedly told him so – that you're the best asset he's got in this force. He's not going to risk losing you over something like this. But, in any case, that's not the way this thing is going to go.'

'Why not?'

'Because the Minister has made what might turn out to be – in terms of short term political expediency

– one tiny error. He agreed to let me run the enquiry.'

'Which means?'

'Which means we do it properly. You and me. We take this as an opportunity really to get to grips with the problems in this team. We can root out the real problems – the real corruption. We make as many heads roll as we need to, knowing that the Minister has to back us up.'

'Why does he have to? He's never been keen on raising his head above the battlements before.'

'Because having announced the enquiry – which he did with as much fanfare as when he announced Muunokhoi's arrest – he can't then be seen not to support it just because the outcome turns out to be rather more radical than he might have expected.'

Doripalam shook his head. He was beginning to suspect that Nergui had been with the politicians too long. 'Are you sure about this?'

Nergui shrugged. 'Not at all. I'll probably be whipped off the enquiry and find myself facing a sudden early retirement. But I think it's worth a shot, don't you?'

He's bored, Doripalam thought, suddenly. That's what this is about. He's bored witless in that comfortable office of his, shuffling his paperwork. All that talk about the nation under siege – well, that was probably sincere, knowing Nergui's distinctive form of patriotism. But it wasn't what was really driving Nergui. What was really driving him was the need to stir the pot again, to get things moving. To raise some sort of hell.

Doripalam smiled. 'As long as it's you facing the

early retirement and not me. Yes, maybe it's worth a shot.'

Nergui sat silently at the desk, listening to Doripalam's footsteps receding down the corridor. He supposed that it might have been possible to have found him a temporary office that was smaller and even more isolated than this one, but probably only by utilising a broom cupboard. Not that he could blame Doripalam. On the whole, Nergui thought that the younger man was taking it all rather well. Nergui was behaving like the very worst kind of manager. The kind who gets kicked upstairs and then just can't tear himself away from the job he's supposed to have left behind. Just can't believe that anyone could do it as well as him.

Was that it? Nergui hoped not. He had enormous respect for Doripalam – he thought Doripalam handled the day to day aspects of this job better than he had, if only because he seemed to have infinitely more patience with all the nonsense involved. No, it was the job he couldn't leave behind. And not just because he liked the pace and the excitement of it, compared with the cerebral challenges of his Ministry role. But also because he thought it mattered. It was important. It was what held the fabric of this increasingly fragile society together.

All the rhetoric he'd trotted out to Doripalam – well, of course it was overblown. How else did you get the Minister to take any notice of this kind of thing? But, nonetheless, it had been sincere. As he saw the growing influx of drugs dealing, mindless violence, not-so-petty theft – the slow but sure seepage of influence from the wider world – he did begin to think that maybe the battle was already lost. All those grand ideological battle-cries – equality, freedom, democracy – and yet it was this mundane criminality, the underbelly of capitalism, that would end up on top of the pile.

So here he was again, dabbling in things that he should have left far behind. If he'd been in Doripalam's shoes, he'd probably have told them precisely where to stick their enquiry. But that was why Doripalam was good in this role. Because he only fought the battles that mattered. Because, much as he might resent Nergui's repeated intrusions, he also recognised that the older man's experience and know-ledge could be useful. Maybe, in the end, it was Doripalam who was exploiting Nergui. At least, Nergui hoped that was the case.

His musing was interrupted by the telephone on the desk in front of him. The sound was startling. Nergui didn't think that anyone yet had this contact number. The Minister would call him on his mobile – probably several times a day once he realised that Nergui wasn't immediately on hand to respond to whatever minor crises were brewing – as would any of his Ministry colleagues. Nergui liked the mobile, partly because he could switch it off when he chose.

He cautiously picked up the receiver. 'Nergui?'

'Sir. I'm sorry to disturb you. I have a visitor down at the reception. She's here to report a crime – a threat of physical assault.'

Nergui shook his head, wondering if the call had been transferred to the wrong extension. 'I'm sorry,' he said. 'I think you want someone else.'

'No, sir. I'm sorry, but she was keen to speak to you.'

'To me? Why should she want to talk to me? Just send her over to the police station.'

'Well, yes, sir, that's what I told her. But she says she knows you. She's a judge.'

'A *judge*?' The dialogue seemed to be drifting into the realms of the surreal. Nergui had become acquainted with a number of judges in the course of his professional life, but he couldn't think of any who might actively seek him out for the purposes of reporting a crime.

'Yes, sir. She says she's been threatened.'

Nergui leaned back in his chair. Through the window, between the angles of the surrounding buildings, he could see a rectangle of pure blue sky. 'Threatened?'

'Yes, sir.'

It sounded like some kind of lunatic. Someone claiming she was a judge, that she'd been threatened, that she knew Nergui. How did she even know he was here? He sighed gently. 'And what's your name, son?'

There was a pause at the other end of the line. 'Sangajav, sir.'

'Well, Sangajav, I suppose you'd better bring her up. But I hope you're not wasting my time.'

There was a second, longer pause. 'I'm sorry, sir, but she does claim she knows you.'

'Bring her up.' Nergui slowly replaced the receiver. He pulled himself upright and walked across to the window. The partial view over the square was not particularly impressive, but at least it was possible to see some real life out there. At the nearest corner of the square there was a cluster of older men, all dressed in traditional robes and sashes, chatting and smoking. Nergui wondered vaguely who they were, and why they were gathered in this way. Beyond there, there was another knot of humanity – this time a group of Japanese tourists, endlessly rearranging themselves to take photograph after photograph of each other standing in front of the government buildings, Sukh Bataar's statue, the post office building.

There was a soft knock at the office door behind him. Nergui turned as the door opened, and Sangajav, a short, colourless figure with his head bowed deferentially, ushered in an attractive dark-haired women in a grey, formal-looking suit. 'Sir,' he said. 'Ms Radnaa.'

She was gazing at Nergui with an amused expression on her face. 'It *is* you,' she said. 'I hadn't quite believed it.'

For a second, Nergui stared at her. He half registered that, somewhere behind her, Sangajav had managed to make a discreet and hurried exit and was closing the door gently behind him. 'Sarangarel,' he said, finally.

She smiled. 'Well, I am relieved. For a moment there, I genuinely thought that you didn't remember me.'

He shook his head, still trying to reconcile all the information that he had received in the preceding minutes. 'I nearly didn't. It's been a long time,' he said, aware of how inane his words sounded. Strange, he thought, how shock propels us back into conventionalities. 'Ten years.'

'Twelve, I think,' she said.

He nodded slowly, gesturing her to take a seat. He lowered himself into the seat behind the desk, still staring at the self-possessed woman in front of him. 'How did you know I was here?'

'I'm glad to see that your ego hasn't diminished over the years,' she said. 'I didn't know you were here. I just came to report a crime.'

'You should have gone to the police station.'

'So I was told by the helpful young man who brought me up here. But I'm glad I didn't.'

'Yes,' Nergui said, after perhaps slightly too long a pause. 'I'm glad you didn't.'

'That sounded almost sincere,' she laughed.

Nergui shrugged. 'No, really, it's good to see you. A bit of a shock, though.'

'I can imagine.'

'You look very different,' he said. 'Still terrific, though.'

'You know, you keep pausing in the wrong places and for just a moment too long.'

Nergui laughed. 'But you haven't changed, have you? Whereas I think my hearing must be going, because I thought I heard young Sangajav say that you were a judge.'

'That's right. I'm a judge. Trying criminal cases. I'm surprised we haven't run across one another.'

He stared at her for a moment, as though trying to make sense of a particularly obscure joke. 'You really are?' He shook his head. 'You always did have a sense of humour.'

'I always did,' she said. 'But I'm deadly serious about this. And I'm good at it.'

'I don't doubt it. You'd be good at anything you put your mind to. But why the judiciary?'

'Well, I think I'd got to know the ways of the law quite well, don't you? Somehow it seemed a natural move.'

'Not to me,' he said. 'And you've not encountered any – problems?'

'As a result of my past, you mean? Why should I? It's not as if I was the criminal. I couldn't help who I was married to. I didn't even know.'

There was a sense that she was protesting too much. But that wasn't so surprising, Nergui thought. She'd no doubt had to rehearse these arguments pretty frequently over the years. He couldn't believe that her past hadn't at some point returned to haunt her.

'Of course not,' he agreed. 'But people can be unforgiving.'

She shrugged. 'I can't pretend it's been easy. After – well, after it all happened, I didn't know what to do. I was completely lost. There was a point when I thought that maybe you and I—' She trailed off, as though suddenly conscious that she might have said too much.

Nergui was watching her intently, his dark face giving nothing away. That had been part of it, she realised. She had never known for sure what he was thinking, could never get quite as close to him as she had needed.

'There was a point when I might have thought the same,' he said, surprising her.

She looked up at him, smiling. 'It's probably just as well then that neither of us knew what the other was thinking,' she said.

'Just as well,' he agreed. 'But what happened to you? I thought about trying to keep in contact afterwards, but it didn't seem appropriate.'

No, she thought, it wouldn't have. And very probably he was right. It wouldn't have been appropriate. 'I floundered for a while. There was nobody. Things could have turned out very badly, I think, if I hadn't got a grip of myself.'

It was difficult now to imagine her having anything less than a very firm grip on herself, Nergui thought. But he knew that hadn't always been the case.

'I managed to get myself a job. Ironically, with the legal firm who'd handled the case—'

Nergui nodded. He recalled the lawyer who had acted for Sarangarel's husband and could imagine that his motives for offering her a job after her husband's death might not have been entirely altruistic. But the lawyer would also have been smart enough to recognise that, whatever else he might or might not get from the arrangement, he would at least get a very capable employee.

'I started doing clerical work. I did well, got myself promoted, and eventually they offered me the chance to take a law degree with the aim of moving into a professional role in the firm.'

'Which I've no doubt you undertook with consummate ease,' Nergui said.

'I'm not sure I'd say that,' she said. 'But I did it, worked as a criminal lawyer for several years and then got the chance to apply for the judiciary. One of the benefits of a burgeoning democracy – it does create a

85

whole new set of employment opportunities. Did you know that over half our judges are women?'

'It just confirms what I've always assumed about female judgement,' Nergui said. 'Considerably more reliable than the male equivalent.'

'And women tend to be less patronising, as well,' she said.

Nergui smiled. 'But, as you say, it is ironic. That you should have ended up passing judgement over—'

'People like my late husband? Well, I suppose you don't need to delve too deeply into the psychology of that.'

'In my experience,' Nergui said, 'it never pays to delve too deeply into the psychology of anything.'

'And what about you, Nergui?' she said. 'I followed your progress for a few years – I suppose I could claim it was a professional interest, as a criminal lawyer. I thought I might bump into you when I was trying the Muunokhoi case. That was one of yours, wasn't it?'

He looked up at her sharply, a glint of suspicion evident in his eyes for the first time. 'You tried the Muunokhoi case?'

'Well, in so far as it was tried. If it was one of yours, it wasn't your finest hour.'

'It wasn't one of mine,' he said. 'Not directly. I'd already moved on by then. But it's why I'm back here now. And, no, it wasn't our finest hour.'

'What went wrong?' she said. 'I've never seen the State Prosecutor's Office look so rattled. Normally they're the ones rattling everyone else.'

Nergui absently straightened the pile of files on the desk, acutely conscious that the entire Muunokhoi case history was spread out on the polished surface between them. 'Are you sure you're here entirely by chance?' he said. 'One hell of a coincidence.'

She sat back and gazed at him coolly, a faint smile on her lips. 'You really don't trust anyone, do you, Nergui? I suppose I should have remembered that. You're always careful to ensure that no-one else is a step ahead of you.'

'I'm not worried when people are a step ahead of me,' he said. 'It's when they're a step behind me that I start worrying what they're up to. I've been caught from behind just once or twice too often. Literally and figuratively.'

She laughed. 'But, no, I am here entirely by coincidence. And only because I went to the wrong place.' She paused. 'But I suppose that wasn't entirely accidental. I came here because I'd been interviewed here so often. I'd assumed this was the station.'

'There's no question that what your husband was involved in were serious crimes,' Nergui said. 'That's why you came here. But – okay, I won't be suspicious – why are you here? What is all this about threats?'

'I don't honestly know. It may well be nothing. It started not long after the Muunokhoi case, actually. Somebody had got hold of my private phone number and I got three or four calls—'

'Threatening?'

She shrugged. 'Not really. Not at first. Just nothing. But with a sense that there was somebody still there, that the line was open.'

'Everybody gets these automated marketing calls these days. Even here. We live in a global economy. Or it could just be someone's mobile playing up. The signals are always poor outside the city.'

'I don't think it's someone I know. The number is always concealed.'

'Marketing calls, then. These predictive dialling machines. The operators can't keep up with them.'

'Of course it could have been. But then more recently I've had some that do seem more threatening. Always late at night. A voice – sounding metallic, as if it's been disguised or treated in some way – repeating a name. My husband's name.'

Nergui stared at her. 'Anything else?'

'Nothing. Just that, over and over. Till I put the phone down. Sometimes even then the line isn't cut so if I pick it up again the voice is still there, still repeating.' She paused. 'Those are the most unnerving times. When I think I'll never stop it – that it'll just keep on and on like that.'

'Does it sound like a recording?'

'It might be. I don't know. Maybe yes. That would explain why it sounds so relentless.'

'And is there anything explicitly threatening?'

'No. Just that. That's why I've been so reluctant to do anything about it.'

'There must be a procedure for you to follow,' Nergui said. 'As a judge, I mean. If you receive threats.'

'I'm sure there is,' she said. 'But I felt foolish invoking something like that unless there was a good reason. And I'm not sure there is.'

'But you were willing to come and talk to the police?' Nergui's blue eyes were watching her intently, and for a moment she realised what it would feel like to be on the wrong end of one of his interrogations.

'I suppose . . .' She hesitated. 'Well, I suppose that's why I came here, though it wasn't particularly conscious. On the whole, I'd been treated well here, in the circumstances. Not least by you. So I thought maybe someone here would listen to me. Just talk it through. See if I'm being ridiculous.'

'Which is what we're doing,' Nergui said. He wondered how accidental her appearance here had really been. She had never struck him, even when she was in the middle of those dark days a decade before, as someone who would engage in a fool's errand. She had thought that Nergui was still in charge here. Maybe she had come intending to have precisely this kind of discussion.

'And do you think I'm being ridiculous?'

'No, of course not. If anything, I think you're probably being too relaxed about the whole thing. It sounds as if this is something specifically designed to unsettle you. It's obviously someone who knows about your background. How widely known would that be?'

'I don't know. I've not lied about it, but I don't particularly go out of my way to publicise it either. But, no, it wouldn't be widely known.'

'And I think we can reasonably assume that it's someone trying to put pressure on you in your judicial role.'

'But not very effectively?'

'Not so far, no. But it's already moved up a gear from the original silent calls, so we can probably assume that they may become more threatening.'

'I'm glad I came to you for an objective opinion rather than comfort,' she said.

'I'm much better on the former.'

'So I recall. But, yes, I suppose you're right. I should report it.'

'Report it as you need to with the judiciary. I imagine they need it on the record in case there are any subsequent questions about your impartiality.'

She looked up at him with a slightly startled expression. 'Impartiality? Yes, well, I see what you mean. It's stupid of me. I should have thought of all this.'

Nergui watched her carefully. As he recalled, she was anything but stupid, or even absent minded. It was difficult to believe that she hadn't really thought through all this before turning up, unannounced and unexpected, at the door of police headquarters. 'You're probably feeling anxious about it all – maybe more than you realise. After all, just hearing that name after all these years will have stirred up a lot that you probably thought was long buried.'

She nodded, as though this idea was also new to her. Nergui thought back to her earlier comment about being patronised. He suspected that she might be someone who tolerated being patronised if this allowed her also to be underestimated.

'I can deal with the police side of it,' he said, wondering even as he spoke whether this was entirely wise. 'We can do some checking on the calls. We might be able to track down the calling number, though I wouldn't be too hopeful on that front. Might be a good idea if we give you some protection too.'

She smiled. 'Is that really necessary, do you think?'

He shrugged. 'I don't want to alarm you unnecessarily. Chances are that this is just some half-baked idiot who's trying to cause a bit of trouble. Maybe someone with a grudge against you. Someone you sent down, maybe?'

'Well, of course, that's possible. But do you think there's any real danger?'

'I doubt it, to be honest. These people usually just like to stir things up. Those who want to do harm will generally just go ahead and do it. But you can never be sure.'

'I bow to your superior knowledge,' she said. 'I hope you're right.'

'So do I,' he said. He paused. 'It's been good to see you again, Sarangarel.'

She nodded. 'It must be fate,' she said. 'I came to the wrong place, and you weren't supposed to be here. Though you never did explain what it is that you are doing here.' She looked around the tiny, sparsely furnished office. 'And this hardly looks like the head man's room.'

'It isn't,' he said. 'I'm not the head man here. Not any more. And, to be honest, I'm not even entirely sure what it is that I'm doing here.'

'That's not like you, Nergui,' she said. 'You usually knew exactly what you were doing.'

'I did, didn't I?' he said. His blue eyes were unblinking. 'And, if I remember rightly, so did you.'

CHAPTER 6

Tunjin was slumped on the bed, looking as though someone had just struck him a hefty blow in the stomach.

He looked again at the open file, the picture of Muunokhoi staring back up at him with its empty smile. If this meant what he thought it did, then he could expect far worse than a blow in the stomach in the near future.

He tried to find some other interpretation, some other explanation for the presence of this photograph. Perhaps it had been in the file all along, an aid to identifying Muunokhoi. There were, after all, no official police mug shots of Muunokhoi – not until his recent arrest, at any rate. The arrest for which Tunjin had been responsible.

But he knew that this picture had not been in the file. He had been through the file dozens of times, collating the genuine evidence, checking the confected material, searching for inconsistencies, searching for anything that would reveal the forgeries. He had been convinced that it had all been perfect, foolproof.

But Muunokhoi had seen through it. And now the only fool here was Tunjin.

And, in any case, even if the photograph had been

there all along, this didn't explain how the file came to be here, in Tunjin's flat. He had been over and over this in his mind in the preceding few minutes. Okay, he remembered little or nothing of the past few nights, but that itself indicated that he had not been in a condition to start stealing files from police headquarters. There was no question – this file had been stolen and placed here by someone in a far more coherent state of mind than Tunjin.

He needed a drink. He really needed a drink. He thought back to the numerous nearly empty vodka bottles in the other room. There was still plenty of booze left. More than enough.

It was tempting. Simply to slip back into oblivion. Just lie there and wait for whatever might happen. Except, of course, that nothing would. He would die of alcohol poisoning before Muunokhoi would do anything to him while he was unconscious. Muunokhoi liked his victims to know precisely what was happening to them and why. Not someone with a great tolerance of ambiguity, Muunokhoi.

Tunjin shook his head. No, for once, the answer wasn't to hide himself away in drink. He shuddered at the thought that, sometime over the last day or two, probably while he lay in a drunken stupor, someone had entered the flat, probably stepped over his comatose body, and placed this file on his bed. That was a fairly powerful incentive to eschewing the booze, at least for a while.

So how close were they? Were they nearby, just waiting for him to wake up, so they could finish things off?

He had to be careful. Fortunately, with the brilliance of the sunshine outside, he had had no need to switch on the lights and the curtains were already drawn back. No-one watching from the outside would have seen any movement so far.

Unless they were listening for the judder of the plumbing as he had turned on the tap to get himself some water.

No, he was being paranoid. The plumbing in this place was so ancient that there was no way of tracing any noise back to any individual flat. But the principle could well be right. They could be waiting for some sign of life. Maybe waiting for him to leave the flat so they could pick him up and take him to some more suitable place. But if that was the case, why hadn't they just snatched him while he was unconscious? They could have taken him where they liked and then waited for him to wake up.

Because they were playing with him. That was why they'd left the file here. That was why they were letting him wait. Because they knew what he'd be thinking. They knew what he'd be thinking about. They knew – because it was now here in front of him – that he'd read Muunokhoi's file.

And that was it. He knew – and they knew he knew – what Muunokhoi was capable of. He couldn't just sit here and wait for it.

He pulled himself to his feet and stumbled over to the window, standing carefully to one side so that he wouldn't be seen from outside. He blinked at the sunlight, noting from the position of the sun that it really was still morning.

The bedroom window gave a view of the main street below. It was certainly nothing impressive. Depressing Soviet-style apartment blocks – just like this one – lined both sides of the street, preventing the sun from penetrating except in the very middle of the day. The occasional puttering car went by, mostly clapped out old Ladas, the only kind of vehicle that could be afforded by the people who lived in these endless anonymous blocks. Tunjin peered out, his eyes flicking across the grey-stained concrete.

There was a figure standing, motionless, a hundred or so metres up the street.

Tunjin pulled back, hoping that no movement had been visible. The figure had been casually dressed – some sort of sweatshirt and loose trousers, a shaved head, cigarette in hand. But watching, definitely watching.

Tunjin shook his head hard, trying to clear the confusion that was gathering there. He needed to think clearly. He needed to concentrate. He needed – he needed a drink, but, no, that was the last thing he needed.

What he really needed was to get out of there.

He looked down at his stained clothes. He couldn't go far dressed like this. He needed to plan this carefully, as carefully as a severely hungover man could.

He moved away from the window, and stepped back over to the built-in closet on the adjoining wall. He slid back the door and looked inside, his expectations very low. To his mild surprise, there were a couple of clean T-shirts hanging up, and at least one pair of the large, elastic trousers that were the only kind suited to his gut. The presence of these clothes was, he suspected, nothing more than proof that he had actually been wearing his current ones for several days.

He quickly pulled off his T-shirt and trousers and tossed them casually into a corner, where they joined several others. After a pause, he pulled off his enormous Y-fronts and threw them in the same direction. There was a pile of apparently clean underwear on the floor of the closet.

He pulled on the new Y-fronts, then quickly donned the new black T-shirt and trousers. Both were perhaps slightly too small and stretched across his fat body, but – he thought, as he caught sight of himself in the mirror – it was a definite improvement on his previous appearance. He thrust his feet into his only pair of boots, kicking off some of the dried mud, and then grabbed his anorak from behind the bedroom door.

Right, he thought, ready for action. The only question now was what he ought to do.

He walked slowly back through into the living room, taking care not to approach the windows. He reached the front door, carefully turned the catch and silently pulled open the door. This was make or break, he thought. If they were watching out in the corridor, this was the end. But he'd bargained on the fact that they wouldn't have left anyone inside the building. Too conspicuous, he thought. Some of his busybody neighbours would have challenged any intruder within moments.

The corridor appeared deserted. He glanced back at

the clock. Eight-forty now. Most of his neighbours would have gone off to work, other than the older ones who tended not to stir from their flats till later in the day. He put the door on the latch, and then stepped quietly out into the corridor.

Nothing.

He walked, as silently as he could manage – and surprisingly so for one of his bulk – towards the head of the staircase that led down to the lobby. Tunjin's flat was on the first floor, so from the top steps he could peer down into the entrance to the apartment block. It was a depressing hallway – a mix of discarded debris from previous tenants, a couple of stacked bicycles, and piles of uncollected mail and newspapers. But it was, at least, apparently unoccupied.

Tunjin made his way slowly down the stairs, trying to ensure that his movement was not visible to any external observer. The main doors to the apartment block contained large glass panels, but the glass was sufficiently filthy and the interior of the lobby sufficiently gloomy that no movement was likely to be visible from outside.

Tunjin moved forward slowly, reaching down as he passed to pick up two items from the pile of discarded items that littered the lobby. The first was an old broom, apparently thrown away because the head was worn out. The second was an old pencil stub. Improvisation was always his strong point.

He stepped slowly across the lobby, still keeping back from the door to ensure that there was no risk of his being seen from outside. Through the grimy glass, he could see the shaven-headed figure he had spotted from the bedroom. There didn't appear to be any other observers that he could see, although it was possible that there was another at the opposite end of the street, out of Tunjin's sight. The man was looking bored, pulling on another cigarette and shuffling his feet. Tunjin waited until he had turned his back, sheltering from the breeze to light another cigarette, then he stepped forward swiftly and jammed the broom handle firmly into the pull handles on the doors, preventing them from being opened from the outside. Then, crouching down so that he was still invisible from outside, he locked the doors with his own set of keys and then forced the pencil stub hard into the lock, breaking off the end to ensure that the lock was solidly jammed.

He felt a little guilty about this. He was undoubtedly going to inconvenience the other residents of the block, and he just hoped that there would be no other, more serious consequences – in common with many of the Soviet-era apartment blocks, this unit had no other escape route in case of fire.

But given that he was unsure when Muunokhoi might decide that he had exercised enough patience, or even when the boredom of the man outside might precipitate him to take some unsanctioned action, Tunjin thought it was prudent to try to buy himself a little extra time. It would be possible to break the glass in the doors, of course, but the glass would be toughened and the act of breaking it would be conspicuous even in this relatively deserted thoroughfare. And there was no other route into the building, other than that which Tunjin was planning to adopt as his exit route, and this, he hoped, would not be immediately obvious to an outsider.

He slipped back from the doors, and then began to climb the stairs as rapidly as his considerable bulk would allow. The worst symptoms of his hangover seemed to have receded now, though he couldn't claim that he felt well, either physically or emotionally.

He passed his own floor, and carried on climbing past the second and third floors, wheezing heavily by now, his breath coming in short spurts. There were definitely times when he thought that a healthier lifestyle might be recommended.

Finally, he dragged himself up the last flight of stairs on to the fourth floor. There were no flats up here, only a couple of storage and utility rooms, mostly filled with junk. His objective lay in the far corner of one of the cluttered rooms – a skylight in the ceiling with a pull down ladder fixed beneath it.

He forced his way through the clutter, pushing aside a rusting twintub washing machine and a couple of broken chairs, until he was standing directly underneath the skylight. As he passed, he reached down to pick up an old screwdriver that had been left on top of the washing machine. Pausing to regain some of his breath, he reached up and pulled on the ladder. It was stiff and a little rusty, but, as he tugged, it eventually juddered down.

Tunjin looked at it carefully, and then looked down at his own bulk. The ladder should be capable of holding his weight, he thought, though he was glad that he wouldn't have to rely on it for too long. He took a deep breath and then slowly began to climb up the rungs. The metal frame of the ladder creaked ominously, but seemed to be holding.

He reached the skylight, pulled on the handle and began to force it upwards. For a moment, he thought that it would fail to open, but eventually, with a little shaking and pushing, it gave. Tunjin climbed the remainder of the ladder and, gasping for breath, he pulled himself up and on to the roof of the apartment block.

He lay for some minutes, feeling nauseous, his breath coming in painful gasps. He really wasn't cut out for this kind of thing. Not any more, at any rate.

The bright sunlight and fresh air hit him almost as strongly as his breathlessness and the after-effects of his hangover. He rolled over on to his back and lay, still gasping, his eyes closed, the brilliance of the sun crimson through his closed eyelids. Thankfully, the sun was still relatively low and the air still chilly, the breeze riffling gently through his sweat-soaked T-shirt.

Finally, he recovered his breath and rolled over to shut the skylight firmly behind him. He looked around to see if there was anything on the flat roof he could use to jam the skylight, in the hope of buying himself a little more time, but there was nothing.

He sat up and looked around. The rooftop was little more than an empty stretch of grey asphalt. A line of identical apartment blocks stretched off down the street, with a similar row opposite.

He had been up here on a couple of previous occasions, with the aim of getting an idea of the layout. The rooftop gave an attractive view of the city. In the distance, he could see the large buildings that dominated the centre – the Post Office, the Parliament house, the Palace of Culture. He could see the pink and black monolith of the Chinghis Khaan Hotel, the wide green spaces of Nairamdal Park, and the Naadam Stadium. In the distance, he could make out the haze and black tangle of buildings that denoted the industrial areas, and the long silver sheen of the railway line. And beyond all that, the wide open green of the steppes and the distant mountains.

He had grown up in this city, known it all his life and – in all honesty – had never thought much of it. But now, just at this moment, it looked genuinely beautiful. But that might, he supposed, have something to do with the fact that he really might not be enjoying the sight of it for very much longer.

He pulled himself slowly to his feet and walked unsteadily across to the edge of the roof above the main street. He lowered himself and peered cautiously down. The shaven-headed man was still there, but was now talking on a mobile phone. There was no obvious sense of urgency in his manner, so Tunjin assumed that his own departure had not yet been noticed.

He pulled back and began to make his way slowly across the rooftop. His aim ought to be to put as much space between himself and Muunokhoi as possible. Or, perhaps more accurately, to give himself the opportunity to try to get a step or two ahead of Muunokhoi. He could perhaps simply flee the city – head off to another town, maybe down into the Gobi. Surely it must be possible to find somewhere where Muunokhoi couldn't track him down.

And it wasn't as if he had much of a future ahead of

him here. He had been deliberately provocative in his meeting with Doripalam, but he assumed that the outcome would be the same – his current suspension would be followed by dismissal. Someone's head was going to have to roll for what had happened, and Tunjin was the only candidate. If he was lucky, he might get to hold on to part of his pension. But he didn't have too many grounds for assuming that he would be lucky. He had been on borrowed time anyway, he knew that, given his drinking and the general state of his health, which was why he'd started all this in the first place.

He'd reached the end of his own apartment block. The rooftop continued on the next block, with a space of about half a metre between them. He peered down – the gap between the two buildings stretched four floors to the ground below. Typical Soviet design, he thought. It would have been too simple and too efficient to have built one large apartment block. Probably building them as separate units created enough additional work to help someone hit their production target.

There was no option but to jump the gap. It wasn't far, and for most people it would have presented no problem. Tunjin had a good head for heights, but his general obesity, not to mention his still mildly spinning head, meant that this was likely to be a challenge. He held his breath for a moment, teetering as close to the gap as he dared. Then, trying not to close his eyes, he leapt across.

He fell flat on his face on the other side, his fingers scraping at the asphalt, his knees and chest stinging from the impact. His feet, he was aware, were still sticking out over the gap. But he seemed to have made it over.

He looked ahead of him. There were two more similar gaps he would have to cross before reaching the final block. And then he would be faced with the problem of how to get down again. But he hoped he had that one sorted.

He continued steadily along the rooftop, until he reached the next block. Then – and this time he did close his eyes – he threw himself forward. Again, he landed roughly but safely. Maybe he was fitter than he thought. He rolled over, pausing to recover his breath. At least this exertion meant that, for the moment, he could postpone thinking further about what the future might hold.

He was dragging himself to his feet again when he heard the sound of some kind of commotion behind and below him. He slowly moved towards the edge of the roof and peered down at the street below, trying to see what was happening without risking being seen himself.

There was no doubt that the disturbance, whatever it was, was happening outside his own block. There was a shouting and a banging. The shaven-headed man, he noticed, was no longer standing in the same position, but had moved into the middle of the street, apparently looking at what was going on.

Tunjin moved himself forward, trying to get a better view, but conscious that – with his equilibrium still disturbed – it would not be wise to lean too far forward. But he could see enough. There were a couple of figures standing outside the door of his block, banging on the glass doors and shouting. Tunjin couldn't recognise them from this distance, but he assumed that they were fellow residents of the block who had discovered that the front door was both locked and firmly jammed.

Perhaps, on reflection, his attempt to buy himself some extra time had not been a wise one. If Muunokhoi's people had tried to make a move straight away, it would have certainly given him an additional respite while they forced their way into the building. As it was, the barring of the door had probably simply highlighted to the shaven-headed man that there might be some sort of problem. Tunjin could see that the man was already drawing closer to the door, and that he was engaged in some sort of dialogue with the locked-out residents.

Tunjin was contemplating his next action when he saw the man gesture furiously to the residents, waving his arms to signal them to move aside. Then – when they had presumably obeyed his instruction – he raised his arm and the sound of a gunshot echoed down the empty street, followed an instant later by the sound of shattering glass.

Tunjin needed no more prompting. He rolled over and staggered to his feet, thinking that, perhaps for the first time in years, he really did have an incentive to lose some weight. He began to jog, as fast as his bulk would allow, towards the next rooftop, this time by some miracle managing to stay on his feet as he threw himself over the gap.

He knew that the end block was identical to his

own, and his original plan had been to use the screwdriver to lever open the skylight. In retrospect, he thought, perhaps this whole scheme would have benefited from a little more thinking through. And now time was definitely not on his side.

He reached the skylight and pulled out the screwdriver, slipping its blade into the gap along the edge of the framework. He pushed it down, but the frame showed no sign of giving. He looked across at the rusted hinges of the window, aware that the screwdriver was already bending under his weight.

Finally, he pulled it out and slammed the blade down into the centre of the glass, which shattered explosively beneath him. He pulled his hand back just in time, avoiding being badly cut. Then he lifted his foot and began to slam down hard on the remaining glass, rapidly clearing the edge of the frame until he felt it would be safe to drop through.

He looked down into the empty gap. There was a ladder, as in his own block, but this one looked to be badly broken. He reached and tried to lower it, but couldn't move it at all. Finally, he looked behind him and, clutching hard on the edges of the frame, dropped through the gaping hole.

There was a battered kitchen table, now only half a metre or so below his dangling feet. He scrabbled for a moment, then dropped, trying to land safely on the polished wooden table top.

His feet hit the table and skidded so that he slipped sideways, his fingers desperately clutching for some kind of purchase. His stomach landed heavily on the table surface and then, just when he thought he had landed safely, he heard the sound of cracking wood as one of the table legs shattered beneath his weight. The table tipped sideways, and Tunjin toppled off to one side, landing heavily among a pile of empty paint-pots, as the table fell across him.

For a moment there was silence, and Tunjin lay breathing heavily, convinced that every bone in his body was broken. It took him a few moments to realise that this probably wasn't the case, and that he appeared to have survived the fall with no more serious consequences than some bruising.

He pulled himself into a sitting position, pushing the table away from him, trying to manoeuvre his body away from the scattered pile of paint tins. For a moment, he felt relief. He was alive. He had – at least for the moment – escaped.

Then his relief vanished, to be replaced by a gut-wrenching fear. He choked, feeling waves of nausea sweeping over him, as though all the symptoms of his hangover, having been suppressed during his traverse of the rooftops, were now returning in redoubled form.

The two barrels of a shotgun were inches from his face, pointing unwaveringly at his forehead.

From behind them, a quiet voice said: 'I do hope you're going to clean all this up.'

CHAPTER 7

'But you know what he's up to. It's what he's always up to. Undermining you.'

Doripalam shook his head, trying to close his eyes. The sight of his wife pacing up and down the room always made his head ache. 'I don't think that's it,' he said. 'I don't think that's really ever been it. But certainly not this time.' He had a small glass of vodka in his hands, chilled from the fridge, and he wanted just to enjoy it, but Solongo, as so often, seemed to have other plans.

'You're just too trusting, that's your trouble. That's always been your trouble. You let people walk all over you.'

He knew she meant well. She always meant well. That was part of the problem. Of course, she was concerned for her own interests – who wasn't? But, deep down, he was convinced that this wasn't simply selfishness, that she really did care about his own interests as well. But then, he reflected, maybe he was just too trusting.

'Why should he want to undermine me? He appointed me into the job.'

'He wouldn't have appointed anyone into the job if he could have helped it, you know that. He'd have been in the job himself. For life.'

'But now he isn't in it. He's in a much bigger job. So why should he care about me?'

'Because you're in the job that he used to do – that he still wants to do – and you're handling it far better than he ever could.'

This was rare. Solongo was generally reluctant to make positive comments about her husband, even when criticising her favourite hate figure – his former boss, Nergui. Maybe this was some sort of positive sign.

He opened his eyes and took a cautious sip of the vodka. 'Well, I'm flattered that you should think so,' he said, trying his hardest not to sound sarcastic.

'Well, it's obvious,' she said. 'You're no fool, Doripalam, even if you quite often act like one. You can do your job very capably. Nergui's going to feel threatened.'

Doripalam found it difficult to envisage Nergui feeling threatened even by physical violence, let alone by the possibility that some youngster might possibly upstage him. 'But even if that's true,' he said, 'it doesn't explain what he's up to at the moment. Why he's been so keen to lead this enquiry.'

'Are you sure he's not going to offer you up as a sacrificial lamb?' Solongo said. She finally sat down and picked up her own glass of vodka, watching him carefully. 'I mean, I know he'd made all these positive noises. But this case with – what's his name? The gangster?'

'Muunokhoi.'

'Yes, Muunokhoi. Well, this case would give Nergui all the ammunition he needs if he wants to get rid of you.'

'And replace me how? There's no one else who could do the job. No one who would want it, anyway.'

She shrugged. 'I don't know. Maybe Nergui would bring it back under his own empire again. I'm sure he's arrogant enough to think he could do both jobs without breaking sweat.'

'You're just paranoid,' he said.

But maybe she was right to be. Doripalam looked around the living room in which they were sitting. A decent-sized room in a decent-sized apartment in one of the better areas of the city. A large leather sofa, thick crimson pile carpets, expensive rugs and a scattering of tasteful ornaments and paintings. It really wasn't too bad. He'd progressed much further in his life and career than he had ever really believed possible, even if it wasn't yet quite as far as Solongo would have preferred. His father – a factory worker under the old regime – wouldn't have believed that his son would ever be living in a palatial residence like this.

So maybe Solongo was right. Perhaps the Muunokhoi case could be the one that stripped him of all this. It had happened on his watch. And arguably he should have been more observant. After the event, he had heard countless rumours about Tunjin. Tunjin's instability since he had split with his wife. Tunjin's insubordination. Tunjin's drinking. Especially Tunjin's drinking. He had obviously kept it well under control during work time, since Doripalam had never seen any signs of it. But it was now clear that, outside working hours, Tunjin was drinking heavily – that he was regularly found semi-comatose in various of the more unsavoury bars around the city. Doripalam suspected that a number of Tunjin's colleagues had covered up for him over the years, getting him home when perhaps, in other circumstances, he would have found himself in a prison cell for the night.

So, yes, perhaps it was reasonable that his neck should be on the block over this. But he still couldn't believe that Nergui would be the one to raise the axe.

He sat back in the crimson leather armchair, sipping on his vodka. 'Anyway, I still think there's more to it than that. This isn't about me. It's about Nergui in some way—'

'It's always about Nergui,' Solongo said. She stretched out her legs, smiling at her husband and shaking her head. She really was a remarkably elegant woman, Doripalam thought, wondering yet again how it was that he'd come to be married to her. She was most definitely out of his league, not just in terms of her beauty but also in terms of her social status. Her father had been a senior party officer under the old regime – one of the small elite who had prospered under the yoke of communism. Doripalam had met him only a few times before his death, and he had never been quite sure what the old man's role had actually been, which was probably ominous enough in itself. But there was no doubt that it had been accompanied by significant wealth and power, most of which he had apparently managed to hang on to even after the arrival of democracy.

He also wondered, in his more suspicious moments, whether the old man had, somewhere in his working life, stumbled up against Nergui. That, he thought, might explain Solongo's antagonism.

'You're far too naïve,' she said, breaking into his thoughts. 'You assume that everyone's as well-intentioned and altruistic as you are.' She gazed at him, with an expression that might have been affectionate, but which was also oddly reminiscent of a young girl's attitude towards her favourite pet or doll.

'Whereas you know differently,' he said.

He swallowed the last of his vodka and moved to pour himself another, gesturing with the bottle towards Solongo. She held up her nearly full glass and shook her head. 'And you drink too much,' she said.

Maybe that was true, too. Doripalam had certainly become conscious of an increase in his alcohol consumption over the last few months, particularly as the Muunokhoi case had collapsed. It was still just a few glasses in the evening, but it had increasingly become a welcome retreat from the pressures of the day. He thought again about Tunjin, and wondered at what point Tunjin's own drinking had tipped over from social relaxation into something much darker and more dangerous. Would Doripalam ever recognise that point if he were to approach it himself?

'So what do you think Nergui's up to?' he said, refilling his glass and slumping back down by her side. 'Other than undermining me. I mean, Nergui's right. There was always going to have to be an enquiry about the Muunokhoi case. The Minister's already taken too much flak in Parliament. He's got to demonstrate that he's doing something.'

'But why does Nergui have to run it?' Solongo said. 'Surely he's the last person who should be involved?'

'That's what I said,' Doripalam countered, defensively. 'I thought there'd be a conflict of interest. But Nergui didn't seem very bothered about that. He obviously wants to use this for his own ends, which seem to be about cleaning up the team once and for all. But I've no idea quite how he thinks he's going to do that.'

'And do you have any idea what all this might do to you?'

Doripalam took a deep swallow of the vodka. 'I'm just hoping that Nergui will protect me more than anyone else might care to do.'

She shook her head slowly, smiling at him. 'I think it's rather sweet that you're so trusting,' she said. 'I just hope that you're right.'

While he waited, Nergui thumbed for the fourth or fifth time through the ring-bound notebook in which he'd jotted down all his thoughts on the Muunokhoi case. He'd spent most of the day sitting in that cramped office working his way through the various relevant files – the case file itself, files relating to various other past cases that he thought might potentially be relevant, Tunjin's personal file, personal files relating to a number of other officers, even Doripalam's own personal file.

The last of these was not stored within police headquarters, in recognition of Doripalam's seniority, but held in the Ministry itself. Strictly speaking, it was accessible only by Doripalam's own line manager within the police hierarchy. But Nergui had quickly discovered that, in the face of his own assumed proximity to the Minister, very few Ministry doors remained closed for very long. Even so, he felt mildly guilty that he had taken advantage of his unofficial authority in this partic-ular case. He told himself that his motives were good, but had also made every effort to ensure that no trace of the file would be found within police headquarters. At the end of the day, he had taken the file back to his own apartment and locked it safely away in his well-concealed strongbox. He would return it to the Ministry in the morning, still unsure whether he had made an error in removing it in the first place.

And now, thirty minutes later, he was sitting among the bright décor of Millie's Café in the Center Hotel, sipping a coffee and wondering if he was about to commit another error.

He looked around him. It would have been difficult to imagine, even five years ago, that places like this would have appeared in the city. Nergui still felt that there was something unpalatable about the existence of such outlets alongside the poverty and deprivation that continued to dominate large parts of the country. It was only a few winters ago that there were people literally dying on the steppes – caught between the natural rigours of the harshest weather in memory and the man-made pressures of the new free market economy. And yet now here were throngs of well-dressed, prosperous people, locals and westerners alike, sipping freshly squeezed orange and fancy coffees to the burbling sounds of American pop music. Nergui had spent enough time in the West to be used to this kind of thing, though he never understood why the Americans deluded themselves they could make coffee. Here, though, he could get the Italian-style coffee he liked. He sipped slowly on his espresso and continued to leaf through the notebook.

It was telling him nothing new, but he had not expected that it would. He was at the stage – which he recalled well from his days as a more conventional investigating officer – when the priority was simply to ensure that he knew the facts as well as he could. He always felt that it was critical that he should be able to piece together all aspects of each case thoroughly in his mind. In this way, if he subsequently stumbled upon some new piece of information, some anomaly, he could isolate it immediately. He had a good memory, but it was far from photographic. Nevertheless, if he worked hard he could embed detail in his mind sufficiently comprehensively that he would know instantly if something didn't fit. It was a useful skill particularly in more complicated cases when key details could easily be overlooked simply because it was assumed that they had already been addressed.

In this case, though, he still wasn't sure quite how much he was investigating, quite how far this went. The immediate concern, of course, was Tunjin's falsification of evidence. There was no real doubt there, though it was far from obvious to Nergui how it had been exposed in the first place. The forged documents were not particularly sophisticated, but they would probably have passed muster with the Prosecutor's Office if someone hadn't started raising questions internally. But where those questions had first arisen, no-one seemed sure.

Lacking any other sense of direction, Nergui had worked his way through the piles of individual staff files for the officers. The majority, including Tunjin's, yielded little that was unexpected. He had asked for the files relating to other cases that had been dropped or abandoned, but had been told that the numbers were so large that it would be easier for Nergui to visit the archives for himself. He had done so, and had spent part of an afternoon ploughing disconsolately through page after page of uninformative paperwork. Somewhere in here might be the single thread that would start everything unravelling, but it would take weeks of work to uncover it.

In the end, with no other way forward, he had returned to the bulging pile of files, dating back nearly two decades, that related to Muunokhoi. The content here was at least moderately interesting. Muunokhoi was a figure well-known to the police in Ulan Baatar, just as, for different reasons, he was familiar to most of the adult population of the country. The files, in accordance with Muunokhoi's status, comprised an odd mix of formal case documentation and endless newspaper clippings.

When had he first encountered Muunokhoi? He had been aware of the name for a long time – nearly twenty years. He had heard the rumours along with everyone else. From time to time, and more frequently as the years went by, he had had reasons to investigate Muunokhoi's activities. But they had finally come face-to-face a decade before.

They had brought him in, initially only as a poten-tial witness, in connection with the torching of a garment warehouse on the south side of the city – a massive blaze that spread into surrounding buildings and resulted in three deaths and the evacuation of a neighbouring residential block. There was little doubt that the cause was arson, and the first assumption was that it was a straightforward case of insurance fraud. But the owner of the warehouse, initially the primary suspect, had been quick to point the finger at Muunokhoi's people. 'We find them importing shoddy versions of our goods – pirated copies – selling them for a fraction of the price. But that is not enough for them. They have to destroy my business, destroy my property, even kill my staff. I know who they are—'

Given that the apparent victim's business was already in trouble as a result of this new competition, it was equally likely that he had himself arranged for the warehouse to be torched. But it had provided Nergui with an opportunity to bring Muunokhoi in for questioning.

Muunokhoi had still been a young man – thirty-two years old according to the files, although Nergui had suspected that this was a conservative figure. But he was already on his way to becoming a legend.

Nergui still remembered his first impressions. A slim, good-looking young man, at ease with himself, exuding a self-confidence that bordered on arrogance. He had been sitting in the interview room, apparently untroubled, one leg slung over the side of the metal chair. It was a room designed to intimidate, but somehow Muunokhoi managed to dominate it.

'You wish to speak with me?' he said, in the manner of one granting an exclusive interview.

Nergui had lowered himself into the chair opposite. 'We wish you to provide a witness statement, yes.'

'Only too happy to be of assistance. I admire the work you people do.'

'We're very grateful,' Nergui said. He raised his eyes and stared unblinkingly at the young man. 'I'm sure the sentiment is reciprocated.'

'I'm sure it is. So what can I tell you?'

Nergui ran through the circumstances of the case, as far as he was able to reveal them. He was aware that there was little here of substance. They had no evidence, other than the warehouse owner's accusations, to link Muunokhoi to the fire. Even if Muunokhoi had been involved, Nergui had little doubt that any connection would have been remote and well-concealed. They were going through the motions, making sure that every stone had been upturned. And, Nergui hoped, recording just one tiny theoretical strike against Muunokhoi's apparently untainted record. Perhaps one day they might accumulate enough strikes to count for something.

Muunokhoi had laughed, as Nergui had known he would. 'This is what you've dragged me in here for?'

Nergui shrugged. 'It's our job. We have to investigate every possibility.'

Muunokhoi had nodded, apparently earnestly. 'Of course. I understand that. You have to eliminate witnesses.' Something about his tone suggested that this was, perhaps, a familiar concept.

'As you say. Of course, we would like to eliminate you.' Nergui's gaze was unwavering.

Muunokhoi nodded. 'I can provide an alibi.'

'I'm sure you can,' Nergui said. 'That is not really the issue. I think there is no suggestion that you started this blaze yourself. The question is whether you might have had an interest in it being started.'

Muunokhoi nodded, a smile playing about his thin lips, as though he were unsure how seriously to take this. 'I understand,' he said. 'Of course that must be a consideration. This was a competitor.'

Nergui had nodded, knowing at that point that there was no likelihood of taking this any further. Muunokhoi had already covered all the angles. Even if he had been involved, there would be no way of proving it.

And so it had turned out. And so it had turned out with every case where Muunokhoi was a potential suspect. At every stage, he was polite, charming, co-operative, occasionally showing just the expected level of irritation as he was called in yet again. But there had been a gleam in his eye that suggested he treated it all as little more than a game. A game he was winning hands down.

Nergui had studied Muunokhoi's history – the kernel of the files that, now, twenty years on, he had in front of him – hoping to find some clue, some chink in Muunokhoi's apparently impenetrable armour. But there was nothing. A first class degree in engineering. An early career as a civil servant in the Ministry of Fuel and Energy, working on the administration of gas supplies from domestic and Soviet Union sources. A rapid progression, leading to a key middle-ranking role in the early 1990s as the USSR disintegrated and democracy made its first impact in Mongolia.

As the state authorities were privatised, Muunokhoi had positioned himself as a Director and major share-holder of one of the newly privatised gas companies. The company had been sold to Russian investors, netting Muunokhoi and his fellow shareholders a substantial profit. It was difficult to imagine that this had occurred without some shady dealing, but the turning of blind eyes had been a characteristic of those early free-market days. It was only when the money finally ran out that anyone thought to ask where it might have gone.

By the time the economy ran into trouble in the mid 1990s, he had established himself in a number of key monopoly positions. Money was scarce, but Muunokhoi was often the only game in town – particularly when it came to energy trading – and could command whatever price he liked. During the harsh winters of the late 1990s, it was probable that Muunokhoi was indirectly responsible for much suffering and some deaths. Nergui did not imagine that Muunokhoi would have lost much sleep as a result.

At the same time, Muunokhoi was a public figure, on the verge of celebrity. He was part of the glitzy new social scene of the city, an extremely eligible bachelor regularly photographed with an attractive woman by his side. He made frequent appearances in the privately-owned scandal sheets, though in practice there was little scandalous about his lifestyle. Or, at any rate, no evidence of the types of scandal likely to be of interest to the popular newspapers. He had a string of supposed girlfriends, but no serious relationships. He was polite to journalists, and friendly and personable with anyone he had dealings with.

But there were claims that Muunokhoi's legitimate trading was only the tip of a much less palatable iceberg. Muunokhoi was an astute businessman, but the size of his wealth did not seem commensurate with the nature and scope of his business. It seemed likely that his visible trading activities were paralleled by other, more covert transactions. There were countless rumours – drugs-, arms-, even people-smuggling.

Nergui consulted endlessly with tax and customs officers to shed some further light on the disparity between Muunokhoi's legitimate business activities and his apparent wealth. But all he had received for his trouble was a repeated shrugging of the shoulders and an increasingly obfuscatory set of technical explanations. Yes, there were inconsistencies, but investigations had uncovered no substantive evidence of wrong-doing. 'It's not impossible,' one said. 'He's a smart businessman. He knows the dodges. People like him don't pay tax anyway, not really, not these days. They're too busy creating wealth for the rest of us. It doesn't mean they're criminals.'

Nevertheless, the Serious Crimes Team built up a substantial dossier on Muunokhoi. Much was hearsay – more of those tiny, unsubstantiated strikes against his record. Once or twice, Nergui thought they might be getting close. There was a recurrent suggestion that Muunokhoi's people had gained access to caches of weapons intended for the Mongolian army or diverted from the Soviet army during the chaotic final months of the old USSR. The police and security services had made a few arrests, picking up shipments on Mongolia's extensive borders with Tomsk, Tyumeny, and Irkutsk, and even managing, in a few cases, to infiltrate the gangs operating in the dark mountains and forests to the north, identifying arms shipments due for exchange with consignments of heroin from Afghanistan.

This was the area that most interested Nergui. Mongolia had no major drug problem – certainly not compared with parts of the former Soviet Union – but the availability and abuse of hard drugs was increasing.

Alcohol remained the drug of choice, but there was growing use of heroin, amphetamines, prescription psychotropic drugs, morphine and other substances. The proportions of serious users were small, but the problem would escalate rapidly if serious commercial interests became involved. Nergui could see that such interests, combined with the relative youth of the population – two-thirds under thirty – and high levels of unemployment and economic deprivation, presented a volatile combination. The prospect that Muunokhoi might be involved was not comforting.

But the evidence never quite held up. Whichever side of the law they might respectively be on, Muunokhoi and the traffickers were in the same business – moving goods and materials across national borders. It was hardly surprising if, from time to time, they should encounter – and even do business with – the same people. It was frustrating but, to Nergui, hardly surprising. He knew enough about Muunokhoi to know that the man made few mistakes. He had a well-paid entourage around him whose role, in large part, was to ensure that their boss's tracks were well covered. He was unlikely to be caught out unless someone got things badly wrong.

In the end, Nergui had scaled down the enquiry, knowing that this covert digging was unlikely to yield any real results. But he kept the files open and encouraged his team to keep their ears to the ground. Because, while Nergui knew that Muunokhoi would have covered all the bases, he also knew enough about humankind to know that, someone – somewhere, sometime, somehow – would eventually make that mistake. And Nergui wanted to ensure that, when it finally did happen, he would not be too far away.

His musing, spurred by his aimless flicking through the notepad, was interrupted by the sight of Sarangarel easing her way through the crowded café towards his table. Nergui glanced at his watch. He had lost track of the time, and she was late, though by only a few minutes. She looked, he had to acknowledge, stunning. Even if he had not been waiting for her, he would have been struck by her extraordinary presence among the chattering crowds. It was not just her physical appearance – though that was certainly striking enough, with dominant features, her long flowing black hair, and the sense of an unconventional beauty. It was also her manner – calm, untroubled, but with a visible sense of purpose. She was going somewhere – figuratively as well as literally – and there was little that would stand in her way.

That, Nergui supposed, was how he remembered her originally, though it had been less obvious in those days. Then it had been her late husband, Gansukh, who was going somewhere. And the place he was going, it seemed all too clear, was prison. That was why her appearance at this moment felt more than coincidential. Because Gansukh, or so Nergui had believed at the time, had been the man who had finally made the mistake.

CHAPTER 8

'Don't move,' the voice said.

Tunjin had no intention of arguing with the instruction. The twin barrels of the gun moved slowly down from his forehead towards his chest. The figure behind them, no more than a silhouette against the light from the open door, leaned forward and Tunjin felt a hand slowly patting his pockets, moving down his body to check whether he was armed. It was hardly a professional search, but it seemed thorough enough. Finally, the figure seemed satisfied and pulled back, gesturing brusquely with the gun. 'Stand up.'

Tunjin staggered slowly to his feet, clutching on to the toppled table. His feet stumbled on one of the paintpots, which clattered off somewhere behind. He still could not make out the face of the man in front of him.

The figure waved the gun vaguely up towards the skylight. 'Quite an entrance,' he said.

Tunjin shrugged, feeling the bruises around his back and legs. 'It wasn't quite how I intended it,' he admitted.

The man with the gun stepped aside and gestured Tunjin to walk in front of him. 'You're either the most incompetent burglar I've ever encountered, or this is something else.'

'This is something else,' Tunjin agreed. He was beginning to relax slightly now. He had initially assumed that this person was one of Muunokhoi's people who had somehow managed to predict his intended escape route. But that didn't seem to be the case. Maybe this was nothing more than a resident who had – reasonably enough – reacted aggressively to the sight of an eighteen stone man falling unexpectedly through his rooftop.

The man nodded, as though this explained everything. 'Downstairs,' he said. 'We can talk there.'

Tunjin made his way slowly down the staircase to the third floor. This block was virtually identical to his own, even down to the colour of the cheap paint on the walls. The view from the landing windows was different, though, looking out beyond the end of the street to one of the *ger* camps that clustered on the outskirts of the city. Tunjin could see the rows of round grey tents, billows of smoke issuing from their central chimneys, whipped away by the strong breeze. There was a man tending a goat, and beyond that – and much more interesting to Tunjin – a row of old but apparently serviceable motorbikes.

'This way,' the man said, waving Tunjin forward towards the door at the foot of the stairs. Still holding the shotgun firmly, he pushed open the door and led Tunjin inside.

The apartment was similar in size to Tunjin's own, although considerably tidier. It was, Tunjin thought, like stepping into a *ger*. There was the usual mix of brightly painted cabinets, rich embroidered rugs and tapestries stretched across the walls and floors, and, by the far wall, a single camp bed. There were two hard backed chairs against the wall, and the man gestured Tunjin to sit in one of them. He spun the other round and sat on it, with his gun resting on the chair back, pointing steadily at Tunjin.

'Now,' the man said, 'why don't you tell me what this is all about?'

Tunjin was beginning to recover both his breath and his presence of mind. He could feel the wooden chair creaking slightly under his weight, and he hoped that he wouldn't soon be responsible for the destruction of yet another piece of furniture.

He reached into his pocket and pulled out his identity card. 'I'm a police officer,' he said, waving the card in front of the man's face. The man calmly held Tunjin's wrist and surveyed the card carefully. After a moment, he nodded, apparently satisfied and lowered the gun slightly, though still leaving it resting on his knees.

He was, Tunjin now realised, a relatively old man – probably mid-seventies. He was dressed in traditional costume, the brown thick felt *del* wrapped around his frail-looking body, heavy brown boots sticking out beneath. He was gazing at Tunjin through untroubled grey eyes, his thinning white hair combed back from his forehead.

The old man nodded slowly. Finally, with a sudden movement, he held out his hand. 'Agypar,' he said.

It took Tunjin a moment to realise that this was the old man's name. He shook the man's hand and said, pointing to himself, 'Tunjin.'

'It is good to see more officers on patrol,' Agypar said. 'But there is no need for you to patrol our rooftops.'

Tunjin smiled obligingly. 'It's a long story,' he said. 'I am being pursued.'

'Pursued?' Agypar said. 'On the rooftop?'

'Well, no. But that was why I was on the rooftop. I live in one of the blocks further down the road. There are intruders. So I escaped on to the roof.'

Agypar nodded as though this was perfectly conventional behaviour. 'These intruders,' he said. 'They are pursuing you because you are a policeman?'

Tunjin nodded. 'More or less, yes,' he said. 'As I say, it's a long story. Let's just say that I have made some enemies.'

'I heard the gunshot,' Agypar said. 'That was them, yes?'

'I think so,' Tunjin said. 'To be honest, I didn't stay to check.'

'You will wish to be leaving shortly,' Agypar said.

'Very shortly,' Tunjin said. 'I don't know how much time I've got. They'll have realised by now that I'm not there, but I don't know how long it will take them to work out where I've gone.'

Agypar nodded, taking in this information. 'And they will be watching the street, I imagine.'

'I imagine,' Tunjin agreed. In all honesty, he hadn't really thought this part through, but Agypar was almost certainly right. By now, they would have stationed someone out on the street, surely, as they tried to understand how Tunjin had disappeared and where he might have gone to. They might also, he realised, have stationed someone at the rear of the blocks in order to cut off his escape in that direction also. All in all, his prospects were beginning to look considerably less positive. Agypar might, he supposed, be willing to lend his shotgun, but it was difficult to see that much else was in his favour.

'These are bad people?' Agypar said.

'These are very bad people,' Tunjin said. 'As bad as they come, I think.'

'You are unable to contact your police colleagues? Surely it must be possible to summon some back-up?' He spoke the words as though an expert in matters of police procedure. Everyone watched the television shows, Tunjin thought. The problem was that life was more complicated.

But Agypar did have a point. Tunjin realised, with a mild shock, that he had almost ceased to think of himself as a policeman. It was as if a thirty year career could just melt away overnight. Suddenly, he was just another civilian. Though even a civilian was entitled to help from the police.

But he knew he would not be calling them. In reality – and this was another shock – he realised that he did not believe that the police could help. At best, they could get him out of his current predicament, and maybe, assuming that they believed his story, they could provide him with some sort of protection. But the truth was that Tunjin did not know who he could trust. There was no doubt that Muunokhoi had unravelled what was going on very quickly, despite all Tunjin's best efforts to cover his tracks. That suggested that he had inside information. If Tunjin were to call the police now, there was no knowing just who might take the call.

'I don't think that's an option,' Tunjin said.

Agypar regarded him silently for a moment, then

nodded. 'Out here,' he said, 'none of us trusts the police. We have seen them do too many bad things to ordinary people. And we remember the old days.'

'We all remember the old days,' Tunjin said. 'Things have changed. But not necessarily always for the better.'

Agypar nodded. 'So,' he said finally, 'you need to get away from here. You will need some help.'

Tunjin stretched out his bulk, feeling the chair again creaking beneath him. He wondered yet again quite how he'd got into this. When Doripalam had interviewed him, he had been deliberately blasé, as if this had been an entirely natural thing for a policeman to attempt as he neared the end of his career. But even if, like Tunjin, you had a suspicion that your career was spiralling out of control already, this had still been an insane move. Not just career suicide, but probably the literal version as well.

He heaved himself slowly up from the chair, conscious of how time was passing. Quite probably he was already too late. His half-baked escape plan was already falling apart. 'I definitely need help,' he said. 'The question is where do I find it?'

Agypar smiled and reached past Tunjin to one of the ornately decorated cupboards. He pulled open the cabinet at the bottom and dragged out a canvas shoulder bag. 'Take this,' he said.

Tunjin looked quizzically at Agypar, then unfastened the top of the bag and peered inside. He reached in and pulled out a handgun, well-polished and in apparently good condition. Below that, nestled in the bottom of the bag, there were several rounds of ammunition.

Tunjin looked back at Agypar, who was sitting, rocking slightly on his chair, looking very pleased with himself. 'What is this?' Tunjin said.

'What does it look like? Don't worry. It's in good condition and it's loaded. Don't forget to take the safety catch off if you want to use it.'

'But where—?'

Agypar shrugged. 'I'm an old soldier,' he said. 'We all kept a few souvenirs. This was one of mine. I've looked after it. You never know when it might come in useful.'

Tunjin opened his mouth to say something, but could think of nothing sensible to say. 'Thank you,' he said, finally.

'Now,' Agypar said, 'we've got to get you out of this place.'

It was likely that, by now, the main road at the front was being carefully watched, and it was probable that similar observation was being carried out at the rear. 'Is there another way out of here?' Tunjin asked.

Agypar nodded, looking as if he'd been waiting for Tunjin to ask precisely this question. 'There's one other way,' he said. 'Come with me.'

Agypar led them out of the room, the shotgun still wedged firmly under his arm. They walked down three more flights of stairs, Tunjin peering cautiously through the landing windows to see if he could see any movement outside. The *ger* camp showed little signs of life, other than the herd of goats munching placidly through a pile of grass and leaves. As they reached the bottom of the final flight of stairs, Tunjin paused to listen, trying to discern any sounds of disturbance from the street outside. He could hear nothing, but that provided only the mildest of comfort. Maybe someone was already waiting for him out there.

The lobby itself was deserted. It was less cluttered and in a better state of repair than that in Tunjin's block, but displayed the same mix of pale wood veneer and beige painted walls. Tunjin began to move nervously towards the glass panelled front doors, but Agypar held up his hand. 'No, this way,' he said.

He turned back behind the stairway. Set into the wall under the stairs was a door with a combination security lock. Agypar adeptly entered a sequence of numbers and then slowly pushed open the door. Beyond, Tunjin could make out a further flight of stairs heading down into a basement.

Agypar reached behind the doorframe and pressed a light switch. There was only a single, low-wattage bulb hanging halfway down the stairs, but it was sufficient to allow a safe passage. Agypar gestured Tunjin in front of him, and the two of them began to make their way down, Agypar carefully closing the door behind them.

'The rubbish bins are down here,' Agypar explained. 'I think the layout of this block is a little different from the others.'

It was certainly different from Tunjin's block, which had concrete floors at ground level and no basement. Tunjin was aware that the land fell away behind the rows of apartment blocks, so he assumed that while the ground floor of this block was at street level at the front, there was room for an additional lower storey at the rear.

At the bottom of the stairs, there was a further

door. Tunjin pushed it slowly open and peered into the gloom beyond. It was, as he had expected, a utility room – there were a couple of large-scale sinks, a workbench with some evidence of recent use, a scattering of household furniture and appliances in varying states of repair, and what appeared to be part of a motorbike. At the far end of the room there were two pale rectangles where daylight shone faintly through two grimy windows.

Agypar moved to stand beside Tunjin and gestured down the length of the room. 'The door there,' he said. 'It has a security lock on the outside, but you can open it from in here. It comes out into the camp, so it's not immediately visible from the road or the back of the apartments.'

He led Tunjin through the dimly lit maze of junk towards the door. 'I will not turn on the lights in here,' he said. 'We do not want to risk giving any prior warning. We need to gain as much time as we can.' It was clear that he was enjoying the experience. This was, Tunjin supposed, the closest he had come to combat since retiring from the army. Tunjin wondered whether he had had a civilian job, or whether, like so many discarded from the army as the Soviet Union imploded, he had found himself without any job or prospects. At least, unlike many others, he had not found himself on the streets.

As they approached the windows, Agypar paused, raising his hand to stop Tunjin moving further forward. The windows were grimy and dust stained, and had clearly not been cleaned for many years. Combined with the bright sunshine, this meant that their movements were unlikely to be visible to any external observer.

Agypar pointed through the window. 'There,' he said, 'you see the row of motorcycles.' It was the same row that Tunjin had observed from the landing windows earlier – a line of aged but apparently serviceable machines. 'The one on the far left, the black one. That is mine.' He reached into his pocket and produced a single ignition key. 'Do you know how to ride a motorcycle?'

Tunjin glanced down at his overweight body. 'I used to,' he said. 'I was a real enthusiast when I was younger. Used to ride out on to the steppes. But I haven't done it for a long while. I guess you don't forget, but I don't know that my body's got as good a memory as I have.'

Agypar smiled. 'I don't think you forget,' he said. 'I still ride it from time to time, But not much now. So take it. It will start perfectly, first time. It always does.'

'Are you sure? I mean, it's—'

'You need help,' Agypar said. 'I am in a position to provide it. That is all. Basic hospitality. And I am sure when you return here, you will return the bike.'

'Well, yes, of course,' Tunjin said. 'But I don't know when that will be. Or even if it will be. I don't know how far I'll get.'

'If you don't get far,' Agypar laughed, 'I will come and collect the motorbike for myself.'

'Okay. Well, thanks. Thank you very much.'

'So,' Agypar said, reverting to his military manner, 'you open the door. You run, as far as you can—' He glanced down at Tunjin's body, tacitly acknowledging that this was unlikely to be particularly quickly. 'Get the bike and get the hell out of here. Do you want me to cover you?'

'Cover me?'

Agypar waved the shotgun in front of him. 'Cover you.'

'No,' Tunjin said. 'You've done more than enough for me. You mustn't do anything to put yourself in danger.' He wondered whether the old man really understood what he was potentially involved in here.

Agypar shrugged. 'A pity,' he said. 'I was always good at providing cover.'

'Thanks, anyway,' Tunjin said. 'For everything.' He had little time to waste, he realised. There was no telling where Muunokhoi's people were by now, no telling how much – or how little – time he might have.

'Okay,' he said, breathlessly, and, twisting the handle of the security lock, he stepped out into the cool sunlight.

The *ger* camp seemed deserted, although there was still smoke rising from one or two of the tents themselves. Off to his left, a flock of chickens in an enclosure was burbling gently, scratching in the dust. Somewhere in the distance, he could hear the faint hum of traffic, the shouts of children.

He looked right towards the main street, but there was no sign of life. To his left, behind the apartment blocks, the land fell gently away into waste ground. Beyond that, there were the remains of some industrial buildings, now unused and collapsing, their roofs open to the sky.

Tunjin took a deep breath and began to jog as

quickly as his bulk would permit. The motorcycles were perhaps a hundred metres away, no more. He clutched the key firmly in his hand and pounded on, his breath already coming in gasps.

He was perhaps twenty-five metres from the bikes when he heard a shout behind him. For a moment he almost paused, tempted to look back in case Agypar was trying to attract his attention. But there would be time enough for that when he reached the bike.

There was another shout behind him and then the sound of a bullet shot. He tensed, poised for the potential impact, but nothing happened. He pounded on. Ten yards. Five yards. The sweat poured from his body. Finally, he grabbed the motorbike handlebars, and pulled the machine towards him. Gasping, he lifted his leg over the seat, slumped down and looked for the ignition, forcing the key into the lock. It turned and, just as Agypar had predicted, the engine fired immediately.

Finally, the machine throbbing beneath him, Tunjin looked back the way he had come. There was a figure running towards him, brandishing a handgun, shouting. Still probably fifty metres away.

Tunjin hesitated a moment, wondering whether to try to flee and risk being shot in the back, or to drive straight at the shouting figure. He was beginning to rev the engine with the intention of doing the latter when a second gunshot echoed around the buildings. The man paused, as though surprised, and then fell forward, clutching his knee, his shouts transformed into screams of pain.

Tunjin looked back behind the man to where Agypar was standing in the doorway of the basement, the shotgun in his hand. Tunjin was too far away to see his face, but he suspected that Agypar was smiling at the accuracy of his shot.

There was no time to ponder the implications of what he had just witnessed. He twisted the bike handlebars, and then – initially unsteadily as his large body grew accustomed to balancing on the narrow seat, but then with growing confidence – he accelerated the motorbike across the waste-ground, down between the walls of the broken down factories, and then out towards the open steppe.

The bike was a smart 1950s British Vincent, which must have been lovingly maintained by the old man. For a brief second, before rationality caught up with him, he almost enjoyed the sensation of power and speed as he pulled out of the dark alleys into the brilliant sunlight beyond. This machine would need looking after, he thought, until he could get it back.

But that, of course, was to assume that he ever could, or that Agypar would be there to receive him. In truth, the future looked bleak. He could scarcely look after himself, let alone the bike. He had no idea where he was heading, or what he was going to do once he got there. Behind him was a ruthless gangster who would, he was sure, now stop at nothing to catch up with him. And, in shooting the man chasing him, Agypar had very probably signed his own death warrant.

It was a mess. It was the biggest mess that Tunjin, never the most fastidious of individuals, had been caught up in. And, this time, he really couldn't see how he was going to extricate himself.

CHAPTER 9

'They were here. Not so long ago,' Doripalam said. 'Look, you can see the marks in the grass left by the tents.'

Luvsan was leaning back against the bonnet of the Daihatsu, smoking a cigarette. 'I feel like the *Lone Ranger*,' he said. Luvsan prided himself on his knowledge of Western popular culture.

Doripalam raised an eyebrow. 'Which would make me Tonto, I suppose.'

'Certainly not, Kemo Sabe,' Luvsan said. 'I'm the sidekick here.'

Doripalam stared at him for a moment. There were times when Luvsan's youthful exuberance bordered on the insolent. 'And you're the one with the tracking skills,' he said, gesturing towards the satellite navigation equipment in the front of the truck. 'I'm trusting you know where we are.'

'More or less,' Luvsan said, in a voice that implied that he was above considerations of geographical precision.

'More rather than less, I hope,' Doripalam said. 'All I know is that we're miles from anywhere.'

This was probably another waste of time, he thought, but there was a risk that everything was slowly spiralling out of his control and he wanted to try to get some purchase on it before it was too late. It wasn't just the Muunokhoi case and everything that went with that. There'd also been the missing youth, Gavaa, a case that had seemed trivial but nevertheless brought them unexpected flak from the press. And then there was the murder of Gavaa's mother, which had come from nowhere and, so far, seemed to be leading them pretty much to the same destination.

Fortunately, for all their previous criticisms of the handling of the Gavaa disappearance, the press seemed more interested in the mystery of his mother's murder than in throwing more mud at the police. For the moment, anyway. Doripalam didn't delude himself that this was anything more than a respite. The truth was that for now the murder story – middle-aged woman found brutally slain in a *ger*, son missing, nomad family apparently moved on – was extraordinary enough in its own right. It didn't need the added spice of routine police-bashing. But as soon as interest in the story began to wane, the press would once again begin to ask how the police had allowed this to happen, why they weren't doing more to solve the crime, whether they could guarantee the safety of other citizens, and – well, any other hook they could find to spin the story out for a few more issues.

His team had been working relentlessly over the last few days – the usual grind of detailed police-work, driven by the ever-present knowledge that, without some rapid breakthrough, the case was increasingly likely to slip through their hands. Doripalam had overseen all the key activities –

setting up a response team close to the crime-scene, allocating the familiar round of essential duties, holding daily briefing meetings with the core team, fending off the gaggle of news and TV reporters. It was all straightforward stuff, the usual well-rehearsed routine. The kind of activity he could handle without thinking. And that was the trouble. He wasn't thinking. Not directly about the murder, anyway. His thoughts kept drifting elsewhere, pulled away from the task at hand, drawn inexorably by the sense that the true story was elsewhere, that there was some link he was failing to grasp.

But the routines of the investigation went on. The first task had been to try to track down Mrs Tuya's missing family. It was still not clear whether their departure was linked to her murder – although the abandonment of the *gers* suggested so – or whether they had already moved on when the killing occurred. Either way, the family of nomads had so far proved surprisingly elusive.

In practice, tracking down nomads was never entirely straightforward, particularly if they did not want to be found. These days, many travellers carried shortwave radios, and there were established procedures for sending and receiving messages through the state radio channels. Some even carried satellite phones, although the cost of these was prohibitive to most. The majority of nomads were now registered within a given region for voting and social security purposes, and some would make regular trips into the local towns to collect benefits or for other purposes. Again, there were standard arrangements for leaving messages through these channels. And, finally, of course, the police and other local services had their own networks within particular regions and could often establish, relatively quickly, the location of a particular individual or group.

Establishing contact with a nomad might be a slow process, but it was usually successful. The message would be picked up by someone locally and, through whatever tortuous means, would eventually make its way to the intended recipient.

In this case, the police had taken all the steps they could to get the message out. The story had been well covered in the press and on the television and radio, and the police had issued an appeal for the family to contact them. They had sent out similar messages through the police and social security networks in the north of the county, with the assumption that, before too long, someone would have identified the party of herdsmen.

But, for several days, there was very little response. There was the usual scattering of crank calls, a few that were well-intentioned but contained no information of substance, and one or two that appeared promising but where the apparent trail very quickly vanished.

They got their first serious lead five days after the body was found. It was a call from one of the provincial police stations up north of the capital, in the rich grasslands in the upper parts of the Bulgan *aimag*. One of the regional nomads had, in the course of reporting some trivial theft, mentioned – with a mild hint of xenophobia – that there were some unknown herdsmen in the area. The implication had been that, even if they were not directly responsible for the theft, they were nonetheless probably up to no good.

The policeman in question, although sceptical of the claims, had made a casual trip out to visit the camp, making enquiries about where the group had come from and to where it was travelling. It had been difficult, he said. The group clearly resented his presence and his questions, no doubt aware of what the locals might be saying about them. They had responded openly, but coolly, that they had travelled from the south looking for better pastureland, but that they expected only to stay a few days. The policeman had wondered about asking for their formal identity documents but could see no justification for a heavy-handed approach. There was no evidence of stolen property in the camp, and he had no grounds for suspecting the group of any crime.

It was only later, when he was re-reading through the various communiqués sent from headquarters during a quiet morning – of which there were many – that it occurred to him that this group might have been Mrs Tuya's family. And finally, after a protracted series of calls around the capital's police network, the information had reached the Serious Crimes Team.

Doripalam had decided almost instantly to travel up here himself with Luvsan. But he had quickly begun to wonder whether they were wasting their time. They didn't even know for sure that Mrs Tuya's family were in a position to tell them anything useful. If they had left, by arrangement, before her murder, then it was quite possible that they were unaware that she was dead, let alone in a position to shed any light on her killing. If that was the case, then Doripalam's role was little more than that of the junior sent to break the bad news. He doubted that the message would be any more palatable because it came from the senior officer.

And, of course, they didn't even know that this was Mrs Tuya's family in the first place. Okay, they had come from outside the region, but then these people were, when all was said and done, nomads. Travel was what they did. Most of them tended to travel within relatively circumscribed boundaries, but it was far from unknown for them to travel further afield.

And, on top of all that, it now turned out that, by the time Doripalam and Luvsan reached the region, the camp had already moved on.

Looking round, Doripalam wondered quite why they had decided to do so. This was a beautiful place. From where they stood, the lush grassland stretched ahead of them, rising up into the gentle hills which formed the start of the Bürengiin Nuruu mountains. In the morning sunlight, the colour of the grass was extraordinary, a shimmering gauze of emerald, shaded by the shifting patterns of the thin fluffy clouds above. Above them, snaking down the foothills, they could see the glittering twisted cable of a mountain stream, which widened into a narrow river and then a broad pool a hundred or so metres across the plain, before disappearing again, presumably back underground. Away across the hills, there were dark shadows of conifers, the first harbingers of the massive Siberian forests that lay beyond the nearby borders.

But, whatever the beauty of the surroundings, it was

clear that the camp had indeed moved on. As Doripalam had pointed out, it was possible to discern the shadows and indentations that showed where the cluster of circular *gers* had been erected. There were some dark patches in the grass where the stoves had stood, and some cropped and scrubby areas of grass where horses or goats had been tethered. Judging from the marks, it looked as if the herdsmen had not been gone for long – perhaps a day, maybe two.

'So what now?' Luvsan said, lighting another cigarette. He had tossed his previous stub carelessly into the grass. Doripalam had watched its arc and landing with some distaste.

He shook his head. 'We've come a long way,' he said. 'We can't go back now.'

Luvsan nodded. 'We'd look stupid,' he said.

Doripalam smiled thinly. 'We wouldn't be doing our jobs,' he said.

'That too,' Luvsan nodded. 'So where do we go?'

'Back to Bulgan, I reckon,' Doripalam said, referring to the regional capital. 'The police there might be able to give us another lead.' The suggestion sounded thin even to Doripalam, but anything seemed preferable to admitting defeat so quickly.

They drove back across the grasslands in silence, Luvsan maintaining his characteristic high speeds, occasionally allowing the rear wheels of the truck to slide gently across the rough ground as they took a corner. Doripalam closed his eyes and tried not to grip the sides of his seat too tightly. He had long since resigned himself to the prospect of writing off the new vehicle at some point before they returned to the capital. He could probably cope with that so long as he didn't live to face the consequences, he thought.

Bulgan itself was a small city – hardly even a town, but dignified by its status as the capital of the region or *aimag*. There was little to the place – just the Town Hall, the Government Building, a few functional and commercial buildings, a couple of hotels. There was a tourist *ger* camp to the north of the city, but otherwise surprisingly few examples of the characteristic round tents. In keeping with the surrounding woodland, the scattering of Soviet-style administrative and commercial buildings was complemented by clusters of comfortable log cabins.

Although still some way south of the Russian border, Bulgan looked like a true frontier town. The image was reinforced by the rows of horses tethered along the main streets and around the market. It was this sight, glimpsed as they had passed through the city on their journey north, that had prompted Luvsan's jocular references to the *Lone Ranger*. The city would not have looked out of place, Doripalam conceded, in the Hollywood Westerns that now found their way on to their televisions in the small hours of the morning.

Far from being a frontier town, Bulgan now gained much of its income from the groups of foreign tourists who used the city as an overnight stopping point on their way to the mountains and lakes of Khövsgöl Nuur in the far north. Because of this, it was a more cosmopolitan place than most of the country's smaller cities. People were accustomed to meeting travellers – locals and foreigners – and were relatively comfortable with the ceaseless traffic of visitors. The positive aspect of this was that the local police were very capable and responsive in dealing with any potential problems on their patch. The downside was that, whereas in most areas outside the capital newcomers would be a source of interest, gossip and possibly anxiety, here their presence would hardly be noticed. Even if Mrs Tuya's family had passed through here, their presence might well have gone unremarked.

Still, it was never wise to underestimate the perspicacity of the local police, Doripalam thought. Although the initial report about the nomadic newcomers had been filed by a local policeman in one of the outlying villages, it had been transmitted rapidly and efficiently by the police in Bulgan down to the capital. It was possible that in the meantime they had gathered some other intelligence that might be worth investigating.

Luvsan turned into the town and passed by the tree-filled parkland around the Achuut Gol river, crossed the river itself, and then turned left into the main street. He was driving with some care, at least by his own unexacting standards. The street itself was relatively busy in the mid-afternoon – largely older people dressed in traditional robes making their way through to the market or simply enjoying the sunshine. As Doripalam and Luvsan approached the hotels at the far end of the street, they saw some clusters of tourists – one Western, one apparently Japanese – walking out to view the limited array of city attractions.

At the end of the main street, Luvsan turned right and drew the truck to a halt in front of the Government

Building which, at its rear, housed the local police headquarters. As he turned off the engine, Luvsan lit another cigarette and sat back casually. 'Are they expecting you, sir?' he said.

Doripalam nodded. 'I called yesterday to warn them that we were coming on to their patch.' This was always a wise move, in Doripalam's experience. However supposedly innocent or uncontroversial the mission, no local officer liked to discover that HQ was trampling over his patch without permission. 'I said I'd probably call in on the way back, just to update them.'

Luvsan nodded, blowing his smoke carefully through the half-opened window of the truck. 'And to pick their brains.'

'As it turns out, yes. Though whether there'll be anything worth picking is an open question.'

Doripalam jumped out of the truck and strode along the pavement past the Government Building, then turned down behind it to the reception of the police offices. He didn't bother to look back to see if Luvsan was following. From past experience, he knew that Luvsan was smart enough to allow his boss to engage in any formal meetings alone, aware that his presence might cramp the senior officer's style. More importantly, Luvsan was also smart enough to make good use of his own time in these situations, putting his personable charms to use to extract whatever other information he could.

Doripalam guessed that, while he was comfortably settled with the senior officer, Luvsan would have casually ingratiated himself with the juniors in the squad room, most likely through the generous donation of the cigarettes that he seemed to carry in unlimited numbers. Doripalam was beginning to recognise that Luvsan was an officer with some potential, maybe even a possible successor in his own role. Doripalam could never claim that Luvsan resembled a younger version of himself – partly because Luvsan wasn't actually all that much younger, but mainly because his casual but streetwise sharpness was almost a diametric opposite of Doripalam's more cautious intelligence. But Doripalam was open-minded enough to recognise ability, even when it took a distinctly different form from his own.

As he turned into the gloomy concrete foyer of the police offices, he paused to gaze down the street. There were two or three more administrative and commercial buildings, then the street opened up to a line of smaller timber-built buildings – a few shops and then houses. Beyond that, there was the green parkland and then the gathering darkness of the trees, brilliant green in the descending afternoon sun. They still had several hours drive back to the capital, Doripalam thought. They would need to conclude their business soon if they were to have any chance even of starting the journey before nightfall.

He turned and made his way into the reception. The layout was familiar, a relic of the old days, with its heavily-built reception desk, the official flags and emblems, the palpably unfriendly atmosphere. Designed to intimidate, rather than to encourage honest citizens to seek official help.

There was a young officer sitting behind a desk, apparently completing some form of official report, though Doripalam noticed, as he leant over the desk, that there was a pile of sports magazines tucked underneath. He had probably heard the door opening and adjusted his reading accordingly.

Doripalam held out his identity card. 'I'm here to see your commanding officer,' he said. 'I spoke to him yesterday and said I'd call in this afternoon.'

The young man took quick account of Doripalam's role and rank, and immediately sat up straighter. 'I'll call him for you, sir.' He picked up the phone and pressed an extension, spoke briefly in a whisper, then looked back up at Doripalam. 'He's just finishing a meeting, sir. Five minutes at most.'

Doripalam nodded. 'Thanks. Is there somewhere I can wait?' He had already noticed an unprepossessing waiting room by the main entrance, presumably designed for potential wrongdoers and other members of the general public.

'You can sit upstairs,' the young man said. 'There's a small waiting area just outside the Chief's office.'

Doripalam smiled and made his way slowly up the staircase that stretched from the centre of the lobby. There was indeed a much more comfortable waiting area, clearly designed for any official visitors, with a couple of armchairs, a low table and even – Doripalam noted with interest – a Western-style water-cooler. This was something they hadn't yet managed to acquire in headquarters, though he noticed that the Ministry now had them in apparent abundance.

He lowered himself into one of the armchairs and sat back to wait. The chair gave a partial view of the lobby below, glimpsed through the stair rails. After a few moments, Doripalam saw Luvsan stride jauntily into the lobby and make his way over to the reception. There would, Doripalam presumed, very shortly be a proffering of both identity card and cigarettes.

'I'm so sorry to keep you waiting,' a voice said from behind him. 'I hope you've not been here long.'

The local police chief was a short, squat man, though Doripalam guessed that his bulk was largely muscle rather than fat. His hair was cut sharp and his bright eyes darted up and down, appraising Doripalam's slim figure, clearly surprised by the senior officer's youth but equally clearly trying hard not to let this show.

'Not at all,' Doripalam said. 'I'm sorry I couldn't let you know more precisely when I was likely to arrive.'

The Chief smiled. 'I am Tsend.'

'Doripalam. Thank you for taking the time to see me.'

'It is a rare honour to meet the head of the Serious Crimes Team.'

Doripalam shrugged. 'Rare, I hope. Honour, I'm not so sure. People don't tend to welcome the implications of our presence,' he said.

'But, fortunately, as I understand it, we are not this time dealing with a serious crime on our territory,' Tsend said. 'Which is a blessing for us, if not for you.' He gestured Doripalam into his office, inviting him to take a seat at a small meeting table.

The office, on the other hand, was relatively palatial, and Tsend's heavy mahogany desk commanded an impressive view of the main street and the parkland beyond.

'A pleasant place to work,' Doripalam commented.

'Well, we have little need to call on the services of your team,' Tsend said. 'Most of what we face here is trivial stuff. The odd theft, drunkenness. Some trouble with tourists, now and again. But nothing serious. Not like your Tuya case.'

'You're aware of the case?' Doripalam said. They had discussed it only briefly during their telephone conversation the previous day.

'A little. I read the newspapers. A dreadful murder, I understand?'

'Dreadful and, to be honest, fairly baffling. From the little we know of Mrs Tuya, there was little obvious motive for her killing.'

'There is a missing son, I understand?'

'It appears so,' Doripalam said. 'Again, we've no idea why he might be missing. Or if he really is. We know he hadn't contacted his mother for some time before her death, but that's hardly an unusual characteristic of young men.'

'But he'd have made contact once he learned of her death, surely?'

'You would assume so,' Doripalam said. 'Though it's difficult to be sure. Their relationship wasn't a strong one in recent years, I understand. And it's possible he's not even aware of her death, I suppose.'

'Though it's been well covered in the media,' Tsend said. 'And you've made appeals for him to come forward?'

'Of course. But who knows where he is? There are still parts of this country where it's possible to escape the media.' Doripalam's tone implied that this was an attractive characteristic.

'And you're trying to track down her remaining family, I understand?'

Doripalam nodded. 'That's why we're here. As I told you, we had a report from one of your outstationed officers about some non-local nomads who had arrived in the area. From the description, it sounded like it might have been the group we're looking for.'

'And was it?'

'I don't know. By the time we got there, they'd moved on and there was no obvious clue as to where they might have moved to. I was hoping you might be able to give me some more ideas.'

Tsend shrugged. 'I doubt it. Out there, they do tend to notice newcomers, if only because they're all competing for the best pastures. But it would only be reported to us if there was anything that required formal action.'

'What about this particular group? I understand that one of your officers visited them!'

Tsend flipped open a manila file on the desk in front of him. There was a small pile of similar files next to it. 'This is the report,' he said. 'It was just a routine visit. There'd been a spate of petty thefts and there were suggestions that this group of incomers might be responsible. People are always keen to blame strangers, though in my experience it's usually the local youngsters who are responsible. But I guess we thought we should check them out.'

'But you found nothing?'

'According to the report, no. The officer just made a casual call, supposedly checking that they were all right. We have a social responsibility towards people as well, of course.' He managed to imply that such considerations would be alien to the Serious Crimes Team.

'But there was no sign of anything wrong?'

'Not really. Though the report does suggest that they were behaving a little oddly. Most herdsmen are really just interested in finding the best pasture for their animals. They don't like to travel too far if they can help it, though of course they can't always control nature. But – judging from the report – this group just seemed to be travelling. They had some animals – some goats, horses – but not a great herd. And they seemed reluctant to talk about where they'd come from or where they were heading.'

'They wouldn't say?' Doripalam leaned forward, growing more interested.

Tsend shrugged. 'The officer didn't feel able to push them too hard, given that he was supposedly there on a friendly visit. But he asked a few casual questions and got deflected every time. As if they weren't keen to talk about it.'

'He didn't ask for any ID?'

'Again, he didn't think it was appropriate. He had no grounds for suspicion. He had a nose around to see if there was anything to link them to the thefts, but there wasn't. And his overall impression was that they were more interested in moving on than in committing any kind of crime here.'

Doripalam nodded, taking all this in. 'If it's true that Mrs Tuya's family did flee for some reason – and we're not at all sure about that – then it sounds as if this group could be them. And that they're still fleeing.'

'You think they were responsible for her death?'

'It's possible,' Doripalam said. 'But it could also be that they're fleeing from whoever did kill her.'

'But that's—' Tsend had clearly been about to say 'ridiculous' or something similar, but then bit this back as an inappropriate response to a suggestion from a senior officer. 'I mean, is that likely?'

'Anything's possible. That's the one thing I've learnt in this role.' Doripalam's mind went back to the extraordinary spate of killings the previous year, the convoluted web of motives that had underpinned the murders. 'But, no, it does seem far fetched.' He paused. 'We really do need to track down this group, though. Do you have any inkling where they might have moved to?'

Tsend shook his head. 'I've been through all the reports from the last few days, just in case there was anything that might be relevant to you. I wasn't specifically looking for information on this group, but I didn't see anything in there that was likely to be of interest. And from where they were – well, they could have gone anywhere. Further north towards the mountains, maybe. If they were looking to hide, that might be the best bet. But other than that, all I can do is ask my people to keep their eyes and ears open and hope we pick up something. I presume you'll ask the same of the other neighbouring *aimags*?'

'Of course,' Doripalam said mildly, biting back his irritation at being told how to do his job. Tsend was, he told himself, simply trying to be helpful. 'And there's nothing else you can tell me?'

'I don't think so. As I say, I've looked through the

files pretty carefully.' He gestured to the pile on the desk. 'But feel free to have a look for yourself if you want to.' He said it as if challenging Doripalam, who briefly felt inclined to accept.

'No, I'm sure you've been through them thoroughly. But if anything comes up – anything you think might be remotely relevant – you'll contact us straight away?' He could at least try to match Tsend in the egg-sucking tuition, he thought.

Tsend smiled. 'Immediately.'

He rose, clearly indicating that the interview was at an end, and led Doripalam towards the office door. 'Thanks for your time,' Doripalam said, as they stepped back out into the corridor. 'I realise how busy you must be.' In the silent building, it was difficult not to make the words sound ironic, but Tsend appeared to notice nothing.

'I am sorry we could not be more helpful,' Tsend said. He gestured towards the stairs. 'Forgive me, but I have another meeting I need to prepare for. You can find your own way out?'

'No problem.' Doripalam gave no real credence either to this meeting or to the one that had supposedly delayed the start of their discussion, but he was happy to get out of Tsend's presence.

He made his way slowly down the stairs and smiled faintly at the sight of Luvsan, perched on the reception desk, chatting amiably to the officer behind it. Clearly, the intimidatory design had little impact on Luvsan.

As Doripalam reached the bottom of the stairs, Luvsan jumped to his feet, waving a cheery farewell to the reception officer. Doripalam noticed that a half-empty packet of cigarettes had been left casually on the desk.

Doripalam made his way back out into the bright sunshine. Luvsan trotted along a few feet behind him, whistling tunelessly.

As they reached the truck, Luvsan said: 'Any luck, sir?'

Doripalam shook his head. 'No. Willing to do anything to help us, apart from actually providing any useful information or support.'

Luvsan smiled. 'That's what you get for mixing with the top brass, if you don't mind me saying so, sir.'

Doripalam paused, his hand on the truck door-handle, looking at Luvsan across the bonnet. 'You're going to tell me you got something more useful?'

Luvsan shrugged, still smiling. 'It's all a matter of who you know, sir.'

CHAPTER 10

'I really don't know how you can drink that stuff,' Nergui said, eyeing the foaming cappuccino as she raised it to her lips.

'I like it,' Sarangarel said simply. She took a large mouthful. It was a testament to her elegance, Nergui reflected, that she could do so without ending up with a large foam moustache. 'It's a comfort drink.'

'I suppose so.' Nergui glanced down at his own intense espresso. 'I suppose comfort's usually the last thing I'm looking for in a drink.'

She smiled. 'I think you look for intensity in all things, Nergui.'

'I'd begun to think you weren't coming,' he said. 'I could have understood why you wouldn't.'

'Could you?' she said. It was a genuine question, he thought. It was as if she really had managed to put all those days behind her. 'But, no, I'm sorry I'm late. Work, you know. Just a trivial case but those are the ones that always run on. And you don't want to adjourn for the next day because it hardly seems worth it.'

He nodded. It was difficult to imagine her behind the bench. Not because she lacked the ability or the presence for such a role, but simply because he had never seen her in that kind of formal setting. It was extraordinary to think that, if the Muunokhoi case had proceeded as planned, he would probably have attended the court as an observer and so would have encountered her, for the first time in years, in that context. If it had been a surprise when she turned up in his office, how much more astonishing would it have been to find her presiding over the trial of a man like Muunokhoi. Particularly given her background.

He had wondered, during their previous discussion, whether there was any perceived conflict of interest in her handling the Muunokhoi trial. But he supposed not. Apart from the fact that she could not be held responsible for her late husband's actions – and there was never any suggestion that she had any knowledge of what he was up to – the suspected links with Muunokhoi had never been identified, much less proved.

He contemplated again his motives for agreeing to this meeting. Of course, he liked her. He had always liked her, and there had certainly been a moment when the liking might have blossomed into something more substantive. But he was conscious that, after all these years, he found it difficult to approach any kind of relationship without at least half an eye on its potential implications, on the ways in which it might be used. Or, conversely, on the risks that it might potentially be used against him. He told himself that this was simply professional caution. As Sarangarel had said, he was used to keeping at least one step ahead.

But part of him recognised that, somewhere at the heart of this, there was also a defence mechanism, something that preserved his solitude, that kept him, not just a step ahead, but a step removed. He couldn't determine where professional caution stopped and emotional cowardice began, but he was smart enough to recognise that it was probably unwise to invite others to join him in the minefield.

But then, only a day or two later, she had phoned him. 'I've done it all by the book now,' she said. 'I've reported the threats. They didn't seem very interested.'

'I don't imagine you're the first judge to receive threats,' Nergui pointed out. 'And there's probably nothing in it. But at least you've put it all on record.'

'Covered my back, you mean.'

'Of course. It's an essential skill if you're to get on in public life.'

'You speak as an expert?'

'None more so. But I've also done what I can at my end, though it's not much. We had no luck in tracing the calls, but I never thought we would, unless it was a real amateur. We've got your phone monitored and your flat under surveillance.'

'A person could feel flattered by all this attention.'

'You're getting priority treatment,' Nergui agreed. 'But that's mainly because you're a member of the judiciary.'

'Mainly?' There was a teasing note in her voice.

'Mainly,' he repeated, his voice giving nothing away. 'We can't keep it up forever. Even for a member of the judiciary.' He paused, and she had time to wonder whether the irony was playful or mocking. 'But if there is any substance to the threat, we should find out soon enough.'

'Try not to lay the reassurance on too thickly, won't you, Nergui?'

He laughed, finally. 'I've told you. I don't do reassurance. I do realism.'

'I suppose that'll have to do, then,' she said. There was another, longer pause, as if both of them had run out of words. Then she said: 'I wondered if you fancied meeting for dinner. For old time's sake. Or I suppose we could convene it as a formal symposium between the Ministry and the judiciary, if that makes it easier.'

'Only in that I could charge the cost to the Ministry, perhaps.' He was laughing more easily now. 'But, yes, that would be good. For old time's sake. And for the future, too.' As he spoke the final words, there had been an ambiguity in his tone that she could not interpret.

They had agreed to meet in fashionable Millie's – probably because it was recognised by both as anonymous neutral ground. Everyone came here, even Nergui from time to time. It would give them time to chat, to reacquaint themselves with each other. And, if none of it worked, for whatever reason, it would give them time to bail out before they were committed to spending the evening together.

But so far it was going okay. The talk, for the moment, couldn't have got much smaller, which always made Nergui feel uncomfortable, but at least they were talking.

'It's busy,' she said, looking round the crowded café. 'Even at this time of the day.'

'I'm told it's very fashionable,' Nergui said. 'I don't

know about that. But they do a decent espresso. About the only place in the city that does.'

'You have decadent Western tastes, these days,' she said.

'I've always had decadent Western tastes,' Nergui said. 'It's because I spent too much time in the decadent West.'

'Well, we're all slowly being corrupted.' She sipped her foaming coffee. 'I imagine I'll learn to live with it.'

'I imagine you will,' he said. 'So – where shall we eat?' The question was out of his mouth almost before he could stop himself, as if his subconscious mind had decided to commit him to the evening before his conscious self could think about preventing it.

She shrugged. 'I'm in your hands,' she said. 'Where's suitably decadent and Western?'

'The Western stuff is mainly pizzas,' he said. 'There's the Café de France. They do half-decent French stuff.'

'Fine by me,' she said. 'Half decent French stuff is probably more decadent than the best cuisine from anywhere else.'

She sat back, watching him closely while he used his mobile phone to make the reservation. It was difficult to tell whether Nergui had actually made an effort in getting ready for the evening. He was wearing his usual dark suit, offset by his trademark pastel shirt and tie, tonight in a pale mauve. He had dressed like this – though perhaps a shade more self-consciously – even when she had known him the first time. She had wondered then, as she continued to wonder now, quite what this was all about. He was, to say the least, very recognisable. The smart suit and distinctive trappings contrasted starkly with his dark, glowering, warrior-like features. He was hardly a public figure, though he had appeared in the media from time to time, but even in this café she could sense people glancing at him, wondering who he was, whether he was some celebrity they didn't quite recognise.

'All sorted,' he said, ending the call. 'Seven thirty.' He looked at his watch. 'We've time for a drink if you've had enough toy coffee.'

They had, fortunately, managed to find overnight rooms at the Bulgan Hotel. The hotel itself was nothing special – typical of the larger hotels outside the capital – but the rooms were at least clean and had hot water. As Doripalam knew from bitter experience, this could not always be taken for granted.

And the Bulgan was situated in the park, with decent views of the scattering of timber houses before the dark encroachment of the forests. Sitting sipping beers in the sparse bar, he and Luvsan looked out over the parkland, the low evening sun scattering stark patterns between the trees. It was, Doripalam was forced to admit, almost pleasant.

'Okay,' Doripalam said, 'you've kept me in suspense long enough. What did you manage to find out?'

Luvsan paused, taking another slow drag on his cigarette. 'I think it's worth investigating, anyway. It sounds like it's probably them.'

'What sounds like it's probably who?' Doripalam said patiently. He knew that Luvsan liked to string this sort of thing out. Tonight, at least, they were in no particular hurry.

'Our band. The ones we're looking for. It sounds like it could well be them.'

'What does?'

'Well—' Luvsan sat himself back in his chair, looking as if he was about to make a lengthy narrative of this. 'There was some sort of disturbance, a couple of nights ago in one of the small villages five or six miles north of here.'

'What sort of disturbance?'

'Something and nothing, apparently. A new bunch of herdsman had arrived, set up camp, put their animals – just a very scanty collection, apparently – out to pasture. But they chose an area that was already being used by the locals, so a bit of a dispute broke out. Then, later in the evening – after a few vodkas, reading between the lines – some of the locals set upon one of the incomers. There was a bit of a fracas, but it didn't last long. The newcomers just backed off, said they'd pack up and be out by morning. Didn't want any trouble, that kind of thing.'

'The Superintendent didn't mention any of this.'

Luvsan gave Doripalam a look that managed to convey, with remarkable eloquence, his profoundly low expectations of any senior officer, Doripalam himself almost certainly included. 'Well, he wouldn't have known, I imagine. By the time the police got there, it was all over. No one wanted to make any kind of fuss in the circumstances. So I don't imagine any kind of report was filed. I only picked it up because I was chatting with a bunch of the officers about any sightings of strangers in the area. As it happened, one of them had been talking to an outstationed officer on the phone that morning, and had picked up this story.'

'But the group had moved on.' Doripalam pointed out. 'So we still don't know where they are.'

Luvsan shook his head. 'No, that's just it. I think I do know where they've gone. The police got there too late to deal with the disturbance, but one of the local officers was intrigued by the behaviour of the newcomers. Thought they seemed just a bit too concerned to make themselves scarce. So he decided to keep an eye on them. Let them get on a bit – they were mainly on horseback though a couple of them had motorbikes and were apparently scouting ahead. Anyway, the officer noted the direction they went in, and then made a point of checking up an hour or so later in his truck. They'd only gone a few miles and then found a sheltered spot, on the edges of the forest, to settle in.'

'But that was – what, the night before last? They could have moved on further since then.'

Luvsan shook his head. 'Apparently not. The officer's been keeping a covert eye on them – he still thinks they might be up to no good and wants to keep them in sight. Anyway, he's checked them out again today and they're still there. It's a decent spot, he reckons – sheltered, sufficiently far from any villages not to be noticed, not treading on anyone else's toes.'

'But do they know they're being watched? If they're trying to be inconspicuous, then the presence of some clumsy local officer might be just enough to send them scuttling for the shadows again.'

Luvsan smiled. 'I took the liberty of calling the outstationed officer direct while I was in the station, just to check up on the story. Seemed a sharp enough young guy. Wasted in the sticks like this. Anyway, he was adamant that he'd been subtle – if they were up to something, the last thing he wanted was to scare them off before he had any grounds to take formal action. So I told him we were interested – that we didn't want them to know they were being observed until we got there and to let us know straight away if there was any sign of them moving.'

Doripalam nodded. 'All very professional. As I'd have expected. But there's still a risk they might decide to do an overnight departure. We should get over there this evening.'

Luvsan sighed gently. 'I thought you'd say that,' he said. 'The truck's all ready. I was just hoping we might get something to eat first.'

Nergui had eaten better in Paris, but the food in the Café de France was good enough, at least by local standards. Sarangarel certainly seemed impressed.

'I didn't know you could get food like this here,' she said, slicing neatly into the steak Roquefort.

'I'm not sure how they do it,' Nergui said. 'I don't know where the food comes from. I've never dared to enquire.'

She smiled, unsure – as she recalled had always been the case with Nergui – whether he was being serious. 'I don't normally get to eat in places like this.'

'Even as a wealthy judge?' Nergui said. He cut carefully into his own rare fillet steak, watching the thin blood spill on to the crisp green of the salad.

She shook her head. 'Wealthy? But, no, it's not so

much that. It's just that I don't often have cause to eat out. Or time, for that matter.'

'So how do you spend your time? Outside work?' This was the closest that Nergui had so far come to enquiring about her personal circumstances.

'I don't seem to have much time outside work,' she said. 'I think I take it all too seriously.'

'I'm not sure you can take that kind of work too seriously,' Nergui said.

'Though from what I remember you wouldn't necessarily be the preferred source of advice on achieving balance in your life.'

He smiled. 'That's true. I've left far too many dead bodies in my wake.'

'Literally and figuratively, no doubt,' she said.

He nodded, noting that she had failed to give any kind of meaningful response to his question about how she spent her time, 'No doubt,' he said. 'But I'm not sure where it gets you in the end.'

She took a sip of the wine which, by some miracle, was not only genuinely French but even quite a decent Burgundy. 'And where's it got you?' she said. 'In the end?'

'I hope it's not the end,' Nergui said. He was watching her closely now, admiring the ease with which she'd evaded his questions and turned the focus of the conversation back on himself. 'I'm not sure I want to spend the rest of my working life in the Ministry. And in any case the shelf life is probably fairly short. If the current Minister goes out of favour – which he will, because that's politics – I don't delude myself that his successor will necessarily be clamouring for my services.'

'I never knew that false modesty was one of your vices.'

'It isn't. But realism definitely is. Though you're right – there would be a demand for my services somewhere.'

'And what are your services, these days?' she said. 'I mean, what is it you're doing in the Ministry?'

Nergui's defences immediately rose. He disliked any direct question about his job. Not necessarily because he had anything to hide, though there were aspects of his role that were certainly not for general consumption. But simply because he was always suspicious of the motives of anyone who showed some interest. And, he was beginning to recognise, suspicion was the last thing he wanted to feel tonight.

'Enjoying myself,' he said, finally, and with a slight shock realised that the statement was true. These days, he really was beginning to enjoy his position and everything that went with it – the challenges and responsibilities as well as the perquisites of power. 'I didn't at first. I hated it. I mean, I'm a frontline person at heart. I like getting my hands dirty. So the last thing I wanted was to become a backroom pen-pusher.'

'So why did you take the job?'

'I don't think I had much of a choice. If a minister – well, certainly if this minister – wants you to do his dirty work, then it's not easy to say no.'

'And is that what you do?' she said, watching him as she brushed back her dark hair. 'His dirty work?'

Nergui smiled, his face as expressionless as ever. 'No,' he said, 'not really. That's just my way of talking. I'm basically involved in running some of the larger scale security investigations – the kind of stuff that sits somewhere between the intelligence services and the police. A kind of co-ordination role, I suppose.'

'Sounds fascinating,' she said.

He shrugged. 'Not really. Most of it is just pen pushing. A lot of bureaucracy. Making sure that everything's done by the book before it gets in front of people like you.'

'You mean as wasn't done in the Muunokhoi case?'

His sharp blue eyes were unblinking. 'I can't comment,' he said. 'It wasn't my case.'

'No,' she said. 'Of course. You've moved on.' She paused. 'So why did I find you in the police headquarters?'

He carved another piece of rare steak and chewed it slowly, enjoying the taste of blood. 'As I say, it's a liaison role. I spend a lot of time there. And elsewhere.'

She shook her head. 'I'm sorry,' she said. 'Too much shop. You can see what I mean when I say I'm not used to this kind of thing. It's not just the food. I'm not used to the socialising.'

He nodded and smiled faintly. 'You never did tell me how you *do* spend your time.'

She placed her knife and fork neatly across the plate. 'It's lovely food. But I think I need to leave a little room for dessert. The crème brûlée sounds excellent.' She paused as Nergui allowed the silence to extend, continuing to chew slowly at his own steak. 'The truth is,' she said at last, 'is that there's nothing really to tell you. I work. That's it, really. I mean, it's a demanding job, though probably not as demanding as I make it. But I work long hours. I go home. I read a book. Maybe I try to watch TV. Then I go to sleep, get up early and go back to work. That's it.'

It was difficult to challenge her words without sounding either patronising or rude. Nergui nodded, placing his own cutlery across his plate. 'It sounds like your life might be even more unbalanced than mine.' Though, really, he thought, her description sounded uncannily like his own typical evening.

'Well,' she said, 'it's not been an easy life.'

'That's true,' he said. 'Though all that was a long time ago. You must have put it behind you.'

She nodded. 'I have. Really and truly behind me. It feels as if all that happened to a different person. Someone I met a few times and then lost touch with. Not me at all.'

'It was a different life,' Nergui said. 'Everything's changed now. You've changed now.'

This was certainly true. It was difficult to relate the elegant confident woman sitting opposite him to the scared figure he had first met that night – ten, eleven years before. Though it had hardly been surprising that she was scared, in the circumstances.

They had made the arrest in the small hours of the morning, in the coldest days of that bitterly cold winter. All of that had been deliberate – to take Gansukh by surprise and prevent him from destroying evidence or making contact with his associates.

There was thick snow on the ground, frozen into the hardest ice, and despite the best efforts of the snow-ploughs the city had been virtually at a standstill for the whole day. By the time the police were ready to make their assault, at around two in the morning, the temperature had dropped again, far below zero. They had positioned their trucks, with their snow chains, at the two ends of the narrow street containing Gansukh's apartment, blocking the exits. The arrest team, bundled up in heavy clothing against the rigours of the frozen night, had made their slow way down the icy street, firearms poised.

They had not known how dangerous Gansukh might prove to be. Forty-eight hours before, a routine customs search on a truck entering the country across the northern border with Russia had uncovered a consignment of classified drugs, including heroin, apparently of Afghan origin. The driver of the truck, who had initially denied all knowledge of his cargo, turned out to be a known associate of Gansukh, a small-time businessman who had been under Nergui's surveillance for some months. The driver had quickly named Gansukh as the instigator of the operation, pulling out the pitifully small handful of US dollars he had been paid upfront for undertaking the assignment. An equivalent sum, he said, would be payable by Gansukh on delivery. He named an abandoned warehouse, on the south side of the capital, as the spot where he had been due to rendezvous with another named associate of Gansukh the following evening. The police had duly arrived at the warehouse at the appointed time and arrested the associate, who without prompting also immediately named Gansukh as the paymaster.

From that point, there was little time to waste. It was only a matter of time before Gansukh realised that the operation had not proceeded according to plan.

And so, there they were, at two a.m. in the depths of winter, making their way slowly down this narrow street, poised for the arrest. Nergui had half expected that Gansukh might have tried to make his escape. But he had overestimated Gansukh's perspicacity. As they stormed in through the shattered front door of his flat, Gansukh stumbled out to meet them, rubbing his eyes, dressing gown pulled around him, demanding in a sleepy voice to know just what the *fuck* was going on. Ten seconds later, he was pinned to the ground, his hands cuffed behind his back, still screaming obscenities.

It was at that point that Nergui had first met Sarangarel. They had discovered her, cowering in bed, like a child trying to hide from her nightmares. Even then, Nergui had been struck by her appearance. But it was impossible to relate that bunched, quaking figure with the poised woman now sitting opposite. He recalled her sitting slumped on the sofa in the small apartment, her head in her hands, staring at the floor, unable to comprehend what was happening.

Under questioning, Gansukh very rapidly admitted his involvement in the smuggling operation but – in what Nergui suspected was one of Gansukh's very rare acts of chivalry – he was insistent that his wife knew nothing of the scheme. Sarangarel herself had expressed only bewilderment. She had had no involvement in her husband's business schemes, no suspicion of any criminal activity.

Nergui would have believed her, even without her husband's insistent corroboration. Their apartment was modest – decently furnished, but with nothing to indicate any unexpected wealth. Nergui initially wondered whether Gansukh had smartly concealed his wealth elsewhere, but then recognised that Gansukh was exactly what he appeared to be – an unsuccessful businessman. It was just that his failed business was on the wrong side of the law.

Then, unexpectedly, the story became more interesting.

Although Gansukh had come clean about his own involvement very quickly, clearly recognising that he had little alternative, he insisted that the real instigator was elsewhere, a big fish, sufficiently removed from the action for his involvement to be deniable.

Nergui had no difficulty believing this, but it made little difference. Gansukh refused to give any more detail even in the face of repeated aggressive questioning and the threat of a lengthy prison sentence.

'You just don't know,' Gansukh said, finally, 'who you're dealing with.'

There was something about the way he said the words that caught Nergui's attention.

'Muunokhoi,' he said, quietly.

Gansukh tried hard to control his facial expression, but the sudden spark of fear in his eyes told Nergui everything he needed to know. He had Gansukh thrown back into custody and ordered a further inch-by-inch search of Gansukh's apartment and of a number of other commercial properties he was leasing.

Meanwhile, he and Tunjin – in those days, one of Nergui's protégés – conducted endless interviews with the nervous young man, trying to get him to acknowledge some link, to provide some evidence. They offered him the prospect of a plea bargain and access to the state's newly-established witness protection programme. They talked and talked, and Gansukh sat, staring at the floor, saying nothing.

After several days of this, Nergui finally thought they were making progress. At heart, Gansukh was a loser. He had always been a loser, and now he was on the point of losing everything. But maybe, as he listened to Nergui talk, he had begun to think that, for once, he might just salvage something.

Late on the third night of interviewing, he dropped his head into his hands and, speaking through his fingers, he said: 'Okay. Okay, maybe I can tell you something more. But I have to be sure—'

'Sure of what?' Nergui leaned back in his seat and watched the man across the desk.

'Sure it's worth it,' Gansukh said. 'You don't know—'

Nergui nodded, indicating that he knew only too well. 'What would make it worth it?' he said.

'How would it benefit me?'

'There are no guarantees,' Nergui said. 'It's not in my power to guarantee, but it is in my power to influence. It will help you in two ways. First, it confirms you're not the lead player in this. And, second, your co-operation will be taken into account. With all that – and it being a first offence, even if a serious one – you should get a minimal sentence. Maybe even suspended.' This was nonsense – regardless of the mitigation, the courts now took drug smuggling very seriously indeed – but it was what Gansukh wanted to hear. Gansukh nodded. 'And what about protection?'

'We have a fully established programme now. Based on best practice from the West. If you go to prison, you'll get full protection there. And if you don't – or when you come out – we can organise an identity change, relocation, whatever it needs.' Again, it was an exaggeration. Nergui had little confidence that he could offer any real protection against Muunokhoi's resources.

It was as if Gunsukh had read his thoughts. 'I don't know what it needs,' he said, his face pale. 'I don't know that anything would be enough.'

'We'll do whatever is humanly possible.' Nergui paused, looking for the final lever that would unlock Gansukh's response. 'And if this person is as fearsome as you say, who's to say you'll be safe even if you say nothing?'

Gansukh stared up at him. 'What do you mean?'

'I mean,' Nergui said, 'that you've painted a picture of a very dangerous individual. Someone who makes you afraid even to open your mouth. To this person, you'll always be a risk. You *know*. You might decide not to speak today or tomorrow or ever, but he can't be sure.' He leaned forward, staring at Gansukh through his hard blue eyes. 'How safe are you?'

Gansukh shook his head. This was clearly a new thought to him. 'I don't know,' he said finally, in a voice scarcely more than a whisper.

'So if you don't speak, you go to prison, a long sentence, with no protection. Do you know how many violent deaths there have been in prison over the last year?' Nergui himself didn't know, but he thought he was unlikely to be required to provide a definitive figure. 'Whereas if you tell us what you can, we give you full protection and support – in prison, if necessary, and outside.' He allowed silence to fall across the conversation, almost able to read the thoughts that were rushing through Gansukh's head.

Finally, Gansukh looked up at him. 'I need to think about it,' he said. 'I don't know—'

'It's late,' Nergui said. 'Think about it overnight. We can talk in the morning.'

This was standard practice, allowing the interviewee to stew with his thoughts. But afterwards Nergui considered it the biggest mistake he had ever made.

He was woken in the small hours of the morning, the telephone in his silent apartment unnaturally shrill in the night. It was the duty officer at the station. There had been an incident. Gansukh was dead.

He had been found in his cell, hanging from the window bars, a bed-sheet twisted awkwardly round his neck. It looked an impossible way to commit suicide, though the pathologist claimed it was not unknown. Nergui bustled around, trying to find out how it had been allowed to happen. Gansukh had not been under any kind of suicide watch – there had been no reason to assume that this was necessary. His cell had been regularly patrolled but was not under continuous surveillance.

Nergui had to acknowledge that, with hindsight, suicide might have been a predictable response. Gansukh had been scared of the consequences whether he spoke out or not. This form of death might be a lot less unpleasant than anything Muunokhoi's people could inflict.

But something nagged at Nergui. He couldn't honestly say that Gansukh was not the suicidal type – how could you judge that? – but Nergui had never seen him that way. And the timing of Gansukh's death, so soon after he had indicated that he might be willing to speak, seemed too convenient.

But only he and Tunjin had been present when Gansukh had been speaking. Nergui quickly found Tunjin and asked him whether he had shared the contents of the interview with Gansukh with any of his colleagues. Tunjin, looking justifiably terrified of Nergui, nodded almost imperceptibly. 'I'm sorry, sir. I didn't realise—' It turned out that he had been transcribing the interview notes, and had chosen to share the contents with a number of colleagues. Quite possibly, by the time Gansukh had died, most of the officers on duty would have been aware of what he had said.

So did Nergui have any grounds to treat the death as suspicious? Only the most circumstantial ones. Gansukh had been under great pressure, was facing a lengthy prison sentence, might be at risk of reprisals. Suicide was hardly an outrageous verdict. This was how the pathologist saw it. After all, what did Gansukh have to live for?

Well, thought Nergui, there was the woman now sitting opposite him delicately eating her crème brûlée. Though by the time he died, he might well have lost her anyway. Certainly, when Nergui had visited her in her hotel room to break the news, she had been – well, upset, certainly, but perhaps also secretly relieved. She would not have to drag forward the legacy of that former life – the trial, her own role as a witness, the endless rounds of visiting Gansukh in prison, the slow and painful progress towards an inevitable divorce. Perhaps, Nergui thought, Gansukh's suicide – if that was what it had been – was less selfish than it might have appeared. Perhaps, after all, he had taken that final step to prove his love for his wife.

And, looking at her now, she had clearly taken full advantage of that freedom. She had made a life and a career for herself. She had a striking presence, a sense of hard-won but powerful authority. And he wondered precisely what it was she had lost, that frozen evening, when he had met her for the first time.

'I was expecting more sparkling conversation than this, if I'm honest,' she said. 'But as I don't get out much, perhaps my expectations are unrealistic.'

He laughed. 'I'm sorry,' he said. 'I was just thinking.'

She raised an eyebrow. 'I think that's been fairly obvious for some minutes. But about what?'

He shrugged. 'I don't know. About the past, I suppose.'

She nodded. 'I don't do that. Far too dangerous. I think about the future. Like the rest of this evening, for example. And beyond.'

He opened his mouth to speak, momentarily disconcerted by her tone. As he did so, he felt his mobile phone, tucked in the inside pocket of his jacket, vibrate twice. A text message.

'I'm sorry—' He pulled out the phone and waved it gently in front of her. 'I'd better check. It might be urgent.'

He thumbed the buttons on the phone and brought up the message on the screen. The number was familiar though it took him a moment to place it. The message simply said: 'Call. Urgent.'

Nergui stared at the phone for a moment, absorbing the message.

'Well?' Sarangarel said, spooning up the last of her dessert. 'Was it urgent?'

Nergui looked back up at her. 'I rather think it was,' he said.

She nodded, amusement playing in her dark eyes. 'Well, then,' she said. 'What a useful device.'

The weather had grown more humid in the course of the evening, and now the first small spots of rain were beginning to fall on the windscreen. Luvsan cursed and switched on the wipers. 'All we need,' he said.

'I take it this won't affect your famed navigational skills,' Doripalam said, gesturing towards the GPS system.

Luvsan shrugged. 'The machine's fine. Whether I can make any sense of it in this darkness is another question entirely.'

Doripalam sat back, knowing that in truth Luvsan was fully in control and enjoying every moment of this trip through the darkness. They were still on the main road at the moment, heading north out of Bulgan towards the mountains. There was no other traffic or signs of life, other than the vanishing glow of the small city's lights behind them. Doripalam watched the progress of their headlights across the road, the monotony almost hypnotic.

'How far do we think it is?' Doripalam said.

'Not far. Twenty kilometres or so. That's where we'll meet the local guy, and he'll take us on to where the camp is.'

The local guy was the outstationed officer who had been keeping an eye on the camp. Luvsan had phoned him again from the hotel and asked for his help in tracking down the camp. He had agreed with alacrity, obviously excited at the prospect of working with the Serious Crimes Team. Doripalam could not help thinking that Luvsan had perhaps rather over-stated the importance of their mission, but it had seemed to have the necessary effect.

Luvsan turned on the radio, and twisted the dial till he found one of the commercial stations playing Western-style pop music. He banged his palm on the steering wheel as they drove in time with the music, occasionally singing along with the choruses. It was irritating, but preferable to the endless silence of the night.

Twenty-five minutes later they saw the few scattered lights of a small village – nothing more than a handful of timber buildings, a couple of prefabricated official blocks, and a filling station with a single petrol pump.

'This is the place,' Luvsan said, pulling to a halt. 'There.' He gestured out of the window towards one of the prefabricated concrete buildings, with the police symbol outside. As he spoke, the main door of the building opened and a figure stepped out into the glare of their headlights, waving to them. It was a young man, with thick dark hair. He was dressed in jeans and an anorak.

Luvsan lowered his window. 'Yadamsuren?' he said.

'That's me,' the young man said eagerly. 'You're Doripalam?'

Luvsan smirked gently and gestured towards the passenger seat. 'This is my boss. I'm Luvsan.'

'Pleased to meet you both,' Yadamsuren said. 'And very pleased to be of assistance.' He peered enthusiastically through the open window, the rain – falling more heavily now – dripping from his hair on to his forehead.

'You'd better jump in,' Doripalam said. 'You're getting soaked.'

Yadamsuren looked almost overwhelmed at the generosity of the suggestion. He pulled open the rear door and climbed in behind them. 'Thanks very much.'

Doripalam twisted in his seat to look back at the young officer. 'How far are we from the site?'

'Not far. A couple of kilometres, no more.'

'They're still there?'

Yadamsuren nodded. 'I checked again after you phoned.'

'And you're sure they've no idea you've been observing them?'

'I was very careful. I parked some way away and then walked up there. I know that terrain very well, so I had no difficulty finding my way up there in the dark.'

Luvsan peered gloomily out through the rain-spattered windscreen. 'I hope we don't have to park too far away,' he said.

'You can drive almost up to it. In this weather, you can probably get quite close before they'd hear the engine.'

'Well done,' Doripalam said to the young man. 'We're very grateful.'

Luvsan turned his head away, smiling faintly. He knew that Doripalam was utterly sincere, but also that this was the most enthusiastic praise that was ever likely to issue from the chief's lips. In this case, though, it seemed to be more than sufficient. Yadamsuren looked almost overwhelmed at Doripalam's words.

'I hope these are the people you are seeking,' Yadamsuren said. It sounded like a genuine expression of goodwill rather than any prompting for more information. Luvsan had given Yadamsuren no indication of why they were interested in these people, although, if Yadamsuren read the newspapers, he might easily have arrived at the answer for himself.

'I hope so, too,' Doripalam said.

Luvsan started the engine and pulled back out on to the road. 'This way?' he said, gesturing ahead.

Yadamsuren nodded. 'Keep going up here a couple of kilometres,' he said. 'I'll tell you when to turn. The last part is over the grassland, but it should be solid enough even in this rain.'

They drove on through the dark. To Luvsan, as he peered out between the sweep of the wipers into the glare of the headlights, the whole landscape looked identical. There was simply the endless passage of the road, clusters of conifers that thickened and then fell away.

Yadamsuren, though, was peering carefully through the window, clearly enumerating every turn in the road and every copse of trees they passed. 'Here,' he said at last. 'Slow down. We're almost there.'

Luvsan obeyed, slowing the truck down to a crawl, staring forward to try to find some discernible landmark.

'Just here,' Yadamsuren said. 'Before that clump of trees. Turn right there, and then drive up slowly past the trees. Take it gently. The ground's okay but a bit rough.'

Yadamsuren's description seemed like an understatement as they slowly bounced their way across the uneven terrain up past the trees. 'How far is it now?' Doripalam said.

'Just a few hundred metres,' Yadamsuren said. 'How close do you want to get in the truck?'

Doripalam shrugged. 'I think in this weather we may as well go all the way. We'll still surprise them – so they won't have much time if they've anything to hide – and they're more likely to take us seriously if we turn up in a dirty great truck.'

'I could turn on the sirens,' Luvsan suggested. The truck had no police markings but carried a siren and lights for use in emergencies.

'I don't think so,' Doripalam said. 'I don't think we want to risk terrifying the life out of them. We don't know how they might react.'

'Do you think they could be armed?' Yadamsuren said, nervously.

'It's possible,' Doripalam said. 'It's always possible. Bear that in mind. With this lot, we just don't know. Assuming it is the people we're looking for, all we know is that we want them as potential witnesses. But we don't know why they're hiding or what it is that they appear to be running from. So who knows?'

'This is connected with that woman?' Yadamsuren said. 'The murder?' So he had been reading the newspapers, Luvsan thought. Smart boy.

Doripalam nodded. 'This is her family. They travelled together. But they'd moved on before her body was found. We don't know why.'

'You think they might have killed her?'

'They might. But they might also be running from whoever did. And maybe they'd left before she was killed. We don't know. That's why we don't know how they're likely to react.'

They had reached the top of the incline now, and the ground fell away before them. In the headlights they could see the tops of a cluster of *gers*, pitched in a low hollow, surrounded on three sides by trees. It was a good hiding place, if that was indeed the intention. The tents were hidden by the trees, as well as by their low elevation in the hollow. They would not be visible from the surrounding terrain until you were right on top of them.

Doripalam saw the door of the closest *ger* swing partly open. It was impossible to disguise their presence any longer – the inhabitants of the camp would have heard the truck's engine, seen the glare of the headlights. Luvsan stopped the truck so that the headlights were shining down fully into the camp, and then killed the engine.

Almost simultaneously, before he had chance to direct their next move, Doripalam felt his mobile vibrating in his pocket. He cursed, pulled it out and glanced at the screen. Headquarters.

'Just wait a moment,' he said. 'Keep an eye on

what's happening down there. If you see any significant movement, we'd better get down.'

He thumbed the phone and took the call. For a few moments, he listened, saying nothing, then said: 'You've got people over there? Search the apartment. Minutely. Anything you can find. Anything that might be remotely relevant. We probably won't be able to get back till morning, but make sure you keep me posted.'

He ended the call and turned back to Luvsan. 'It's Tunjin,' he said.

'Tunjin? I thought he was suspended.'

'He is,' Doripalam said, noting that, despite all their efforts at keeping this information under wraps, it was already common knowledge. 'That's just it. There was some sort of disturbance outside his apartment block. Gunfire. His flat looked as if it had been ransacked. And Tunjin's gone missing.'

'Gone missing? But how—!' Luvsan was about to make some joke about the difficulty of losing eighteen stones of solid fat, but he didn't finish the sentence.

It took them all by surprise. There had been no apparent movement from the camp below them. But then, suddenly, all at once, Doripalam caught the glare of gunfire, the sound of a shot, and the nerve-shattering explosion as their windscreen collapsed into countless tiny shards, brilliant in the glare of the headlights. And then there was screaming and the smell of blood and burning, and the sound of all hell breaking loose.

CHAPTER 11

He had his back to the wall and was watching intently, waiting for something to happen. Outside night had fallen and the darkness was thickening.

He needed to relax, he knew that. He couldn't keep up this pace, this intensity for long. He just wasn't built for it. And he knew, rationally, that as yet they could have no idea where he was. For the moment, at least, he was safe. The only question was for how long.

He breathed deeply, trying to calm himself down, trying not to think too hard about the implications of being found. He had bought himself some time, at least. Now he needed to make use of it. He needed to force himself to think, to work out what he was going to do next.

He looked about him, trying to rationalise his position, trying to think about what he needed to do. Okay, he thought, first things first. Work it all out, step by step. The position is straightforward. He had found himself a haven. As long as he stayed here, he was likely to be safe. The only problem was that he couldn't stay here for very long.

He was sitting in the corner of a storeroom in an abandoned shop on the south side of the city. It was one of the industrial areas that had been redeveloped with the emergence of capitalism, where dozens of supposedly entrepreneurial businesses had sprung up apparently overnight. As the grand old monolithic communist enterprises gradually ground to a halt, the westerners had been quick to tell them that this was where the future lay, in the energetic play of the free market. Let a thousand self-employed flowers bloom.

But of course it hadn't lasted. Tunjin had had friends and relations whose lives had collapsed during those fateful years, who had lost whatever security and savings they might have had. And he recalled the dreadful winters that had accompanied those years of depression, as if nature and the heavens had chosen to conspire with man's worst instincts.

The place was a wreck. The display window at the front had long been shattered, and large shards of glass still lay scattered across the tiled floor. Any remaining items of stock had been looted almost immediately, and all that was left now were a few broken shelves and display cabinets, faded printed notices advertising long obsolete electronic goods.

Behind the shop itself was a small network of rooms – a living area with a small bed-sitting room, a kitchen and a lavatory, and then, behind that, the small storeroom where Tunjin was currently sitting.

There was no furniture in any of the rooms, other than a discarded broken table lamp and a few tattered remains of what had presumably once been blinds. The storeroom contained a few empty cardboard boxes, some scattered unidentifiable electrical components, and little else.

Tunjin had come to the storeroom simply because it represented the point furthest removed from the front of the shop and the outside world. He had come to the shop in the first place because – well, because he could think of nowhere else to go. His journey out of the city on the motorbike had been utterly terrifying, because he did not know how closely he was being pursued. The shots had faded behind him, but he did not know whether Muunokhoi's people would have other observers or pursuers stationed around the area. He half expected that, at any moment, another shot might bring him or the bike down, or that some car or truck would appear to block his route or sideswipe him.

But it didn't happen. He kept on, making his way through the ruined factories and warehouses, and then between the camps of semi-permanent *gers* that surrounded the city, until finally he was away from the buildings and heading out on to the open steppe.

Finally, at that point, he felt able to stop and look back. Even if he were not being pursued, he was acutely aware of his potentially lethal ineptitude on the bike. In his younger days, he'd been a pretty skilled motorcyclist, having bought and maintained an old Russian bike when he was a teenager. He'd ridden that for years, around the city, out into the country, taking girls for dates on the back of it. It all seemed a very long time ago.

He'd even had a police bike for a while, and had received full professional training on how to ride it. So he should have known what he was doing. They said it was one of the things you never forgot. And that was probably the case, or he wouldn't have made it this far.

But the young man who had ridden that old Soviet bike as if it was a part of his own body was long gone, replaced by this overweight old slob. When he'd first set off on Agypar's bike, Tunjin's sheer bulk had been a problem – he could feel his weight wobbling around the bike's centre of gravity as he struggled to maintain his balance. But he'd eventually come to grips with that and felt much more comfortable. Even then, though, he was aware that his reactions were not what they once had been, and that the nerve and lack of fear that characterised his younger biking were long gone. Left to his own devices, he would have ridden as slowly as possible until his confidence returned. But there had been no question of that – he simply had to get out of there as quickly as possible.

And somehow he'd made it. He was out in the grassland, looking back at the city's jumble on the skyline. There was no evident sign of pursuit. It was a bright clear day, with only a few dark clouds clustering on the horizon. Everything looked beautiful and peaceful.

But out here, Tunjin felt exposed. Rationally he was safe. If anyone was pursuing him, he would see them from miles away. But, equally, they would see him. And perhaps someone was already watching him. Perhaps they had watched him the whole way, knew exactly where he was, but had not bothered to give chase. Perhaps they did not need to.

He looked up at the empty sky. Muunokhoi was a

wealthy man. He would have access to aircraft, helicopters. He or his people could be out here in a matter of minutes if they so chose. Suddenly, the vast wasteland of the steppe seemed much less like a sanctuary.

It was that thinking that had led him back into the city, and back here. He had twisted the bike round and, taking a convoluted route back around the city, entered it again from the west side and made his way down here. He had used all his police skills and training to try to lose any possible pursuit, twisting and turning up and down alleyways, between and through abandoned buildings, jumping red lights, taking narrow passages so that pursuit by car was impossible. And finally he'd arrived here.

For the moment, then, he was safe. But he knew that this state could not last long. He would soon have to emerge to find some food and drink – he had managed a single stop on his way here to get some bread, fruit and bottles of water from one of the small new supermarkets, but hadn't dared to linger. And he was conscious that he already presented a conspicuous figure, with his heavy weight and dishevelled appearance. People would notice him, and he was sure that, sooner or later, the message would get back to Muunokhoi.

He wondered whether he'd made a mistake in coming back. Maybe he should have just carried on, maybe got a flight down into the Gobi or up into the north. Taken himself as far away as possible from the capital and from Muunokhoi, tried to make himself a new life somewhere else.

But he knew that this was impossible. Muunokhoi would track him down no matter how far he fled.

So what options did he have? Precious few, it seemed. Hide out here like a terrified rabbit for as long as possible, then emerge and take the consequences? It didn't seem much of a prospect.

Or he could try to take the initiative. He could at least try to use what few resources lay at his disposal. He could go down fighting.

It was his own fault, his own responsibility that he was in this mess. But there was one other factor that had contributed, one other person who was, at least peripherally, involved. One other person who had the same drive, the same motivation in this, as he did.

He looked at his watch. It was nearly nine. Outside, the sun had set and the deserted streets and alleyways were in darkness.

Tunjin reached into his pocket, pulled out the mobile phone he had not yet dared to use, and very carefully began to dial.

Doripalam was out of the truck and had pulled out his pistol almost in one movement, rolling across the wet grass until he was standing upright, facing down into the camp. He moved himself quickly back behind the truck's bulk, and stared out ahead of him.

There were four of them, standing in a row, all apparently holding rifles. They had all fired in sequence, round after round, the echoes still reverberating around the distant hillsides. It seemed, though, that only one bullet had found a target, shattering the windscreen of the truck.

Doripalam saw that Luvsan had followed his example, and was now moving back to join him.

'How's Yadamsuren?'

'Okay, I think,' Luvsan said. 'Bullet just grazed his shoulder. Fair bit of blood, and we need to get it bandaged, but it's not serious. Lucky, though. Could have got any one of us.'

'Unlucky, I think,' Doripalam countered. 'I don't think they actually meant to hit us at all. That was just a stray shot.'

'Oh, that's okay, then,' Luvsan said. 'When I get hold of those bastards, I'll make sure one of my boots strays into their teeth.'

Doripalam carefully pulled open the back door of the truck, and lifted out a loud-hailer which he raised to his lips.

'Armed police. I repeat, armed police. Put down your weapons. Otherwise, we will open fire.'

There was a long pause. The four figures below them, little more than black shadows in the truck's headlights, remained motionless. And then, like a soldier breaking ranks, the figure on the far left stepped forward and threw down his rifle. There was a further pause, and then, one by one, the others did the same.

Doripalam glanced at Luvsan. 'I'll go down there,' he said. 'Cover me. If there's any sign at all of trouble, start firing.'

Luvsan nodded. He had pulled a medium range rifle out of the truck, and now set it down carefully across the roof, the sights trained on the figures below. 'Good luck,' he said.

Doripalam stepped out from behind the truck, holding his pistol out in front of him in both hands. The rain was still falling heavily, and the cold water ran down his arms, dripping off the steel of the gun.

The four men still stood motionless. Doripalam stopped and called out: 'Put your hands on your heads. No other movements.'

The men obeyed silently, watching his descent. He moved slowly, watching them carefully, alert for any movement.

He moved closer, reaching the point where the discarded rifles lay in the sodden grass. Moving carefully, his eyes still fixed on the four men, he kicked the rifles back to ensure they were out of the men's reach.

'Okay, you,' he said to the man on the far left – the first to discard his weapon. 'Take off your jacket – very slowly and throw it on the ground. Then turn out your pockets. Slowly.' The four men were all dressed in Western clothes, anoraks and jeans.

The man hesitated for a moment and then obeyed, throwing his anorak down on to the grass. He pulled out the pockets of his jeans – a wallet, a few coins, nothing else.

Doripalam repeated the process with the other three men, then beckoned Luvsan down to join him. Luvsan held his rifle trained on the men while Doripalam talked.

'I've an injured officer in the truck,' he said. 'Injured by one of you. I'm planning to arrest you all and charge you with assault, maybe even attempted murder. I'll go through all the formal procedure in a moment. In the meantime, any of you want to tell me what this is all about?'

Luvsan glanced across at him in mild surprise. But it was as clear as it could be that these men posed no serious threat. All four of them looked scared out of their wits, trembling not just with the rain and the cold, but also from the unwavering sight of Luvsan's firearm.

The men looked at each other in some confusion. Then, finally, the man on the left spoke. 'I'm sorry,' he said. 'We have been very foolish. We did not realise you were police. We were terrified. We thought you were—' He stopped.

Doripalam waited a moment, but when it was clear that the man did not intend to continue, he said: 'Who did you think we were?'

The man looked around at his companions, as if looking for support. 'It's a long story,' he said at last. 'You said your companion was injured. Can we do anything for him?'

Doripalam hesitated, not wanting to lose control of the situation, but recognising that Yadamsuren did need attention. He looked at Luvsan. 'He's right. There's a first aid kit in the truck. Go and get Yadamsuren bandaged up as best you can. I'll look after this bunch.'

One of the men leaned forward. 'I have some medical skills,' he said. 'I trained as a nurse. I can help.'

The situation was, Doripalam thought, drifting towards the surreal. But he found it hard to believe that these cowering men constituted any kind of a threat. 'Okay,' he said to Luvsan. 'Take him with you.'

He turned to the man on the left of the group. 'We're investigating a murder,' he said. 'In a nomadic camp close to the capital. Does that mean anything to you?'

'My sister,' the man said. 'We saw it in the newspapers a few days ago. It was not a surprise but it was – a shock. I did not really believe it.'

'You didn't know she was dead?'

'Not for sure. Not until we saw the report. We thought she might have escaped somehow. But we did not really believe that she would.'

'Escaped what? What's this all about?'

'It is a long story,' the man repeated. 'We do not even know the whole story.'

Doripalam was becoming irritated with the cryptic responses. 'You'll have plenty of time in custody to go through it all,' he said. He began to intone the formal charges of attempted murder, following the prescribed procedure and wording, while the three men stared at him aghast.

'But we are not criminals,' one of them said, as he finished.

'I would advise you not to say more until you're in custody,' Doripalam said. 'We can organise legal representation for you.'

'We are not criminals,' the man repeated.

'You have fired repeatedly on officers of the law, with no warning or provocation. You have injured a police officer. You have – and I mention this in passing – damaged a police vehicle. Whatever your motivations, these are serious crimes.'

'But we did not intend—'

'That will be for the courts to decide. I can only work on the outcomes.'

Doripalam sighed and pulled out his mobile phone. He was going to have to call backup from the local police to take these characters into custody in Bulgan. All this would take time, and the rain was continuing to fall.

'If you're prepared to co-operate, we can perhaps short-circuit some of the formalities. And I may be prepared to reconsider the charges, so long as my young companion does not wish to press charges.' This, he thought, was all very unorthodox. Still, pouring rain in the middle of the steppe was not conducive to orthodoxy.

'Let's get inside and talk,' he said, gesturing with his pistol towards the nearest *ger*.

The three men filed slowly into the tent. Doripalam followed them, still holding his gun at chest height, keeping them all carefully in view. It might be worth being unorthodox, but it certainly wasn't worth being reckless.

Inside, the *ger* was comfortable enough but very sparsely furnished, as if the men were travelling with the minimum of equipment. The first man gestured Doripalam to sit on one of the two wooden seats, while he and his companions crouched on the floor. The *ger* was lit dimly by two oil lanterns, but the tent was well enough illuminated for Doripalam to discern the anxiety on the men's faces. Doripalam held his gun casually, but kept it trained on the three men.

'Okay,' he said at last, 'so what's the story?'

'It's my sister,' the first man said.

'Mrs Tuya?'

The man nodded. 'I'm Tseren.' He gestured. 'Damdin is also my brother. Kadyr is our cousin. Another cousin, Ravhjik, is assisting your colleagues.'

Doripalam nodded. 'Tell me about your sister,' he said.

Tseren hesitated, as if unsure where to begin. 'I suppose it starts with her husband,' he said.

'The soldier?'

Tseren nodded. 'Khenbish. The great war hero,' he snorted, ironically. 'Yes, with him.'

'You did not have a high opinion of him?' Doripalam watched Tseren quizzically, wondering quite where this was going.

'He was a bad man,' Tseren said, simply. 'In every way. I have been amused reading the press coverage. The great war hero.' He laughed, bitterly. He glanced at the other two men who looked back at him, stony-faced.

'What do you mean?' Doripalam said.

'You name it. He was a violent man. He drank too much.'

'He was violent with your sister?'

Damdin began to speak but Tseren cut him off. 'I think he was. She always denied it, but I have seen her with bruises. I am sure he was.'

Doripalam looked at Damdin, wondering whether he was about to contradict his brother. Damdin shrugged. 'I do not know,' he said. 'I do not like to condemn people without evidence. But I think Tseren is right.'

'You are too generous,' Tseren said. 'Khenbish was

a bad man. He was trouble for our sister. He was involved with bad people.'

'What sort of bad people?' Doripalam looked between the three men. He had the impression that Tseren was keen to talk, but that the others were uneasy about saying too much.

Tseren looked at the others. 'I cannot name names,' he said.

'This is a murder enquiry,' Doripalam said. 'If you have information, it is your duty to give it to the police. If I think you're withholding evidence, we may once again need to revert to the formalities.'

Tseren shook his head. 'I am not trying to withhold evidence. I genuinely don't know the names of these people. I've no desire to know them.'

Doripalam decided to let that one go for a moment. 'So what kinds of people are we talking about?' he said.

Tseren shrugged. 'Mostly small-time crooks, I think. Organised crime, though not on a grand scale – protection rackets, smuggling, robbery. Some pretty unsavoury types. I met them occasionally when I went to visit my sister. Some of them were ex-soldiers, which I guess is how Khenbish had got to know them.'

Doripalam nodded. Once the USSR had withdrawn its support, the military, like most other parts of the economy, had collapsed. There were many soldiers who found themselves back out on the street, with no pension, no skills and few prospects. It was also common knowledge that a substantial proportion of the military armoury had found its way back on to the street with them.

'But I think there were other things he was involved in. Deals he got involved in during his time in Afghanistan—'

'You mean drugs?'

Tseren shrugged. 'Well, he certainly had access to them for his own use. Openly boasted about it. So, yes, I think he was probably involved in some sort of operation.'

'Drug smuggling?' It sounded far-fetched to Doripalam. Would it be possible for a soldier, even in those chaotic post communist days, to be involved in smuggling drugs into the country?

'I don't know for sure,' Tseren said. 'I just know that he seemed to get himself caught up with some unpleasant people. I was frightened for what might happen to his family—'

'You met these people?'

'Sometimes. Again, when I went round there, he'd be engaged in what he described as business meetings, though he'd never tell us what kind of business was involved. But I got the impression that the meetings weren't always comfortable ones. If I know Khenbish, he'd have promised more than he could deliver. I don't know for sure, but there were a couple of occasions when I thought he was in serious trouble.'

'He died in combat?'

Tseren laughed. 'Is that what the records say?'

Doripalam shook his head. 'I've not looked at the records myself,' he said, 'but that was what I understood.'

'He was drunk,' Tseren said, 'and maybe more than drunk. Fell into the path of a truck. They hushed it up, but that was the real story. The best way it could have ended, really. The family got an army pension – not a great deal but something – and were rid of him. That was when they moved back out to live with us.'

'But what does this have to do with Mrs Tuya's death?' Doripalam said. 'He'd been dead for a long time by then.'

'Gavaa idolised his father,' Tseren said, as though changing the subject.

'Gavaa? The son? The one who went missing?' Doripalam said.

Tseren nodded. 'Thought his father was marvellous. Well, I suppose every son has a right to do that, though not every father deserves it. Wanted to follow in his father's footsteps.'

'As a soldier?'

'Yes. At first. But he wasn't cut out for it. But he saw his father as the great hero. Thought that everything he did was marvellous.'

'What are you saying? That he followed his father—' For the first time, Doripalam lowered the gun and stared at Tseren.

'I don't know for sure what happened, but his mother thought he'd fallen in with a bad crowd in the city—'

'Mothers always think that,' Doripalam pointed out. 'Mine thought it when I joined the police.'

'No, it was more than that,' Tseren said. 'She didn't say so to me, but I think she knew some of the people he'd got in touch with. I think he was trying to make contact with some of his father's business contacts.'

'Mrs Tuya said nothing about this when she came to us about his disappearance,' Doripalam said.

'No, well, I don't think she wanted to believe it,' Tseren said. 'She didn't really have any concrete evidence – just hints he'd dropped on the few occasions when he'd spoken to her.'

'I understand they didn't get on at the end,' Doripalam said. 'Surely that's the kind of thing that any teenager might say to bait his mother?'

'That's what she thought at first.' Tseren paused. 'It's certainly what I told her. It was only when he disappeared that she thought there might have been something more in what he'd said.'

'And what had he said?'

'Something about job prospects. She was saying the usual stuff about wasting his life in some dead end job, and he started telling her that he had real prospects. Stuff she couldn't even dream of.'

'Doesn't sound very plausible,' Doripalam said. 'We've no evidence he did get another job. And his mother didn't mention it when she spoke to us.'

'I don't think any of us took much notice of it, even when Gavaa went missing. We all thought it was just teenage bravado. To be honest, my concern was simply whether Gavaa could survive in the city. He had a high opinion of himself, but I'm not sure many other people shared it.'

'Including you?'

'Including me. And, I think, even including his mother. He treated her badly – knew she hadn't really got on with his father and thought that was her fault. But he saw his father as a hero, whereas we all saw him as a drunken bully. But she was his mother. She loved him. I think that was why she was so worried when he vanished. Because she just thought that he wouldn't be able to cope.'

'Did you take his disappearance seriously?'

Tseren shrugged. 'Not at first. I don't imagine the police did, either. I was a bit embarrassed by the press coverage. But when we continued to hear nothing from him, I began to get more concerned.'

'You'd have expected him to contact you?'

'If only to ask for money. He was always short. And then, when the men came—'

Doripalam looked up sharply and stared at Tseren across the dim expanse of the tent. 'Men?'

'I wasn't there myself. We'd all made a trip into the city and left Bayarmaa – Mrs Tuya – by herself looking after the animals.'

'When was this?'

'I don't know. A couple of weeks before her murder, I suppose.'

'And you never came forward—'

'No. We should have done, I know. But we were afraid.'

'Who were these men?'

'We don't know. They apparently arrived in a truck, two of them. Large, threatening men. The kinds of people that Bayarmaa's husband used to associate with, she told us. They were asking for Gavaa. Said he was in some serious trouble. They tried to give the impression that they wanted to help him, but Bayarmaa's impression was that if he was in trouble, they were probably the cause of it.'

'But they didn't know where he was?'

'No, they were trying to track him down. They said it was some business deal that he'd been involved in but they wouldn't say more. They were clearly convinced that he was hiding out with his mother.'

'She told them he wasn't?'

'Of course. But it wasn't clear that they believed her. From the way they spoke, it sounded as if they thought that, at the very least, she was in contact with him.'

'Did they threaten her?'

'Not overtly, I don't think. She was a tough woman – I don't think she was scared of them herself. But she was worried about Gavaa.'

'And what about you? Were you worried?'

Tseren nodded, crouched down on the rugs that were spread across the floor of the tent. 'Yes, I knew the kinds of people that Khenbish had associated with. If those were some of those people, then – well, yes, I had reason to be worried.'

'And you thought they might be?'

Tseren shrugged. 'I began to put two and two together. Remembered what Gavaa had said about having prospects. I thought he might well have approached some of his father's old associates and got sucked into something that was over his head.'

Doripalam had lowered the gun. 'I wanted to get out of there,' Tseren continued. 'Move on. I know these kinds of people. They don't take no for an answer. If they thought Gavaa was hiding with us, then they'd keep watching us. If they thought we knew where he was, then they'd take whatever steps they could to get the information out of us.'

'So you moved on? Without Mrs Tuya?' It was hard not to make the question sound accusatory.

Tseren shook his head. 'Not immediately. I told myself I was just being paranoid, that there was no reason to be frightened. Then the following evening, I came out of the tent to see a truck parked some way away across the grassland. It was them. They were watching us. I could even see the binoculars. Worst of all, they weren't making any effort to hide themselves. They wanted us to know they were there. They didn't stay there long. But then a day or two later they were back again. Just watching. And that was when I knew that it would go on like that, that we really didn't have a choice, that we really should get away.'

'So you did?'

'We did. The four of us left as quickly as we could to look for new pastures, somewhere far enough away that they wouldn't easily be able to find us.'

'Why didn't you take Mrs Tuya with you?'

'She wouldn't come. She thought there would be some news soon of Gavaa, and she didn't want not to be there. And there was a policeman coming to talk to her—'

'That was me,' Doripalam said quietly.

'She thought you might have some news.'

Doripalam shook his head. 'I had nothing to tell her.'

Tseren nodded. 'I assumed that would be the case. I told her so. But she was desperate for any information.'

Doripalam nodded, thinking back to how lightly he had treated Gavaa's disappearance. 'And none of you stayed with her?'

Tseren dropped his head and stared at the floor. 'We told ourselves that nothing would happen to her before we returned. She told us the same. And she said that the police were coming to visit her so the men wouldn't dare do anything. But I think we were just cowards.'

'And you didn't go back?'

Tseren nodded. 'We started to. We found a good pasture for the family. We left the rest of the family there – another cousin and her husband, their two boys – and then we went back for Mrs Tuya and the rest of the equipment. But when we got within sight of the camp, we saw that it was surrounded by police vehicles.'

Doripalam looked up and stared at Tseren. 'So why didn't you come forward? Why didn't you tell us what you knew?'

'I don't know. We were scared. We didn't know what had happened. We thought – maybe that Bayarmaa had called you in or that she'd spoken to you about the men when you visited. But I think we knew from all the activity that – well, that that wasn't really what had happened. So we panicked and fled. We've been running ever since.'

Doripalam shook his head, watching the three cowering men in front of him. It was, he thought, a sight far removed from the Mongolian martial ideal. 'You should have come forward,' he said. 'We would have protected you.'

'You were not able to protect Bayarmaa,' Tseren said. The statement was factual rather than accusatory. 'You were not able to protect Gavaa.'

Doripalam could hear the faint thudding of the rain on the roof. 'We do not know that anything has happened to Gavaa,' he said.

Tseren shook his head. 'I do not believe we will see Gavaa again,' he said. 'I think he is dead.'

CHAPTER 12

Nergui, working his distinctive brand of bureaucratic magic, had managed to organise an official car to take them home. He had originally assumed, without making any definite plans, that they would go on somewhere after the restaurant. Maybe just to a bar for a nightcap or two. He imagined that both of them were getting a little old for nightclubs.

He had not thought what might happen beyond that. Quite probably nothing. He still wasn't sure about the nature of this relationship, or where it might lead. He was enjoying the companionship, and Sarangarel seemed to have enjoyed the evening, if only because she so rarely socialised. Nergui was reluctant to look any further forward than that. He couldn't imagine that romance was seriously on the cards for either of them, and he was still concerned about his own, possibly darker motives for re-establishing this relationship.

Even so, he found himself disappointed that the text message should have cut the meeting shorter than he intended.

The large black official car pulled to a stop outside her apartment block. Nergui was pleased to note that a police officer was positioned discreetly in the shadows, ensuring protection in case the threats should turn out to have any substance.

Rain had swept in from the north, falling in heavy windswept sheets down the dimly lit street. This was, he noted, one of the more upmarket parts of town, not far from his own apartment.

She peered out through the car window. 'I'm going to have to make a run for it,' she said. 'I didn't expect this kind of weather tonight.'

'It's cold, too,' Nergui said. 'Look, I'm really sorry I've had to bring you straight back. I was hoping we could have had another drink.'

'Probably not the weather for it, anyway,' she said. 'But, yes, I'm sorry too. I've enjoyed the evening. It's a rare pleasure for me – eating out, someone else paying, and not even on official business. And I imagine that urgent phone messages are an occupational hazard for someone in your position.' She paused, smiling. 'Mind you, if it had come earlier in the evening, I would have assumed you were looking for an excuse to bail out.'

He laughed. 'On the contrary,' he said, 'I was trying to find an excuse not to bail out. But it really is urgent.'

'Oh, well. I suppose that means I'm off to bed, while you're back off to work.'

'Something like that,' he said.

They made their goodbyes, even a polite European-style kiss on the cheeks, and then she was gone, out into the rain, holding her coat over her head. Nergui watched her run into the lobby of the apartment block, shaking off the rain and standing waiting for the lift.

The driver turned, blank faced. 'Back to headquarters now, sir?'

Nergui hesitated. 'No,' he said. 'Take me home. I've got some calls to make but I can make them from there.'

Nergui's own flat was only another ten or fifteen minutes away. He dismissed the driver, and then walked slowly across the pavement to the doors of the apartment block, perversely enjoying the slow drip of the rain through his hair and down his face. He was, he realised, delaying the moment when he would have to return home and start to deal with all of this. Even though he didn't know yet what all this might actually turn out to be.

He shook the rain from his hair then hurried into the lobby of the apartment block, and made his way rapidly up the stairs to his first floor flat.

The flat was, as always, warm and comfortable, a haven that Nergui had created for himself away from the bustle of his daily business. He'd pulled strings to get some of the furniture, shipping heavy mahogany items in from Russia and the West. Unmarried, no dependents, with a high ranking government job, he could afford to spend money on this kind of thing. But there were times when it seemed a poor substitute for human company.

He poured himself a small glass of vodka and then sat down on one of the plush crimson armchairs. He pulled his mobile out of his pocket, thumbed the keys and looked again at the text message that had been sent earlier. The number had not been concealed, which might have been a mistake. Nergui had no idea how easy or difficult it might be to monitor mobile phone calls.

He hesitated for a moment longer, then dialled in the call back sequence. There was a long moment's silence then the ringing tone. The ringing tone ran on, and at first Nergui thought that no one was going to answer. But, finally, just when he was on the point of giving up, the call was picked up.

'Yes?' The voice was hoarse, little more than a whisper.

'Tunjin?'

A pause. 'It's you,' Tunjin said, finally.

'Are you all right?' Nergui said. Tunjin's voice was faint, static ridden.

'For the moment, yes. But they're on to me—'

Nergui nodded, slowly. 'It was inevitable,' he said. 'You should never have got caught up in this. Especially not the way you did.' He cursed himself inwardly. There was no point in berating Tunjin about this now. Tunjin's intentions were good, but he'd done a stupid thing. He just hadn't realised what he was up against.

'Where are you—? No, don't tell me,' Nergui said. 'I don't know how secure this line is. Are you somewhere safe?'

'I think so,' Tunjin said. 'But I don't know how long I can stay here.'

Nergui sat back in his chair, trying to decide on the best way forward. His own enquiries were going too slowly, making too little progress. He didn't have enough information to protect Tunjin. He still didn't know who was on the inside. But if they were after him, Tunjin was unlikely to have much breathing space.

'Can you get to the usual place?' Nergui said. 'Just say yes or no.'

There was another audible hesitation. 'Yes.'

'Can you be there in an hour? Again, just say yes or no.'

'Yes.'

'Well meet there,' Nergui said. He looked at his watch. Ten thirty. 'Eleven thirty. Don't say anything else. Just hang up.'

As instructed, the line went dead and Nergui sat for a moment, listening to the silence. Maybe he was just being paranoid. He would certainly be wary of the phones in headquarters, and maybe even of those in his own office in the Ministry, even though those were regularly swept for listening devices. But he really didn't know what was possible with a mobile phone. He understood that digital phones were more secure, but didn't know what that really meant. And the one thing he had learnt from this whole sorry affair was not to underestimate the opposition. They had got on to Tunjin's schemes quickly enough, and then even more quickly had got on to Tunjin. They undoubtedly knew what Nergui was up to, even though his enquiry was supposedly confidential. Indeed, Nergui's logic had been that, since the chances of keeping his involvement quiet were effectively zero in any case, he might as well try to use his presence to try to smoke them out. But quite possibly they were too clever for that.

Nergui swallowed the last of his vodka. The next question was whether he could get to their designated rendezvous safely. The last thing he wanted was to draw Tunjin into an ambush. They had used the same spot as a meeting place for years – the legacy of a surveillance case they had been involved in years before. It had become almost a private joke between them, no need to spell it out. And Tunjin was even more streetwise than Nergui, so he would surely have spotted any pursuer. But there was always the risk that somewhere, somehow, they had been spotted.

Nergui poured a second vodka and strolled over to the window. He pulled back the heavy tapestry curtain and peered out into the night. The rain was still falling and the street below looked deserted. Nergui stared out into the pale slick of the streetlight spread across the rain-drenched street, trying to discern any sign of movement.

The meeting place was relatively close by – only a few minutes away by car, half an hour or so to walk. Probably best to drive, he thought. The car would be more conspicuous but would allow them the prospect of an immediate getaway if anything went wrong. In this situation, Nergui wanted to avoid vulnerability at all cost. He wanted to be in control. Or, at least, as in control as it was possible to be.

He walked into the bedroom and pulled out a drawer from the heavy dark wood dressing table by his bed. Then he crouched and reached into the drawer space. Concealed at the back was a built-in gun safe, which he had had installed following the kidnapping of the English policeman the year before. Prior to that, Nergui had never kept firearms in his apartment, believing that it was appropriate only to keep firearms in his official capacity where they could be safely stored. But the kidnapping had unnerved him and he had suddenly recognised the vulnerability of his own position. He had increased the security on his apartment, and had decided for the first time to store one of his licensed handguns at home.

He clicked open the safe and pulled out the pistol, feeling its cold weight in his palm. He knew he was unlikely to deploy it. Although he was fully trained in its use, all his instincts were against using a weapon in any context other than a formal police exercise. And this, he thought, was anything but.

He slipped the gun into his pocket, closed the safe and carefully replaced the drawer. Then he looked around him, as if he were being watched. The security on this place was as tight as it could be, but it was difficult to shake off the paranoia. There was no knowing who could be trusted here. He couldn't even have risked having his flat swept for bugging devices, because he wasn't sure he could trust those who would be doing the sweeping. He was prepared to take that risk in his office environment because he could manage the potential consequences. But he needed this place to be genuinely safe, a haven.

He shook his head. All this was getting to him. Maybe that was what had happened to Tunjin in the end. Maybe the paranoia had got to him, and that was what had forced him into that ridiculous plan. If so, who knew what state he might be in by now?

He looked at his watch. Just after eleven. Probably still slightly early to be setting out, but he was finding the waiting too much. He paced up and down again, and then made his way to the front door of the apartment. He paused for a moment and leaned forward to peer out through the tiny spyglass. The distorted image of the corridor showed it to be empty.

He hesitated for a moment, then turned and walked back into the kitchen. He picked up a loaf of bread, some pieces of fruit that were sitting in the bowl on the table, a couple of bottles of water. It wasn't much, but it was all he had easily available. Back in the hallway, he retrieved a canvas rucksack from under the coat-rack and threw the items inside. Then he unlocked the door, pulled it open and stepped out into the empty corridor. Time to face the rain and the night, he thought, and whatever else might be waiting.

'You're sure you're okay?' Doripalam said, peering into the truck.

Yadamsuren nodded weakly. He looked pale and very shaken, curled up in the back seat of the truck.

'Serves you right for mixing with us city folk,' Luvsan said. 'We always bring trouble.'

Yadamsuren smiled weakly. 'Thanks for patching me up,' he said. 'It hurts like hell but at least it's not bleeding.'

'I didn't do much,' Luvsan said. 'It was the old chap over there knew what he was about. Ten times more than my basic first aid.' He gestured to where Ravhjik had now re-joined his cousins. It was still raining, but the four men were sitting outside the *gers*, the rain pouring on to them, as if they were performing some kind of penance.

'Do you want to press charges?' Doripalam said. He

was also still standing out in the rain, his head peering in through the truck window, though he was well wrapped in a police-issue waterproof coat. 'I'm very happy if you want to. I played softball with them in there to get them to talk, but I made it clear that it's your call. We're not normally too keen on allowing people to get away from shooting police officers.' He had already outlined to Luvsan and Yadamsuren the content of his discussion with Tseren.

'From what you say, they were scared to death,' Yadamsuren said. 'I'm not hurt – well, not seriously anyway. Don't think we'd achieve very much by putting them through the legal mill.'

'Increase your arrest tally,' Luvsan said. 'That always looks good.'

'I don't think so,' Yadamsuren said.

Doripalam nodded, mildly impressed by the young man's fortitude. 'For what it's worth, I think you're right. But it's your decision.'

Yadamsuren nodded. 'I can live with the pain,' he smiled.

'We'll take them in, anyway,' Doripalam said. 'I think they'll be happy to volunteer. We need them as witnesses – I don't want them getting away again. And we can offer them some protection.' He looked at Yadamsuren. 'How long do you think it will take your people to get here?'

'Twenty minutes. No more.'

Doripalam looked at his watch. 'They should be here any minute then. I'll go down and prepare our friends. They might want to bring a change of clothes with them.'

He walked back across the sodden grassland to where the four men were sitting crouched. There was an almost palpable sense of misery and shame hanging over the group, as if the reality of their relative's violent death had only now hit them. Tseren looked up as Doripalam approached.

'Truck should be here in a few minutes,' Doripalam said. 'Get yourselves a change of clothes if you can. You'll freeze to death otherwise. You'll be relieved to know that my colleague has very generously decided not to press charges. But we would like you to come into the local station with us.'

'How long will you need to hold us?' Tseren said.

Doripalam shrugged. 'I don't really want to hold you at all,' he said. 'I could arrest you and require you to assist with our enquiries, but I'd much rather you came voluntarily. We may need you as witnesses – you certainly have new information about Mrs Tuya's death and possibly also about Gavaa's disappearance. More importantly, though, we want to ensure that you're safe.'

'Do you think you can do that?'

'If you're not safe with us, you're not safe anywhere,' Doripalam said, recognising that this didn't entirely answer their question. 'We don't know if someone really is after you, but if they are you're safer with us than you are out here.'

Tseren nodded and glanced at the others. 'That sounds reasonable,' he says. 'I am very happy to come with you.' The others nodded slightly in agreement, still crouched in the pouring rain.

'Thank you.' Doripalam could see the lights of an

213

approaching truck, some way distant across the plain. 'They'll pick you up and take you to the local station,' he said. 'I've got other business now, but I'll send someone up in the morning to talk to you properly.'

The truck pulled up a few minutes later. There were two local officers, bemused at this summons late in the night. Doripalam had explained the situation briefly to the senior officer, but it was not clear how much of this explanation had reached the officers now standing before him. The older of the two – a tall, skinny individual with an apparently permanent expression of disdain – emerged from the truck and stood in front of Doripalam.

'Who're we taking in?' he said.

Doripalam eyed him. 'A "sir" would be nice,' he said. 'This group. They're not under arrest. They've volunteered to come in to help us with our enquiries. And, in this case, that's not a euphemism. They want to help us, and I want them to be treated accordingly. Look after them. Give them a hot meal. Find them somewhere to sleep. I'll get one of my men up to talk to them in the morning. And I don't expect him to find that they've got anything to complain about in the way they've been treated. Is that clear?'

'Very clear. Sir.' The officer looked down at him lazily. Doripalam recognised the all too familiar sight of the junior local officer determined not to be intimidated by the big boys from the city. But it didn't make him feel any less tempted to kick the gangling idiot's feet from under him.

'Good. One more thing. There's a possibility that these men might be in physical danger. I want them kept under close observation at all times. And, again, I'll be deeply unhappy if anything should happen to them while they're in your keeping. And you wouldn't want that, would you?'

'No. Sir.' The officer turned and gestured to the four men to make their way to the back of the truck, studiously paying no more attention to Doripalam, who watched him with barely concealed amusement. His primary concern had been that, despite Yadamsuren's intention not to take the matter further, his colleagues might decide to take a little informal revenge once they got the four men back to the station. His confidence wasn't increased by having met this character, but he hoped that his warnings would be sufficiently authoritative to prevent any reprisals.

The two officers helped the men into the back of the truck. Yadamsuren was to join them in the front with the intention of taking him to the hospital in Bulgan so he could be given a full examination.

Yadamsuren paused, as he was about to climb into the front of the truck, turning back towards Doripalam. 'I am glad that your journey wasn't wasted,' he said. 'That these were the men you were seeking.'

'So am I,' Doripalam said, sincerely. 'And I'm very grateful for your help. You did well in identifying these people. I'm sorry the night was more eventful than we expected.'

Yadamsuren shrugged. 'It could have been much worse.'

It could indeed, Doripalam thought. He watched Yadamsuren climb slowly into the truck, clearly troubled by his injury. And it raised the question. What were the four men so afraid of that they were prepared to shoot indiscriminately simply because a truck turned up unexpectedly in the night? Was there something more they knew or suspected? Something they hadn't so far chosen to share with him?

He would have to make sure that whoever he sent up here was appropriately skilled in questioning, someone who could take whatever steps might be necessary to find out if there was something more, something that had not yet been said.

But now Doripalam had other matters to concern him. In all the excitement of the shooting and its aftermath, he had almost forgotten the call that he had received shortly beforehand. A disturbance at Tunjin's apartment building. Tunjin's flat ransacked. Tunjin apparently missing. What the hell was all that about?

He turned and made his way back across the grass to the truck. Luvsan was standing by its side, working his way slowly through another packet of cigarettes.

'Back to the hotel?' Luvsan said.

Doripalam shook his head. 'No. I'd thought we could stay up here to deal with whatever we found here – interview our four friends. But I need to get back.'

'Tunjin?'

'Tunjin. It may be something and nothing. He's a strange character at the best of times. But given his current – status, I'm a little worried. I think we need to get back. Are we okay to drive in this thing?' Doripalam gestured to the shattered windscreen.

Luvsan had punched out the shards of glass so the interior of the truck was now open to the air.

'No choice,' Luvsan said. 'Even if we were staying up here, I doubt we'd be able to get it repaired locally. It'll be cold, but if we wrap up warm we should be okay.'

Doripalam nodded and thumbed a number into his mobile. He waited a moment for the call to be answered, then asked to be put through to the officer who had called earlier. 'Sorry for the delay in getting back. We had a bit of an incident up here, but it's okay now. Any more news on Tunjin?' He listened for a moment then said: 'Well, keep us informed. We're heading back, but it'll be a few hours before we reach the city. If anything happens in the meantime, call us straight away.'

He ended the call and turned back to Luvsan. 'Nothing. No sign of Tunjin. They're searching the flat. It's a mess – though they suspect that it was probably a mess anyway. Tunjin's domestic life seems to have been everything that you might have expected. But it also looks as if it's been searched pretty thoroughly already.'

Luvsan pulled open the passenger door of the truck. 'What would Tunjin have that would be worth searching for?'

Doripalam shrugged. 'Who knows? But nothing would surprise me about Tunjin.'

They climbed back into the truck. Luvsan turned it round, and slowly pulled back up on to the road and then turned left back towards the south. 'Was there any sign of a struggle?' he said.

'What?' Luvsan was having to keep the truck's speed fairly low, but even so the continuous blast of cold air filled the truck with noise.

'At Tunjin's flat. Any sign of a struggle?' Luvsan shouted.

'Difficult to tell, apparently,' Doripalam shouted back. 'Whole place was turned over. No way of knowing if there'd been a struggle in the middle of it.'

'So we don't know whether Tunjin's just gone to ground for some reason, or whether something's happened to him?'

Doripalam shook his head. 'But as you were no doubt about to point out so politely earlier, someone like Tunjin doesn't go missing easily. He's a big person to lose.'

CHAPTER 13

The basement always made Nergui feel uneasy, though it was as secure as all other parts of the apartment block. This place mainly housed government officials, and, although Nergui had taken additional steps to address security in his own flat, the whole place was designed to offer substantial protection to a potentially vulnerable group. The concerns had been greater during the early days of democracy, when there seemed to be a permanent fear that some form of revolution, or perhaps counter-revolution, was brewing just around the bend. Now, things had calmed and most of those who lived here paid little heed to the security trappings that this place offered. But Nergui was grateful, now as much as ever, that the block offered at least some protection.

Even so, the basement felt more vulnerable. It was mainly just that the lights were dim and the place was riddled with shadowy corners, as well as the potential hiding places offered by the rows of residents' cars. It wouldn't be an easy place to penetrate, but if anyone did get in, there would be plenty of places for them to hide.

And tonight who knew what might be waiting? Nergui crossed the concrete floor cautiously, his hand resting on the steel of his pistol, his eyes watchful for any sign of movement. He knew he was being paranoid. But he also knew that, on a number of occasions, it was paranoia that had kept him alive.

His own Mitsubishi 4x4 was parked a little way along the row. He reached it without incident, unlocked it and climbed in, throwing the canvas bag into the rear seat. He started the engine, reversed out and turned back towards the entrance. Still no sign of anything.

As he approached the entrance, he lowered the window to wave the electronic tag near the monitor. There was a moment's pause and then the heavy metal gates that enclosed the entrance slowly drew back. He noted, in passing, that the slow movement of the gates might well allow an intruder on foot time to slip through once a car had departed. He had not thought about this before, and the revelation of this minor weakness in the block's security increased his unease.

And, he realised, his unease was feeding upon itself. The very fact that he was feeling so uncomfortable was unusual – the last time he had experienced this kind of sensation was when they had faced the series of brutal killings the previous winter. Then, as now, he had had the sense that his unconscious mind was telling him something that his conscious brain had not yet learned to interpret. That there was something more going on than he'd so far identified.

Nergui was smart enough and experienced enough to be able to assess realistically the risks involved in his journey tonight. As long as he was careful, they were likely to be minimal. But still something was nagging at him. There was still a sense that he was – not out of his depth, exactly. The waters would have to be very deep indeed before Nergui's limits were reached. But certainly that he was much closer to those limits than his rational mind might suggest.

And Nergui had learned to trust his instincts. Not as something supernatural or magical, but simply as the expression of all his years of experience. However slight the apparent risk, he would take no chances tonight.

He pulled out from the apartment block and turned into the main street. He hesitated just for a moment and then took a right, heading in the opposite direction from his intended destination, travelling west along Peace Avenue, out of the city. He continued for two or three miles, the long strip of the railway prominent on his right, the Onion Mountain visible on the left. At this hour, there was no other traffic and no sign that he was being followed.

As the road straightened out, he did a sharp U-turn and headed back, passing clustered *ger* encampments and then industrial areas until he once again entered the central area of the city. He passed no other vehicles. Driving at this time of night was a mixed blessing in terms of security. On the one hand, it would be difficult for any pursuer to remain concealed. On the other, Nergui's own car was highly conspicuous.

He drove back along Peace Avenue, and then turned right down towards Nairamdal Park. There were a few more people around here – drinkers tumbling out of the Khanbrau and East West Bars, a scattering of late-night pedestrians. Above to his left, he could see the clustering temples that formed the Monastery

Museum of Choijin Lama. And then he was past that and the vast dark space of the parkland opened up beyond the road.

To his right, opposite the park, there was the squat tower of the Bayangol Hotel.

He turned into the hotel and parked his car inconspicuously alongside a row of others. Grabbing the bag from the rear seat and ensuring that the handgun was safely in his pocket, he jumped out of the car and crossed the road to the entrance to the park.

He looked around. There was no one in sight, and even the hotel lobby looked closed and deserted. The park gates were locked for the night but it was easy enough to climb over into the darkness beyond. He wondered quite how Tunjin would manage to negotiate the fence, but knew from experience that Tunjin would have identified his own entrance route.

He stepped away from the fence and walked a few metres into the shadow, listening hard for any sound of movement. The rain had long ceased, but he could hear the dripping of water from the trees as a faint breeze rippled through the foliage. Otherwise, there was nothing.

He began to walk slowly across the park, heading from memory in the direction of the lake. He had brought a flashlight, but wanted to avoid using it unless absolutely necessary.

There was no sign yet of Tunjin. In the near blackness, he could just make out the shapes of the aged ferris wheel and other rides in the amusement area across the park.

He found the lake without difficulty, its dirty water

giving a faintly luminous glow. The surrounding trees clattered quietly in the soft wind. He glanced at the luminous dial of his watch. Almost exactly eleven thirty. Perfect. The only question now was whether Tunjin would make the rendezvous.

The question was answered almost immediately. A larger patch of blackness suddenly emerged from the shadows further along the lake. Nergui walked forward and said, only just audibly, 'It's me.' He didn't give his name but knew that Tunjin – assuming that it was Tunjin – would recognise the voice. His hand slipped into his pocket, firmly gripping the pistol handle. He glanced briefly around him, keeping his back towards the lake so there was no danger of being surprised from behind.

Within seconds, he had no doubt that it was Tunjin. The ungainly movement of his large body was unmistakable. Nergui relaxed slightly, suddenly aware that he had been holding his breath. But he continued to grasp the gun, conscious that, if they had been followed, it was at this moment of exposure that they were probably most vulnerable.

'You made it,' Tunjin said, drawing up closer.

'It wasn't that difficult for me,' Nergui said. 'The more important thing is that you made it safely. You're sure no one spotted you.'

'As sure as I can be,' Tunjin said. He glanced down at his heaving body. 'You wouldn't think it to look at me, but I'm actually quite good at giving people the slip.'

Nergui smiled, pleased at least that some signs of the old Tunjin were still in evidence. And the greatest miracle was that, as far as he could tell, there was no hint of alcohol on Tunjin's breath.

'What about you?' Tunjin said. 'You're sure you weren't followed?'

'In any other circumstance,' Nergui said, 'I'd have you disciplined for impertinence.'

'You can't,' Tunjin pointed out. 'I'm already suspended.'

'So you are,' Nergui said. 'And your own bloody fault too.'

'You're not the type to say "I told you so",' Tunjin said. 'If you were, you'd be insufferable.'

Nergui laughed, softly. 'Glad to see that this mess hasn't entirely dampened your spirits.'

'I haven't had time for my spirits to be dampened, other than by that bloody rain. Though I wasn't feeling too pleased with myself, holed up in the back of a semi demolished shop.'

'How are you?' Nergui said. 'I mean, really.'

Tunjin shrugged. 'As well as can be expected. I've been suspended from the only job I've ever known, a year off retirement. I've been exposed as the thorn in the side of the most dangerous criminal psychopath in the city. And I'm on the run, with no obvious prospect of salvation. In the circumstances, not so bad.'

'At least it's got you off the drink.'

'And where the bloody hell am I supposed to find booze? It's not for lack of wanting it, I can tell you.'

'So what are we going to do?' Nergui said. 'How are we going to get you out of this mess?'

'I was rather hoping that you might be able to tell me that.'

'I don't think it's going to be easy,' Nergui said. 'The problem is knowing who to trust.'

'That's been the problem throughout this whole bloody affair,' Tunjin said. 'Everywhere you turn, he's got people. I mean, I know I was bloody stupid and it was half-baked, but I'd never expected that it would leak like that. No one knew.'

'Someone knew,' Nergui said. 'Assuming that you're not informing on yourself.'

'At least that would have been simpler,' Tunjin said. 'Cut out the middleman and all that. No. Everywhere you turn there's someone. I'm not even sure about you, sometimes.'

'To be honest,' Nergui said, 'I wasn't at all sure about you till you pulled this little stunt. And even now I'm wondering if it isn't some kind of double bluff.'

'If you knew what I'd been through today, you wouldn't have any doubts. And I guess I know that, if you're not on the side of the angels, then the whole bloody police force might as well pack up and go home.'

'It may come to that,' Nergui said. 'I'm getting nowhere in rooting out what really is going on there.'

'What about Doripalam?' Tunjin said. 'You think he's straight?'

Nergui hesitated. In any other circumstances he would be reluctant to express any views about a senior officer, particularly to the likes of Tunjin. But these were far from ordinary circumstances. 'I'm pretty sure so,' he said. 'But that's the difficulty. All my instincts tell me he's straight. But even with him I can't be absolutely certain. And in any case there are too many others I don't trust. I've started to get together some pretty damning evidence on one or two characters, but in most cases there's just no way to be sure. We just don't know how far this goes.'

'Further than you can imagine,' Tunjin said.

'I thought about trying to organise you police protection,' Nergui said. 'But there's no way.' He thought about what had happened to Sarangarel's husband, a decade before. The tentacles were in place already, even at that time. There was no way of knowing how far they might stretch by now.

'I'll happily decline,' Tunjin said. 'As things stand.'

'It might be feasible to organise some sort of safe house through the Ministry,' Nergui said. 'But even there, even in the intelligence services—'

'You don't know for sure.' It was a statement rather than a question.

'I don't know for sure,' Nergui agreed. 'It would be your risk.'

Tunjin turned. 'I'm tired,' he said, in a tone that suggested that his weariness was more than merely physical. 'Let's find somewhere to sit down.' He began to trudge slowly across the silent park, Nergui following behind him, his senses alert for any other sign of movement. Ahead of them there were the floodlit façades of the Buddhist temples and then, beyond that, all the scattered lights of the city. By contrast, in the darkness, the park seemed inhospitable, a lifeless wasteland, its shadows containing who knew what kinds of threat.

They reached the play area. The rides were all

firmly closed and locked, but there were benches where they could sit. The skeletal shape of the ferris wheel towered above them, black bones against the cloudy night sky.

Tunjin slumped heavily on to one of the benches, the wood and metal creaking beneath his weight. Nergui sat carefully beside him.

'It's not a risk I want to take,' Tunjin said, continuing their previous conversation.

'In your place, I'd feel the same,' Nergui said. 'It's one thing to be out here, keeping an eye out for yourself, however great the risk. It's another to hand yourself over to someone else's safe keeping, if you don't have confidence in them.'

'And you're saying you wouldn't have confidence in the intelligence services?'

'I don't know. No. Not entirely. '

'So, no, I don't think so.'

'But what's the alternative?' Nergui said. 'You can't stay on the run forever.' He paused. 'It's outrageous. After all these years. All my supposed authority. And I can't even provide adequate protection for a police officer in trouble.'

'I'm still a police officer, then?' Tunjin said. 'I wasn't sure.'

'Of course you're still a police officer,' Nergui said. 'And as far as I'm concerned you'll stay a police officer till you retire.'

'Assuming I live that long.'

'Assuming you live that long. And, at the moment, I don't know how we ensure that. You can't keep running.'

'I'm not exactly built for it,' Tunjin agreed, looking down at his vast bulk.

'So what do we do?' Nergui said. 'I can try to find you somewhere to hide out. Somewhere only we know about. I'd take you back to my flat, but I can't believe that it's not at least under some kind of surveillance. That's why I was afraid of being followed tonight.'

'I'm best where I am at the moment,' Tunjin said. 'It's not comfortable. But no one but me knows that I'm there. It'll buy me two or three days at least. But I can't stay there forever.'

'I brought you some food and water,' Nergui said, remembering the canvas bag he had slung over his shoulder. 'Nothing much. I just grabbed what I had, but it'll keep you going for a while. If we arrange another meeting, I can get you some more.'

'I could do with losing a pound or two, anyway,' Tunjin laughed.

'But it doesn't solve the problem,' Nergui said. 'All we're doing is buying time. I'm out of ideas.'

'As I see it,' Tunjin said, 'there's only one way forward.'

Nergui looked across at the man sitting next to him. In the gloom, he could not make out his expression. 'And that is?'

'I've got to finish what I started,' Tunjin said. 'Only this time I've got to make sure I do it properly.'

There was a faint breeze rustling through the trees. For a moment, Nergui fancied that he could discern some other sound, maybe someone moving. He held his breath for a second, listening, but could make out nothing more.

'What do you mean?' he said, at last.

'What I say,' Tunjin leaned back on the bench which creaked alarmingly under them. 'I need to finish what I started, but make less of a mess of it this time.'

Nergui shook his head. 'I don't know what you've got in mind,' he said. 'But you're hardly in the best position to start collating more evidence. And you presumably didn't find it all that easy last time, which is why you're in this mess.'

Tunjin shrugged. 'Maybe I was too complacent last time. I thought I'd covered all the angles, but I clearly hadn't. I didn't realise how far this thing went.'

'I don't think any of us really did,' Nergui said. 'I was taken aback by what you tried to do, but I was even more startled that – with all your natural talents – you didn't manage to get away with it.' He paused, as if wondering quite how many metaphorical cards to put on the table. 'It scared the hell out me, actually. I mean, I always knew he had people on the inside. But then I also knew how smart you'd have been in trying to pull all that stuff off. And if you got caught out – well, it doesn't bear thinking about.'

'That's the trouble,' Tunjin said. 'I tell you, nobody knew what I was up to. One or two would have had inklings, and I had some professional help with the forgeries, but there was no individual I confided in. And all the evidence was held confidentially, even within the team, because of its sensitivity. If they got to the bottom of that, well – anybody could be involved.'

'Even Doripalam?' Nergui said.

Tunjin shrugged. 'You can judge that better than me,' he said. 'But he was one of the few people with a real overview of all the evidence. If anyone was going to spot flaws or inconsistencies – well, he wasn't the only one, but there weren't many.'

'I still don't think so,' Nergui said. 'I still think he's straight.'

Tunjin made no response. After a pause, he said: 'So maybe I'm in a better position to do something now than I was before. At least now there's nobody going to expose me. So maybe I can finish it off.'

Nergui turned and stared at the grey silhouette of the large man beside him. 'Finish it off?' he said. 'What have you got in mind, exactly?'

'I don't know. But as long as he's there, he's going to want my blood.'

'It's insane,' Nergui said. 'You know who we're talking about. We've never got close to him.'

'No,' Tunjin said, slowly. 'But before we've all – even me, for the most part – have had to do it by the book. I don't have that constraint any more.'

'You're still a police officer,' Nergui said.

'So you tell me. It doesn't feel like it. It didn't feel like it this afternoon.' He paused. 'Look, Nergui, all I know is I can't just sit here waiting for him to come to me. So I've got to go after him. If I decide to adopt methods that are – well, the kinds of things that might be unacceptable to you, I wouldn't dream of troubling your conscience by sharing them.'

'I could arrest you now if I thought you were going to commit an illegal act,' Nergui said.

'Yes, but you don't. And neither do I. But I do know that I haven't got much to lose. In fact, given what might happen to me if they catch up with me, I'm better off with the prospect of something quick and clean.'

'It sounds like a fantasy to me,' Nergui said.

'I'm in need of fantasies right now,' Tunjin said. 'I don't have much else.'

Nergui looked around them. He was beginning to feel exposed, sitting motionless in this dark parkland. It was not a rational anxiety – if anyone was watching them, then they would just wait until Nergui was gone before tackling Tunjin. But there was something about the vast silence of this place that made him uneasy.

'We need to find a way out of this,' he said finally.

'From where I'm sitting, I don't see too many options,' Tunjin said. 'You carry on with your investigations, but how much progress do you really expect to make?'

'I don't know,' Nergui said. 'Some. There are some I know are bent, some I know are on his payroll. I'll get them eventually. But whether I'll get them all—'

'There'll be no way of knowing, unless we take him down.'

Nergui knew that he was right. There had been a time, even when he had started his enquiry, when he had thought that now finally he was in a position to deal with this properly. He had thought that Tunjin's actions and their fallout might have given him the opportunity and the ammunition he had been seeking for all those years. But he should have realised that Tunjin would not have messed up so easily. He should have realised quite how deeply ingrained the problem would be. He could catch a few bent officers – maybe even most of them – but unless he was confident he had identified them all, the problem would never be resolved.

Tunjin climbed slowly to his feet, hoisting the canvas bag over his shoulder. 'Thanks for the food,' he said. 'I'll keep in touch. I don't want to use the mobile any more than I can avoid because I don't know how traceable it might be. And I want to save the battery for as long as possible. But if I want to make contact, I'll just send you a text – just "Meet" and that'll mean – let's stick with the same time – that'll mean 11.30p.m. here.'

'I'll bring some better food next time,' Nergui said. 'If I've got a bit of notice.'

'Glad to hear it. This selection's not very impressive.'

'Tunjin,' Nergui said, 'I don't know what you've got in mind, but whatever it is, good luck.'

Tunjin shrugged. 'I don't know either,' he said, 'but thanks anyway.'

He turned and began to trudge slowly back in the direction of the lake. Nergui sat, unmoving, watching Tunjin's bulk disappear into the enveloping blackness, ready to draw his gun if there was any sign of trouble. But the sound of Tunjin's soft footsteps faded, lost in the faint rustle of the breeze, and there was no indication of any disturbance.

Nergui sat for a few moments, listening hard, wondering whether Tunjin had made his way out of the park safely. For a moment, he considered trying to follow him but he knew that this would be madness. There was little he could do to protect Tunjin, who could look after his own interests as well as anyone.

Finally, Nergui rose and made his way slowly back

across the park, past the square block of the State Youth Theatre. He lifted himself back over the fence and out into the street. It was nearly half past midnight. The road was deserted, and even the Bayangol Hotel looked as if it was closed for the night. There were dim lights in the foyer, and the occasional bedroom light, but otherwise little sign of life.

Nergui's car was as he had left it. He unlocked it and climbed inside, mulling over his conversation with Tunjin. What about Doripalam? Could he be trusted? Nergui was as confident as he could be that Doripalam, of all people, was straight. But someone had betrayed Tunjin. Someone had realised what was going on, and had fingered Tunjin as the individual responsible. And there was no question that, as one of the most sensitive cases they had handled for years, the details of the Muunokhoi would have been available only to a selected few – certainly to none of those whom Nergui had so far identified as potentially corrupt.

So who was it?

Nergui jammed his car into reverse and pulled slowly back out of the parking space, and then drove forward out of the hotel car park. As he passed the entrance, his eye was caught by two figures, both wearing long rain coats and hats, standing in the shadows outside the lobby of the hotel.

Something about the figures struck him as incongruous, out of place in the scene. They didn't look like hotel staff. He pulled out into the street and up towards the junction with Peace Avenue, hoping that Tunjin had managed to get away safely.

CHAPTER 14

It was already growing light by the time they reached the outskirts of the city. Doripalam was glad to complete the journey, after hours of the beating cold and noise from the open windscreen. Conversation, other than the occasional shouted exchange, had been virtually impossible. In the end, Doripalam had simply closed his eyes, though far from any possibility of sleep, and listened to the endless roar of the engine and the wind.

'Where to?' Luvsan shouted. 'Back to HQ?'

'I think we have to,' Doripalam said. 'Get this thing in for repair, for one thing.'

They came into town, driving with the river on their right and then, above them, the majestic Chinese-style temple of Gesar Süm, turned left past Liberty Square and the taxi stand, and then right down towards Sukh Bataar Square. The rain had long passed and it looked set to be a fine day, just a few wisps of cloud in the translucent sky.

They parked the truck behind Headquarters and Luvsan went in to organise the repair of the windscreen. Doripalam stood for a moment by the front entrance, looking out across the Square, empty and silent in the early morning sunlight. He felt momentarily overwhelmed, struggling to come to grips with the responsibilities that were facing him. He understood his job as a police officer, as a detective. He knew what that was all about. Carrying out investigations, trying to get to the truth. That was – not exactly straightforward, but at least comprehensible. But now, in this job, he was never sure of his priorities. It was the political stuff that confused him – the constantly shifting balance of interests and demands. The kind of thing that Nergui had managed with his eyes closed.

And at the moment it was just one problem after another. The whole Muunokhoi debacle. All the publicity around Gavaa's disappearance. The horrific murder of his mother – so far, ironically, accorded less attention than the apparently much more mundane absence of her son. The possibility that she was being threatened – but by whom and why? And now, on top of everything, Tunjin going missing. It was as if a whole year's worth of serious cases had descended on him at once, with no clear rhyme or reason.

And then there was Nergui and his supposed enquiry. What was that all about? An attempt to use the Muunokhoi mess as an opportunity to root out whatever corruption there was in this squad? Doripalam knew that, if he had any dignity, he should have offered his resignation already in the face of Nergui's interference. But he also knew – because he knew Nergui – that there was likely to be more to this than was immediately apparent.

'Where now?'

Luvsan was standing behind him, holding two

plastic cups of steaming coffee. For the first time, it occurred to Doripalam that he'd been up all night. And a pretty stressful night at that. The sense of tiredness swept over him like a wave, and he felt suddenly removed from everything around him.

He took the coffee from Luvsan. 'Thanks. You must be exhausted. I know I am, and you did all the driving.'

Luvsan took a sip of his own drink. 'Can always manage without much sleep. One of my few talents.'

Doripalam yawned. 'Wish it was one I shared,' he said. 'I guess we should go and have a look at Tunjin's apartment. I take it there's no more news.'

'Doesn't seem to be. I checked quickly with the duty officer. We've got the flat all cordoned off. Spoken to the neighbours and to those who witnessed the original disturbance, but it's not much clearer. We can get the full story once we're there, I guess.'

Luvsan had procured them an alternative police vehicle, a marked car. Inevitably, he turned on the siren as they made their way through the centre of the city, even though it was still early morning and the streets were largely deserted. Doripalam regarded him with amused disapproval but said nothing.

Tunjin's flat was only a few minutes away and they were able to park without difficulty outside the apartment block. Even if Doripalam hadn't known the address, it would not have been difficult to identify the building. The glass fronted doors to the lobby had both been shattered, the doors now covered with temporary boarding.

'They told me on the phone that there'd been some

shooting,' Doripalam said. 'It looks as if they were shooting their way in.'

There was a uniformed officer stationed at the door, who recognised Doripalam without having to be shown any ID. 'There's one of your people upstairs, sir,' he said.

Doripalam gestured to the doors. 'This was where the shots were fired?'

'Yes, sir. It looks as if the doors were locked or jammed in some way, and the intruders shot at the glass to make their entry.'

Doripalam glanced at Luvsan. 'The doors were locked or jammed? This was in the middle of the day?'

'Yes, sir. Late morning.'

'That wouldn't have been normal, then? The doors being locked, I mean.'

'No, sir. I mean, security here is normally pretty lax, apparently. Nothing to stop anybody entering the building during daylight hours.'

Doripalam nodded. 'Thanks. Who are you letting in at the moment?'

'Residents only, that's my orders. Not making ourselves very popular because we're not even allowing in residents' guests for the moment.'

'Keep it that way. I don't want the press in here just yet. And I wouldn't put it past some of them to try to do a deal with some of the residents to talk their way in.'

'That's what I thought, sir. We've been very rigorous.'

'Glad to hear it. Keep it up.' As always, Doripalam was uncomfortably aware that this commanding officer stuff was far from natural to him. The young officer didn't appear to notice anything, though, even if Luvsan looked mildly amused.

'Come on,' Doripalam said. 'Let's go and see the flat. First floor.'

They made their way up the open, faux marble stairs to the first floor. It was far from a smart address. The lobby area had been full of junk, all of which, other than the scatterings of broken glass, presumably pre-dated the disturbance. The whole place could do with a new coat of paint, he thought, looking around at the scuffed walls, the worn floor tiles, the chipped woodwork.

It was, again, not difficult to spot Tunjin's flat. A bored looking uniformed officer was sitting on a hard wooden chair outside, a folded newspaper in his hand. He looked up quizzically as the two men approached.

'Doripalam.' He flicked open his ID and waved it in front of the seated officer. 'Serious Crimes Team. I understand one of my people's inside.'

It took the uniformed officer a moment to take all this in. Then he jumped to his feet, scattering the newspaper untidily to the floor. 'Yes, sir. Please go in.'

Doripalam smiled and pushed open the door. His smile faded almost immediately. Partly it was the smell. Not an overwhelmingly unpleasant smell – Doripalam had had all too frequent cause to enter rooms containing corpses, and this was nothing like that. But it was there, nonetheless. A scent of decay, of organic matter left too long in the spring warm, a smell of sour milk and rotting vegetation, underpinned with a strong smell of alcohol.

The appearance of the apartment matched the

smell. It was clear that, however much the flat might have been ransacked by the intruders, it had hardly been a model of organised living beforehand. There were plates of half-eaten food scattered on every surface, buzzing with flies. There were several empty or nearly empty vodka bottles. Clothes – presumably dirty – were scattered about the floor.

But, on top of all that, the room had been systematically turned over. Drawers from the cabinets lay emptied across the floor and sofa. Pictures had been pulled from the walls. A cupboard stood with its doors agape and its contents tossed, apparently casually, to the ground.

In the middle of all this, a young officer stood, a clipboard in his hand, apparently making an inventory. He looked up as Doripalam and Luvsan entered. 'Good morning,' he said. 'Sorry it's not more homely.'

Doripalam carefully made his way through the scattered debris towards the young officer. 'Good morning, Batzorig. You pulled this one, then?'

'Looks like it,' Batzorig said. 'Not quite sure what I did to deserve it.'

'Something pretty bad, clearly,' Doripalam said. 'So this is how Tunjin lived, then?'

'Well, not entirely, to be fair,' Batzorig said. 'He can take responsibility for the food and the booze, but probably not for the emptying of the drawers and cupboards.'

'No.' Doripalam looked around carefully. 'It's been ransacked pretty thoroughly. So they were after something. Do we have any idea what?'

Batzorig shook his head. 'It's difficult to know what

Tunjin might have had that they would have been interested in,' he said.

'Unless it was something he'd taken from HQ,' Luvsan said, from behind.

Doripalam turned. 'Like what?'

Luvsan shrugged. 'No idea. Files, paperwork? Who knows?'

'The last time I saw Tunjin,' Doripalam said, 'he didn't give me the impression he was intending to follow up assiduously on his paperwork.' He turned back to Batzorig. 'And we've no idea what might have happened to Tunjin?'

'None at all,' Batzorig said. 'He's just vanished.'

'With the intruders?'

'We don't think so.'

'So what's the story?' Doripalam said. 'Walk me through it.'

'It's an odd one,' Batzorig said. 'From what we've been able to piece together from talking to neighbours and passers-by, there was some sort of disturbance yesterday. One of the residents of this block – coming back from the market, I think – discovered she couldn't get in the front entrance. It's normally left unlocked during the day. She tried to unlock it with her own key, but the door was jammed. She asked a passer-by for some assistance, but he couldn't do anything. It looked as if, as well as locking the doors, someone had jammed a broomstick into the handles.'

'To stop it being opened from outside?'

'Exactly. Anyway, a bit of a crowd started to gather. The general consensus was that it was kids – you know, youth of today, all that stuff. Then, in the middle of all that, with this small group milling about outside the doorway, two men came up, dressed in dark glasses, baseball caps, leather jackets, you know the kind of uniform—?'

Doripalam looked up at him. He knew the uniform. The hard men, the hired help, all over the seamier side of the city.

'These two guys came up, gestured for the crowd to move aside, and then pulled out a handgun each and shot out the glass in the doors. I think the crowd dispersed pretty quickly.'

'And no one thought to call us?' Luvsan said from behind.

'Well, yes, they did eventually. But I think they were all a bit shocked. Anyway, from what we can tell, the two men cleared and opened the doors, made their way up here, kicked down Tunjin's door and got in here. We don't know quite what happened after that because no one was getting too close to find out. But we assumed they didn't find Tunjin and they went through the flat pretty quickly – probably only a few minutes. We've got some witnesses who then saw the two men exit the front of the block, probably five minutes or so later. There was no one with them so we presume they didn't find Tunjin. The two men then ran down to the far end of the block. There was the sound of more gunfire, and somebody reported the sound of a motorbike speeding away. Nothing more after that. It looks as if the two men had a car parked somewhere, but nobody seems to have seen them leave. We've got one witness down in the end block who thinks he may have seen something.'

'So we think Tunjin might have made an escape on a motorbike?' Luvsan said, incredulously. He was clearly struggling to picture the image.

'Who knows? The motorbike might have just been a coincidence. But it certainly looks as if – well, either he escaped or he wasn't here in the first place.'

'The gunshots at the far end of the blocks suggest that they were trying to stop someone,' Doripalam pointed out. 'Has anyone had a look down there yet?'

Batzorig nodded. 'Yes. There's a patch of waste ground out there. And an encampment – one of the permanent ones. We found an old man—' He stopped to glance at his notebook. 'Agypar, apparently. Lives in the end block and happened to be down in the utility room in the basement at the time. Said he heard some gunshots and peered out. Saw two men, one of them apparently injured. Looked as if he'd been shot in the knee.'

'Tunjin?'

Batzorig shook his head. 'Definitely not. I think Tunjin's build would have been unmistakeable. This man was nothing like that. More likely to have been one of our two intruders. The old man thought he was wearing a leather jacket, but he was too far away to see anything for sure. When the old man realised it really was gunfire, he made himself scarce.'

'What about the motorbike?'

'Knew nothing about it,' he said. 'Said he didn't see or hear anything of that kind. There were a few bikes chained up there, but most of them looked as if they'd been standing there a long time. There were some tyre tracks, but it was difficult to be sure how recent they were.'

'Any sign of blood?' Doripalam said.

'We found a few traces on the ground. We've sent a sample to be analysed, see if it matches Tunjin's records.'

'If the old man's right, it sounds as if Tunjin might have been doing the injuring, rather than the other way round.' That wouldn't have been particularly surprising, Doripalam thought. For all Tunjin's failings, he knew how to look after himself.

He looked round the room. 'I take it the scene of crime people have done their stuff?' he said.

'Pretty much so,' Batzorig said. 'The only clear prints we can find match Tunjin's, but there are smeared prints that would indicate the intruders were wearing gloves. Not much else. No evidence of any kind of struggle – not easy to be sure given the state of the place, but there's nothing to contradict the assumption that Tunjin wasn't here when they arrived.'

'I guess in that case,' Doripalam said, 'we can do Tunjin a favour and get the place cleaned up. Don't suppose he'll object if we get someone to do his washing up for him.'

'I still wasn't sure if it was an excuse,' she said. 'I mean, as I said, it seemed a little late in the evening for a bail out call, but I suppose that depends on what it was you thought you might be bailing out of.'

He put down his espresso and looked at her. 'I don't think I'm even going to try to follow that,' he said. 'I had a late night last night, and I'm not at my sharpest.'

Sarangarel laughed. 'Well, so long as you really

were working, I won't be too offended. But thanks for the offer of lunch anyway.'

Nergui nodded, wondering what it was that had prompted him to make the call that morning. Partly just straightforward guilt. He had felt genuinely bad about terminating their date the previous evening, even if he hadn't been entirely clear what it was he was terminating. Also, he thought – and this was another distant echo of the less admirable part of his character – there was still some curiosity, reignited by his midnight conversation with Tunjin. It was strange, almost a little too strange, that these ghosts from his past should have re-emerged now.

That icy midnight raid. Sarangarel terrified and confused. The small hours phone call that told him that Gansukh was dead. The sense, following that call, that a prize that had been almost within his grasp had suddenly vanished, like some cheap conjuring trick. And the realisation that, if Gansukh's death had really not been an accident, then Nergui's team was more corrupt, had been infiltrated further, than he had ever imagined possible.

Gansukh's death had marked the start of what Nergui now felt to be the longest sustained period of failure in his career. This was not to say that Nergui had carried out his role badly. The Serious Crimes Team had gone from strength to strength, and – certainly by comparison with other parts of the civilian police – developed an enviable reputation for both integrity and effectiveness. Nergui had been promoted to the Ministry simply because he was one of the few senior police officers who was respected and trusted by all parts of the political establishment.

But Nergui himself felt that this was all a sham. As the years went by, he increasingly felt as if he was operating with one hand tied behind his back. It was as if he had been given a licence to operate so long as certain unspecified boundaries weren't transgressed. Ordinary crime was fair game, organised crime was off-limits. And whenever he got close to the boundaries, whenever he might have the makings of a case against Muunokhoi or one of his wealthy cronies, somehow things fell apart. Evidence went missing. Confidential information suddenly appeared on the front pages of the newspapers. Witnesses disappeared or refused to speak. Every time, he somehow found himself standing on quicksand.

For Nergui, who had been accustomed to playing by his own rules even in the dark days of communism, this was a shock. But he was a pragmatist. All he could do was fight the battle, make whatever inroads he could, bide his time until an opportunity presented itself.

Others, he suspected, had been less stoic. He could never be sure, but he suspected that Tunjin's personal and professional decline had started with his unintentional mistake over Gansukh. Though he had never said so, Nergui believed that Tunjin had blamed himself for Gansukh's death. Though he had always been a very capable officer, he had never seemed the same, never displayed the same commitment and focus as in those days. For years, Nergui had never been sure whether Tunjin's guilt was that of the perpetrator or the victim – that is, whether Tunjin himself had already been corrupted. Over the years, he had investigated

Tunjin repeatedly but – although his increasing drinking and dissolute behaviour might have made him a natural blackmail victim – there had never been any evidence, substantive or even circumstantial, that he was bent. But it was only with the recent debacle over Muunokhoi's trial that Nergui had finally been convinced that Tunjin had been waging his own quiet vendetta over the years. And maybe now when Nergui finally trusted Tunjin fully, it was all too late.

And that brought him back here, full circle, with the woman who had been here at the start of all this and who had been there, incredibly, as the trial judge when it all came to a head. Who said that ghosts didn't exist?

And now they were sipping coffee and eating American-style club sandwiches in the Casablanca café, only yards from where he had met Tunjin the previous night.

She finished her caffè latte and smiled at him over the table. 'You keep doing this,' she said. 'You take me out and then you sit staring moodily into space. It's company of a kind but it's not particularly flattering.'

He shook his head. 'Sorry. I've a lot on my mind. I should stay indoors until I provide better company.'

'Is this about your call last night? It must have been a late night for you.'

He shrugged. 'I've had a lot worse. And, yes, it's partly about that. But it's about a whole stack of things actually.' He paused, wondering whether to go on. 'But mainly about Muunokhoi.'

She put down her glass slowly and stared at him. 'Muunokhoi? What about him?'

'I'm not entirely sure about the ethics of this,' he said, 'given your professional role.'

'I don't see an issue,' she said, 'unless you're going to draw my attention to some misadministration of the trial, in which case this isn't the appropriate forum, I don't think. But, otherwise, the trial is over. If there's any subsequent trial, I won't be involved. So I don't think there's a problem.'

He nodded, as if thinking this over. 'It's nothing to do with the trial,' he said. 'Well, not directly. It's broader than that. It's – well, in part, it's about Muunokhoi and Gansukh.'

'Gansukh?' But she spoke the name without surprise, almost as if she had been waiting for the subject to arise. Perhaps waiting for a long time.

Nergui swallowed the last of his espresso. 'Maybe we should go for a walk,' he said.

CHAPTER 15

After the previous day's rain, the new day dawned bright and chilly. Tunjin pulled his coat more tightly around him and hunched himself into the corner of the desolate room.

The cold of the night and the unyielding hardness of the floor had kept him from sleep. Instead, he had propped himself against the wall, his eyes fixed on the empty doorway, his ears straining for any sound of movement.

Someone had been watching Nergui and himself in the park, he was convinced of it. He was not really surprised. Nergui's flat would be under surveillance by these people – they would be trying to keep tabs on his enquiry as best they could, though Tunjin knew that Nergui would make this very difficult. Nergui would have done his very effective best to ensure that he was not being followed to the park, but it would not have been very difficult to keep track of a solitary car travelling through the city at that time of night. Tunjin was unsure what kinds of resources Muunokhoi would have access to, but he knew they would be plentiful.

It was fortunate, therefore, that no action had been taken against them in the park. They would not have known, initially, that Nergui's rendezvous was with

Tunjin, and their priority was probably simply to keep Nergui under observation rather than confirm his suspicions that he was being followed. So if – or, more likely, when – they had recognised Tunjin, they would not have wanted to take action until the two men had parted.

And that was where Tunjin had been too sharp for them. He had banked on the fact that the observers would not be particularly close at hand, since they would not have wanted to risk being spotted. On leaving Nergui, Tunjin had moved with surprising agility and light-footedness to hide himself in the thick bushes surrounding the play area. He had watched Nergui as he sat waiting – clearly wondering whether he himself should follow Tunjin, which thankfully he had not chosen to do – and then as he had slowly left across the park. Nergui's hesitation had been helpful, buying Tunjin some time before the pursuers were able to step into the open.

They had appeared a few minutes later. Two men, dressed in leather jackets, one carrying a mobile phone, the other carrying what Tunjin assumed to be a gun. The two men had stopped and looked around, obviously concluding that Tunjin had departed and unsure which direction he had taken. Tunjin had wondered, nervously, whether the two men might be armed with night sights or infra-red gear but it appeared not. People always tended to underestimate Tunjin's abilities, and not for the first time he was profoundly grateful for this.

One of his great qualities was his patience, and this once again proved his saviour. He remained concealed in the bushes, scarcely breathing, for long minutes, as the two men looked around, spoke on the mobile and then departed, taking what they thought to have been Tunjin's path.

He was tempted to emerge then, but he knew that could prove suicidal. When the men failed to find him further out across the park, they might well return. So, instead, he remained concealed in the bushes, watching carefully, remaining as motionless as he could. As expected, after ten or fifteen minutes, the men reappeared, talking to each other in a whisper, seeming mildly agitated. They paused, looked around, then set off in the opposite direction. Tunjin waited another thirty minutes or so, having lowered himself to the earth, and then, when he was sure that they were not returning, he eventually emerged. He made his exit from the park and walking silently though the city streets, his senses alert for any sign of pursuit, he had made his way back here.

The experience had confirmed his view that he couldn't stay here for much longer. Apart from the sheer physical discomfort, he did not know for how long this place would be secure. Sooner or later, someone would stumble across him – maybe a police patrolman making a routine examination of this run-down area. And at that point he would no longer be confident of remaining undetected.

No, as he had told Nergui the night before, the only way forward was to take some positive action, to take the initiative. He still had no idea what he meant by this, but he needed to do something. Even if he failed at least he would feel in control, at least he would feel that he was making the running.

He dragged himself slowly to his feet, looking down at his stained and grubby clothing. How long was it since he had had a drink? It seemed like an eternity. It was difficult to tell whether he felt better as a result. His life was in so much of a mess that any kind of oblivion seemed attractive as an alternative.

But he had to be positive. He opened the canvas bag that Nergui had given him, and took a large gulp of the water. He began to chew slowly on the end of slightly stale bread. Access to food – even food as primitive as this – began to make him feel slightly more human. Outside, the day was brightening, sunlight beginning to stream in through the doors and windows. There was no sound other than an occasional rustling, presumably of mice or rats.

Okay, he thought. Another day. Maybe his last day on earth. But surely, surely there was something he could do, some positive action he could take.

All he had to do was think of it.

By day, the park looked more welcoming. It had seen better days, certainly, and even in the bright spring sunlight its facilities were clearly worn and run-down. But at least it looked like a place that had been designed for pleasure, rather than the vast black waste-land it had seemed the previous night.

They had entered the park by the entrance opposite the Bayangol Hotel, and had walked slowly across to the play area. Neither had spoken for some minutes, Nergui unsure where to begin and Sarangarel suffi-ciently patient to wait until he had found the words.

Nergui led them across to the row of benches by the

play area, and they both sat down. It was not, he thought, the bench where he had sat with Tunjin the night before, but maybe two or three along.

'I'm not sure I know where to begin,' Nergui said.

'I think I'd guessed that,' she said, 'from the fact that you hadn't done so.'

'I suppose I need to begin with Gansukh.'

She nodded. 'I thought you might. I've put all that behind me. It's a different life. A different person.'

'I know it is, and the last thing I want to do is drag you back there—'

'But you're going to.'

'I suppose I am,' he said. 'I don't know if you remember, but – well, when we were questioning Gansukh, I asked you some questions about any relations he might have with Muunokhoi.'

'I remember,' she said. 'I thought you were insane.'

He nodded, looking up at the slowly turning ferris wheel. He had been up there only once, a long time ago, enduring the agonisingly slow elevation, seeing the breadth of the city slowly opening out before him, the texture of the streets and buildings, the untidy sprawl of the *ger* camps, the vast expanse of the steppes and mountains beyond. 'I know you did,' he said. 'Do you still think that?'

There was a long pause. So long, in fact, that Nergui became convinced that she was not going to respond. Above them, the ferris wheel continued its silent motion.

'No,' she said at last. 'No, I don't.'

He looked at her. 'You think he was working for Muunokhoi?'

'I know he was.'

It was Nergui's turn to be silent. There were some young children, scarcely more than toddlers, playing on the swings and roundabout off to their left. The sound of their high pitched voices carried faintly across the grass. Behind them, there was the deep blue of the lake, glittering in the midday sun. 'How do you know?' he said at last.

'I know,' she said. 'I don't mean just – oh, you know, women's intuition, that sort of thing. I mean evidence. Of a sort, anyway.'

'You should have told us, if you knew. You might have helped save his life.' The words were out of his mouth before he could stop them.

She laughed. 'Do you think that would have been an incentive? At the time, that was the last thing I wanted. But, no, in any case, I didn't know then. But I do know now.'

'How do you know?'

'As far as I'm concerned,' she said, as though embarking on a different narrative, 'I'm not that person any more. I'm not the person who married Gansukh. I don't think I would be anyway, even if – all that hadn't happened. Our marriage wouldn't have survived. When you arrested him, I realised that I wasn't surprised and that – other than worrying about what might become of me – I wasn't that sorry.'

Nergui nodded, wondering where all this was leading.

'But, of course,' she went on, 'that's not quite how the world out there sees it. I'm still Gansukh's widow. I haven't remarried. We're still – in some people's eyes –

a couple.' She paused. The breeze ruffled her dark hair, toying with the folds of the long silk dress she was wearing. 'He had a cousin who died recently, down in the Gobi. Someone I'd met – well, only once or twice, as far as I can remember, years ago. But he'd left some possessions – originally intended for Gansukh. But when Gansukh died, he apparently changed his will and left them to me. So, a couple of months ago, I received an unexpected parcel through the post.'

Nergui was watching her closely now, struck by the intensity with which she was recounting the story.

'The parcel contained a stack of different things. Some petty trinkets that, for some reason, he'd decided to leave to Gansukh and then to me. A small amount of money – there were few other living relatives, apparently. And, with all of that, a stack of papers and documentation.'

'What sort of papers?'

'These were, as far as I could tell, things that Gansukh had deposited with his cousin, years ago, presumably for safe keeping. Do you remember that, not long after Gansukh's death, our apartment was burgled?'

This was news to him. 'Burgled? I never knew that. You must have reported it?'

'Of course. But this was – what? – two or three months after Gansukh had died. I'd started to move on. I didn't associate the burglary with Gansukh's death – just put it down to another instance of the bad luck that seemed to be following me around. So I just reported it to my local station. They took down all the details, but told me it was probably just an opportunist robbery. Not much chance of catching the perpetrators, they said.'

'No wonder the general public has such faith in us policemen,' Nergui said. Inwardly, though, he was cursing. The robbery had never been reported to him. Probably just oversight – no one had thought to link this incident with the arrest weeks before. And he was all too aware that, given any opportunity, the local forces were often only too keen to withhold information from the arrogant bunch in headquarters. Or maybe, once again, there was a more sinister explanation.

'I didn't take it too seriously,' she continued. 'They ransacked the place but by then there was very little worth stealing. Bit of old jewellery, a few dollars in cash. Not much more.'

'But you think they were looking for something else?'

'I don't know,' she said. 'But what I do know is that, before he died – before he was arrested – Gansukh had made a point of packaging up a stack of formal documents and sending them, in a sealed package, to a cousin he'd scarcely met.'

Nergui nodded. If you were looking to hide something, then an unknown cousin, across the other side of the country, might well be a better bet than any conventional safe deposit box. Particularly if you were looking to hide it from someone like Muunokhoi.

'I'm not sure why he did it,' she said. 'I think it was some sort of insurance policy – but it's typical of Gansukh that he wouldn't really have thought it through.'

'What kind of papers are we talking about?' Nergui said.

'Well, it's not really a smoking gun,' she said. 'At least not in the sense that it provides any definitive evidence of Gansukh's dealings with Muunokhoi. But, as far as I can understand it, there are copies of notes and paperwork that do at least show there were commercial dealings between Gansukh's businesses and Muunokhoi.'

'Legitimate dealings?' Nergui stretched out his legs and leaned back on the bench. Today, his characteristic dark suit was offset by pale blue socks.

'It's difficult to be sure,' Sarangarel said. 'I mean, yes, in the sense that the paperwork includes – you know, invoice copies, payment details, that kind of thing, relating to what look like legitimate transactions. Import–export business, mainly, as far as I can see. But it's all relating to goods that Gansukh had no involvement in, as far as I know.'

Nergui straightened up in his seat and looked at her. 'How do you mean?'

'Well, for example, there are invoices relating to the import of various foodstuffs. That was never a business that Gansukh got involved in – too difficult, all that perishable stuff. He was always very clear about that – liked to get things that had a decent shelf life. Not surprising, given how useless he was at selling it.' She smiled.

'So you think the paperwork was a cover for something else?'

She shrugged. 'That sort of thing's more your line. But it doesn't make much sense as it stands. So, yes, I think there's something of that sort. I think he needed some sort of cover to justify the money that was being paid over, and that was it.'

'It doesn't prove much in itself,' Nergui said.

'Not in the legal sense, no,' she said. 'I don't think I'd be very impressed by it if it was presented as evidence in a case I was presiding over. But I went through it very carefully and did a little checking. There were various companies involved and all of them were either directly owned by or closely associated with Muunokhoi. There's little doubt in my mind that he commissioned many of Gansukh's shady operations.'

Nergui nodded. 'It's probably more than we've been able to get on Muunokhoi before, even if it's not exactly definitive. I wonder why he was so lax in dealing with Gansukh.'

'I don't think he was, particularly. I imagine that he'd have had dealings of this kind with countless suppliers. All this material was well presented and would have just got lost in the records of most companies. You wouldn't notice anything odd about it. I think Muunokhoi made the same mistake that everyone did in dealing with Gansukh.'

'Which was?'

'He overestimated him. Gansukh was brilliant at the front, at the bluff. People were only too ready to believe that he was a world-class businessman, a big operator. But he wasn't at all.'

'Muunokhoi would have had him checked out.'

'Of course, and that's probably why he only got some limited, pretty risky business. Probably the stuff that no one else was keen to touch. But even so, I'm willing to bet that Muunokhoi thought that Gansukh had more substance than he really did. I think Gansukh's dealings with Muunokhoi's companies would have been notice-able simply because there wouldn't have been a lot else. But I also think that, as always, Gansukh was just trying to be a bit too clever. He'd have known that Muunokhoi wasn't one for leaving any traces, so he gathered up all the relevant paperwork and hid it – sent it off to this cousin. Then he had some kind of insurance policy if things went wrong.'

'As they did. So why didn't he use it?'

She shrugged. 'Maybe he was just about to. I suspect it was intended as a last resort, for when he was really in trouble. This was his way of trying to shift the responsibility – he was always very good at that – of having at least some evidence that he wasn't the big noise behind all this.'

'So that would have been part of the deal he would have offered us?'

'I think so. But he didn't get the chance.'

'No.' Nergui looked out across the sunlit park. There were children on the playground. A group of old men in traditional robes – looking far too hot for the warm spring day – were sitting smoking on one of the benches, apparently content simply to enjoy each other's company in silence. It all seemed a world away from these machinations.

'Do you think Muunokhoi knows that this paper-work exists?'

'He knows that something exists.' She spoke with a calm certainty that startled him.

'What do you mean?'

She didn't answer immediately. Instead, she climbed slowly to her feet, the bright silk dress shaking softly in the breeze. 'Let's walk down to the lake,' she said.

Nergui rose and followed her without speaking, assuming that she would begin to talk in her own time. She said nothing until they reached the edge of the grey water. 'It needs cleaning,' she said.

Nergui came to stand beside her in silence. The water rippled gently in the sunshine, scattering glittering reflections of the midday sun.

'You're as sharp as ever, aren't you? You knew there was something.'

It was only as she spoke that Nergui realised that she was right. He had known that there was something. That was part of the reason – though only part – why he had been keen to spend time with her again. That was, he thought, why all these ghosts kept rising unbidden into his mind.

'I suppose you're right,' he said. 'I did know that there was something. But I don't know what it is.'

'I was lying, earlier,' she said. 'When I claimed that I was a different person, that I'd put all of that behind me. Of course, it's true in some ways. But in other ways – probably more important ways – it's not true at all. I'm still the same person I was that night when you came barging into our flat.'

Nergui said nothing. There was very little he could say about that, after all this time, all these years.

'And I suppose,' she went on, 'the other thing that I haven't wanted to admit to myself is that – despite everything – I loved Gansukh. I mean, I know he was a crook – a small time petty crook, at that. And what he did – well, at the time it felt as if it had destroyed my life. Though in the end the opposite was probably true. But because of that I spent a long time trying to persuade myself – and probably everyone else – that I really didn't care for Gansukh at all.'

Nergui looked across at her, standing at the edge of the lake. She suddenly looked, he thought, much more like the woman he had met ten years before – vulnerable, confused, lost.

'But I did. There was a lot about him to like – he was good company, lively. And I think he genuinely cared for me. Part of what drove him to do the things he did was to try to make a better life for the two of us. So I did care about him. And I did care that he died.' She paused. 'And most of all I did care that he was killed.'

'He killed himself,' Nergui said. 'That was the verdict.'

She turned and looked at him. 'You didn't believe that, even then,' she said. 'You certainly don't believe it now.'

Nergui shrugged. 'I've no evidence,' he said. 'But, no, his death was always too convenient.' He wondered, in the light of what she had just said, whether his words sounded unduly callous.

'Muunokhoi had him killed,' she said, simply. 'And it was one of your men killed him.'

Nergui nodded. The logic was inescapable, as it always had been. If it was true that Muunokhoi was responsible for the death, then it had indeed been one of Nergui's men who had betrayed and killed him.

'It's been eating away at me,' she said. 'For years. That knowledge. I thought I'd managed to put it behind me, but then when I came face to face with Muunokhoi in court, it all rose up again – it all rose up again, as potent as ever.'

'Surely it wasn't appropriate for you to be the presiding judge in Muunokhoi's case?' Nergui said.

'Of course it wasn't. But nobody but me – not even Muunokhoi himself – had made the connection. Why would they? It was a long time ago. I don't look like the same person. My name is different.'

'You should have declared an interest.' It was, he realised, a fatuous thing to say. But if you're a policeman, you try to uphold the law.

'Of course I should. But I didn't want to. I wanted – not revenge, but justice. I wanted to make sure that justice was done.'

'But it wasn't.'

'No. That was the worst point of all. To be so close, and then to have it all snatched away by what – incompetence? There I was, having to play the impartial judge, acknowledging Muunokhoi's case, badgering the poor man from the Prosecutor's Office who was clearly trying to defend the indefensible – and, well, in the end there was no choice. The trial had to be abandoned. You can't imagine how I felt.'

Nergui nodded. 'I think, in a way at least, that I can. I've been trying to bring this man to justice for nearly two decades.'

'I told myself that it was probably just as well,' she said. 'I'd put myself in an impossible position. It was insane. I mean, there was nothing wrong in principle with my presiding over the trial, given that there's no proven link between Muunokhoi and Gansukh. But in any case I don't think I'm entirely rational about all this.'

There was something about the way she spoke the final words that caught Nergui's attention. 'And what about since then?' he said. 'When you received these papers?'

There was a long pause. She stared out across the lake, watching the movement of the trees in the wind. 'I was – I don't know, thrown by the outcome of the trial. It had come so close and then – nothing. Back where we started and no way forward. And then, just a couple of weeks later, I received that package in the mail. It was as if all my unspoken prayers had been answered. I recognised that it wasn't hard evidence, but I began to think that it might provide some leverage—'

'What did you do?' Nergui asked quietly.

'I don't know what I was trying to do,' she said. 'I told you, I'm not rational about this. I'd received this material, but didn't know what to do with it. So I wrote, anonymously, to Muunokhoi – just addressed to him as Chief Executive of one of his companies – and told him I had some material linking him to Gansukh's death—'

There was a long silence. Nergui watched a flock of birds launch itself, with impressive synchronisation, from one of the trees at the far end of the park. 'You're sure he couldn't have traced the letter back to you?' he said.

'I don't see how. I mean, it was just a word-processed letter. I sent it from somewhere across town.'

'Why did you send it?' Nergui asked. 'I mean, what did you think you might achieve?'

'I don't know. I suppose I was just trying to provoke some sort of reaction. Make something happen. I didn't know how to make use of the information I had. I thought about taking it to the police, but I didn't think you'd take it seriously. I mean, there's no real substance to it.'

'You're probably right,' Nergui said. 'Though if you'd brought it to me, I'd have taken it seriously.'

'I thought about that afterwards. It was one reason why I turned up on what I thought was your doorstep. But I'm getting ahead of myself. The reason I sent the letter to Muunokhoi? Well, I didn't know how else to use the material. I suppose I thought it might shock him, jolt him out of his complacency. At least make him aware that there was someone out there who *knew*.'

'I don't think Muunokhoi's likely to be too jolted by a single anonymous letter,' Nergui said.

'No, well, neither did I. That was why I followed it up.'

He looked at her. 'Followed it up?'

'I know. But I sent – well, three letters in all. Including some photocopies of what I felt were likely to be the most suspicious of the materials I had, but hinting that this was just the tip of the iceberg. That it was only a matter of time before everything was exposed—'

Nergui whistled softly. 'And you were still confident that he couldn't track the letters back to you.'

'I don't know. I didn't think so, but I've only just begun to realise quite how much influence he has. And it's possible he'd made the link between me and Gansukh. I mean, between Judge Radnaa and Gansukh.' She paused. 'And I suppose that might really have rattled him. He might have realised that, for all his power, he could actually be vulnerable.' She paused, as if reluctant to follow through the logic of her own words. 'It was shortly after that that I received the first of those threats I told you about. It might have just been coincidence. I can't prove that there was any link with Muunokhoi—'

'But it was a coincidence,' Nergui said. 'Another one. Always another coincidence.' He paused. 'That would be Muunokhoi. One step ahead.' He looked around, realising that even in the bright spring morning he was feeling nervous, wondering if someone might be watching them. 'And if it's true, that's a serious matter. You need protection. Real protection. Not just a uniformed officer standing outside your apartment.'

She nodded. 'That's why I came to see you originally. I mean, all that stuff about looking for the police station. That was all nonsense. I was looking for you. Didn't realise you'd moved on. You were one of the few people I thought I could trust.'

That, he thought, was perhaps even more true than she realised. 'So why didn't you tell me?'

She shook her head. 'I don't know. I was embarrassed. I'd behaved stupidly. Maybe even compromised my position.' She hesitated. 'And I suppose, knowing you, I thought you'd work it out for yourself. As you seem to have done.'

'I'm not sure about that,' he said. 'But we've got there in the end, between us. And maybe you're right about him being rattled.' He thought about Tunjin, living who knew where, on the run from the same Muunokhoi. And he thought about Muunokhoi, engaging in apparently pointless vendettas with those who had tried and failed to bring him to justice, perhaps risking more than he knew.

'We need to take care of you,' he said, finally. 'We need to keep you safe. Where are the papers?'

'I think they're safe,' she said. 'I took them to my lawyer first, made sure everything was recorded, and then I lodged them in my bank, in a safe deposit box. Even if Muunokhoi somehow knows where they are, he won't be able to get at them without my co-operation.'

Nergui looked at her. 'Don't underestimate Muunokhoi's influence. I don't welcome the idea of him trying to secure your co-operation. Look, let's get you back to police headquarters. I'll speak to my contacts in the Ministry, try to find you a safe house where you can stay.' He didn't add that he could not trust the police to provide her with an uncompromised guard.

He began to lead her back from the lake, over towards the park entrance opposite the Hotel Bayangol where his car was parked. He felt genuinely nervous, aware of the possibility that they were being observed. Inwardly, he cursed her for not being open about this before, as he realised for the first time quite how vulnerable she had been for the preceding days.

They reached the gates in silence and hurried out into the street. Nergui's car was parked in the hotel car park, over the road. The street itself was deserted. He looked around then gently bundled her in front of him across to the hotel entrance, his hands already closing on the keys in his pocket.

The car came from nowhere. It had been parked parallel to Nergui's own, facing forwards, just a few yards closer to the car park entrance. Its engine started suddenly, and the car was thrown forward as if the handbrake had just been released. Its front wing hit Nergui a glancing blow and he was thrown across the car park, landing roughly on the concrete. At the same moment, the rear door of the car opened, the car slowed momentarily, and two hands grabbed Sarangarel, who was standing transfixed by the unexpected drama. Without a sound, she was dragged into the back of the car, the rear door slammed shut, and with a loud screech of tyres, the car spun round and back out into the street.

Nergui lay on the ground, semi-conscious, an agonising pain in his left leg, his brain scarcely working but his aching head telling him, over and over again, that it was too late, that it was all over, that he had failed.

CHAPTER 16

Doripalam was at home when the message came through, but he would rather have been almost anywhere else. It was unusual for him to take a day's leave in the week, and he had known right from the start that it was a mistake. But it was hardly as if he had a choice.

'I mean,' Solongo had said, 'they can surely manage without you for one day. It's not as if you don't put in the hours.'

He had wondered, momentarily, about pointing out the inconsistency in her position. It was Solongo, after all, who was always suggesting that his job was under threat, that everyone around him was waiting only for the opportunity to see him fail. It was Solongo who, without ever quite uttering a word on the subject, had persuaded him that he needed to be in the office every waking hour – and possibly some sleeping ones too – in order to demonstrate his indispensability.

But that, of course, was when she wanted him out of the house so that she could get on with living her own life. Today, she needed him in the house for the same reason.

Doripalam had known it would be excruciating from the moment she had first raised the idea. As it turned out, it was even worse than he had envisaged. And now, here he was, at four o'clock in the afternoon, sipping weak coffee while listening to what was quite possibly the most boring lecture he had ever been compelled to endure. Even the worst rigours of university and police training had not prepared him for this. And, more to the point, Solongo had certainly not prepared him for it.

In advance, she had made it sound almost interesting. As part of her continuing quest for social advancement – or, perhaps more accurately, her quest to combat the almost inevitable social decline she associated with Doripalam's chosen profession – Solongo had accepted an invitation to become a trustee of one of the city's major museums. It was an honour, as Doripalam was happy to acknowledge, and it carried certain responsibilities. One of which, apparently, was to play occasional host to the trustees' bimonthly committee meetings which rotated between the members' homes.

Doripalam had been willing to go along with the idea for Solongo's sake, and had been quite happy to throw his home open to any number of his wife's cultural associates. But he had failed to take account of her expectation that he should be present for the occasion.

As soon as they had begun to arrive that afternoon, Doripalam had recognised the type. They were precisely those who, twenty years before, would have been senior Party apparatchiks, and who had somehow made a seamless transition into the new order. Doripalam had nothing in common with these people. Except of course that, in his elevated role, he was now on the verge of becoming one of them.

He found himself, on his second glass of vodka, standing talking to Solongo and a tall, middle-aged man who was apparently some bigwig in one of the former state energy companies.

'Solongo tells me you're a policeman,' the man said, with a clear implication that Doripalam should really be out patrolling the streets.

'Sort of,' Doripalam said.

'Doripalam is Head of the Serious Crimes Team,' Solongo said. Doripalam was quite sure that she would have provided this information already, possibly several times, but for once he felt no qualms about her reaffirming his status.

The man nodded slowly, sipping his vodka. 'Were you the bunch behind the Muunokhoi debacle?'

Doripalam bit back his immediate response. 'We were involved in the arrest, yes. Those kind of charges fall under our jurisdiction.'

'He was only doing his job,' Solongo said. Doripalam glanced at her, slightly annoyed at her unnecessary defensiveness. On the other hand, in the circumstances, there was probably some need to be defensive.

'It's a scandal,' the man said. 'The whole thing was politically motivated.'

Doripalam raised an eyebrow, and took a deep swallow of his vodka. 'You think so?'

'Of course. It's the same as the way Putin's been behaving in Russia. You can't control the likes of Muunokhoi, so you persecute them.'

'I've persecuted nobody,' Doripalam said, trying to subdue his irritation.

'I don't mean you personally,' the man said, in a tone which indicated that Doripalam himself was below any kind of serious consideration. 'You're just an agent. But there are forces in the government that would want to bring Muunokhoi down, I'm sure.'

Doripalam shrugged. Perhaps the man was right, but it wasn't his own impression. From what he'd seen – and from what he'd heard from Nergui – the government largely just kowtowed to money and power, regardless of its source. Yes, the Justice Minister had tried to gain some political capital out of Muunokhoi's arrest, but that was only because the Minister had assumed that Muunokhoi's power was on the wane. Doripalam could easily imagine the Minister's subsequent flailing to regain the ground he had lost.

'If that was the case,' Doripalam said, 'they weren't very successful.'

'Just as well,' the man said. 'It's people like Muunokhoi who are the future of this country. He's smart, he's a step ahead.' He smiled, jabbing a finger towards Doripalam. 'And, as we all know, he's got people like you in his pocket.' The man rubbed his thumb and finger together in an unambiguous gesture.

Just for a moment, Doripalam gave serious consideration to the potential consequences of a senior police officer punching one of the great and the good on the nose. Even accepting those consequences, the idea was a tempting one.

He opened his mouth to respond – if only to point out the inconsistency of the man's arguments – but

Solongo was clearly one step ahead of him and was already steering the man off towards another group. She glared back at Doripalam, daring him to speak. Doripalam nodded and then smiled at her, suddenly recognising that she hated all this nonsense almost as much as he did.

It was a moment of unexpected warmth between them, not quite dissipated as she moved to engage in another tiresome conversation. It had struck him for the first time quite how hard she was working on his behalf. For a moment, he was tempted to break into her conversation, to make some acknowledgement of how much he appreciated, if not the effect, at least the good intentions behind what she was doing.

But as he moved forward he felt his mobile phone vibrate in his jacket pocket. He pulled it out, thumbed the keyboard and glanced at the message, feeling a chill down his spine as he did so.

When he did break into Solongo's conversation, his words were very different from those he had planned only moments before.

'I'm sorry,' he said. 'I've got to go. It's Nergui. He's been in an accident.' He turned away quickly before she could respond.

Minutes later, he was making his hurried way out of the flat and down the stairs. It would probably be a while, he thought, before he and Solongo would be able to recapture that brief moment of mutual warmth and support. For that matter, it would probably be a while before she was prepared to speak to him again.

*

The house wasn't quite what Tunjin had expected. It was an impressive enough place, but he had expected – well, something more grandiose, more impressive. Something in keeping with Muunokhoi's status. This was, admittedly, only one of several residences Muunokhoi possessed, although, from Tunjin's recollection of the files, this was the place he was most likely to call home.

There had been something in the files, too, about the history of the place. As far as Tunjin could recollect, the house had originally belonged to one of the bigwigs in the Party, in the days when communist grandees lived in places like this. It was, Tunjin supposed, a summer house, a dacha, located a few miles outside the heat and fumes of the city centre, but close enough to allow the occupier to continue working in the city.

It was a wooden construction, a chalet design, with long sweeping rooflines, tucked away amongst the trees, designed to be cool and shaded through the warmth of the summer. Tunjin had taken the Vincent motorbike around the house, keeping his distance, ending up on the undulant hillside and woodland that overlooked the house from the rear. From here, he could gain a good vantage point of the layout of the building and its surroundings.

Tunjin wished he had binoculars so that he could get a better view of the estate. As far as he could see, there was no obvious security, though he was under no illusions about how well protected the house and gardens would be. The garden itself was not particularly large and mostly laid to grass, scattered thickly with fir trees. A curving drive swept from the imposing front gates to the house itself.

There was no sign of life. There was a single car – a large black Mercedes – parked to one side of the building, but Tunjin had seen no one enter or leave. He didn't even know for sure that Muunokhoi was staying here at present. The files had indicated that he had another house up in the north of the country, in the picturesque Khövsghöl Nuur region, as well as a flat in the city centre. But Tunjin's impression had been that the second house was used largely for holidays – or possibly for more clandestine meetings – while the apartment was used as a place to bunk down when Muunokhoi was engaged in his characteristic long working days. He might not be back here tonight, but he typically spent only one or two nights a week in the apartment.

And even if Muunokhoi wasn't here, it was likely that the house was staffed with both domestic and security people. Someone would be down there.

Tunjin had sounded confident enough, in his conversation with Nergui, talking about the need to take Muunokhoi out of the picture. And there was no question that, in principle, he was right. If he wanted to regain his own security, his own peace of mind – no, forget that, if he wanted to live – then that was the only option.

But he didn't have a clue about how he might bring it about.

What was it that he had had in mind? Was he planning to break into Muunokhoi's house and perhaps steal some incriminating documents, some perfect piece of substantive evidence which Muunokhoi happened to have left handily lying about on his dining room table? He would probably have a better chance of success if he just tried to talk Muunokhoi out of killing him.

No, like everything else Tunjin had attempted in respect of Muunokhoi, this was worse than half-baked. He didn't even have a clue what the ingredients might be, let alone how to start cooking up anything. He had no equipment, no support, no resources and – above all – no ideas. Perhaps he should just walk up to the front door, hand himself over, and invite Muunokhoi to do his worst.

Tunjin slowly lifted himself off the bike, kicking down the stand as he did so. He was positioned near the top of the low hill, up amongst the thickening fir trees, where he hoped that he was invisible to any observers below. There was always a risk that the chrome on the motorbike might reflect the sun, but as far as Tunjin knew this was open land so it would not be unusual to find walkers, and perhaps even the occasional biker, up here.

It was another beautiful spring day, only a few wisps of cloud in the sky. From the hillside, the grass-land fell away, a patchwork of emerald green and darker shadows, down to the house and garden below, then across to the road. Beyond that, there was more grassland, a few houses, and nothing but the open steppe until the distant blue haze of the city.

Tunjin slumped down on to the ground and took stock of his position. All he could do was to keep watching, in the vague hope that inspiration would strike. He scrutinised the layout of Muunokhoi's house carefully. From here, he was at a diagonal angle to the house and could see both its front and rear elevations, though not its far side. It looked to be a fairly simple layout. At the rear he could see large double patio windows, which opened out onto a paved area arranged with an array of tables, chairs and other garden furniture. There was another window to the left of that, which Tunjin assumed was probably a kitchen. Above were lines of windows on the first and second floors, presumably bedrooms, with the occasional frosted window indicating a bathroom.

The front was similar. There was an imposing double door as the main entrance, with a substantial pine-built porchway over it, studded with lamps. And then lines of large windows, presumably of bedrooms and reception rooms.

Tunjin was surprised that, other than what looked like a standard domestic burglar alarm, there were no obvious security measures. He guessed that, somewhere around, there would be CCTV cameras, though he could see no sign of them from up here. He'd also presumed that some of Muunokhoi's security staff would be located on site, but again he had so far seen nothing.

Tunjin might be aware of the true nature of Muunokhoi's operations, but to the world at large he was simply a very successful businessman. People would expect him to have some security in place, but would not expect to see his domestic residence swarming with hired hitmen. Muunokhoi had an image to sustain.

But none of this was helping Tunjin. He needed some idea, some spark of thought that would give him a way forward. Anything.

And, as if in answer to this plea, there was finally some movement in the panorama spread out below.

Tunjin heard it before he spotted it. A car engine, distant, but unmistakeable in this silent landscape. He looked up and scanned the scene in front of him, and finally made out the rapid movement of a car, still miles away, heading away from the hazy fog of the city out in this direction.

He watched the car's progress, fully expecting that it would bypass the house and head on out north into the steppes. As it came closer, he saw it was a large black vehicle – a saloon car rather than a 4x4, probably Western. A Mercedes, maybe, or a BMW, but it was too distant to be sure.

To his mild surprise, as it approached the house, the car slowed. In almost perfect synchronisation, the large wrought iron gates at the end of the drive began slowly to open, clearly operated by someone from inside the house. The car turned into the entrance and made its way, at a much slower speed now, up the driveway towards the house.

At the same time, Tunjin noticed that the large double doors at the front of the house had been opened, and two men – both dressed in the standard leather jacket and dark glasses that seemed to be the uniform for Muunokhoi's hired help – stepped out into the sunlight. Both were holding something. In one case, this seemed to be a mobile phone, as the man was holding it close to his ear. In the second case, Tunjin caught the glint of sunlight on the metal. A handgun of some sort.

Tunjin watched in some fascination as the car

pulled to a halt. The two men stepped down to greet it, as the two front doors of the car opened. Two further men, dressed in identical fashion to the first, emerged and conversed briefly with their colleagues. Finally, one of them opened the rear door of the car, reached inside and, with assistance from his colleague, he pulled out what Tunjin at first took to be some kind of bundle – a parcel or a roll of cloth.

Then Tunjin realised that it was a body – a woman. She had dark hair, and was wearing a brightly coloured silk dress which fluttered gently in the breeze as the two men lifted her carefully towards the door of the house.

The other two men watched him for a moment. Then the one holding the gun slipped it back into his pocket, said something to the other, and they followed their colleagues and the woman into the house.

Tunjin watched for a few more moments, trying to take all this in, wondering whether anything else would happen. But the house remained as silent as before, the scene unchanged except for the addition of the new car parked on the drive.

Finally, Tunjin slumped backwards and lay on his back on the damp grass, watching the slow movement of the scattered clouds across the empty blue of the sky.

Okay, so something was happening here. Something that perhaps required some response, some action. Tunjin still had no idea what he was going to do. But at least now he had a positive motive for trying to do it.

*

'You don't believe in a quiet life, do you?'

'I don't recall it being part of the job description—' He hardly knew what he was saying. He was engaging in badinage on automatic pilot. It was like being in a dream, or perhaps just waking from a dream, except that he was unsure whether he was awake or still sleeping.

'Not of yours, certainly.' The volume of the voice faded in and out, so that he was still unsure whether or not he was really hearing it or whether it was just imagined. His dreams were so vivid. Sarangarel. The car. The abduction.

Nergui opened his eyes suddenly. 'Where is she?'

'Where's who?' The response was soothing, as though patronising a child or someone mentally ill.

Nergui sat up in the bed. 'Where is she?'

It was Doripalam sitting by the bed, anxiety etched into his features. 'Who? Who are you talking about?'

Nergui shook his head, trying to clear his fogged brain. 'Her. Sarangarel. Where is she?'

Doripalam stared at him. 'Who's Sarangarel?'

'She's – she's the judge. Judge Radnaa. Where is she?'

Doripalam was looking at Nergui as if, finally, after all these years, he really had lost his reason. 'You've been injured,' he said at last. 'Concussion. You really need to rest.'

Nergui's eyes were wide now. He was beginning to distinguish between dream and reality. He was beginning to work out where he was. 'No,' he said. 'It's true. She's been kidnapped. She's in danger.' He paused, taking in the implications of this statement.

'No. Really. In real danger. Muunokhoi.' Even saying the name seemed to exhaust him.

Doripalam blinked. 'Muunokhoi? What do you mean?'

Nergui leaned forward, forcing himself to think clearly, trying to sort fact from – whatever else was clouding his brain. 'She was with me. When the car – whatever it did – when it hit me. She was with me. And they took her into the car. They kidnapped her—' He stopped, feeling exhausted by the explanation.

'We don't know what happened to you,' Doripalam said. 'We don't know how you were injured. We don't know what the story is.'

This was finally making sense to Nergui, though he was not yet in a state to work out the implications. 'I was attacked,' he said. He paused, trying to get the narrative straight in his mind. 'It was like this. I was having lunch with her. With Sarangarel. Judge Radnaa. She's a judge—' he added, perhaps unnecessarily, but knowing that the narrative would be making little sense to Doripalam. And then there was the question – which his damaged, sleep-raddled mind hadn't begun to come to terms with – of whether it was wise for him to make sense to Doripalam in the first place. 'We went for a walk in the park,' he went on, 'and then came back to the hotel car park. I was going to give her a lift because—' What should he say? What version of the truth was it appropriate to share with Doripalam? How far – because this is what it came down to – could he be trusted?

Nergui paused, partly to regain his breath, partly to work out how much he should say. But his mind was still confused. He could not come to grips with the idea of not trusting Doripalam. 'We were having lunch together,' he repeated, finally. 'We went back to the hotel car park. The Bayangol. And then this car – it came from nowhere. It was parked. Drove out. Hit me. But – no, this is the point. The back door of the car opened and – they grabbed her—'

'Who? They grabbed who?'

Nergui knew that Doripalam was an intelligent man. He seemed to be being almost wilfully obtuse. 'Sarangarel,' he repeated patiently. 'Judge Radnaa. They kidnapped her.'

'They kidnapped a judge?'

Nergui breathed out, like a runner who had finally reached his destination. 'Yes. Exactly. They've kidnapped a judge. Judge Radnaa.'

Doripalam was staring at him. 'You said Muunokhoi. What did you mean?'

It was Nergui's turn to stare, all his doubts returning. 'I don't know,' he said. 'What did I say?'

Doripalam sat back, looking at his former boss, sitting propped up in the hospital bed. 'I think I'd better tell you what I know. How we found you.' He paused. 'All we know is that you were found in the Hotel Bayangol car park. One of the hotel staff found you. You were bleeding from the head and he assumed – rightly, as far as we can tell – that you were hit by a car. An accident—'

'It wasn't an accident.'

'No, well, that wouldn't be a surprise. Anyway, he called for medical help. You were brought in here. And they found your Ministry ID and so contacted us.'

'I wasn't alone,' Nergui insisted. 'When I was hit by the car.'

'Yes, well, I'm beginning to understand that. You were with Judge—'

'Radnaa. She's been kidnapped.'

'Judge Radnaa. Why do I—?'

'She was the judge in the Muunokhoi case. The aborted case.'

'Is that why you think—?'

'It's a long story,' Nergui said. 'But, yes, I think she's been kidnapped by Muunokhoi's people.'

There was a long silence. Finally, Doripalam said: 'You do know what you're saying? I mean, you were concussed.'

Nergui was sitting bolt upright in bed now. 'I know exactly what I'm saying. The only question in my mind is whether I ought to be saying it to you.'

The silence was even longer this time.

'What do you mean?' Doripalam said at last.

Nergui shook his head. He realised, only now, that his head was aching, very intensely, a dull numbing ache that still seemed to cloud his reason. His normally razor sharp instincts seemed blunted, and he felt unable to trust his judgement. 'This is a very long story,' he said. 'How badly hurt am I?'

'Hardly at all,' Doripalam said. 'I've always suspected you were indestructible and this proves it. Not many people get into an argument with a car and walk away.'

'I didn't exactly walk away,' Nergui pointed out, 'and it wasn't really an argument. More like a very brief exchange of views. And it doesn't really feel like I'm hardly hurt at all.' As his senses had slowly returned, Nergui was becoming increasingly aware that some parts of his body – his hip, one of his arms – were in considerable pain.

'Even so,' Doripalam said, 'I checked with the doctor. You suffered some bruising – some of it very painful but not serious. You hit your head, but they've done a scan and there's no lasting damage. Not that I could have deduced that from the way you've been talking.'

'No,' Nergui said. 'So when can I leave?'

'I think they'll sign you out as soon as you think you're ready,' Doripalam said.

'I think I'm ready. I think I'm more than ready.' Nergui twisted himself across the bed with some difficulty and sat up on the edge. He was wearing a hospital issue gown. 'Where are my clothes?'

'I really don't think you ought to—'

Nergui looked up at the younger man. His dark face was as impassive as ever but his blue eyes were blazing with an emotion which Doripalam could not read. 'Listen, Doripalam. There isn't time. Sarangarel's been taken by Muunokhoi's people. We don't know where. We don't know what might happen to her. But we have to assume the worst.'

'But you don't know for sure—'

'That Muunokhoi's behind this. I do know. But, no, I can't prove it. And if Muunokhoi is true to form, he'll make sure that he's a long way away from whatever might happen. Although—' He stopped and stared at Doripalam, as though trying to fathom some intricate puzzle.

'What?'

'It doesn't feel right for Muunokhoi, all this. All these years of caution. All this time we've never been able to lay a finger on him. And now—'

Doripalam was watching Nergui, clearly wondering whether the concussion had been more serious than he had originally imagined.

'Now,' Nergui went on, 'he seems rattled. He seems almost to be panicking. It's—' He stopped, still perched on the edge of the bed and looked back up at Doripalam. 'I need to know,' he said. 'I need to know whether I can trust you.'

Doripalam opened his mouth to speak, but no words emerged. Finally, he said: 'What are you talking about?'

'Find me my clothes,' Nergui said. 'We need to get out of here. We need to talk.'

CHAPTER 17

It was nearly dark outside.

Tsend's main office window faced north and the setting sun was already invisible, lost behind the endless forests and low hills, the last crimson rays draining from the sky. He could almost see the movement of the night's shadows spreading across the rolling grassland.

The call would come soon, he knew. The second call since the young man from the city had been here. Doripalam. So confident and cocksure. So patronising. And so much further out of his depth than he could ever have imagined.

Tsend smiled, standing by the window, staring out at the darkening landscape. It was amusing, he thought. Ironic. Left to himself, he would have never made the connection, never realised who the four men were. He had been following, with some detached amusement, the news stories of the missing son and then the murder of the mother. And he had noted, with no real interest, the official request that any new arrivals in the area should be reported back to headquarters.

But he had not taken the request seriously. And he had certainly not registered its deeper significance to his own position.

So it was thanks only to some over-enthusiastic local rookie that the men had been spotted. And – even more amusingly – it was thanks only to Doripalam's own assiduousness that the four men had been positively identified and then brought back here. Into Tsend's safe-keeping.

It was only then that Tsend finally learned who the men were. And who else was interested in them. And just how much that interest might enhance his own standing. For the first time, he had the opportunity to prove himself, to show that he was more than just another local hick on the take.

The only question now was what happened next. The first call had simply told him to keep hold of the men, ensure they were kept safe. Someone would be coming up from the city to question them, but that was okay. That was all in hand.

But once that was out of the way, the matter would have to be finished off. Tidied up. Tsend should await further instructions.

He was still gazing fixedly out of the window when the mobile phone vibrated in his pocket. He pulled it out and thumbed the call button. 'Yes?' Use only this phone, they had said. Never give your name.

'Someone will be coming up from the city tomorrow morning,' the voice said. Tsend thought the speaker sounded familiar, but immediately put the idea from his mind. He didn't want to know. 'Make them welcome. They will question the men. You should co-operate. That's all under control.'

Tsend had never doubted it. 'And then—?' he breathed.

'Then the men should be released,' the voice said.

'But I was told to keep—'

'The men should be released,' the voice repeated, as if Tsend had not spoken. 'They should be sent back to their camp. They should be told that there is nothing to worry about. That they are safe and under your protection. You will keep them under observation until we contact you again.'

'And then—'

'Then, with your assistance, we will take care of things,' the voice said, evenly. 'We will take care of everything.'

'This is outrageous,' she said. 'I've never been treated like this.' The words were automatic. She hardly knew what she was saying, her mind still struggling through the fog of semi-consciousness. But already she was recognising the need to assert her will, to try to gain some control of the situation.

The man sitting opposite her merely nodded and shrugged. He was watching her closely, but it was clear that he had no intention of engaging in any kind of conversation or offering any kind of response.

'How long are you intending to keep me here?'

The man shrugged again, this time smiling faintly. His impervious calm was almost the most infuriating aspect of the situation in which she found herself.

She was still half-asleep, her mouth was dry and her head was aching. She was lying uncomfortably on an overstuffed sofa, a blanket draped decorously across her, although she was still fully clothed. She had no idea how long she had been unconscious, but her stomach felt empty and nauseous, as if she hadn't eaten for days. She pulled herself upright and looked around her.

In other circumstances, this would have seemed a very comfortable environment. It was a large, well-appointed living room, clearly the property of someone possessing both good taste and the wealth needed to express it. The furniture was expensive and well-chosen – mahogany woodwork, plush upholstery, delicate splashings of gold and silver here and there. At the far end of the room was something she had never seen before – a large, flat-screen television. There were shelves of books – all leather bound, apparently unopened.

Through the window beyond the television, she could see a large expanse of grass, dotted with some pots of apparently exotic flowers. The garden was bounded, at the far end, by a large fence, fronted by rows of dense fir trees.

There was no way of knowing where she was. As soon as she had been pulled into the car, she had been blindfolded and moments later she had felt the prick of a syringe in her arm. She had fought hard against the blankness that began to overwhelm her, trying to maintain consciousness. Her last recollection had been a brief exchange of words that had told her there were two men in the front seats, and then she had remembered nothing until waking up in this room.

How long had she been unconscious? She had no watch and no idea of the time. But the sunlight streaming through the windows was low, and something about the quality of the light suggested that it was morning rather than evening. Was it possible that she had been unconscious overnight?

'Won't you at least give me an idea what this is all about?' she said. 'I mean, is it some kind of joke?'

It was a ridiculous question. What sort of joke could this be? What sort of joke would involve seizing a member of the judiciary, while apparently in the process also running over a senior officer from the Ministry of Security?

The last question sent her thoughts back to Nergui. Could he possibly be all right? The sound of the car hitting his body had been indescribably awful – all the more dreadful for its softness. She had seen him – only for a moment before she was dragged into the car – fall backwards, his head thudding against the concrete of the hotel car park. It was possible, she supposed, that he was badly injured or even dead, though she rapidly pushed the thought to the back of her mind.

She looked back at the blank-faced man sitting opposite her. They were seated like prospective diners or perhaps chess players, facing one another across the polished mahogany table.

She rose slowly from her seat and made her way towards the rear window. The man watched her movement with no apparent interest.

As she had expected, the view from the window told her nothing more. There was a well-tended garden at the rear of the house, largely laid to grass, scattered with conifers and potted plants. The concept of a garden was not widely appreciated in this land of vast open plains and desert, and she could only assume that the owner of the property had spent some time in the

West – or, she supposed, in Japan, although the style of the garden was essentially European. She wondered quite how expensive it would be to maintain this kind of garden in this extreme continental climate, with its sub-zero winters and dry summers.

The rear boundary of the garden was marked by a high solid fence lined with tall conifers. She could see nothing beyond – no sign of the mountains or forests, no clue as to where this house might be located.

She moved away from the window, and wandered back across the room, pausing to glance at the glass fronted bookshelves that lined the adjacent wall. The books were all antiquarian, leather bound, virtually all of them – other than an ornate edition of *The Secret History of the Mongols* – with titles she did not recognise. The library looked like the kind of anonymous collection that might be held by any rich man as an investment or perhaps simply as an indicator of his wealth. There was no sign that any of the books had been read. There was also no clue even to the personality, let alone the identity, of the owner of the house.

She turned back from the bookshelf as the door opened and a figure stepped quietly inside. For all the absence of evidence, she had been assuming – on the basis of her discussion with Nergui – that she had been brought here at Muunokhoi's behest. She had similarly assumed that Muunokhoi would appear to greet her and carry out whatever purpose had been behind her apparent abduction.

But, she realised, this was naïve. Muunokhoi had not revealed his hand so far, and there was no reason to assume he would start now. She could not even assume that this was Muunokhoi's house – it was far more likely that he would find some anonymous location to take whatever action he had in mind, rather than have her taken to his home. Not that there was anything obviously anonymous about this place.

Certainly, the man who now entered the room was not Muunokhoi, and did not look like one of his henchmen. He was a short, relatively young man – probably in his early thirties – dressed in a smart dark suit. His hair was trimmed short, and he wore angular black framed glasses which Sarangarel presumed were some kind of fashion statement rather than simply an optical aid. In his hands, he carried a small silver tray, with a plate of bread and cold meats and a jug of water.

He moved softly across the room and placed the tray carefully on the table. Then he sat down opposite the first man, who nodded and left the room.

The young man gestured Sarangarel to take the vacated seat. 'Mrs Radnaa,' he said. 'Will you join me?' It was a voice which carried no expectation of a negative response.

She nodded to him and walked slowly back across the room, but made no move to sit down. 'I presume you're going to tell me what this is all about?'

He smiled. 'Please sit down, Mrs Radnaa. It is very awkward holding this conversation with you standing up. If it's any reassurance, I think that even sitting down you are likely to be taller than I am.'

She watched him for a moment, then nodded and sat down on the chair. 'So, Mr—'

He smiled. 'I don't think that the name is important,' he said.

'That rather depends,' she said, 'on what you have in mind. I don't think it's unreasonable to want to know the name of my abductor.'

'"Abductor" is rather a strong term,' he said. 'I'd rather think of myself as your host.'

She stared at him for a moment. 'Well,' she said at last, 'I think you leave me speechless.' She paused. 'So this place is yours?'

He shrugged. 'I live here,' he said.

She nodded. 'I see. So this belongs to someone else. Who presumably shares your eccentric view that dragging someone involuntarily into the back of a car doesn't constitute abduction.'

He smiled. 'You're a lawyer,' he said. 'I am sure you know best. But – however you arrived – you are here as our guest. You will not be treated badly.' He gestured towards the tray. 'You must be hungry.'

For a moment, she contemplated refusing the food, but realised that her hunger was too great. She pulled the tray towards her and took a slice of bread and meat, trying not to appear too eager. As she ate, the man poured her a glass of water.

After a few moments the food and water dispelled the worst of her nausea. Her mind was still fogged, but she felt more in control. 'Guests are normally free to leave when they wish,' she pointed out. 'I take it that is not the case here.'

'Not at present, no,' he admitted. 'But I hope that we can conclude our business relatively quickly.'

She sat back in her chair and regarded him. 'And that business would be?'

He hesitated for a moment, as though seeking the

most appropriate words. 'We believe,' he said, 'that you are in possession of some material, some – paperwork, that rightly belongs to us.'

'I don't think so,' she said. 'Though of course it's difficult to be sure without knowing who you are.'

'I don't think there is much point in playing games, Mrs Radnaa,' he said, calmly. 'We know more than you can imagine.'

'I'm sure you know things I couldn't begin to imagine,' she said. 'But I am not sure where that gets us. I am not playing games. I really don't know what you're talking about.'

The man leaned forward across the table, staring at Sarangarel. 'I have told you,' he said. 'We know. We know about your husband. We know that you recently – and unexpectedly – received a legacy indirectly from your husband.'

If Sarangarel was surprised by this announcement, she did not allow it to show. She smiled faintly. 'You're very well informed,' she said. 'But I fail to understand why this information should be of interest to anyone but myself.'

The man gazed at her for a moment, as though – against his expectations – it was he who had been surprised by her words. 'We know about your husband,' he repeated.

'What do you know about my husband?' she said. 'You know that he was a businessman? Not a very successful one, I should say.' She looked around as though seeing the room for the first time. 'Much less successful than you, if you really are the owner of this place. And what else do you know? You know that he was arrested, supposedly for smuggling, but that he was never brought to trial? You know that he died in police custody?' She paused. 'I'm not sure what else there is for you to know. I can tell you his shoe size and probably several more intimate facts about him, but then you're probably ahead of me there as well.'

The man looked down at the table, as though Sarangarel's attempts to embarrass him had succeeded.

'But,' she went on, 'all of this is public knowledge. Perhaps you thought it would cause me difficulties, as a member of the judiciary, but, no, I've been able to put all that history well behind me. So, you see, I really don't know what it is you're talking about.'

The man made no immediate response and at first it seemed as though he had no response to give. If it was the case that he was acting on Muunokhoi's behalf, then he was really now facing something of a dilemma. He had clearly hoped to intimidate her into handing over the papers immediately. Instead, all he had succeeded in doing was confirming that there was – or at least he thought there was – something significant in the papers. And if he were to say anything more, he would at the very least confirm that fact and might risk revealing something more. Even the issue of her husband's identity had no significance unless it really was the case that he was somehow linked with Muunokhoi.

Finally, the man looked back at her, his dark eyes revealing nothing. 'All I can say to you, Mrs Radnaa, is that while we do not, for the moment at least, intend you any harm, you cannot be released until you give us what we seek.'

'In that case,' she looked around her, 'I am glad that you have provided me with such a comfortable prison.'

Even at the time, Tunjin had no idea how it happened. But that was the story of his life.

He had stayed on the hillside all night, initially with some half-idea that he might try to break into the house under cover of darkness. But he didn't fool himself that the security would be any less tight at night, and he still had no idea how he could gain entry. Eventually, he had wrapped himself in an old blanket he had found in the pannier of the motorbike, and settled down to try to get some rest. He had expected that sleep would be elusive, but in fact he had succumbed very quickly, cushioned by the soft grass and exhausted by the travails of the previous days.

When he awoke, the sun was already rising over the hills to the east. It was another fine spring day. He was cold and hungry, but beginning to recognise what sobriety felt like. It was years since he had felt this alert on first waking. He dragged himself to his feet, and dug out the last remnants of the bread and water that Nergui had given him. As he ate, Tunjin made his way back along the hill, trying to gain a good vantage point over the house, wanting to get as clear an understanding as he could of its layout, likely security protection, and anything else that might assist him in the – as yet unknown – activity in which he was about to engage.

He moved slowly, his eyes fixed on the estate below. Before him, the slope dropped gently away, a smooth contour of grassland which became progressively steeper as it swept down towards tall blank fences that surrounded the house. The wind rippled gently through the grass, a brilliant green in the spring sunshine, and some way off before the trees a cloud of butterflies scattered into the shadows.

It was, perhaps, the butterflies that distracted Tunjin, though he had thought his attention was entirely fixed on the house. He stepped on – what was it? A loose stone, a more slippery area of grass? He wasn't sure. He knew only that, suddenly, his feet went from under him and his considerable weight toppled him, at first slowly then with increasing speed, down the hillside. His feet skidded on the grass, still wet from the morning dew. The next moment, he was, quite literally, rolling, his hands flailing to try to obtain some purchase. He saw the darkness of the trees, the brilliance of the clear blue sky, the dazzling sunshine, strobing through his vision as he fell, completely out of control now, spinning down towards the wooden fence.

His tumbling body hit the steeper part of the hill and bounced into the air, knocking the breath from his large body, and then he was rolling again, spinning faster, his flesh bruised and scraped despite the softness of the ground.

The end came suddenly and brutally, as his body slammed into the brown wooden fence. All the breath was expelled from his body and he lay on his back, gasping, assuming that at any moment his heart would give out and relieve him from the agonising pain that coursed through his limbs.

It took him some minutes to register that, despite the pain, he did not appear to be seriously injured. His breathing slowed, and he lay on his back, staring at the blue of the sky, watching the slow drift of the white clouds above him. He could move his limbs. He stretched out his arms, feeling the ache of the bruises, but grateful that nothing seemed to be broken.

He was lying pressed against the wooden fence, still lacking the energy to move. He had struck the fence with a deafening crash. So much for his idea of approaching the place surreptitiously.

Finally, he pulled himself up to a sitting position. He looked back up behind him. At the top of the hill he could see the sun glinting on the Vincent motorcycle. Was there nothing he could do right? He hadn't even managed to conceal his transport.

But then he realised that his fall had actually achieved something. The impact of Tunjin's weight against the wood had cracked several of the slats, leaving a gaping opening. The fence was, Tunjin now realised, rather less substantial than it appeared. He sat forward, gasping slightly, and pulled gently at the wood.

The first slat came away very easily, and Tunjin tossed it away on to the grass. Behind it, he could see dark undergrowth, thick trees and, beyond that, more grass. He climbed up on to his knees, and began to pull at the wood. Two, then three more slats were pulled back, and thrown on to the grass. Very shortly, Tunjin had cleared a space large enough for even his body to squeeze through.

He kneeled in front of the hole, hesitating,

wondering what kind of security protection might lie beyond it. There was no way of knowing. It was likely that there would be some kind of camera arrangement, perhaps even alarms. But what were the options? He could turn and climb away – not that the prospect of climbing the hill was particularly attractive – or he could continue.

He pushed himself forward through the hole, squeezing with some difficulty through the limited space. On the far side he found himself in shady undergrowth, thick conifers towering above him. The sun barely reached here, shaded by the trees and the fence itself. Through the undergrowth he could see an expanse of grass and a network of paths.

Once through the fence, he climbed slowly to his feet, still feeling the bruises across his body. The garden was silent, apart from the faint whisper of the wind through the trees.

Tunjin pushed forward, feeling the thick conifers brushing against his face. Across the grass, he could see the solid wooden bulk of the house. He still didn't even have the beginnings of a plan, had no idea what he might be about to do now he had managed to enter this place.

There was no sight or sound of any alarm, though that didn't necessarily mean that strident sirens weren't sounding within the house.

Finally, Tunjin emerged on to the path, feeling an unaccountable sense of release as he entered the open light and air. He paused on the path, wondering precisely where he should proceed next.

But, almost immediately, the choice was taken from

him. As he straightened up, he heard a voice behind him.

'Well, I suppose it cuts both ways. You're fat enough to break through the perimeter. But you're not hard to track down.'

Tunjin turned slowly. A man was standing on the path behind him, having apparently appeared from nowhere. But all Tunjin really saw was the shining black barrel of a gun, pointing steadily towards his chest.

CHAPTER 18

Earlier in the day, in the brightness of the spring after-noon, the place would have been heaving with people, locals and tourists alike, perhaps looking for a dose of spirituality or simply seeing the extraordinary sights. Now, though, as the afternoon came to an end, the grounds had emptied and provided a perfect backdrop to the uneasy conversation between Nergui and Doripalam.

'Are you all right?' Doripalam said solicitously as they made their way slowly up the steep hill.

Nergui nodded, though the honest answer would have been negative. He was not entirely all right, either physically or mentally. Perhaps not even spiritually, he thought, in which case they had at least come to the right place.

'I used to come here a lot,' Nergui said, looking around as they reached the summit of the hill. He was breathing heavily, his limbs still aching from the cuts and bruises. 'But not for a while. Perhaps it's been too long.'

Nergui was not a religious man. Or at least not religious in a way that any conventional faith would appreciate. But he had always found that the Monastery of Choijin Lama, with its clustering of ornate temples, provided some kind of sustenance, something which, he supposed, could be described as spiritual. Perhaps it was the history. Perhaps it was the way that this faith, these rituals, had managed to survive through all the days of suppression. Or perhaps it was simply the rituals themselves, the sights, the sounds, the sonorous music, all redolent of something greater than anything merely human.

Even now, as they strolled among the gaudily coloured buildings, scattering pigeons as they walked, they could hear the clattering of the dazzling prayer wheels, the repetitive chanting of the monks faintly discernible from inside. Beneath the brilliant blue of the sky, it was as if they were somehow connected with a world with more significance than anything found in the hazy shadows of the city spread out below them.

Not that this improved the connection between the two men themselves. They had barely spoken as they made their slow way up the hillside. Doripalam had insisted that Nergui's departure from the hospital should be handled by the book, and Nergui had reluctantly acceded. They had had to wait until the doctor in charge had appeared and then had to spend further time persuading him to release Nergui. He was initially reluctant. He acknowledged that there was nothing seriously wrong with Nergui, but felt that he needed more rest. It was only as it became increasingly obvious that, inside or outside the hospital, rest was the last thing on Nergui's mind that the doctor finally agreed to his departure.

They stopped at the top of the hill, the temple behind them, and looked down at the sprawl of the city.

'So,' Doripalam said finally, 'are you going to tell me what this is all about?'

'I'm not sure I can tell you what it's *all* about,' Nergui said, still staring down at the streets and buildings beneath them.

'And are you sure now that you should?' Doripalam said. 'These things are difficult for me to understand, given that I don't normally move in your exalted circles.'

Nergui turned and stared at the young man, and then burst out laughing. 'Is that what you think this is all about?' he said. 'My over-inflated sense of my own importance?'

Doripalam shrugged. 'As I say, it's difficult for me to judge.'

Nergui turned his back on the view below. 'Doripalam. I want to talk about Muunokhoi.'

'I know all about Muunokhoi,' Doripalam said. 'He almost cost me my job.'

Nergui laughed again. 'And you accuse me of having an over-inflated sense of my own importance?'

'You put those words in my mouth,' Doripalam pointed out. 'I didn't say it.'

Nergui smiled. 'But how much do you really know about Muunokhoi? What do you know of the history?'

'I know you were after him. I know you've been after him for a long time.'

'It was that obvious, then?' Nergui said. 'Yes, I suppose it was. I've been after him for – what, the best part of two decades. Probably not particularly rational. Except that he's one of the biggest crooks this country's produced.'

'Do you know that? I mean,' Doripalam said, 'are you sure? We've never laid a finger on him. You've never laid a finger on him. He's one of our more respectable citizens. You admit you've not been entirely rational about this.'

Nergui was watching a flock of pigeons sweeping softly across the sky, attracted by the scatterings of bread crumbs left by tourists in the heart of the temple. 'There's a history to it, of course. Of course there is. And for Tunjin as well.'

'Tunjin? What do you know about Tunjin?' Doripalam looked at him sharply.

'It's a long story. But there's history there, too. Tunjin's been after Muunokhoi as long as I have.'

'So is that why he pulled that stupid stroke?'

'Trying to forge the evidence against Muunokhoi? Yes, of course. He was getting near the end of his career, running out of chances. He thought it was worth a try.'

'That was how he explained it to me,' Doripalam said. 'I thought he was mad.'

'He probably was,' Nergui said, smiling faintly. 'Or, at least, not entirely rational.'

'But you're sure it's true? You're sure that there's a case against Muunokhoi?'

Nergui regarded the young man closely. 'You keep asking me that. Have you some reason to question it?'

'You trained me. You'd expect me to challenge you on this. He's one of our more respectable citizens.'

'And respectability never goes with criminality?'

Doripalam laughed. 'You should know. You're the one who mixes with politicians.'

'That's better,' Nergui said. 'You're finally beginning to sound like the Doripalam I know. You know—' He stopped.

'What?'

'I even thought it might have been you. Just for a moment. I really thought even you might have been one of them.'

'One of who?'

Nergui paused and then carried on slowly. 'The reason why we have never managed to lay a finger on Muunokhoi is because he has people – I don't know how many people – on the inside.'

Doripalam stared at him. 'You're the second person today who's implied I'm on Muunokhoi's payroll. I nearly punched the first one.'

Nergui shrugged. 'He seems to know everything. Why do you think Tunjin's plan failed? Not because it was half-baked. I don't condone what Tunjin did but I have to concede that he did it well. His forgeries were simple but good enough to do the job. He pitched it just right. It should have worked. But it didn't. And the reason it didn't work was that Muunokhoi found out what was going on. Almost immediately.'

'And you really think that I—?'

Nergui shook his head. 'No. No, of course not. Not really. But we're talking about someone – maybe more than one – who has access to the most sensitive information. When I started the enquiry—'

'So that's what it was all about, the enquiry. Not just cleaning out the stables. You wanted to know how Muunokhoi knew what Tunjin was up to.' He paused. 'Does that mean you knew about Tunjin's scheme?'

Nergui nodded. 'I suppose I can't be too offended about that question, given what I've just said. But, no. I didn't. If I had, I'd have stopped it. But once the whole thing collapsed, it was obvious to me that Muunokhoi knew.'

'So you persuaded the Minister to let you head the enquiry to find out how?'

'"Persuaded" is perhaps a bit strong. But, yes, I did.'

Doripalam paused, staring out over the city. There were a few fluffy clouds in the sky now, drifting slowly out towards the rich green of the steppes. 'And you investigated me?'

Nergui shrugged. 'I investigated everyone. Including you.'

'And found nothing, I trust?'

'If you really had been on Muunokhoi's payroll, I'd have found nothing anyway. But, no, I found nothing.'

'So why don't you think I am? On Muunokhoi's payroll, I mean.'

Nergui shrugged. 'I'm a policeman,' he said. 'I trust my instincts. Don't you?'

'Not as much as I should, probably,' Doripalam said. 'But, okay, you trust me, and I suppose I should be flattered, though I'm not sure that's exactly how I feel at the moment. But where does that get us? What's this all about?'

'It gets us into an almighty mess,' Nergui said. 'We've still got nothing on Muunokhoi. Sarangarel – Judge Radnaa – has been abducted. Tunjin is missing. And we don't have a clue how any of this fits together.'

'And Mrs Tuya was brutally murdered,' Doripalam said. 'And her family are terrified.'

Nergui had been watching the slow movement of a freight train through the centre of the city. Now he turned back to look at Doripalam. 'What do you mean?' he said. 'What does that have to do with Muunokhoi?'

'I don't know. Possibly nothing. But I somehow made the link in my mind as you were talking. Maybe I'm finally trusting my instinct. Anyway, you remember the story. Gavaa had moved to the city. Boasted he'd got some impressive job, but nobody knew what. Then he went missing. And then we found his mother's body—'

'And you think this might somehow be connected with Muunokhoi?' They had turned back towards the temple now, and were walking back down towards the cluster of buildings. A line of orange-clad monks emerged from the temple and walked slowly ahead of them. The rows of prayer wheels glittered and clattered in the early evening sunshine.

Doripalam shrugged. 'It wasn't a connection I'd made till just now. I had a sudden image in my mind of the mother's mutilated body.' He paused. 'I've heard all the stories about Muunokhoi and what he's capable of. Those four terrified men up in the mountains—'

Nergui nodded. 'Did you get anything out of them?'

'I sent someone up there, but they clammed up, apparently. Nothing at all. Nothing to add to what they told me.'

Nergui nodded. 'It may depend on who you sent.'

Doripalam turned and looked at him. 'Did your

enquiry give you any idea who we can trust? Or who we can't?'

'No. I've identified one or two junior officers who I'm pretty sure are on the take, but even there it's hard to find real evidence. But among the senior officers – no. I wouldn't even want to guess.'

Doripalam stopped walking. They were looking out over Nairamdal Park, where Nergui had held his midnight meeting with Tunjin. 'You really think it's that serious?' Doripalam said. 'You really think we've been infiltrated that deeply?'

'I'm sure of it,' Nergui said. 'Muunokhoi does what he likes.' He paused. 'But there's something else happening here. We've never got close to Muunokhoi before, never got anywhere near to laying a finger on him, other than Tunjin's doomed effort. And Muunokhoi's never needed to get his hands dirty. And yet now—'

'What?'

'Now we have Tunjin missing, on the run from Muunokhoi—'

'How do you know he's on the run?' Doripalam was watching the older man closely, realising that as always he was several steps ahead in his thinking, already playing with thoughts that Doripalam had not yet begun to conceive.

'He called me,' Nergui said. 'I met him. Here.' He gestured out towards the green sweep of the parkland, the distant blue sliver of the lake. 'The night before last.'

'But why didn't you say? Why didn't you do something?'

Nergui looked back at Doripalam. 'What should I have done? I did not – do not – know who to trust. I could not even offer Tunjin the protection of the police. Think of that.'

'But he's safe?'

'For the moment. Tunjin is no fool, despite appearances. He can look after himself.'

'I hope so,' Doripalam said. 'I wouldn't wish to be on the wrong side of Muunokhoi.'

They had resumed walking, making their way down from the Monastery grounds out towards the park. 'But why is this happening?' Nergui said. 'Why is Muunokhoi risking playing his hand? Why is he bothering to pursue Tunjin? Why has he had Sarangarel abducted?'

'You don't know for sure that he has,' Doripalam said. 'I mean, you don't know for sure that Muunokhoi is behind this.'

'I know,' Nergui said. His voice, as always, carried an absolute authority. 'And I think you're right. That he was also behind the murder of Mrs Tuya. And quite possibly behind the disappearance of her son. But why are these things happening? This is not Muunokhoi. This is not his way of working.'

'Maybe it's not Muunokhoi,' Doripalam suggested. 'Maybe it's – I don't know – maybe someone in his organisation. Some loose cannon. Taking things into his own hands.'

'I don't think so,' Nergui said. 'That wouldn't be Muunokhoi's way of working either. It might happen once – perhaps an over-enthusiastic servant. But it would not happen twice.' He paused. 'There is something wrong here. We need to find Sarangarel. Quickly.'

'That won't be easy,' Doripalam said. 'Even assuming you're right, and Muunokhoi is behind this—' He raised his hand to cut off the older man's objections. 'I'm not disagreeing with you. But we have no evidence. Muunokhoi is an important man. We can't simply have him arrested. We can't even go and search his property, unless we have a far more substantive reason than anything that's emerged so far.'

'There are things we can do—'

'I know, and I've already set them in motion while you were negotiating your way out of hospital. I've got surveillance on all of Muunokhoi's houses and business premises. I've got Muunokhoi himself under surveillance. And of course I've set all the standard processes in place to try to find Mrs Radnaa. The kidnapping of a judge would still be a serious offence even if she weren't a friend of yours.'

Nergui nodded, accepting the mild rebuke as justified. 'Of course,' he said. 'You know your job.'

'But you're worried.'

'I'm worried. And if you've set all this in motion, then Muunokhoi will already know we're after him.'

Doripalam shrugged. 'There was no way of avoiding that,' he said, 'if your suspicions about infiltration are correct.'

'And it may not be a bad thing. There is something happening here. Perhaps Muunokhoi will feel the pressure.'

'Perhaps,' Doripalam said, 'but I do not think we should place much faith in that possibility.'

They had entered the park now, the children's play area ahead of them. In the late afternoon the park was crowded with families, teenagers eating ice creams, old men in traditional robes talking the day away.

Nergui stopped walking and looked at Doripalam as though a thought had just struck him. 'What happened to Mrs Tuya's family?'

Doripalam looked at him. 'What do you mean?'

'You spoke about the four men. Up in the mountains. Afraid they were being chased. What happened to them?'

'They—' Doripalam stopped, his mind suddenly pursuing the train of thought that Nergui had presumably already followed. 'I left them up there. Told the local police to keep them under surveillance. Give them any necessary protection. But I didn't really think—'

'That they needed it?'

Doripalam hesitated. 'No. I mean, they were clearly afraid. But I couldn't see why anyone would want to pursue them. Even given Mrs Tuya's murder. They had nothing that anyone might want—'

'Except that we don't know that,' Nergui said. 'We don't know anything.'

'And if you're right,' Doripalam said, 'by offering them police protection, I might have sentenced them to death.'

Nergui shook his head. 'We don't know that,' he said. 'But we can't take anything for granted.' He stood silently for a moment, watching the carefree crowds spreading out across the green of the park. 'We can't trust anyone.'

Doripalam nodded and took out his mobile phone. He flicked through the saved numbers and dialled the direct line for Tsend, the police chief up in Bulgan. He found himself redirected through to a secretary.

'I'm sorry,' she said. 'He's tied up in meetings all day. I can take a message.'

'Tell him it's Doripalam of the Serious Crimes Team. Ask him to call me back urgently.' The tone was more peremptory that usual for Doripalam, but he had little expectation that Tsend would return his call quickly.

He ended the call, looked at Nergui and shrugged. 'I'm not sure how far I'm going to get through official channels,' he said. 'Tsend was hardly co-operative when I was up there before. I assumed it was the usual cynicism about visitors from the capital, but who knows?' He began to flick through the saved numbers again. 'There's one other route I can try.'

He dialled the number for the local station where Yadamsuren, the outstationed officer, was located and, after a few moments, succeeded in being put through.

'It's Doripalam,' he said. 'From the Serious Crimes Team. You remember?'

'I'm not likely to forget quickly,' Yadamsuren said. 'My shoulder's still sore.'

'I've been trying to get through to the main station in Bulgan,' Doripalam said, 'but I can't raise anyone who might be able to give me any information. I just wanted to know what happened to our four nomads. They're still around, I take it?'

There was a long silence at the other end of the line, so that Doripalam began to think that the signal had been lost.

'I don't really know,' Yadamsuren said, finally. 'I've not really had any contact since it all happened.'

There was something in Yadamsuren's voice that made Doripalam uneasy. 'What about their *gers*?' he said. 'Have they been back there?'

There was another pause, less extended, but somehow more freighted with meaning than the previous one. 'No,' Yadamsuren said. 'I've not seen them here. The *gers* are still there—' There was a hesitation. 'Some of the officers from Bulgan came out,' he said. 'They conducted some sort of search through the tents.'

'A search?' Doripalam said, looking up at Nergui. 'For what?' He had, he thought, made it very clear that this was a Serious Crimes case. The local brief was simply to provide protection, not to get involved in any kind of investigation.

'I don't know,' Yadamsuren said. 'They didn't give me any kind of explanation. Well, there was no reason why they should. I mean, I assumed – well, I assumed that it was your people behind it.'

'What did they say?'

'Well, not much. They told me that I should just keep an eye on the *gers* until they were dismantled. And to find someone to look after the animals, temporarily.'

'When the nomads returned, you mean?'

'Well, that wasn't very clear. I had the impression it would be the police who would do it. Presumably just to keep the tents safe. I assumed that the nomads were under protection of some sort.'

'They are,' Doripalam said, deciding that there was no point in raising Yadamsuren's interest further.

There was no reason to suspect Yadamsuren, but any information could potentially get back to those who were perhaps less trustworthy. 'Just seems to be a bit of confusion, that's all. That's why I've been trying to find out what's going on. Thanks for your help.'

He ended the call. Nergui was watching him closely, having apparently followed the gist of the conversation.

'I think we need a trip to the mountains,' Nergui said.

Doripalam nodded. 'I'll go,' he said. 'You need to be here. In case there are any developments on the kidnapping.'

Nergui shrugged. 'There is nothing I can do here except worry. It is better that I'm taking some action.' He paused, still scrutinising Doripalam closely. For a moment, Doripalam wondered whether Nergui really did trust him, or whether he was reluctant to allow the younger man to make the trip on his own. But he also knew that Nergui, ever the pragmatist, was right. There was little they could do here for the moment, except make sure that the usual investigatory processes were in place.

'And if you're right,' Nergui went on, displaying his usual uncanny ability apparently to follow Doripalam's train of thought, 'if there is some link between Muunokhoi and the Tuya murder, then perhaps this is another thread we can begin to pull. Let us hope that something of this begins to unravel before it's too late.'

CHAPTER 19

'Well,' the voice said, 'it's always pleasing to welcome an unexpected visitor.'

The tone was surprisingly relaxed in the circumstances. After all, even Tunjin had to acknowledge that he did not, just at the moment, present the most prepossessing sight. His usual shambling overweight figure was clad in a T-shirt and trousers which were quite clearly showing the impact of his brief period of living rough. His always-greasy hair was matted down on his head. And, on top of all that, he was covered in grass and bruises from his tumble down the hill.

He might have expected a rather less calm response from the man facing him. On the other hand, he also had to recognise that the man in question was holding a handgun, pointed unerringly at Tunjin's heart. Perhaps the man could afford to be relaxed.

Tunjin looked behind him at the broken fence, wondering precisely what kind of explanation he might offer for his presence. 'Um, I'm sorry,' he said. 'I slipped.' It didn't sound particularly appropriate.

The man was dressed in a plain dark suit, with a pale grey tie. He was Mongolian, but otherwise had few obviously distinguishing features. His hair was slicked back and he wore a pair of mirrored sun glasses, providing Tunjin with a disconcerting convex view of his own disarray. Tunjin noted irrelevantly that the effect of the curved mirrors did little to flatter his already obese figure.

The man, unsurprisingly, ignored Tunjin's offer of an explanation, and instead gestured with the barrel of the gun. 'I think you had better come this way,' he said. 'So that we can welcome you properly.'

Tunjin walked forward in the direction indicated by the gun barrel. The house was ahead of them, a rear door open in the spring sunshine. Tunjin hesitated, wondering if he should enter.

'Keep going,' the man said. 'Inside.'

Tunjin nodded, noting that the man's voice had become less welcoming. Tunjin found this oddly reassuring. At least, that was closer to what he understood.

He followed the path towards the door, glancing momentarily around at the tidiness of the garden. The grass was well-trimmed, the conifers neatly pruned. It hardly looked organic, he thought. It was as if someone had sculpted it from stone or wax. Even the colours seemed too bright.

'Inside,' the man said, again. His tone was definitely less friendly now, almost aggressive. Tunjin obeyed, and stepped through the doorway into the gloomy interior.

He wasn't sure what to expect beyond the door. Perhaps a hallway, or a kitchen. Instead, though, he found himself in a blank, empty room, probably originally intended as a scullery or cloakroom. Tunjin stopped, hearing the footsteps of the man with the gun behind him.

'Turn round,' the man said.

Tunjin turned, taking the opportunity to look around the room. There was little to see. The room was painted grey, with a floor of heavy stone tiles. There was no window, and the only light came through the door by which they had entered. There was a further door at the far end of the room, a solid-looking wooden edifice which appeared to be closed and, perhaps, locked. There was no furniture, and no decoration on the walls. Even as an entrance hall, the room looked bizarrely bleak and inhospitable.

The man reached behind him and pressed the light switch. Tunjin glanced up. There was a single bare lightbulb, which gave a harsh glare that served only to expose the asceticism of the room. The man smiled thinly, and then reached behind him to pull closed the outer door. It was a duplicate of the interior door – just as solid, just as impenetrable. It slammed shut with a dull thud, and the man carefully turned a large key in the lock. Still smiling, he slipped the key into his trouser pocket.

'There,' he said, 'now we're secure.' He was still smiling, but there was no warmth to the smile. It was as if the expression was a mask, painted on his face.

He walked forward slowly, still holding the gun pointed steadily at Tunjin's chest. For the first time – as though, up to that point, he had somehow managed to resist the evidence of his own eyes – Tunjin realised that his predicament was serious. He was in trouble.

Deep trouble. And he had walked – or, more accurately, fallen – into it entirely of his own volition.

The sun was setting behind them, staining the western sky a deep crimson. Blood, Nergui thought. It does really look like blood. It was as if a tide of blood was pouring down on the city. As if chaos really had arrived. As if all control was lost.

'I'm getting old,' he said to Doripalam, sitting beside him. 'I'm getting melodramatic. Sentimental.'

Doripalam laughed. He was leaning forward, concentrating on the road. He wondered whether they should have brought another officer, someone who could at least have done the driving. Luvsan, for example. He loved this kind of trip. Loved the buzz of driving these new 4x4s up on to the steppe. But Nergui had insisted they make this trip alone.

'I look forward to the day when you're sentimental,' he said. He paused, wondering whether to point out that, to take just one instance, Nergui had preferred to make this trip to the mountains rather than to stay in the city and wait for news of Sarangarel. It was a rational decision – of course it was, there was little that Nergui could do in the city – but it was not one that many men would have taken in the circumstances. But perhaps that thought was better kept to himself. 'Melodramatic,' he went on, 'perhaps, yes, I can see that. But you've always been that. It's nothing to do with growing old.'

Nergui grunted, although it was unclear whether this sound represented assent. 'It's as if,' he said, after an extended pause, 'as if we lost control a long time ago, but didn't know it. As if everything had spiralled out of our grip, and now we're flailing around trying to hold on to something—'

'Yes, melodramatic,' Doripalam nodded, his hands gripping the steering wheel. The empty road stretched ahead of them. In the distance, they could see the mountains, a dark strip against the translucent mauve of the evening sky. 'That's definitely the right word.' The truck hummed beneath them, echoing the repetitive pounding of the road. 'It's strange, though, isn't it?' Doripalam went on. 'Okay, if you're right, things have been out of our control for a long time. Or, at least, we've had nothing like as much control as we thought. But maybe that didn't matter too much—'

Nergui snorted – a sound which somehow managed with absolute eloquence to express his disgust. 'How can you say that?' he said, staring out of the passenger window at the hypnotic passing of the landscape. 'You see why I was suspicious of you?'

Doripalam sighed. 'You understand my point,' he said, 'even if you choose to misinterpret it. If Muunokhoi really had infiltrated the police to the extent you suggest—'

Nergui turned his head slowly towards Doripalam. 'There is no question,' he said. 'Muunokhoi had – has – infiltrated the police to the extent I suggest. If not more.'

'But my point is,' Doripalam said, 'that even if that is true – I'm sorry, yes, I accept it, I know that it is true – Muunokhoi was simply protecting his own interests. He may have constrained our work – or, at least, made sure that we didn't constrain his work too much – but he wasn't concerned to disrupt our work generally. We were able to police serious crime—'

'So long as it was serious crime not perpetrated by Muunokhoi,' Nergui pointed out.

'I'm not trying to excuse or justify it,' Doripalam said. 'I'm not – I'll keep repeating this till I'm absolutely sure you believe me – I'm not on Muunokhoi's payroll. I'm saying only that – well, it was a controlled situation. It was an explicable situation. It might even – I shouldn't say this – it might even have been a manageable situation.' He paused, still watching the curves of the road. 'But now things have changed.'

Nergui looked across at him, nodding slowly. He smiled faintly. 'You're right,' he said. 'Of course you're right. You're always right.'

'I thought that was your prerogative,' Doripalam said, barely able to contain the edge of smugness in his voice. It was strange how, even now, after all this time, and despite his own seniority, their relationship remained that of master and pupil.

Nergui smiled. 'Not now,' he said. 'Not at all now. I think I have not been right for a long time. Not in this matter. But, yes, on this occasion, you are certainly right. Things have changed. But I don't know why.'

Doripalam clutched the wheel. 'That's the point, isn't it?' he said. 'Whatever the situation before, it was rational. It was possible for us to respond to it. We could handle it.'

'And now we don't know what's happening,' Nergui said. 'We have a brutal murder – perhaps, though let us hope not, more then one. We have kidnapping – certainly one, perhaps more. We don't know about Gavaa. We don't even know now about Tunjin.' He paused. 'They may have caught up with him,' he said, finally.

Tunjin had been expecting it, at least in theory. Nevertheless, when the blow came, it took him by surprise. The man moved suddenly, an unexpected jerking motion, the gun barrel abruptly raised, then thrust across his face.

The metal barrel was cold and hard against his flesh. Tunjin fell backward, gasping for breath, startled less by the pain than by the suddenness of the action. The pain was slow in coming, but when it came it was sharp and agonising. He staggered backwards, trying to suppress a scream, and then his own substantial weight dragged him off his feet, and he fell backwards on to the floor.

He floundered for a moment, rolling around on the cold stone like a turtle toppled on to its shell. The man moved forward, the harsh light of the bare light bulb glittering on the mirrored lenses of his sunglasses. He drew back his foot and kicked savagely out at Tunjin's ribs. Tunjin rolled, avoiding the worst of the blow, which glanced across his shoulders. The man struck out again, forcing Tunjin back against the wall, this time absorbing the kick painfully against his stomach.

Tunjin gasped for breath, cowering back in expectation of the next blow. But the man paused, holding the gun barrel steadily towards Tunjin. 'Now,' he said, 'perhaps you will tell me the truth. I have to confess that, after your unexpected disappearance, we were not expecting to encounter you again so soon.'

Tunjin rolled over, still cowering against the wall, and stared at the man. It was difficult not to imagine that Muunokhoi had some powers that were more than merely human. He had managed – through who knew what kind of inside information – to see through Tunjin's half-baked attempt to frame him. He had managed to identify Tunjin as the perpetrator of this idiotic scheme, almost before he'd had time to admit his guilt to Doripalam. And, now, when Tunjin had harboured vain hopes of taking him at least momentarily by surprise, this operative had recognised him almost straight away. How was that possible? If the explanation was not supernatural, he could assume only that his picture – the policeman who had dared to threaten Muunokhoi with prison – was hanging up as a dire warning all around Muunokhoi's properties. The thought was not comforting.

'You look surprised,' the man said, echoing Tunjin's own thoughts. 'You should not be. We have a very good memory in this organisation. And good communications. It is helpful of you to have made yourself available so readily, but you would not have escaped us for long.'

The man smiled, the smile all the more terrifying for the blankness of his mirrored gaze. 'Though I confess I do not understand why you have chosen to come here. You are clearly more accommodating than we imagined.'

Tunjin said nothing, staring up at the towering

figure of the man. Even if he had wanted to, he did not think that he could have provided any coherent explanation. Like so much of his life, it had seemed a good idea at the time.

The only question now was what would happen to him. He could not believe that Muunokhoi's people had in mind to furnish him with a simple clean death. There would be more to come.

Again, with almost telepathic precision, the man echoed his thoughts. 'So,' he said, 'what are we going to do with you? There is nothing complicated about this. You know what you've done. You know what is likely to happen to you.' He paused, the smile, like the gun barrel, unwavering. 'For my part, I am curious to know what prompted you to come here. I am not sure whether to admire your courage or despise your stupidity. Quite possibly both, I suspect.'

Tunjin couldn't really argue with this judgement, which largely replicated his own. In any case, he was hardly in a position, or a state, to offer any kind of meaningful response. There was a part of him that hoped that, if he just kept still – if, for once, he just kept his mouth shut – he might still be allowed out of all this.

'You don't seem to have a lot to say,' the man observed. 'Perhaps I should offer some encouragement.' He stepped forward, and aimed another kick at Tunjin. Tunjin wrapped his arms around himself, pressed into the corner of the room, awaiting the blow.

Even so, its ferocity took him by surprise. He rolled just in time, taking the force of the impact on his arm. The blow was agonising. It felt as though his arm was broken. It was fortunate that the kick had not hit him in a more vulnerable part of his body, though for the moment that seemed little consolation.

'Now, do you feel encouraged?' the man said. 'Would you like to be a little more talkative?'

In truth, Tunjin felt precisely the opposite, though he suspected that this would not be a welcome response. He gasped, trying to grunt out some kind of answer, some words that might at least momentarily stay any further violence.

'I'm sorry,' the man said. 'I'm having difficulty following you. Perhaps you need a little more prompting.'

He stepped back, lifting his foot, preparing to aim another kick at Tunjin. Tunjin twisted awkwardly, feeling the agonising pain from his arm, the underlying pattern of bruising from the previous assaults and from his tumble down the hillside. This, he realised, was simply going to continue. Blow after blow. Kick after kick. Pain following pain, until he could bear it no longer. With any luck unconsciousness would follow, but he imagined the man would keep him awake for as long as he could. And then at that point he might introduce some more imaginative form of torture.

Afterwards, he remembered seeing the man raise his foot. He remembered tensing, his body poised for the impact. And he remembered somehow twisting suddenly, his body moving purely through instinct, his legs moving with an agility unexpected for someone of his bulk.

It was as if, up to that point, Tunjin's streetwise

skills – the instincts that had enabled him to survive through thirty years of hard policing – had deserted him, as if he had suddenly become a victim. And then, just as unexpectedly, all those instincts, all that unconscious savvy, suddenly returned.

His movement clearly took the man by surprise. Tunjin spun over, ignoring the agonising pains coursing through his body, and hooked his foot behind the man's leg. The man had been in the process of kicking, one foot raised, the other anchored to the floor. Tunjin dragged his foot around the latter, pulling the man off balance. Caught by surprise, the man staggered, toppling backwards. Tunjin took his momentary advantage and kicked out with his other foot, hitting the man at the top of his thigh. Then he kicked again, savagely, as the man fell, aiming for the groin.

The effect was better than he might have dared hope. The man fell, his arms flailing, his pistol clattering into the far corner of the room. He staggered backwards, trying desperately to regain his balance, slipping on the smooth flagstones, and then finally fell, his head hitting the solid stone floor with an appalling thud.

There was a long silence. Tunjin lay, gasping for breath, waiting for the man to sit up, to resume or increase his assault. But nothing happened. The man lay motionless, apparently unconscious.

Tunjin sat up, wondering what to do next. He clambered on to his hands and knees, his breath still coming in agonising bursts.

There was blood spreading from the man's head,

seeping out from beneath the splayed skull. The stain, crimson as the spring sunset across the steppe, expanded slowly across the grey stone, stark against the unrelenting flags.

CHAPTER 20

It was like another world, Nergui thought. Like an alien planet.

He always felt like this, away from the city. He was an urban creature, a creature of the twenty-first century. For all its faults, for all its shortcomings, the capital was part of the modern world, part of everything he associated with the West.

Nergui was hardly typical of his countrymen. Indeed, he was probably close to unique here. He had travelled widely in the West. He had lived in the US. He had lived in Europe. He was able to compare all this – everything his fellow citizens took for granted – with something different.

Not necessarily something better. He was no apologist for the West. He recognised, and was happy to acknowledge, its shortcomings. It was a godless place, he thought, a faithless place, with an emptiness at its heart. It was – ironically, given the nomadic culture of this place – a rootless civilisation. Here, for all the privations and suppression of the communist era, something spiritual had survived, some sense of contact with the land, the past, community and family.

But, out here, out in these rural spaces, it was difficult to feel that. They had driven through mile after mile of empty grassland, the rolling plains abolishing all sense of distance, as though this landscape might simply continue forever. In the clear spring evening, they saw no other vehicles, no other sign of life. Ahead, there was the dark shadow of the mountains, sharp against the crystalline sky. And before that they could see the black shading of the forests, though the shapes of the trees were too far away to discern.

Eventually, they saw the small scattering of hazy lights that revealed the presence of Bulgan in the distance. From here, it looked like a solitary beacon in the fading light, a single indication that human life had not abandoned this landscape.

It was another forty minutes or so before they reached the outskirts of the town. The woodland had thickened around them as they drove, and they began to see a scattering of log cabins and other buildings.

'Where's the place we're looking for?' Nergui said.

Doripalam turned. 'The camp. Just a few miles north of Bulgan. I hope I can find it again.'

'Assuming that the *gers* are still there.'

'Yadamsuren said the tents were still there yesterday. He's obeyed his orders and not gone near them, but he's been keeping an eye on them from a distance.'

'Assiduous of him,' Nergui commented.

'He's a good officer,' Doripalam said. 'We could use more like him in the team. He's wasted up here. Perhaps worse than wasted.'

Doripalam had wondered whether to make another effort to contact Tsend, to see whether he could glean anything more about what had happened to Mrs Tuya's family. But, despite the supposed urgency of the message Doripalam had left, Tsend had not so far returned his call. In the circumstances, they had to proceed with caution. If Tsend's behaviour was suspect, there was little point in giving him any further warning that they were heading up here.

'You should make him an offer,' Nergui said. 'See if you can tempt him into the big bad city.'

'I don't know whether he'd want to go.'

Nergui looked out of the truck window. They were passing through the centre of Bulgan. Even though it was the *aimag* capital, in the evening it looked like a ghost town. The streets were largely deserted, other than the occasional knot of bored looking teenagers drifting aimlessly through the central square. There were a few parked cars, but little traffic. 'If I was in his position,' Nergui said, 'I'd go tomorrow.'

'With respect,' Doripalam said, 'I'm not sure your views are representative.'

They passed through the town, and the buildings began to thin out again as they headed north into the forests. Once the city was behind them, Doripalam slowed, keeping alert for the turn off to where the *gers* were situated. It was dark now, and there was little to distinguish any part of the tree-lined road in the sweeping glare of their headlights.

At first, he thought he had missed it. Then, finally, when he was convinced they had gone too far, he spotted the angled track leading off the metalled road up towards the trees.

He slowed right down. 'There it is.'

'I'm impressed,' Nergui said. 'It looks just the same as the last four or five miles of forest to me.'

Doripalam turned the truck so that the headlight beams shone up through the trees, illuminating the rough track. 'No, that's it, I'm sure.'

'Where was the camp?'

'Over the hill. There's a kind of hollow beyond that. The tents are well concealed. You can see nothing at all from the road. You wouldn't know they were there unless you went looking for them.'

'Or unless someone had told you they were there,' Nergui said.

Doripalam nodded grimly. 'That's what worries me,' he said.

The two men emerged from the truck and stood for a moment breathing in the clear woodland air. It had been a warm day and the evening air was still temperate, rich with the scent of the pine trees. Other than the occasional rustling of the trees, the silence was complete.

Doripalam flicked on his flashlight and shone it up the path. 'This way,' he said. 'It's not far.'

He began to walk slowly up the incline, mindful of his last visit here – the pouring rain, the unexpected gunshots, the fear in the eyes of the four men. In the soft warmth of the night, it was hard to believe this was the same place.

They reached the top of the hill and stared down into the hollow beyond. There were no lights other than the flickering beam of the flashlight and for a moment Doripalam thought that the *gers* had gone. Then he shone the beam a little further back and found the grey shape of the foremost tent.

'There they are,' he said. 'Still there.'

Nergui moved beside him and nodded. 'No sign of life, though,' he said.

'I hope that's all it is, though,' Doripalam said. 'An absence of life rather than the presence of death.'

Nergui glanced at him, seeing the silhouette of Doripalam's face. 'You're getting philosophical,' he said. 'Maybe you've been in the job too long.'

Doripalam said nothing but began to make his way slowly down into the hollow, approaching the door of the first *ger*. He shone the flashlight carefully along the wall of the tent. The two other *gers* stood behind, as silent and dark as the first.

Doripalam reached out and pulled open the ornate wooden door. It was not locked and swung open easily to his touch. Beyond the door, there was only blackness. Doripalam stepped forward and shone his light into the interior, recalling the similar search he had conducted with Luvsan in Mrs Tuya's *ger*.

It was immediately clear that the tent was empty. The interior had a slightly stale smell, with an undertone of soured milk – maybe someone had spilt some *airag*. But there was nothing more unpleasant than that. Doripalam shone the flashlight around the enclosed space.

'Looks as if they conducted a pretty thorough search,' he commented. All the cupboards were pulled open, clothes and personal goods scattered across the floors. The bed had been pulled out, and the coverings torn from it. Drawers lay upended on the floor. Various containers – jars, tins, bottles – that had contained dried foodstuffs had been emptied with no concern for their contents.

'They were policemen,' Nergui said. 'Professionals. What would you expect?'

'The question is,' Doripalam said, 'did they find what they were looking for?'

'If they did,' Nergui said, 'they clearly didn't find it quickly. Let's have a look in the other *gers*.'

They stepped back out into the night. The sky was clear above them, studded with stars. There was a yellow moon rising over the horizon, enormous and swollen. They made their way around to the remaining two gers and systematically entered each one, looking carefully around at the contents. All of the *gers* were in the same state, clearly resulting from a painstaking search of their interiors.

'They've made no attempt to clear them up,' Nergui said. 'Just left them as they were.'

'Which is a serious dereliction of their duty,' Doripalam smiled grimly. 'But more importantly—'

'Suggests that they didn't have a high expectation that the owners would be returning to the tents anytime soon.'

'So what's happened to them?'

'Perhaps we do now need a conversation with your friend, Tsend,' Nergui said. 'It will be interesting at least to hear what story he comes up with.'

Doripalam nodded and pulled out his mobile. He dialled the number of the station in Bulgan. After a couple of rings, the call was answered, clearly by a desk officer on night duty.

'I need to speak to your Chief,' Doripalam said. 'Yes, I do know what time it is. I wasn't aware the police up here ran an office-hours only service. No, it is urgent. This is Doripalam, Head of the Serious Crimes Team in Ulan Baatar. I'm up here in your territory. I left an urgent message for your Chief earlier this afternoon, but he hasn't deigned to call me back. Now, I'm standing out in the night at what may be a crime scene and I need to speak to him. Immediately. And, no, I don't care what your orders are. I'm standing here with Nergui, representing the Ministry of Security, and I don't think either of us will be very pleased if we don't receive a response in the next – well, shall we say the next two minutes? Yes, you do that.'

He ended the call and looked back at Nergui. 'Tsend will call back immediately.'

Nergui raised an eyebrow. 'Let us hope so. We Ministry types do not like to be kept waiting.'

As if in response to his sardonic comment, the mobile rang immediately. Doripalam smiled faintly and answered the call. 'Very good of you to call back,' he said. 'No, I wouldn't dream of it. But I think you may very well be risking wasting ours.' He went on, his voice rising, clearly overriding whatever Tsend was saying at the other end of the phone. 'No – frankly, I don't care what you think about my behaviour. You can complain to whoever you like. I'm sure my colleague from the Ministry will be only too pleased to expedite your complaint. In the meantime, I'd like to know why my orders have been disregarded.'

There was a moment's silence, which clearly extended also to Tsend at the other end of the phone.

'I left four men in your custody,' Doripalam went on. 'Potential material witnesses in a murder case. In need of police protection, which I asked you to provide. I also made it very clear that this was a Serious Crimes case which fell outside your local jurisdiction.' He paused, waiting to see if Tsend made any response, but the silence at the far end of the line continued. 'I'm now standing at the site of the men's camp. And I discover that their tents have been thoroughly searched, apparently by your men. I would be very interested to know why. I am also concerned to know where the men are now.'

Again, there was no response. Doripalam had almost begun to wonder if Tsend had hung up, though he thought he could hear the other man's breathing. He stopped speaking himself, determined to offer no further prompt.

Finally, Tsend spoke, sounding almost out of breath. 'The men left,' he said. 'We couldn't hold them. They were not under arrest, you made that very clear. We could not hold them against their will.'

'And why were they suddenly so keen to leave?' Doripalam said. 'They were desperate for protection.'

'I do not know.' There was another prolonged pause. 'We had organised some accommodation for them. A safe house. I was about to contact you to seek further orders—' There was an implied reproach in Tsend's tone which Doripalam knew was at least partially justified. He had not followed up the men's situation as he should have done. Things had moved too quickly since then, but that was no excuse. 'But then, overnight, they vanished. I do not know why. That was why I sent my men out to check their camp. To see if the tents had been removed. To see if there was any clue where they might have gone.' There was another slight hesitation and then Tsend continued, more confident now. 'I thought that you would want me to have all the facts before I advised you of the situation.'

It sounded plausible enough, if you accepted the suggestion that the four men had simply disappeared. It would not have been surprising if this local police chief had wanted to be pretty sure of his ground before he reported back on the situation. Maybe that was why he had taken so long to return Doripalam's call. On the other hand, this still did not explain why the men had suddenly chosen to leave.

'And you've no idea why they left? Or where?'

'None at all,' Tsend said. 'But then I had little knowledge about the significance of these individuals in the first place. This was, of course, a Serious Crimes matter.' He was sounding much more confident now, Doripalam thought, having negotiated his way successfully through this discussion. It was even possible that Tsend's role in this was entirely innocent. If the nomads had felt under threat from within the police service – or, even worse, if anything had actually happened to them – then the culprits might well sit at more junior levels. And maybe this was all just paranoia, another Muunokhoi-inspired ghost.

'As you say,' Doripalam acknowledged. 'But these people are important witnesses – even more important now, perhaps, than we originally thought. We need to have them found. I want to put as much resource as you can on this.'

There was only the briefest grudging pause before Tsend said, 'Yes, of course. My men are already on to it. But I will treat it as a priority.'

'I would be very grateful,' Doripalam said, trying hard to keep any edge of irony out of his voice. 'I'm sorry for disturbing your evening.'

'No problem. As I said, I am always pleased to assist the Serious Crimes Team.' Tsend made less effort to moderate his tone. 'Goodnight.'

Doripalam stood for a moment, looking at the silent phone. He looked up at Nergui through the darkness and repeated the gist of the conversation.

Nergui shrugged. 'As you say, it sounds convincing enough. But it does not explain why the men suddenly decided that police protection was not for them.'

'We have to assume that they did not feel sufficiently protected.'

'Either that,' Nergui said, 'or they learned that from experience.'

Doripalam nodded grimly. 'Let us hope not,' he said. 'Let us hope that their departure was voluntary.'

Nergui took some steps forward into the thickening darkness and peered at the cluster of *gers*. 'Do you think there is anything more for us to learn here?'

'Probably not,' Doripalam said. 'If there was anything here, I'm sure the locals would have found it. They searched the place pretty thoroughly.'

'All the same,' Nergui said, 'I'm reluctant to leave the hunt for our friends solely to the local force.'

'I'm not sure we have much option,' Doripalam said. 'We've little chance of making progress here on our own.'

As if not listening, Nergui switched on his own flashlight and began to walk slowly around the *gers*, his eyes fixed on the ground as if searching for some discarded item. Through the trees, the moon had risen higher, casting pale light across the steppe.

'Nergui,' Doripalam said. 'I don't think—'

Nergui raised his hand, as if silencing Doripalam. He was little more than a silhouette against the paler star-filled sky, the torchlight jumping in his hand. For a moment, Doripalam lost sight of him as he disappeared behind the *gers*. He reappeared unexpectedly, shining the torch directly at Doripalam. 'There is something,' he said, his voice little more than a whisper, 'something not quite right here.'

'What do you mean?' Doripalam said.

'If the local police really are looking for these men,' Nergui said, 'surely they would have kept this place under observation. If the men really are missing, surely there is a good chance they will return, if only to collect their possessions.'

'Maybe not. There are lots of possibilities. If they're as scared as we think, then they might well think it's not worth coming back here, regardless of what they've left behind.' Doripalam paused. 'And of course it's possible that they're not simply missing. That they're in no position to return anywhere. And, on top of all that, you're assuming that Tsend was telling the truth about having started looking for them.'

'You're right, of course,' Nergui said. 'But I think he would have – at least to the extent of staking out this place. It doesn't make any sense that he would have sent his people out to search the place and then just left it.'

'Unless he knew that they were never going to return.'

'Of course, but – even if we assume that Tsend is involved in all this – unless we assume the whole force is corrupt, he'd want to go through the motions if only so it would look convincing to you.'

Doripalam nodded, unsure of the logic of all this. 'But in any case,' he said, 'how do you know the place isn't being staked out?' He looked around uncomfortably. 'We could be being watched.'

'We could,' Nergui said. 'But if he saw two men hanging around here, wouldn't he have called for back-up by now? And either back-up would be on its way or – if he managed to get hold of Tsend – he'd know who we are and come out to introduce himself.' Doripalam could just make out Nergui's dark face in the moonlight. He seemed to be smiling. As so often with Nergui, Doripalam was wondering both how seriously to take all this and – at the same time – quite where it might all be leading.

'I don't know,' Doripalam admitted. 'I'm not sure I have quite your faith in the rationality of other people's thought processes.'

'The thing is,' Nergui said, 'I know that the place was being staked out. Until quite recently.'

Doripalam looked up sharply at Nergui. 'What do you mean?'

'I'm sorry,' Nergui said. 'I have just been trying to work out the logic in my own mind.'

'What logic?'

Nergui had begun to wander back around the tents, gesturing Doripalam to follow him into the dark shadow of the trees.

'The logic,' Nergui said, 'of precisely who this is and how he came to be here.'

He shone his torch, with a vaguely melodramatic action, into the darkness. But there was no need for any further melodrama. Lying on the rough grass, his head twisted awkwardly towards the sky, blank eyes glittering in the thin moonlight, was a dead man. And not just any dead man, but a police officer, his uniform dark with his own recently-shed blood.

Sarangarel was staring out of the window. There had been some commotion out in the garden, just a few minutes before, but she had been unclear about its significance. Someone – one of the staff, she assumed, one of the heavies – had run across the pristine lawn, a startled expression on his face. She had seen that, as he ran, he had been pulling out a handgun, so she assumed that this interlude, whatever it might be, had not been planned.

But, sadly, she had lost sight of him after that. He had run briefly past the window, a determined expression on his face, his eyes lost behind mirrored sunglasses that momentarily caught the glare of the late evening sun. Then he was gone, and she was left to wonder what had happened and what this might portend for her position here.

She was unclear precisely what that might be. But she was at least clear that the short man, the man who had questioned her, had been unhappy with her responses. It was clear that she had not given him what he wanted, what he had expected. It was clear that these people, whoever they might be, thought she had something, some information. And perhaps she did. Perhaps she knew something, but did not know that she knew it.

Something connected to the papers she had received and to her husband, that was for sure. Well, of course, what else would be interesting about her life? Even though she was a member of the judiciary, even though she held a senior legal position, it was obvious that she couldn't leave all that behind. She had thought she had turned into someone different. She had thought that it was possible to recreate herself, to forget everything that had gone before. But of course that was not possible. She was, underneath it all, the same person who had entered into that marriage all those years ago. She was the same person who had lived with the consequences. And she was – and this was the really unnerving part – the same person who was living with those consequences now.

She stood for some more moments, staring out at the silent empty garden, watching the play of the setting sunshine on the treetops, crimson against the brilliant green of the leaves. Then she turned back to look at the luxurious room behind her. Her original guardian had returned and was sitting as he had before, motionless, apparently uninterested in her presence. He looked across the room at nothing in particular, his expression blank.

'How long will this go on?' she said.

He turned his head to look at her, as if seeing her for the first time, but did not respond.

'This is ridiculous,' she said. 'It's quite clear that I can't answer any of your questions. It's equally clear that you can't keep me indefinitely.' She paused, wondering about that. They could keep her here as long as they chose. It depended on what they were willing to do. 'It would be much simpler if you let me go now. It's clear that there's been some misunderstanding. Of course, I appreciate that. I know how these things happen. But it would be simplest if you were just to let me go. Take me back.' She was babbling, she thought, keeping only just this side of desperation.

The man said nothing, but continued to stare at her, as if she was speaking some foreign language. Perhaps she was, she thought. This man looked like a local, but perhaps he wasn't. Or perhaps he was deaf. Or perhaps . . .

She shook her head. This was ridiculous. These were just mind games that they were playing with her. Toying with her. Keeping her waiting. Leaving her with this man who seemed incapable of responding to her in any way. They were hoping that, if she did know something – if she did know whatever it was they wanted to hear – that eventually she would break down and tell them. And very probably they were right. She would be only too happy to talk right now. If only she knew what it was they wanted.

She was about to try again with the guard – not because she expected any response but simply to keep her mind alert – when the door of the drawing room opened. She was expecting to see the short man again, but instead there were two men, both dressed in dark suits and wearing similar mirrored glasses to those she had seen on the man outside. Clearly, this was some sort of uniform in this household. It was possible that one of these men was the figure she had seen through the window, but she thought not. Although they all looked similar – Mongolians, with slicked back dark hair, with their identical dark suits – she was fairly sure that these men were different from the individual she had seen previously.

The two men stood silently in the doorway for a moment, watching her. Then one of them gestured to her to follow. 'This way,' he said, in a quietly spoken but authoritative tone.

She hesitated for a moment, wondering where all this might be leading. The man at the table had remained motionless, hardly acknowledging the presence of the two figures at the door.

'I'm not sure I—' she said, unsure quite how she was intending to finish the sentence.

In the event, she had no need to. One of the men walked forward and seized her roughly by the arm. He dragged her across the floor and over to the door. She opened her mouth to protest and then, seeing the expression on his face, thought better of it.

She was pulled violently out of the room and into the hallway beyond. She barely had time to glimpse the vast size of the hallway before she was pulled through another doorway.

Beyond the doorway, at first there was only darkness. Then, just in time, her eyes grew accustomed to the gloom and she realised that, at the end of a short landing, a set of stone stairs fell away into deeper darkness. The man on her left pulled at her arm and dragged her forward, virtually dragging her on to the stairway. She tried to protest but the words jammed in her dry throat. And then she was being pulled down the stairs, her feet in their high heels stumbling on the hard stone risers. At one point, she almost fell but was dragged back to her feet by the two men.

Within seconds, they were at the bottom of the stairs. Immediately, the room was filled with an eyeball-burning glare. She blinked, unable to see for a moment, then slowly her vision cleared.

They were in some kind of cellar, she supposed. It was an empty space, the opposite of the well-appointed room she had occupied upstairs, with a blank stone floor and bare brick walls. There was no furniture, other than some functional metal-framed chairs and a line of benches along the wall, and no other sign of occupancy. There were no obvious windows or doors other than the stairway by which they had entered.

The men waited a moment, then, suddenly and unexpectedly, one of them pushed her. She stumbled and fell, grazing one of her knees on the hard stone floor, tearing her tights, feeling her silk dress ripping slightly. She landed awkwardly on her side, momentarily breathless.

Then, her spirit not quite yet destroyed by her predicament, she rolled out and began to shout expletives at the two men, with a sudden outburst of the anger that had been building in her since she had first been dragged into the car.

There was no response. The two men turned on

their heels and began to climb the stairs. She staggered to her feet to try to follow them, but it was too late. They reached the top of the stairs and pushed open the door. Then, as a final act, one of the men reached out and turned out the lights, throwing the cellar back into pitch darkness. Sarangarel stood, not daring to move, her mind as blank as the darkness around her. From somewhere above, she heard the click of a key turning in the lock.

Tunjin was still lying half on his side, scarcely able to recover his breath. The man who had brought him here, the man with the mirrored sunglasses, was motionless. Tunjin could see the blood seeping from the man's skull and thought that it looked as if the man might well never move again.

Finally, still gasping, Tunjin dragged himself to his knees and looked at the figure sprawled on the stone floor. He reached out and gingerly took the man's wrist, alert for any sign of sudden movement or response. The figure lay, inert, while Tunjin tried to see if there was any pulse.

There was none. It was difficult to be absolutely certain – these were hardly ideal circumstances for a medical examination – but Tunjin was sure that he was dead. In the circumstances, he found it hard to be too regretful.

So where did this leave things? Did anyone else know he was here? Had the man been responding to orders, or had he contacted others in the household to let them know what he had found? It seemed likely. How else would the man have known who Tunjin was? Perhaps Tunjin had simply been unlucky and stumbled upon someone who happened to recognise him. But it seemed more likely that Tunjin had been spotted on some closed circuit television screen and a collective identification had been made.

Still, even if that was the case, Tunjin had at least managed to buy himself some time. Even if others knew he was here, they now presumably thought he was safely under lock and key. They would not know the truth until his captor was missed. Which, Tunjin was forced to acknowledge, might not take very long.

He crawled across to the wall, and pulled himself slowly to his feet. As so often, he wished that he was fitter, or at least less completely corpulent. Still, the way things were going, he might be destined to leave his corporeal self fairly definitively behind before too long, so there was no point in fretting too much. If he ever got out of this, he thought, he would lose some weight. He would give up drinking. All that. And how often had he made those promises?

He looked about him, taking in the blank empty room. Which way should he go? He could head back outside, which felt safer. But was it really? They had spotted him quickly in the garden. And, more to the point, what could he achieve outside?

If he penetrated further indoors – well, there was every chance that they would apprehend him quickly, but then that was true outside as well. And at least he might have a chance of finding out what was going on here, perhaps identify the woman he had seen being brought into the building.

It sounded pretty thin, even to the ever-optimistic

Tunjin. But, still, here he was, one of Muunokhoi's heavies lying dead at his feet. There was no obvious way of going back. All he could do was go forward, wherever that might lead.

At least half-convinced, he stepped forward, his heart beating heavily, and began to turn the handle on the door that led into the house.

'He's dead,' Doripalam said, dropping the wrist in which he had been trying to detect a pulse.

Nergui nodded. 'Thanks for your perseverance,' he said. 'Though I think you are only confirming what I had assumed.'

Doripalam shrugged. 'I'm nothing if not scrupulous. If it adds anything, he's not been dead for long. There is still some warmth in the body. It is not a cold evening, but – well, who knows? Maybe two or three hours.'

'Our pathologists would not be more precise,' Nergui conceded. 'Recent, anyway.'

'Recent,' Doripalam agreed. He rose from his crouching position and looked around at the surrounding trees, their dark shadows visible only against the pale moonlight. 'And shot. Which means that he could have been shot from some distance away.'

'Which means,' Nergui said, 'that we could also be targets.'

'I always like to be cautious,' Doripalam said, switching off his flashlight.

Nergui followed suit. 'I suppose you're right,' he said, 'though it does little to alleviate my feeling of vulnerability. The prospect of a sniper is never an attractive one.'

Doripalam nodded. This was ridiculous, he thought. There's a killer out here. We don't know who he is or why he's killed. All we know is that, so far, his one victim is a policeman. We should get out of here, come back in daylight. On the other hand, this was the only lead they had.

His cogitations were cut short by the sudden, shattering sound of a gunshot. Nergui dropped instantly, and for a moment Doripalam thought he had been hit, but then he saw him roll over and throw himself against a tree. At the same moment, he saw the silver glimmer of a handgun in Nergui's hand. Not for the first time, Doripalam was left wondering how a man twenty years his senior could move so rapidly. Almost as an afterthought, he dropped himself, reaching for his gun, wondering what the hell was happening.

He lay pressed against the cold damp grass, looking feverishly around, trying to spot their assailant, but there was no sign of movement. He looked across at Nergui.

And then they heard the voice calling, thin and tremulous in the chilly night air. 'Please don't move,' it said. 'Please stay still.' There was a pause, and they could almost hear the nervous intake of breath. 'I don't want to have to kill you too.'

CHAPTER 21

For long minutes she stood in the darkness, wondering what the hell was going to happen now. The blackness seemed complete, and there was no sound that she could detect, once the tiny echoes of the locking door had died away.

She dared not move. As far as she could recall, the room had been empty of furniture so there was no real risk in walking through the darkness till she reached the walls. On the other hand, there was little point, either. She sighed and slowly lowered herself to the cold stone floor, feeling the sharp pain from her bruised knee.

She realised that her optimism – never more than half-hearted in the first place – had been entirely without foundation. Having brought her here, in search of whatever arcane piece of information, there was no way that they were simply going to let her go. What had she imagined? That they might just acknowledge that they had made a mistake, that she would simply shrug it off as a misunderstanding?

No. Having embarked on this route, there was no obvious way they could turn back. And she had no choice but to go with them all the way. Wherever that might lead.

She sat back on the cold floor, feeling the despair sweeping over her. There was no way out of this, she thought. Wherever this might be leading, it was nowhere she wanted to go. This darkness might as well go on forever.

But, of course, it didn't. Even in the midst of that thought, the light suddenly came flooding back, blinding her with its unexpected brilliance. She sat motionless on the stone floor, feeling its unyielding pressure on her back and buttocks, wondering what might happen next.

'Mrs Radnaa,' the voice said. 'Or, rather Judge Radnaa.'

She blinked, still unable to see, wondering who was speaking, thinking that she had heard the voice before.

'I'm sorry,' the voice said. 'I had not intended that things would reach this point.'

She continued blinking, not able to see, not really trying to see, unsure whether she wanted to face whatever might meet her gaze. The light seemed too bright, as if she might never be able to see again.

'But here we both are,' the voice said. 'There is nothing we can do. We have to live with it.'

She dropped her head into her hands, still trying to see, noting that way that the speaker, whoever it might be, had somehow managed to implicate her in the situation, as if she was partly responsible for this.

Finally, as she rubbed her eyes, her vision began to clear. She could see the blank emptiness of the room, the bare brick walls, the stone floor. And then, there at the far end of the room, a solitary wooden chair. And on the chair a figure.

She recognised him, she thought. She knew him from somewhere. But her mind was barely working, was barely able to compute any information.

'Good afternoon, Mrs Radnaa,' the voice said. 'I'm sorry I was unable to greet you earlier.'

The figure was relaxed, slumped on the hard wooden chair. He was dressed in an expensive looking striped shirt, open at the neck, and blue denim jeans. He was shaven headed, an earring dangling from his left ear lobe. And he was smiling.

She sat up, conscious of her undignified position sprawled on the hard stone floor. Rather different from the last time they had met. 'It is you then?' she said, conscious of how ridiculous her words sounded, echoing round the empty room.

'Well, of course,' Muunokhoi said. 'Though you never really doubted that, did you?'

'I suppose not,' she acknowledged. She paused. 'Though I have no idea what it is you want.' She stumbled to her feet, trying hard not to show any sign of weakness, though her efforts were hardly convincing.

He nodded, his limbs sprawled relaxedly. 'I appreciate the difficulty of talking about these things.' He hesitated. 'I'm sorry,' he said. 'I am hardly being a gentleman. You will want to sit down.' He gestured beside him. There was a second chair, a few yards from his own. 'Please.'

For the first time it occurred to her to wonder where these chairs, not to mention Muunokhoi himself, had come from. Still half-dazzled by the glare, she looked around her. The room looked as blank and empty as ever. There was no obvious entrance other than the steps down which she had been brought. Muunokhoi had, it seemed, come from nowhere.

But all of that was nothing more than showmanship, designed to disconcert her. It didn't really matter where Muunokhoi had come from. He was not a ghost. He was a solid, living man. He had come from somewhere. There was some other way in, some other concealed entrance.

She was surprised how difficult it was to convince herself of this.

'I cannot talk to you like this,' Muunokhoi went on. 'Please, Mrs Radnaa, I ask you to sit down.'

She stumbled forward, still not entirely steady on her feet. She had wondered vaguely whether she might gain some sort of psychological advantage by remaining standing. But she realised now that this was not a serious option. She could barely manage to stay upright.

She took three steps forward and slumped on to the hard wooden chair, looking up at Muunokhoi. 'Okay,' she said, trying to sound uncowed. 'Talk to me now. Tell me what this is all about.'

Muunokhoi shrugged and paused, as if not knowing how to begin. 'It is a long story,' he said.

'I don't doubt it,' she said, gathering some courage. 'But I'd expected better of you, Muunokkoi. I wasn't brought here to listen to fairy stories.'

He smiled faintly. 'You are right,' he said. 'I should not be subjecting you to stories that begin "once upon a time". We Mongolians are always storytellers.'

'I hear plenty of Mongolian tall tales in court,' she said. 'I'm not sure I want to hear yours.'

He nodded, as though seriously taking account of this comment. 'I do not wish to bore you,' he said. 'But my story is an interesting one. Especially to you, I imagine.'

She shrugged, tired already of this interchange, suddenly feeling the sharp pain in her knees and all the weary aching of her body. 'Tell me,' she said. 'You clearly intend to.'

He looked at her, no longer smiling, and paused as though now, at this point, he was suddenly unsure whether he really did want to share his story. Then he said: 'Okay. Indulge my storytelling. This is not quite "once upon a time" but it begins fifteen years ago—'

She nodded, determined to strip any shreds of melodrama from his story. 'When else?'

He shrugged, smiling again. 'You are clearly ahead of me,' he said. 'Perhaps I should ask you to tell the story. But, no, you claim not to know all the details. That is the point. Fifteen years is, after all, a long time.'

'At the moment,' she said, pointedly, 'five minutes is beginning to seem like a long time. If you have something to tell me, please get to the point.'

His smile was unwavering, his eyes fixed on hers, their dark pupils glittering in the brilliant cellar light. 'I had not intended to try your patience. But I have to start fifteen years ago. You were, I believe, married then?'

She stared at him, refusing to give any acknowledgement of his question. He knew full well that she had been married then, and to whom, just as he presumably knew equally well that she was not married now.

Nevertheless, Muunokhoi nodded as if she had responded to his question. 'Your husband, as you have probably surmised, worked for me.' He paused. 'He was not one of my more effective associates. But then, I imagine that is also not a surprise to you.' Again, he paused, as though expecting some sort of response. This is, Sarangarel thought, a man used to playing to an appreciative audience.

'Your husband was a fool in many ways, Mrs Radnaa. Let me enumerate some of them for you.' He smiled faintly, watching her closely. It was all an act, she thought. Every word, every gesture. This was no more the real Muunokhoi than the silent figure who had sat opposite her in court. His eyes were blazing, staring at her unblinking, but there was nothing behind them, no sense of life or personality.

'Some would say,' he went on, 'that your husband's first foolish act was accepting my offer of work in the first place. But he did not know that the offer was mine, any more than I knew, initially at least, that it had been made. It was simply an offer of a commercial contract from one of my companies for the handling of some import work. The terms were generous, as they always are with my suppliers. I think loyalty is always worth buying, don't you?' He smiled and waited a moment, as though seriously expecting her to answer the question. 'As you can imagine, I had no personal awareness of your husband at that point. He was recommended to us by some mutual contact. We were told that he was already running a successful import and export business.'

It was Sarangarel's turn to offer a thin smile. 'I hope

that your sources are better informed today.' She paused, wondering how far to take this. 'But perhaps not, given that you've brought me here in the hope of obtaining some information.'

Muunokhoi ignored her comment. 'You are right, of course. We had been misled. Though I believe that your husband was always skilled at creating the illusion of success.'

'One of his few talents,' she said. 'A fatal one, as it turned out.'

'We realised very quickly that your husband's business was less prosperous than he might have led us to believe. That did not necessarily worry us unduly so long as he was capable of fulfilling our contract – which did not initially appear to be a problem. After a trial, we offered him more work which he carried out to our satisfaction, and he became a regular supplier to us. More than that, he introduced us to some of his own contacts – notably, Khenbish, the soldier, who was able to offer us some useful, ah, overseas relationships. We were very pleased with your husband at first. His contacts opened up some useful seams of business for us. Some profitable areas.'

'I never met Khenbish,' Sarangarel said. 'He had served in Afghanistan, I understand.' She paused, regarding Muunokhoi closely, trying to read his expression. There was nothing to read.

She remembered this period of their marriage, shortly before Gansukh's arrest and death. Gansukh had finally thought that things were coming right for him. There was the prospect of ongoing work, money was coming in. For the first time, the business was something more than merely hand to mouth. He told her little about the nature of these new contracts, and she had not wanted to enquire too closely. She hadn't really believed a word of it. Gansukh had always been full of pipe-dreams – an apposite description given the kind of business he was probably involved in. She knew he had, at that moment, been making some good money, but she had assumed it would just fizzle out like all his previous schemes.

Even now, she was not entirely sure what Muunokhoi was talking about, but she could easily envisage the nature of these illicit imports best handled by some disposable third party. Probably, despite what Muunokhoi now said, they had selected Gansukh precisely because his business was struggling. He would have done anything for these people, and he was the kind of small fry who could be dropped at a moment's notice if anything went wrong. As, of course, it had.

As though reading her thoughts, Muunokhoi went on: 'But it was then that your husband began to demonstrate quite how foolish he could be. First, we discovered that he was handling other, similar consign-ments alongside our own. Not necessarily a problem in itself. We do not demand exclusivity from our suppliers – that would not be realistic – but we do expect that they exercise some discretion and care. We have our own interests to protect. And it soon became clear to us that your husband was less discreet and careful than we might have liked.' He paused. 'So we began to pay a little more attention to him. And we discovered that his foolishness was really quite considerable. Not only was he handling other consignments alongside ours, but it appeared that, on occasions, he was substituting inferior product for ours.' He stopped again, as though allowing Sarangerel an opportunity to appreciate the enormity of this behaviour. 'In other words,' he continued, 'there were occasions when our customers received inferior goods from those they had expected. Whereas presumably your husband was selling our products on to his own customers. Not good for our business reputation.'

Sarangerel was beginning to find the circumlocution very wearying. 'What are we talking about here?' she said. 'Drugs?'

Muunokhoi smiled at her. 'We supply a wide range of import needs,' he said. He sounded as if he was giving evidence to a government committee.

'So why didn't you do something about Gansukh at that stage?' she said. 'I'm sure you have means of dealing with those who don't meet your exacting commercial standards.'

He nodded. 'We would have taken some action. Some disciplines are needed in business. But it was rendered unnecessary by your husband's own continuing foolishness.'

'He was arrested,' she said. She hesitated as another thought struck her. 'Were you behind that?' After all, she thought, there was really no need for Muunokhoi to engage in strong arm tactics. A quiet word in the right quarters would presumably be sufficient.

'I run a very efficient business, Mrs Radnaa. I have good contacts. I maintain high commercial standards. If someone – one of our suppliers – was behaving inappropriately, I would certainly consider drawing this to the attention of the appropriate authorities. But in this case it was not necessary. Your husband was not only dishonest. He was also incompetent.'

Sarangarel wondered whether Muunokhoi thought that all these disparaging references to Gansukh were likely to have an impact on her. If so, he knew little about either her or her marriage.

'We have a range of operating procedures. We have developed these over years as the most effective and secure methods of handling our business. We asked your husband to follow these procedures. He chose not to. He was arrested. No action was needed on our part.'

It was easy to believe, she thought. Gansukh had been capable of making many enemies, but none worse than himself.

'I'm sorry,' she said. 'I still don't understand why you're telling me all this. It was all a very long time ago. I knew nothing of it. I still know nothing of it.'

'I understand that,' he said. 'But this was only the beginning of your husband's foolishness. As I say, we do look for a little discretion from our suppliers, particularly if things go wrong. That is partly why we pay them so well. We organise things very carefully so that the nature of our business relationships does not become too explicit.'

I bet you do, she thought. 'You mean so that no one can link you to the poor bastards who do your dirty work,' she said.

'Not quite the words I would use,' Muunokhoi said. 'But, yes, a reasonable summary.'

'But you must have contracts? Written arrangements of some kind?'

He nodded. 'But the nature of the contracts – the companies involved – do not always fully reflect the nature of the business transacted.'

Sarangarel wondered where Muunokhoi had picked up this kind of Western business speak. Was this how all the gangsters talked these days? Concealing the reality of their activities under this shell of meaningless verbiage. Another triumph of Western capitalism. 'So how do you make sure your – suppliers adhere to your real terms?' she said, despising herself for adopting the same kind of euphemistic language.

He shrugged. 'Most of our contracts are verbal,' he said. 'It does not matter. Our suppliers – and our customers – fully understand the implications if they fail to adhere to our terms. It is a matter of honour.'

She almost laughed out loud. Did Muunokhoi really believe all this? Had he become so lost in the tangle of his own commercial transactions that he no longer recognised what he was really involved with? It was quite possible, she thought. And arguably this was no different from any other business – just a difference in scale, perhaps. Those at the top didn't allow themselves to reflect on the realities of their activities. 'And I take it Gansukh was not so honourable?' she said. For the first time, she almost began to feel a trace of admiration for her late husband.

'You might say that. I think he had tried to take out some insurance. He knew he was playing a dangerous game, but I'm afraid that greed got the better of him.'

Muunokhoi was shameless, she had to give him that, lecturing others on the perils of greed.

'So he tried to pre-empt what we might do. He had recorded some of the conversations he had had with my people – both telephone and face to face. Probably not good quality, but enough to be potentially incriminating. And then there was Khenbish. We built up a rather more substantial relationship with Khenbish than we did with your husband, as he was able to put my companies in contact with some lucrative overseas opportunities. Our relationship was a little more – formal. We hadn't realised – at least, not initially – that Khenbish was also working closely with your husband and was involved in some of his petty scams. A pity. Khenbish could have worked very successfully with us without getting involved in that kind of sordid enterprise, if only he'd played straight.'

In her professional life, Sarangarel never ceased to be astonished at the subtle gradations of criminal morality. In other circumstances, she would have been blackly amused at Muunokhoi's contempt for those engaged in less successful criminality than his own.

'We hadn't realised – not until a little later – that Khenbish had shared some of these formal arrangements with your husband. We don't know precisely what was disclosed, but we have reason to believe that your husband copied at least some of the material.'

To her own surprise, she found that this time she did laugh out loud. For the first time, Muunokhoi showed some reaction, opening his blank eyes wider in surprise. 'You find something amusing in this?' he said.

'You've gone to great lengths to illustrate how

foolish my late husband was – which, I have to tell you, was scarcely news to me. But it seems to me that he was probably smarter than you gave him credit for.'

Muunokhoi nodded. 'There was a degree of – street cunning there, I admit,' he said. 'He was a different creature from those we were used to dealing with.'

'Anyway,' she went on, looking to press home some sort of psychological advantage, even though she was still unsure where this discussion was heading, 'how do you know he tried to take out this – insurance? Did he try to – make a claim?' This euphemistic nonsense was disturbingly catching, she thought.

'He did not have a chance,' Muunokhoi said.

'That was why you had him killed,' she said simply, watching for his reaction.

He threw up his hands and laughed. 'Mrs Radnaa, I am not a murderer. I cannot deny that your husband's suicide was convenient for me, in that it removed a risk. But it required no intervention from me. He had nowhere else to go.'

She stared at him, trying to detect some sign of emotion, some revelation in his expression, but there was nothing.

'So why do you think he had this material?' she repeated.

Muunokhoi shrugged. 'Some of it we learned from Khenbish, who was rather more co-operative once he realised what we knew about his dealings with your husband.'

'I bet he was,' she said. 'I hope that you looked after him well in return.'

'Sadly, we did not have the opportunity.'

'You killed him as well.'

'Mrs Radnaa, you really do have a low opinion of me, don't you?'

'You've no idea,' she said.

'He was a soldier. He died in action. Or, at least, on duty.'

'You really are an unfortunate man, Muunokhoi. People are dying all around you.'

He smiled icily. 'Then you should be concerned at being in my presence, Mrs Radnaa. Especially as I believe that some of your husband's insurance policy is now in your possession.'

'You think I have materials that might incriminate you?'

'I don't know what the content of these materials is,' Muunokhoi said, 'but I believe that your husband thought they might offer him some protection.'

'And that was why he sent them off for safe-keeping with some cousin on the other side of the country?' she said. 'If so, it was another smart move. So he was one step ahead of you there as well.' She recalled the break-in at her flat, shortly after Gansukh's death, when her world was still in turmoil. She had had few possessions of any value, and nothing had been stolen other than a small amount of loose cash. But the apartment had been left in a mess, presumably – or so the police had suggested – because the intruders had tried to find something else worth stealing. Now, though, she was sure that Muunokhoi's men had been behind this, hunting for these mysterious documents.

Muunokhoi nodded his head. 'Smarter than we thought, certainly. It is a pity that he never had the

opportunity to exploit such intelligence. A pity also –
for him, that is – that he never had the chance to use
the insurance policy he had so carefully arranged.'

'The police thought he was about to make a deal,'
she said. 'Just before his death. It seems a strange time
for him to have committed suicide.'

'Who can fathom the workings of the disturbed
mind?' Muunokhoi said piously.

'I'm certainly having great difficulty just at the
moment,' she said. She leaned forward. She was still
feeling deeply anxious, trapped here in this bare room
with a very dangerous individual, but somehow she
had been able, for the moment at least, to push her
fears to the back of her mind. The only way out of this
was to reason her way out, somehow persuade
Muunokhoi that it was not in his interests to harm her.
It was the longest of long shots, but she saw little alternative. No one else knew she was here. Quite probably
no one other than Nergui knew that she had been
kidnapped, and she had no idea what kind of state
Nergui was in. If he was safe and unharmed, then he
would probably assume that Muunokhoi was behind
her kidnapping, but she did not fool herself that
mounting a search of Muunokhoi's properties would
be a straightforward task, even for Nergui. In the
meantime, the only option she could see was to keep
probing, in the hope that she might uncover some
means of justifying her release.

'What I don't understand,' she went on, 'is what
you're really worried about. Even if Gansukh did
somehow manage to cobble together some potentially
incriminating papers – and, even if he turned out to be

360

smarter than you expected, you shouldn't over-estimate his abilities – surely the threat went away once he was . . . after his death.'

Muunokhoi nodded, as though absorbing new information. 'We thought that was probably so,' he said. 'But we couldn't be sure. If your husband really was smart, he would have wanted some bargaining counter in place in case he was threatened. He would need some means of releasing the incriminating material even if he were incapacitated or dead. Otherwise – and I speak only of what might have gone on inside your husband's fevered mind, you under-stand – the material would only have increased his vulnerability to threat.'

'So why wasn't the material released after his death, then?' she said. This all sounded far-fetched to her. She couldn't imagine Gansukh having the wit or the energy to engage in anything so sophisticated.

Muunokhoi shrugged. 'I suspect that your husband didn't have his plans in place in time. He was concerned about what we might do to him. He wasn't expecting to be arrested. That probably took him by surprise.'

That sounded plausible enough. The story of Gansukh's life. Even if he had been foresighted enough to arrange this supposed insurance, it was almost inevitable that his plans would come to nothing. 'But he'd already got rid of the documents.'

'I suspect he would have done that at the earliest opportunity, just so there was no evidence against him if we should become suspicious. Probably just sent them to his cousin – perhaps without much explanation

– saying he'd come to sort out the materials shortly. But he didn't get the opportunity to do it. Or to find anyone who might be prepared to release the documents if anything happened to him.'

'I can see why that wouldn't be an attractive role,' she said.

'Which may be why you refused to do it?' Muunokhoi said.

She looked up and him. 'You think he asked me?'

'Who else could be trust?'

'Probably nobody,' she said. 'But, by the same token, he wouldn't have trusted me either. Not with that. He never shared any of his – business dealings with me. He knew what I thought of them.'

'But you were happy to turn a blind eye and live off the proceeds?' Muunokhoi said, with a trace of amusement.

'I earned my own living,' she said, 'Not a great deal in those days, but then Gansukh was hardly rolling in money either. It sounds stupid now but I was in love with Gansukh. I didn't approve of what he did, and I told him so, but I didn't take much advantage of it either.' She didn't know why she felt any need to justify herself to Muunokhoi, except that perhaps she recognised that, even allowing for her youthful lack of judgement, there was some truth in his comment. 'But I would be the last person he'd have trusted with something like that.'

'So perhaps he had difficulty in finding anyone,' Muunokhoi said. 'Which is why the material remained unused.'

'Did it ever occur to you that Khenbish might have

just exaggerated things to ingratiate himself with you and maybe try to shift your attention on to Gansukh?'

'I'm sure he did,' Muunokhoi said. 'But I'm equally sure that the documents existed. And that they still exist.'

'I still don't see how I can help you, or why you felt it necessary to bring me here against my will. So I've received some material that used to belong to Gansukh, which for some reason he deposited with his cousin. And some of that material undoubtedly relates to his business dealings. But I've been through it all. I didn't see anything that might incriminate you. And I've no doubt that if you had just wanted to get hold of those papers, you could have found a means of taking them.' She paused, her mind working. 'After all, someone must have informed you that I'd received them in the first place.' She shook her head, marvelling at her own naivety. She had thought she was being smart, registering the papers with her lawyer, keen as always to ensure that anything associated with Gansukh should be handled as formally and transparently as possible, so that her own professional position could not be compromised.

'It was important to keep a close eye on you, Mrs Radnaa. Even after all this time. Just in case.'

So it looked as if Nergui had been right. Muunokhoi had indeed infiltrated everywhere. Whichever way you turned, his associates were there, passing on information. No wonder that Gansukh had been unable to trust anyone with the papers.

She shrugged. 'It doesn't seem right that we should both be paying for my lawyer's services. I must ask for a refund. But then surely all this is unnecessary. If my lawyer's on your payroll, the papers – or copies of them – must already be in your possession.'

Muunokhoi nodded. 'And you are also right that there is nothing incriminating in the papers. Nothing significant, anyway. One or two things that might potentially cause me a little commercial embarrassment – or might have done at the time, anyway. But nothing major.'

'So why am I here, then?' she said. Maybe this whole situation was less rational than she had thought. Perhaps Muunokhoi wasn't simply after the documents. Perhaps there was something else. For the first time, she began to wonder about Muunokhoi's state of mind. She had seen him as a calculating businessman – not an attractive figure, but amenable to rational negotiation. Now she was less sure.

'I think you know more than you are saying, Mrs Radnaa. I think that you knew that you might be under observation. I think you found something more in those documents which you chose not to deposit with your lawyer.'

'Why would I do that?' she said. 'I don't want anything to do with all this. Apart from anything else, I've my own professional position to maintain. That's why I placed all Gansukh's materials with my lawyer in the first place, so no one could ever accuse me of hiding anything. If I'd found anything important in those papers, I'd have handed it over to the police.'

Muunokhoi smiled faintly, sitting back in his chair. 'Ah, but would you, Mrs Radnaa? Would you have even trusted the police with this material? You are an intelligent woman, and I think you would have recognised that there might have been risks in handing over such material. Even to the police.'

She stared at him, astonished at the calmness with which he was confirming Nergui's worst suspicions.

Again, it was as if he were reading her thoughts. 'And, interestingly, Mrs Radnaa, we now know who was with you when we – picked you up. One of my people recognised him but couldn't initially put a name to his face. When he told me, my first thought was that this was a very intriguing companion for you. Nergui and I go back a long way. He is one of the senior officers whom you could certainly trust.'

'Nergui is a friend,' she said. 'We also go back a long way, as you no doubt recall.'

He nodded, smiling now. 'It is always good to reinvigorate an old friendship. But don't take me for a fool, Mrs Radnaa.'

She was, finally, beginning to feel angry now, her rising fury driving out her gnawing anxiety. 'I'm not sure what to take you for,' she said. 'I suspect you're insane. Pursuing some decade old – well, I'm not even sure what. A vendetta? Because, for all your ruthlessness, my husband managed to make more of a fool of you than you'd care to admit? Is that it? For once, someone was a step ahead of you, and you didn't manage to tie up every last loose end?'

She was aware that her temper was getting the better of her, that she might be losing whatever chance she might have had of talking her way out of this. But the words kept tumbling out of her mouth as she struggled to make some sense of her absurd predicament.

'I don't know what Gansukh did,' she said, 'and after all this time I don't much care. Maybe for once he was smart. Maybe he did really have something on you. All I do know is that there was no sign of it in the papers I received.' She paused, recovering her breath and trying to recover her composure. 'You're chasing ghosts, Muunokhoi. I think the truth is that you are going to end up in jail. But not because of anything that Gansukh might have had on you. Just because you're running out of time. You're not the man you were. Someday, somehow, someone's going to catch up with you.'

Muunokhoi seemed untroubled by her diatribe. 'Your friend, Nergui, has been chasing me for twenty years and never got close. I don't think he's going to catch me now.' He paused, the empty smile playing again across his pale face. 'But we are really wasting time, Mrs Radnaa. I admit that, in your current position, you perhaps have plenty of time to waste. But I do not. I want to know what else was in those papers you received.'

She stared at him, unable to come to grips with what appeared to be little more than monomania. 'I've told you, there was nothing else. Everything was placed in the hands of my lawyer. And so, it appears, was handed directly over to you.'

'I have told you, Mrs Radnaa, do not take me for a fool. You're an intelligent woman. You would not have trusted your lawyer. You would not have trusted the police. You would have disposed of the materials in some other way. If you've handed them over to Nergui then I will need to arrange for their recovery.'

'Recovery?'

His smile grew wider, somehow emphasising the emptiness of his eyes. 'Ah, I see. You are concerned about Nergui's safety. Quite understandable, given the views you have expressed about my own morality. But you will not be placing Nergui in any greater danger by acknowledging that he now has the relevant material. You will merely be simplifying matters.'

'Don't you understand?' she said. 'I've nothing to tell you. I've handed nothing to Nergui.'

He shook his head slowly. 'Everything would be so much easier if you were to co-operate. But I can see that that would be difficult for you. You accused me of conducting a vendetta. But it seems to me that it is you – and, over the years, Nergui – who have been conducting the vendetta. Nergui has his own reasons for wanting me behind bars – not least, I think, because he sees me as the symbol of everything he has failed to achieve in his professional career. He is an honourable man and I've no doubt he has the best interests of our nation at heart, but he is a man out of time. He has been unable to hold back the tide of Westernisation, and every day he sees our country embracing more and more of those corrupt decadent ways. It is a tragedy, no doubt, but it is not my tragedy.' He paused, as though daring her to interrupt. 'As for your motives, Mrs Radnaa, well – I don't know. A mixture, I imagine. In part, you hold me responsible for the death of your husband.'

'If you think—'

'And, in part,' he went on, overriding her, 'it is no doubt a matter of professional pride to you. You had to oversee a trial which was – well, frankly, a fiasco. Not through any fault of yours, I understand. But it must have been deeply frustrating to see a figure of my supposed criminal stature slip through your fingers in that way.'

'You really don't understand anything, do you?' she said, feeling her anger rising again at the presumption of this man. 'You've no understanding of my feelings – or my lack of feelings – for Gansukh. And you don't even understand that my role as a judge is to ensure a fair trial, not to indulge some ancient, non-existent vendetta.'

'Even when faced with a conflict of interest as great as this? Believe me, even if the prosecutor's office had not messed things up so spectacularly, I would have ensured that your own position in the trial would have come under close scrutiny.' His smile now looked as if it were painted on his face.

'What position? What conflict? I've told you, I didn't even know that Gansukh worked for you. Can't you understand? I don't care about you or what you might have done. I've no interest.'

Even as she spoke, she knew that the words were untrue. There was an obsession there, still, somewhere buried deep in her mind. That was why she had behaved so irrationally after the trial. That was why she sent the anonymous letters to Muunokhoi, trying to provoke some response, not suspecting that, by then, he had already learned of the existence of the legacy. Not suspecting that all she was doing was reinforcing a paranoia that had been building for more than a decade.

But this was what she had been seeking. This confrontation. This opportunity to challenge, face to face, the man who had killed her husband, who had thrown her life into chaos. A chance, after all these years, for some kind of resolution, some kind of closure. Some kind of ending to that part of her life.

And so here she was. But, of course, the closure would be Muunokhoi's alone. Her actions had simply led her straight into his hands, allowing him finally to tie up the one loose end that had always trailed behind his apparently unstoppable ascent.

Still, though, he showed no reaction. His mouth was twisted in an expression which would have resembled a smile only if his eyes had been concealed. The eyes themselves were as blank as ever, as if all expression, all emotion, had been stripped from them.

'I am sorry, then,' he said, at last. 'Your co-operation would have made things much more straightforward. For me. For you. And for Nergui.' He shrugged. 'But so be it. I cannot waste more time talking to you. I will leave you to think. Perhaps you will have a change of heart. But, if so, I fear that by then it will be too late.'

He climbed slowly to his feet, as though wearied by their conversation. Sarangarel wondered whether he was going to exit as mysteriously as he had entered – she could imagine that he would enjoy the showmanship – but instead he simply walked past her across the room towards the stairs.

She wondered, briefly, whether she could take some action. Perhaps try to use one of the chairs as a weapon. But both chairs, she realised then, were tightly bolted to the concrete floor. It was, she reflected, probably not the first time that Muunokhoi had used this bleak venue for this kind of purpose.

There were no other weapons to hand, and in any case Muunokhoi had already reached the bottom of the stairs. She contemplated running after him, but it was too late. He began to climb, pausing halfway up to turn and look down at her. 'Think about it,' he said. 'I do not know how long I may leave you down here. Or what I will do when I return. But there is no way now that you can help Nergui. It may be too late to help yourself. But you may still be able to co-operate.'

It sounded like an invitation and she wondered whether she might be able to buy herself some time by offering her co-operation, even though she had nothing to tell him. She half opened her mouth to speak, but then Muunokhoi turned and, as if someone had responded to a signal, the heavy door opened to let him out.

The slamming of the door behind him had a terrifying finality. She'd blown it, she thought. She was smart and articulate. She should have been able to talk her way out of this somehow, or at least bought herself some time. Maybe Muunokhoi really was out of his mind, but she should have been able to handle that. Instead, she'd just tried to argue rationally and then, when that hadn't worked, she'd allowed him to goad her into losing her temper.

And she was still trapped in this featureless room, with no knowledge how long she would be left here, and no idea of what might be facing her at the end of that time. For the first time, she allowed herself to face the reality of her position. Muunokhoi was never going to allow her to leave this place alive. She was going to die. The only questions were when and how. From what she had heard and seen of Muunokhoi, it could not be assumed that her death would be either quick or humane.

And, on top of all that, there was something else – something, she realised, that terrified her almost as much as her own impending death. Somewhere out there, Muunokhoi and his people were waiting for Nergui. The way Muunokhoi had spoken at least gave her some hope that Nergui had at least survived the impact of the car, though it was quite possible he was lying injured or incapacitated, a helpless potential victim. And, she thought, whatever his current position, his well-being was likely to be substantially worsened in the very near future.

CHAPTER 22

Doripalam lay, as motionless as he could, on the cold earth, holding his breath, trying to detect some movement in the darkness around them.

He knew that Nergui was lying similarly, his hand gun poised, a few metres to his left, although in the blackness he could no longer see him.

After the tremulous voice had died away, he had heard nothing. No footsteps or movement, nothing that revealed any human presence. The only sound was the faint whisper of the breeze through the firs. The moon was higher now, skimming the trees, scattering pale silver across the woodland and steppe. But Doripalam could see nothing but a filigree of grey and shadow, with no solid shapes other than the triangular silhouettes of the *gers*. He could conjure up all kinds of ghosts in this near darkness, but he had no idea about the location of the sniper.

He looked across, trying to locate Nergui, but the grass between the trees was empty. Nergui had already changed his position, though his movements must have been as silent as the breeze. Doripalam glanced around, trying to spot Nergui among the trees, but could still see nothing.

He twisted around, positioning his back against a

tree to minimise the chances of the sniper catching him from behind. He could still see and hear nothing.

And then, suddenly, he saw a movement, little more than a shifting shadow against the trees, a momentary blackness against the glimmer of moonlight. He eased out his own pistol and waited, holding his breath, watching the spot. Was it the sniper, or was it Nergui circling round the *gers*?

The silence extended, and then, somewhere further round the clearing from where he had detected the movement, there was a noise. It was little more than a faint rustling, possibly no more than some wild animal making its way through the trees and under-growth, but Doripalam tensed, watching for any further sign of life.

Then there was a much more distinctive sound. First, a thud of footsteps across the grass, a clattering as if something had been dropped, and a sudden sharp cry, immediately stifled.

Doripalam rose, pressed himself behind the tree, peering out into the dark, trying to work out what was happening. There was definitely movement now, a bundling of shadows beneath the faintly moonlit trees, then suddenly a whisper of voices and the movements ceased.

Doripalam raised his gun, poised to fire as soon as there was some positive indication of a possible target.

'I think you'd better hold fire,' he heard Nergui's voice say. 'It would take some explaining if you were to hit me by mistake. You can switch your flashlight back on now, though.'

Doripalam fumbled in his pocket for the torch

which he had extinguished, as soon as the shot had sounded. He pointed it in the direction of Nergui's voice, flooding the woodland with sudden light.

Nergui was lying on the ground, his arm clutched firmly round the neck of a young man, his pistol pointing unwaveringly at the man's head. The young man himself looked terrified, his eyes blinking frantically as he tried to take in the scene. His own handgun lay on the grass, several metres away, presumably where he had dropped it as Nergui had launched himself at him.

'If you've got your handcuffs with you, that would probably be helpful,' Nergui said. 'I'd rather talk to this individual in a standing position.'

Recovering his composure, Doripalam pulled his handcuffs from his pocket and crouched down to snap them on the young man's wrists. There was no attempt at resistance. Looking at the young man's frightened expression, Doripalam suspected that he would have been compliant even if there had been no cuffs on his arms or gun pointed at his temple.

Doripalam dragged the young man to his feet and thrust him against the side of the nearest *ger*. He quickly searched the man's pockets for any sign of a further weapon, but there was nothing. Behind them, Nergui climbed slowly to his feet, brushing the dew from his clothes. 'This suit's going to need cleaning,' he said. 'Another strike against this young man.'

'Along with the murder of a police officer, you mean?' Doripalam said, still holding his own gun against the man's back.

'Alongside that, yes,' Nergui said, his expression

strangely casual. Doripalam glanced at him. In the normal run of things, there were few crimes more serious than the murder of a serving officer.

Doripalam pulled the young man round to face him. He should begin the formalities, arresting the man on suspicion of the murder of the officer they had found in the woods. Not to mention, he thought, the possible attempted murder of himself and Nergui.

He opened his mouth to speak, shining the torch up at the young man's face, and then he stopped. He turned slowly to Nergui. 'We've already met,' he said. 'You were one of the four men here when we came before. One of Tseren's cousins.' He stopped, searching for the name.

'Kadyr,' the man stuttered. 'Yes.' He paused as though seeking some adequate form of words. 'I'm sorry,' he said, at last.

'Sorry?' Doripalam stared at him. 'You – or one of your kinsmen – injured one of my colleagues before. Tonight, you've completed the job on another officer. And, quite frankly, I've had my fill of you taking pot shots at me.'

'I'm sorry,' Kadyr said again. 'It's not—' He stopped. 'It's not how it looks.'

'How else can it be?' Doripalam said. 'There's an officer dead. Another injured.'

'I know,' Kadyr stammered, 'but—' He stopped, clearly at a loss now, looking as if he were trying to offer some sort of coherent explanation but lacking the language.

Doripalam was about to respond, but Nergui cut in from behind him, speaking with his usual calm authority. 'He's right,' he said. 'It's not how it looks. But then we know that. I think you can put the gun away, Doripalam. Kadyr's not going anywhere, not as long as we're here, anyway. There's no one else he can trust. Not any more.'

Doripalam turned to look at the older man, trying to work out – as so often – what precisely was going through his mind.

'We should get back to the truck,' Nergui said. 'There'll be others out here soon. We need to get away from here while we've still got time.'

'Others? You mean—'

'More police. More of Tsend's people.'

'But—'

'And if they find us here I think we may find that the local force have little respect for intruders from the big city, even if they're as senior as we are. Let's get moving. We've got a lot to talk about with – what did you call yourself? – with Kadyr here.'

There was something about the way that Nergui uttered the last sentence. He knows something, Doripalam thought. It's the same as ever. He's a step or two ahead, working out something that I'm only just beginning to grasp. It was clear that, for whatever reason, Kadyr thought so too. He was staring at Nergui with an aghast expression, his terror clearly even greater than before.

'Come on,' Nergui said, with greater urgency. 'We need to move.'

He grabbed Kadyr's arm, and began to drag the young man back down the slope towards their truck. The moon was higher above them now, casting its cool light down along the path, exaggerating the shadows and potholes in the ground. Nergui began to move faster, almost running, as if he had suddenly noticed some change in the landscape. 'Come on,' he said again.

And then Doripalam, following a few steps behind, heard it. The sound of a car engine, still distant but approaching rapidly. Despite Nergui's urgency, Doripalam paused momentarily, trying to locate the vehicle. Finally he saw it, two dim lights coming closer across the undulating steppe, obscured partly by the distance and partly by the fact that, despite the darkness, the vehicle was using only its side-lights. The driver had obviously hoped to delay being spotted for as long as possible, knowing that full headlights would carry for miles across the empty landscape.

Doripalam began to hurry down the slope behind Nergui and Kadyr, trying to calculate how far away the vehicle might be. Two or three kilometres, probably. And it would take them four or five minutes to reach their own truck, even running. Even if they reached the truck, there was no guarantee that they could get away easily, assuming that the new arrivals were as dangerous as Nergui was assuming.

Nergui was virtually dragging Kadyr now. It was as if the young man had finally given way, as if all the energy had drained out of him. Doripalam tried to hurry forward so he could assist the older man, but, even supporting Kadyr's weight, Nergui was moving too quickly. Doripalam considered himself reasonably fit, but he was already becoming breathless and could barely keep up with the pace.

By now, the slope had taken them below the level of the trees and Doripalam could no longer see the lights of the approaching vehicle. He had no idea how much time they had, or what might happen when they reached their own truck. There was something irrational, almost superstitious about their running, as if Nergui believed that, if they reached the truck, everything would be all right.

And perhaps it would have been. They were never to find out since, just as they came within sight of their own truck parked by the roadside, the dim lights of the second vehicle appeared ahead of them. Nergui staggered to a halt, still clutching the young man as if he might otherwise float away. Doripalam followed behind, scarcely able to breathe.

The approaching vehicle – another off-road vehicle, Doripalam thought – slammed on its brakes and skidded to a stop, angled across the road. Its headlights came on, blazing on full beam, and for a moment Doripalam could see nothing for the glare. He stumbled on down the slope, catching up finally with Nergui and Kadyr. Kadyr by now looked little more than semi-conscious, his eyes staring blankly into the dazzling light.

Slowly, Doripalam was able to make out two figures emerging from the vehicle. The first figure stepped into the light, and Doripalam let out his breath in relief, realising that Nergui's assumptions had for once been wrong. There shouldn't have been any doubt, he thought, given that unique approach to stopping a car.

'Luvsan,' he called out, 'thank—'

And then he stopped. The second figure had stepped forward, and, suddenly, like a camera coming into focus, the whole picture became clear in Doripalam's mind. Nergui was staring down into the light, as if he had known this all along.

Luvsan was smiling up at them, a powerful handgun clutched in his hand. Not police issue, Doripalam noted irrelevantly, his brain still trying to make the connections. Behind him, holding an assault rifle, was Tsend, the local police chief.

'Good evening. Sir.' Luvsan nodded slowly to Doripalam and then to Nergui. 'Though I imagine we can dispense with the hierarchical conventions in the circumstances.'

'I find myself in illustrious company,' Tsend said from behind him. 'But then I have always been happy to co-operate with requests from headquarters.' He glanced, still smiling, at Luvsan. 'As your colleague here will be only too pleased to confirm, I am sure.'

'And I hope,' Luvsan said, 'that you will find it equally easy to co-operate with our requests.' He gestured with his gun. 'It would be most disrespectful of me to have to use this on a senior officer or indeed—' He bowed slightly towards Nergui, '—on a Ministry official.'

'This way, gentlemen,' Tsend said. 'We have an appointment to keep.'

Tunjin had begun to open the inner door, but then he stopped, walked back across to the man on the floor. There was no doubt now that he was dead, his head lying crushed in a rapidly darkening pool of blood.

Tunjin had seen plenty of dead bodies in his career, but had never previously been personally responsible for the death. It was an odd sensation. He knew that he wasn't to blame – his action had been legitimate self-defence, and the death itself had been an accident. Moreover, from what he knew of Muunokhoi's heavies, the death was unlikely to be a major loss to society.

Even so, as he leaned over the body, Tunjin felt a shudder of – what? Guilt? Disgust? Both of those, he thought, along with a quite understandable tremor of fear. He didn't imagine that those who killed Muunokhoi's henchmen normally survived for very long themselves. On the other hand, given his broader predicament, he couldn't imagine that this would have significantly worsened his life expectancy. He contemplated briefly whether it would be possible to conceal the body in some way, but decided that it was impossible. There was nowhere to hide the body in this room. He could perhaps drag it outside and hope to hide it among the trees, at least to delay its discovery, but the risk of being spotted on the security cameras would outweigh any possible benefits.

Tunjin looked around and saw the man's pistol lying in the corner of the room. It was the thought of this that had made him hesitate at the door. He had suddenly realised that his own handgun, the one that Agypar had given him, was no longer in his pocket. He couldn't recall if he had left it up on the hillside with Agypar's motorcycle, or whether it had tumbled from his pocket during his fall down the slope. Either way, he had just been about to enter Muunokhoi's house unarmed. Probably not the smartest of moves, but typical of his approach so far.

He picked up the gun, weighed it gently in his hand, and checked it was loaded. He had to do everything carefully from here on. Think it through. Not just go blundering in his usual manner.

His resolve in this respect lasted only slightly beyond his cautious opening of the inner door into the house. He peered carefully out, and saw that the door opened into a long passageway, its ornate wallpaper and thick carpeting contrasting starkly with the bare room he had just left. He stepped out into the hallway and let the door close behind him, hearing it shut with a solid click. He realised, just too late, that it had locked itself. He gently tried the door and discovered that it could not be opened without a key. Brilliant. His one known exit route and he'd just managed to seal it. At least it reduced his options. He was hardly spoiled for choice.

He began to make his way slowly down the hallway, feeling desperately exposed. There were a couple of doors opening off each side of the passageway, but it would be too risky to explore at this stage – there was no way of knowing who or what lay on the other side of them. He had to try to get an understanding of the layout of the place.

At the end of the hallway, the passage opened out into a broader area. Tunjin cautiously peered around the corner, where the thick carpeting gave way to a polished light wood floor. An entrance hall with, some metres away, what Tunjin took to be the main front door of the house. To the right, an imposing stairway rose to the upper floors.

Across the hallway, another door stood half-open and Tunjin could hear voices coming from inside. He took another step or two forward to glimpse the interior of the room, and then he froze. He could see, in side view, a figure he recognised instantly.

Muunokhoi. There was no doubt about it. The short, stocky but somehow imposing figure. The shaved head. And, though the face was currently turned away from him, Tunjin had no doubt about the dark, empty eyes. He made a movement backwards, praying that those eyes would not be turned in his direction.

So Muunokhoi was here. And presumably his presence was in some way connected with the woman whom Tunjin had seen being led into the building earlier in the day.

Tunjin took a further step forward, keeping out of the line of sight of the door, hoping desperately that no one would decide to emerge. He tried to hear what might be being discussed, but could make out no clear words. Muunokhoi's authoritative tones sounded anything but happy.

Tunjin looked down at the gun in his hand. It would be easy, he thought. He could just walk in there now and, without a word, gun down Muunokhoi. He would be shot himself almost immediately by Muunokhoi's henchmen, but that would be a small price to pay. Tunjin was not a man with any future. He could at least make sure that the same was true of Muunokhoi. Few people – maybe only Nergui and a handful more – would recognise the worth of what he had done, but the nation and society would be immeasurably improved. Nevertheless, whatever its potential merits, the prospect of cold-blooded murder did not come easily, especially to one who, for all his personal peccadilloes, had devoted his life to upholding the law.

But, before he could think any further, Tunjin heard another sound that, momentarily, made his heart freeze. It was the sound of a key turning in the lock of the massive front door. He realised that, while he had been straining to hear the conversation going on in the opposite room, his mind had somehow filtered out the sound of a car arriving outside, although now the sound of the running engine was all too clear.

Tunjin backed away rapidly down the hallway. Whatever the morality of taking Muunokhoi out, there was no merit in being caught at this point. Hearing the key turning, he looked frantically behind him for some point of concealment.

The only options were the various doors lining the passageway. The majority of these looked like the doors to internal reception rooms which might harbour any kind of peril. But one, at the far end of the corridor next to that through which he had entered, looked different. Like the neighbouring door, it had a substantial lock which suggested that it might lead outside the house. Unlike the lock in the neighbouring door, however, this one still contained a key.

There was no time to hesitate as the front door was already opening. Tunjin leapt two or three steps backwards, his agility again belying his impressive bulk. In one movement, he turned the key, opened the door and stepped inside, pulling the door to behind him but leaving a small gap so that he could see out.

He glanced behind him, trying to ensure that he had not simply stepped into further peril.

It looked safe enough. He appeared to be in the entrance to some sort of cellar. A set of stone steps descended away from the landing on which he stood. There was a light, but he could see only a few metres beyond the bottom of the steps. Still, it was safe to assume that no one was down here, since there had been no reaction to his entry.

Secure for the moment, he pressed his eye to the narrow gap he had left between the door and the frame, and peered out at the group entering the hallway. For a second his breath died in his throat and he could scarcely believe what he was seeing. The first two men were unknown to him. There was a young man who looked terrified – not an unreasonable reaction for someone entering Muunokhoi's residence, Tunjin thought, especially if the entry was not entirely voluntary. Behind him, there was a heavily built middle-aged man who, on second glance, appeared vaguely familiar though Tunjin could not think where he might have encountered him.

It was the remainder of the group, though, that had left Tunjin breathless. There was Nergui, his dark face as impassive as ever. Close behind him was Doripalam, his face also for once unreadable. And then, behind the two senior officers, was the supposed high flyer, Luvsan, the one everyone thought of as Doripalam's protégé.

So was that it then? Had Muunokhoi's influence penetrated much further than anyone had dared to believe? If even Nergui was on his payroll, then there really was no hope. It didn't matter whether Tunjin, or any police officer, lived or died, whether they did their duty or not. Whatever happened, Muunokhoi was in control.

Despair almost swept over Tunjin at that point. He had, he realised, given up on his own life, his own future, long before. From the moment that his half-baked scheme against Muunokhoi had collapsed, he had known that the death sentence had been pronounced, that he was effectively dead. He could flee. He could try to fight back. And maybe, somewhere, somehow, he might have some success, but it was difficult to see how all this would end other than in his own killing.

But his faint hope, the smallest glimmer that had kept him going through all this, was that, just maybe, he might succeed in taking Muunokhoi with him. It was true that, if Muunokhoi was out of the picture, others would eventually come along to take his place. But there was no one – not yet, not in this country – like him. There was no one with the same power, the same network, the same wealth, the same influence – or, most important, the same ruthlessness. There would be pretenders, but it would be a long while before anyone else occupied the throne with equivalent authority.

And then the hope briefly came back, as he watched the group file across the hallway. Muunokhoi's henchmen were holding pistols, pointed firmly at the backs of Nergui, Doripalam and the young man. They weren't Muunokhoi's guests. They were his prisoners. For a moment, the position seemed almost reassuring.

These senior officers – these few men he had been sure he could trust – were not corrupt. There was still some sanity left in the world.

But his relief was short-lived. Nergui and Doripalam might be straight, but they had somehow fallen into Muunokhoi's power. And Tunjin had no illusions as to how wide-ranging that power might be. If Muunokhoi had brought them here, he would not be allowing them to leave. Worse still, he realised, as the group moved past, not all the police officers were prisoners. Luvsan had been one of those holding a gun.

But none of that, he thought, invalidated the simple plan he had formulated while standing in the hallway. Here he was, undetected in the heart of Muunokhoi's house, a loaded gun in his pocket. There would never be another opportunity like this. All he had to do was move swiftly and silently out there and make sure that he acted before anyone could stop him. He could gun down Muunokhoi and then – well, take the chance to shoot anyone else he could before he was finally stopped. If all those people were on Muunokhoi's payroll, then, as far as Tunjin was concerned, they were legitimate targets. He should feel no compunction – even about Luvsan.

He peered out into the hallway again. The group had disappeared into the room where Muunokhoi had been waiting. He could hear the sound of voices – largely Muunokhoi's, he suspected, though it was difficult to be sure – carrying down the hallway.

Tunjin took the opportunity to reach out and remove the key, ensuring that he would not find himself accidentally locked in the cellar, then stepped back and allowed the door to close fully, while he thought through his actions. He needed to move quickly, he thought, while the group was still together in that room. If he allowed them to separate, or if any of Muunokhoi's heavies stumbled across the dead body, his task would become impossible.

He straightened up and took a deep breath. It was a long time since he had had any kind of a drink. There would have been a time – a very recent time, he realised with a shock – when he would have thought that an impossible achievement, the pinnacle of his ambition. Now, it seemed irrelevant. Not that the craving for alcohol had vanished. On the contrary, he would have given almost anything for a drink just at the moment.

He reached out to open the door. And then there was another heart stopping moment, as he heard a clear footstep on the concrete floor of the cellar behind him. He spun round, cursing himself for not having checked properly that the cellar was empty.

As he turned, a voice, softer than he would have expected said, 'So you've come for me, then? At last.'

CHAPTER 23

'It has been a long time,' Muunokhoi said. 'I presumed that even your persistence had its limits.'

Nergui shrugged. 'I take the long view,' he said. 'But I rarely give up.'

Muunokhoi nodded, his mouth smiling, his eyes as dead as ever. 'As you say. Though I think your investigations have always proved fruitless. I have considered bringing a formal complaint before now. But I understand that you and your colleagues—' He nodded vaguely towards Doripalam, '—have a job to do.'

'We do our best,' Nergui said. His gaze rested, just for a moment, on Luvsan. Then he looked back at Muunokhoi. 'Now,' he said, 'perhaps you will tell us what this is all about.'

'I think you know what it's all about, Nergui,' Muunokhoi said, quietly.

Nergui nodded, as though giving serious consideration to this assertion. He looked around the plush reception room. It looked, at the moment, like some bizarre house party. He and Doripalam had been seated on a large, over-stuffed sofa, with Kadyr hunched beside them, his face knotted into an expression of pure fear. Muunokhoi sat opposite, in a comfortable looking armchair. Luvsan and Tsend, along with what were presumably a couple of Muunokhoi's security staff, were seated on hard chairs around a mahogany table, watching the interchange.

'I know what some of it's about,' Nergui said at last. 'But by no means all. I suspect that I know rather less than you think I do.' He paused, his gaze fixed on Muunokhoi. 'Though, in some respects, perhaps also rather more.'

'Opaque as ever, Nergui,' Muunokhoi said, with a touch of harshness in his tone. 'But I'm sure we will be dazzled by your insights.'

'I have limited skills,' Nergui said. 'I used them as best I can. Shall I tell you what I think I know?'

Muunokhoi sat back in his chair. 'I am keen to hear.'

'I know quite a few things,' Nergui said. 'It is really a question of where to start. I know, for example, that yours is the most destructive, corrupt regime that has ever gained any kind of power in this country. Which is quite an achievement, when you consider the kinds of power that have been wielded here over the centuries. I know that despite that – or, to be frank, because of that – you exercise enormous influence in all aspects of our daily lives, both through your legitimate business dealings and through the more – sordid aspects of your activities. I know that more people are in your pocket than I could begin to conceive—' He gestured elegantly towards Luvsan at the table. 'Though I am not sure that you always pick your servants wisely. Luvsan's taste for fast cars – for expensive fast cars – had already made him a prime candidate in my investigations.'

'Though too late as always, I note,' Muunokhoi said. 'Your views on my business influence are most interesting, but I am not sure that they are entirely pertinent.'

'They are no doubt entirely impertinent,' Nergui said. 'But they are sincerely held and, I think, very relevant to our – presence here today.' He paused, his face as expressionless as ever, his eyes firmly fixed on Muunokhoi's blank gaze. 'We are here because, for the first time in twenty years, you feel vulnerable. You think your regime is under threat.'

Muunokhoi laughed suddenly, though there was no humour in his expression. 'Really? And yet I think it is you who are here, at my behest, betrayed by one of your own officers.'

Nergui shrugged. 'That seems to be the case. But the question is why you brought us here in the first place. And why you kidnapped Mrs Radnaa. And, for that matter, why you had Mrs Tuya killed.'

For the first time, Muunokhoi looked at Nergui with something approaching interest. 'Who is Mrs Tuya?'

It was Nergui's turn to laugh, and he seemed genuinely amused. Doripalam glanced across at him, as astonished by his apparent good humour as by what he was saying. Sometimes he wondered quite what it would take to shake Nergui's confidence.

Nergui turned, still smiling, to the young man sitting cowering next to them on the voluminous sofa. 'Mrs Tuya,' he said, 'is this young man's mother.' He paused, enjoying the silence while those around absorbed this information. 'And this young man,' he said, turning back to Muunokhoi, 'is of course your son.'

The silence was even more protracted this time. Doripalam stared at Nergui, wondering just what kind of complex game he was playing. Kadyr was looking more terrified than ever, his body twisted as though he hoped that the bulk of the sofa might swallow him up.

'I'd heard you were smart, Nergui,' Muunokhoi said at last. 'But I never knew you had such an imagination.'

'Perhaps I am simply making a fool of myself,' Nergui said, still smiling. 'But since you are not planning to allow to us leave here alive, I think that is a fairly minor consideration.'

Muunokhoi looked between Nergui and Doripalam. 'We can reach some accommodation,' he said. 'Things are not so absolute.'

Nergui shook his head. 'I don't really see what accommodation is possible. We know the truth about you, or at least something approaching the truth. And you have already committed a serious offence simply by bringing us here. I don't see that you can let us go.'

'I'm sure we can reach some accommodation,' Muunokhoi repeated. 'Once things have been resolved.'

'I don't think so.' He glanced across at Luvsan. 'Not everybody has a price.'

He's right, Doripalam thought. We're dead. If we were different people, Muunokhoi might be able to walk away from this. We might be able to walk away from this. But Nergui would never do that. And, Doripalam realised, neither would he.

Muunokhoi stared at Doripalam, as though expecting him to disagree with Nergui. But Doripalam simply shook his head. 'He's right,' he said. 'There's no accommodation.'

Muunokhoi shook his head. 'Perhaps you are right,' he said. 'In which case, I am sorry. I simply want what is mine.'

'Nothing is yours,' Nergui said. 'Everything you have is stolen. Or corrupt.'

'You know nothing. You have been pursuing a vendetta for twenty years. You see me as a symbol of all that you think is wrong in this country. But you have never been able to lay a finger on me. You know nothing.'

Nergui smiled. 'You've always been a step ahead. Perhaps you still are. You will walk away from this and we will not. But it's not true that I know nothing. I don't know everything. But I know a lot.'

Muunokhoi stared at him, his eyes as blank as ever. 'Go ahead,' he said. 'What do you know?'

'Your story,' Nergui said. 'Which begins a long time ago. Sixteen, seventeen years ago, I guess. It is difficult for us to remember now. You have been so good at building your own mythology. But you were not quite then the power you are today. You were small time.'

For the first time, Doripalam thought that Nergui might have got under Muunokhoi's skin. 'I was bigger than you'll ever be, Nergui. What were you in those days? A secret policeman?'

'Something like that, I suppose. But you were – what? A small time crook with a lot of ambition. Protection rackets. Smuggling from Russia and China.

Small scale drug dealing. Prostitution. Illegal gambling. Anything where you could turn a quick buck.' He paused. 'We could have had you then, but we didn't take you seriously enough.'

'Not usually one of your failings, Nergui.'

'We had other things on our minds,' Nergui smiled. 'The state was more concerned with what was happening in the Soviet Union than with petty criminals. Except that, for exactly that reason, you weren't going to be petty much longer. All those changes across the border would start to open doors for you. And then you made what probably seemed to others a pretty dumb business decision. You went into partnership with Gansukh.'

Muunokhoi raised his eyebrows, as though about to challenge this assessment of his business acumen, but he remained silent.

'Perhaps I'm giving you too much credit,' Nergui went on, 'but I don't think you were taken in by Gansukh's bravado. You saw him for what he was. Small-time, no brains, a risk-taker. Gansukh was dispensable. But he had one thing that you didn't. He – or at least his associate Khenbish – had good contacts in the drugs trade. I'm not entirely sure how he acquired them even now – I don't imagine, even in those confused days, that it was easy to develop those kinds of networks as a soldier in Afghanistan. But Khenbish *was* smart. He *was* like you. If you'd let him live, he might be sitting in your place today.'

'You've no idea what you're talking about, Nergui. I'm not the only one skilled at myth-making.'

Nergui leaned forward in his seat, staring at

Muunokhoi. 'I got close to the story at the time, but not close enough to pin you down. You brought Gansukh and Khenbish on board. They didn't have the resources or expertise to take advantage of their contacts, but you did. You tried to muscle in, but Khenbish was too smart for that. He insisted on a deal.' Nergui paused. 'And for the first and probably last time in your business career, you were forced into the open. You knew how important this was. You knew the opportunity that was out there. And you knew it couldn't be left to intermediaries. This had to be face to face, with them and with their contacts.'

Nergui's voice was hypnotic in the silent room. Doripalam watched him in something close to awe. Muunokhoi was a charismatic figure, capable of dominating a room without obviously trying. But Nergui was matching him easily.

'And it was worth the risk,' Nergui said. 'You established a dominance in the drugs field just at the right time. The iron curtain was crumbling, the borders were opening and chaos was spreading across eastern Europe. By the time the game might have been open to other players, you had it sewn up. It's been the foundation of your empire ever since, the base on which everything else – the energy interests, the media empire, everything – has been built.' He paused. 'But it's also your one area of vulnerability.'

'I should simply kill you now, Nergui,' Muunokhoi said, dismissively. 'It would save us from listening to this nonsense.' But there was something in his tone that belied the words, as if, finally, he wanted the story to be told.

'You exposed yourself too much,' Nergui said. 'Gansukh and Khenbish weren't to be trusted. I imagine they tried to blackmail you, tried to squeeze out a better deal. Even then, you had a lot more to lose than they did. You were building a public profile, making friends in the right places, developing the networks that have served you ever since. You needed Gansukh and Khenbish, or at least you needed what they could bring you, but you couldn't afford to be held to ransom by two small-time crooks.' Nergui hesitated, as though he were just at that moment working out the final details of his story. 'So you had Khenbish killed. Not difficult. He was a serving soldier. He drank heavily. He'd made enemies in the army and outside. And, before he was killed, you tried to make him tell you what information he had. But Khenbish, being the smart one, tried to buy his own life by laying the blame on Gansukh – it was him behind the black-mail attempt, he had the incriminating material, all that. It didn't matter whether you believed him or not. When you couldn't get anything else from him, you had him killed anyway. Then you went after Gansukh.'

'It was your people who went after Gansukh, if you remember,' Muunokhoi said.

Nergui nodded. 'Gansukh's usual inept sense of timing. You were coming to get him, but instead he managed to get himself arrested. And then, like Khenbish, he tried to talk his way out of trouble by claiming that he had useful things to tell us.' Nergui stopped again, and then continued almost wistfully. 'And maybe he had. I really thought, just for a moment, that I might have had you then.'

'So where does this leave you, Nergui? All this nostalgia for two decades ago, and the vendetta you've waged against me ever since?'

Nergui smiled. 'I don't know where it leaves me. But it left you, Muunokhoi, in a very interesting place. There's one part of the story we haven't touched on yet. Your affair with Khenbish's wife. Mrs Tuya. A very attractive woman in those days, I imagine, though I don't know if that's what you were interested in. If I'm not drifting too far into the realms of psychology, maybe it was a power issue. You'd given a lot of ground to Khenbish. Perhaps you wanted to get some back. And, traditionalist that you are, you did it in the way that would have most impact on an old-fashioned Mongolian male. Possibly you even took steps to ensure that he knew, or at least suspected. And one side effect, if you'll excuse me—' Nergui gestured apologetically towards the cowering young man, '—is this poor individual, who was introduced to us as Kadyr, one of Mrs Tuya's cousins, but who is, of course, Gavaa, her son. Who has spent the last few weeks on the run from you. No wonder he looks terrified.'

'He's no son of mine,' Muunokhoi said.

Nergui shrugged. 'I don't see any strong resemblance at the moment. But you believed he was. And it suited you to allow his mother to think so.'

Muunokhoi shook his head. 'You're rambling, Nergui.'

Nergui continued as though Muunokhoi hadn't spoken. 'Gansukh and Khenbish were both dead. But you still didn't know whether there was anything incriminating out there. You searched Gansukh's flat. I imagine you did the same with Khenbish's. But you found nothing. For a while, you lived with the fear that they might somehow have arranged for the material to be released posthumously. But it didn't happen. And you'd put in place an insurance policy of your own. You encouraged Mrs Tuya to believe that Gavaa was your son, and you offered to pay her a very generous continuing allowance. If she had the materials, or if she knew where they were, there was a strong incentive for her not to use them. And, over time, nothing happened, and you allowed yourself to relax a little, assuming that now nothing ever would.'

Muunokhoi smiled. 'So tell me why, eighteen years down the road, I should suddenly take an interest in all this?'

'Well, that is the question, isn't it?' Nergui said. 'As I see it, a combination of things all happened at once. The most important one, I'm sure, is that young Gavaa here found himself on the brink of adulthood. His mother realised that, before long, the allowance was going to cease. So she made one last request. Or was it a demand? She asked you to take him into the family business.'

Gavaa sat forward, looking as if he had suddenly returned to life. 'She didn't do that. It was nothing to do with her. I made the contact. She always thought she had to do everything. But it was me. I wasn't going to be stuck out there forever, herding sheep. I wanted to be—'

'Like your father?'

The young man nodded, his face reddening. 'I

suppose so. He'd talked to people – to my uncles and others – years ago about how he was working with Muunokhoi – this was when Muunokhoi was just beginning to become a public figure – about how he had Muunokhoi just where he wanted because he had evidence that would bring him down. Nobody believed him. They thought it was just the drink talking. And, years later, when Muunokhoi became really famous, my uncles used to tell the stories, laughing at what my father had claimed, making a fool of him—'

'But you thought he had been telling the truth?'

'I knew he'd been telling the truth. He was a clever man and a brave one.' He stopped and looked at Muunokhoi. 'Worth ten of this—'

'So you approached Muunokhoi?'

'Yes. I made contact. It wasn't easy. But when he realised who I was he agreed to see me. I didn't threaten him or anything—'

Muunokhoi laughed harshly. The words sounded absurd coming from the mouth of the trembling teenager, but Nergui seemed to be taking him seriously.

'Of course you didn't,' Nergui said. 'You just talked about your father and how he'd worked with Muunokhoi. And you asked whether Muunokhoi would be prepared to give you a job.'

'That's what happened,' Gavaa said, miserably. 'I just thought that – well, that he must have respected my father. That he'd want to help.'

'You didn't know that he'd been paying an allowance to your mother all your life? That he might be your father?'

'He's not my father,' the boy said indignantly. 'But, no, I didn't know any of that. I was just using my initiative. Following up my father's networks. And it worked. He took me on. Said he wanted me to be his—'

'Protégé?' Nergui prompted.

'Something like that. He wanted to honour my father's memory—'

Nergui turned to Muunokhoi. 'It was just another lever for you. Another insurance policy. Make sure he was with you, implicated in everything you did. Even if his mother did have any dirt on you, she couldn't use it.'

Muunokhoi opened his mouth to say something but the boy interrupted before he could speak.

'That's exactly it,' he said. 'Exactly what he did. I thought he was going to involve me in the business but he didn't. He put me with his heavies, his – security team—' He stopped, almost sobbing now, then continued, barely in control. 'We killed someone. The second day I was there.' His eyes were wide, staring at the ground, but it wasn't clear what he was actually seeing. 'They called it discipline,' he said. 'Someone who'd – I don't know – but they were going to punish him. I had to go, they said, so I'd understand how things were done. I thought – I thought they were just going to burn the car. I thought it must be his car – the person they were punishing.' He paused, hardly able to continue. 'But he was inside, locked in the boot. They told me later, but I already knew. And they said it should be a lesson to me if I ever did anything—'

Muunokhoi shook his head and climbed slowly to

his feet. 'Enough of these stories,' he said. 'Why do you think I am interested? Why do you think I brought you here?'

Nergui shrugged. 'I presume for the same reason you brought Mrs Radnaa here. Or wherever you've taken her.'

Muunokhoi laughed. In other circumstances, Doripalam thought, it would have been fascinating to watch this clash of egos. Muunokhoi was standing, looking as if it was he who was out of his familiar element, trying to regain some ground.

'You're right, of course, Nergui,' Muunokhoi said. 'I wanted you here initially because of Mrs Radnaa. I thought she might have given you – whatever she had.' For a moment, he looked confused as if suddenly even he was unsure where all this was heading. 'But that is unimportant now. If you and your colleague—' He glanced down at Doripalam 'If you and your colleague are out of the picture, then I no longer need to have any concerns about what incriminating material might be out there.'

'What makes you think that?' Doripalam said, speaking for the first time. 'Nergui and I are just two small parts of the machine. If there is something out there to incriminate you, it will see the light eventually.'

'Do you really believe that?' Muunokhoi said. 'You're even more naïve than you look. Do you really understand the nature of the team you supposedly lead? I think Nergui knows better.'

'You don't own everyone,' Nergui said. 'Not every officer is in your pocket.'

'Of course not. I would not be so presumptuous. But I own, as you put it, most of those who matter. Yourselves excluded, of course.' He glanced across at Luvsan, who avoided his gaze. 'Luvsan is one of my most loyal and pro-active servants, but he is by no means the only one. I think that now I can be reasonably confident that, even if some material does emerge, it will be handled with – discretion.'

'So what are you planning to do with us?' Doripalam said. 'Even you wouldn't dare to kill two senior government officials.'

Muunokhoi smiled. 'You really don't understand this, do you? You really don't understand me. I can do anything. I'm the power in this country now. Me and people like me.'

There was a moment's silence. Then Nergui said, his face as expressionless as ever: 'I haven't finished telling the story yet. Perhaps I should.'

'There's no need, Nergui,' Muunokhoi said. 'I think we all know how the story is going to end.'

'Go on, then. You may as well get on with it,' she said.

Tunjin stared down at the woman, wondering what she was talking about. 'I don't—'

'Are you the best they could find?' she said. 'Still, I don't imagine they expected much resistance. Maybe I should try to prove them wrong.'

She looked vaguely familiar, he thought. A very elegant middle-aged woman, now slightly dishevelled. Perhaps she was one of Muunokhoi's girlfriends, maybe a celebrity of some kind. But, if so, what was she doing in the cellar? Perhaps she'd just been down here for some reason and had assumed him to be – what? A burglar? It was as if she had been expecting him.

Tunjin held up his hands, realising too late that he was holding a gun in one of them. 'I'm sorry,' he said. 'I'm not going to hurt you.'

Her eyes opened in surprise. 'You aren't? Then why are you here? I told Muunokhoi, I don't have anything. I can't harm him. He's made a mistake.' She paused, thinking that it was worth one last effort. 'He can let me go. I mean, I'm not pleased about any of this. But I'm not going to make an issue of it. Not if he just lets me go.'

Tunjin blinked at her, trying to work this out. 'Muunokhoi is holding you against your will?'

'Well, of course he is.' She looked around the empty cellar. 'Did you think I was enticed by the comfortable environment?'

'No, but—' He was finally beginning to work out the misunderstanding here. 'I don't work for Muunokhoi.' He smiled, finally, with the recognition that he and this woman might be potential allies. 'I'm a stranger here myself,' he said. 'That is, I'm an intruder. I broke into the house.'

'A brave intruder, then,' she said, trying to understand this. 'I don't imagine many people choose to break in here.'

'It's a long story,' he said. 'But I'm not a thief. I'm a policeman.' He paused. 'Or at least I was.'

She nodded, trying to behave as if this was the most natural conversation to have while locked in an empty cellar. Or rather, she thought suddenly, reflecting on

Tunjin's presence, now apparently not locked in a cellar. 'Well, that's obviously destiny,' she said, 'because I'm a judge.'

'A judge?' He stared at her for a moment, as his brain made connections. So that was why she'd looked familiar. She'd been pointed out to him – before everything fell apart – as the judge in Muunokhoi's aborted trial. 'Is that why you're here?'

She shook her head. 'Not exactly. It's another long story. And one I'm not sure I understand myself.' She looked behind him at the stone stairs rising up to the cellar entrance, conscious that at any moment they might receive another, less welcome visitor. 'Look, I don't know why you're here,' she said. 'But can you get us out of here? The cellar, I mean.'

Tunjin produced the heavy key from his pocket. 'From the cellar, yes. But I don't know that we'll be able to get out of the house. It's very secure. Cameras. Guards. You name it. They'd stop us before we'd got five metres.'

'What about you?' she said. 'How were you planning to get out?'

He shrugged. 'I wasn't, really. I'd resigned myself to the fact that I wasn't going to.'

She stared at him. 'What do you mean? What were you going to do?'

'I was going to kill Muunokhoi,' he said, simply. 'I thought it would be a public service. If I don't, he'll kill me anyway. So I might as well try to get a two-way deal. But—' He paused, as if a new thought had struck him. 'I don't know what will happen to the rest of them.'

'The rest of them?'

'You're not the only captive here. Muunokhoi has more upstairs.' He stopped. 'He's gone mad. He really must be insane.'

'What captives? Who?'

He shook his head. 'Police officers. Senior officers. Ministry officials. He's insane.'

She was staring at him aghast. 'Ministry officials? Who do you mean?'

'It's unbelievable,' he said. 'You know Nergui? Used to be our chief. And Doripalam. He's our chief now. They're both there.'

'Nergui?' she said, with a look more despairing than he might have expected. 'That must be because of me. That's my fault. He warned me. Muunokhoi warned me. But I never imagined he could do it so quickly.'

'I think none of us know what Muunokhoi is capable of,' he said. 'Some of us thought we knew. But we've always fallen short. He's always been one step ahead.' He looked at the elegant Mrs Radnaa, wondering how it could be that Nergui's imprisonment here could be her fault.

'We have to do it,' she said. 'You're right. Nergui wouldn't want us to hesitate. If we don't do it, they're dead anyway. We're all dead anyway.'

He nodded. There was no question really. The only issue was whether, talking like this, they had now left it too long, missed their opportunity.

And that question was answered almost immediately by the sound of the cellar door opening above them.

*

'I think it is time,' Muunokhoi said, 'for you to be reunited with Mrs Radnaa. It will be very touching.'

Nergui said nothing, and his face gave nothing away. His pale blue eyes were blazing but there was no way of reading his emotions. Doripalam, a step or two behind, tried to emulate the older man's apparent lack of emotion, but feared that he was far from successful. Perhaps Nergui had some plan up his sleeve, but it was difficult to conceive what it might be. There could be no way out of this. He glanced back at Luvsan who was standing holding his gun, apparently casual, but careful not to catch Doripalam's gaze. I hope he feels it's worth whatever he's getting for this, Doripalam thought.

They were standing outside the door of the cellar. Muunokhoi reached forward and then stopped, looking quizzically around at his henchmen. 'Who's got the key? I left it here.'

There was a moment's silence. Muunokhoi turned the handle, clearly not expecting the door to open. He stepped back in surprise as it swung back easily. 'Who's been in here?' he said. He looked at each of them in turn. 'One of you idiots forgot to lock it.'

Again, there was no response. Doripalam looked around at the group. It wasn't difficult to gauge what they were thinking. It was Muunokhoi who had come out of that door last. It was Muunokhoi who had failed to lock it behind him. It was Muunokhoi – they were thinking but dared not say – who was losing it.

'She can't have got out, anyway,' Muunokhoi said, as if to reassure himself. 'Just be more careful next time, whoever it was.'

He pulled open the door and then stared down the stairway. At the bottom, just visible, Mrs Radnaa was standing. He could see little more than a silhouette. She stood, apparently calmly, as though awaiting an expected visitor.

Muunokhoi stepped aside and gestured Nergui, Doripalam and Gavaa to step forward on to the top landing. Doripalam hesitated on the threshold, recognising that there was likely to be no way back from this point, wondering how it might be possible to resist.

There was, it turned out, no opportunity. Seeing Doripalam's hesitation, Muunokhoi gestured to Luvsan who stepped forward and, raising his gun, slammed it hard against his former chief's head. Doripalam collapsed forward, staggering onto the top of the steps and then fell half way down the stone flight, hitting his head against the wall. He lay, sprawled and motionless, halfway down the flight of stairs, his body twisted. There was no way of telling whether he was still alive.

There was a moment's pause, as if everyone had stopped breathing in sympathy. Then, moving with extraordinary speed, Nergui grabbed Luvsan's gun arm and twisted it painfully. Somehow managing to remove the gun in the process, he turned and threw Luvsan past Doripalam's prone body down the stairs. Luvsan hit the concrete floor with a sickening thump and lay still. This time, there seemed little doubt about his mortality.

Nergui turned, grabbed Gavaa and pulled him behind him, trying to keep the boy safe. There was confusion as Muunokhoi's henchmen struggled to pull out their guns. Nergui shot one before he could move and the man fell back, pumping blood thickly on to Muunokhoi's thick carpet. The second had his gun out but Nergui was close enough to slam Luvsan's pistol hard down on the man's arm. He screamed, dropped the gun, and let out a painful, half-swallowed shout as Nergui thrust the pistol hard against his head. The man reeled back, tripped over his colleague, and fell in a heap on the floor, barely conscious.

For a second, there was no sound. Nergui looked back at Muunokhoi, expecting to find that Muunokhoi's weapon was pointed firmly at his own head or heart.

But it wasn't. Instead, Muunokhoi was staring down into the cellar, his gun pointed towards Sarangarel. He began to walk slowly down the steps. 'Don't try anything, Nergui. I'm too quick for you. If you shoot me, Mrs Radnaa will be dead before I am. You would not want that on your conscience.'

Nergui hesitated, unsure whether Muunokhoi was capable of carrying out this threat. But he knew from bitter experience the risks of underestimating Muunokhoi's capability in any field.

Muunokhoi moved slowly and smoothly down the steps until he was a metre or so from Sarangarel. 'Kill him,' she said, calmly. 'It doesn't matter what he does to me. It's worth it.'

Nergui raised his gun, but could do nothing, his finger frozen on the trigger. 'Nergui,' she called out, 'if you don't, he'll kill me anyway. He'll use me as a hostage as long as it suits him. He'll get away again. So kill him now. It doesn't matter about me.'

She was right, of course. He knew she was right. But Muunokhoi, one step ahead as always, had judged that this was the one thing that Nergui would not be able to do. The one thing he could not have on his conscience.

Muunokhoi stepped behind Sarangarel, raising the gun-barrel towards her head.

She was right, of course. Of course she was. In any moment, the last chance would have gone and they would be back to playing Muunokhoi's game.

In the final moment before Muunokhoi raised his gun to Sarangarel's temple, Nergui finally lifted his own gun. And a shot echoed round the empty cellar.

CHAPTER 24

The prayer wheels were spinning somewhere behind them and they could hear the sonorous chanting of the monks. It was a hypnotic sound, at one with the breath of the wind and the cries of the children from the park below. The pure blue sky seemed endless, echoing the eternal sweep of the green steppe beyond the city.

'I could get used to this,' Doripalam said. 'So long as you were doing the pushing.'

'You do realise quite how vulnerable you are up here?' Nergui said, taking the wheelchair to the edge of the slope down to the park. 'I could simply let go and you'd roll all the way down till you hit something.'

'Solongo's already pointed that out,' Doripalam said. 'Quite forcibly, in fact. I think it's her way of expressing her affection for me.' Her reaction had been a characteristic mixture of concern for his condition and disapproval of the fact that he had allowed it to happen. He was hoping that, for the moment at least, the concern would remain paramount.

Nergui nodded, watching the flight of some bird of prey across the empty sky. The weather was finally warming up. It would be summer soon. 'You'd better keep on the right side of her, then,' he said. 'We need you back at work as soon as possible. Now especially. The Minister isn't happy at losing my services while I cover for you.'

'There's no one else, though, is there? No one we can trust, I mean.'

'There are some I think we can. But nobody with enough experience to cover for you while we start to clean things up.'

'And we don't know who's straight and who isn't. We don't know how much Muunokhoi was exaggerating.'

Nergui shrugged. 'Muunokhoi had countless faults. But he had no need to exaggerate his influence. It's a hard one. I've got some clues from the enquiries I was already conducting. And it should be easier now, with Muunokhoi out of the picture. There's no one to protect them.'

'But there's also nothing to protect. With Muunokhoi gone – well, they're not corrupt cops any more. Not active ones, anyhow. There may be nothing to find.'

'If they've been corrupt once, they'll be corrupt again. Integrity's like virginity. You can't get it back.'

'Very philosophical,' Doripalam said, wondering if this was an apposite moment to ask about Mrs Radnaa.

Nergui had described those final moments in the cellar, but even now Doripalam could barely imagine what it must have felt like. When, at the sound of the single gunshot, Mrs Radnaa had fallen, leaving Muunokhoi standing over her. Nergui had stared at his own hand, certain that he had not yet fired, but certain also that Muunokhoi had not shot Sarangarel, that the bullet had come from somewhere else. He glanced behind him, but there was no sign of movement from the two henchmen.

And then, just as the horror was rising in Nergui's throat, Muunokhoi had finally staggered forwards, his body twisting, and Nergui had seen the blood pouring from his back. It was as if, in those few seconds, Muunokhoi had been focusing every last ounce of will in a desperate effort to deny the inevitability of his own death. But then there was a second shot and Muunokhoi's head had exploded as his body crashed down on to the stone floor. By then, mercifully, Sarangarel was already unconscious.

As so often, it was as if Nergui had read Doripalam's thoughts. 'I saw her – Mrs Radnaa – this morning. She's recovering well. There was no serious physical hurt. Her collapse was mainly shock.'

Was it corruption, Doripalam wondered, to bury the disciplinary charges against Tunjin? The shooting of Muunokhoi had been unavoidable, but Tunjin had been a long way from following any established procedures. And there was also the indisputable fact that, at the time of the killing, Tunjin had still been formally suspended from duty.

But Nergui had had no concerns about these niceties, and had applied his ministerial authority accordingly. Tunjin had saved their lives. Tunjin was unquestionably straight, one of the few about whom they could be certain. He was the kind of man they needed in the force. Tunjin himself – or so Doripalam had been told – had celebrated his return to duty by downing a bottle of vodka. Or possibly two.

'You never did finish the story,' Doripalam said.

'I never did, did I? But you will have worked it out for yourself.'

'Humour me,' Doripalam said.

Nergui smiled. 'So what did we have? We had Muunokhoi trying to terrify the life out of poor Gavaa. Who, to do him credit, didn't go along with – all the things that Muunokhoi was showing him, but made his exit as soon as possible. And did the only thing that an eighteen-year-old boy can do in those circumstances.'

Doripalam raised an eyebrow. 'Which is?'

'Go home to his mother. Whatever's gone on between them, his mother will always take him back in. He tells her the whole story, and she's scared out of her wits. She knows Muunokhoi. She knows what he's capable of. She knows how paranoid and vindictive he is and that he's not going to let the boy out of his clutches. So she hides Gavaa, hoping that she'll be able to look after him till Muunokhoi's wrath subsides. And she even makes a lot of fuss about going to the press and the police about her poor missing boy, just so that Muunokhoi will never think that the boy's being hidden as part of her family.' Nergui stops and smiles. 'She was a resourceful woman, gives nothing away even when Muunokhoi's heavies turn up. But then, maybe inevitably, one day Muunokhoi himself arrives. Maybe he tries to remind her of old times, tells her again that Gavaa is probably his son. Maybe he threatens all kinds of things.' He paused.

Nergui began to push the wheelchair back up the slope towards the temple. 'But she's smart. When she sees the way the conversation is going, she starts to intimate that maybe she's got some evidence that Muunokhoi wouldn't like to see the light of day. She threatens Muunokhoi with exposure if he doesn't forget about her son. And Muunokhoi's response is—'

'To murder her in cold blood.'

'Indeed. But not, as we know, before he also subjected her to some dreadful abuse, trying to force her to reveal her son's whereabouts. Which, of course, being a mother she did not.'

'An interesting way to treat your ex-lover. And the supposed mother of your son. And Gavaa himself had already gone off with the rest of the family, pretending to be a cousin.'

'Exactly. Which is why they were so terrified about anybody – that is, Muunokhoi – catching up with them. Which, with a little help from our friend in the north, he eventually did.' They had still not managed to track down the bodies of Gavaa's three relatives. Gavaa had told them how a team of police officers, apparently from Tsend's team, had arrived in the camp in the middle of the night, dragging out the three men. Gavaa himself had been hidden away from the main camp, just in case of such an eventuality. He had heard the cries of the men being dragged away, supposedly under arrest, and had hidden himself further into the woods, emerging only once the team had gone leaving behind a solitary sentinel in case Gavaa should return. But it was the guard himself who had been taken by surprise as Gavaa had obtained at least some small revenge.

Tsend had been arrested and was being questioned, but to date had denied all knowledge of the men's supposed arrest, as had all other officers in the Bulgan force. Maybe they would find the bodies one day, Doripalam thought, though Tsend was likely to have covered his tracks well.

Doripalam looked up at the line of monks crossing the path, still chanting. 'But what about this supposed evidence? Do you think Mrs Tuya really had it?'

Nergui shrugged. 'Who knows? Maybe it never existed. Gansukh and Khenbish were quite capable of living in a fantasy world and helping others to do the same. I can easily imagine that, having tried to gather meaningful stuff, Gansukh just faked some more serious evidence to keep Muunokhoi at bay. Maybe they really were just a bit too smart for Muunokhoi. And a bit too smart for their own good.'

'So all this was for nothing?'

'I fear so. But I think Muunokhoi had hit the paranoid stage long before this. He saw everything as a threat. All of this must have seemed – well, preordained. Muunokhoi found himself sitting in court for the first time in his life. A court overseen by the wife of the man he killed. I imagine he would have been scarcely able to believe it. Even though the trial collapsed, it might have been enough – with all of this going on – to tip him over the edge.'

'You think he went mad?'

'I think his world was much less stable and secure than he had imagined. I think he saw some cracks beginning to show. There was probably some justification to his paranoia. But, yes, in the end, I think he went mad.'

They had stopped at the edge of the temple ground, looking out over the windy spaces of Nairamdal Park. Below, the weathered amusement rides glittered faintly in the early afternoon sun. Children were racing across the grass, shouting and playing games. Clusters of old men smoked and talked, wrapped in their unseasonable *dels*. Beyond the park, there was the endless grassland, the distant mountains, the land without boundaries. Life continuing.

'So what now?' Doripalam said.

'We have a job to do,' Nergui said. 'Muunokhoi is gone. Most people won't know why or how. A lot of people will mourn him.' No one had challenged Nergui's account of events – people did not tend to challenge Nergui on such matters – but there had been no desire, from the Minister upwards, to make the circumstances of Muunokhoi's death public knowledge. He had, it appeared, died unexpectedly of natural causes after a short illness. Which, Doripalam acknowledged, was at least a version of the truth.

'And there will be other Muunokhois coming to fill the vacuum. It's the way of things. Our world here is changing. We can't stop that. We can even welcome it. But we have to hold a line, make sure we retain control.' They listened to the distant sound of the monks enacting their ancient rituals in the ornate buildings behind them. 'We have a job to do,' he said again.